Fibbed

RAZORBILL
An imprint of Penguin Random House LLC, New York

First published in the United States of America by Razorbill,
an imprint of Penguin Random House LLC, 2022

Visit us online at penguinrandomhouse.com.

LIBRARY OF CONGRESS CATALOGING-IN-PUBLICATION DATA
Names: Agyemang, Elizabeth, author, illustrator.
Title: Fibbed / Elizabeth Agyemang.
Description: New York : Razorbill, 2022. | Audience: Ages 8–12 years. | Summary: After telling too many far-fetched tales, Nana Busumuru is sent to spend the summer with relatives in Ghana, where she must join forces with the trickster spider Ananse to prevent an evil corporation from stealing the magic in the village forest.
Identifiers: LCCN 2022001473 | ISBN 9780593204887 (hardcover) | ISBN 9780593204900 (trade paperback) | ISBN 9780593204894 (ebook) | ISBN 9780593352342 (ebook) | ISBN 9780593352335 (ebook)
Subjects: CYAC: Graphic novels. | Anansi (Legendary character)—Fiction. | Tricksters—Fiction. | Americans—Ghana—Fiction. | Family life—Fiction. | Magic—Fiction. | Ghana—Fiction. | LCGFT: Graphic novels.
Classification: LCC PZ7.7.A326 Fi 2022 | DDC 741.5/973—dc23/eng/20220304
LC record available at https://lccn.loc.gov/2022001473

Manufactured in China

3 5 7 9 10 8 6 4 2

TOPL

Design by Danielle Ceccolini

Text set in Mikado Regular, Mandrian Whispers, Attaboy, and Gill Sans

*To my parents, who flew across the ocean with one
suitcase and a dream for their children.*

To my siblings, who inspire me every day.

*To my grandparents, and all my family in Ghana and the United States,
whose smiles and stories will forever be ingrained in my heart.*

And to God. Every day is a blessing.

Thank you.

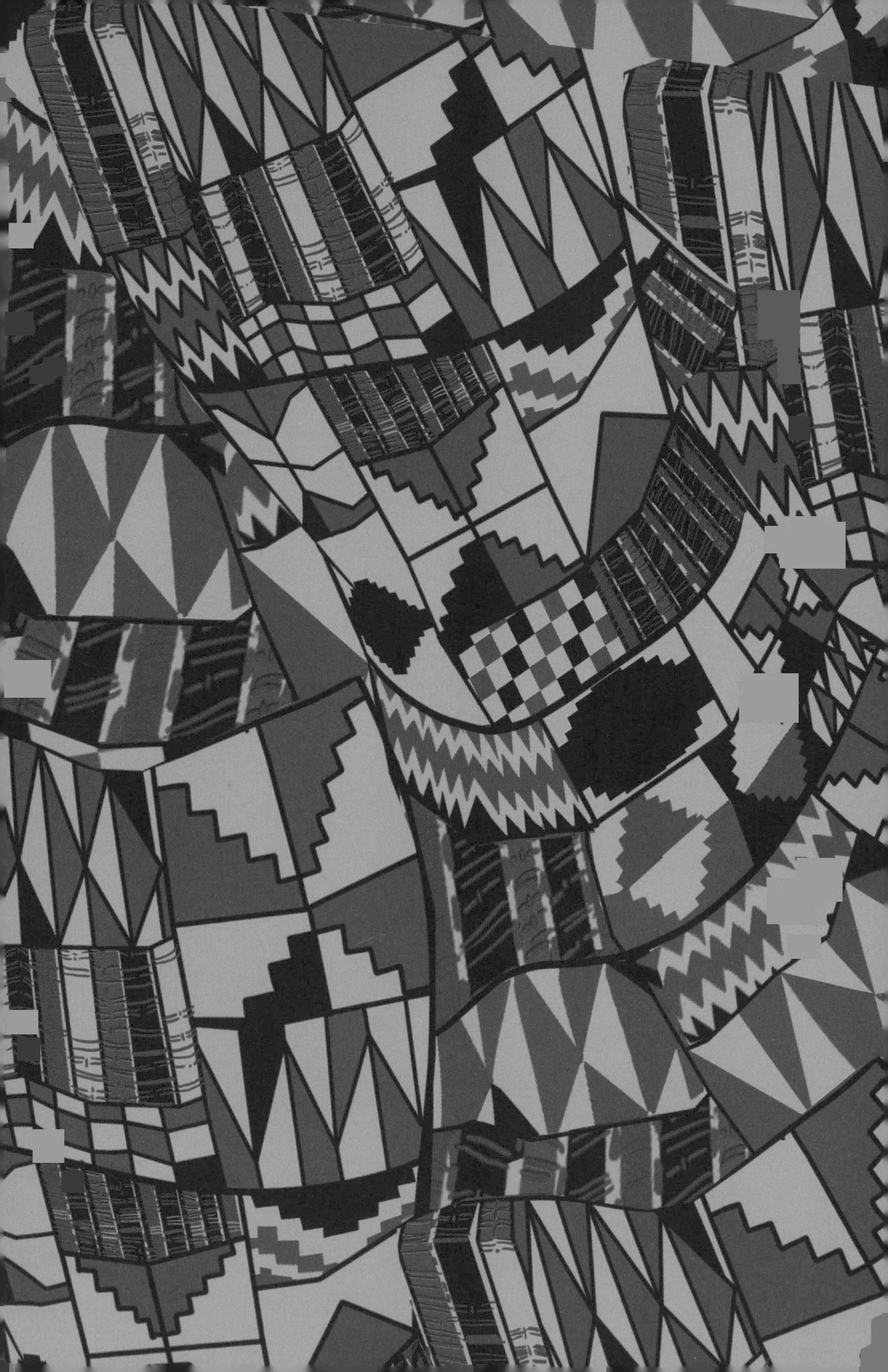

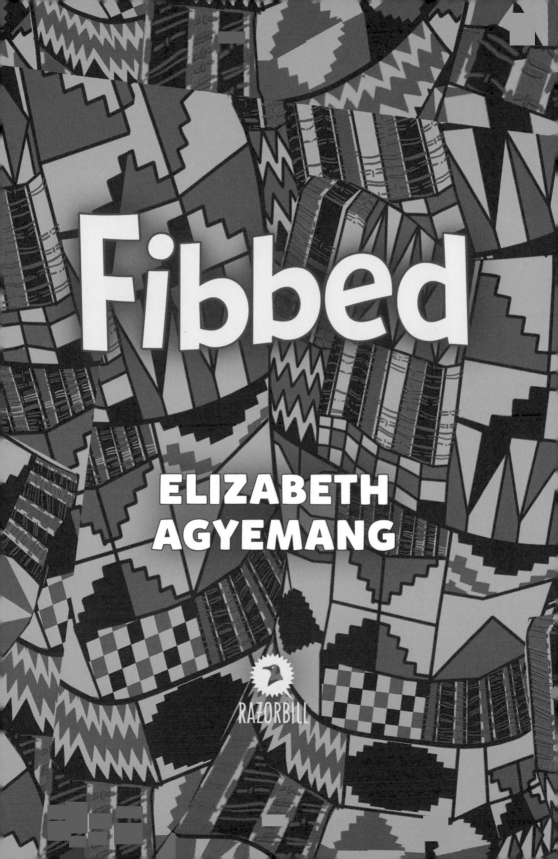

Fibbed

ELIZABETH AGYEMANG

RAZORBILL

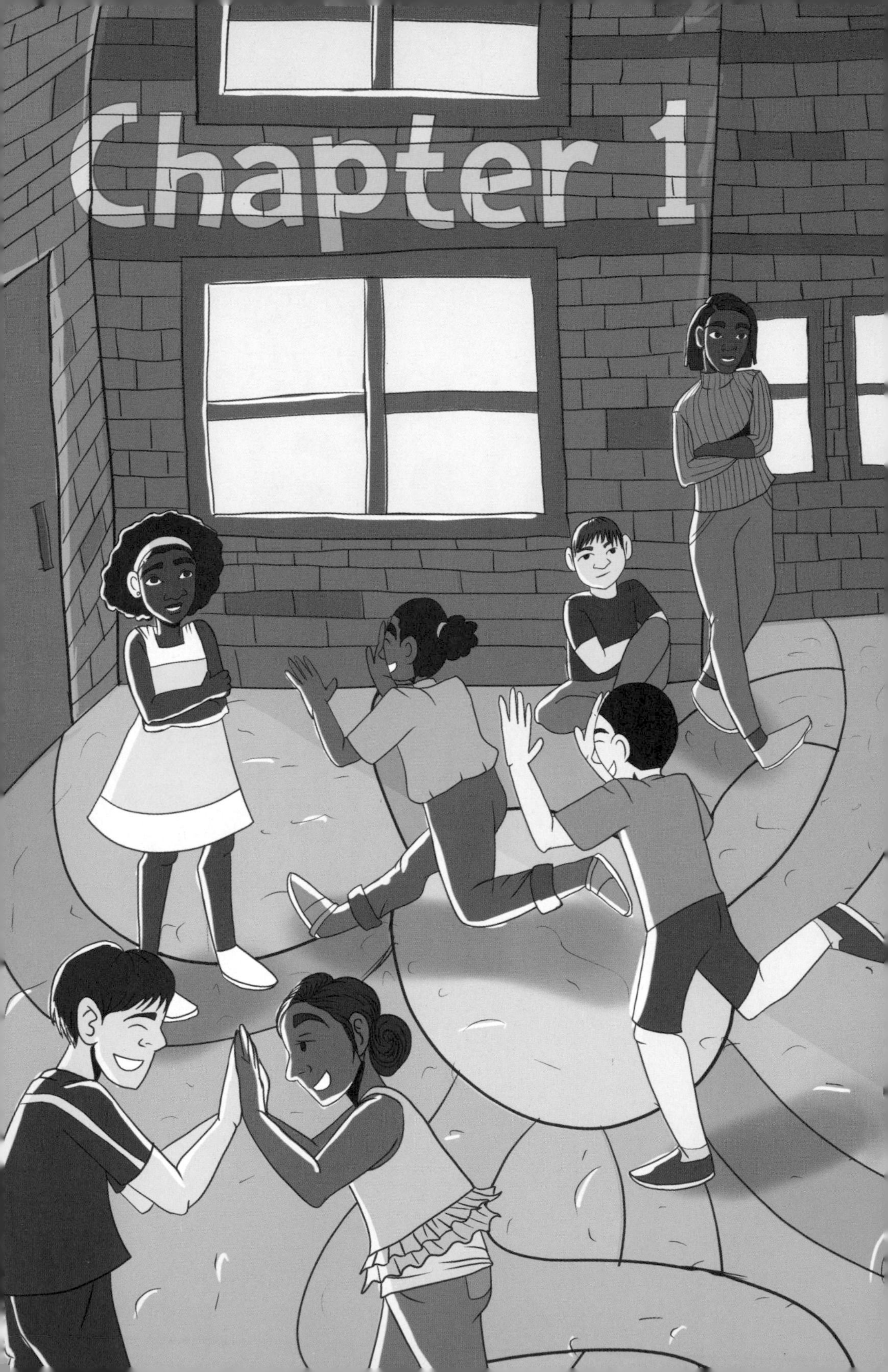
Chapter 1

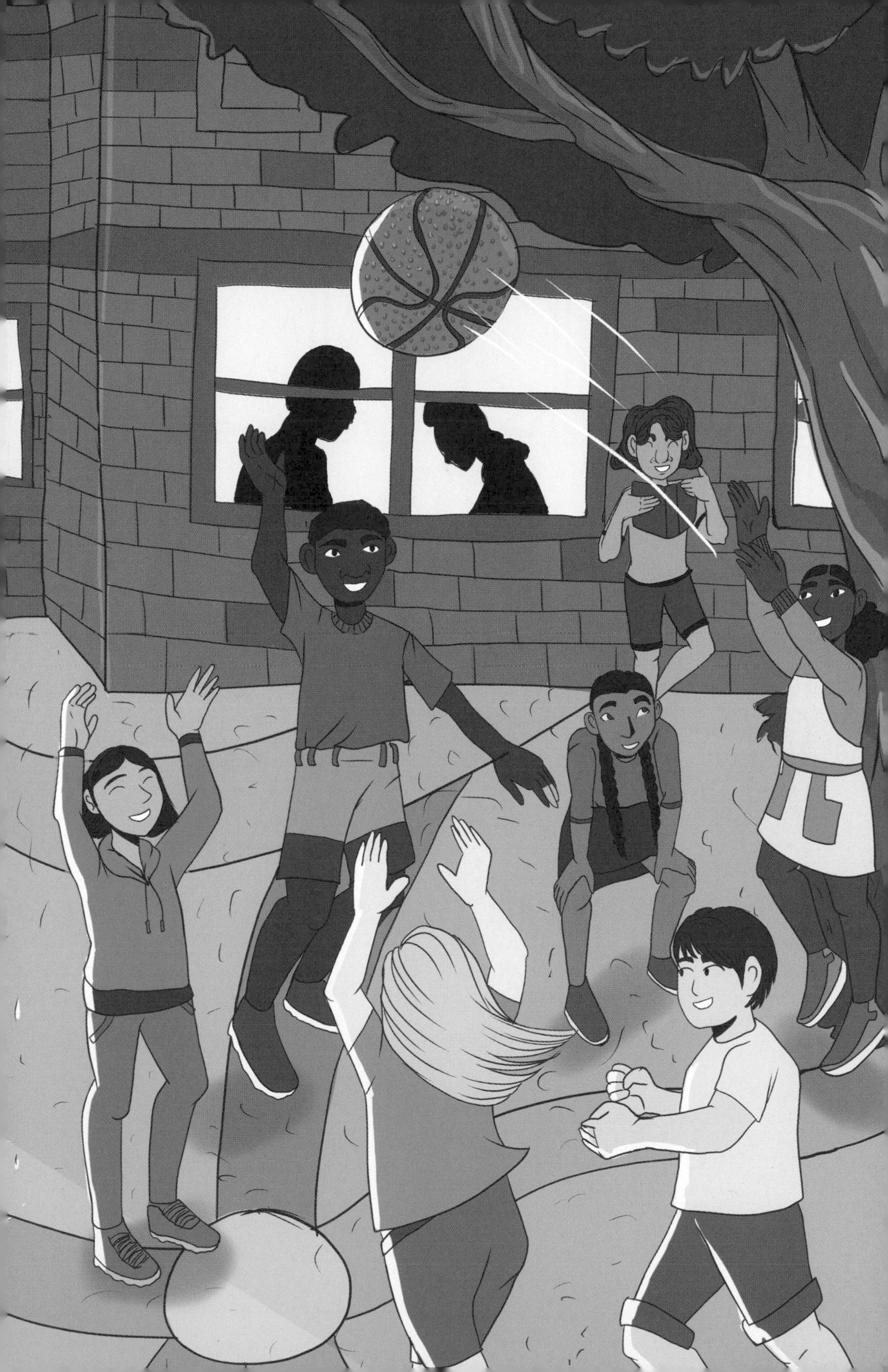

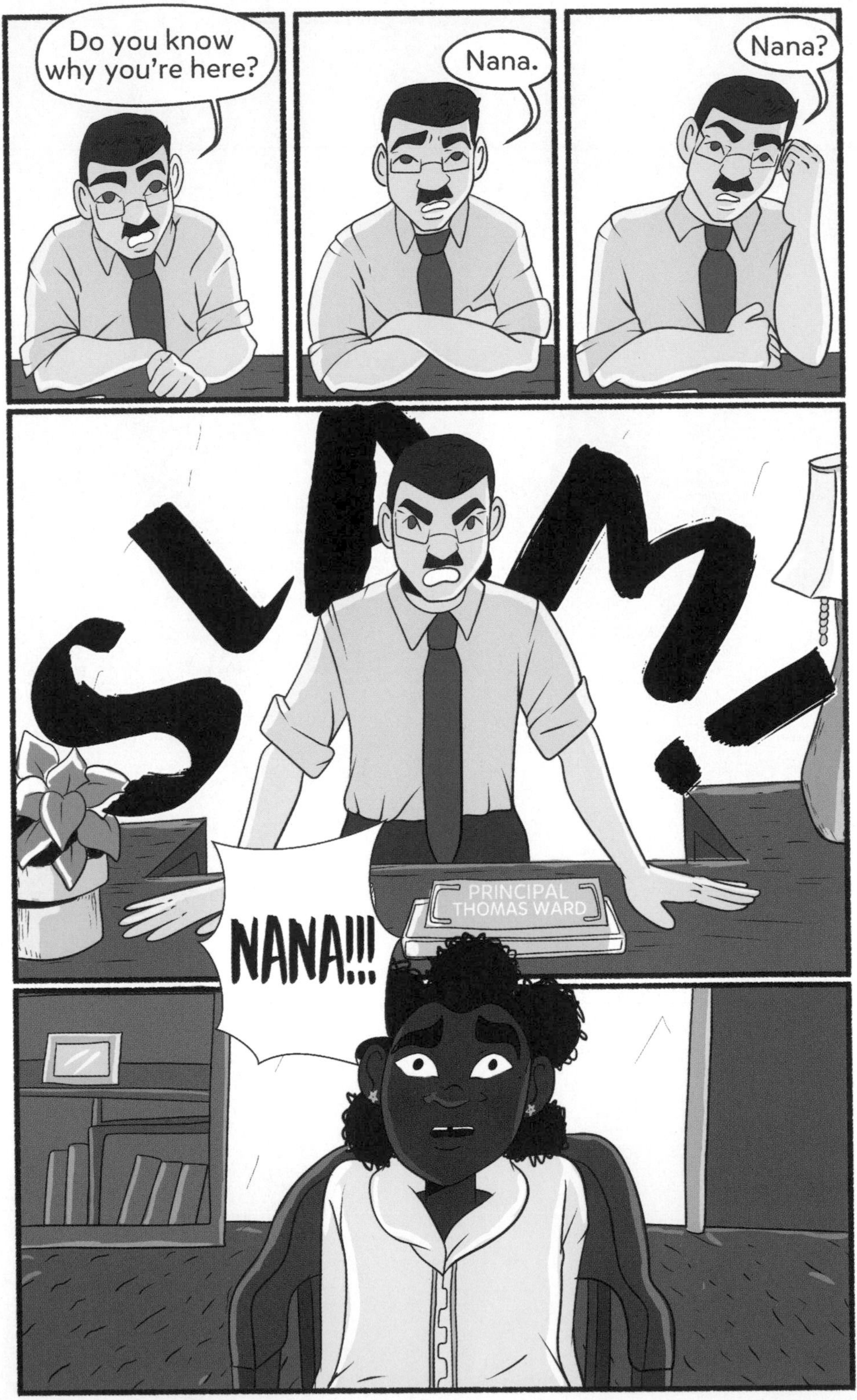
Do you know why you're here?
Nana.
Nana?
SLAM!
PRINCIPAL THOMAS WARD
NANA!!!

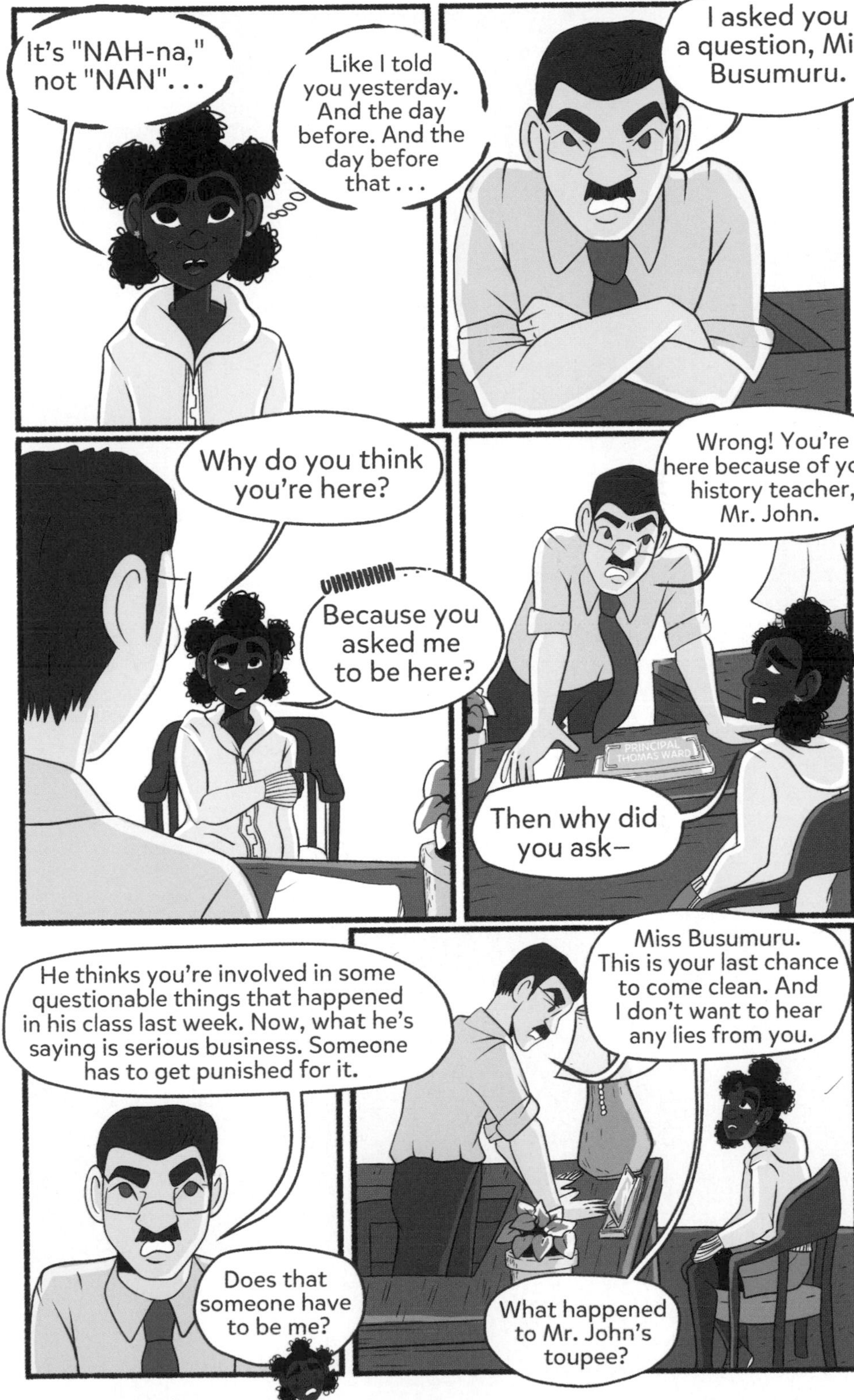
It's "NAH-na," not "NAN". . .
Like I told you yesterday. And the day before. And the day before that . . .
I asked you a question, Miss Busumuru.
Why do you think you're here?
UHHHHHH . . .
Because you asked me to be here?
Wrong! You're here because of your history teacher, Mr. John.
PRINCIPAL THOMAS WARD
Then why did you ask—
He thinks you're involved in some questionable things that happened in his class last week. Now, what he's saying is serious business. Someone has to get punished for it.
Does that someone have to be me?
Miss Busumuru. This is your last chance to come clean. And I don't want to hear any lies from you.
What happened to Mr. John's toupee?

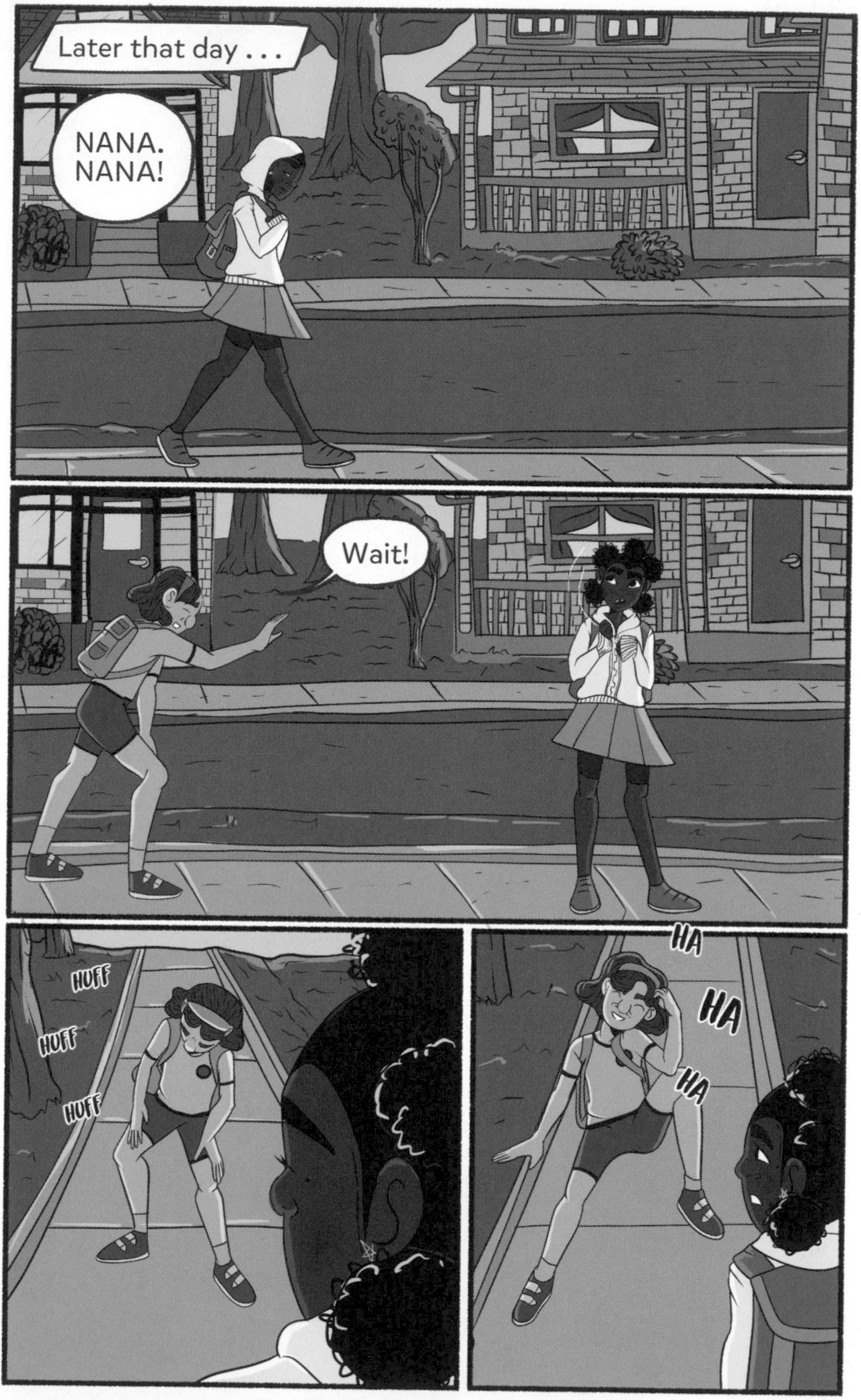
Later that day . . .
NANA. NANA!
Wait!
HUFF
HUFF
HUFF
HA
HA
HA

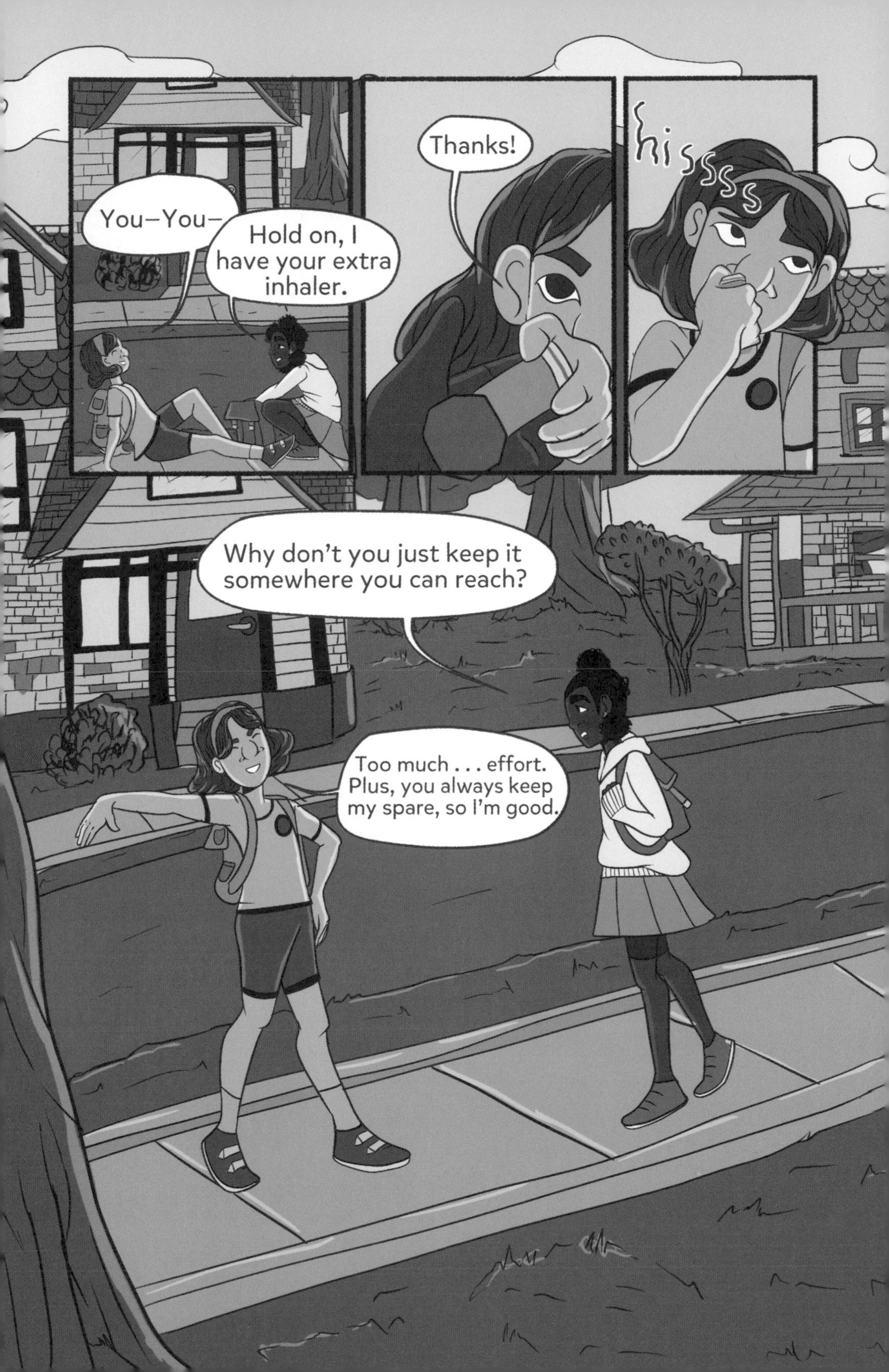
You—You—
Hold on, I have your extra inhaler.
Thanks!
hissss
Why don't you just keep it somewhere you can reach?
Too much . . . effort. Plus, you always keep my spare, so I'm good.

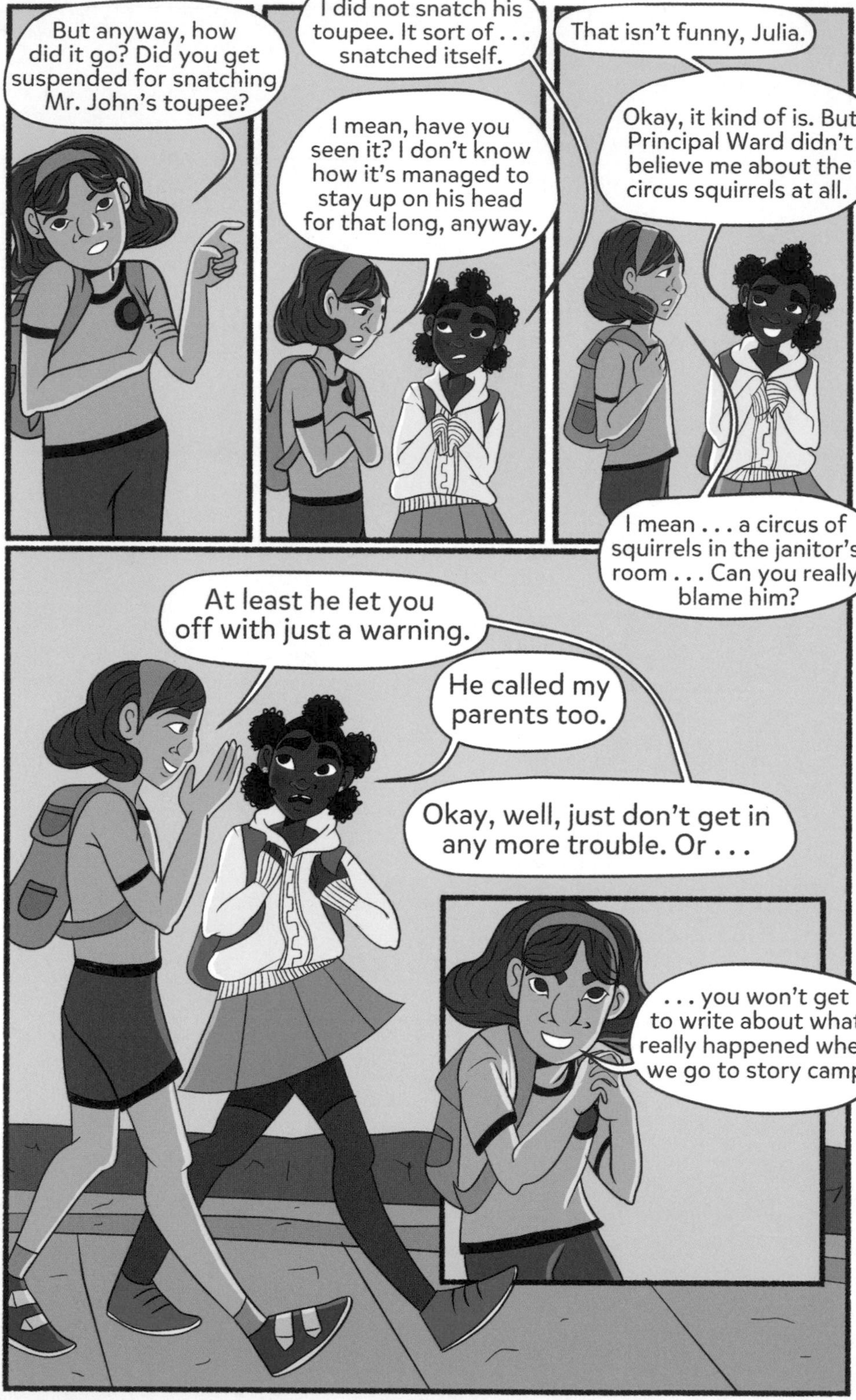
But anyway, how did it go? Did you get suspended for snatching Mr. John's toupee?
I did not snatch his toupee. It sort of . . . snatched itself.
I mean, have you seen it? I don't know how it's managed to stay up on his head for that long, anyway.
That isn't funny, Julia.
Okay, it kind of is. But Principal Ward didn't believe me about the circus squirrels at all.
I mean . . . a circus of squirrels in the janitor's room . . . Can you really blame him?
At least he let you off with just a warning.
He called my parents too.
Okay, well, just don't get in any more trouble. Or . . .
. . . you won't get to write about what really happened when we go to story camp!

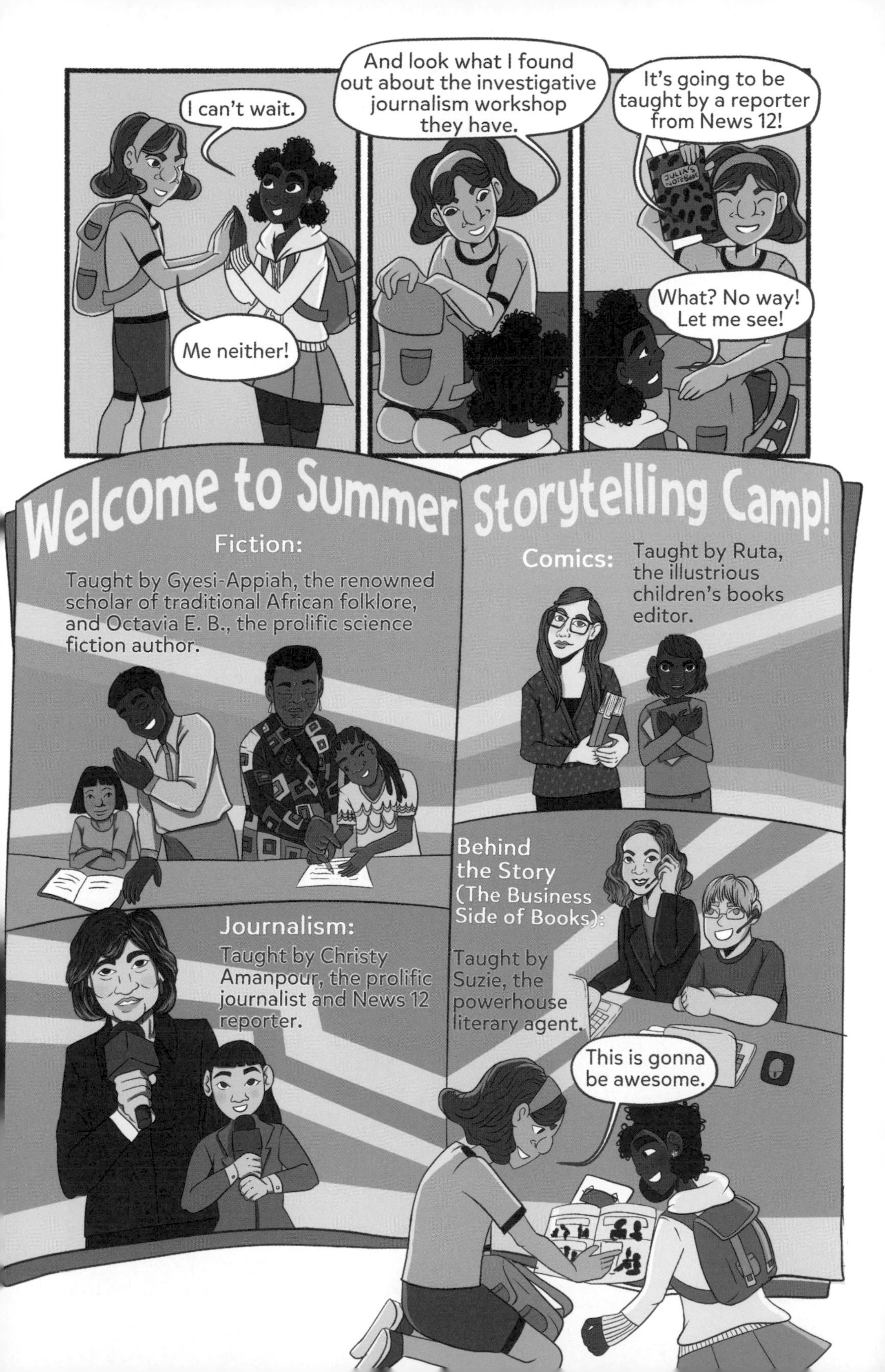
I can't wait.
Me neither!
And look what I found out about the investigative journalism workshop they have.
It's going to be taught by a reporter from News 12!
JULIA'S NOTEBOOK
What? No way! Let me see!
Welcome to Summer Storytelling Camp!
Fiction:
Taught by Gyesi-Appiah, the renowned scholar of traditional African folklore, and Octavia E. B., the prolific science fiction author.
Comics:
Taught by Ruta, the illustrious children's books editor.
Behind the Story (The Business Side of Books):
Taught by Suzie, the powerhouse literary agent.
Journalism:
Taught by Christy Amanpour, the prolific journalist and News 12 reporter.
This is gonna be awesome.

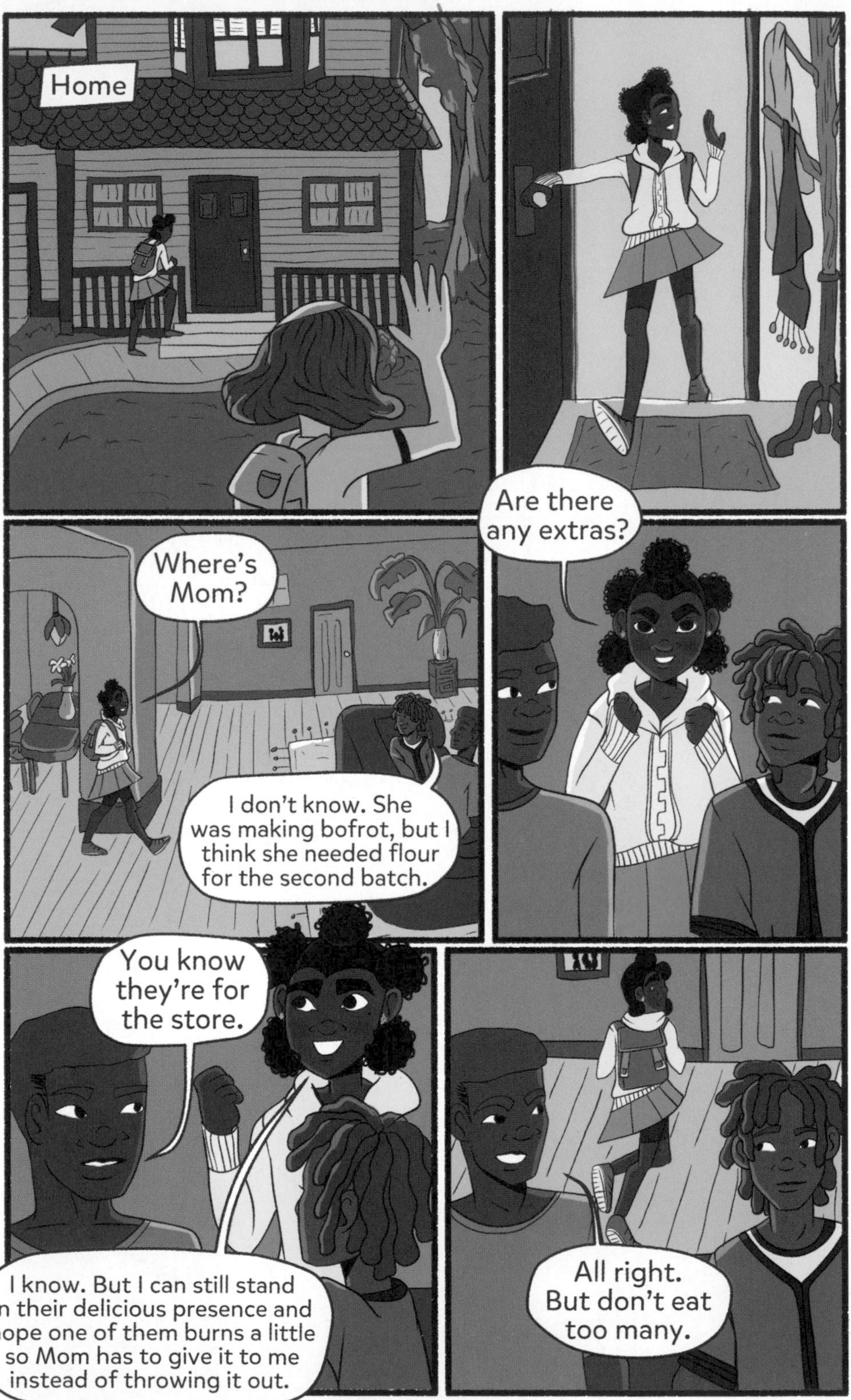
Home
Where's Mom?
I don't know. She was making bofrot, but I think she needed flour for the second batch.
Are there any extras?
You know they're for the store.
I know. But I can still stand in their delicious presence and hope one of them burns a little so Mom has to give it to me instead of throwing it out.
All right. But don't eat too many.

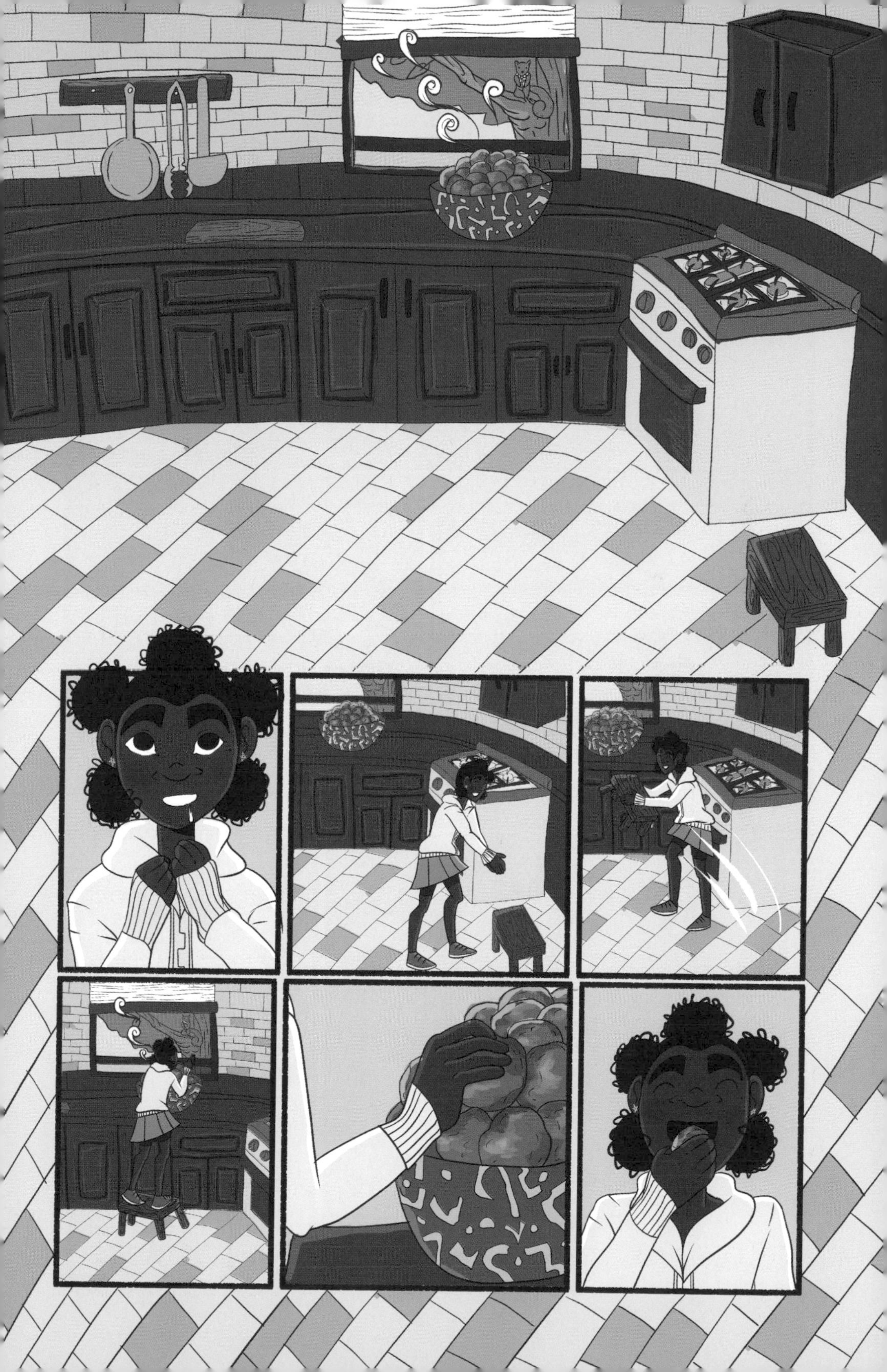

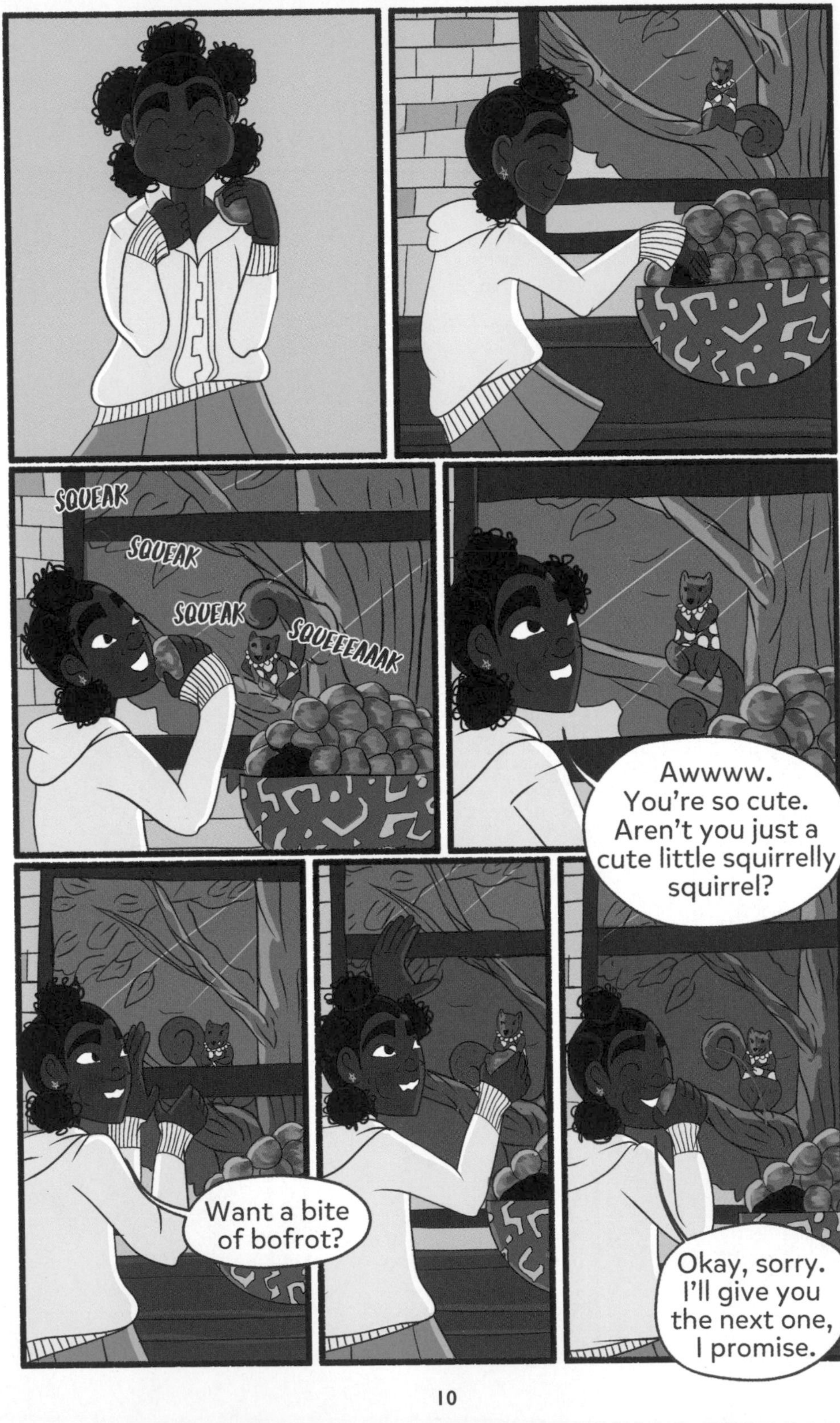
SQUEAK
SQUEAK
SQUEAK
SQUEEEAAAK
Awwww. You're so cute. Aren't you just a cute little squirrelly squirrel?
Want a bite of bofrot?
Okay, sorry. I'll give you the next one, I promise.

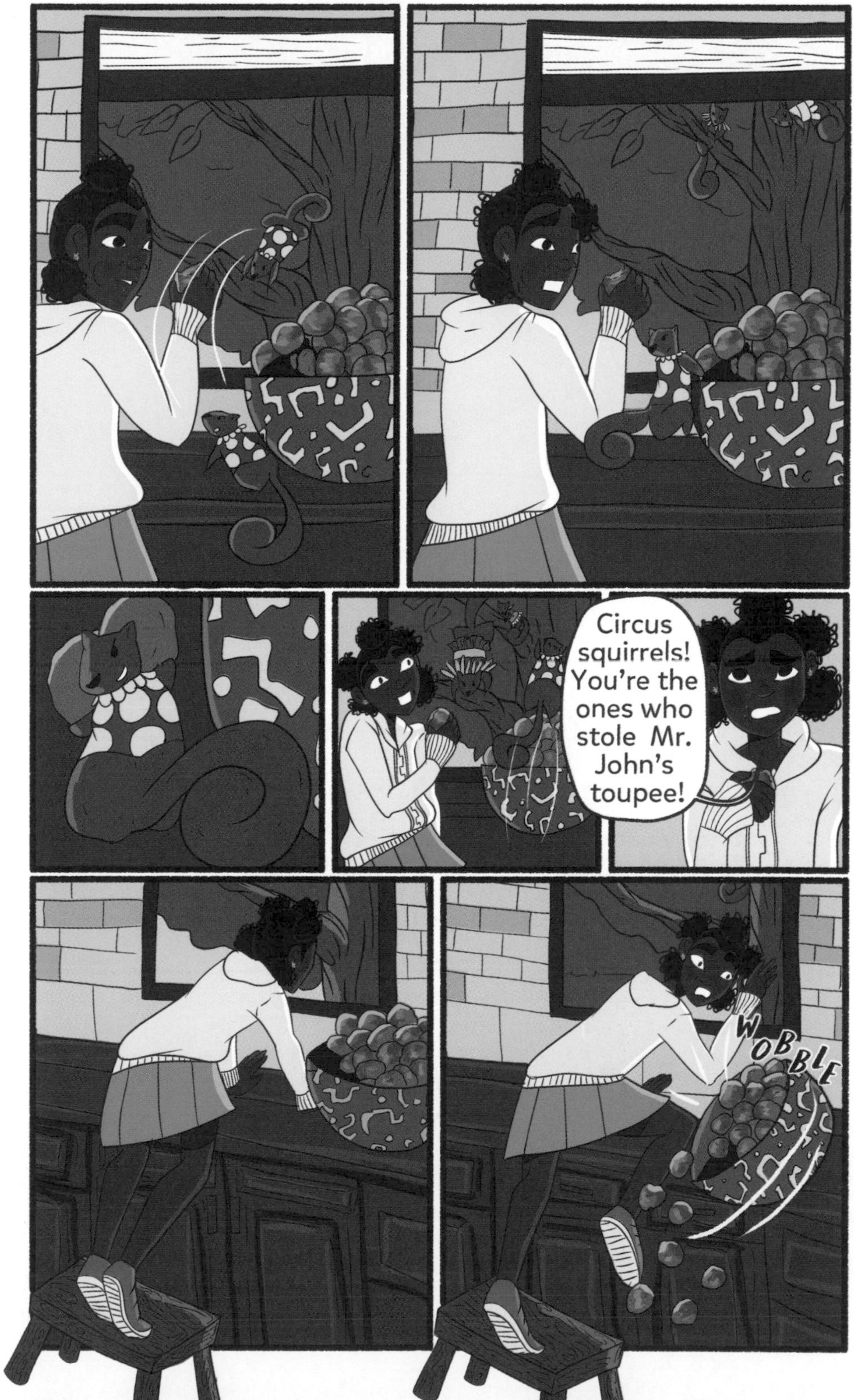
Circus squirrels! You're the ones who stole Mr. John's toupee!
WOBBLE

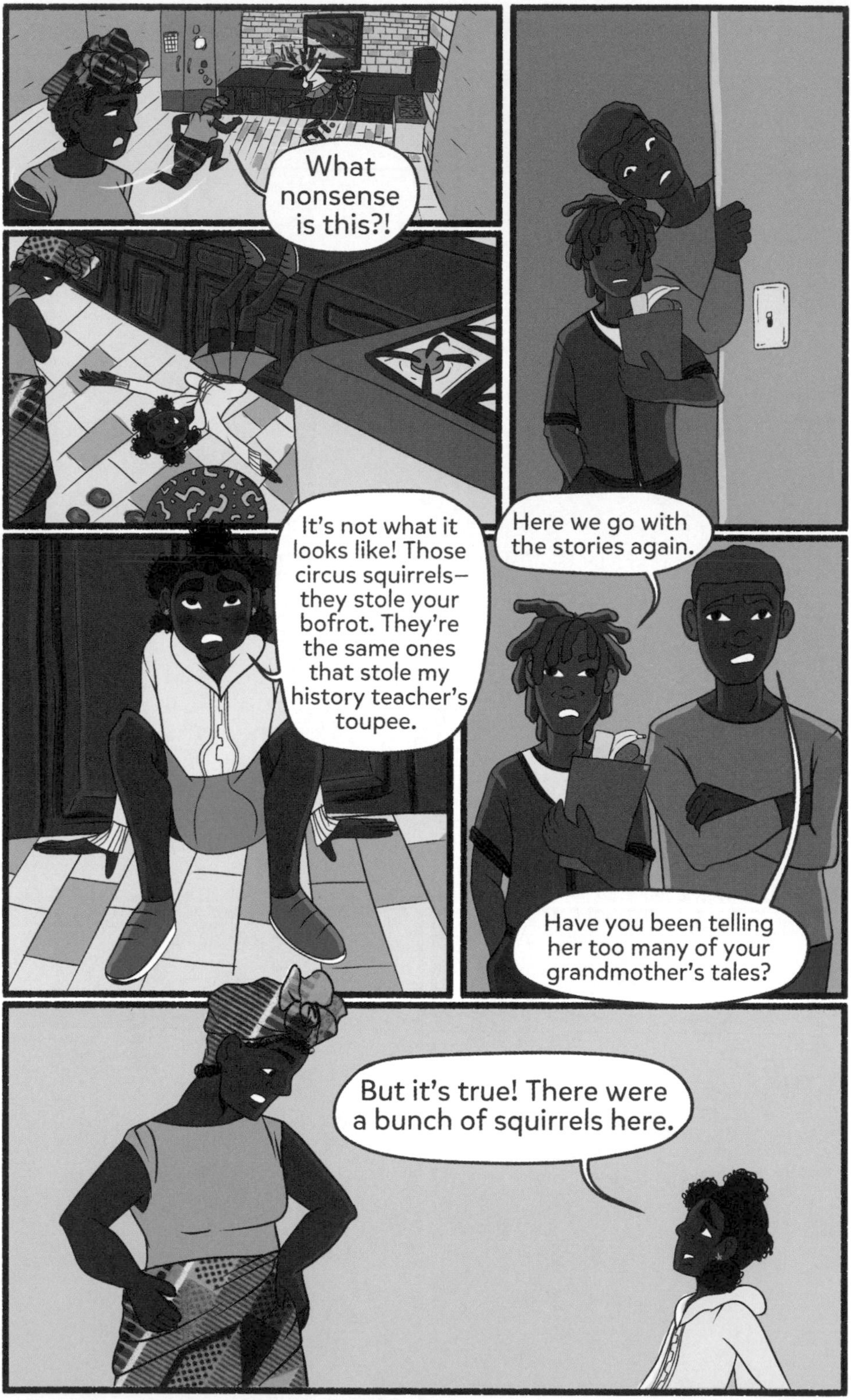
What nonsense is this?!
It's not what it looks like! Those circus squirrels—they stole your bofrot. They're the same ones that stole my history teacher's toupee.
Here we go with the stories again.
Have you been telling her too many of your grandmother's tales?
But it's true! There were a bunch of squirrels here.

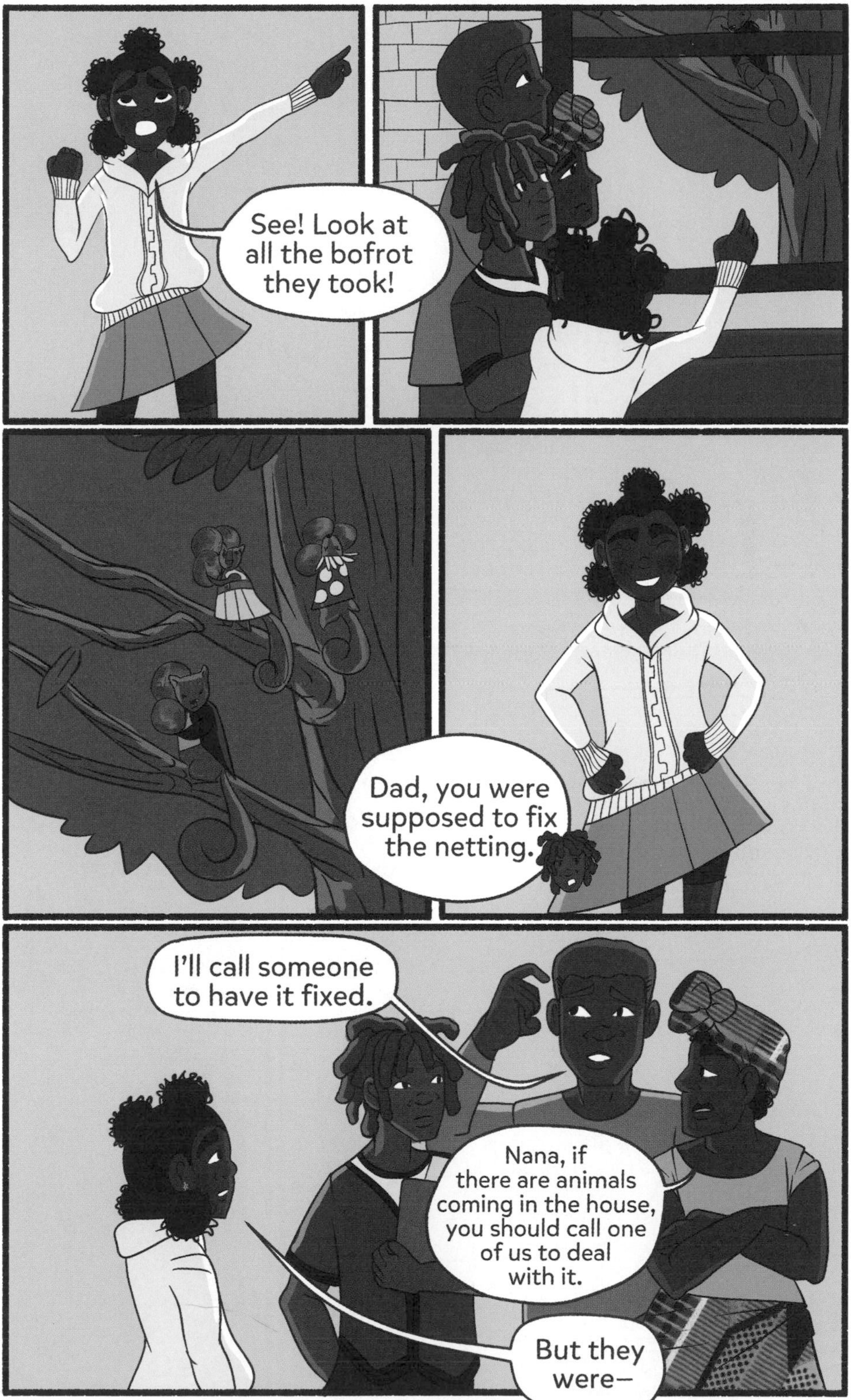
See! Look at all the bofrot they took!
Dad, you were supposed to fix the netting.
I'll call someone to have it fixed.
Nana, if there are animals coming in the house, you should call one of us to deal with it.
But they were—

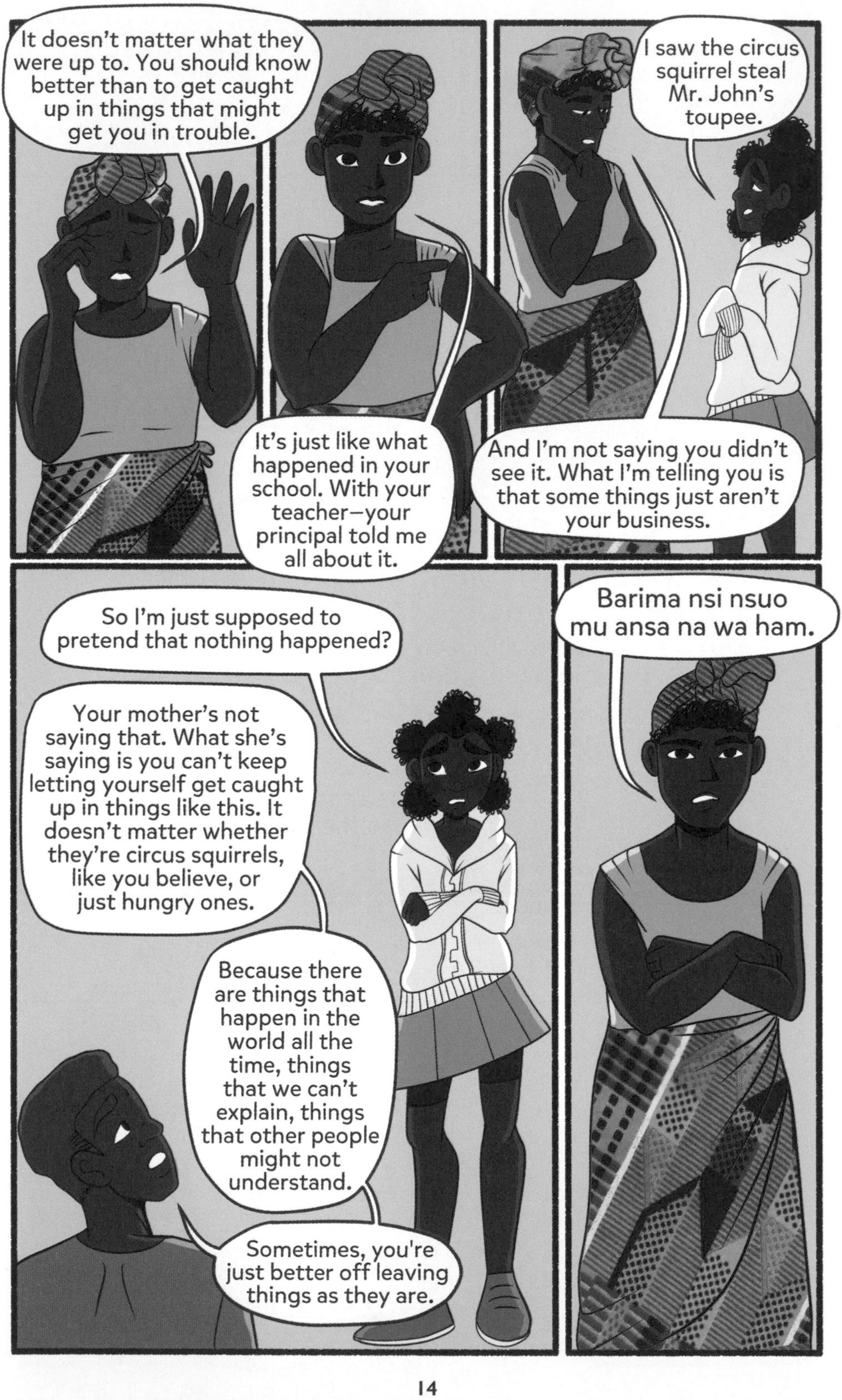

It doesn't matter what they were up to. You should know better than to get caught up in things that might get you in trouble.
It's just like what happened in your school. With your teacher—your principal told me all about it.
I saw the circus squirrel steal Mr. John's toupee.
And I'm not saying you didn't see it. What I'm telling you is that some things just aren't your business.
So I'm just supposed to pretend that nothing happened?
Your mother's not saying that. What she's saying is you can't keep letting yourself get caught up in things like this. It doesn't matter whether they're circus squirrels, like you believe, or just hungry ones.
Because there are things that happen in the world all the time, things that we can't explain, things that other people might not understand.
Sometimes, you're just better off leaving things as they are.
Barima nsi nsuo mu ansa na wa ham.

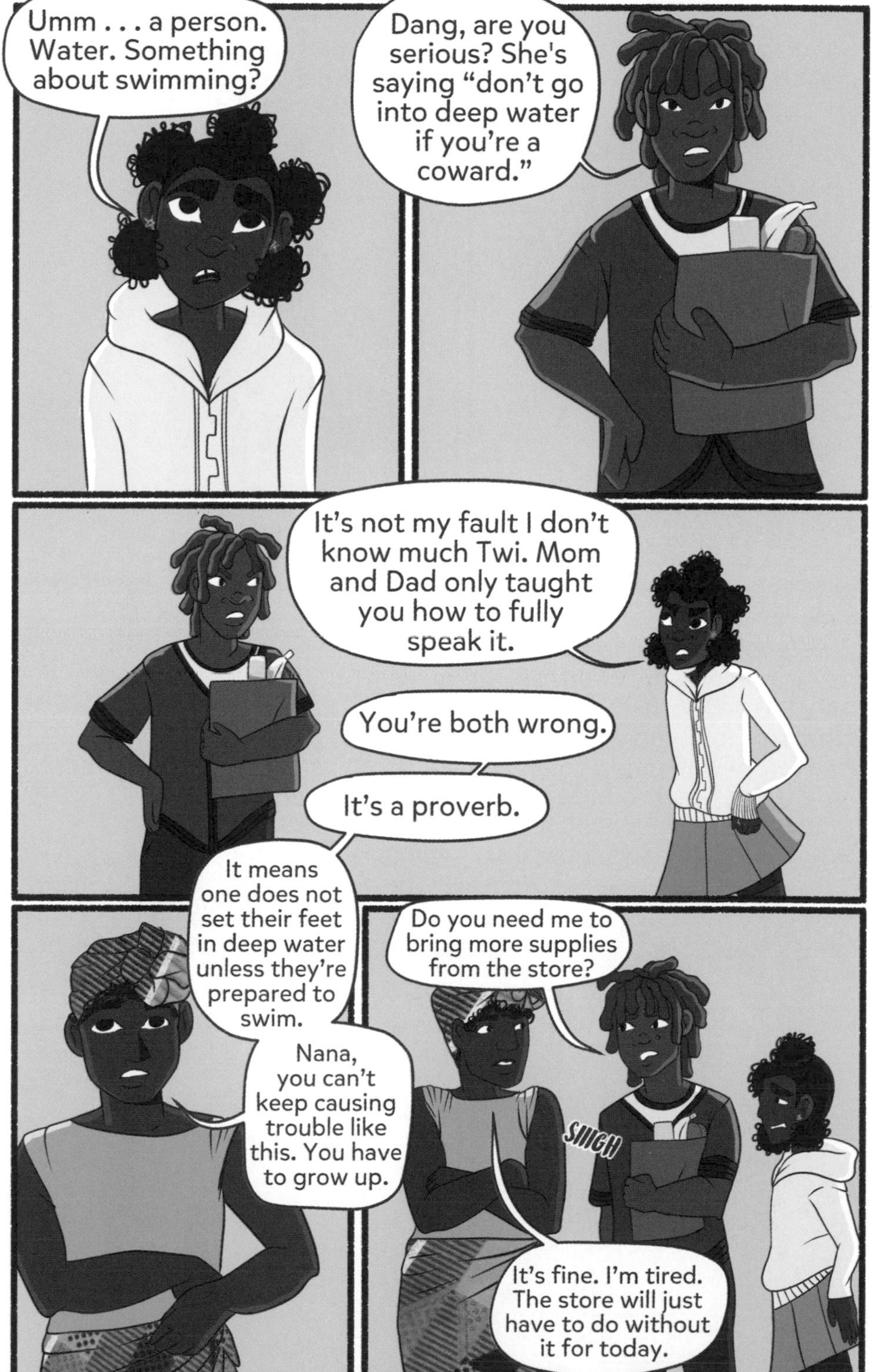
Umm . . . a person. Water. Something about swimming?
Dang, are you serious? She's saying "don't go into deep water if you're a coward."
It's not my fault I don't know much Twi. Mom and Dad only taught you how to fully speak it.
You're both wrong.
It's a proverb.
It means one does not set their feet in deep water unless they're prepared to swim.
Nana, you can't keep causing trouble like this. You have to grow up.
Do you need me to bring more supplies from the store?
SIIIGH
It's fine. I'm tired. The store will just have to do without it for today.

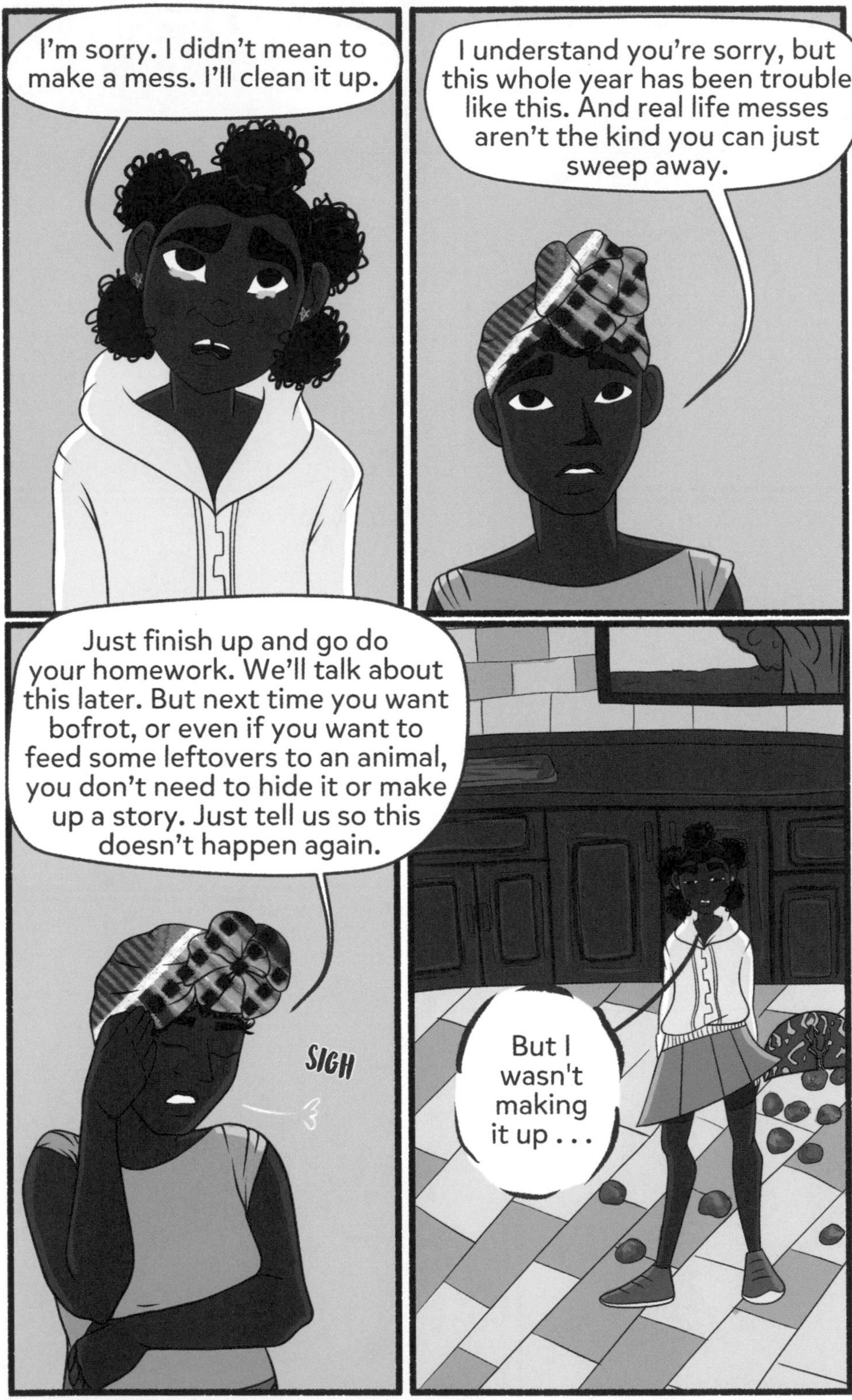
I'm sorry. I didn't mean to make a mess. I'll clean it up.
I understand you're sorry, but this whole year has been trouble like this. And real life messes aren't the kind you can just sweep away.
Just finish up and go do your homework. We'll talk about this later. But next time you want bofrot, or even if you want to feed some leftovers to an animal, you don't need to hide it or make up a story. Just tell us so this doesn't happen again.
SIGH
But I wasn't making it up . . .

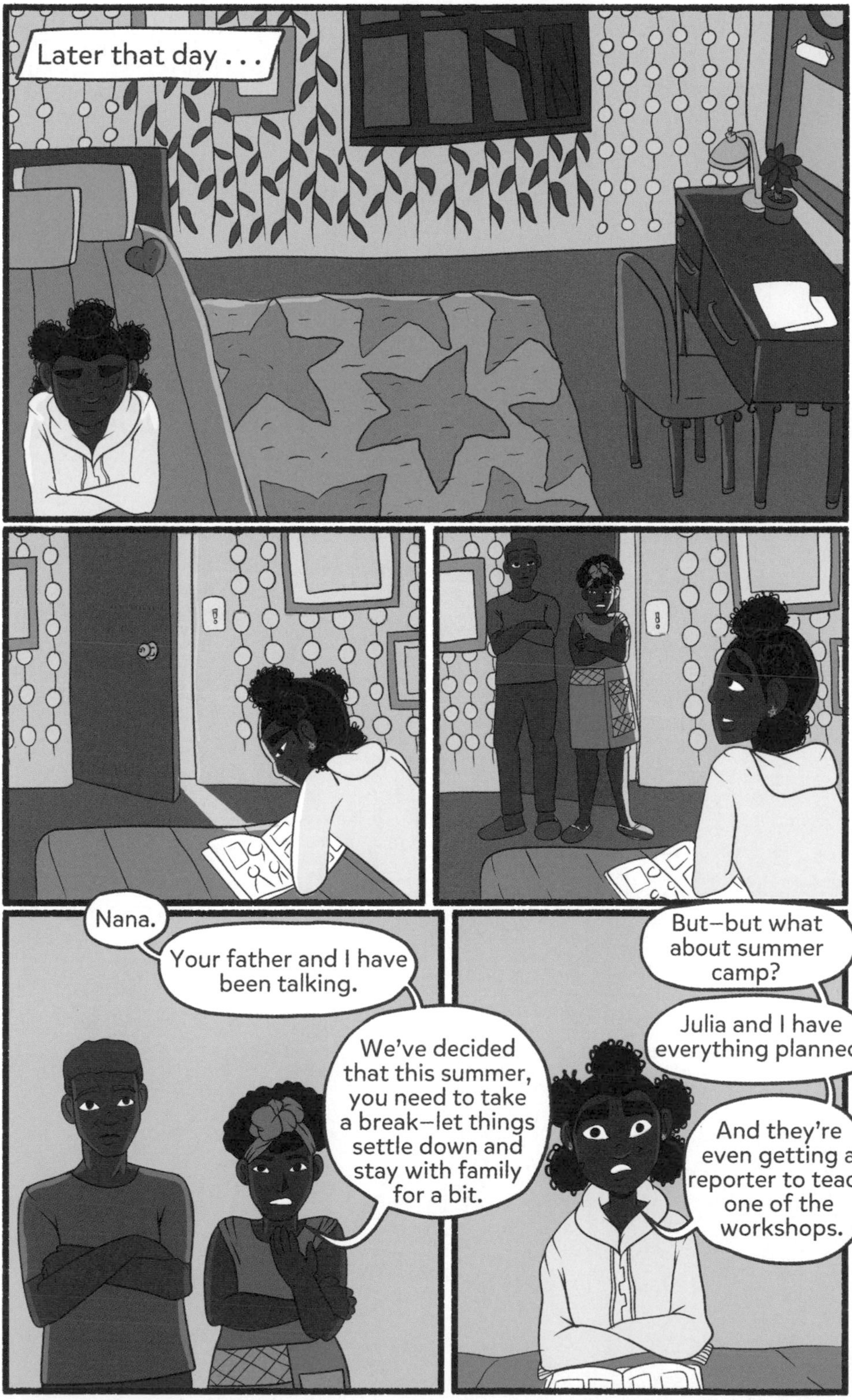

Later that day . . .
Nana.
Your father and I have been talking.
We've decided that this summer, you need to take a break—let things settle down and stay with family for a bit.
But—but what about summer camp?
Julia and I have everything planned.
And they're even getting a reporter to teach one of the workshops.

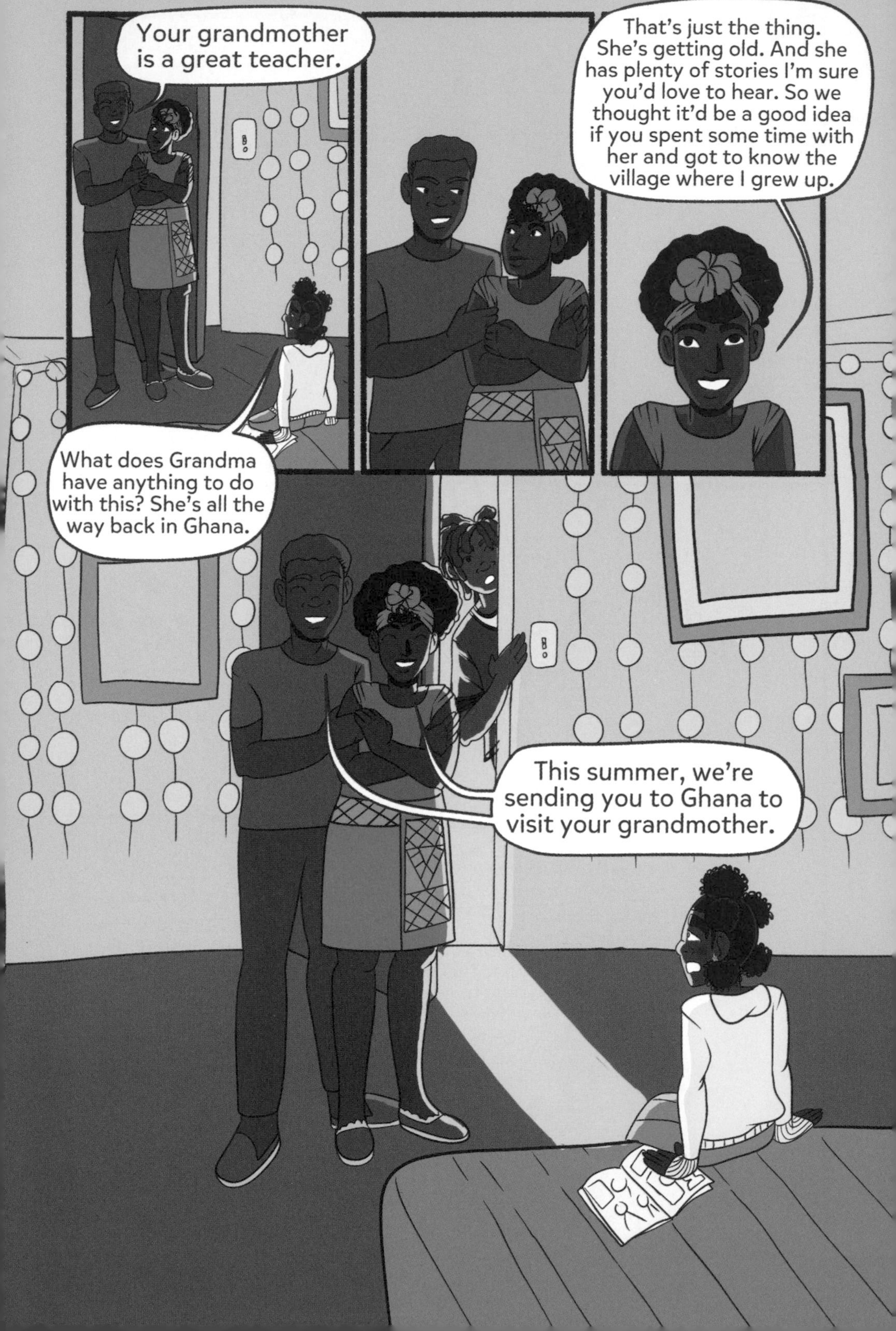
Your grandmother is a great teacher.
What does Grandma have anything to do with this? She's all the way back in Ghana.
That's just the thing. She's getting old. And she has plenty of stories I'm sure you'd love to hear. So we thought it'd be a good idea if you spent some time with her and got to know the village where I grew up.
This summer, we're sending you to Ghana to visit your grandmother.

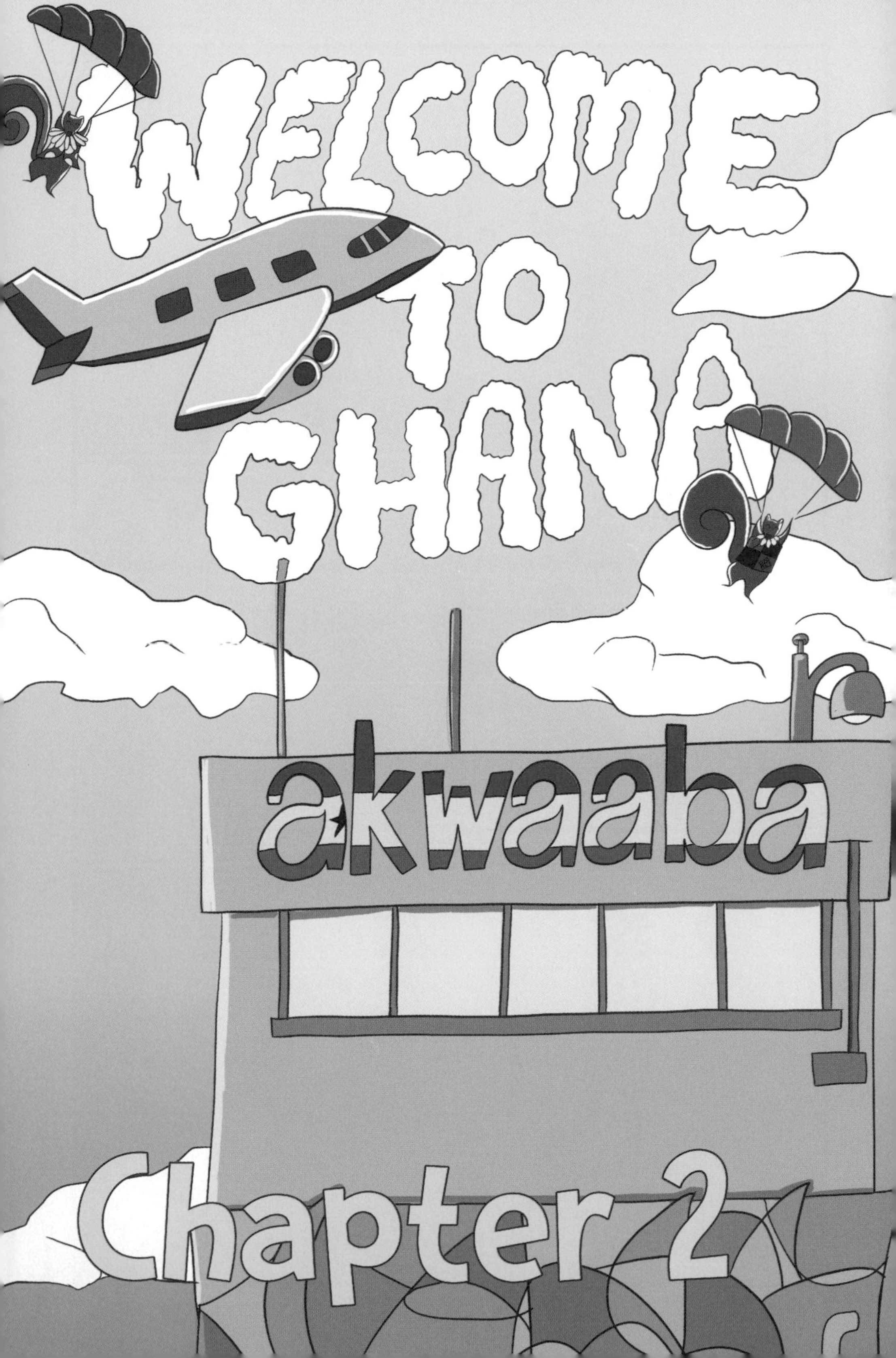

WELCOME TO GHANA
akwaaba
Chapter 2

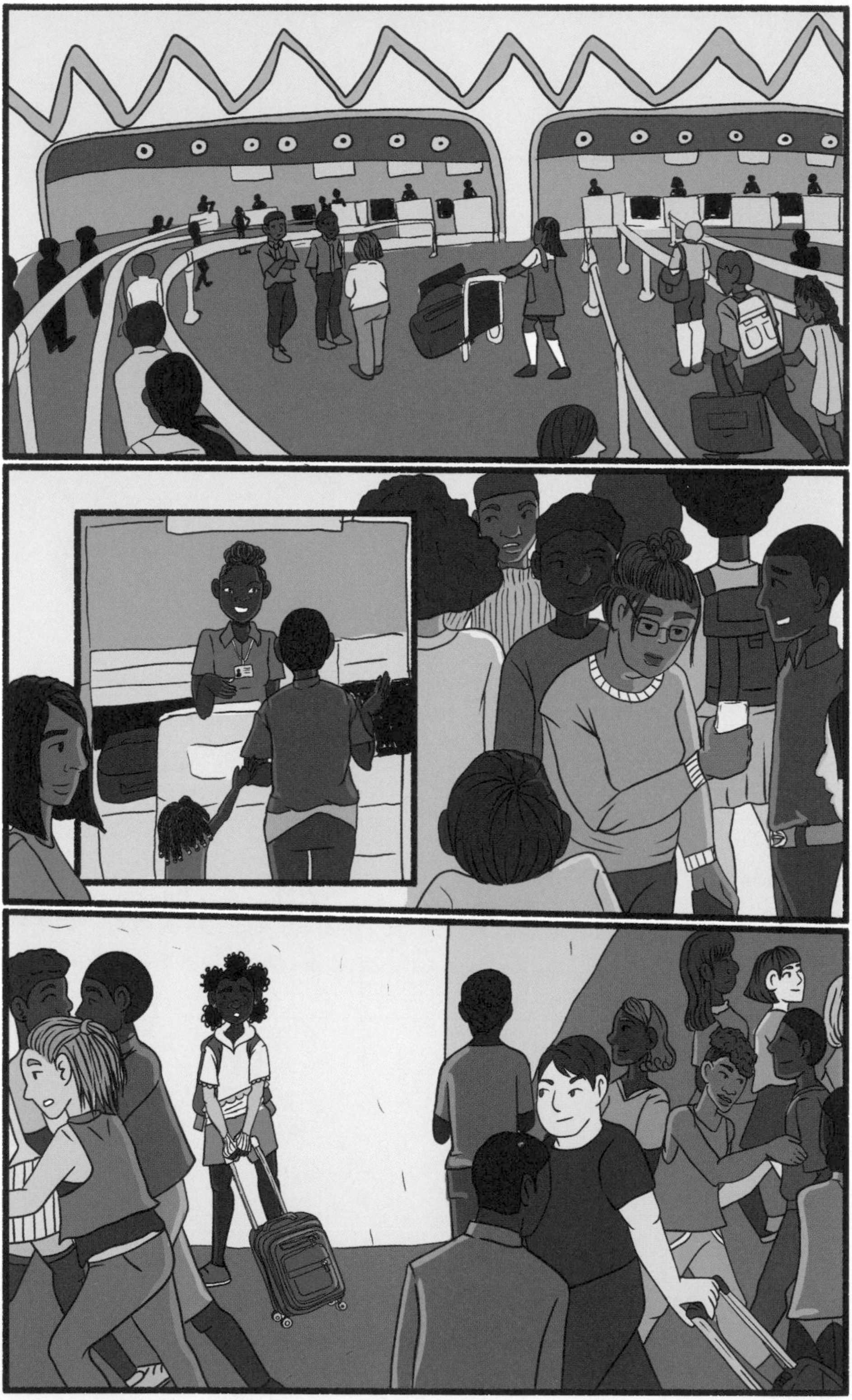

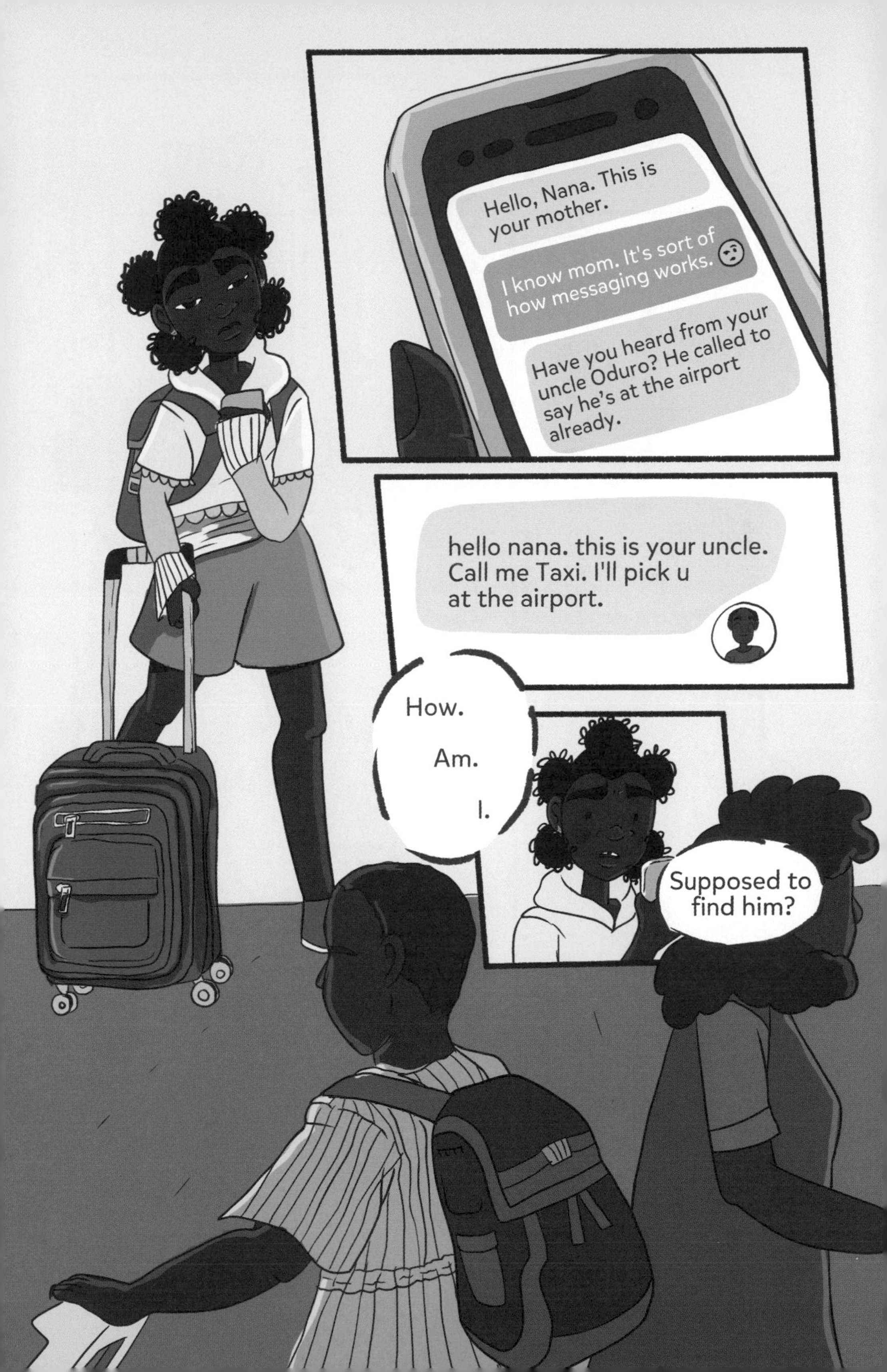
Hello, Nana. This is your mother.
I know mom. It's sort of how messaging works.
Have you heard from your uncle Oduro? He called to say he's at the airport already.
hello nana. this is your uncle. Call me Taxi. I'll pick u at the airport.
How. Am. I.
Supposed to find him?

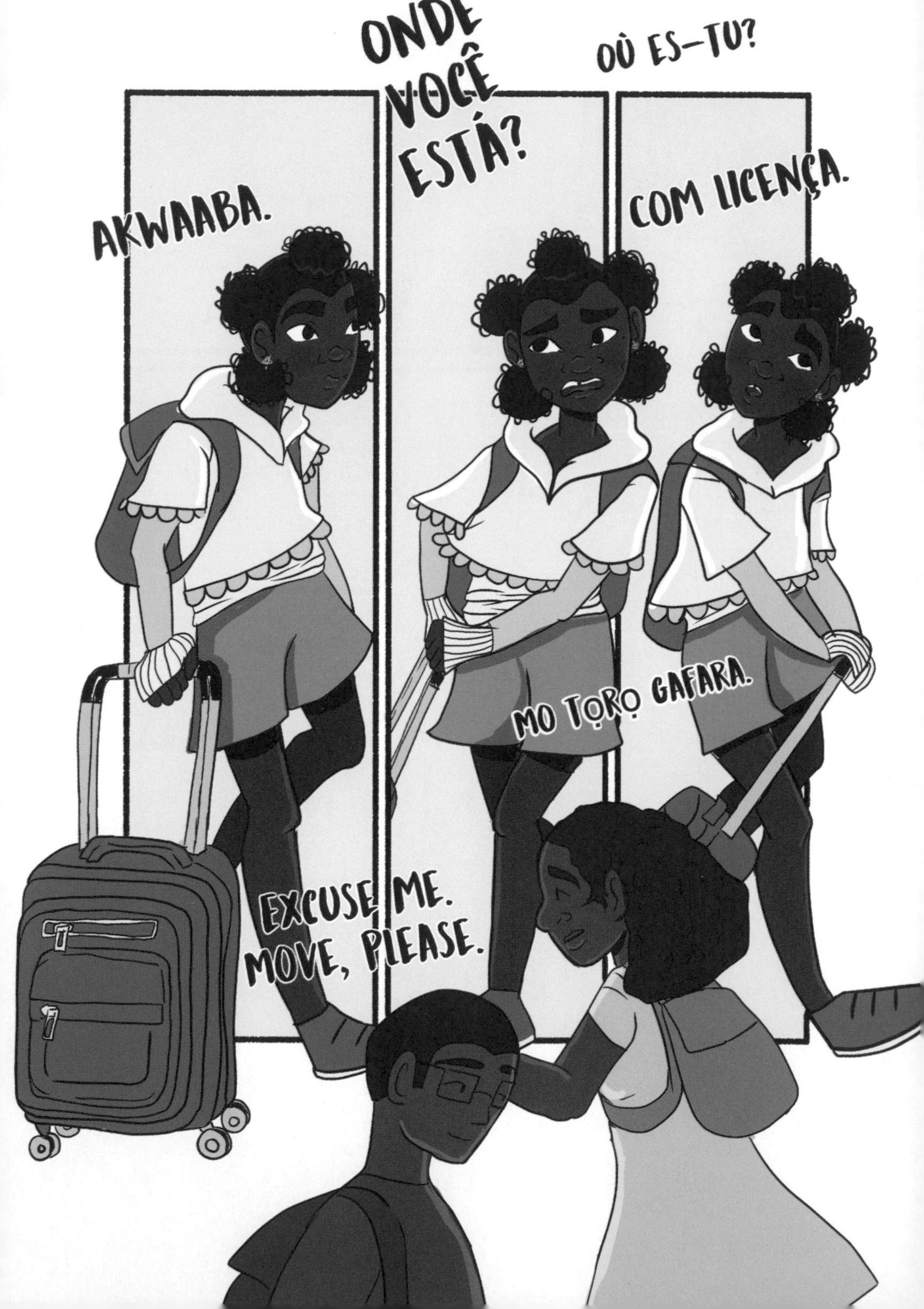
ONDE VOCÊ ESTÁ?
OÙ ES-TU?
AKWAABA.
COM LICENÇA.
MO TỌRỌ GAFARA.
EXCUSE ME. MOVE, PLEASE.

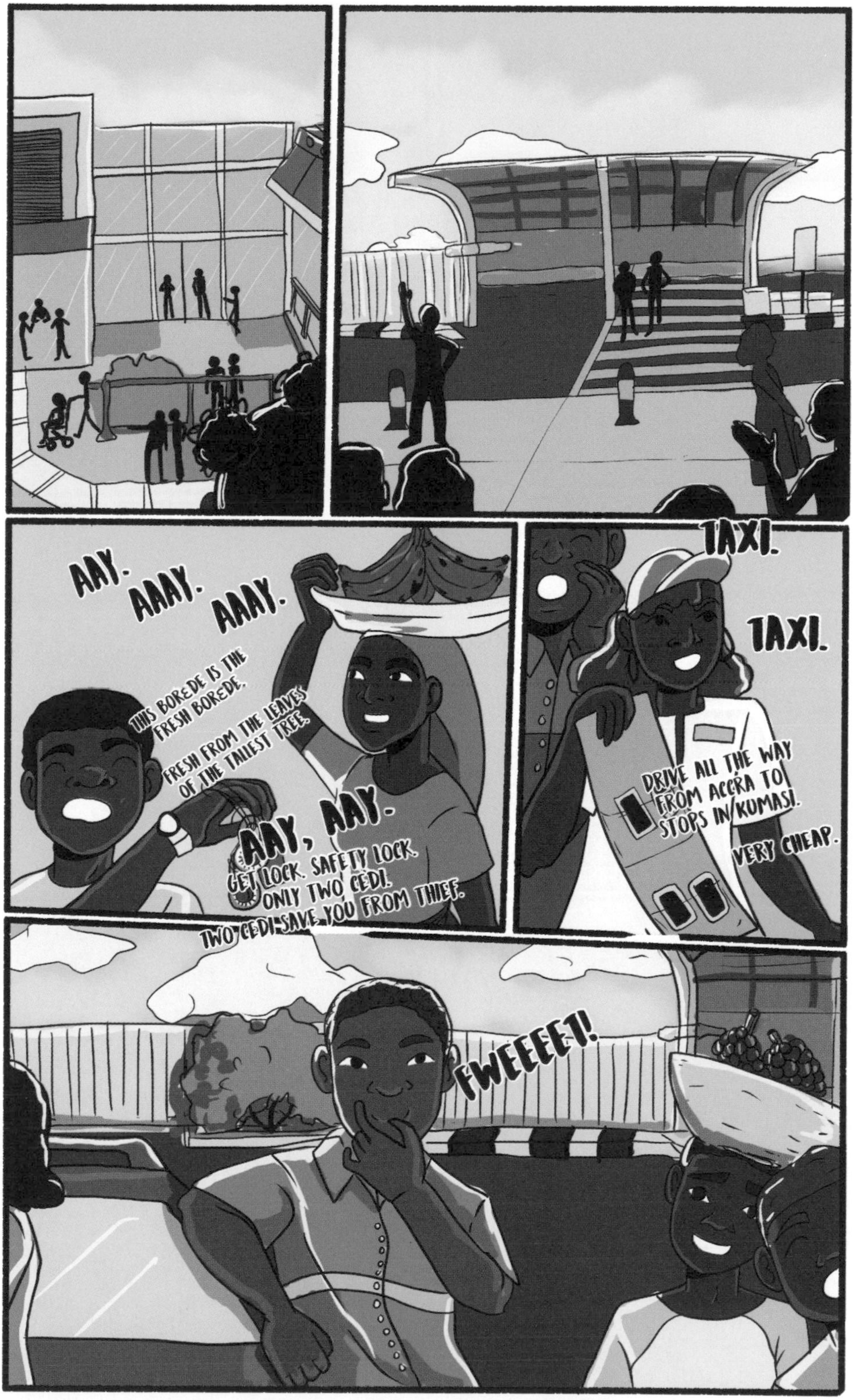
AAY.
AAAY.
AAAY.
THIS BOREDE IS THE FRESH BOREDE.
FRESH FROM THE LEAVES OF THE TALLEST TREE.
AAY, AAY.
GET LOCK. SAFETY LOCK. ONLY TWO CEDI.
TWO CEDI SAVE YOU FROM THIEF.
TAXI.
TAXI.
DRIVE ALL THE WAY FROM ACCRA TO STOPS IN KUMASI.
VERY CHEAP.
FWEEEET!

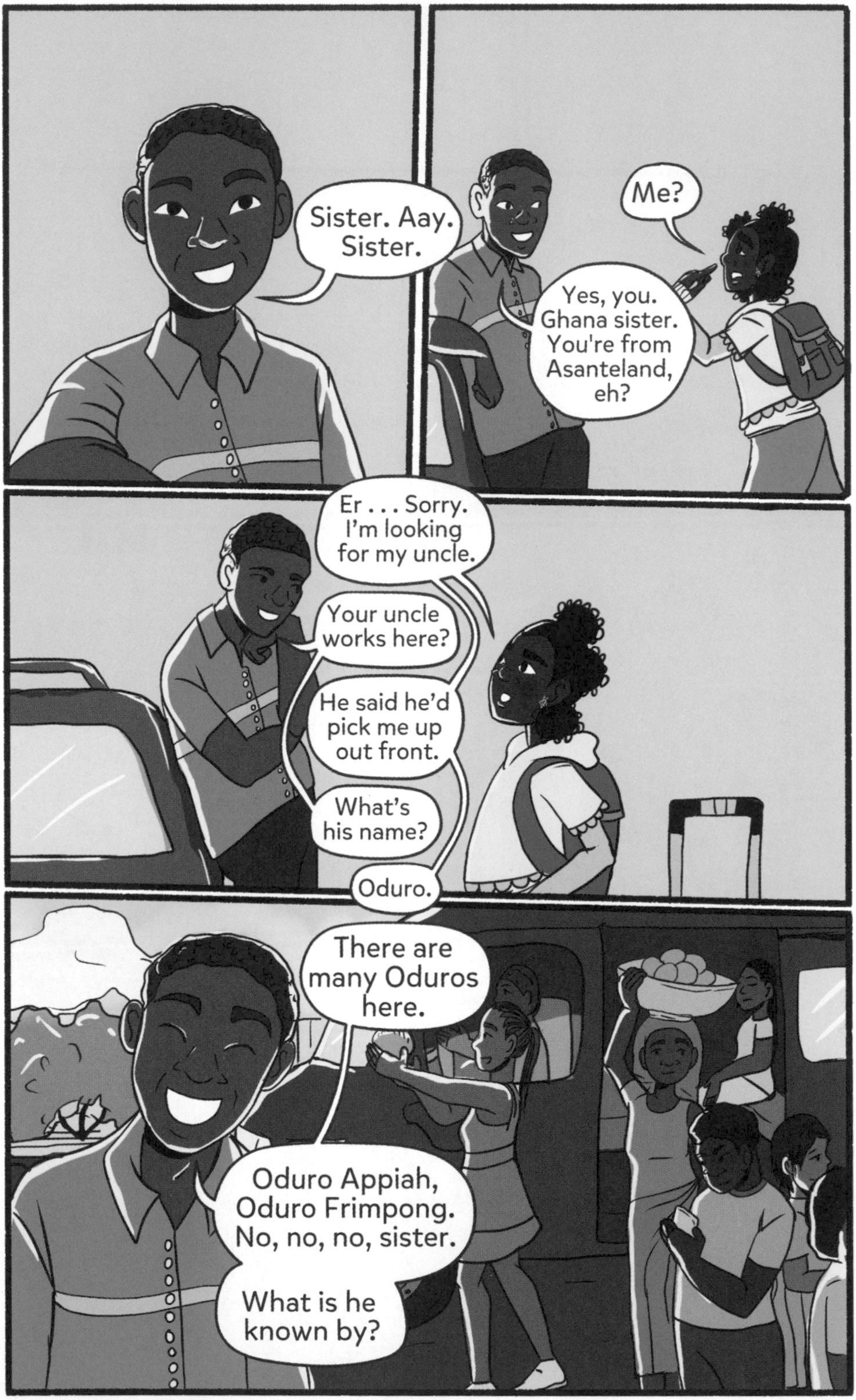

Sister. Aay. Sister.
Me?
Yes, you. Ghana sister. You're from Asanteland, eh?
Er . . . Sorry. I'm looking for my uncle.
Your uncle works here?
He said he'd pick me up out front.
What's his name?
Oduro.
There are many Oduros here.
Oduro Appiah, Oduro Frimpong. No, no, no, sister.
What is he known by?

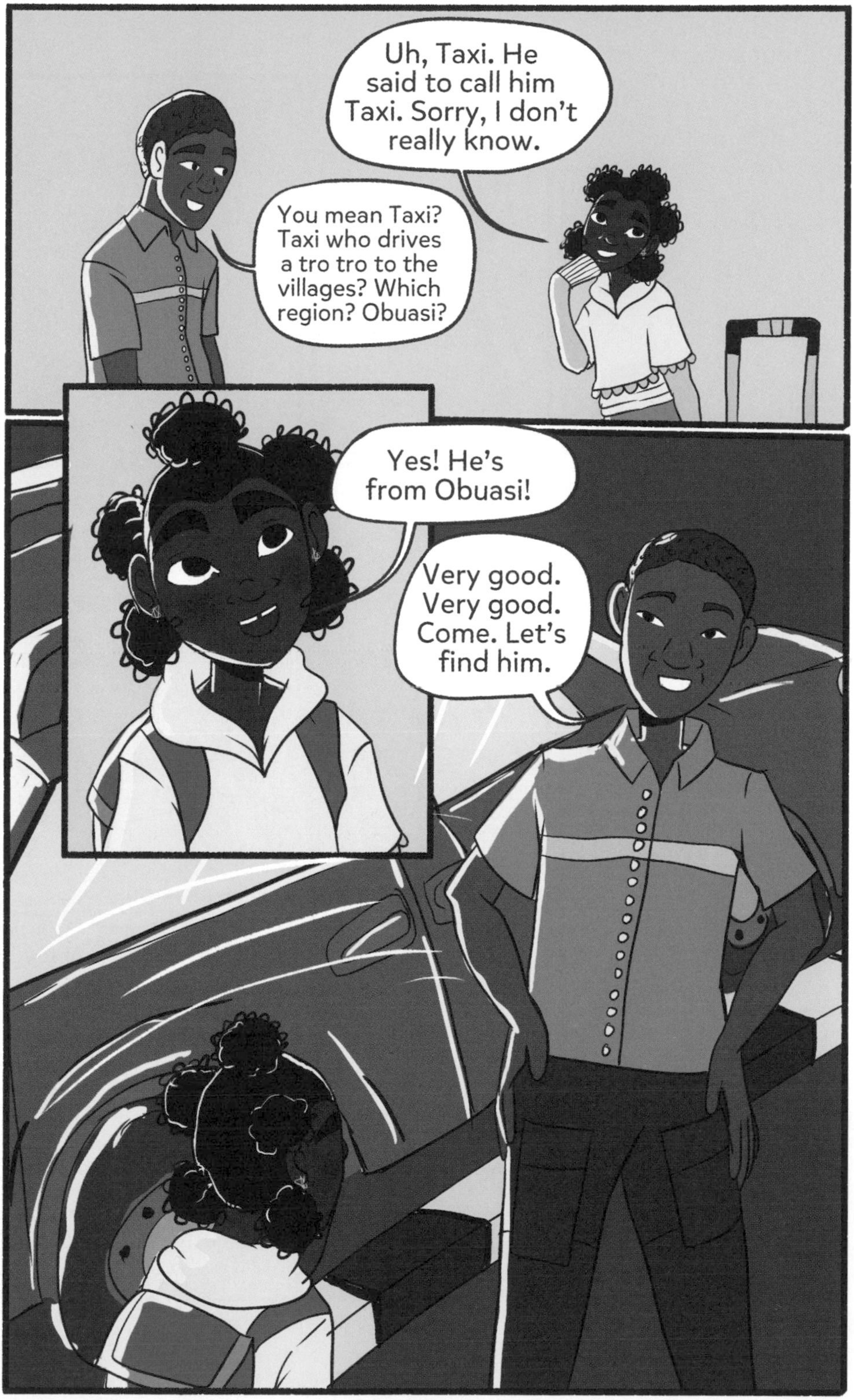
Uh, Taxi. He said to call him Taxi. Sorry, I don't really know.
You mean Taxi? Taxi who drives a tro tro to the villages? Which region? Obuasi?
Yes! He's from Obuasi!
Very good. Very good. Come. Let's find him.

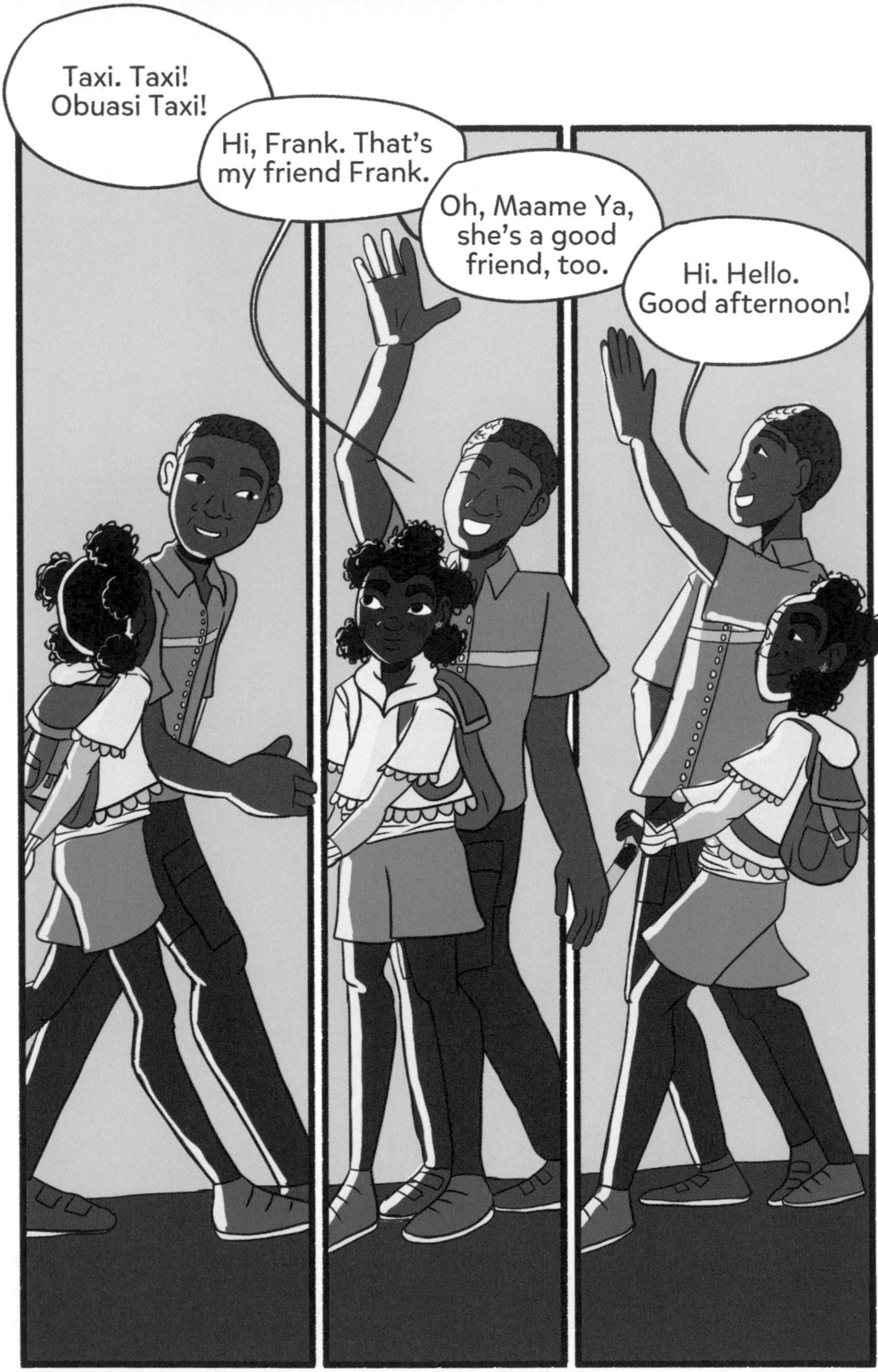
Taxi. Taxi! Obuasi Taxi!
Hi, Frank. That's my friend Frank.
Oh, Maame Ya, she's a good friend, too.
Hi. Hello. Good afternoon!

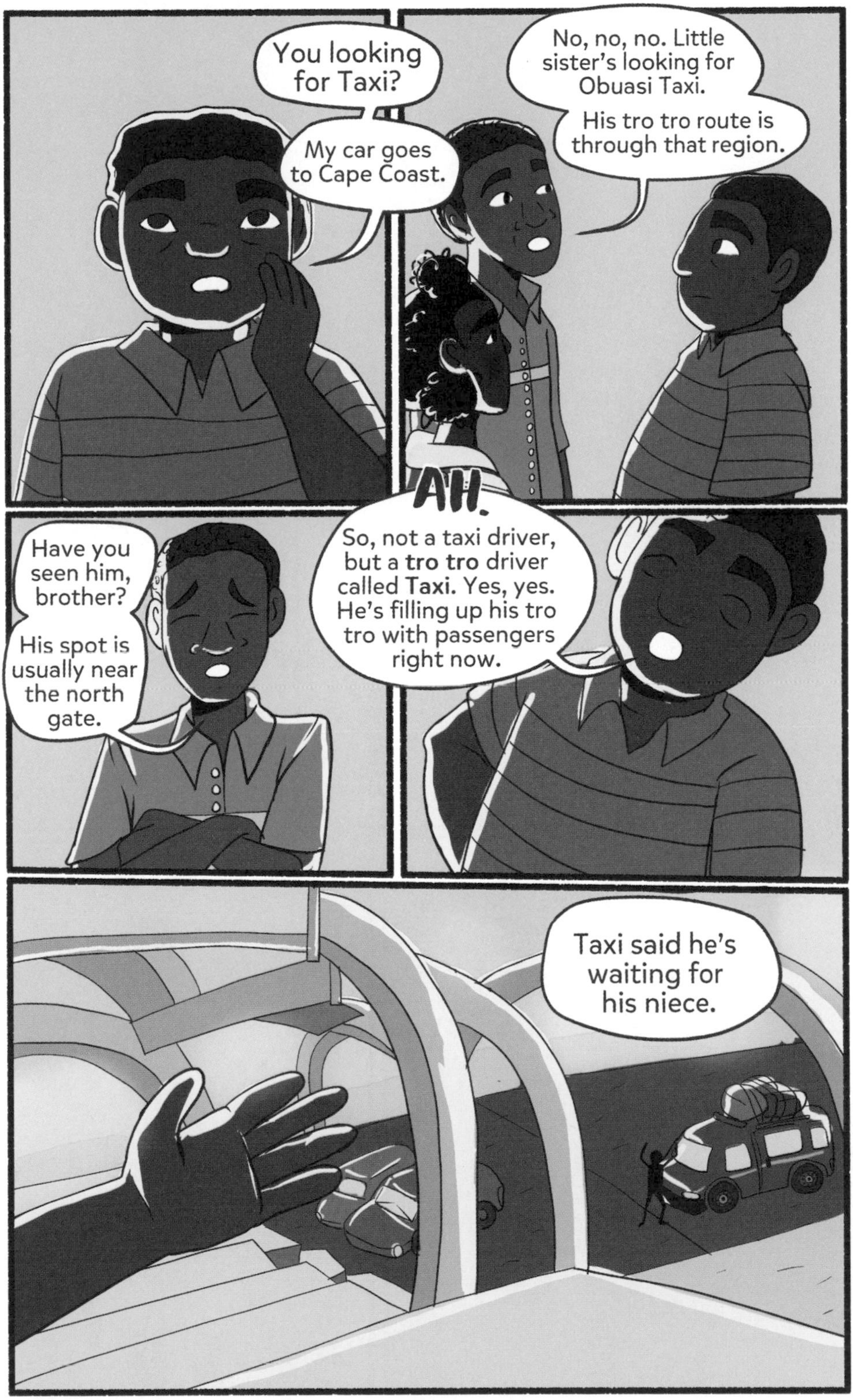
You looking for Taxi?
My car goes to Cape Coast.
No, no, no. Little sister's looking for Obuasi Taxi.
His tro tro route is through that region.
AH.
Have you seen him, brother?
His spot is usually near the north gate.
So, not a taxi driver, but a **tro tro** driver called **Taxi.** Yes, yes. He's filling up his tro tro with passengers right now.
Taxi said he's waiting for his niece.

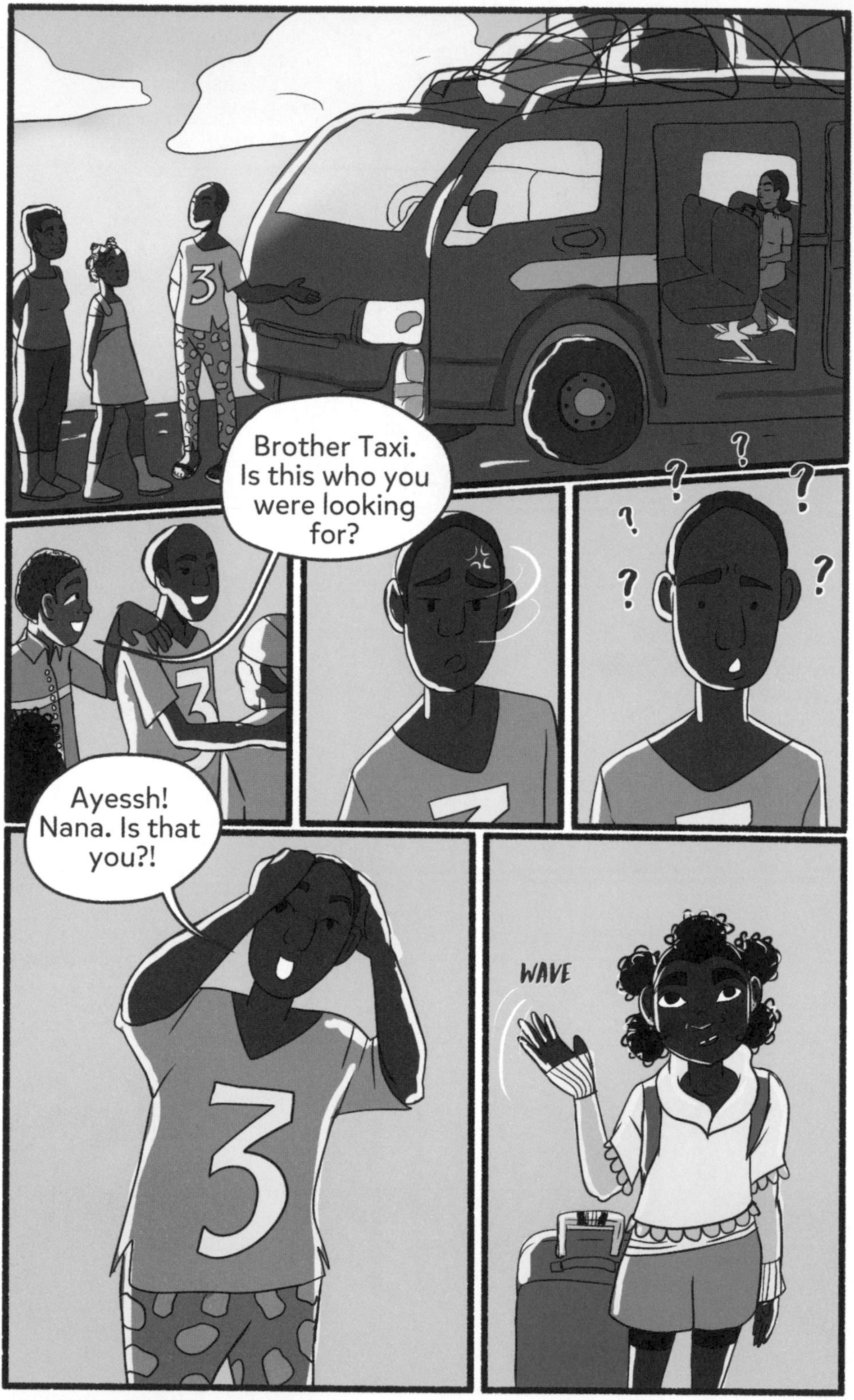

Brother Taxi. Is this who you were looking for?
Ayessh! Nana. Is that you?!
WAVE

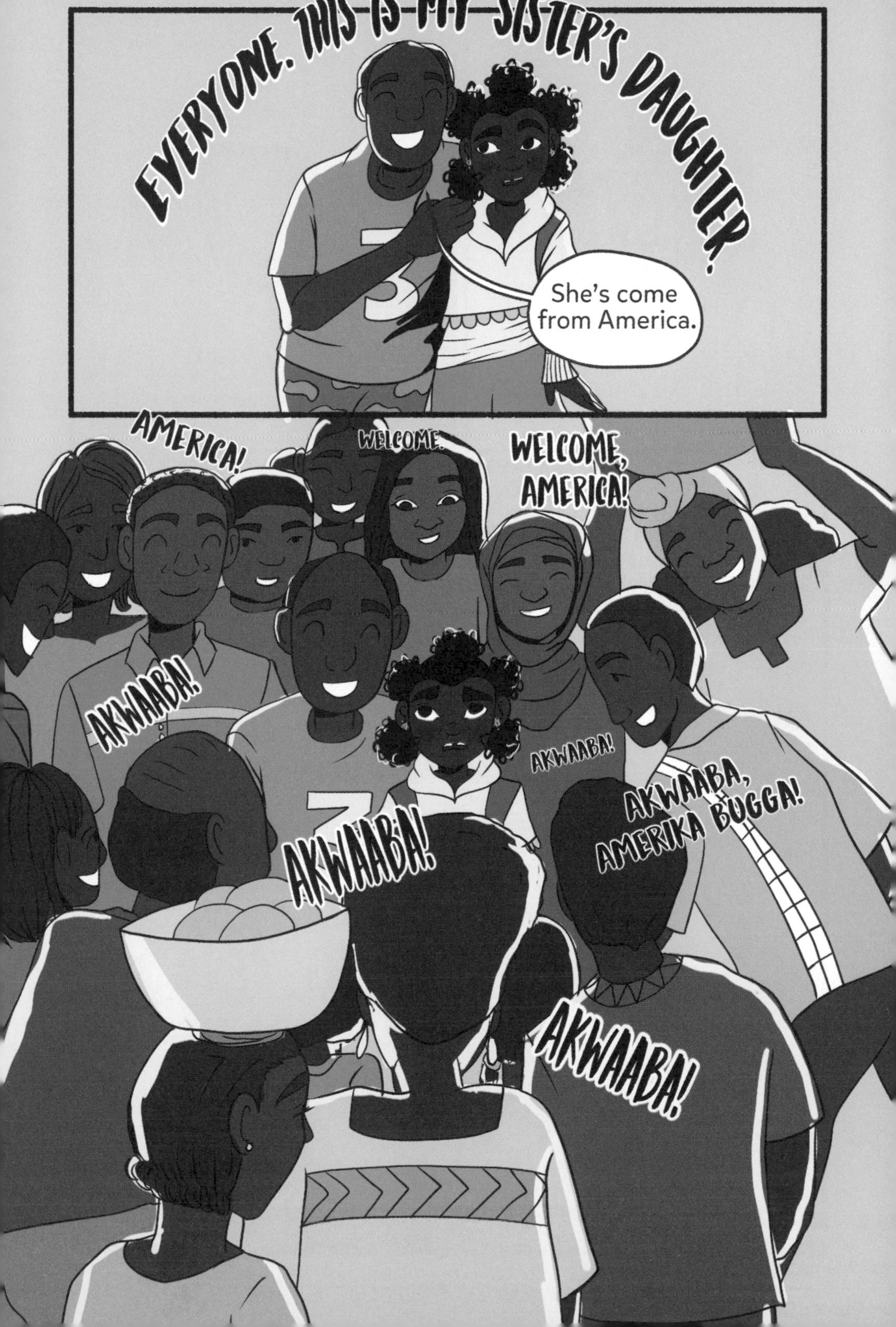
EVERYONE. THIS IS MY SISTER'S DAUGHTER.
She's come from America.
AMERICA!
WELCOME.
WELCOME, AMERICA!
AKWAABA!
AKWAABA!
AKWAABA, AMERIKA BUGGA!
AKWAABA!
AKWAABA!

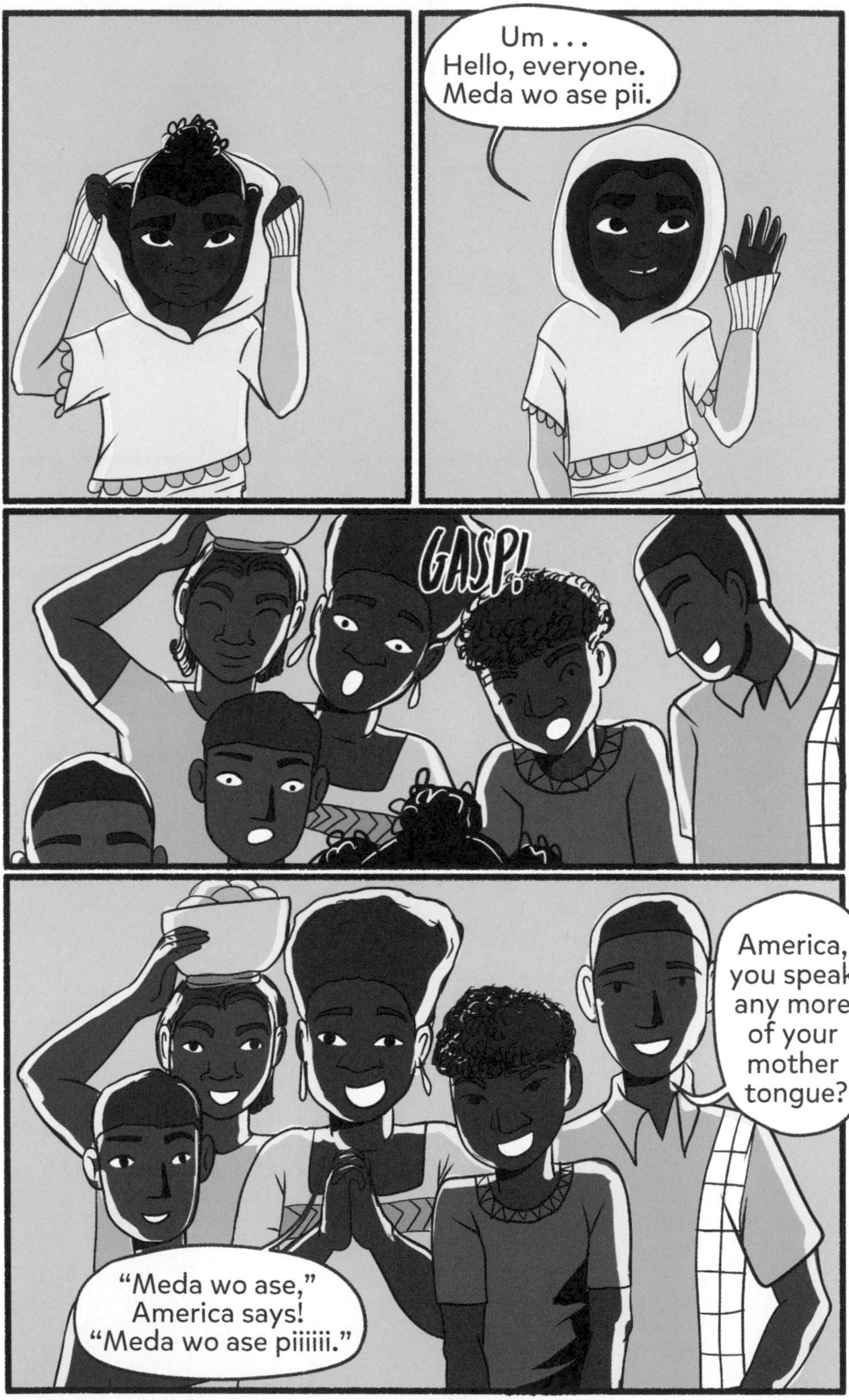
Um . . .
Hello, everyone.
Meda wo ase pii.
GASP!
America, you speak any more of your mother tongue?
"Meda wo ase," America says! "Meda wo ase piiiiii."

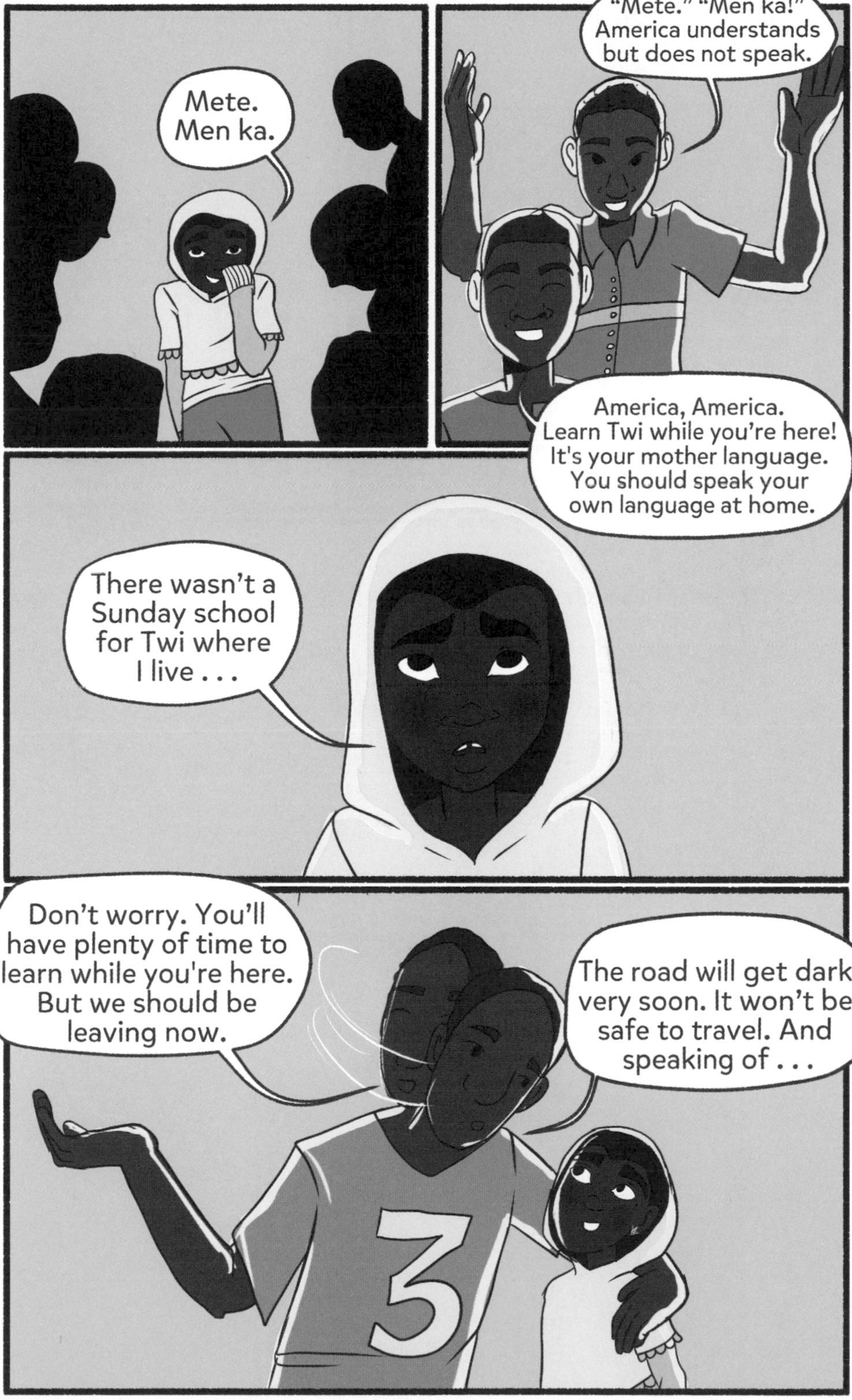
Mete.
Men ka.
"Mete." "Men ka!" America understands but does not speak.
America, America. Learn Twi while you're here! It's your mother language. You should speak your own language at home.
There wasn't a Sunday school for Twi where I live . . .
Don't worry. You'll have plenty of time to learn while you're here. But we should be leaving now.
The road will get dark very soon. It won't be safe to travel. And speaking of . . .
3

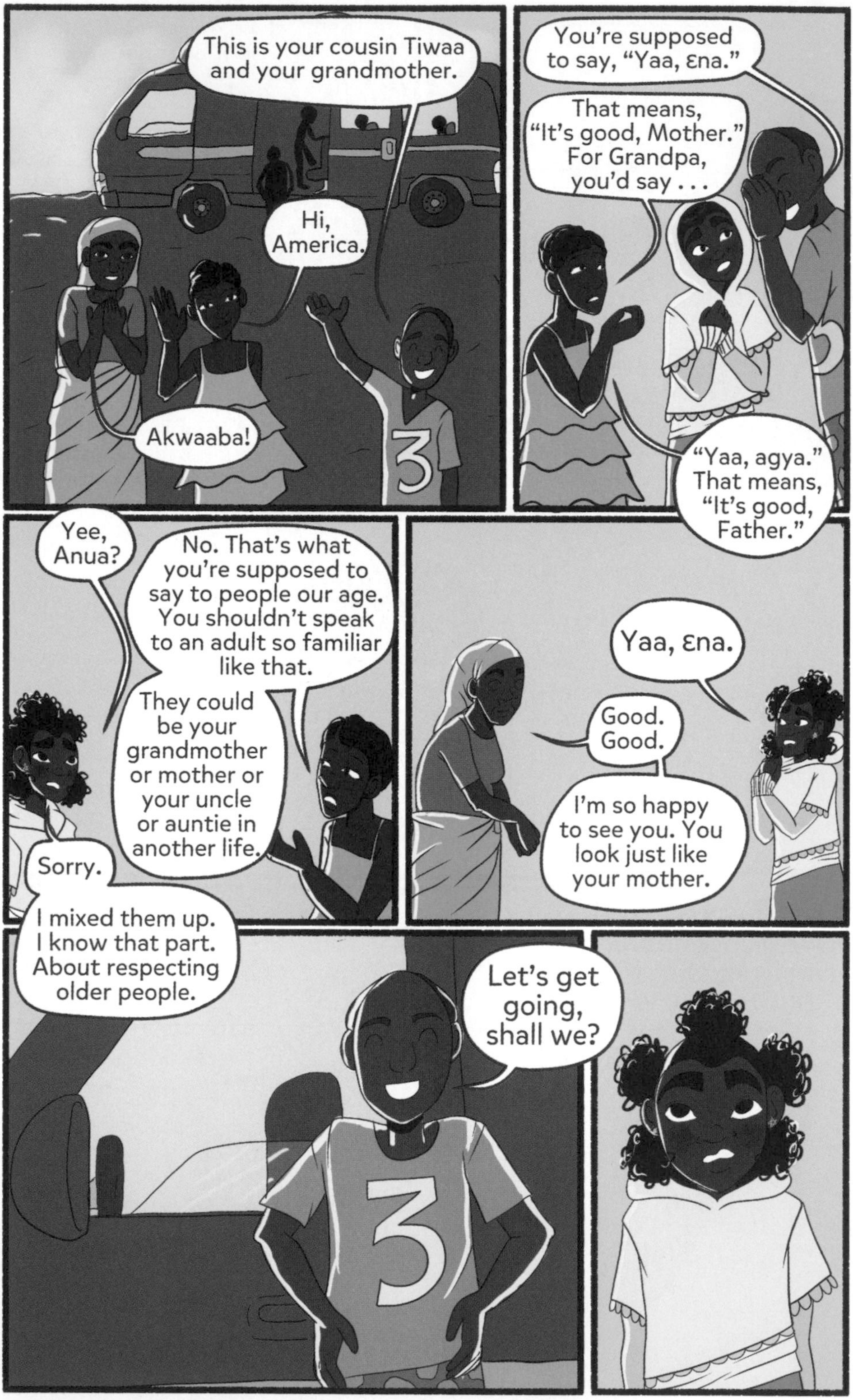
This is your cousin Tiwaa and your grandmother.
Hi, America.
Akwaaba!
You're supposed to say, "Yaa, ɛna."
That means, "It's good, Mother." For Grandpa, you'd say . . .
"Yaa, agya." That means, "It's good, Father."
Yee, Anua?
No. That's what you're supposed to say to people our age. You shouldn't speak to an adult so familiar like that.
They could be your grandmother or mother or your uncle or auntie in another life.
Sorry.
I mixed them up. I know that part. About respecting older people.
Yaa, ɛna.
Good. Good.
I'm so happy to see you. You look just like your mother.
Let's get going, shall we?

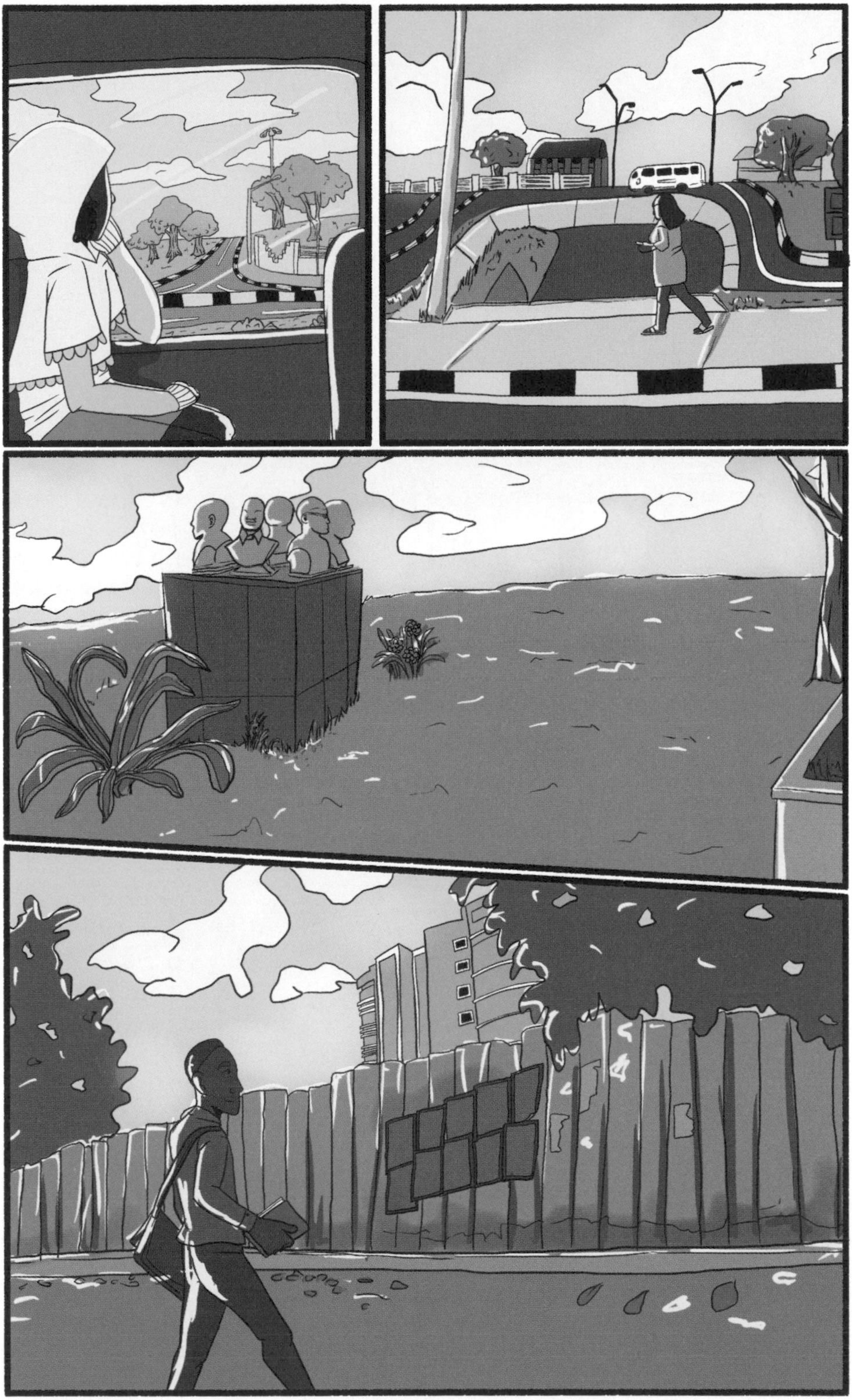

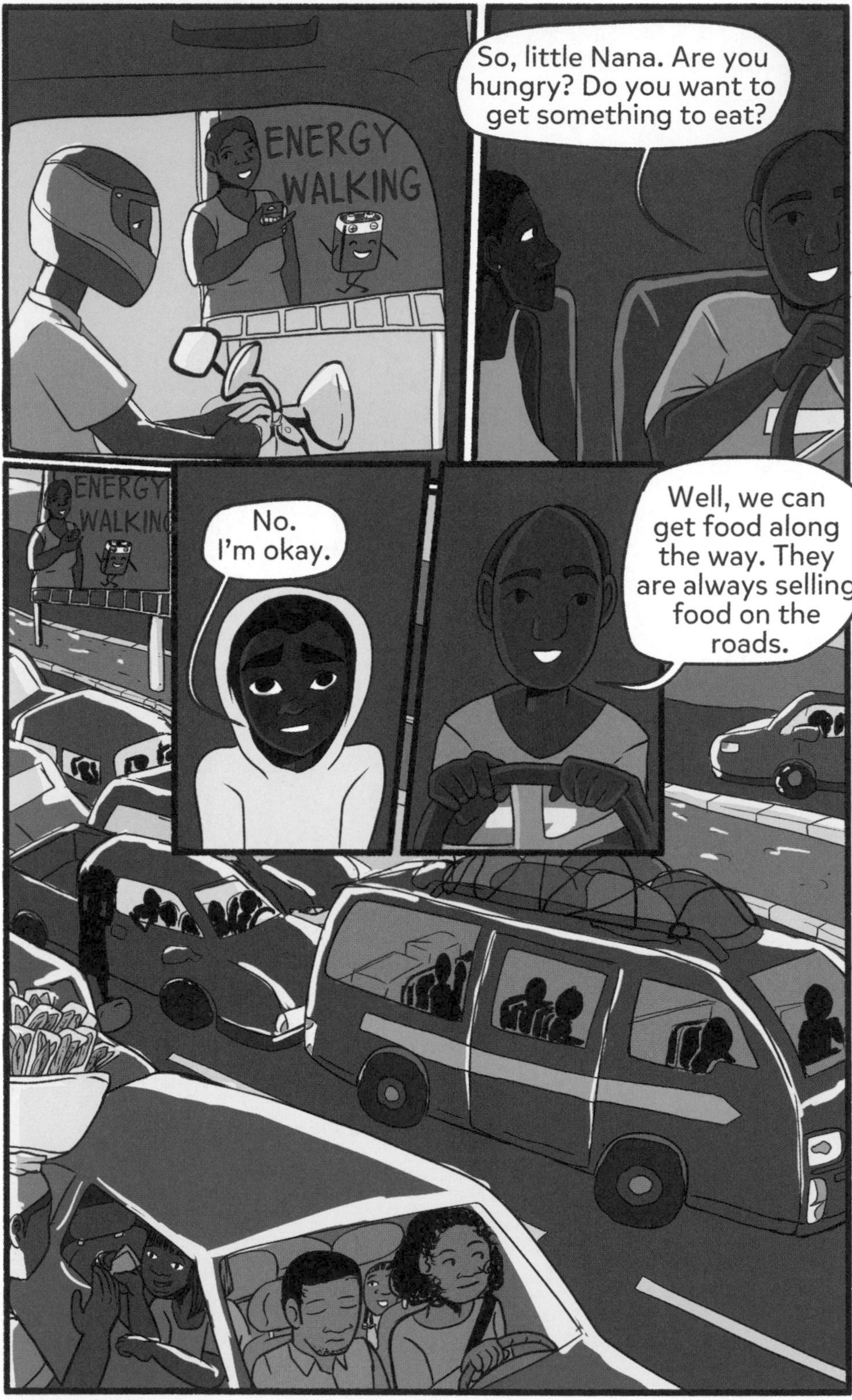
ENERGY
WALKING
So, little Nana. Are you hungry? Do you want to get something to eat?
ENERGY
WALKING
No. I'm okay.
Well, we can get food along the way. They are always selling food on the roads.

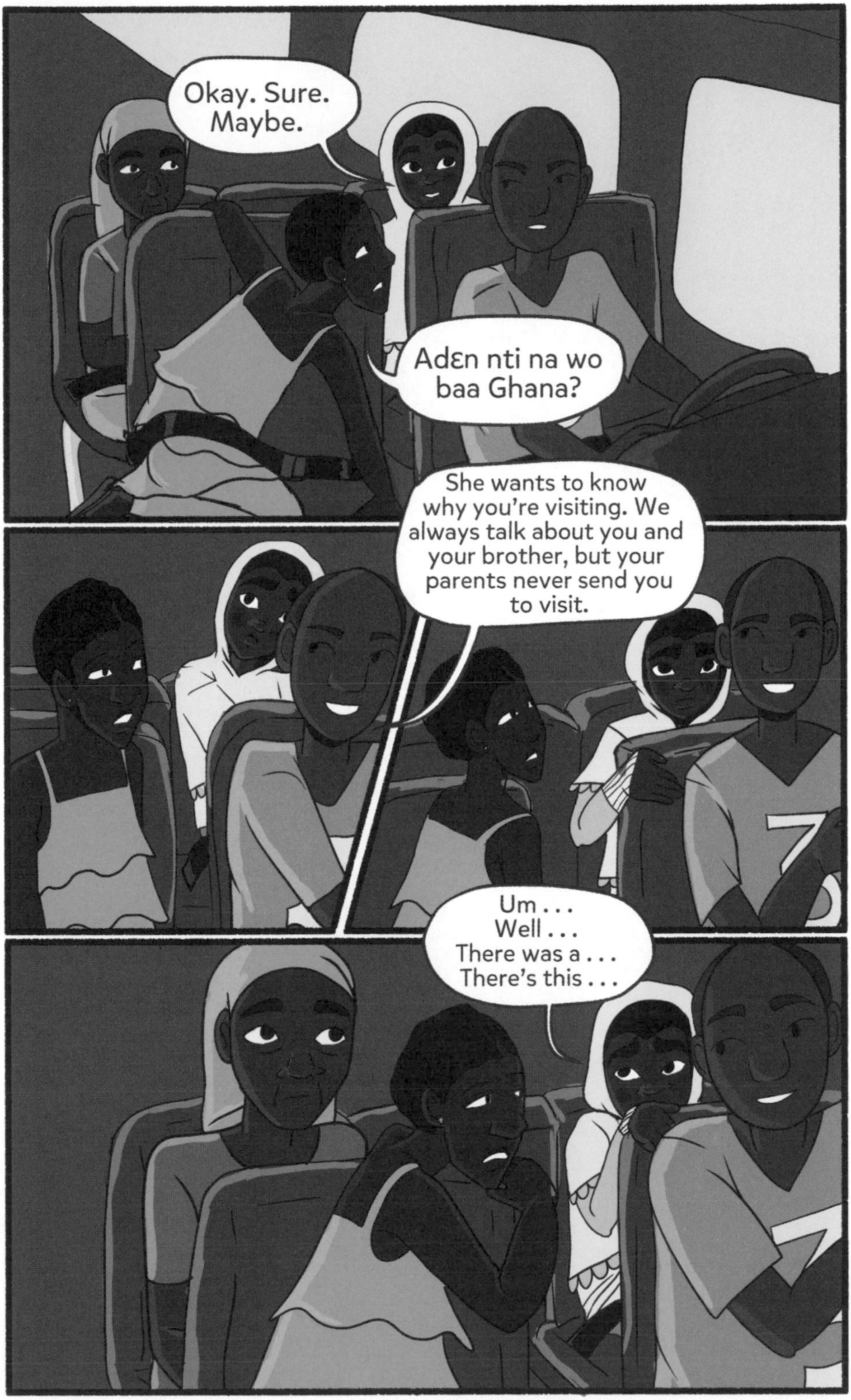
Okay. Sure. Maybe.
Adɛn nti na wo baa Ghana?
She wants to know why you're visiting. We always talk about you and your brother, but your parents never send you to visit.
Um . . . Well . . . There was a . . . There's this . . .

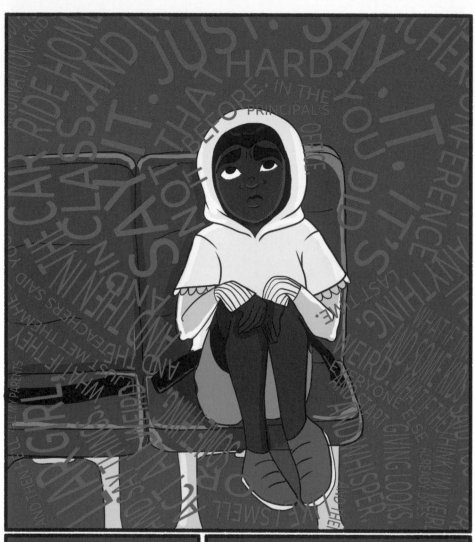

I don't feel like talking.

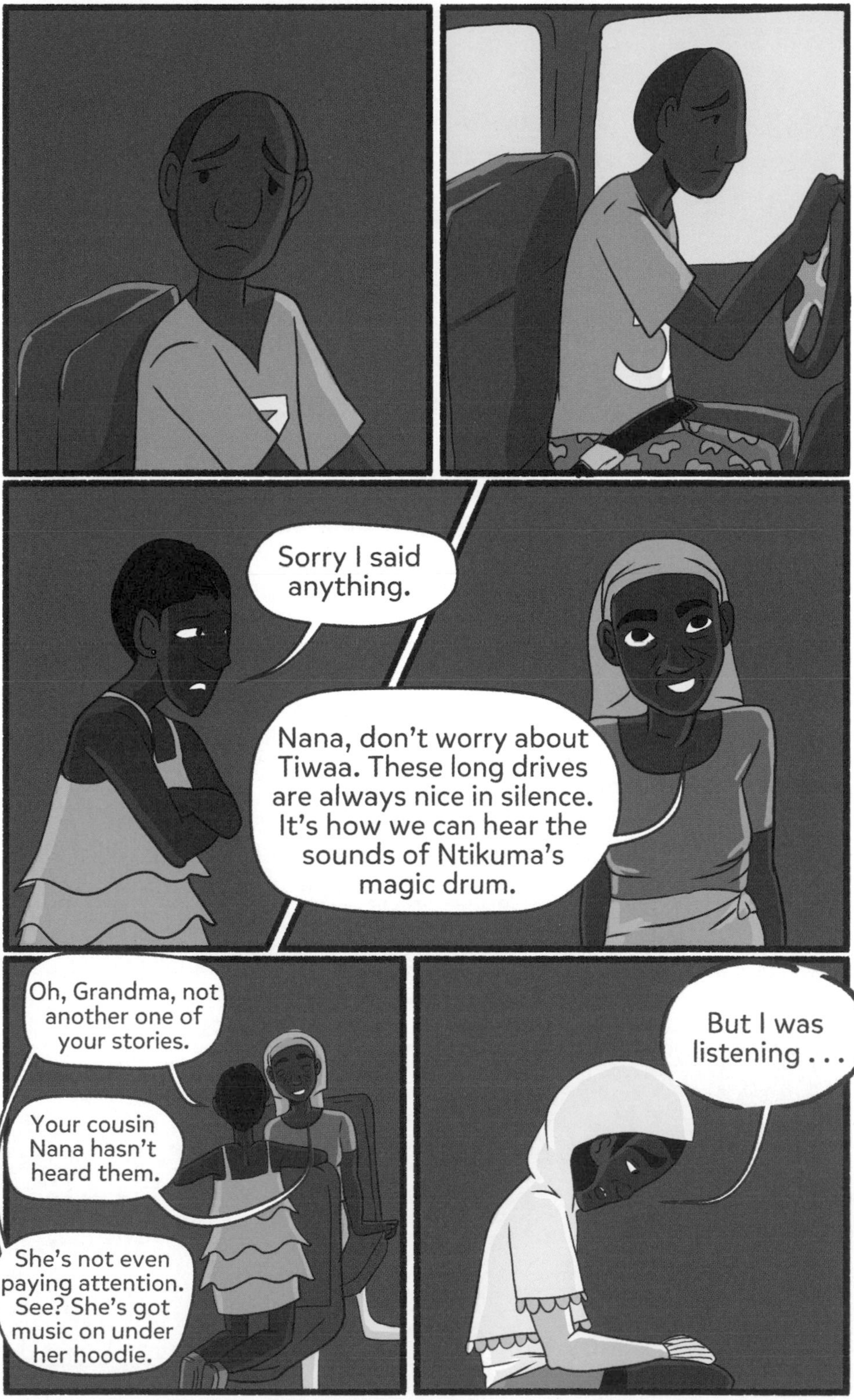
Sorry I said anything.
Nana, don't worry about Tiwaa. These long drives are always nice in silence. It's how we can hear the sounds of Ntikuma's magic drum.
Oh, Grandma, not another one of your stories.
Your cousin Nana hasn't heard them.
She's not even paying attention. See? She's got music on under her hoodie.
But I was listening . . .

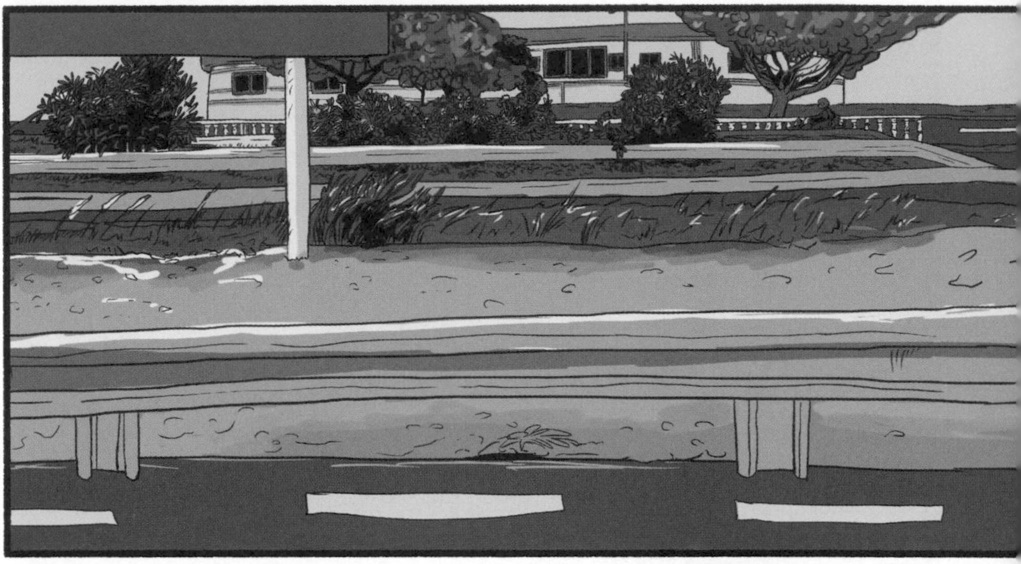

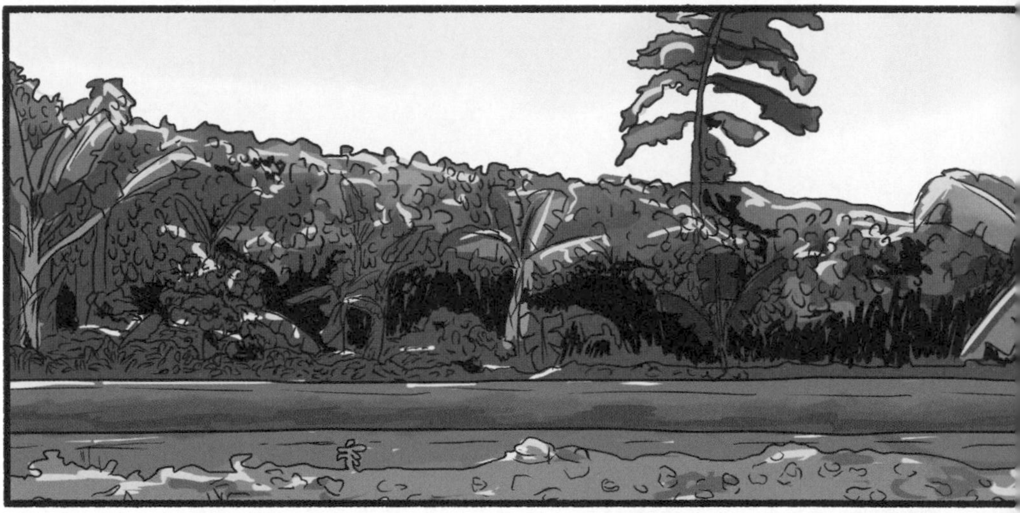

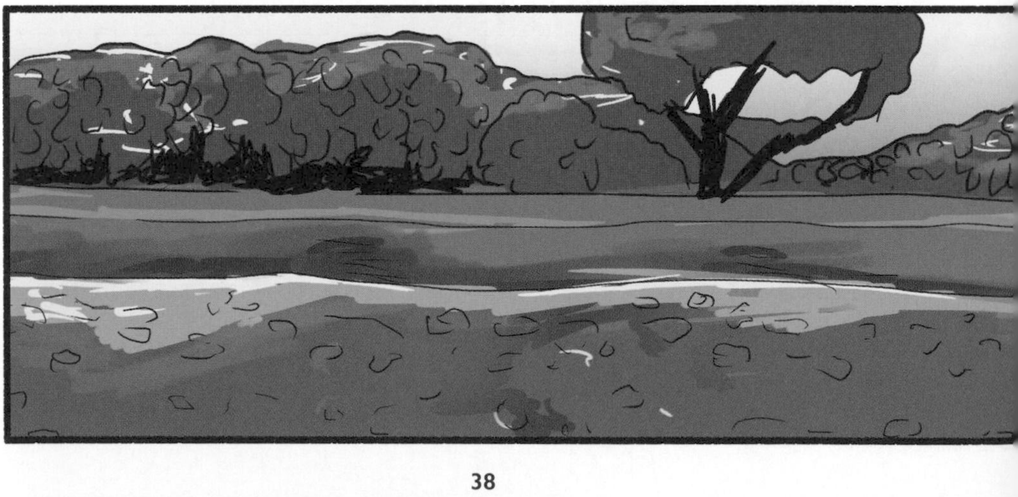

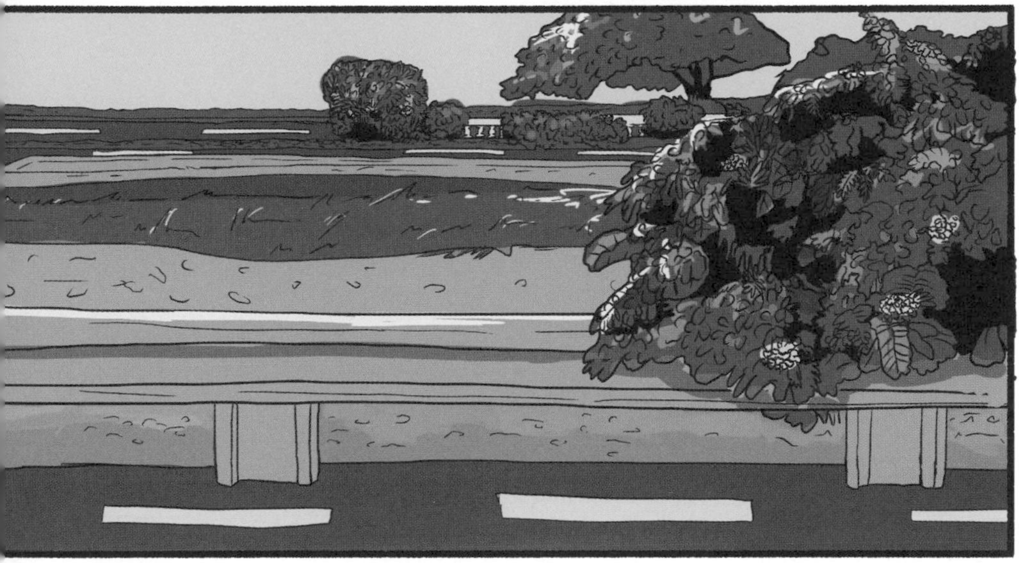

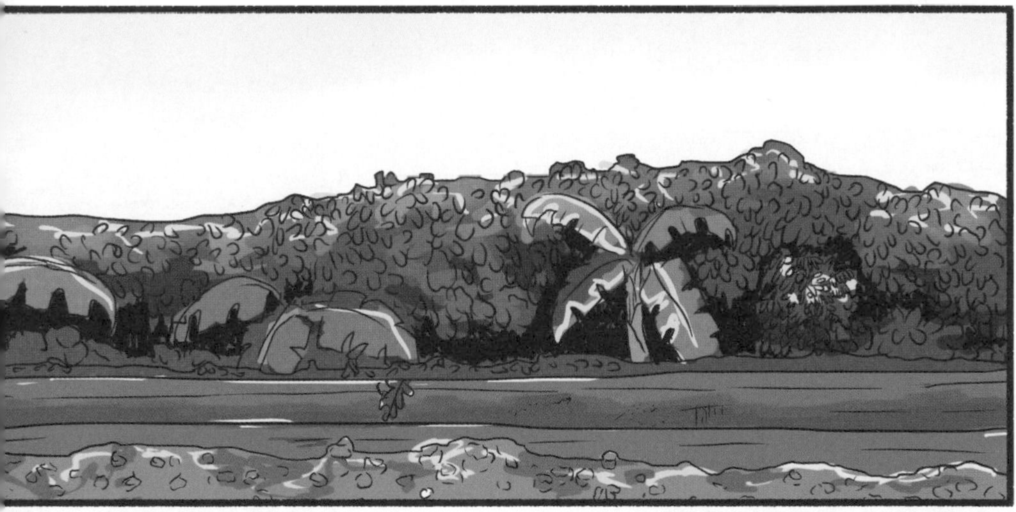

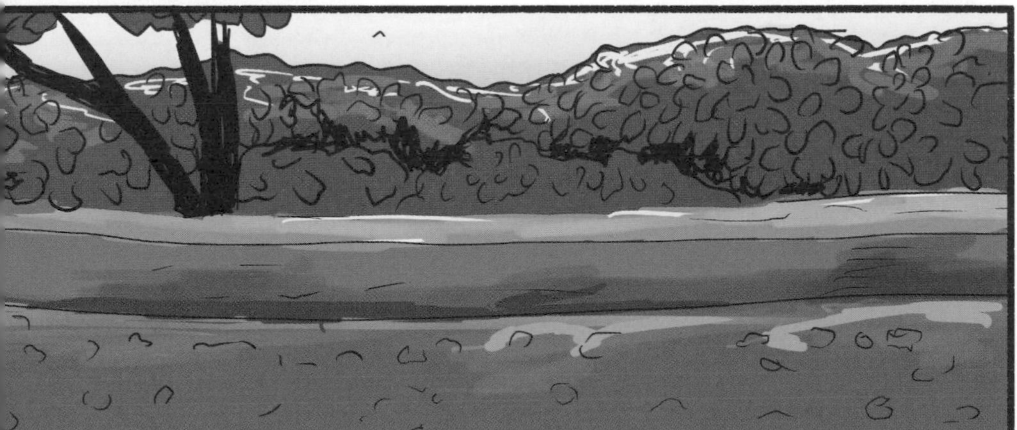

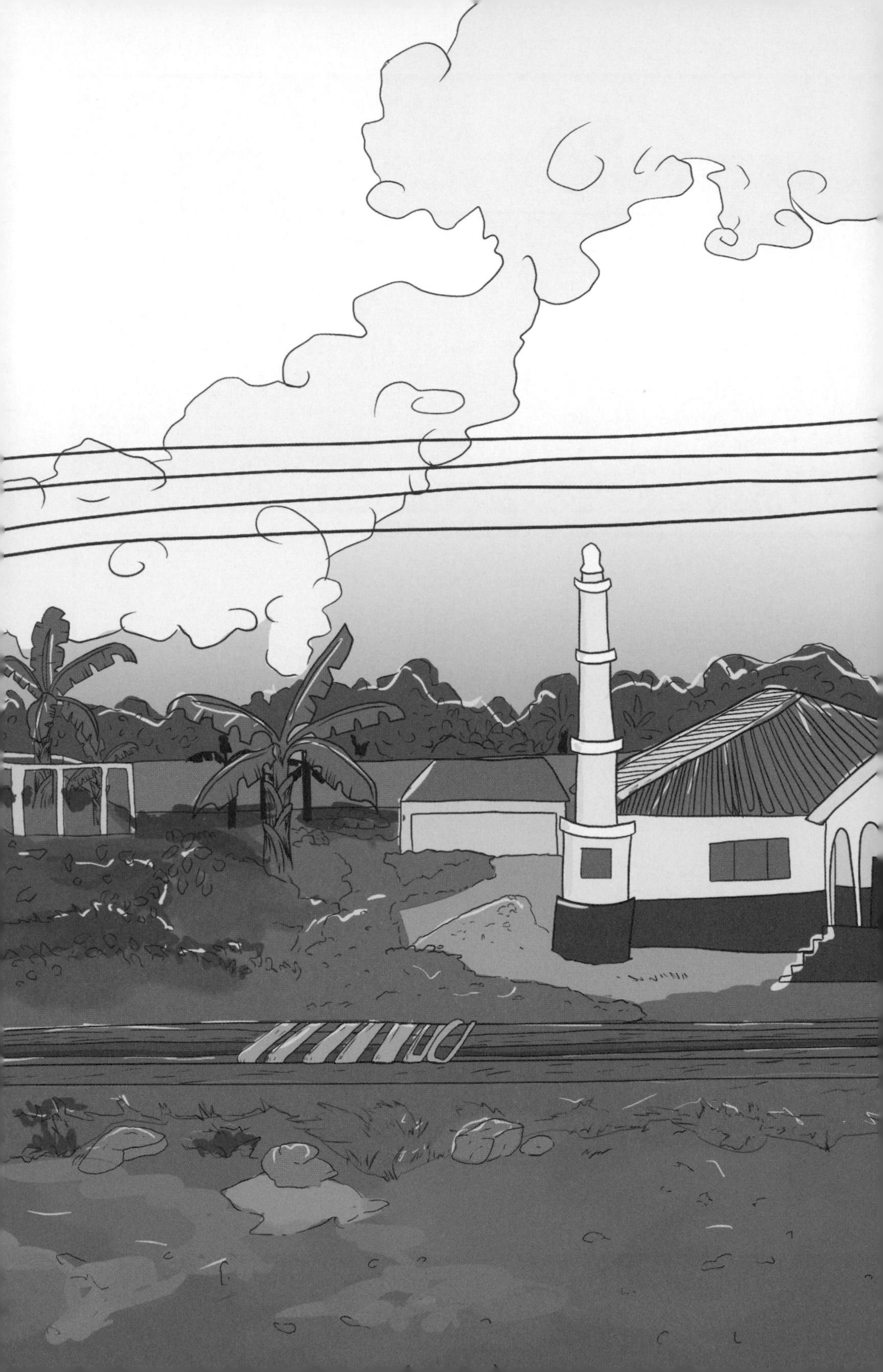

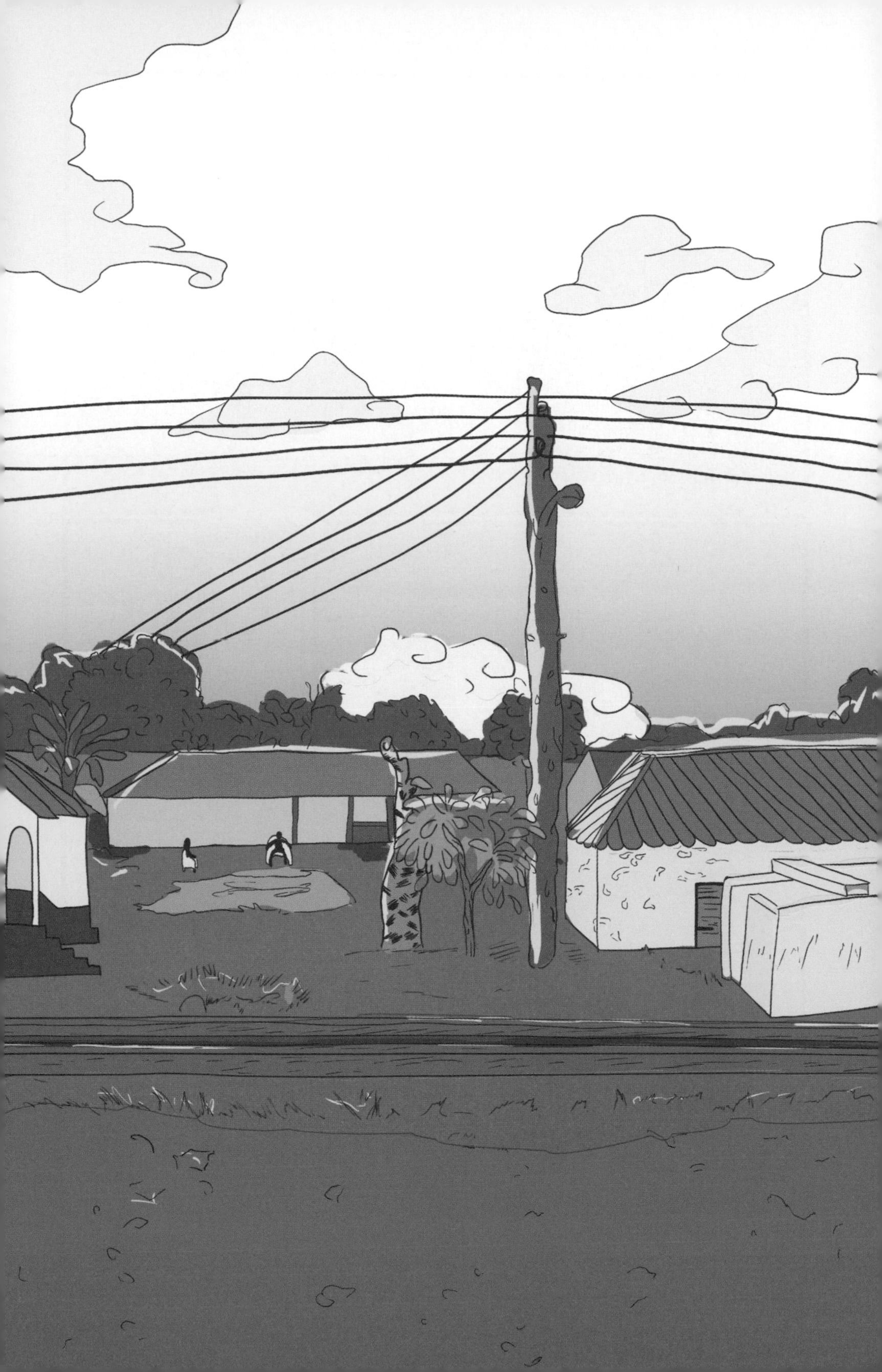

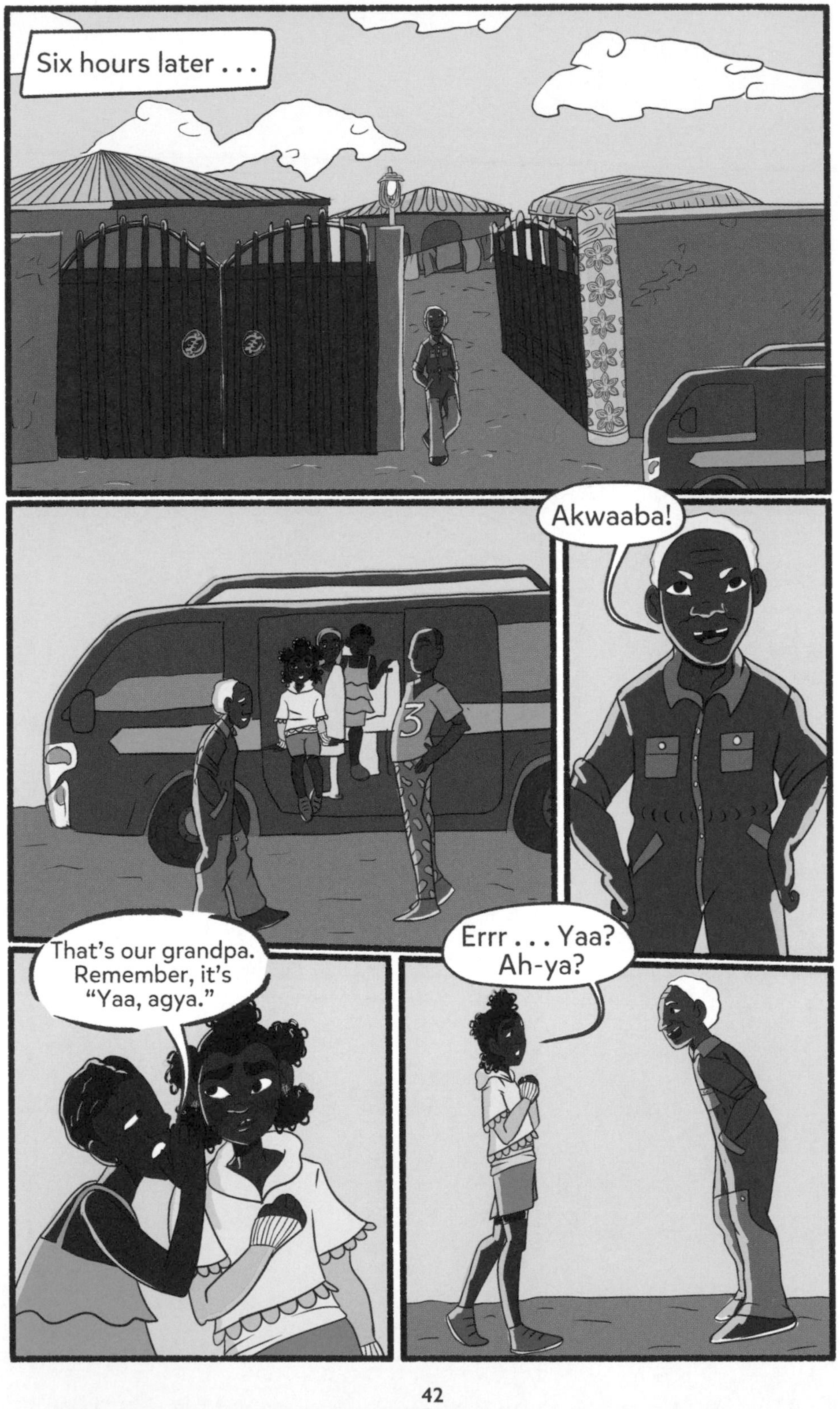
Six hours later . . .
Akwaaba!
That's our grandpa. Remember, it's "Yaa, agya."
Errr . . . Yaa? Ah-ya?

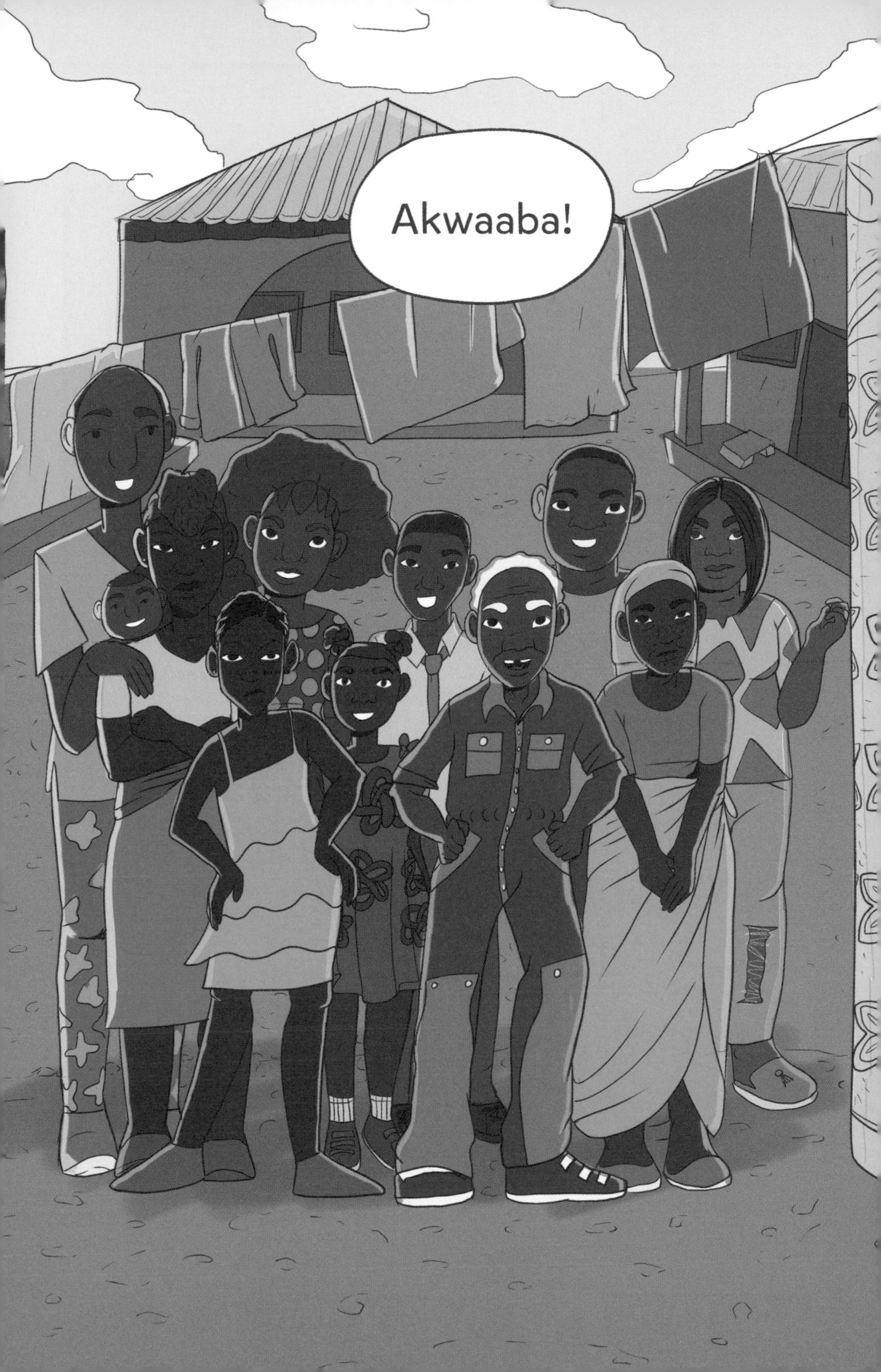
Akwaaba!

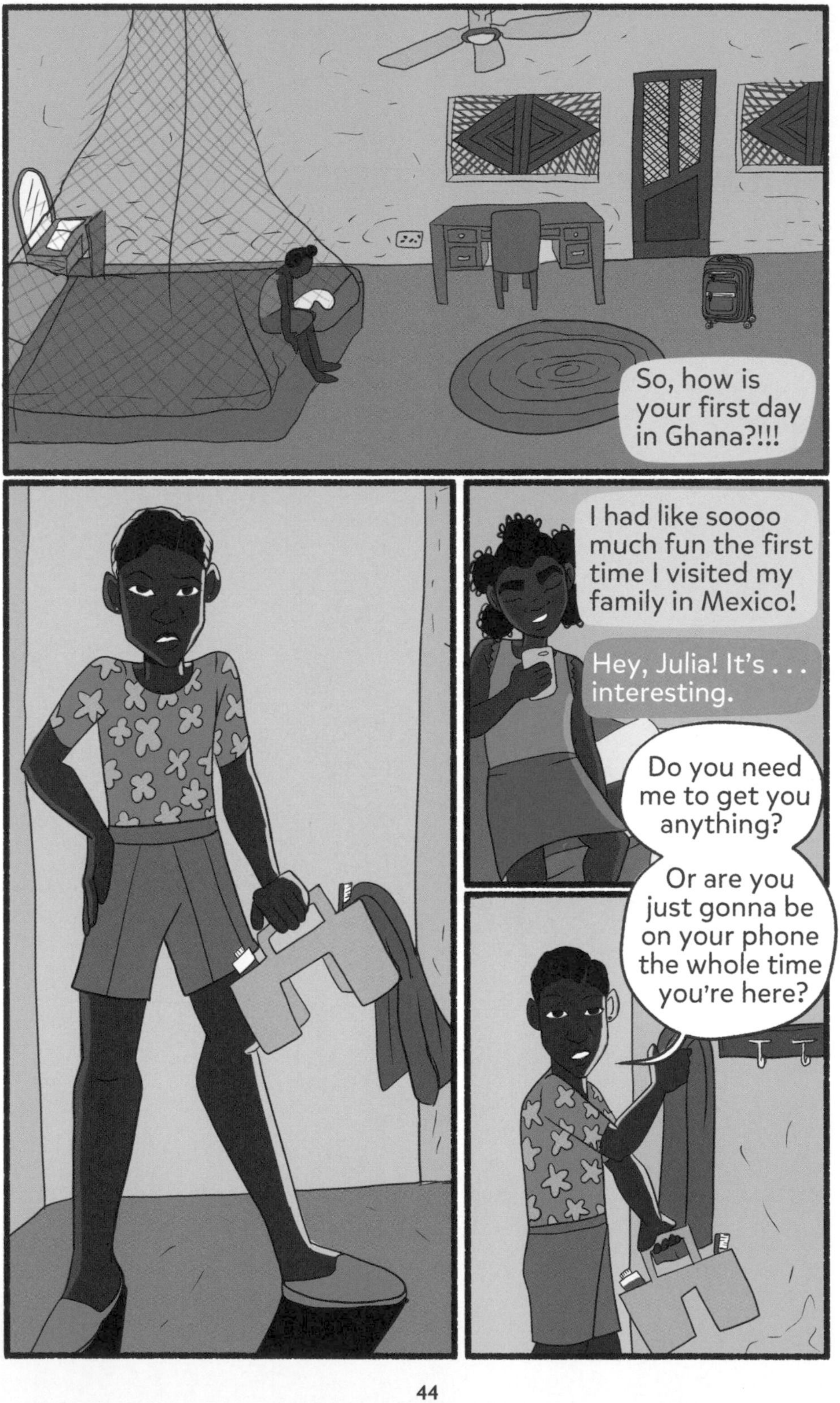
So, how is your first day in Ghana?!!!
I had like soooo much fun the first time I visited my family in Mexico!
Hey, Julia! It's . . . interesting.
Do you need me to get you anything?
Or are you just gonna be on your phone the whole time you're here?

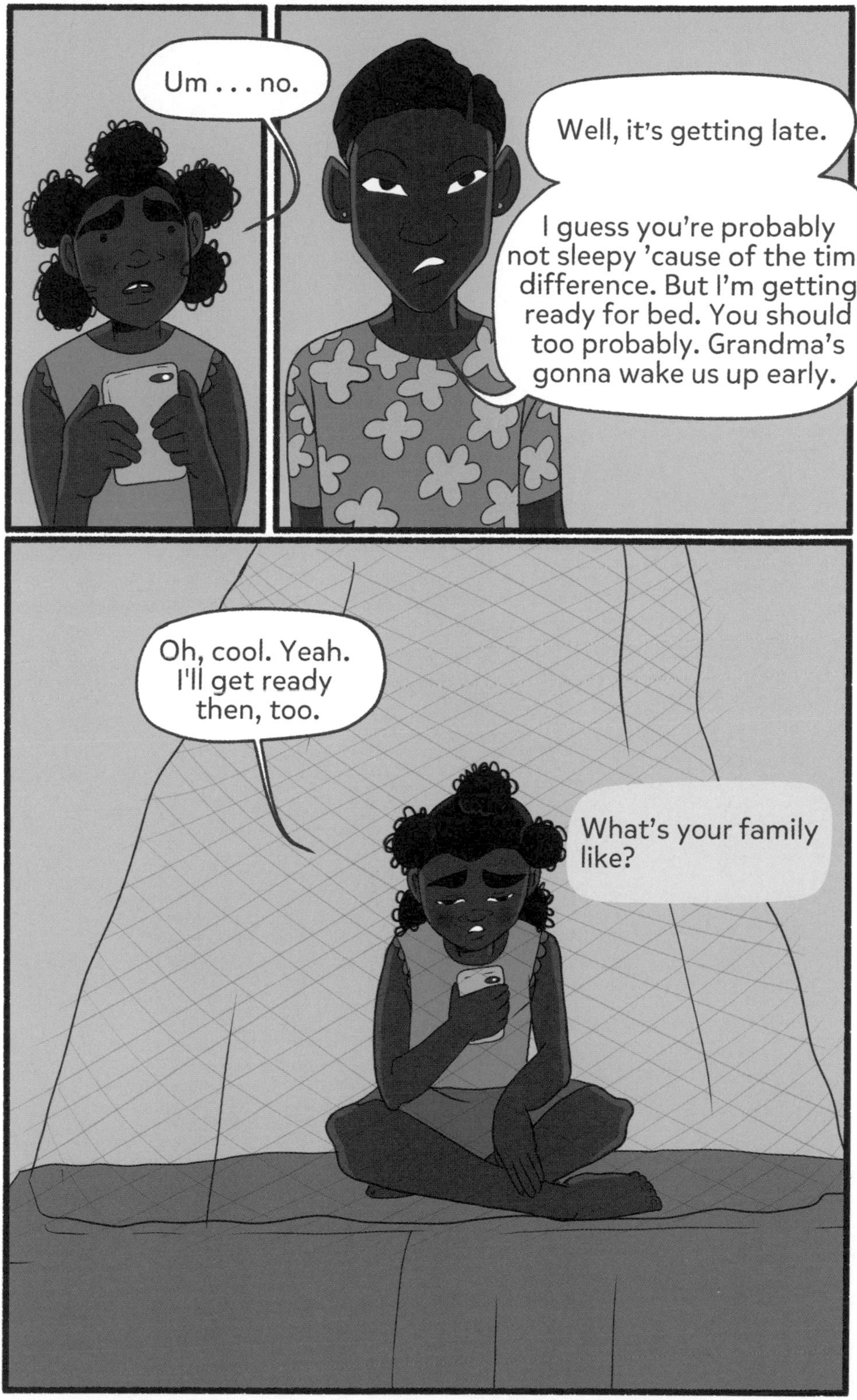
Um . . . no.
Well, it's getting late.
I guess you're probably not sleepy 'cause of the time difference. But I'm getting ready for bed. You should too probably. Grandma's gonna wake us up early.
Oh, cool. Yeah. I'll get ready then, too.
What's your family like?

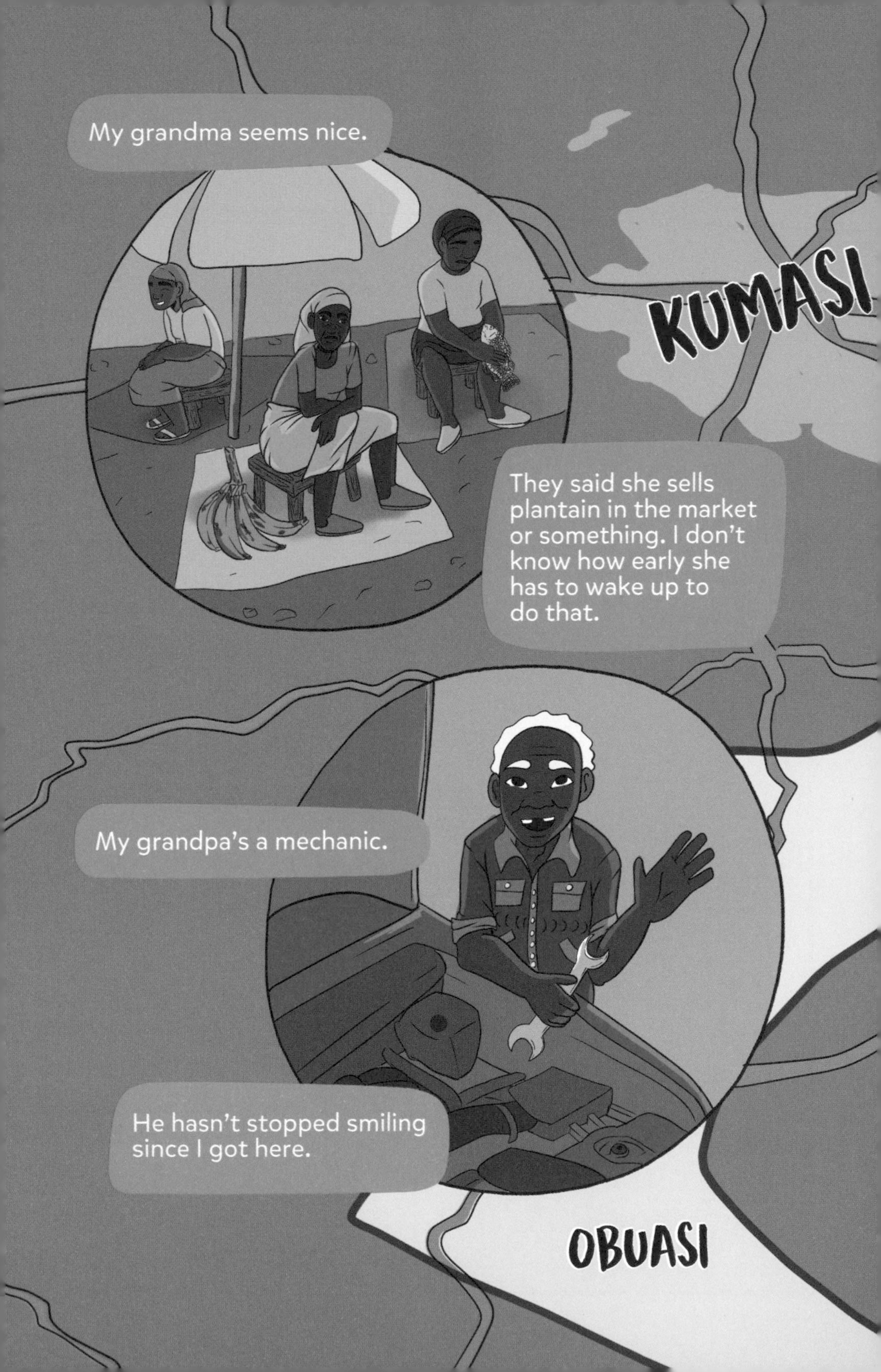
My grandma seems nice.
KUMASI
They said she sells plantain in the market or something. I don't know how early she has to wake up to do that.
My grandpa's a mechanic.
He hasn't stopped smiling since I got here.
OBUASI

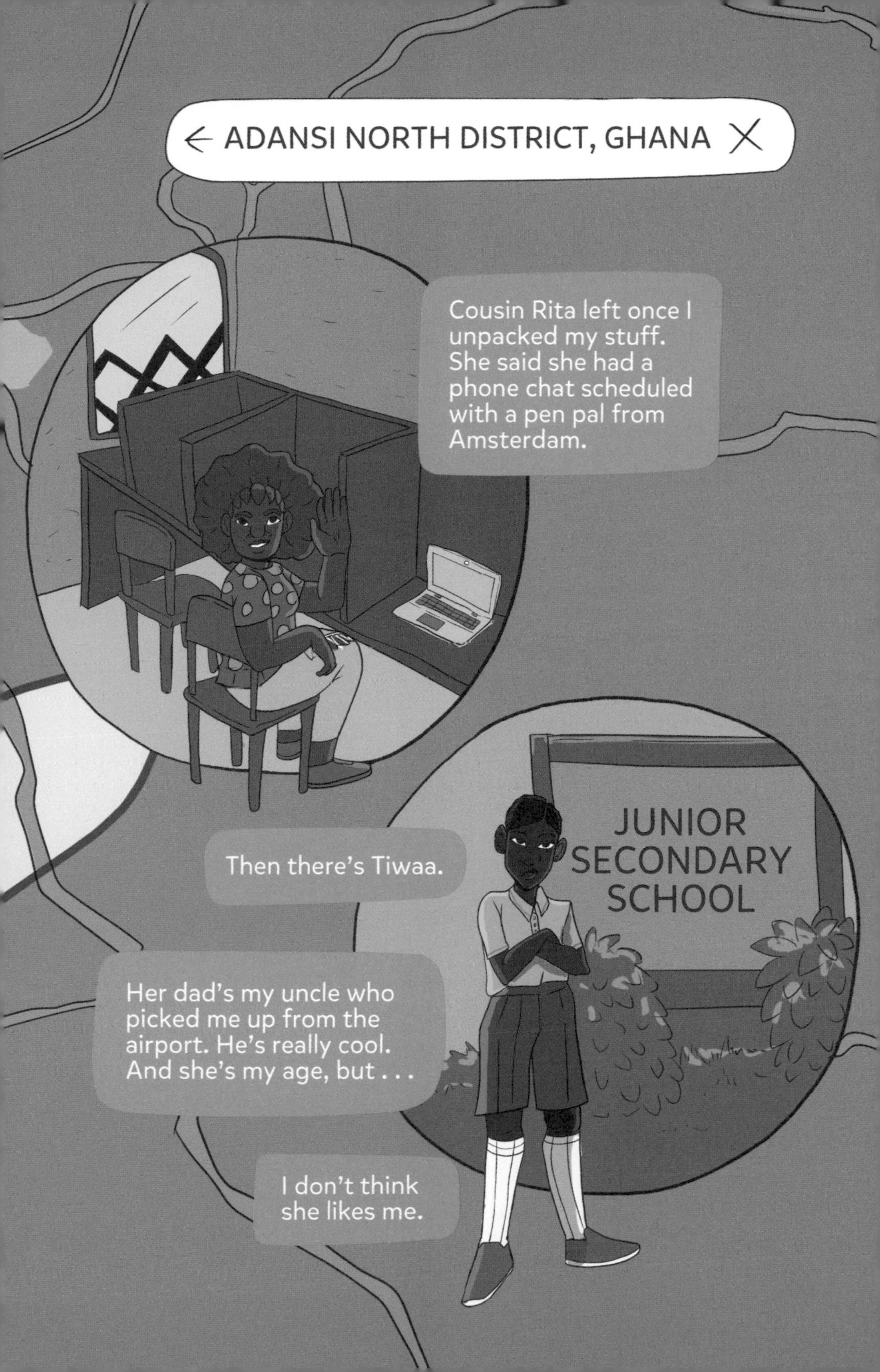

← ADANSI NORTH DISTRICT, GHANA X
Cousin Rita left once I unpacked my stuff. She said she had a phone chat scheduled with a pen pal from Amsterdam.
JUNIOR SECONDARY SCHOOL
Then there's Tiwaa.
Her dad's my uncle who picked me up from the airport. He's really cool. And she's my age, but . . .
I don't think she likes me.

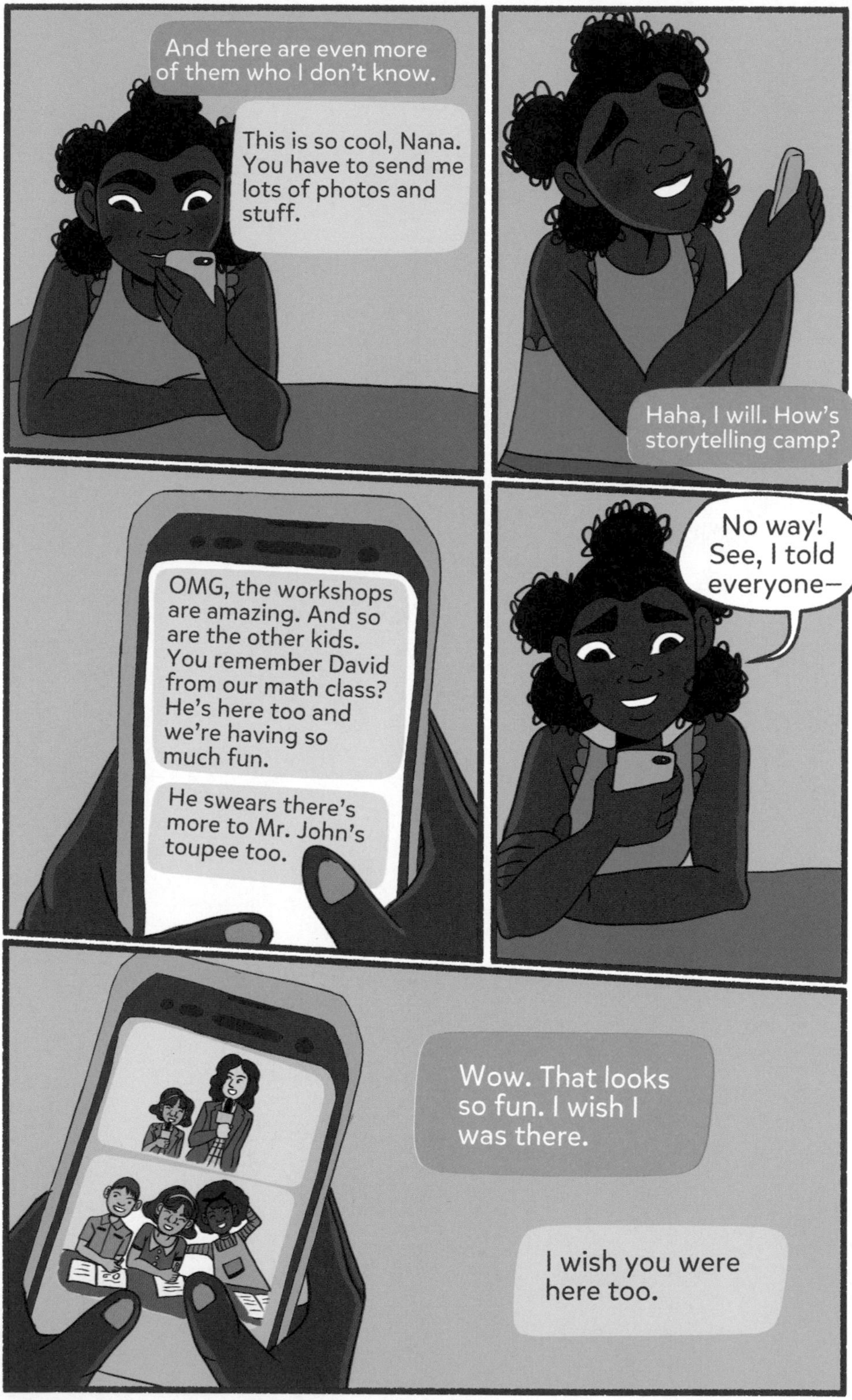
And there are even more of them who I don't know.
This is so cool, Nana. You have to send me lots of photos and stuff.
Haha, I will. How's storytelling camp?
OMG, the workshops are amazing. And so are the other kids. You remember David from our math class? He's here too and we're having so much fun.
He swears there's more to Mr. John's toupee too.
No way! See, I told everyone—
Wow. That looks so fun. I wish I was there.
I wish you were here too.

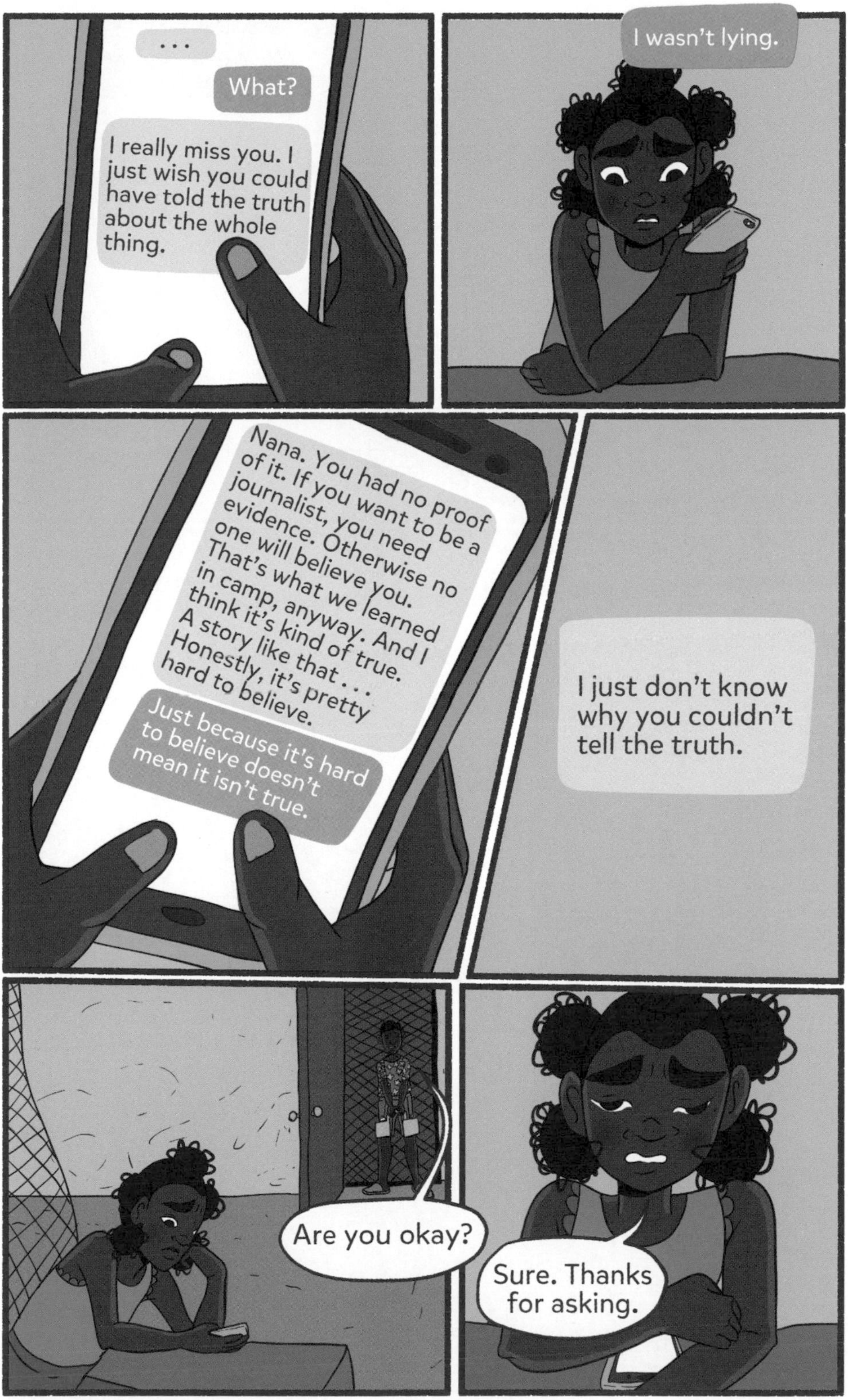
...
What?
I really miss you. I just wish you could have told the truth about the whole thing.
I wasn't lying.
Nana. You had no proof of it. If you want to be a journalist, you need evidence. Otherwise no one will believe you. That's what we learned in camp, anyway. And I think it's kind of true. A story like that . . . Honestly, it's pretty hard to believe.
Just because it's hard to believe doesn't mean it isn't true.
I just don't know why you couldn't tell the truth.
Are you okay?
Sure. Thanks for asking.

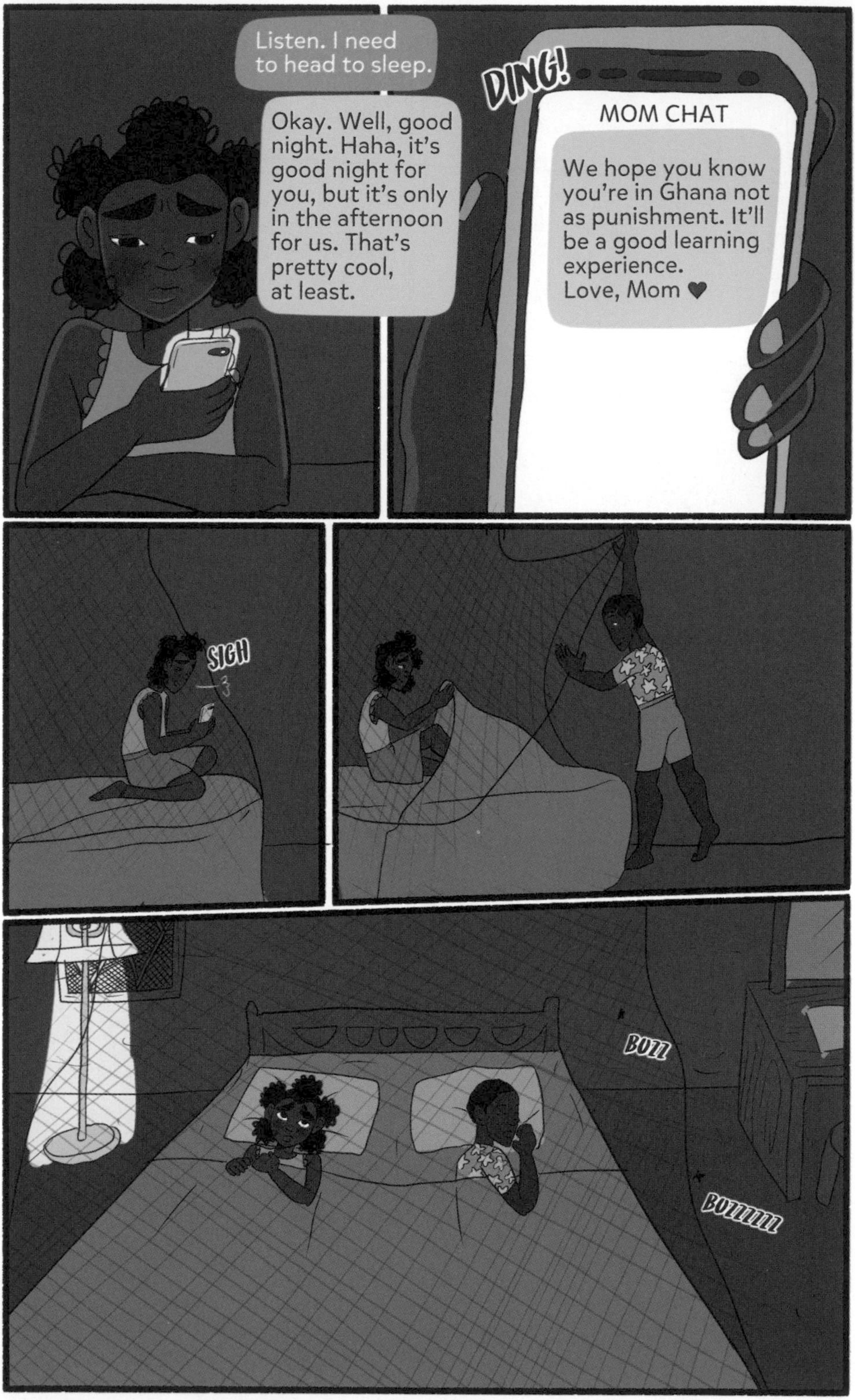
Listen. I need to head to sleep.
Okay. Well, good night. Haha, it's good night for you, but it's only in the afternoon for us. That's pretty cool, at least.
DING!
MOM CHAT
We hope you know you're in Ghana not as punishment. It'll be a good learning experience. Love, Mom ♥
SIGH
BUZZ
BUZZZZZZ

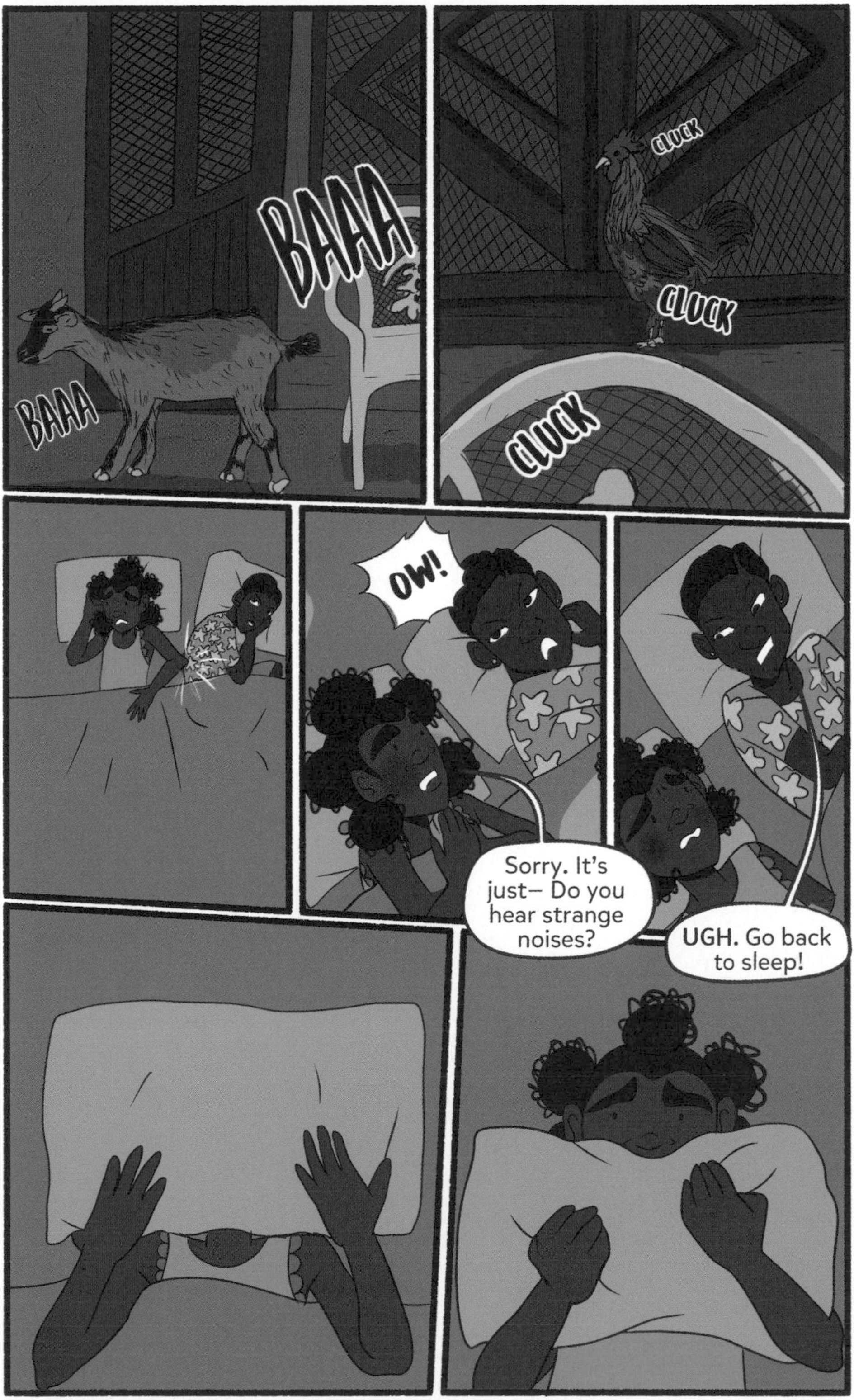
BAAA
BAAA
CLUCK
CLUCK
CLUCK
OW!
Sorry. It's just— Do you hear strange noises?
UGH. Go back to sleep!

Chapter 3

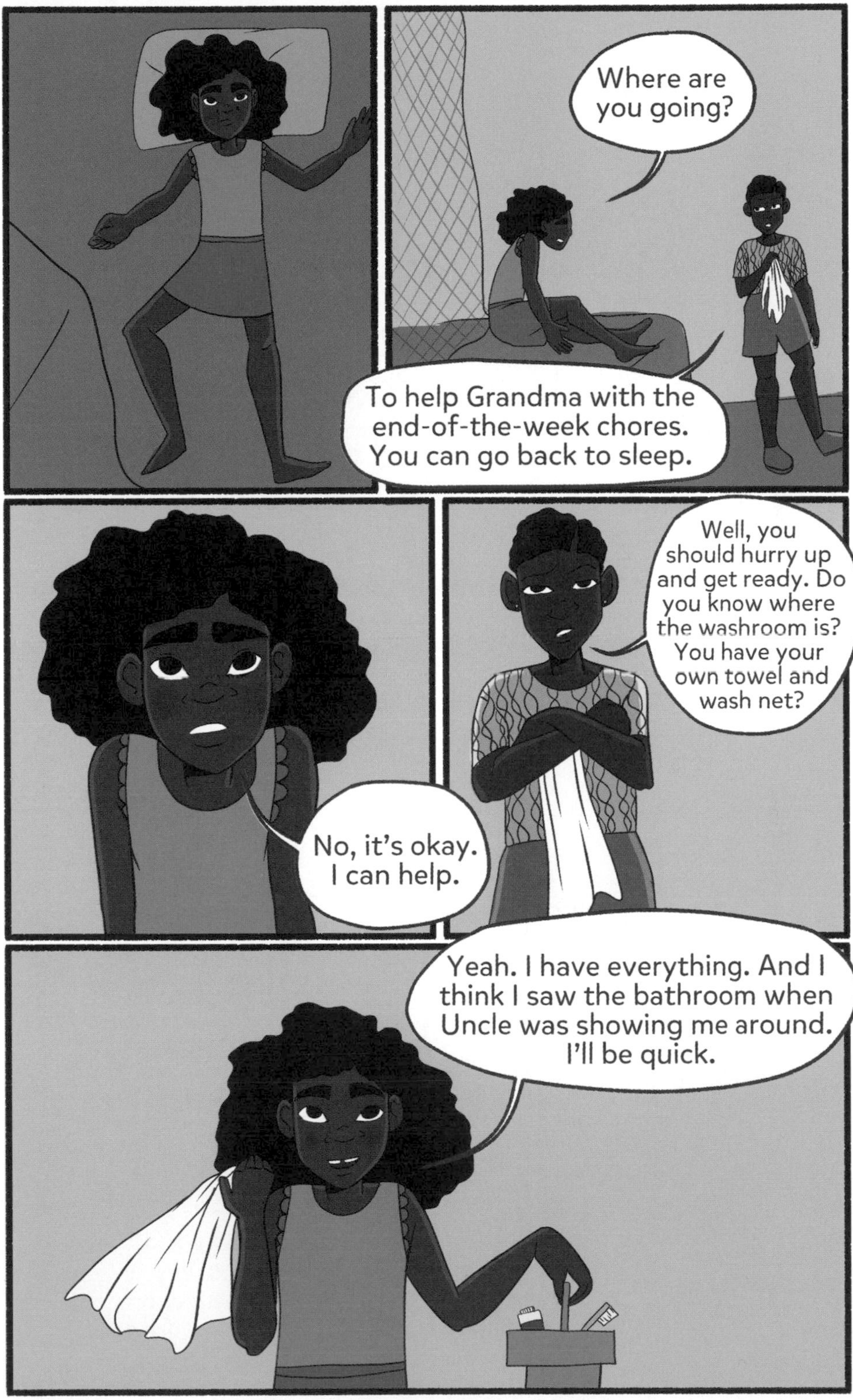
Where are you going?
To help Grandma with the end-of-the-week chores. You can go back to sleep.
No, it's okay. I can help.
Well, you should hurry up and get ready. Do you know where the washroom is? You have your own towel and wash net?
Yeah. I have everything. And I think I saw the bathroom when Uncle was showing me around. I'll be quick.

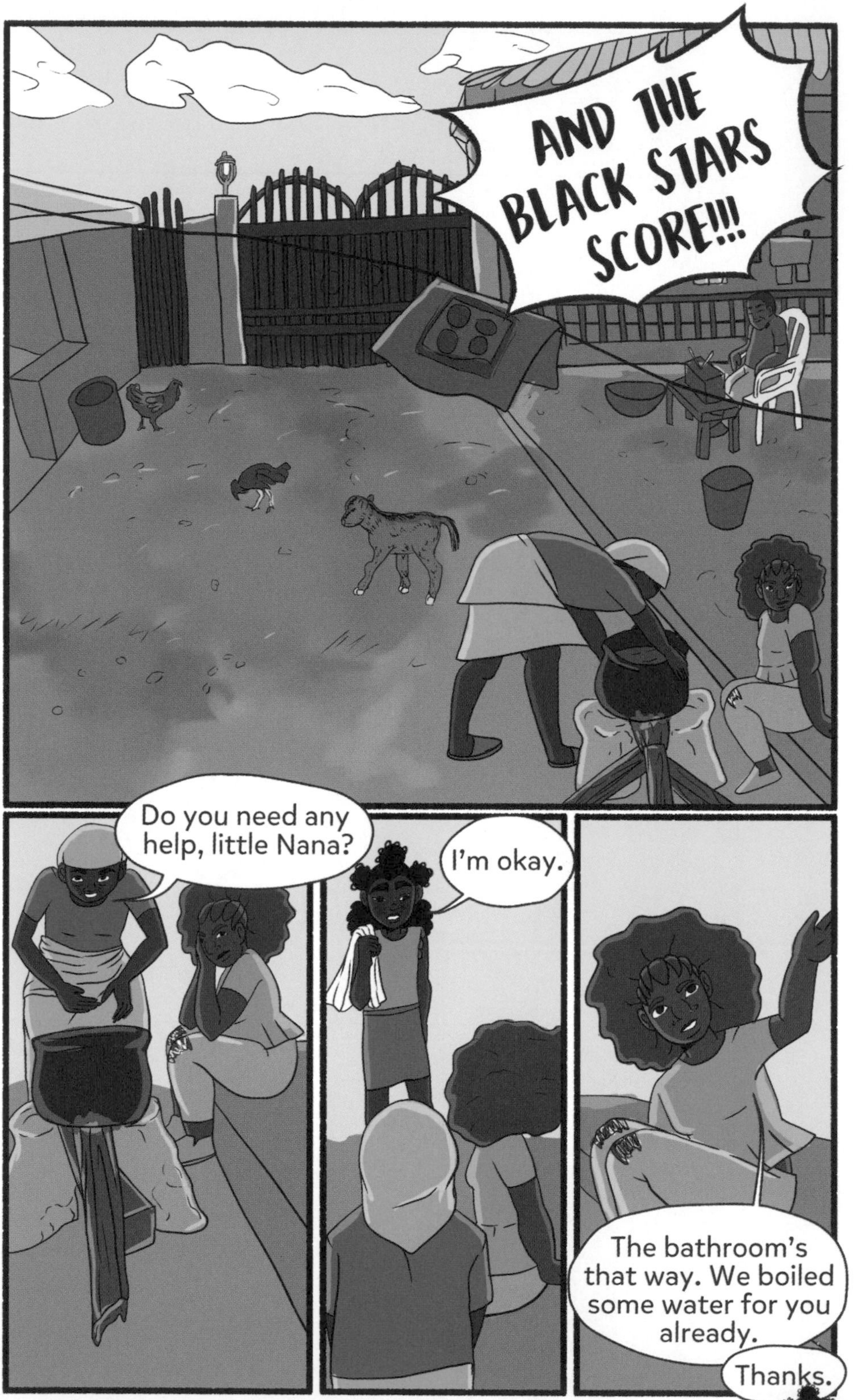
AND THE BLACK STARS SCORE!!!
Do you need any help, little Nana?
I'm okay.
The bathroom's that way. We boiled some water for you already.
Thanks.

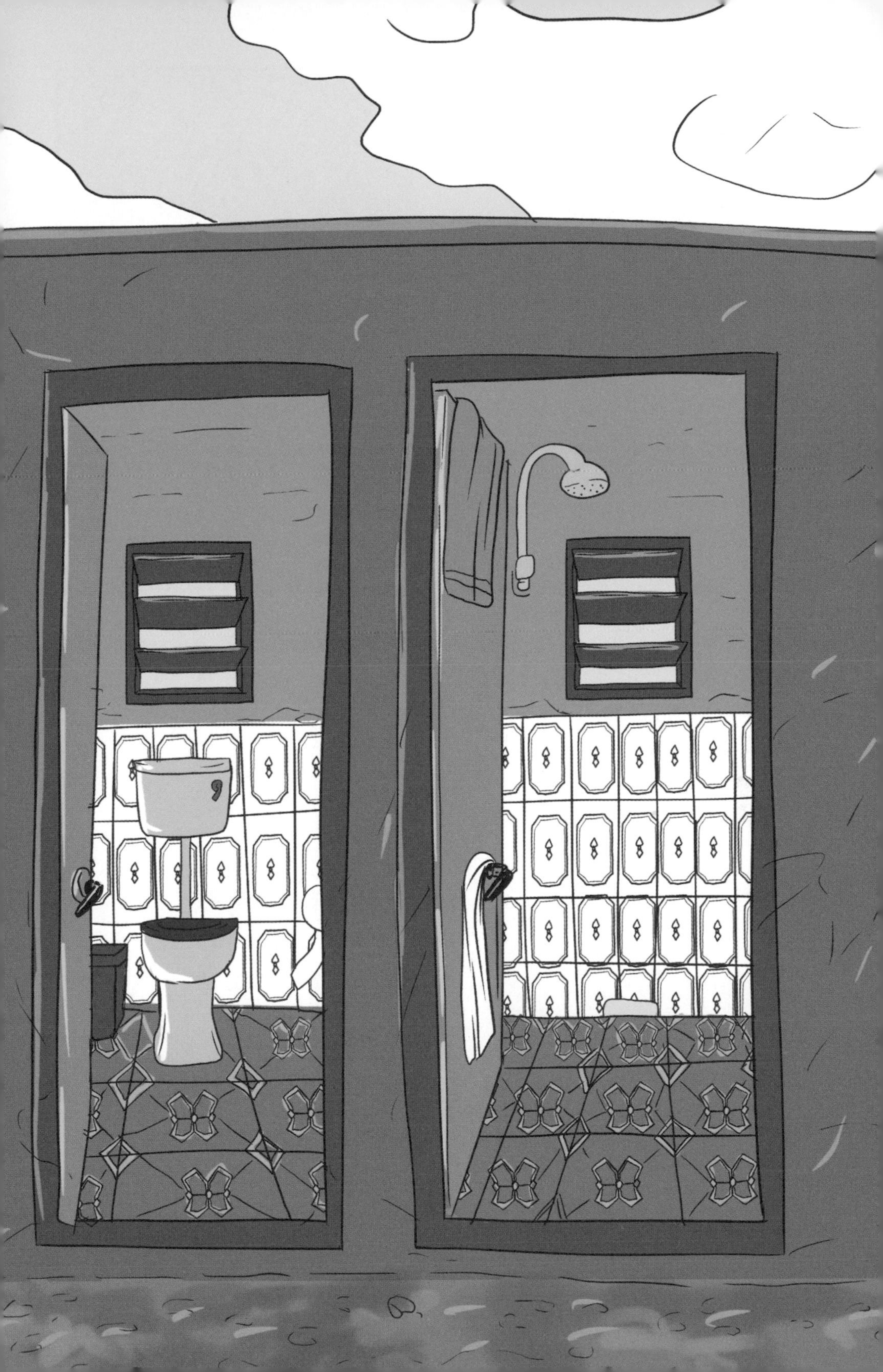

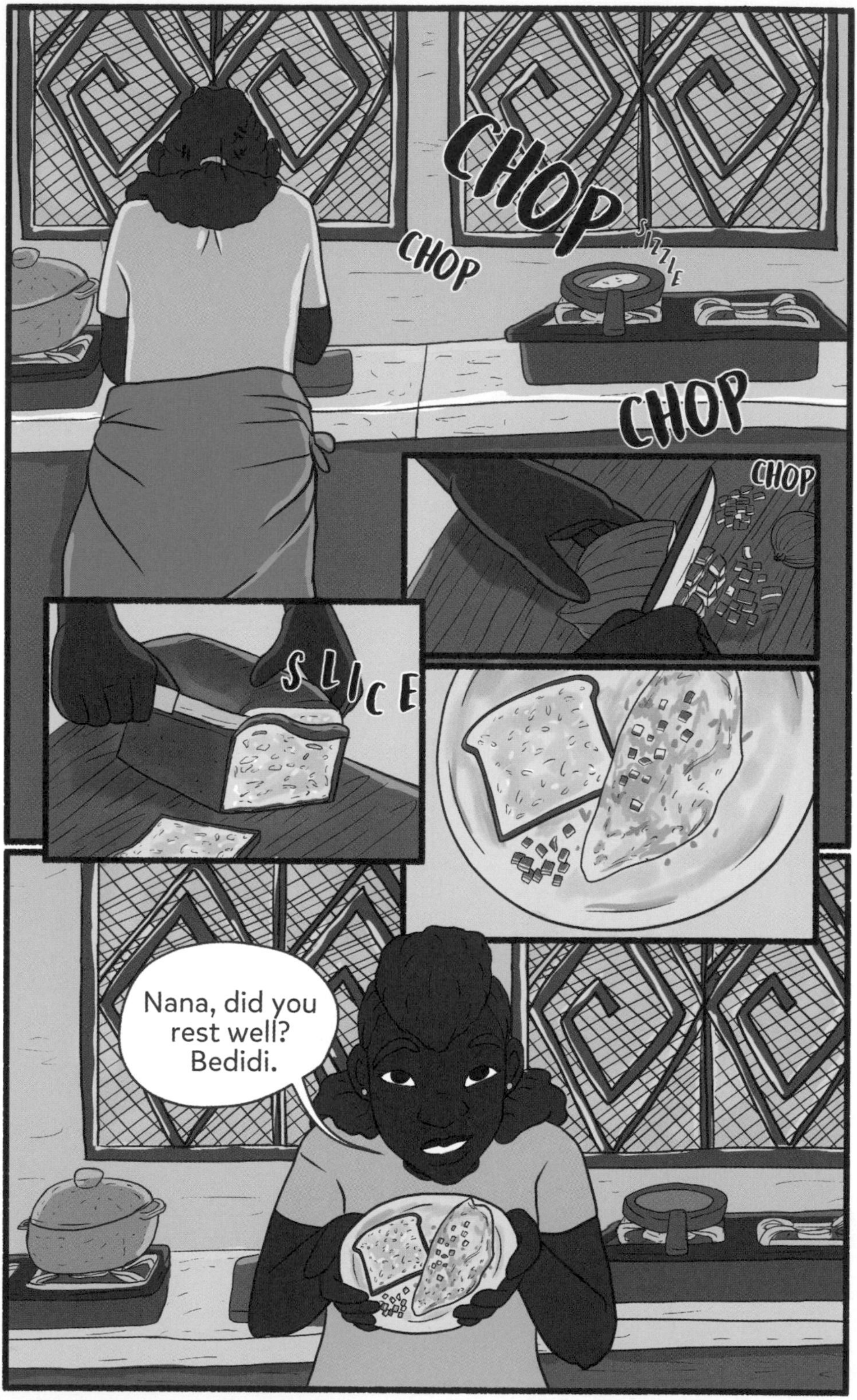
CHOP
CHOP
SIZZLE
CHOP
CHOP
SLICE
Nana, did you rest well? Bedidi.

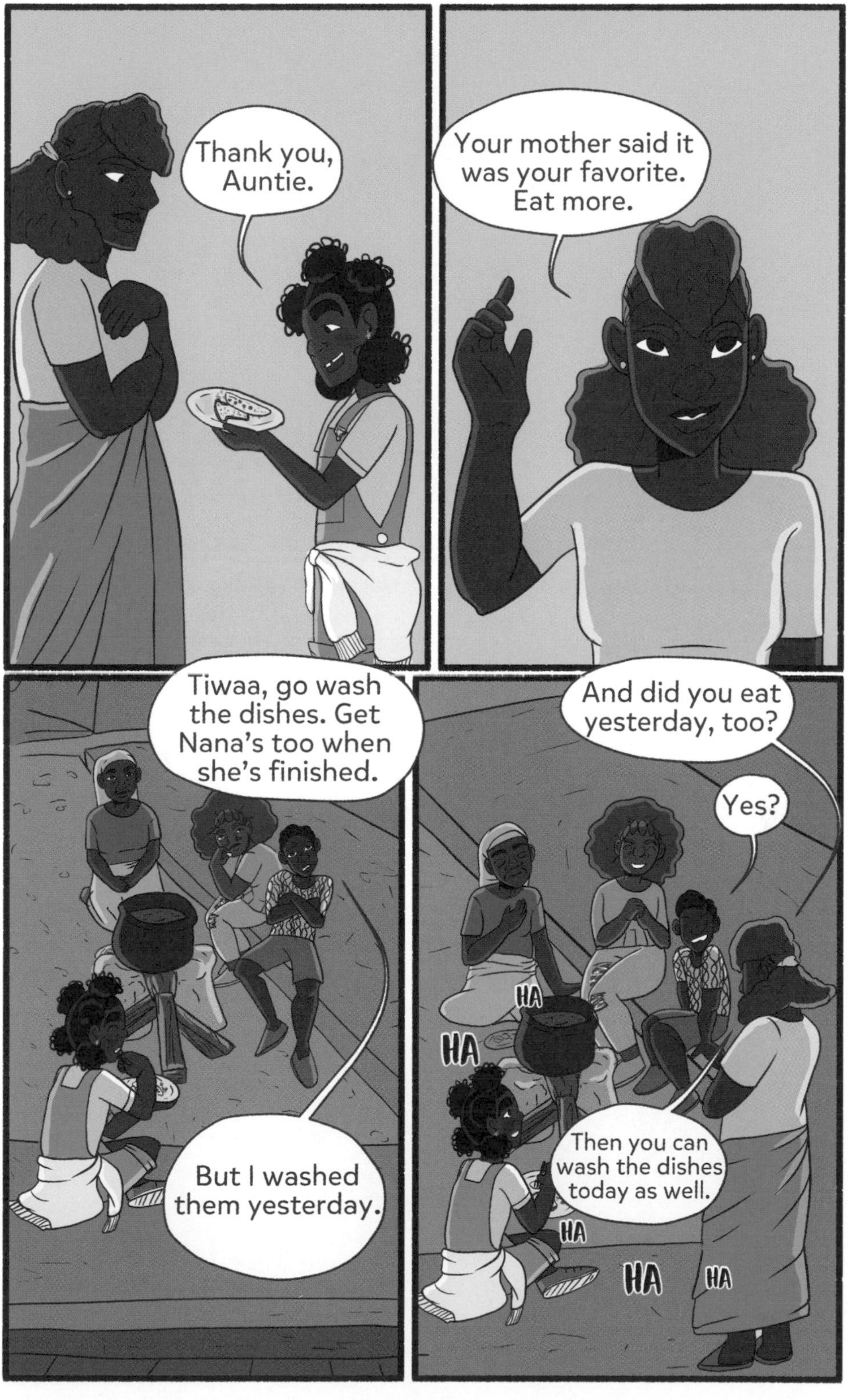
Thank you, Auntie.
Your mother said it was your favorite. Eat more.
Tiwaa, go wash the dishes. Get Nana's too when she's finished.
But I washed them yesterday.
And did you eat yesterday, too?
Yes?
HA
HA
Then you can wash the dishes today as well.
HA
HA
HA

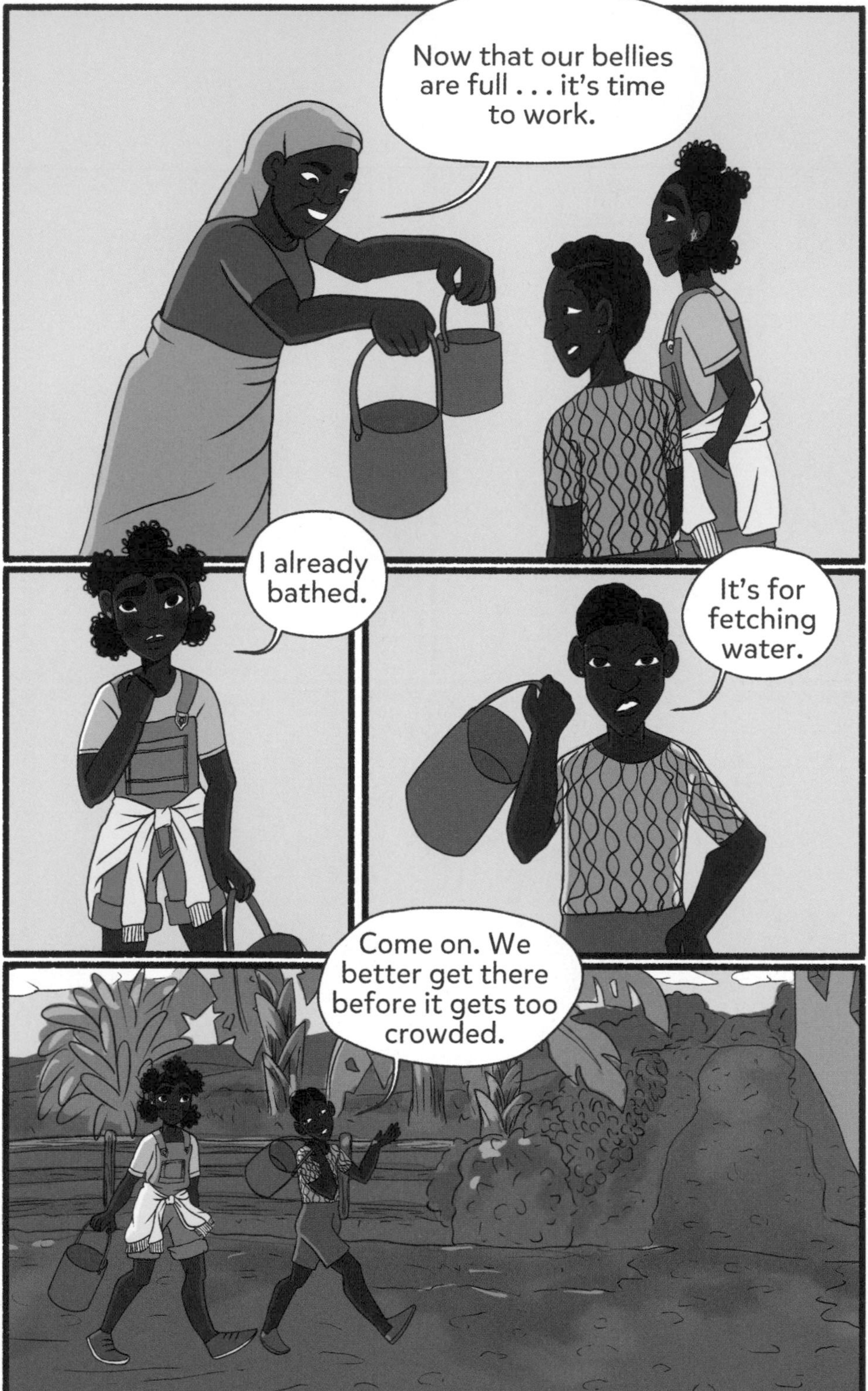
Now that our bellies are full . . . it's time to work.
I already bathed.
It's for fetching water.
Come on. We better get there before it gets too crowded.

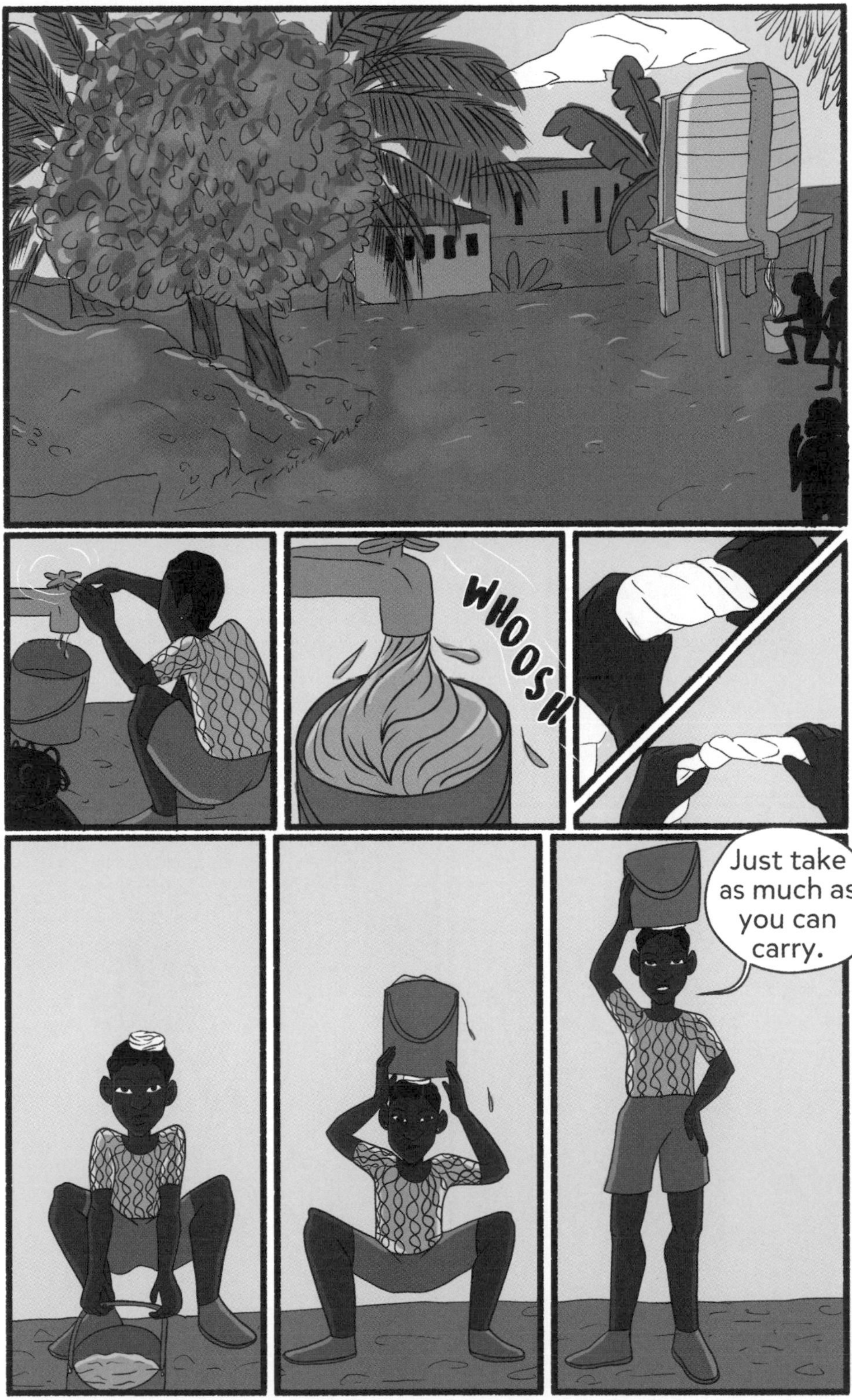
WHOOSH
Just take as much as you can carry.

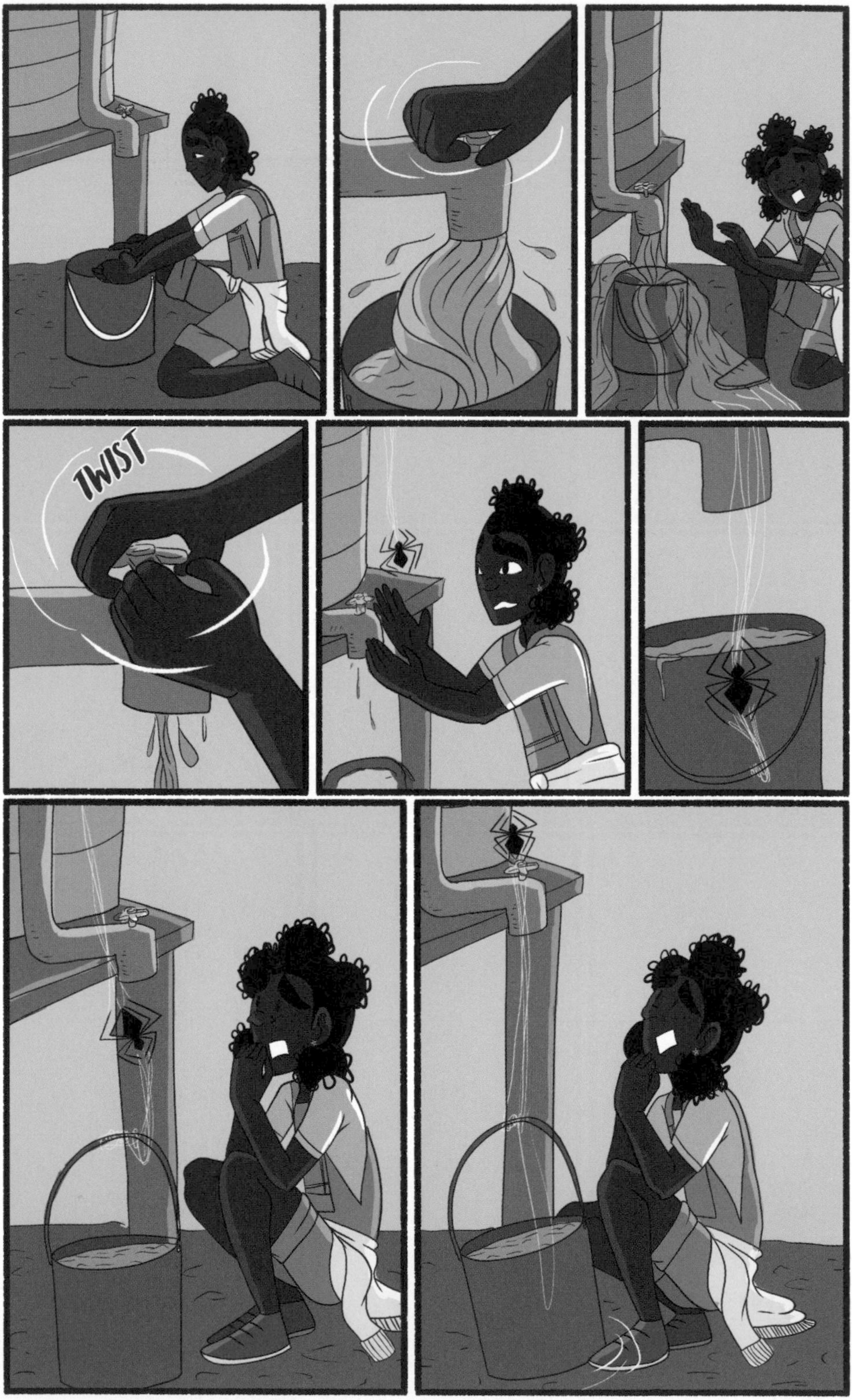
TWIST

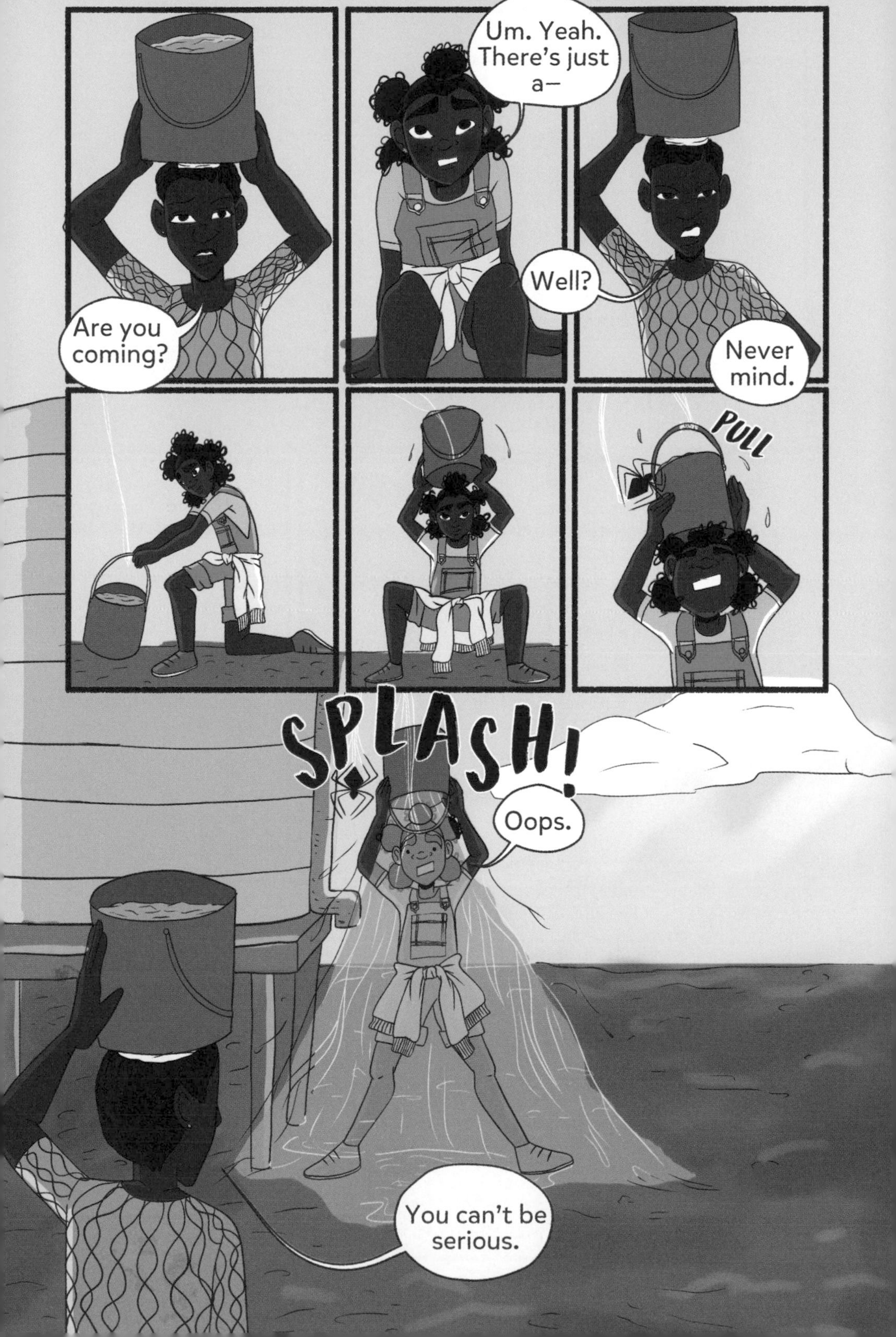
Are you coming?
Um. Yeah. There's just a–
Well?
Never mind.
PULL
SPLASH!
Oops.
You can't be serious.

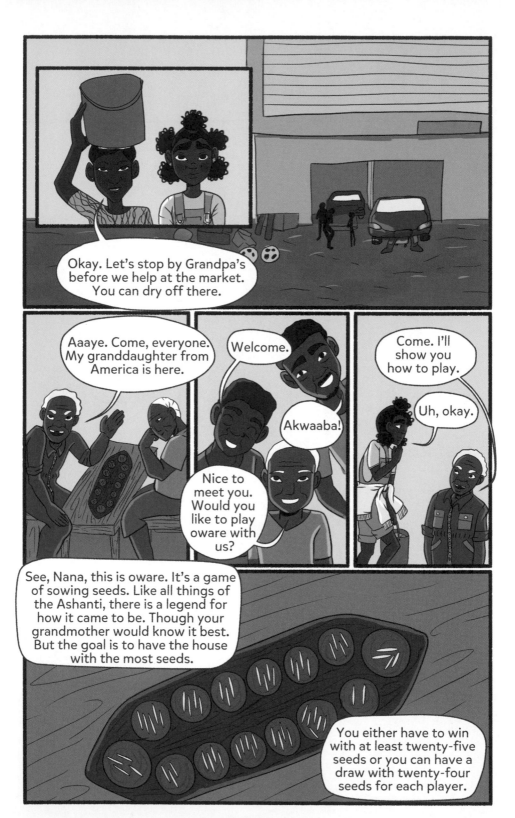

Okay. Let's stop by Grandpa's before we help at the market. You can dry off there.

Aaaye. Come, everyone. My granddaughter from America is here.

Welcome.

Akwaaba!

Nice to meet you. Would you like to play oware with us?

Come. I'll show you how to play.

Uh, okay.

See, Nana, this is oware. It's a game of sowing seeds. Like all things of the Ashanti, there is a legend for how it came to be. Though your grandmother would know it best. But the goal is to have the house with the most seeds.

You either have to win with at least twenty-five seeds or you can have a draw with twenty-four seeds for each player.

Ummm . . . Well . . . Should I move here? How many does this count as again?

See? Isn't this great?

Ha ha, looks like Ananse wants to play as well.

Ananse?

It means "spider" in Twi.

He's also a trickster. Your grandma will know many of his stories.

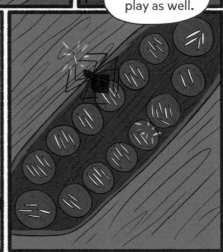

It just took my seed! You saw that. You all saw, right?!

HA HA HA HA HA HA HA

Oh, don't worry, Nana. Ananse is just playing a trick on you. Next time for sure you can win.

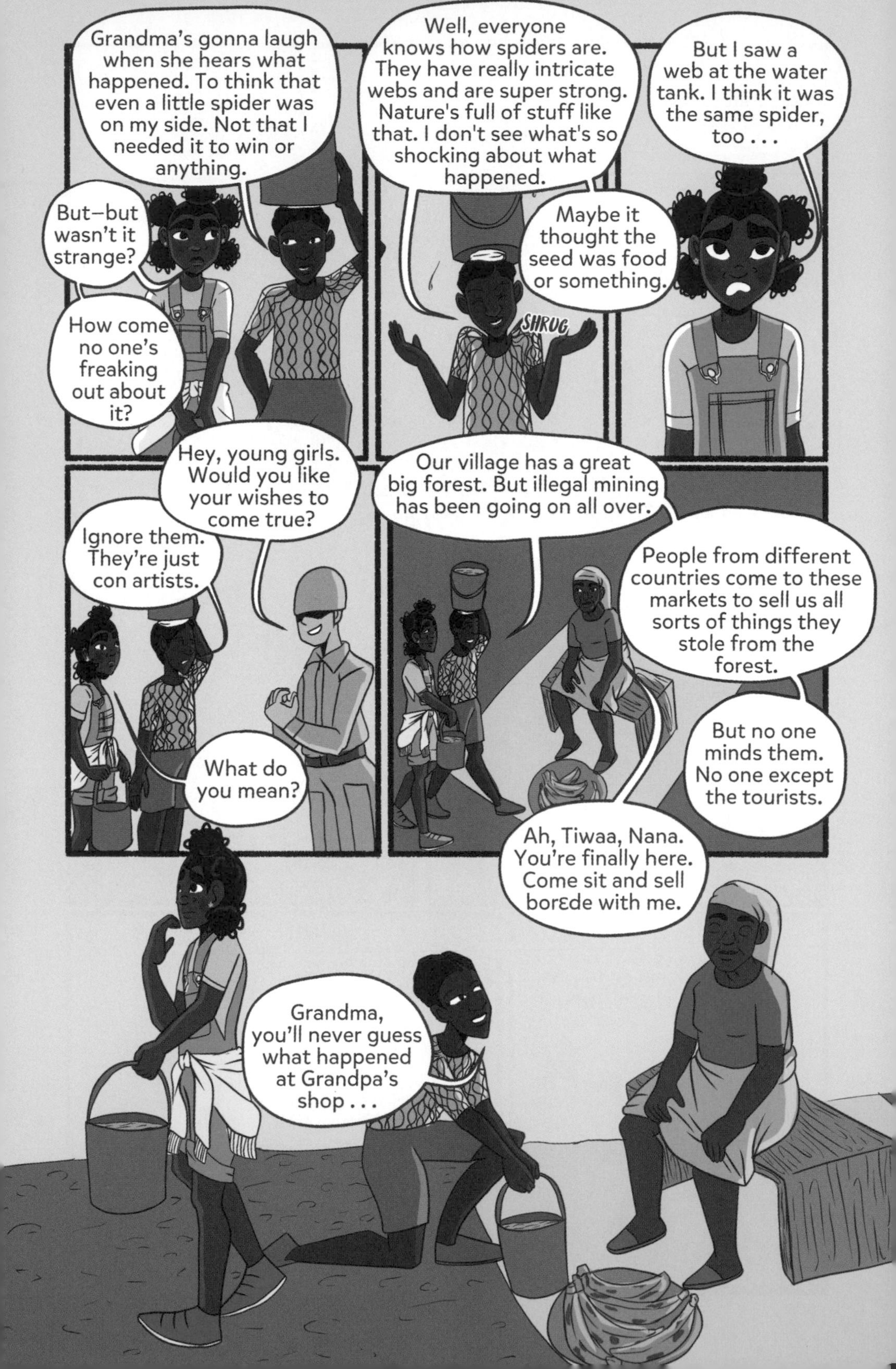
Grandma's gonna laugh when she hears what happened. To think that even a little spider was on my side. Not that I needed it to win or anything.
But—but wasn't it strange?
How come no one's freaking out about it?
Well, everyone knows how spiders are. They have really intricate webs and are super strong. Nature's full of stuff like that. I don't see what's so shocking about what happened.
Maybe it thought the seed was food or something.
SHRUG
But I saw a web at the water tank. I think it was the same spider, too . . .
Hey, young girls. Would you like your wishes to come true?
Ignore them. They're just con artists.
What do you mean?
Our village has a great big forest. But illegal mining has been going on all over.
People from different countries come to these markets to sell us all sorts of things they stole from the forest.
But no one minds them. No one except the tourists.
Ah, Tiwaa, Nana. You're finally here. Come sit and sell borɛde with me.
Grandma, you'll never guess what happened at Grandpa's shop . . .

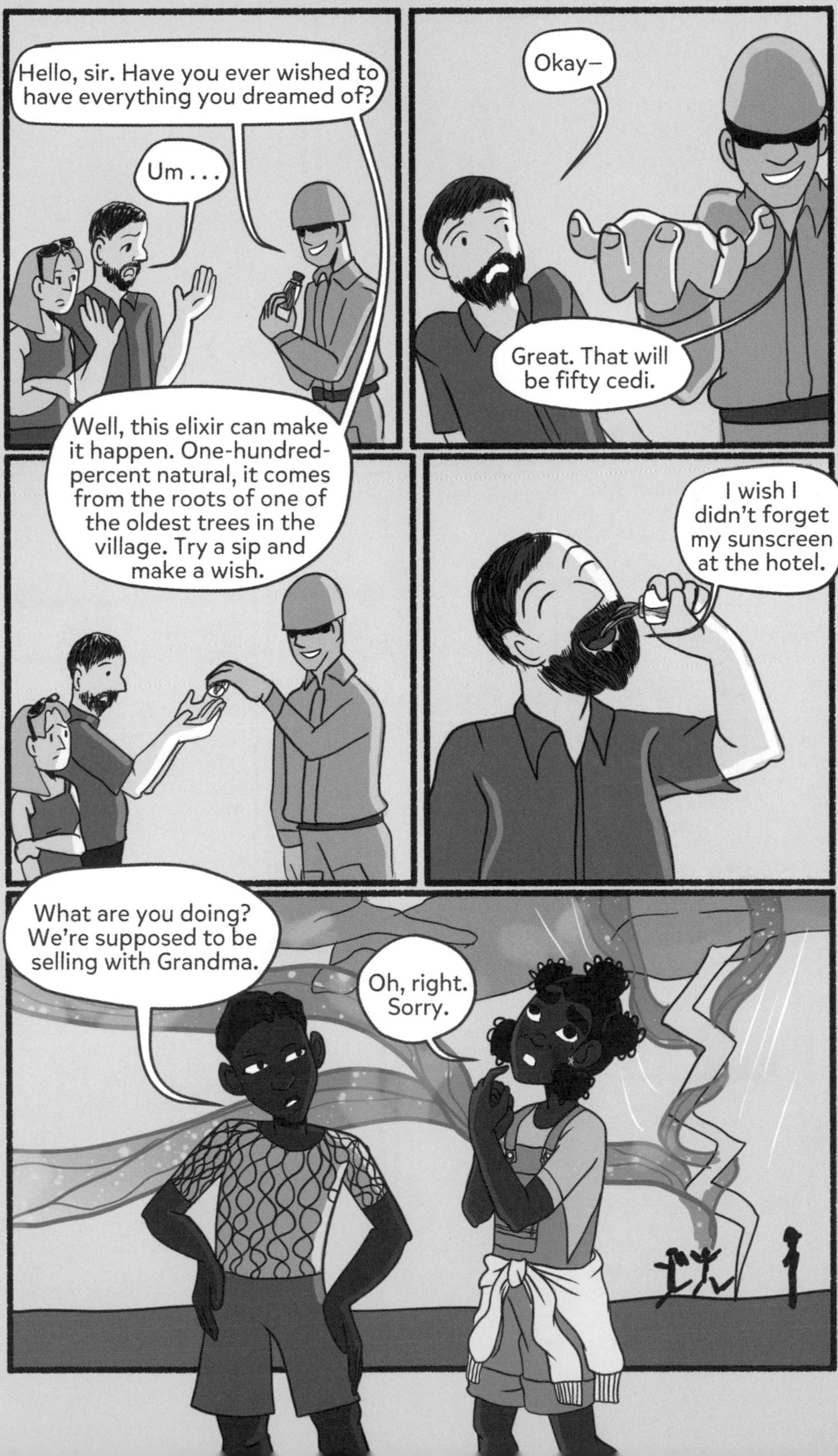
Hello, sir. Have you ever wished to have everything you dreamed of?
Um . . .
Well, this elixir can make it happen. One-hundred-percent natural, it comes from the roots of one of the oldest trees in the village. Try a sip and make a wish.
Okay–
Great. That will be fifty cedi.
I wish I didn't forget my sunscreen at the hotel.
What are you doing? We're supposed to be selling with Grandma.
Oh, right. Sorry.

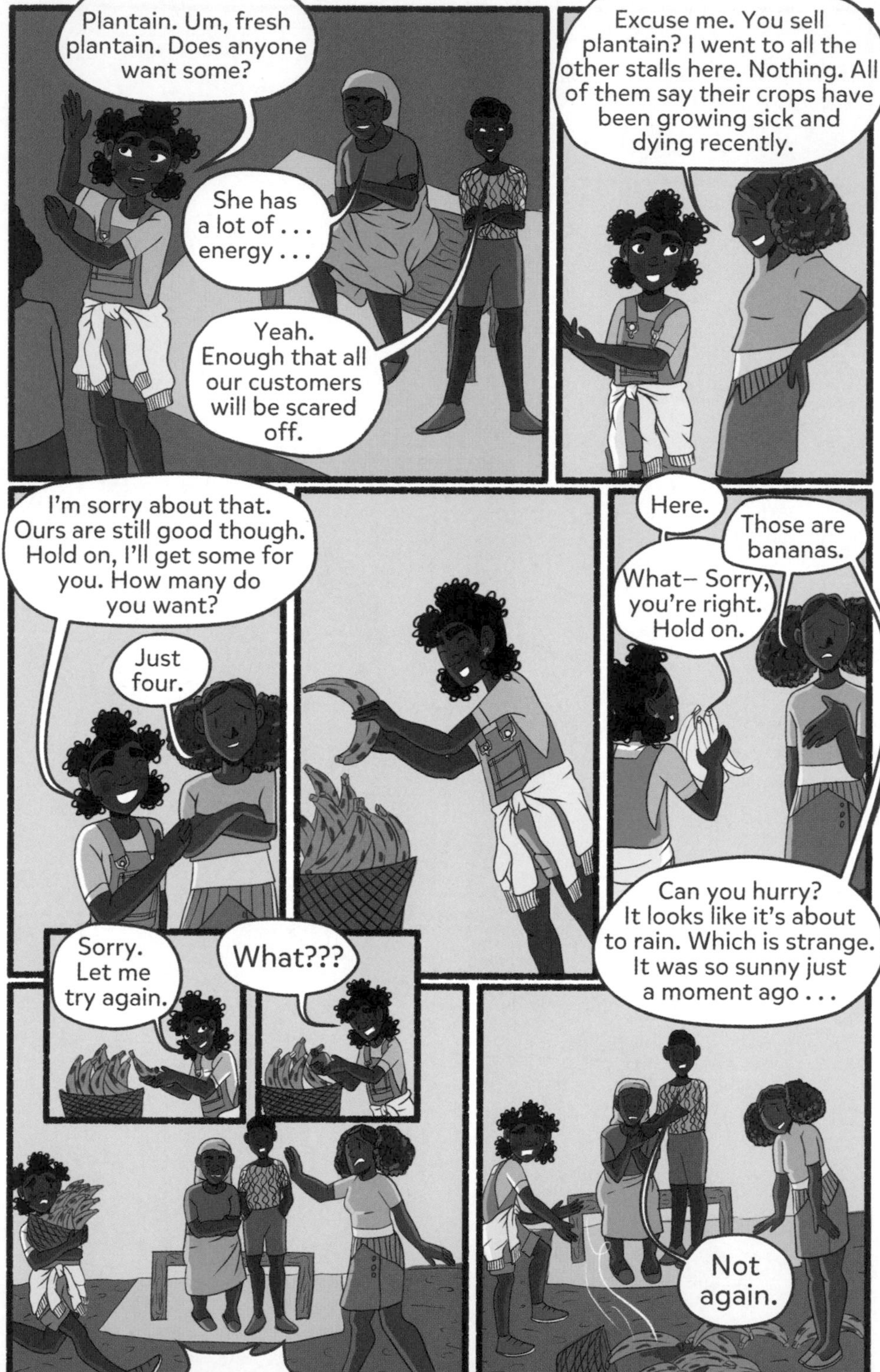
Plantain. Um, fresh plantain. Does anyone want some?
She has a lot of . . . energy . . .
Yeah. Enough that all our customers will be scared off.
Excuse me. You sell plantain? I went to all the other stalls here. Nothing. All of them say their crops have been growing sick and dying recently.
I'm sorry about that. Ours are still good though. Hold on, I'll get some for you. How many do you want?
Just four.
Here.
Those are bananas.
What– Sorry, you're right. Hold on.
Can you hurry? It looks like it's about to rain. Which is strange. It was so sunny just a moment ago . . .
Sorry. Let me try again.
What???
Wait–
Not again.

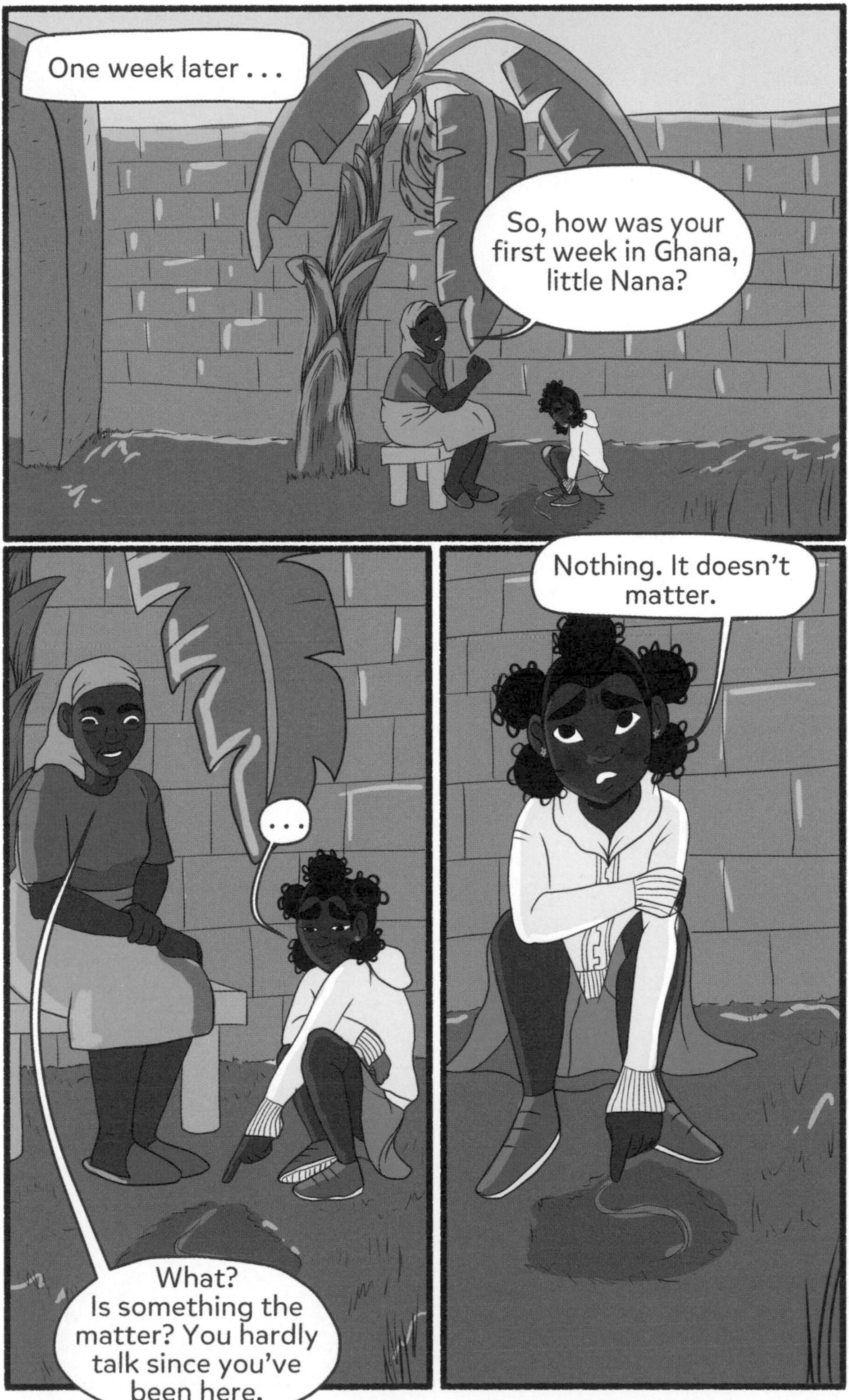
One week later . . .
So, how was your first week in Ghana, little Nana?
. . .
What? Is something the matter? You hardly talk since you've been here.
Nothing. It doesn't matter.

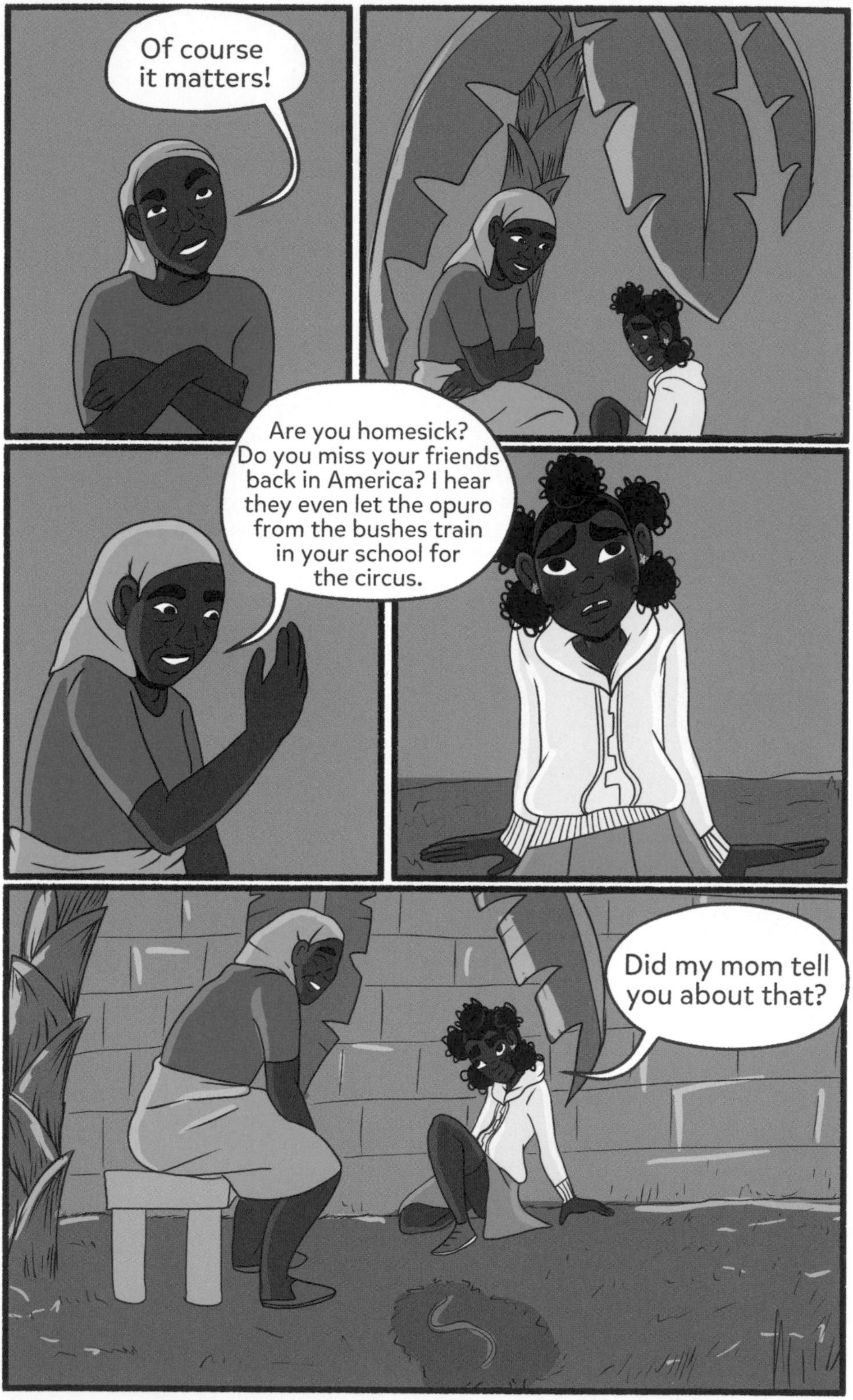
Of course it matters!
Are you homesick? Do you miss your friends back in America? I hear they even let the opuro from the bushes train in your school for the circus.
Did my mom tell you about that?

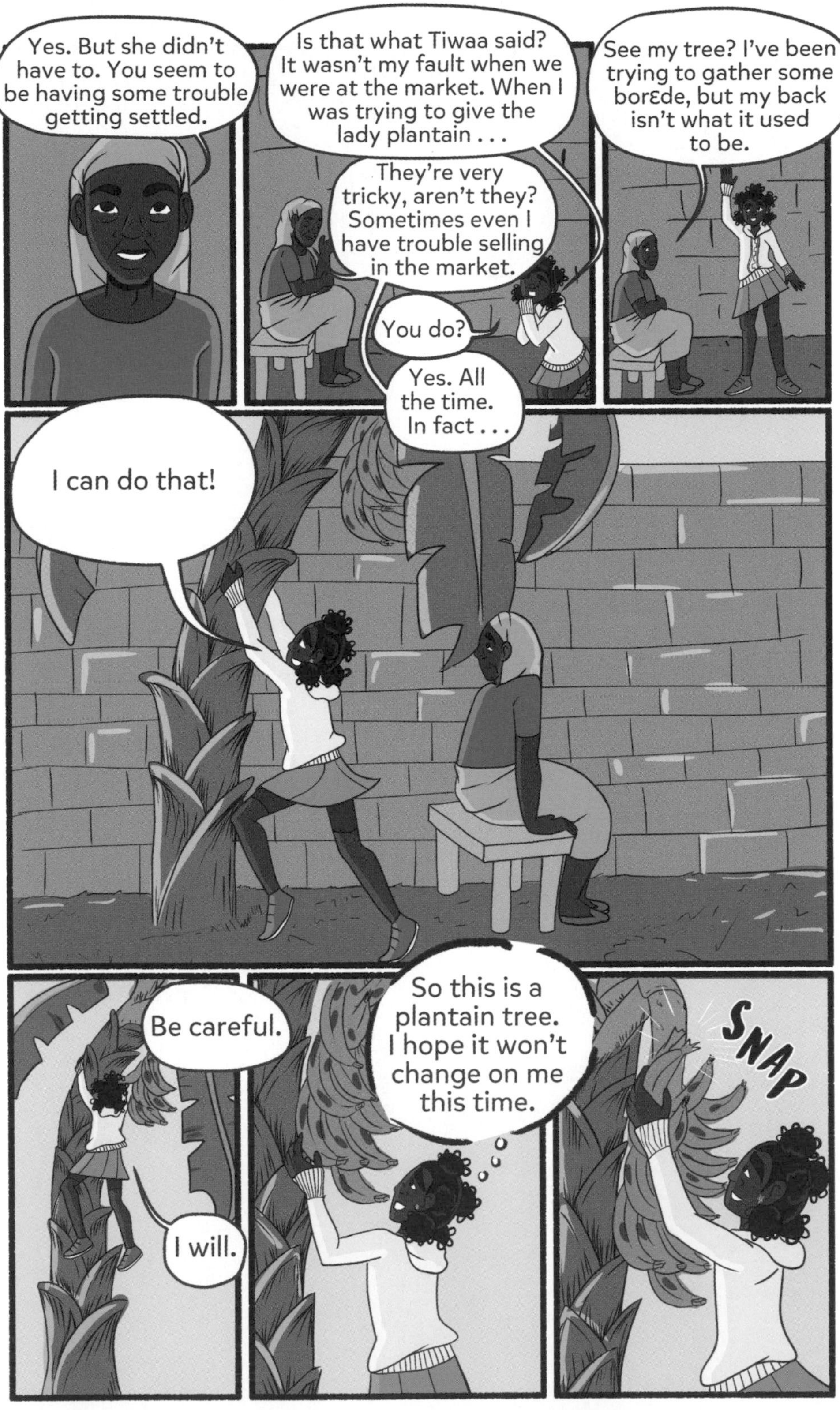
Yes. But she didn't have to. You seem to be having some trouble getting settled.
Is that what Tiwaa said? It wasn't my fault when we were at the market. When I was trying to give the lady plantain . . .
They're very tricky, aren't they? Sometimes even I have trouble selling in the market.
You do?
Yes. All the time. In fact . . .
See my tree? I've been trying to gather some borɛde, but my back isn't what it used to be.
I can do that!
Be careful.
I will.
So this is a plantain tree. I hope it won't change on me this time.
SNAP

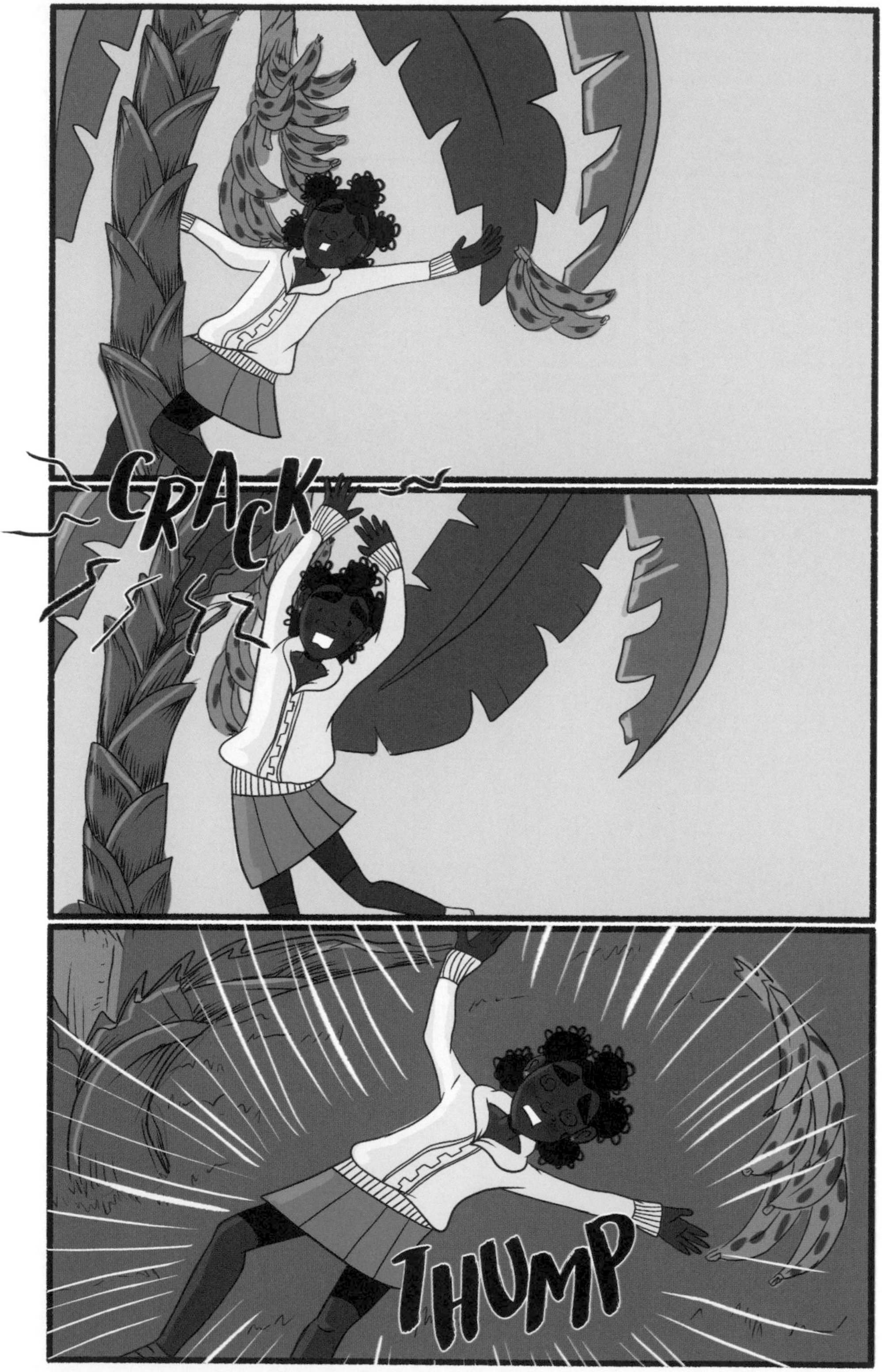
CRACK
THUMP

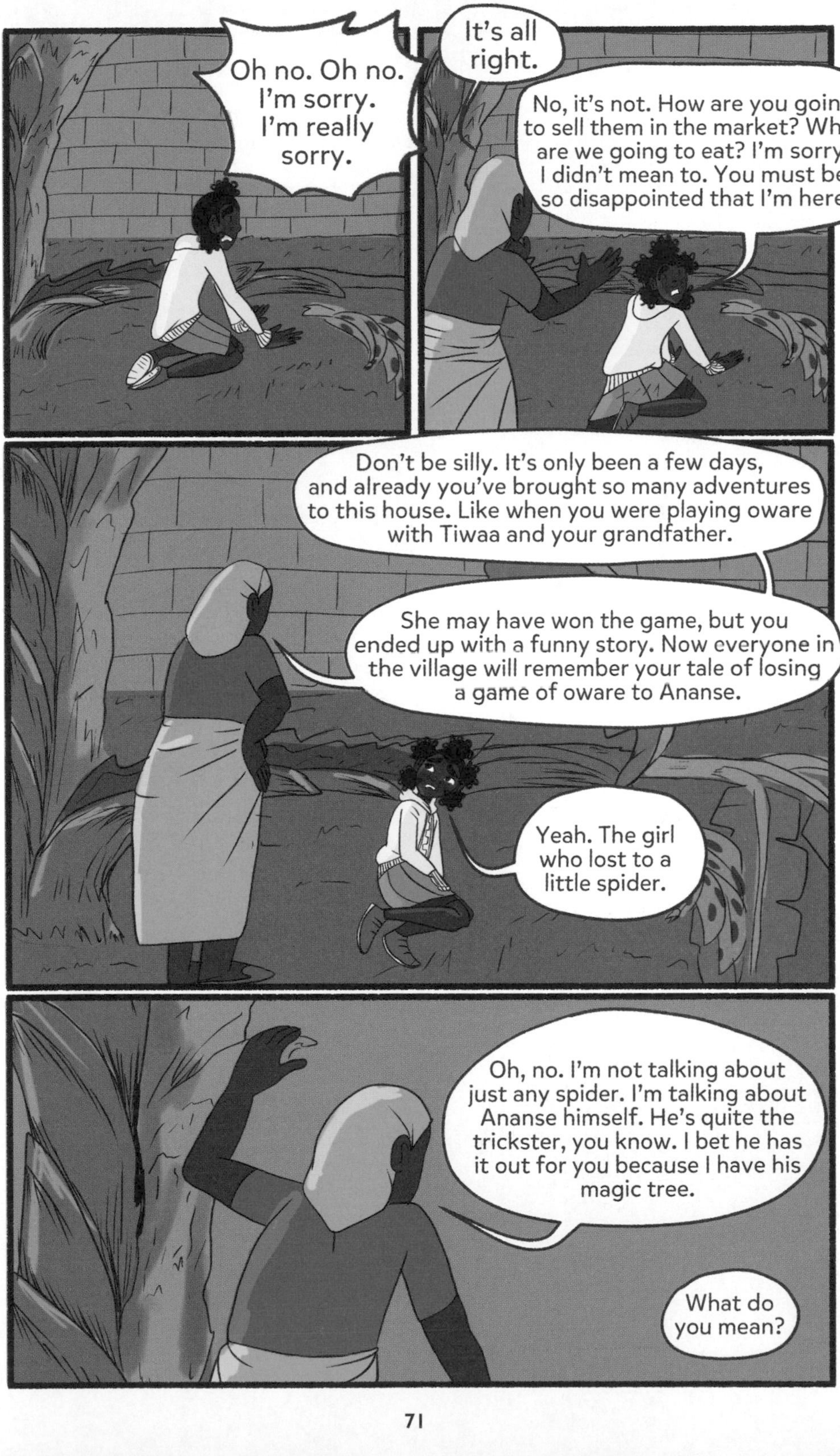

Oh no. Oh no. I'm sorry. I'm really sorry.
It's all right.
No, it's not. How are you going to sell them in the market? What are we going to eat? I'm sorry. I didn't mean to. You must be so disappointed that I'm here.
Don't be silly. It's only been a few days, and already you've brought so many adventures to this house. Like when you were playing oware with Tiwaa and your grandfather.
She may have won the game, but you ended up with a funny story. Now everyone in the village will remember your tale of losing a game of oware to Ananse.
Yeah. The girl who lost to a little spider.
Oh, no. I'm not talking about just any spider. I'm talking about Ananse himself. He's quite the trickster, you know. I bet he has it out for you because I have his magic tree.
What do you mean?

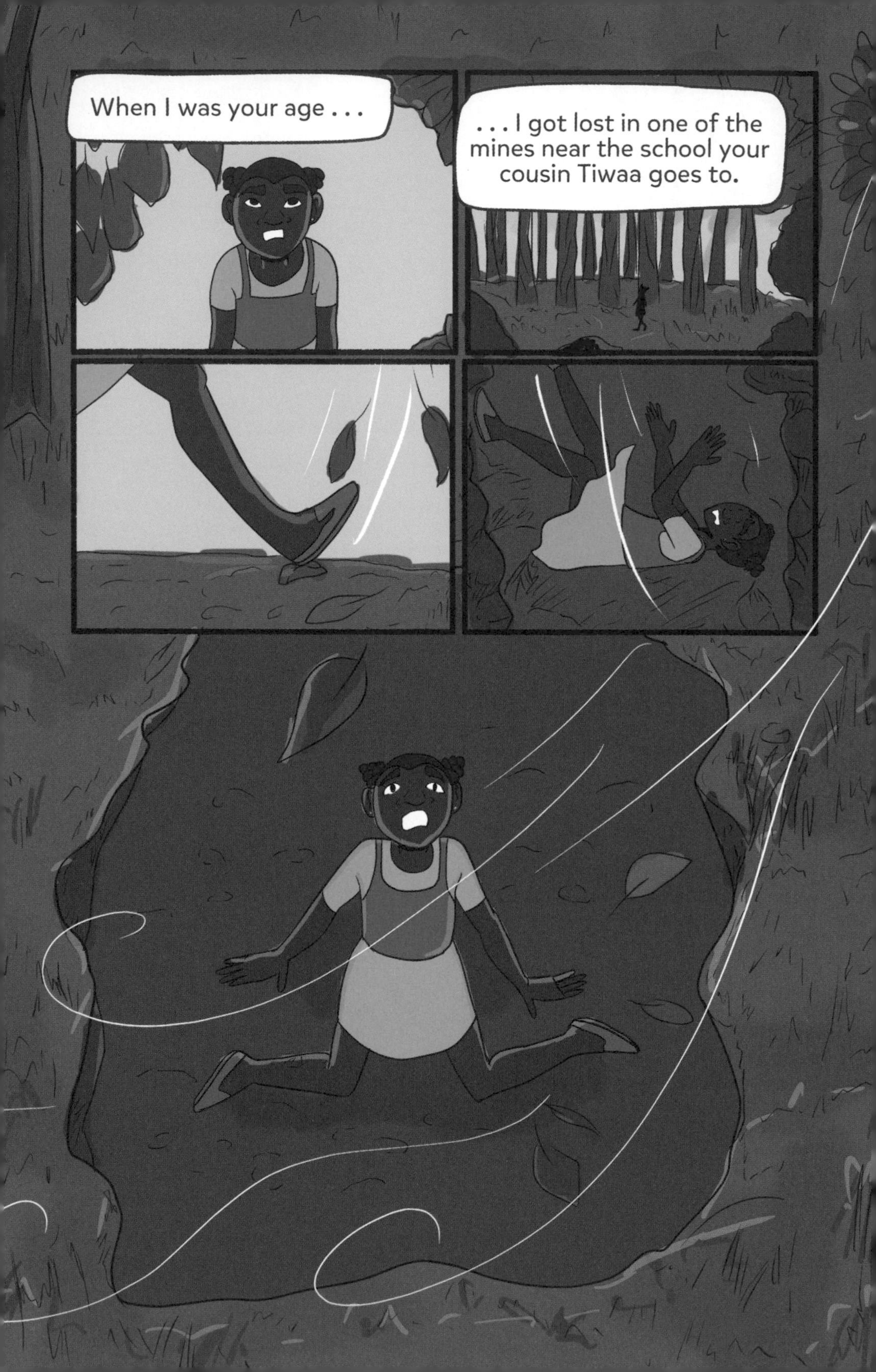
When I was your age . . .
. . . I got lost in one of the mines near the school your cousin Tiwaa goes to.

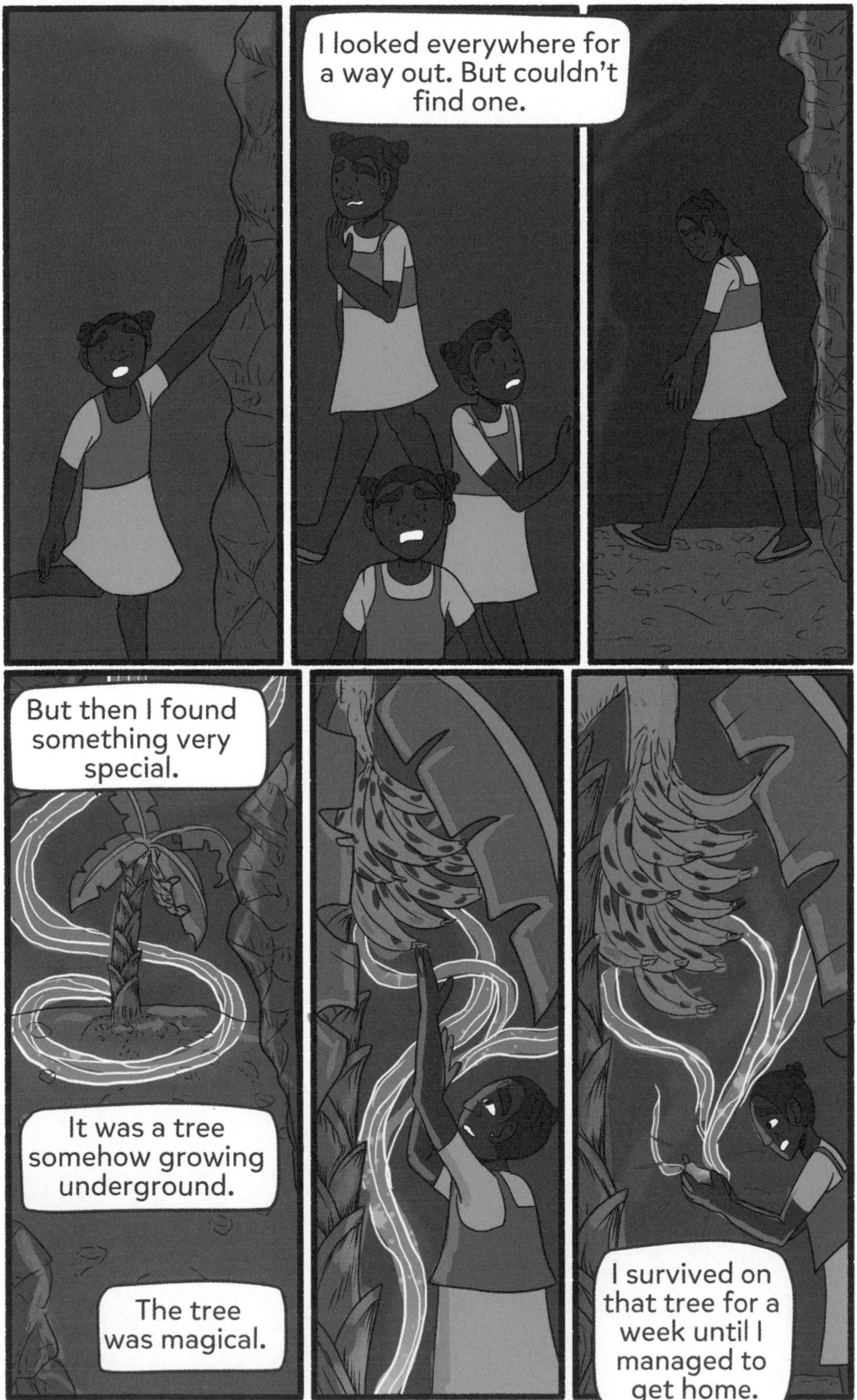
I looked everywhere for a way out. But couldn't find one.
But then I found something very special.
It was a tree somehow growing underground.
The tree was magical.
I survived on that tree for a week until I managed to get home.

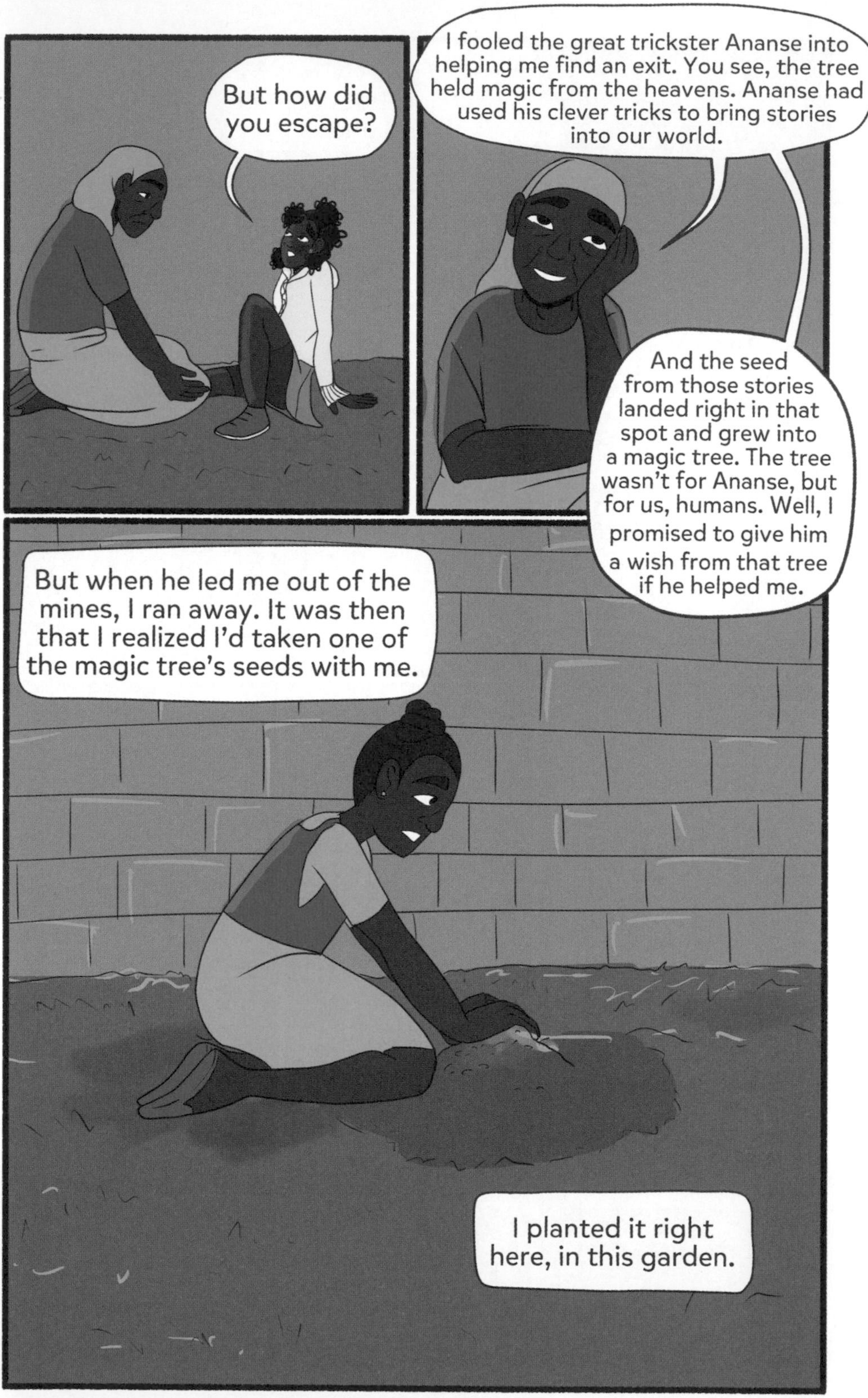
But how did you escape?
I fooled the great trickster Ananse into helping me find an exit. You see, the tree held magic from the heavens. Ananse had used his clever tricks to bring stories into our world.
And the seed from those stories landed right in that spot and grew into a magic tree. The tree wasn't for Ananse, but for us, humans. Well, I promised to give him a wish from that tree if he helped me.
But when he led me out of the mines, I ran away. It was then that I realized I'd taken one of the magic tree's seeds with me.
I planted it right here, in this garden.

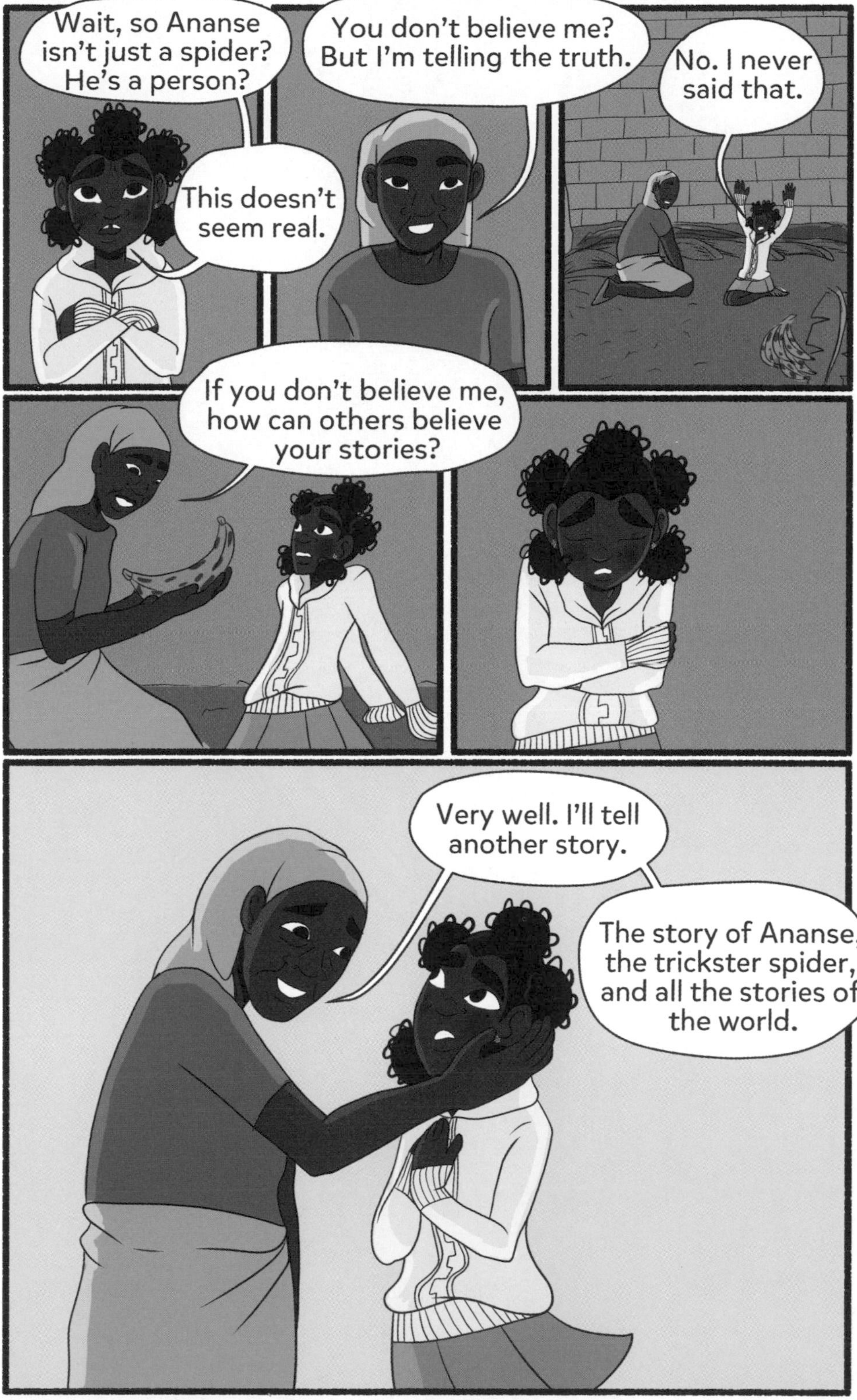
Wait, so Ananse isn't just a spider? He's a person?
This doesn't seem real.
You don't believe me? But I'm telling the truth.
No. I never said that.
If you don't believe me, how can others believe your stories?
Very well. I'll tell another story.
The story of Ananse, the trickster spider, and all the stories of the world.

ANANSE AND ALL THE STORIES OF THE WORLD

Chapter 4

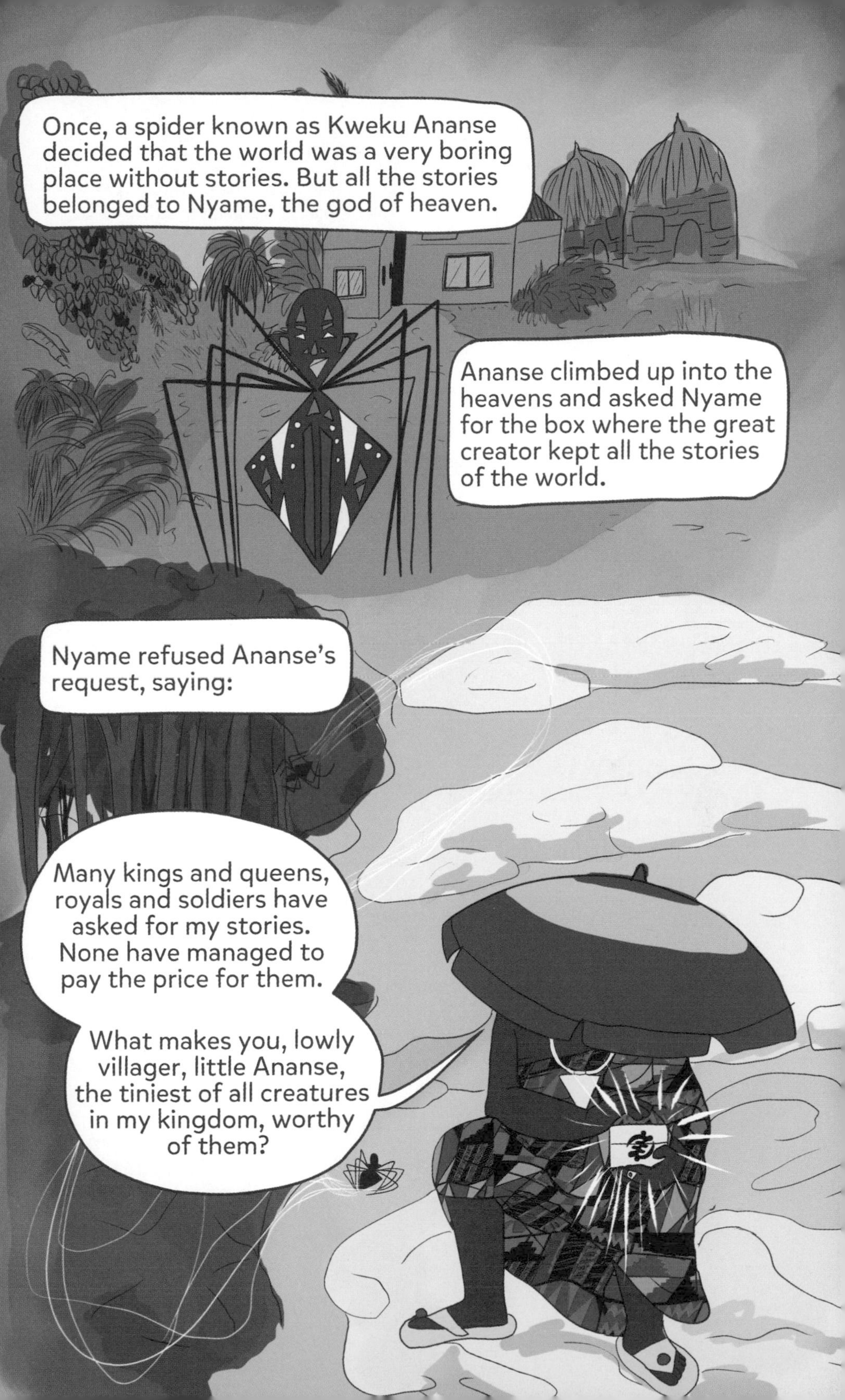
Once, a spider known as Kweku Ananse decided that the world was a very boring place without stories. But all the stories belonged to Nyame, the god of heaven.
Ananse climbed up into the heavens and asked Nyame for the box where the great creator kept all the stories of the world.
Nyame refused Ananse's request, saying:
Many kings and queens, royals and soldiers have asked for my stories. None have managed to pay the price for them.
What makes you, lowly villager, little Ananse, the tiniest of all creatures in my kingdom, worthy of them?

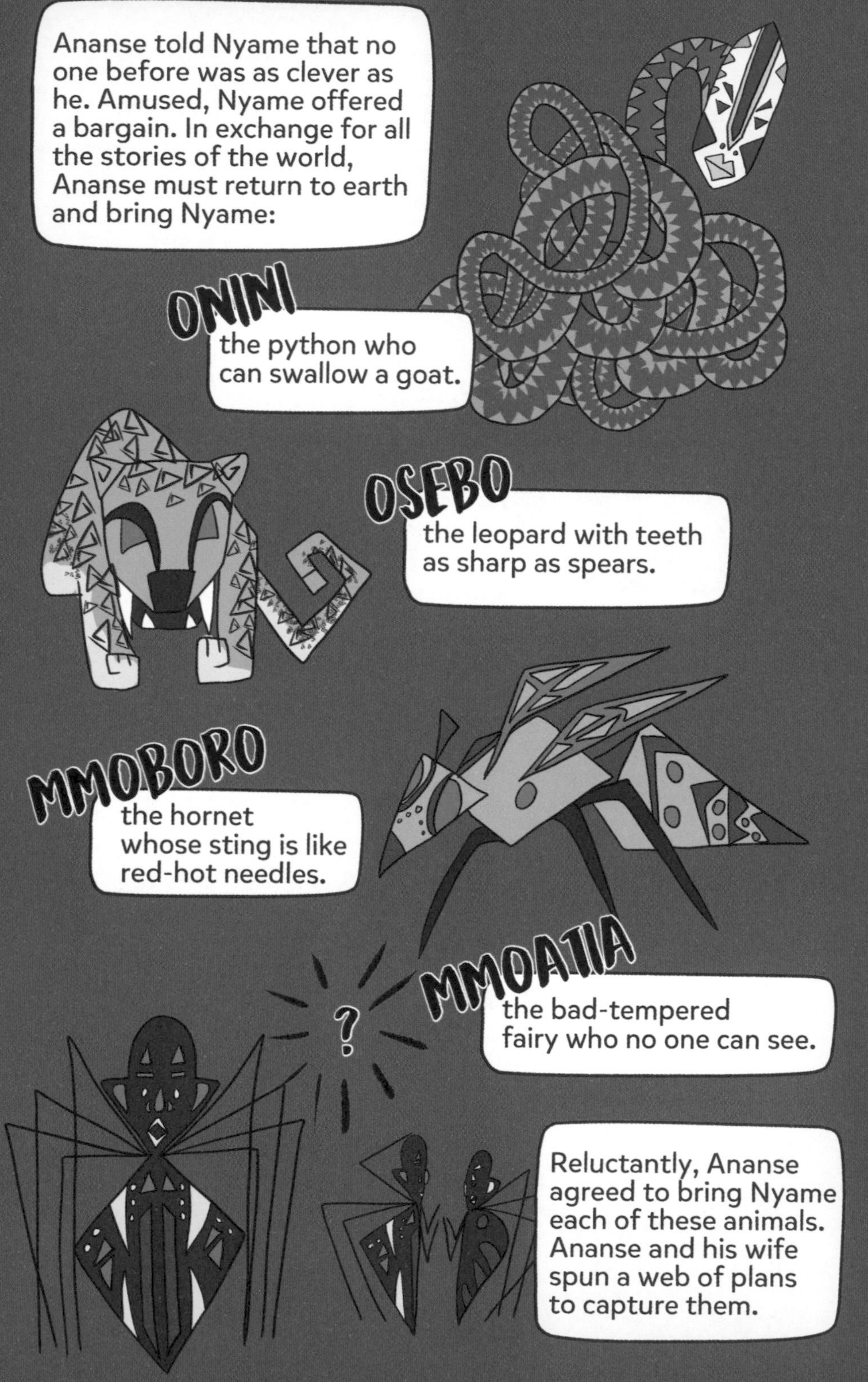
Ananse told Nyame that no one before was as clever as he. Amused, Nyame offered a bargain. In exchange for all the stories of the world, Ananse must return to earth and bring Nyame:
ONINI
the python who can swallow a goat.
OSEBO
the leopard with teeth as sharp as spears.
MMOBORO
the hornet whose sting is like red-hot needles.
MMOATIA
the bad-tempered fairy who no one can see.
?
Reluctantly, Ananse agreed to bring Nyame each of these animals. Ananse and his wife spun a web of plans to capture them.

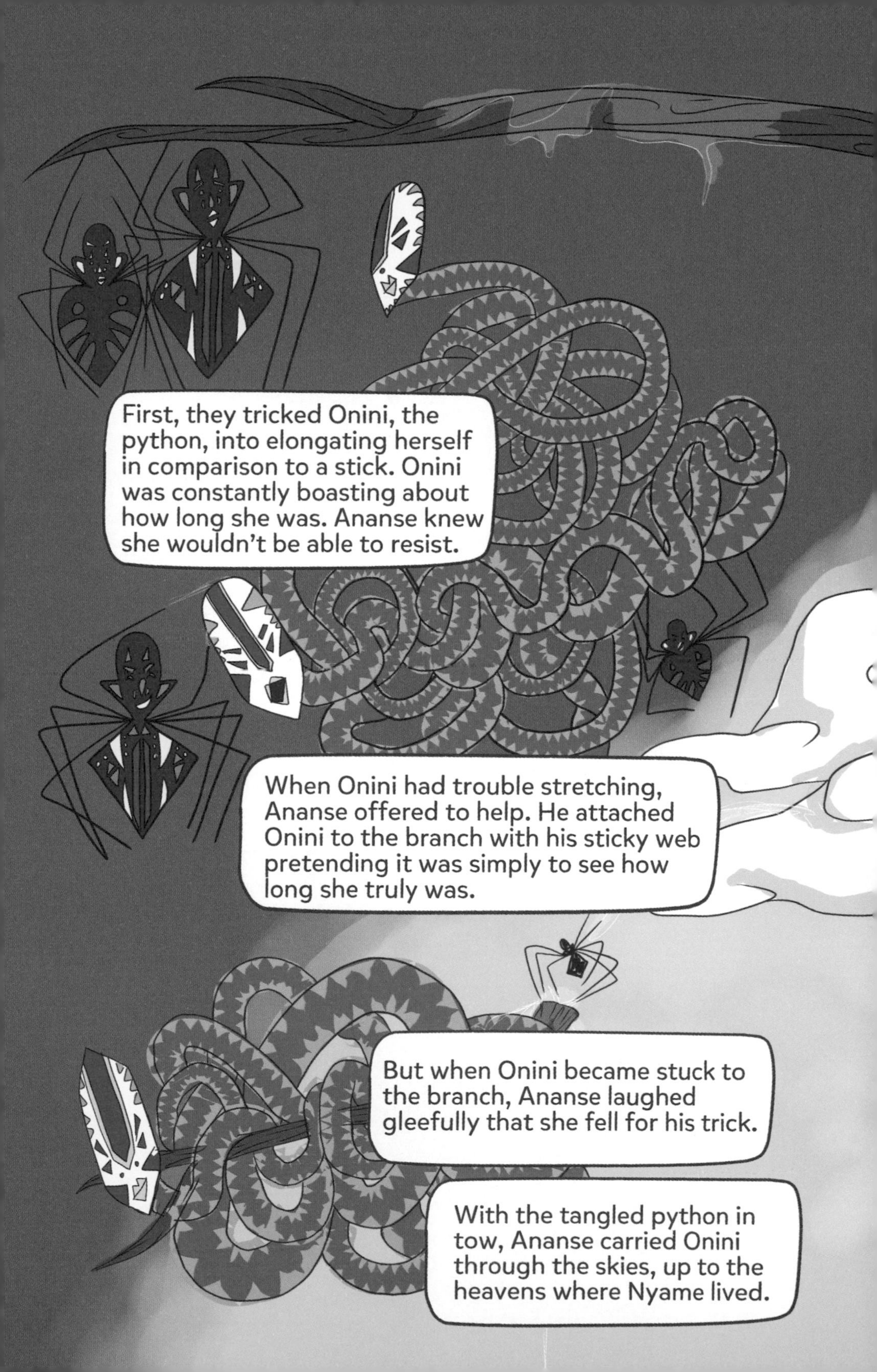
First, they tricked Onini, the python, into elongating herself in comparison to a stick. Onini was constantly boasting about how long she was. Ananse knew she wouldn't be able to resist.
When Onini had trouble stretching, Ananse offered to help. He attached Onini to the branch with his sticky web pretending it was simply to see how long she truly was.
But when Onini became stuck to the branch, Ananse laughed gleefully that she fell for his trick.
With the tangled python in tow, Ananse carried Onini through the skies, up to the heavens where Nyame lived.

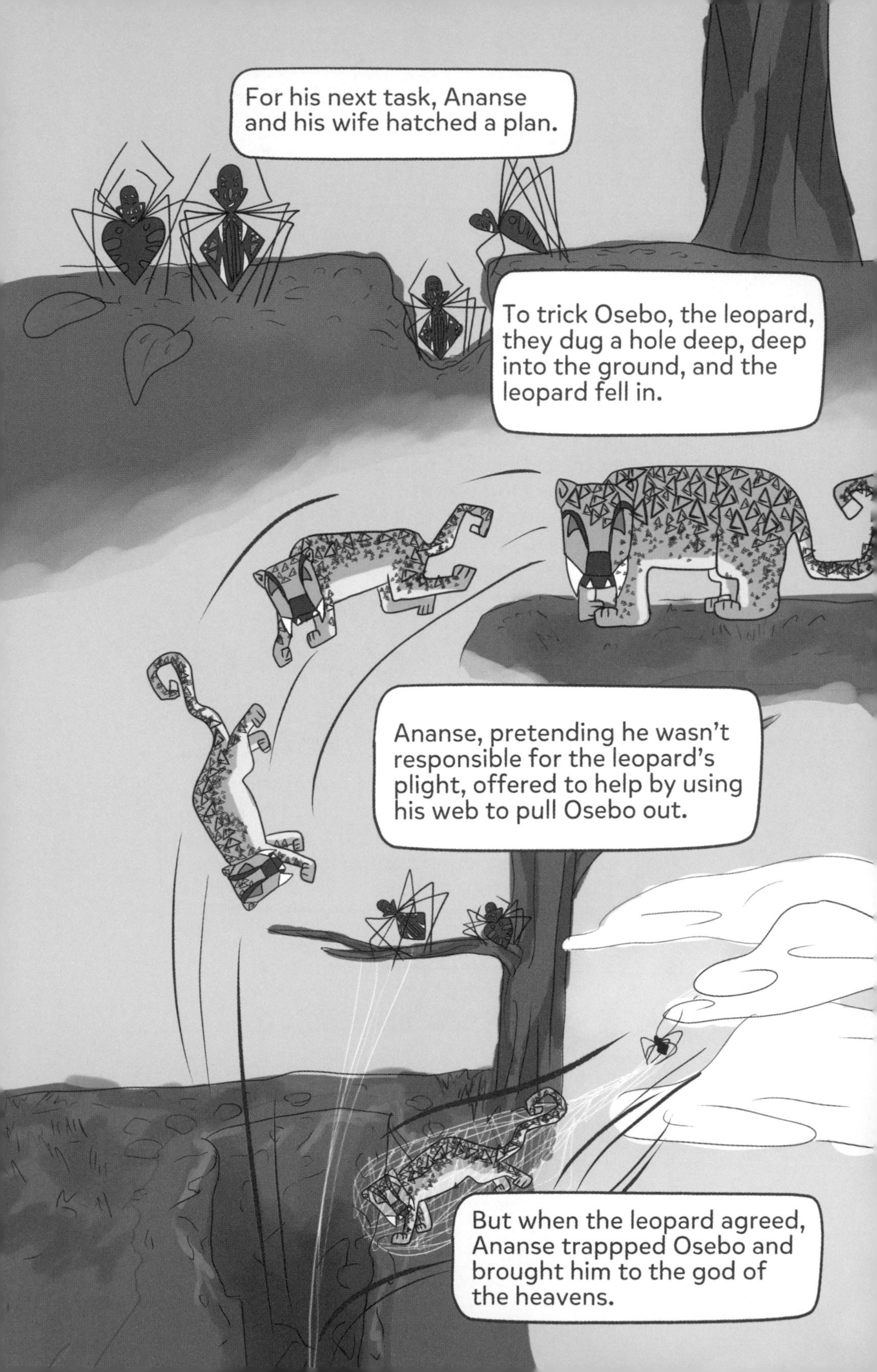
For his next task, Ananse and his wife hatched a plan.
To trick Osebo, the leopard, they dug a hole deep, deep into the ground, and the leopard fell in.
Ananse, pretending he wasn't responsible for the leopard's plight, offered to help by using his web to pull Osebo out.
But when the leopard agreed, Ananse trappped Osebo and brought him to the god of the heavens.

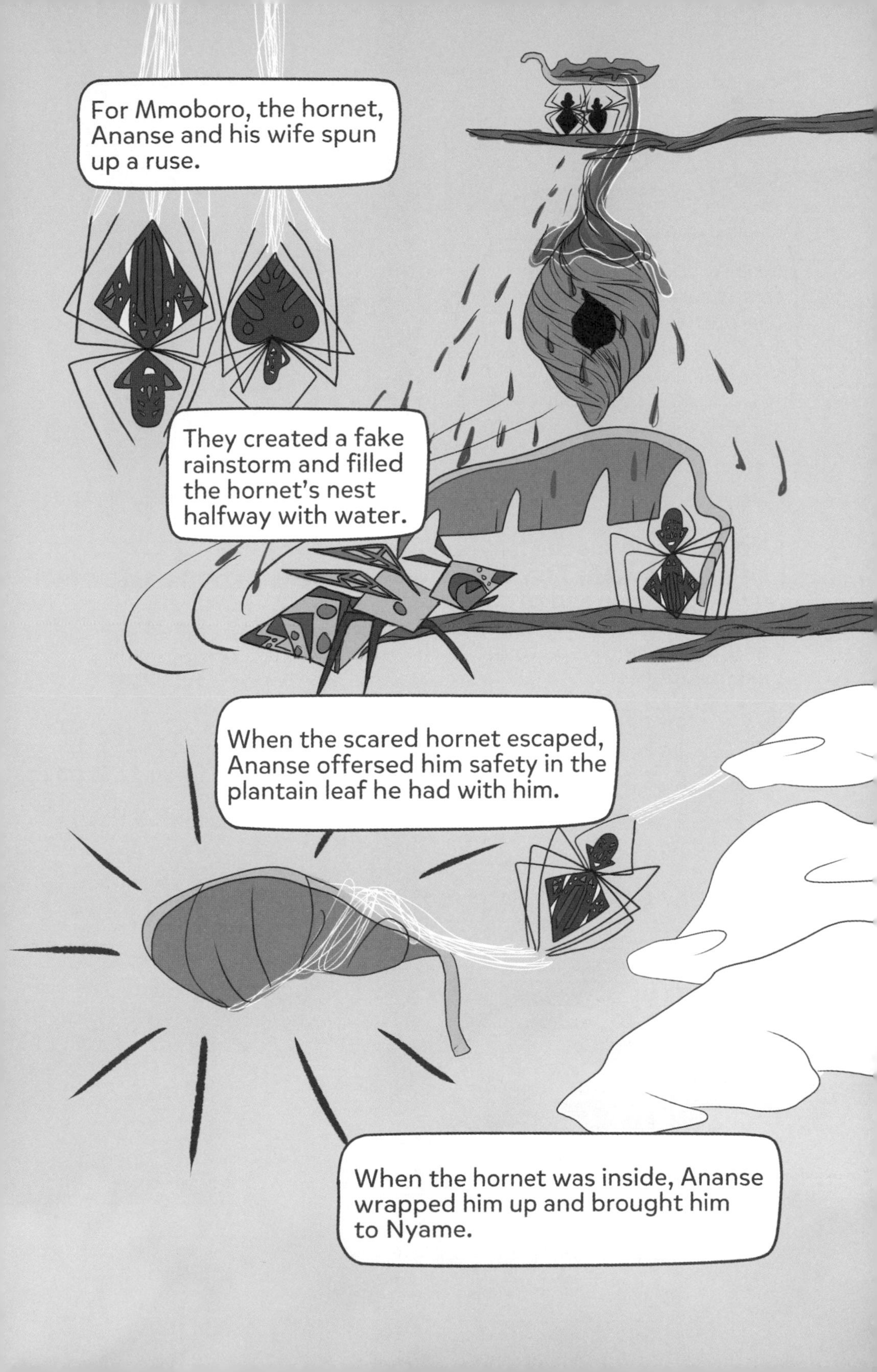
For Mmoboro, the hornet, Ananse and his wife spun up a ruse.
They created a fake rainstorm and filled the hornet's nest halfway with water.
When the scared hornet escaped, Ananse offersed him safety in the plantain leaf he had with him.
When the hornet was inside, Ananse wrapped him up and brought him to Nyame.

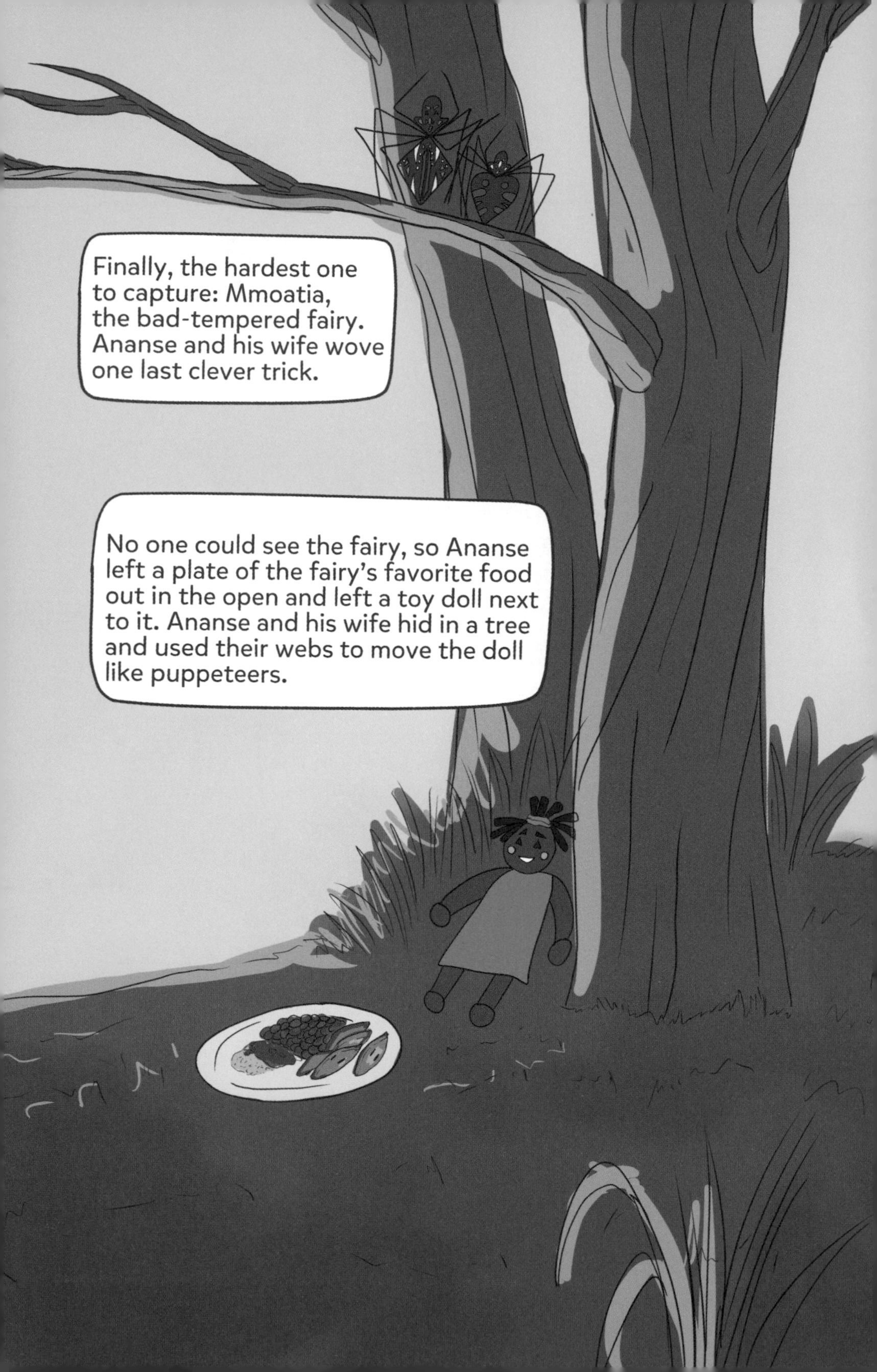
Finally, the hardest one to capture: Mmoatia, the bad-tempered fairy. Ananse and his wife wove one last clever trick.
No one could see the fairy, so Ananse left a plate of the fairy's favorite food out in the open and left a toy doll next to it. Ananse and his wife hid in a tree and used their webs to move the doll like puppeteers.

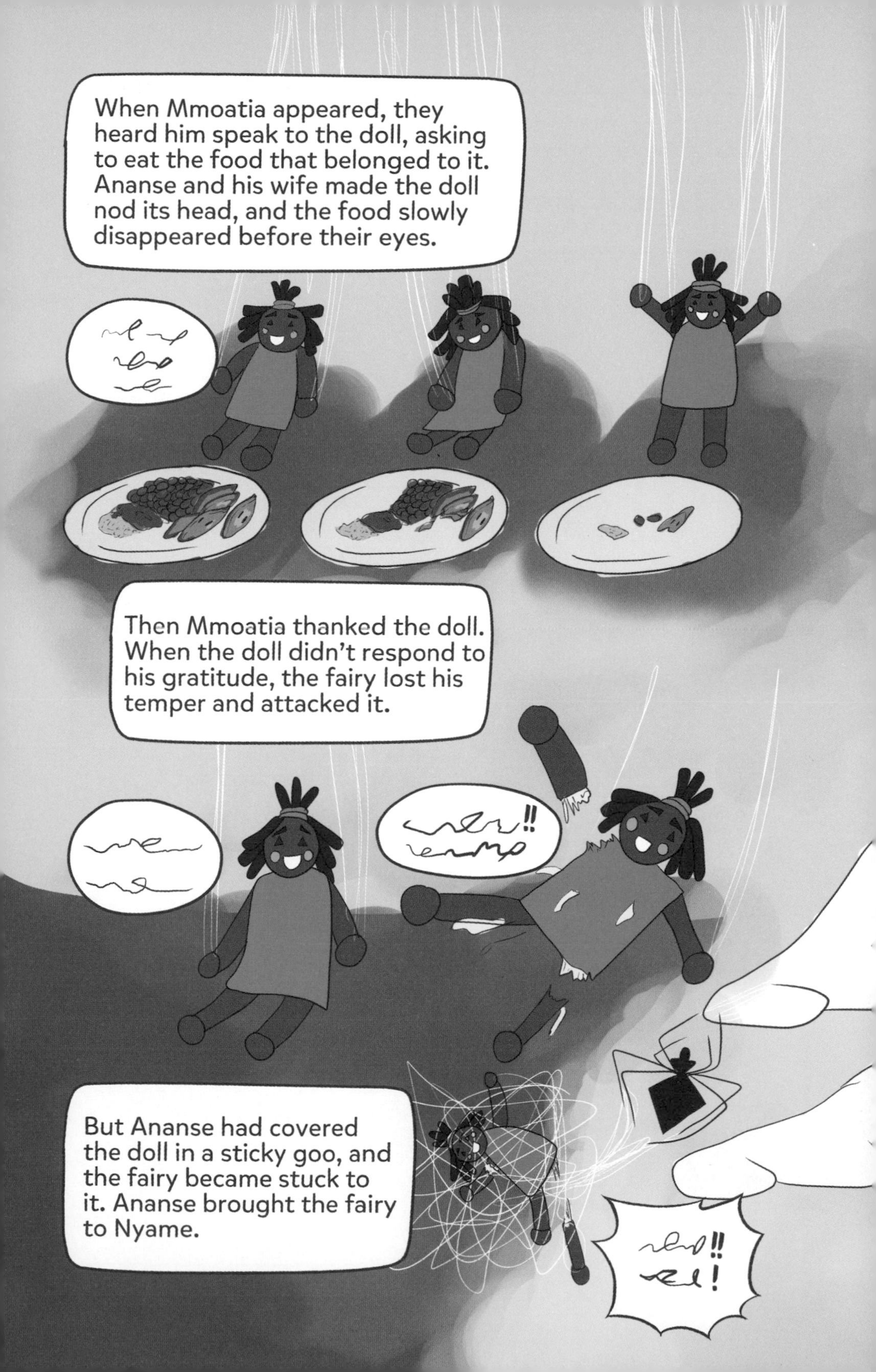
When Mmoatia appeared, they heard him speak to the doll, asking to eat the food that belonged to it. Ananse and his wife made the doll nod its head, and the food slowly disappeared before their eyes.
Then Mmoatia thanked the doll. When the doll didn't respond to his gratitude, the fairy lost his temper and attacked it.
But Ananse had covered the doll in a sticky goo, and the fairy became stuck to it. Ananse brought the fairy to Nyame.

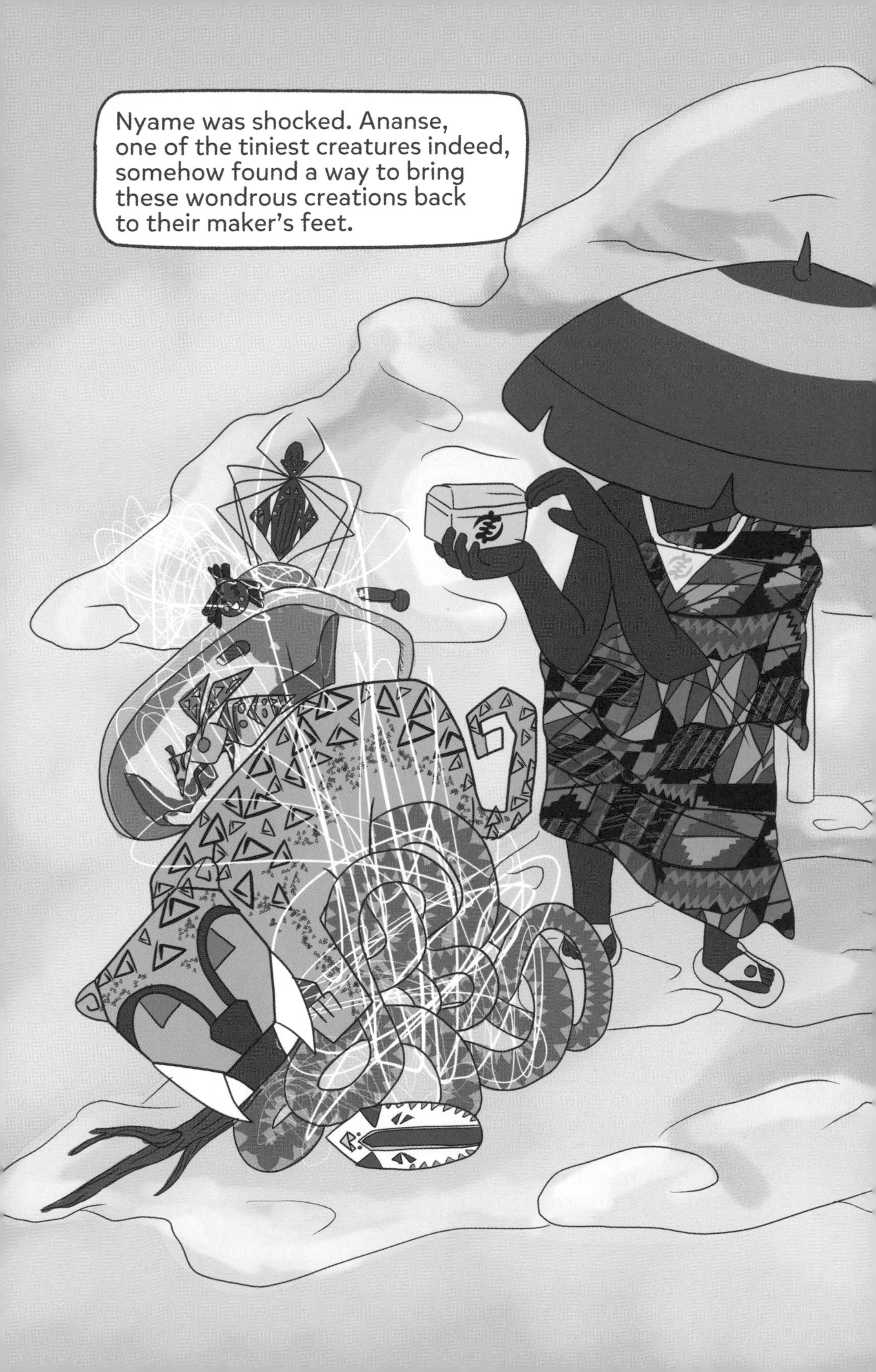
Nyame was shocked. Ananse, one of the tiniest creatures indeed, somehow found a way to bring these wondrous creations back to their maker's feet.

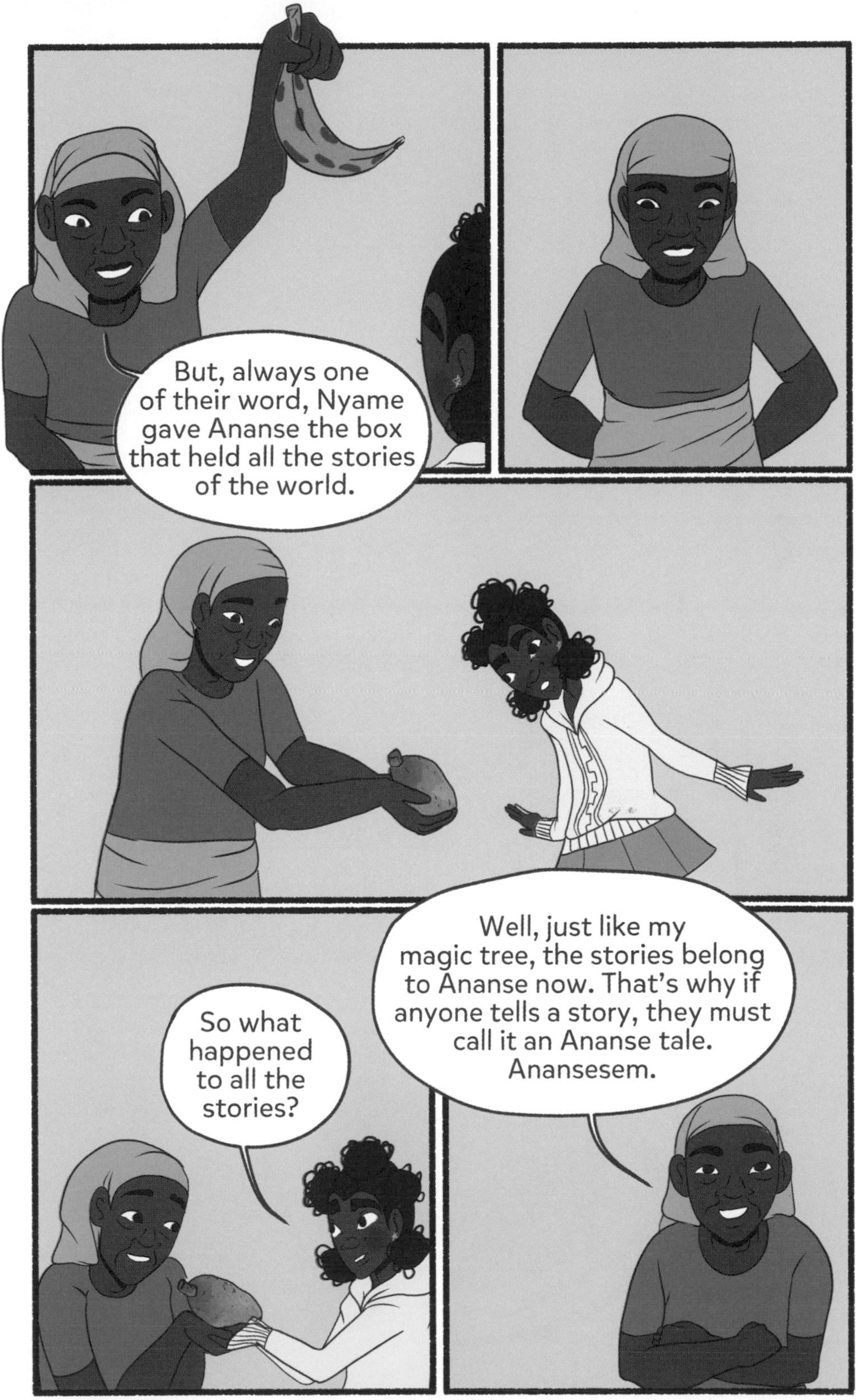
But, always one of their word, Nyame gave Ananse the box that held all the stories of the world.
So what happened to all the stories?
Well, just like my magic tree, the stories belong to Ananse now. That's why if anyone tells a story, they must call it an Ananse tale. Anansesem.

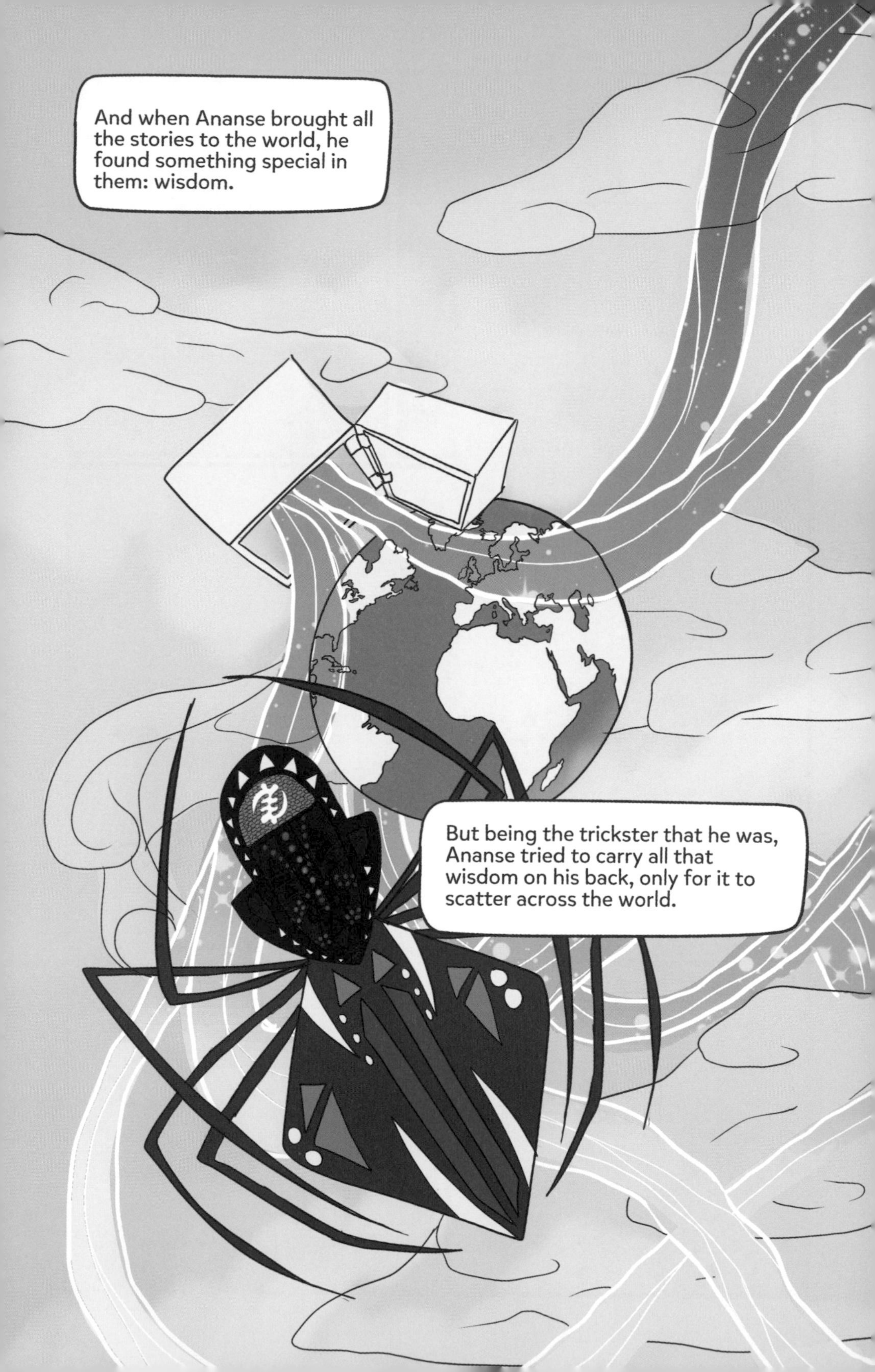
And when Ananse brought all the stories to the world, he found something special in them: wisdom.
But being the trickster that he was, Ananse tried to carry all that wisdom on his back, only for it to scatter across the world.

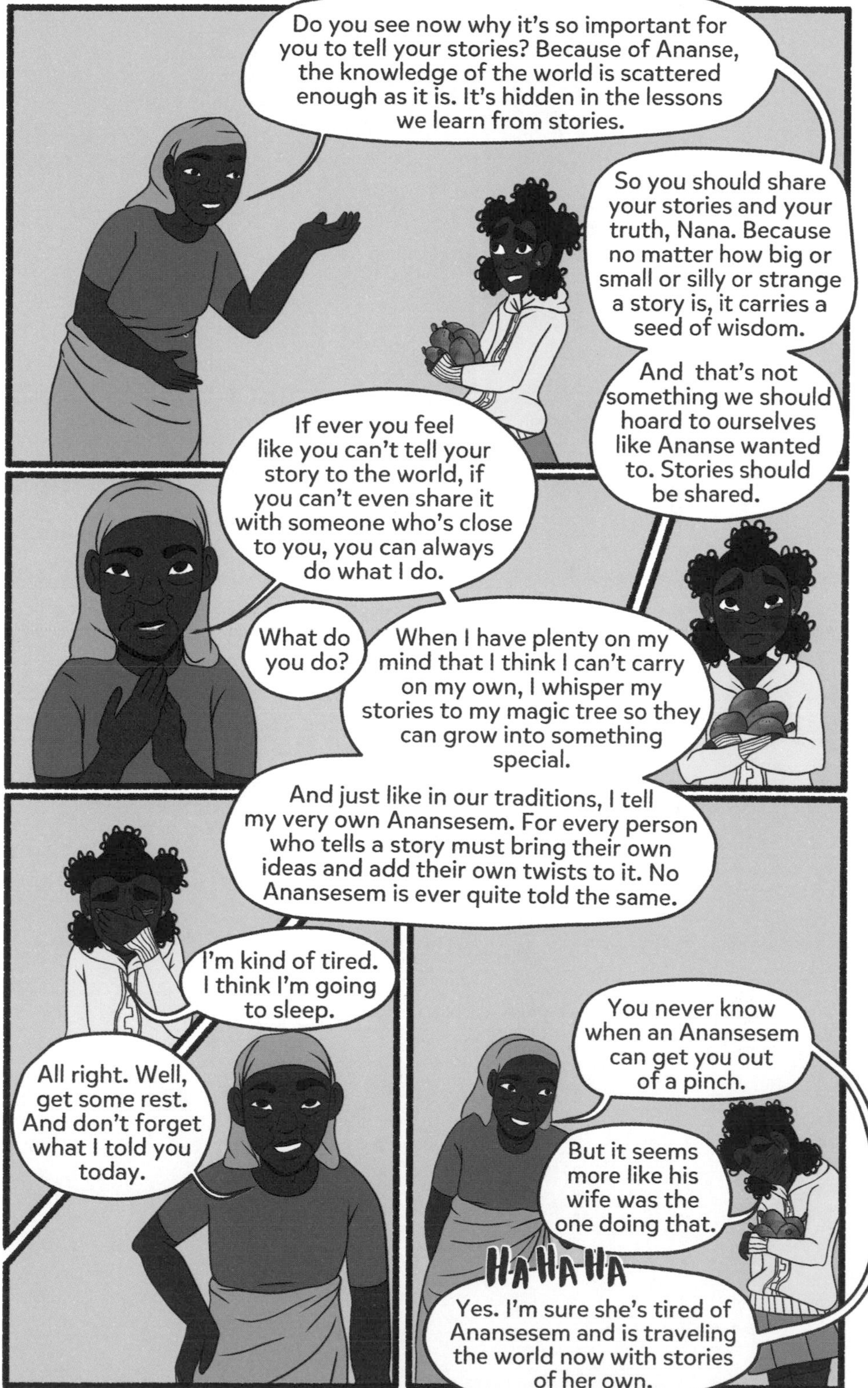
Do you see now why it's so important for you to tell your stories? Because of Ananse, the knowledge of the world is scattered enough as it is. It's hidden in the lessons we learn from stories.
So you should share your stories and your truth, Nana. Because no matter how big or small or silly or strange a story is, it carries a seed of wisdom.
And that's not something we should hoard to ourselves like Ananse wanted to. Stories should be shared.
If ever you feel like you can't tell your story to the world, if you can't even share it with someone who's close to you, you can always do what I do.
What do you do?
When I have plenty on my mind that I think I can't carry on my own, I whisper my stories to my magic tree so they can grow into something special.
And just like in our traditions, I tell my very own Anansesem. For every person who tells a story must bring their own ideas and add their own twists to it. No Anansesem is ever quite told the same.
I'm kind of tired. I think I'm going to sleep.
All right. Well, get some rest. And don't forget what I told you today.
You never know when an Anansesem can get you out of a pinch.
But it seems more like his wife was the one doing that.
HA HA HA
Yes. I'm sure she's tired of Anansesem and is traveling the world now with stories of her own.

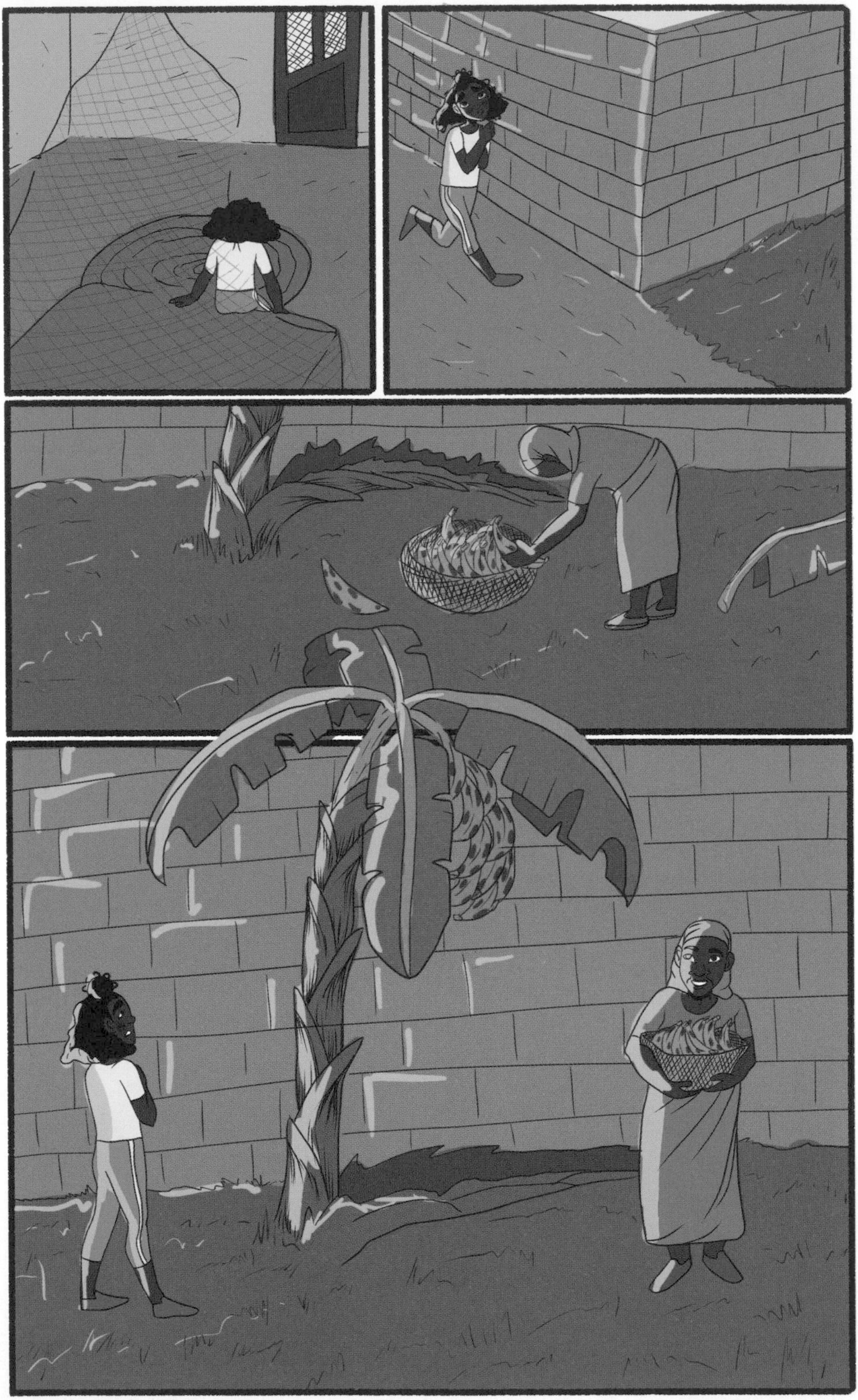

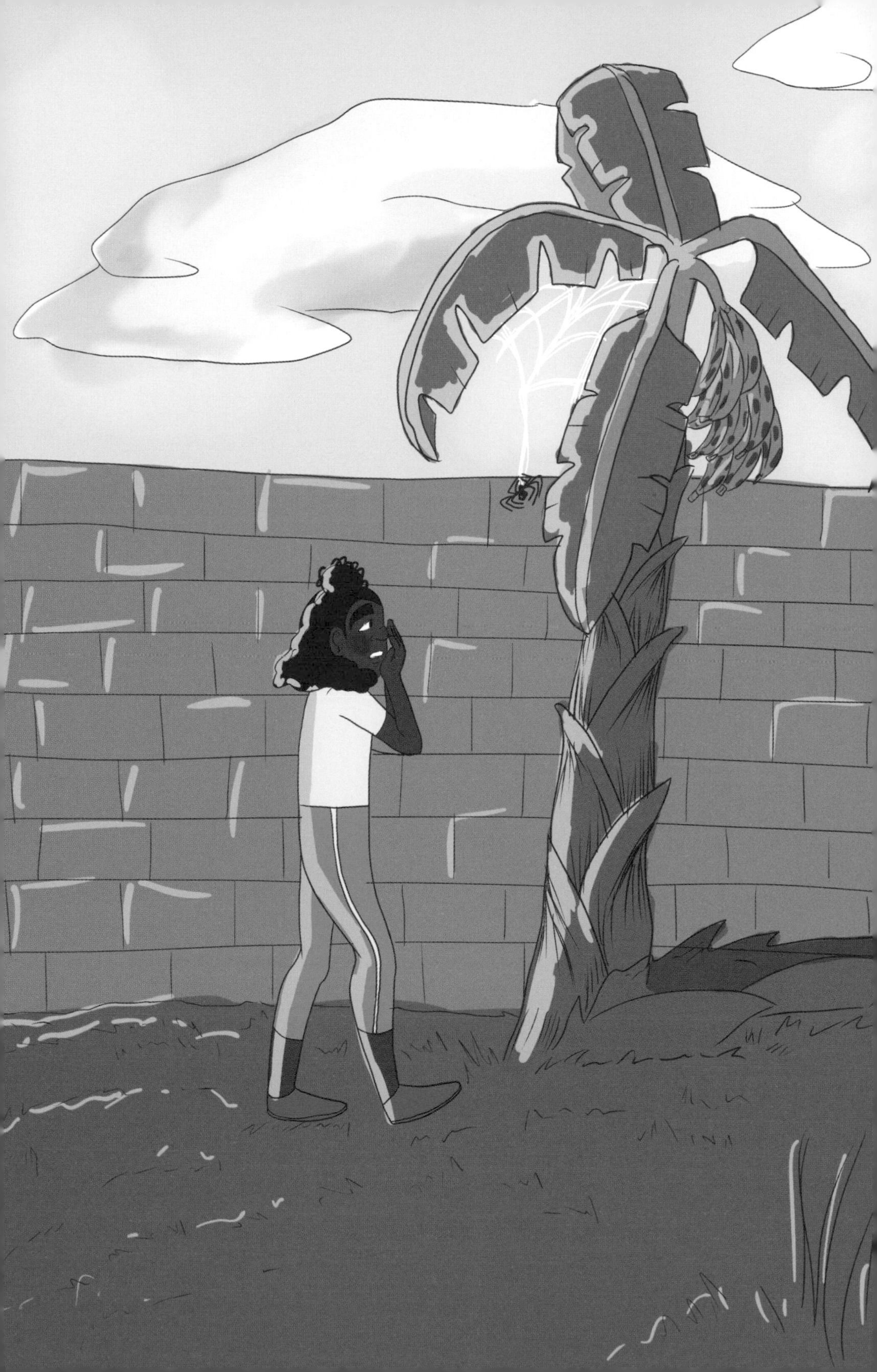

Chapter 5

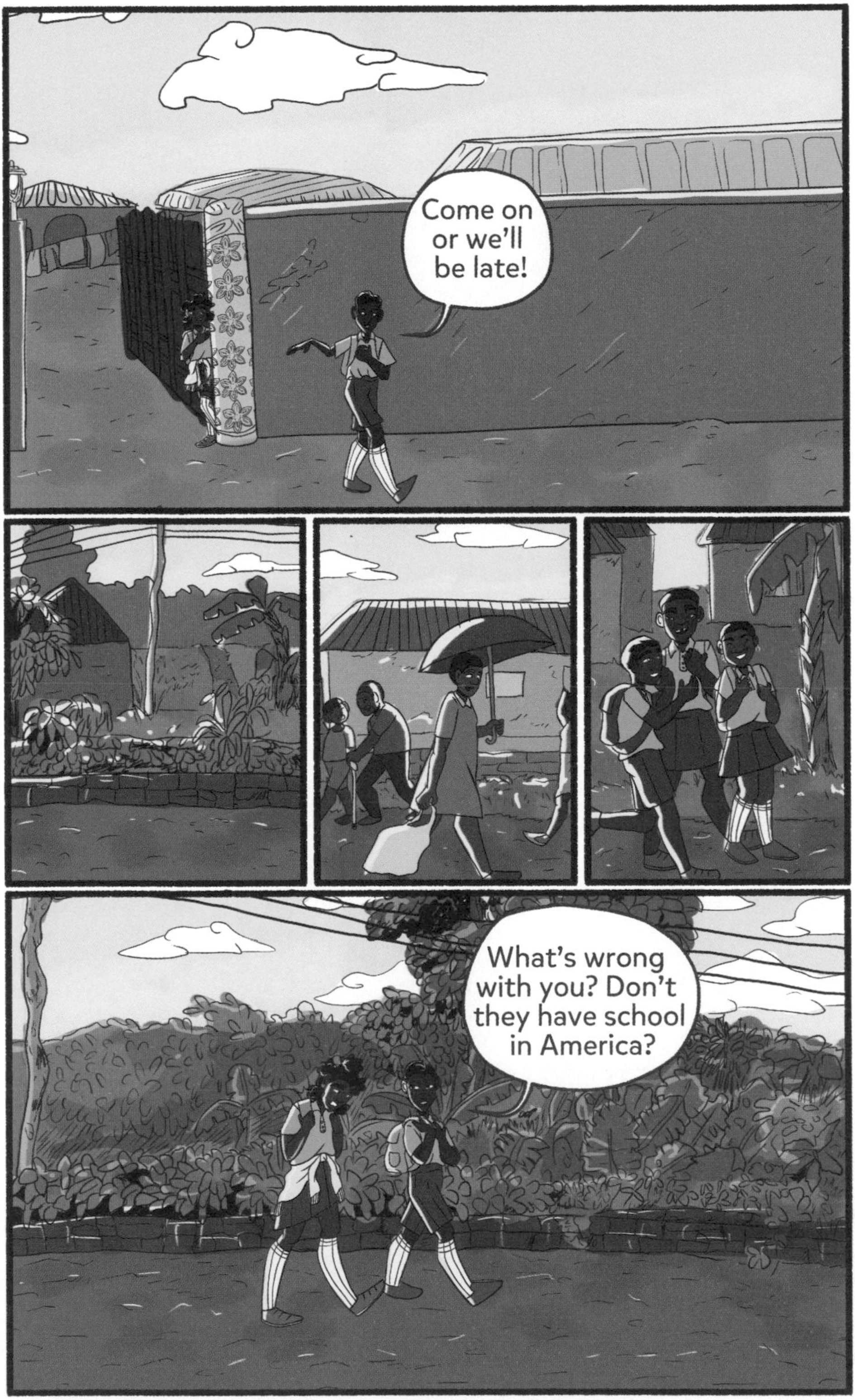
Come on or we'll be late!
What's wrong with you? Don't they have school in America?

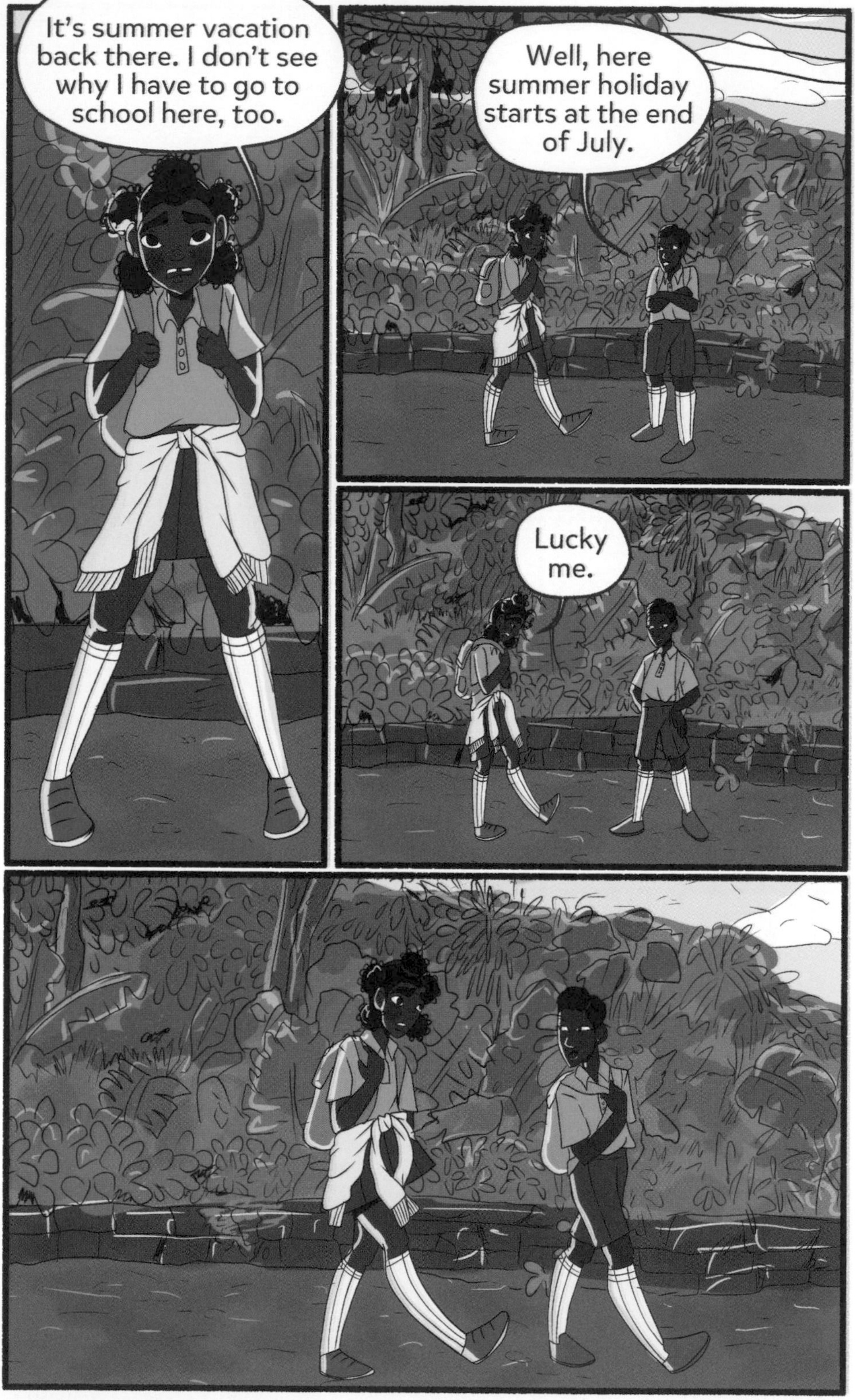
It's summer vacation back there. I don't see why I have to go to school here, too.
Well, here summer holiday starts at the end of July.
Lucky me.

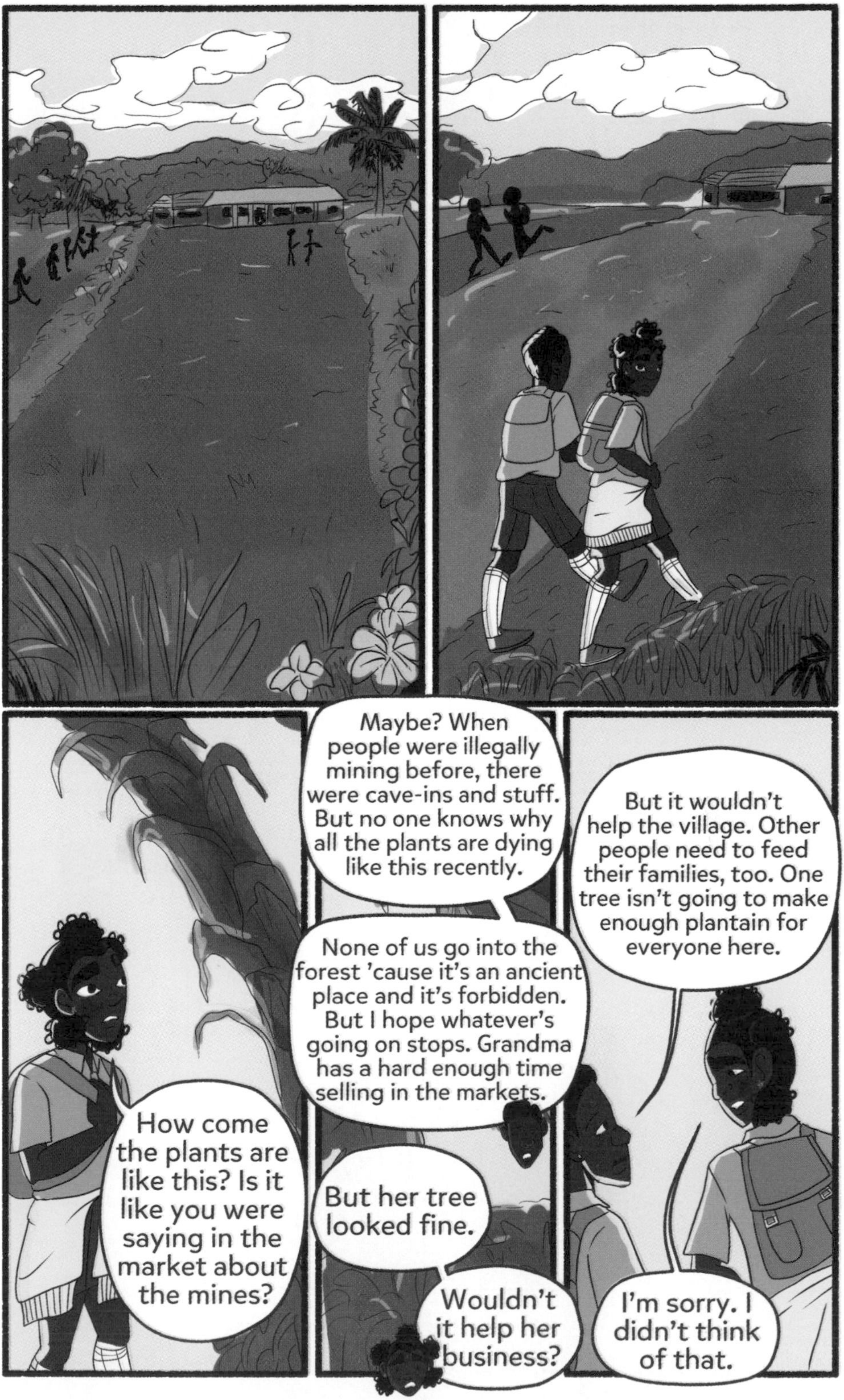
How come the plants are like this? Is it like you were saying in the market about the mines?
Maybe? When people were illegally mining before, there were cave-ins and stuff. But no one knows why all the plants are dying like this recently.
None of us go into the forest 'cause it's an ancient place and it's forbidden. But I hope whatever's going on stops. Grandma has a hard enough time selling in the markets.
But her tree looked fine.
Wouldn't it help her business?
But it wouldn't help the village. Other people need to feed their families, too. One tree isn't going to make enough plantain for everyone here.
I'm sorry. I didn't think of that.

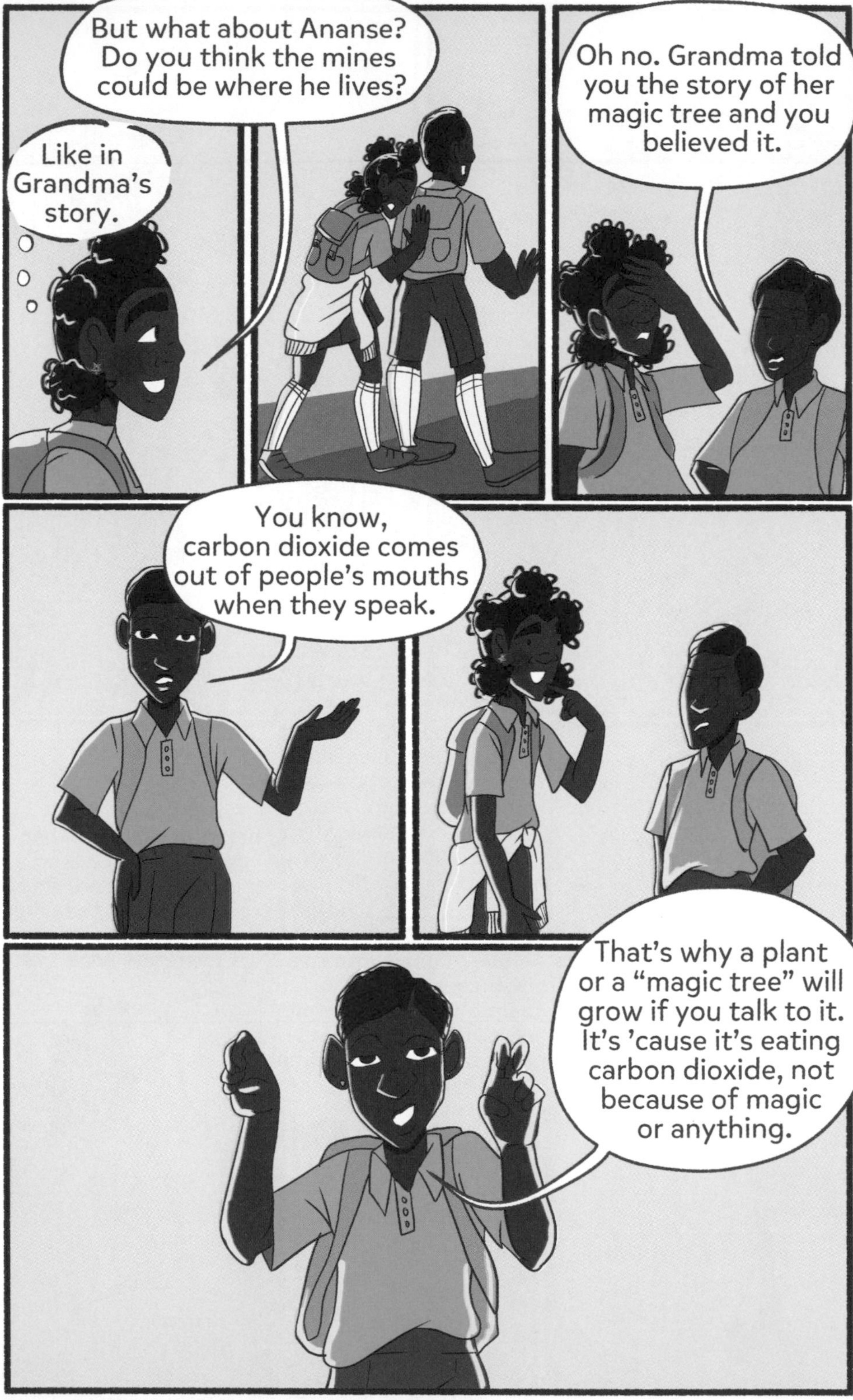
Like in Grandma's story.
But what about Ananse? Do you think the mines could be where he lives?
Oh no. Grandma told you the story of her magic tree and you believed it.
You know, carbon dioxide comes out of people's mouths when they speak.
That's why a plant or a "magic tree" will grow if you talk to it. It's 'cause it's eating carbon dioxide, not because of magic or anything.

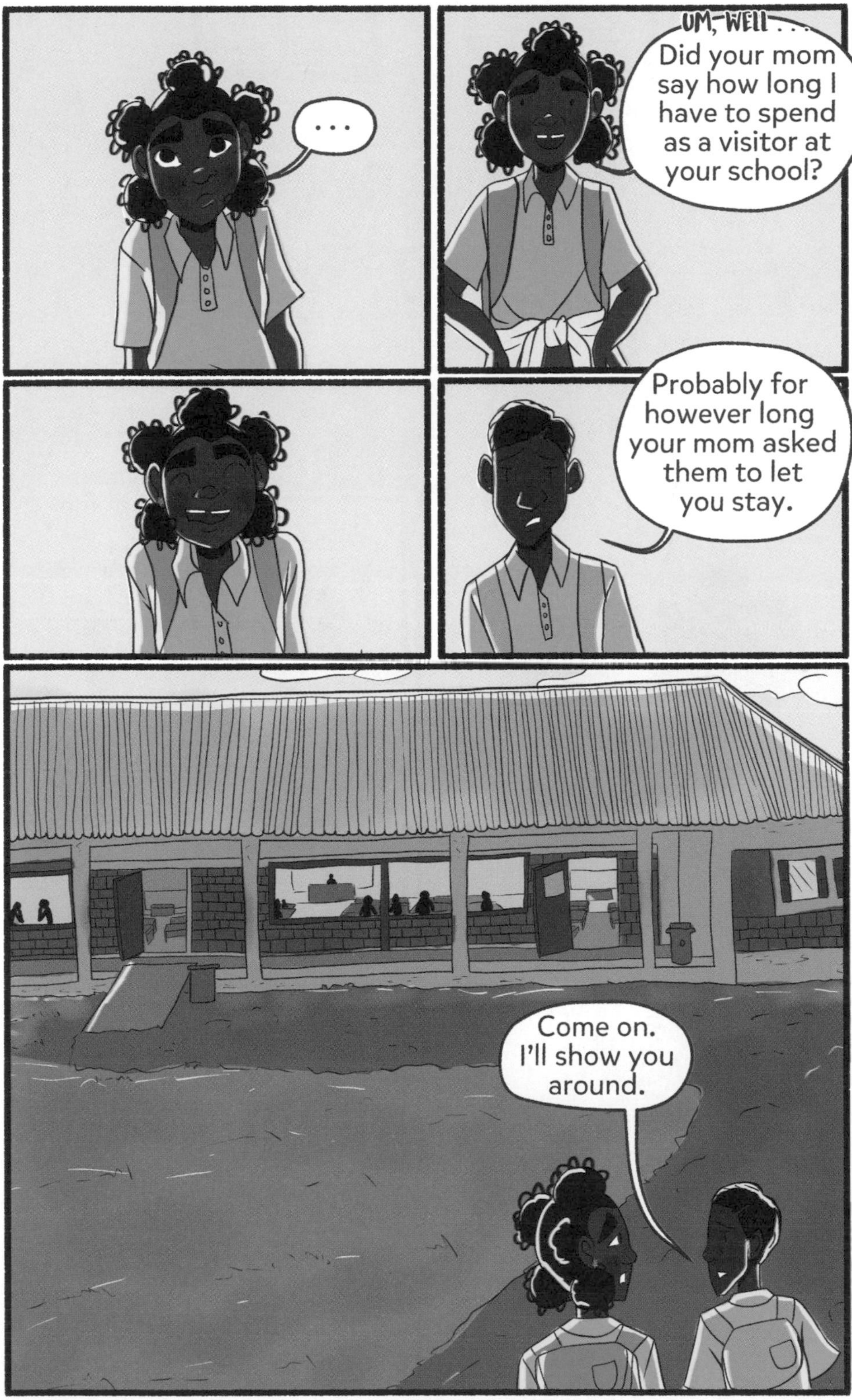
. . .
UM, WELL . . .
Did your mom say how long I have to spend as a visitor at your school?
Probably for however long your mom asked them to let you stay.
Come on. I'll show you around.

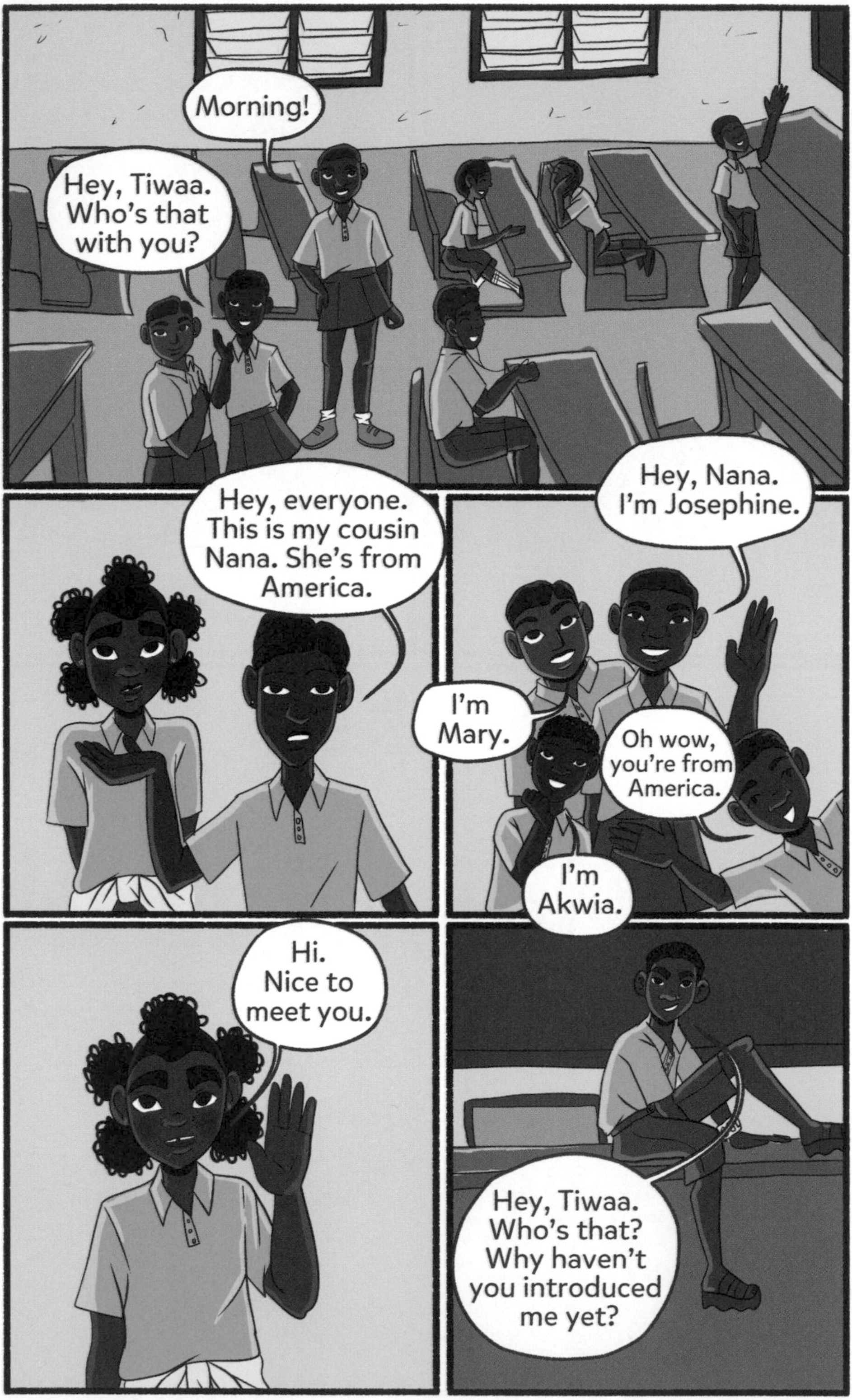
Morning!
Hey, Tiwaa. Who's that with you?
Hey, everyone. This is my cousin Nana. She's from America.
Hey, Nana. I'm Josephine.
I'm Mary.
Oh wow, you're from America.
I'm Akwia.
Hi. Nice to meet you.
Hey, Tiwaa. Who's that? Why haven't you introduced me yet?

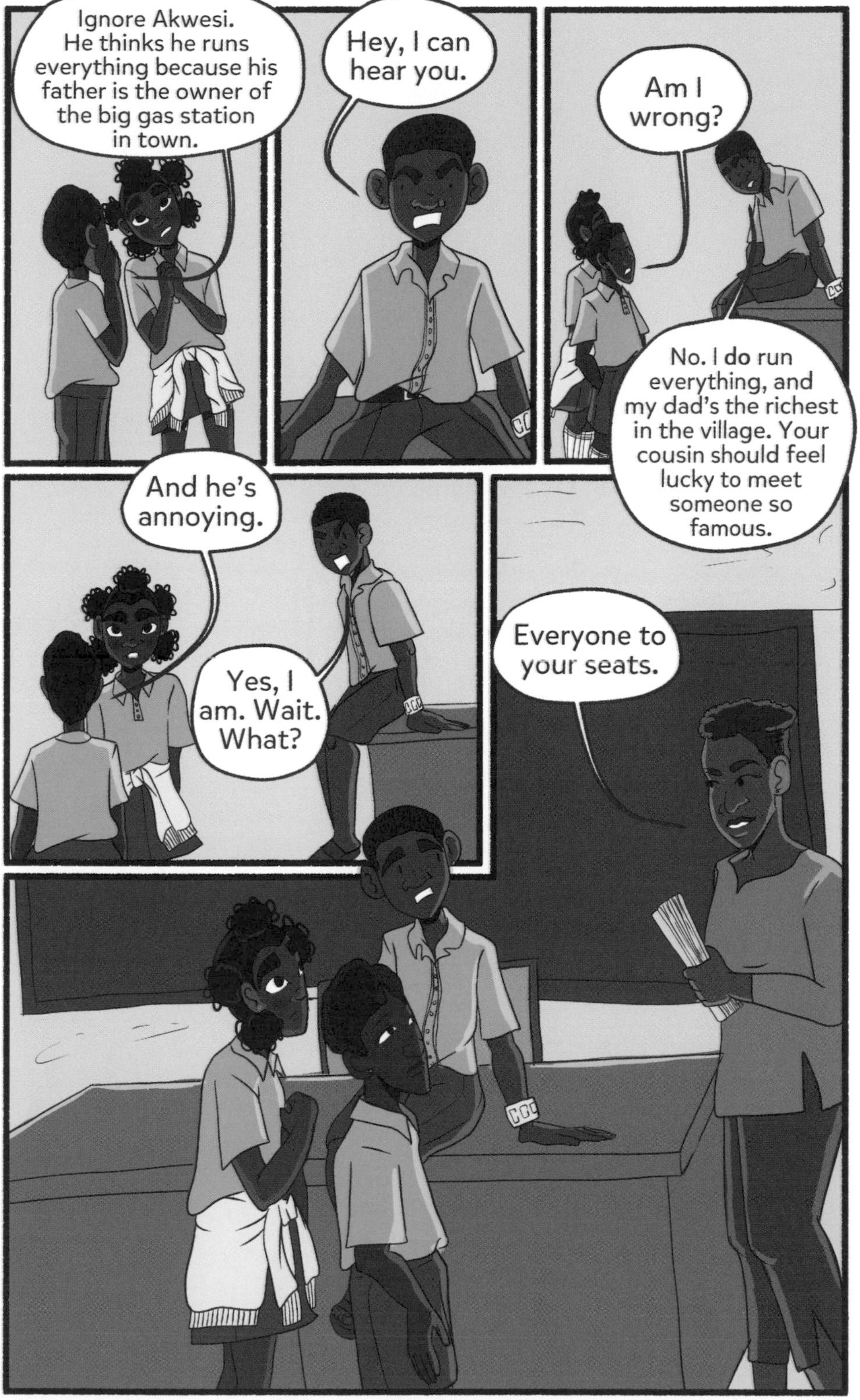
Ignore Akwesi. He thinks he runs everything because his father is the owner of the big gas station in town.
Hey, I can hear you.
Am I wrong?
No. I **do** run everything, and my dad's the richest in the village. Your cousin should feel lucky to meet someone so famous.
And he's annoying.
Yes, I am. Wait. What?
Everyone to your seats.

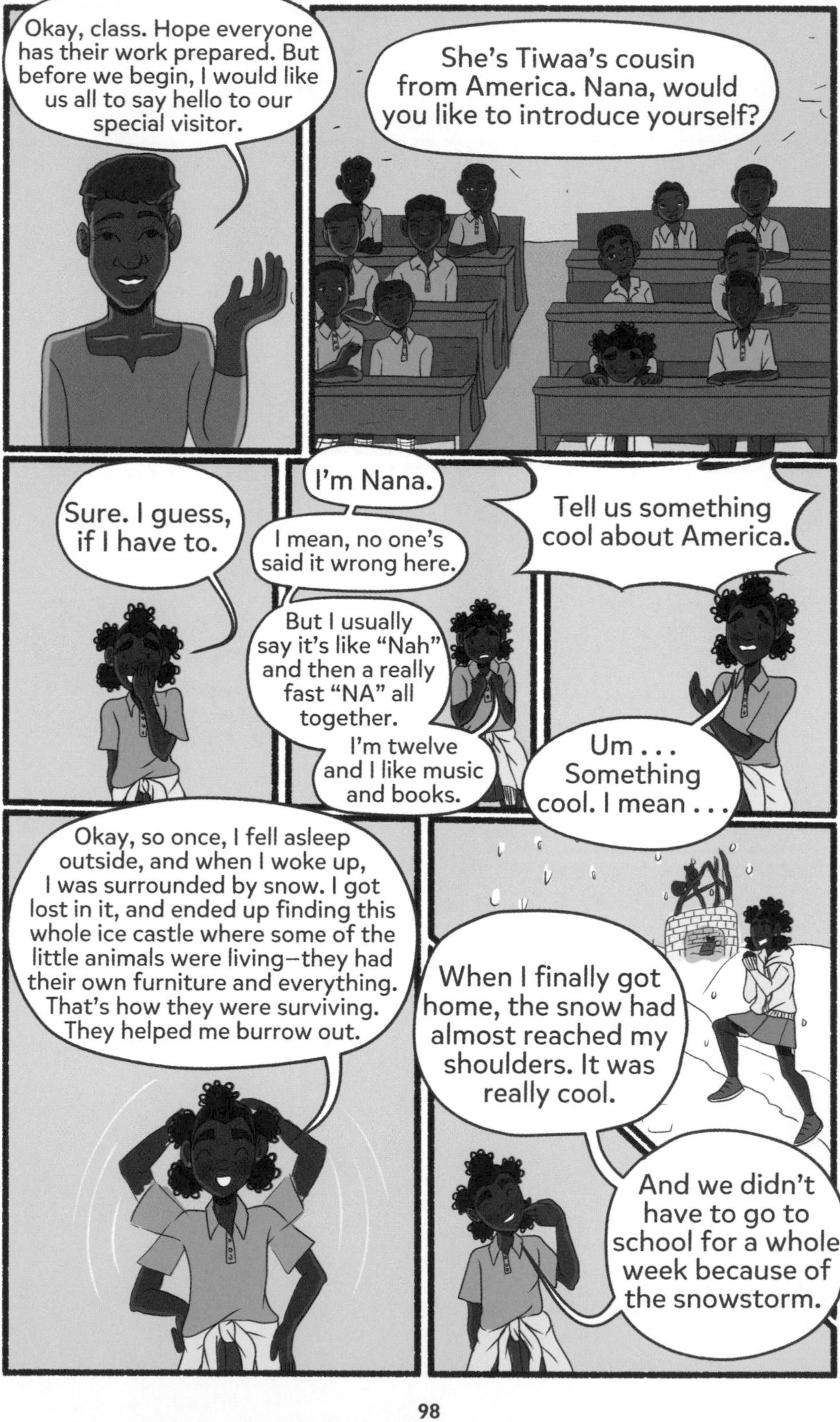
Okay, class. Hope everyone has their work prepared. But before we begin, I would like us all to say hello to our special visitor.
She's Tiwaa's cousin from America. Nana, would you like to introduce yourself?
Sure. I guess, if I have to.
I'm Nana.
I mean, no one's said it wrong here.
But I usually say it's like "Nah" and then a really fast "NA" all together.
I'm twelve and I like music and books.
Tell us something cool about America.
Um . . . Something cool. I mean . . .
Okay, so once, I fell asleep outside, and when I woke up, I was surrounded by snow. I got lost in it, and ended up finding this whole ice castle where some of the little animals were living—they had their own furniture and everything. That's how they were surviving. They helped me burrow out.
When I finally got home, the snow had almost reached my shoulders. It was really cool.
And we didn't have to go to school for a whole week because of the snowstorm.

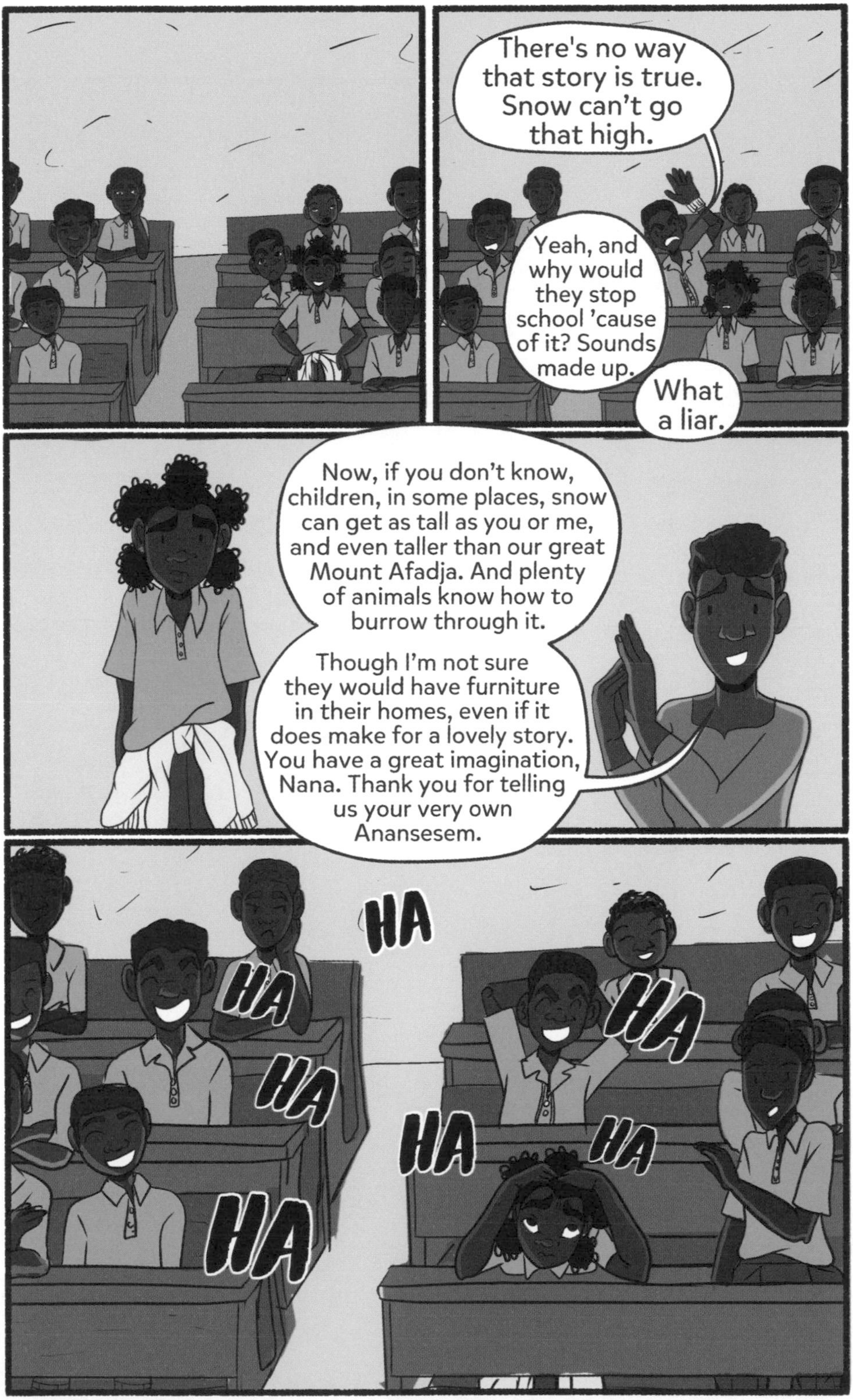

There's no way that story is true. Snow can't go that high.
Yeah, and why would they stop school 'cause of it? Sounds made up.
What a liar.
Now, if you don't know, children, in some places, snow can get as tall as you or me, and even taller than our great Mount Afadja. And plenty of animals know how to burrow through it.
Though I'm not sure they would have furniture in their homes, even if it does make for a lovely story. You have a great imagination, Nana. Thank you for telling us your very own Anansesem.
HA
HA
HA
HA
HA
HA
HA

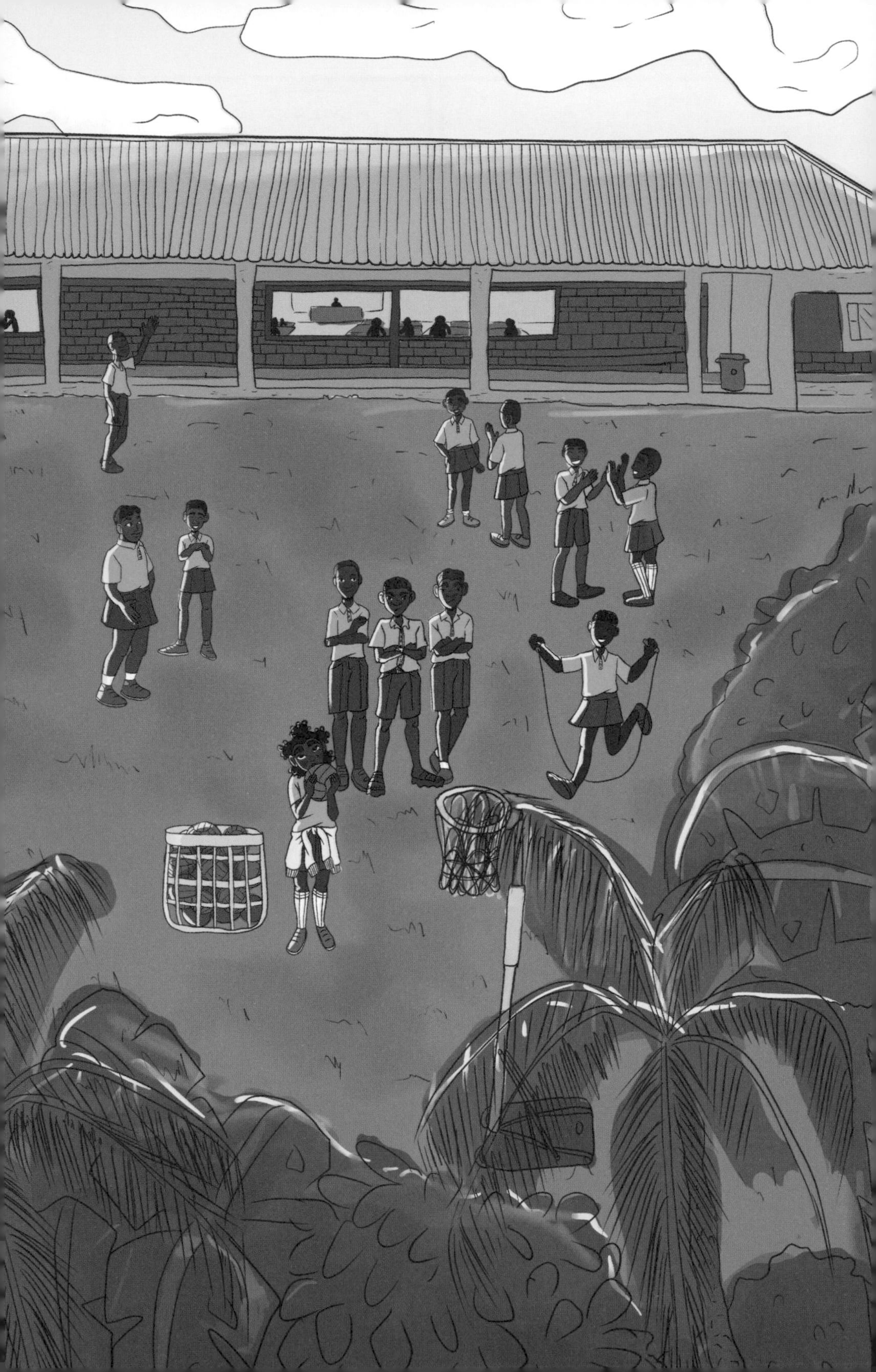

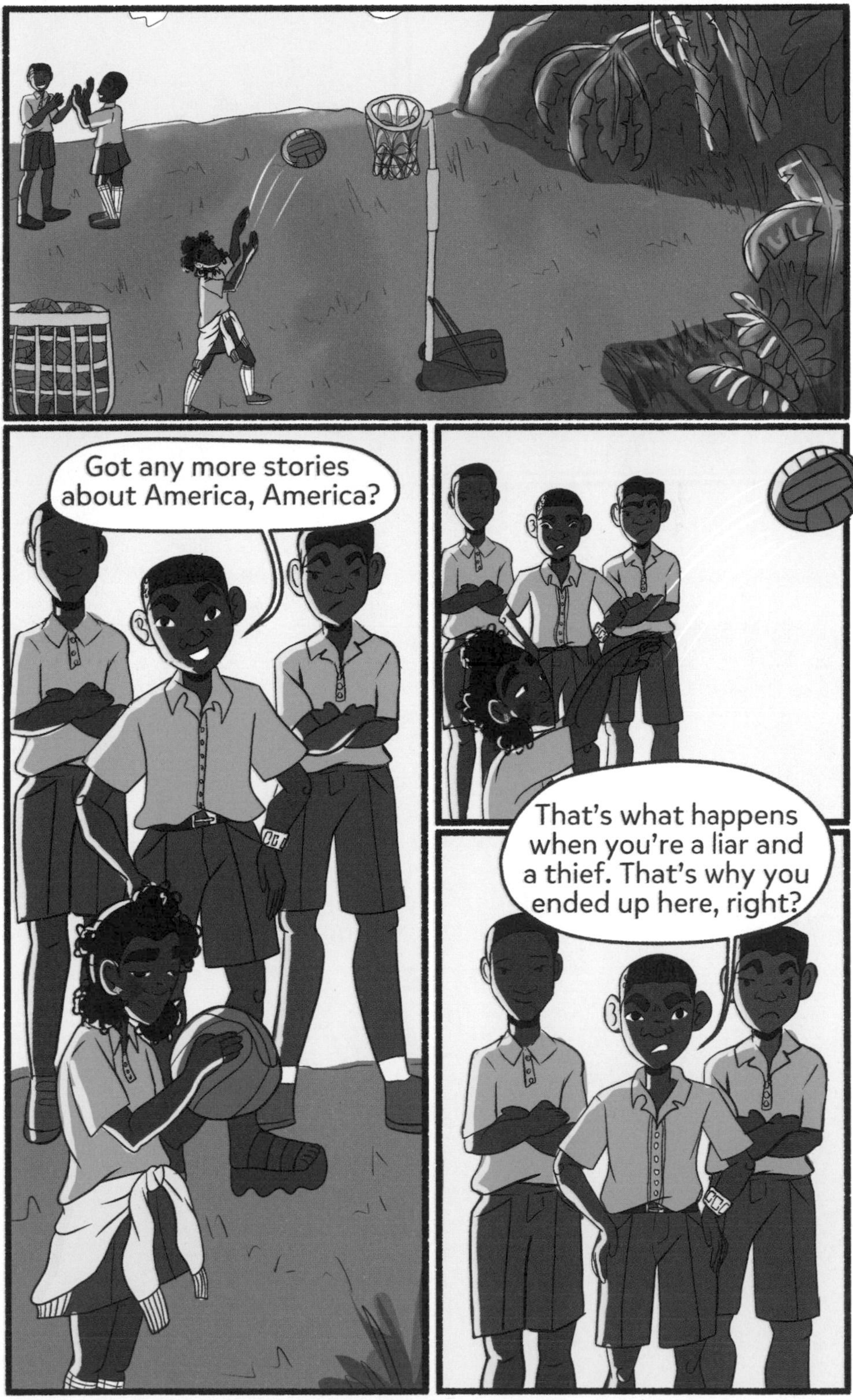

Got any more stories about America, America?
That's what happens when you're a liar and a thief. That's why you ended up here, right?

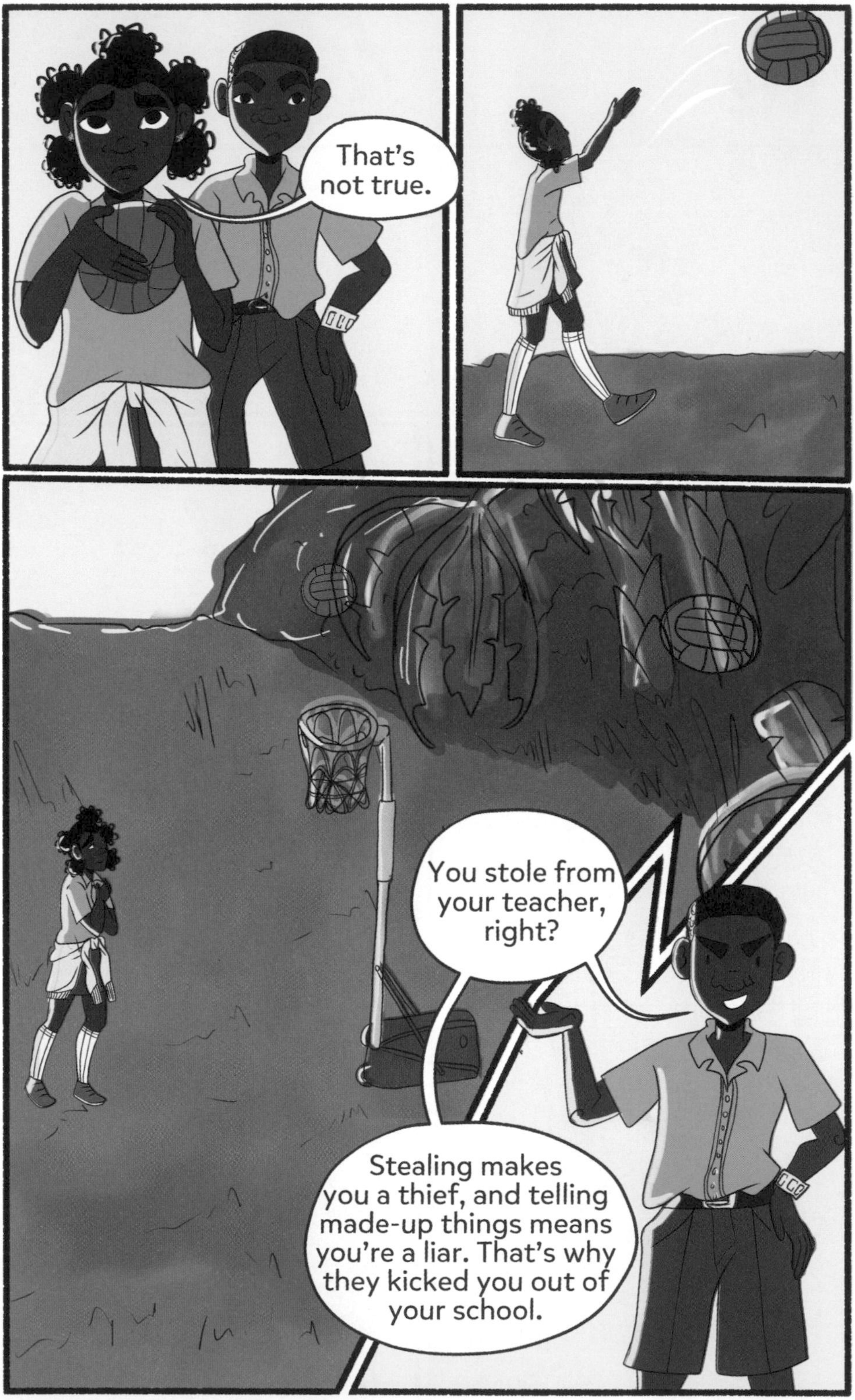
That's not true.
You stole from your teacher, right?
Stealing makes you a thief, and telling made-up things means you're a liar. That's why they kicked you out of your school.

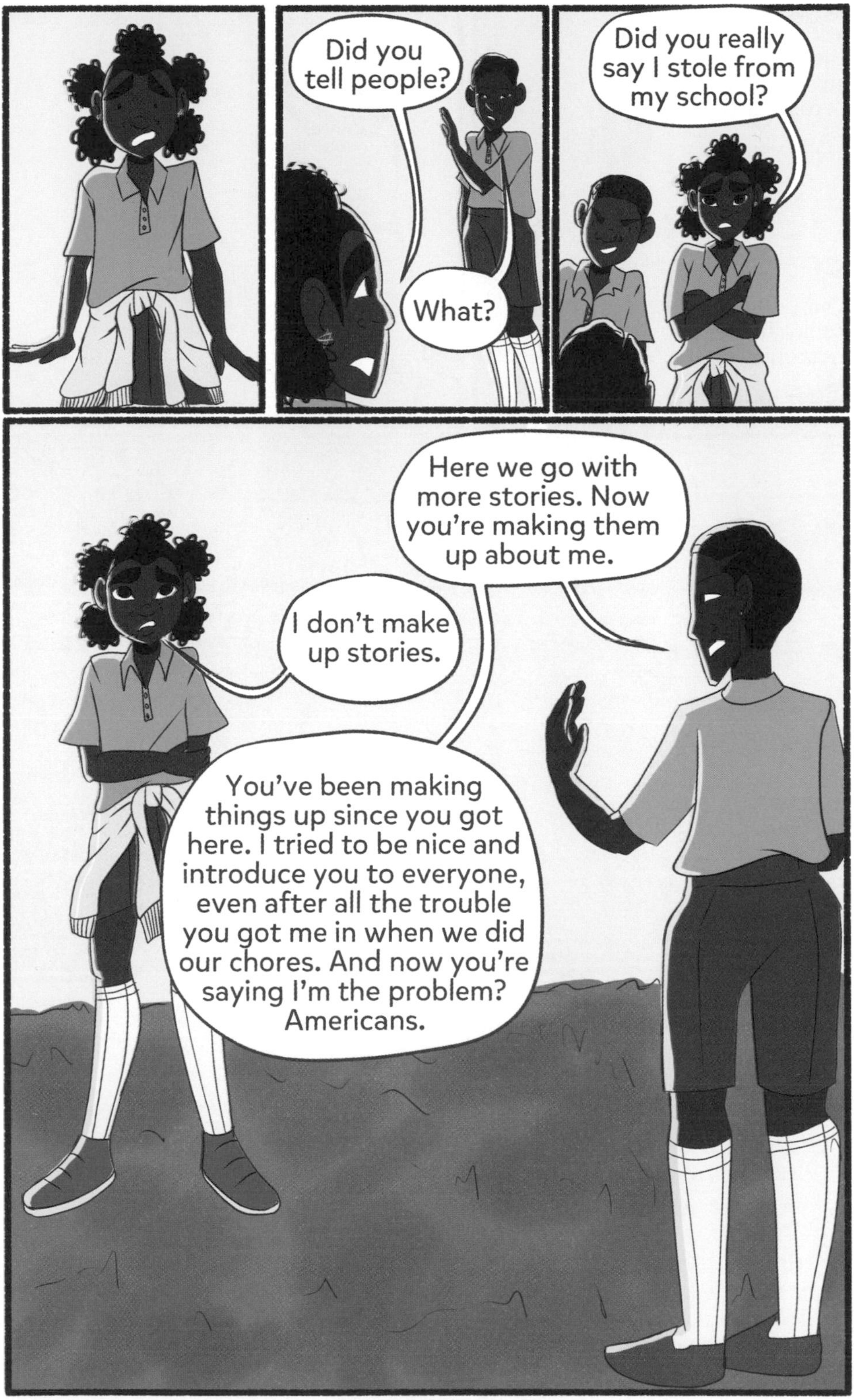
Did you tell people?
What?
Did you really say I stole from my school?
Here we go with more stories. Now you're making them up about me.
I don't make up stories.
You've been making things up since you got here. I tried to be nice and introduce you to everyone, even after all the trouble you got me in when we did our chores. And now you're saying I'm the problem? Americans.

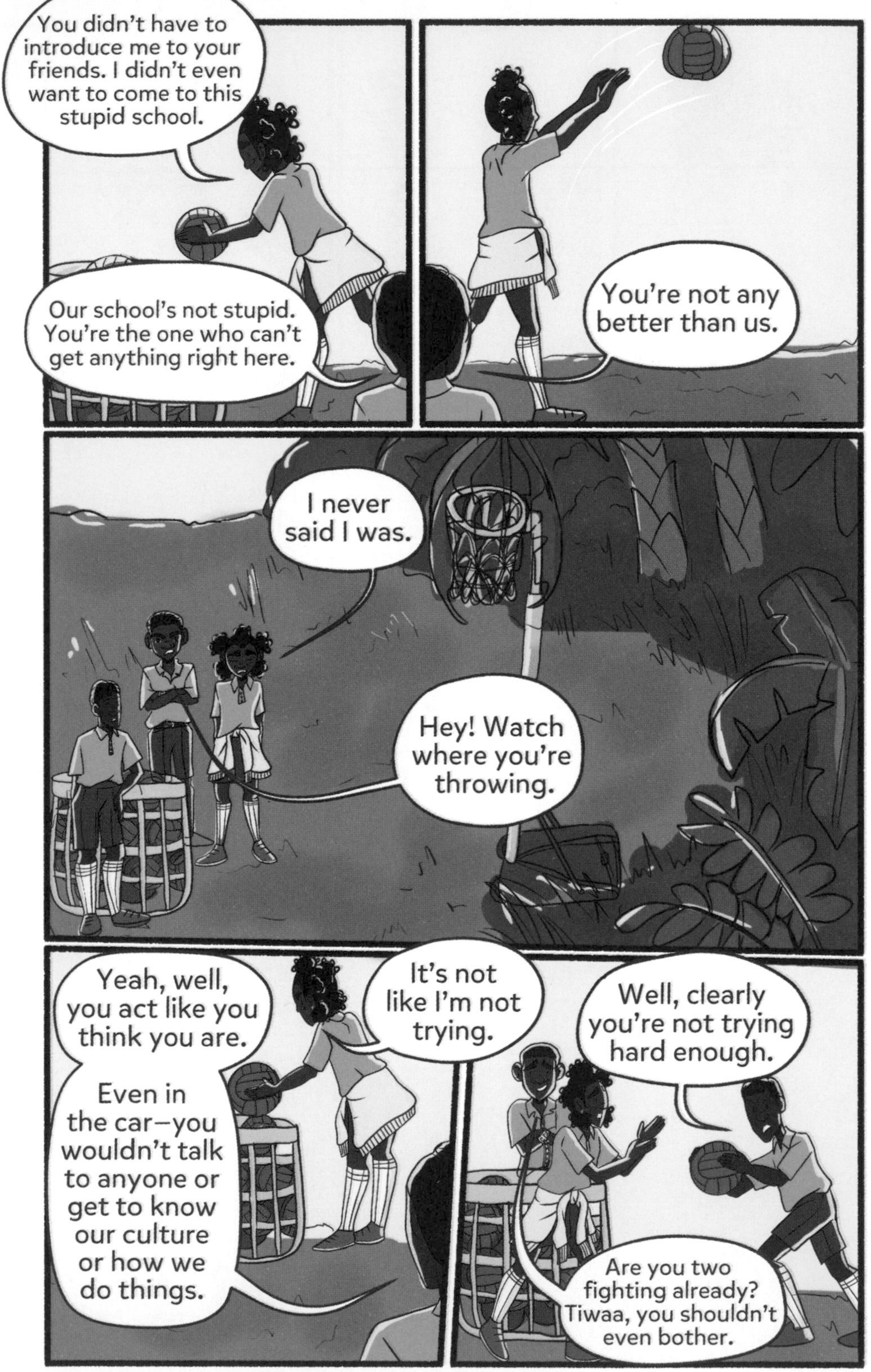
You didn't have to introduce me to your friends. I didn't even want to come to this stupid school.
Our school's not stupid. You're the one who can't get anything right here.
You're not any better than us.
I never said I was.
Hey! Watch where you're throwing.
Yeah, well, you act like you think you are.
Even in the car—you wouldn't talk to anyone or get to know our culture or how we do things.
It's not like I'm not trying.
Well, clearly you're not trying hard enough.
Are you two fighting already? Tiwaa, you shouldn't even bother.

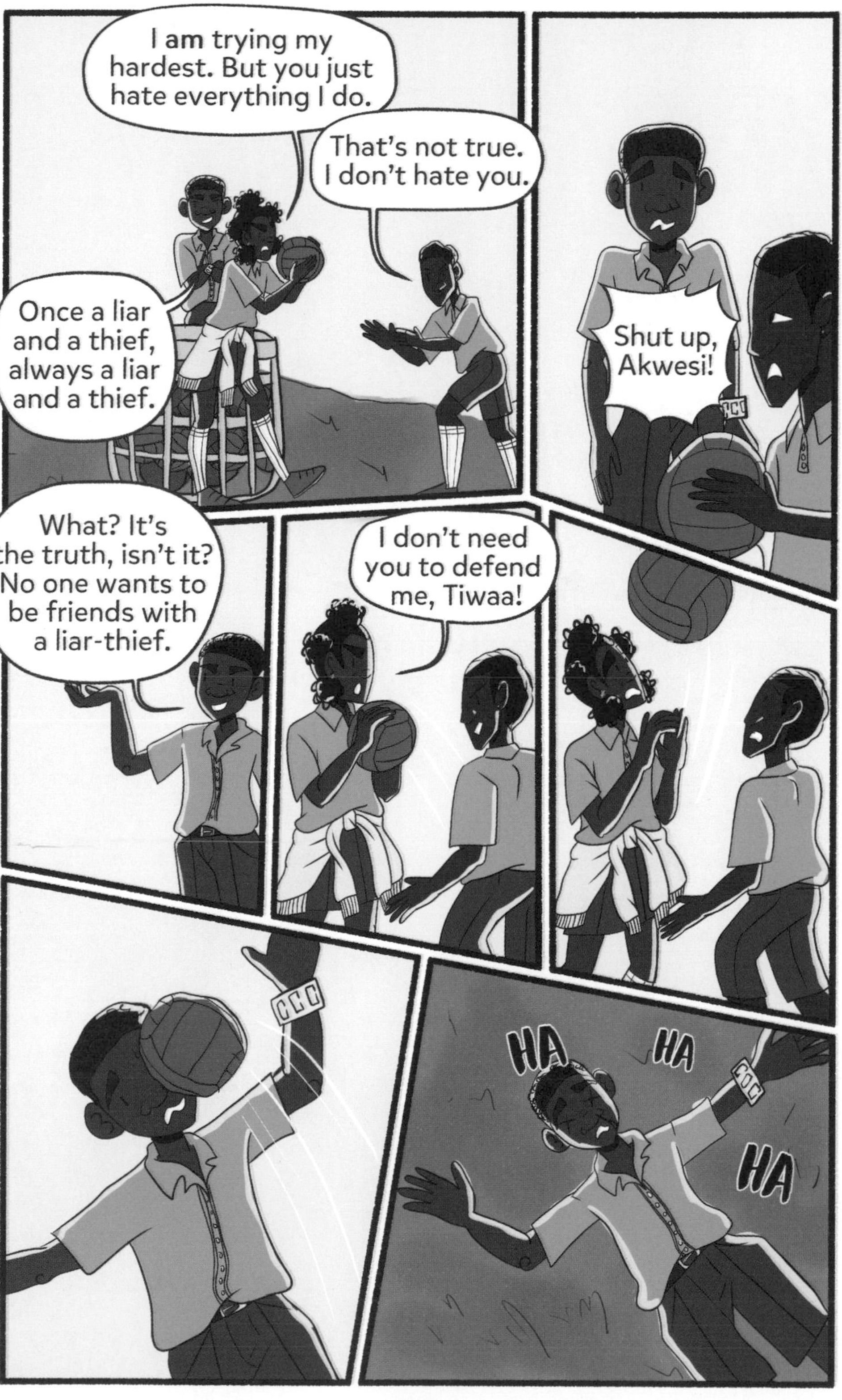
I am trying my hardest. But you just hate everything I do.
That's not true. I don't hate you.
Once a liar and a thief, always a liar and a thief.
Shut up, Akwesi!
What? It's the truth, isn't it? No one wants to be friends with a liar-thief.
I don't need you to defend me, Tiwaa!
HA
HA
HA

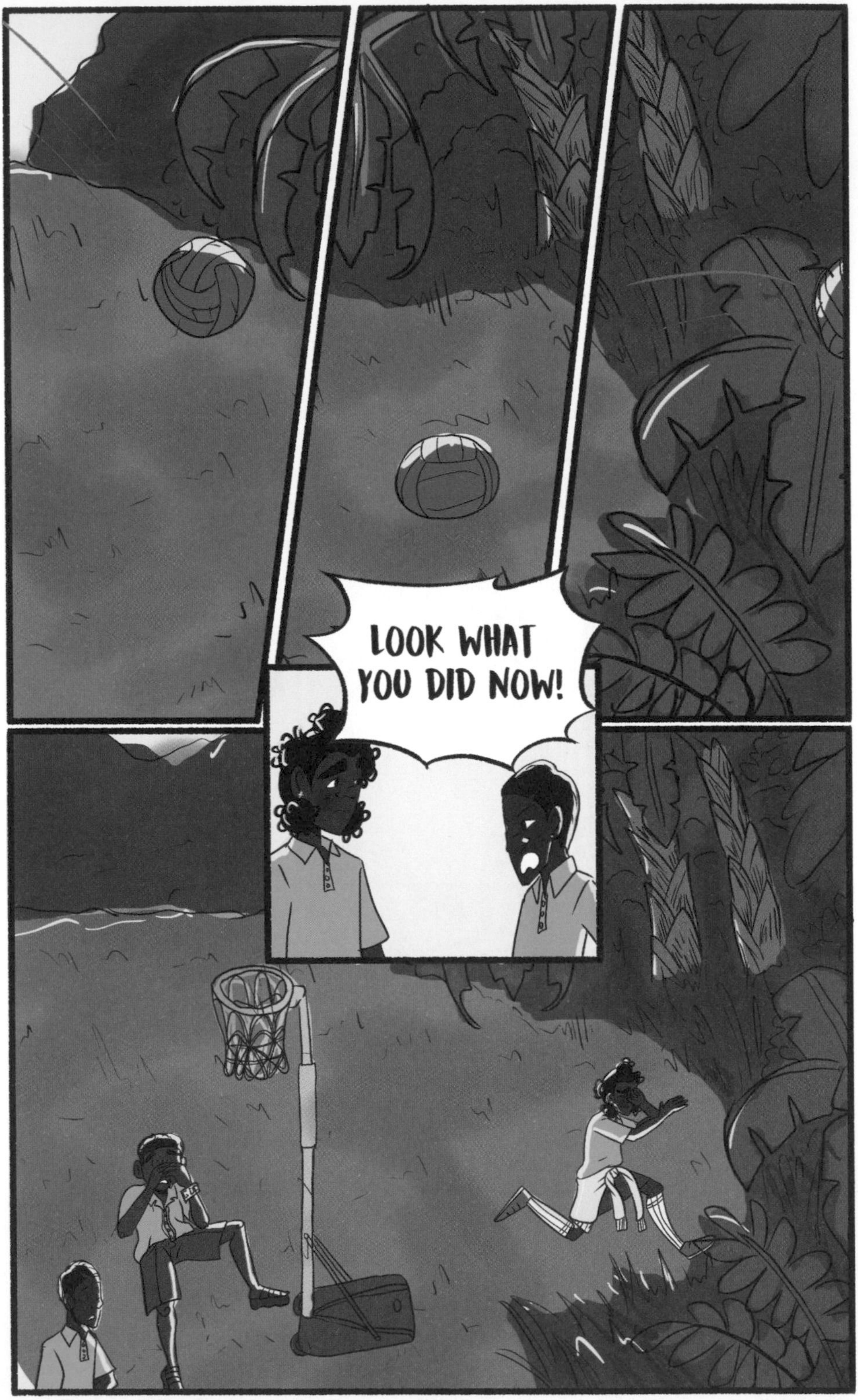
LOOK WHAT YOU DID NOW!

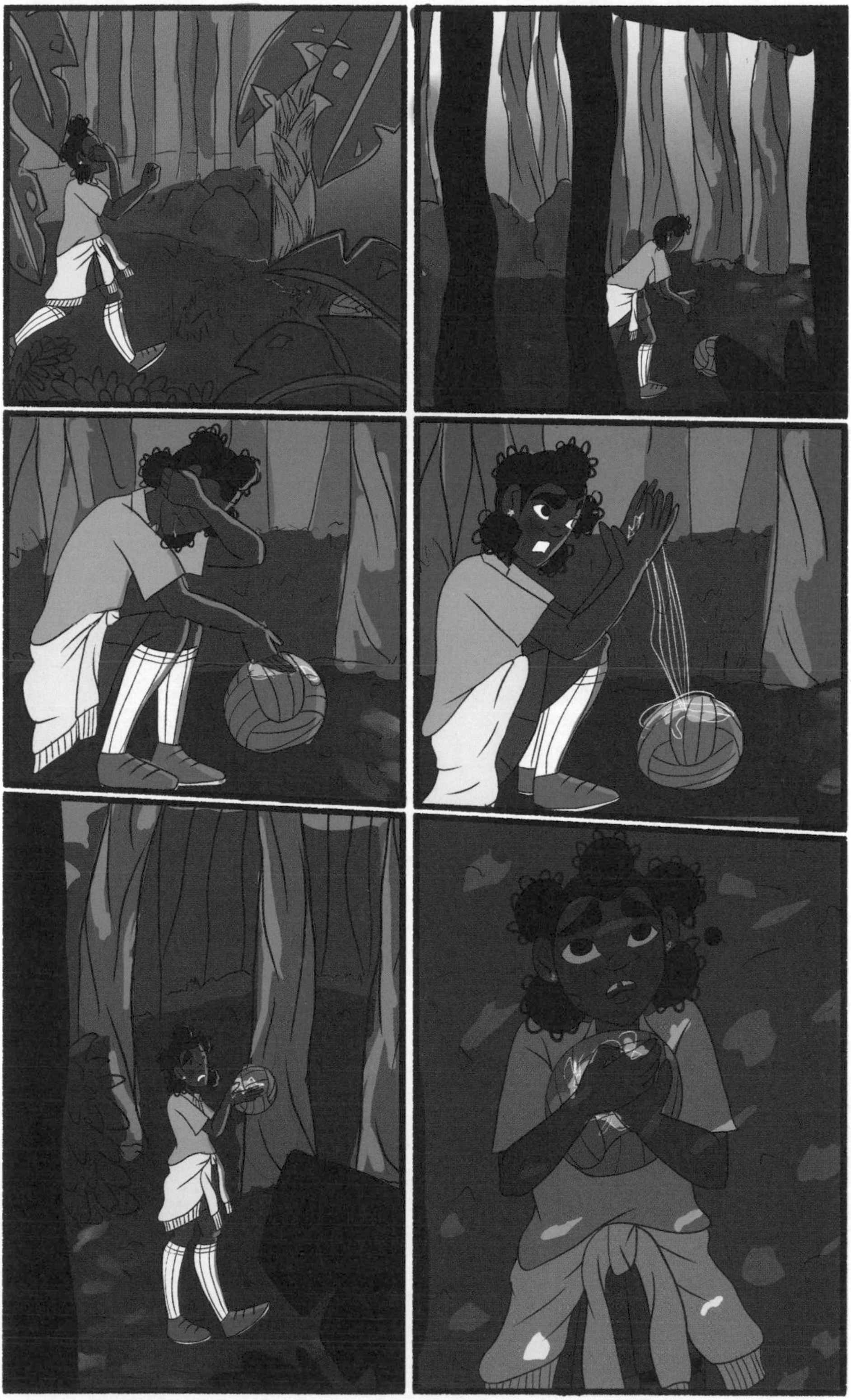

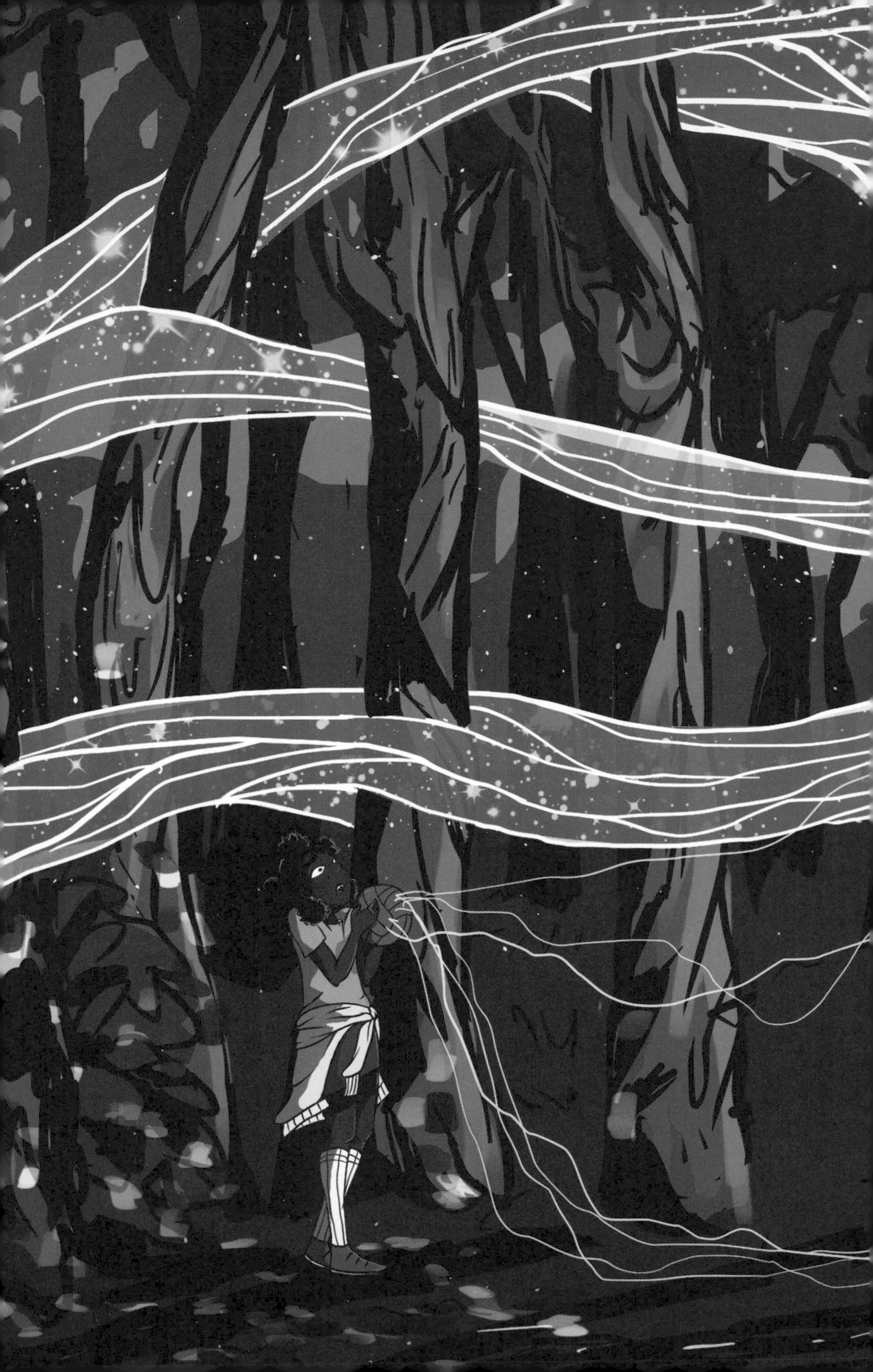

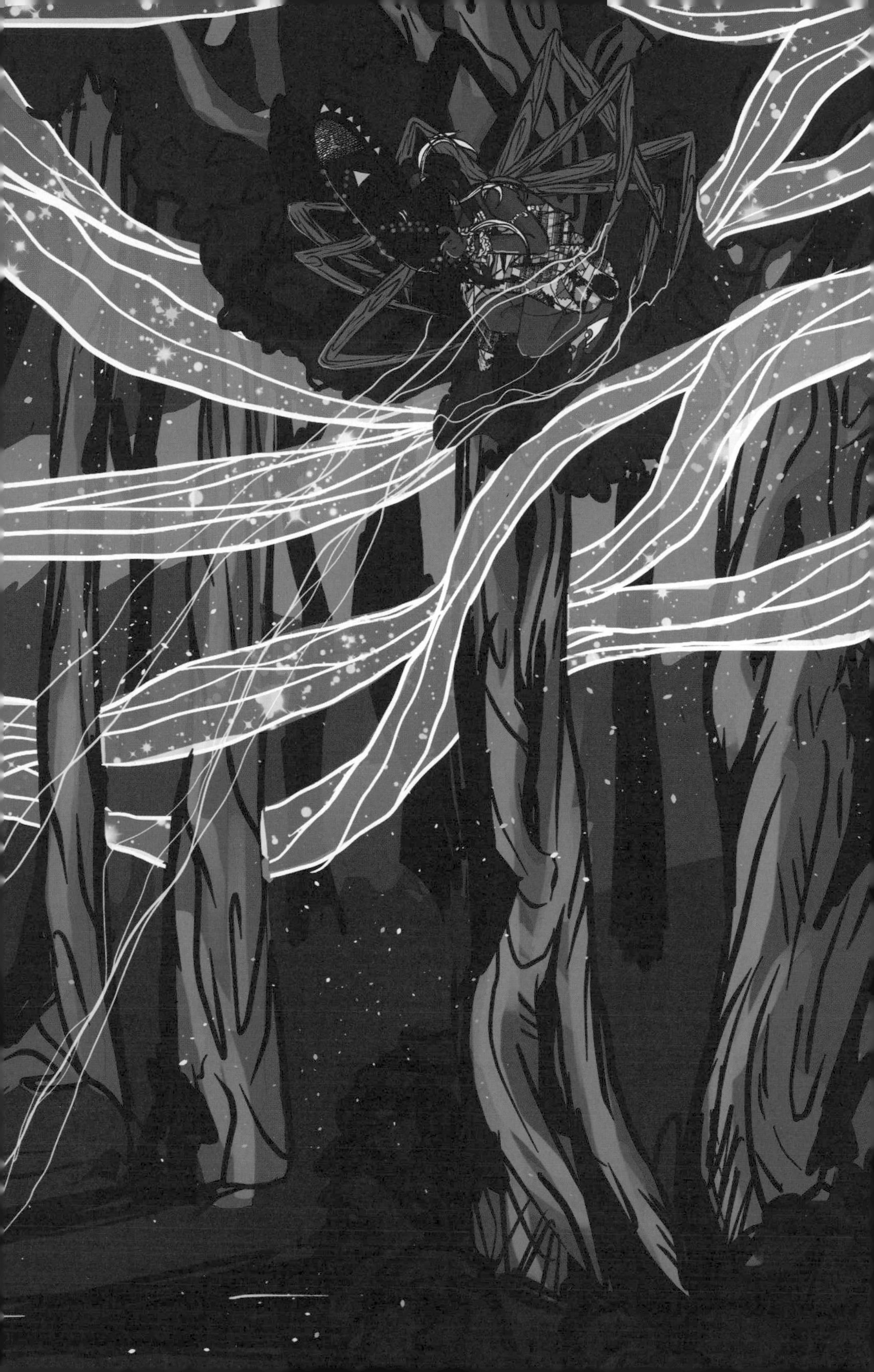

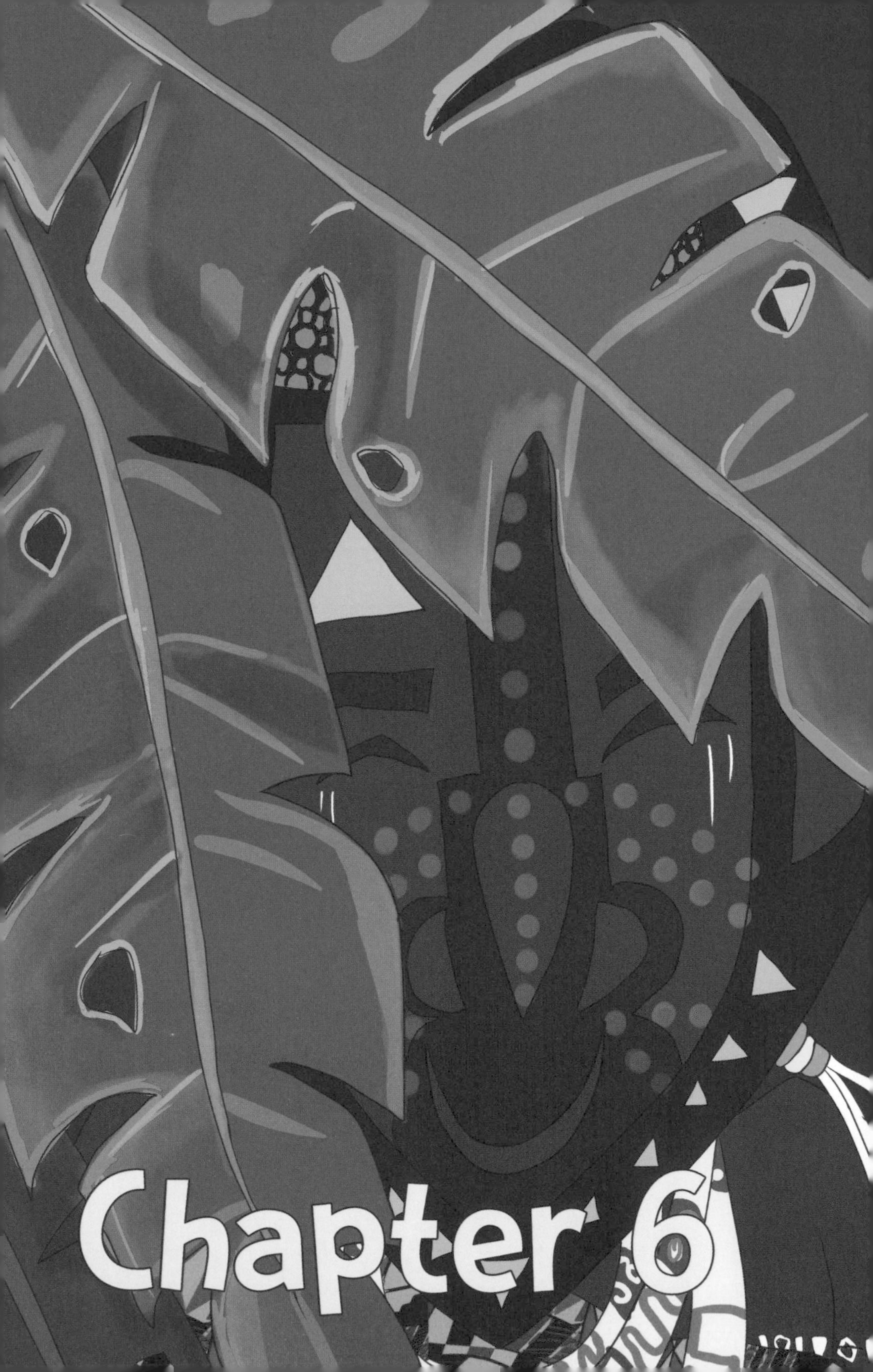
Chapter 6

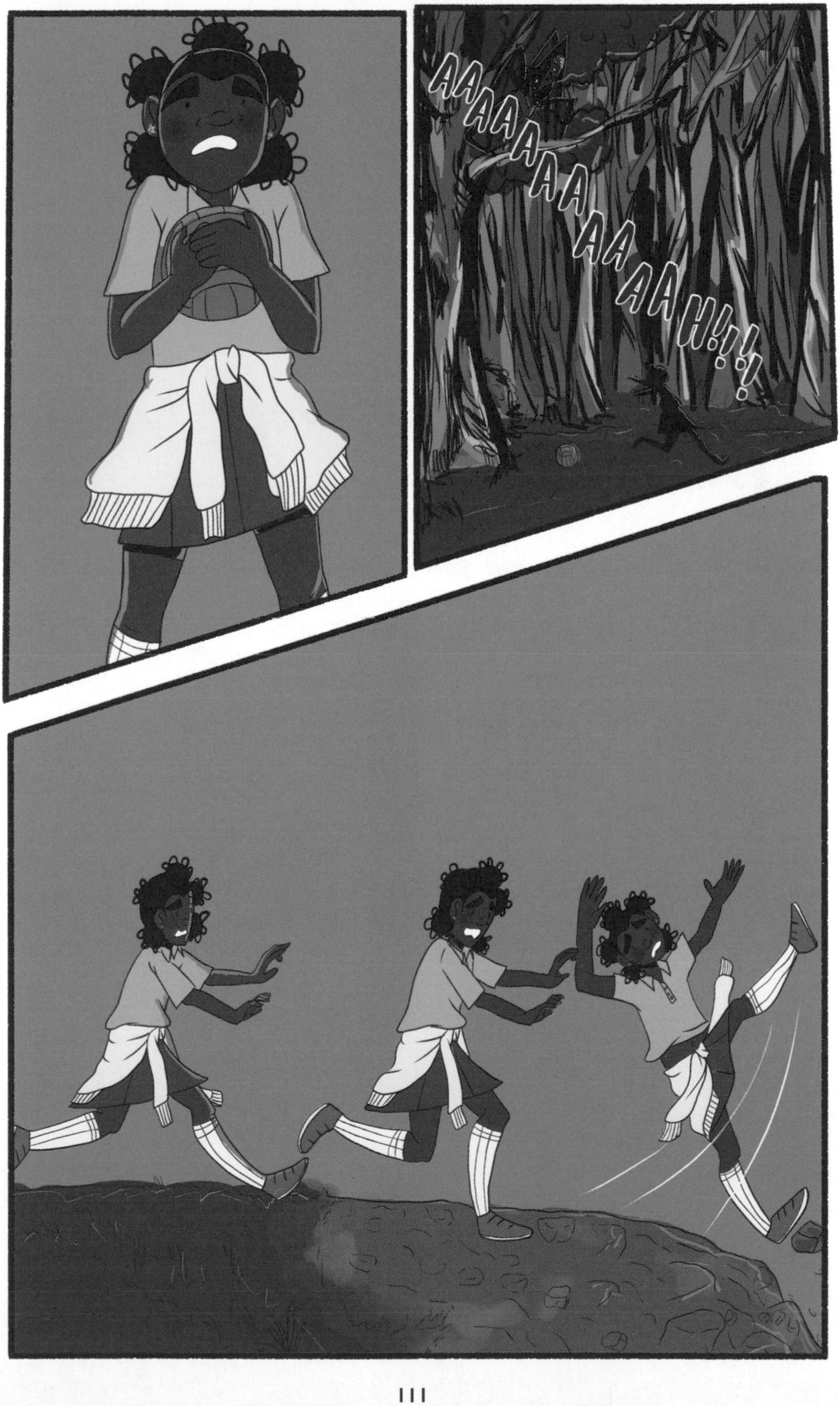
AAAAAAAAAAAAAH!!!!

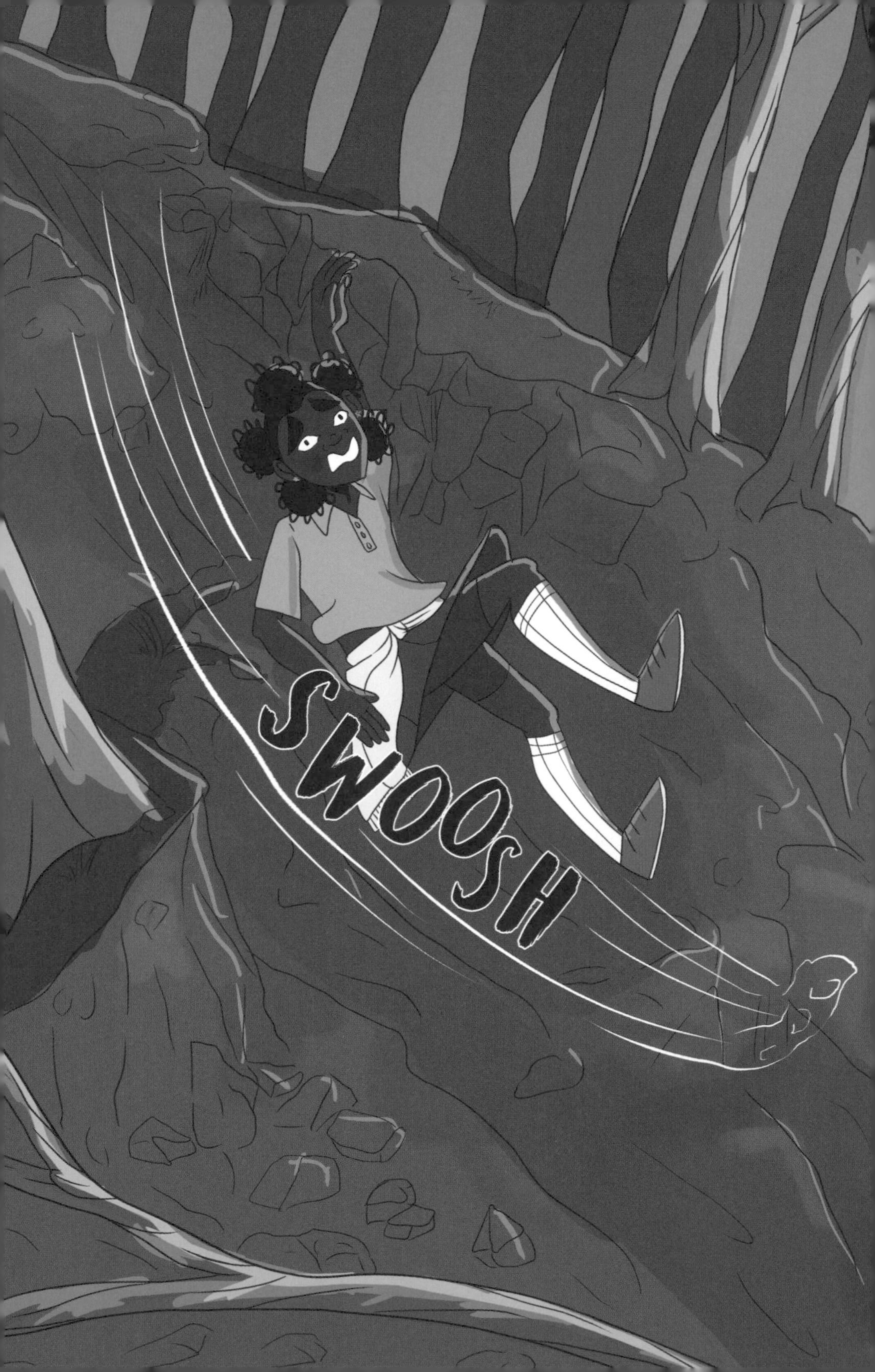
SWOOSH

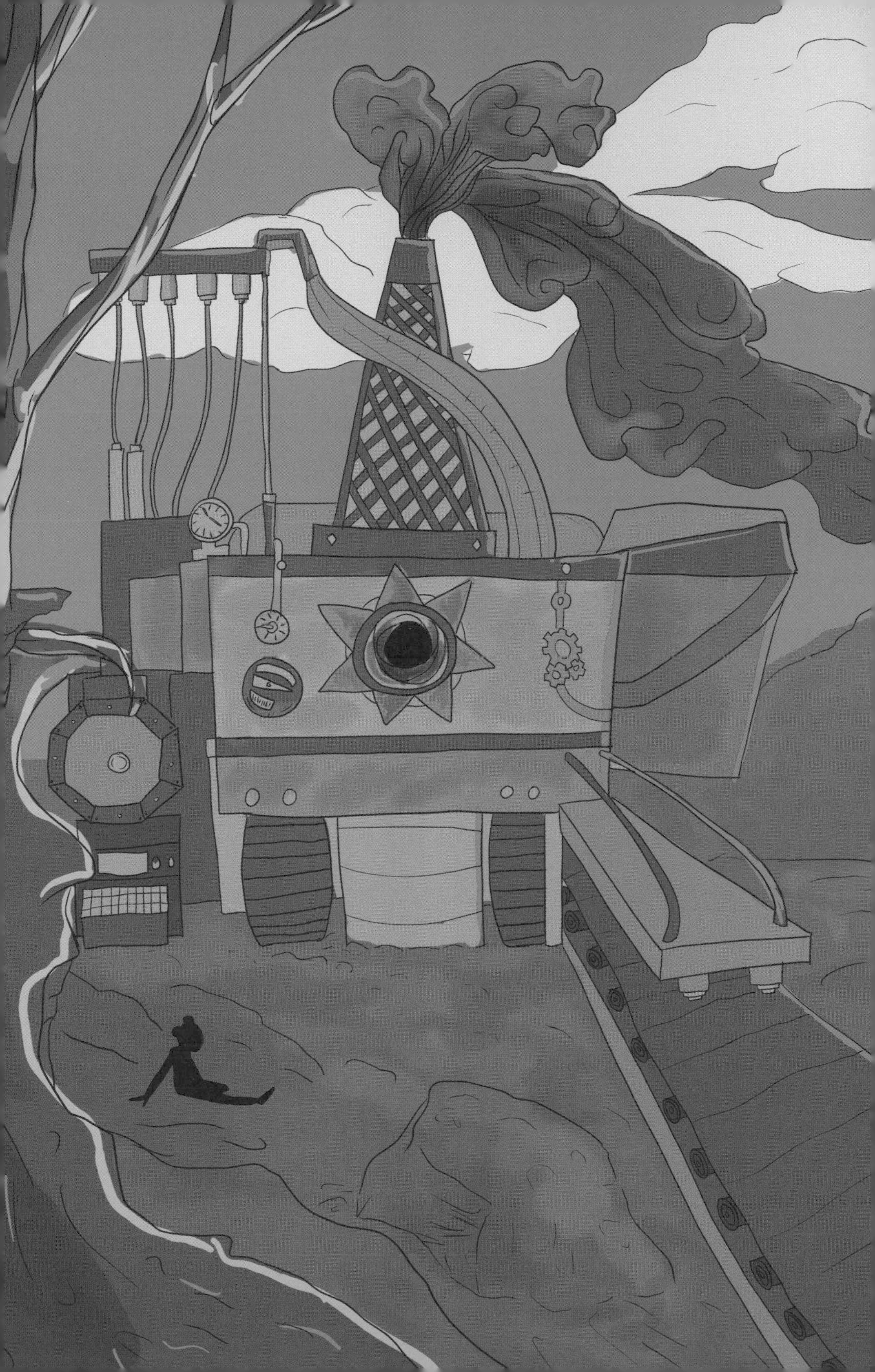

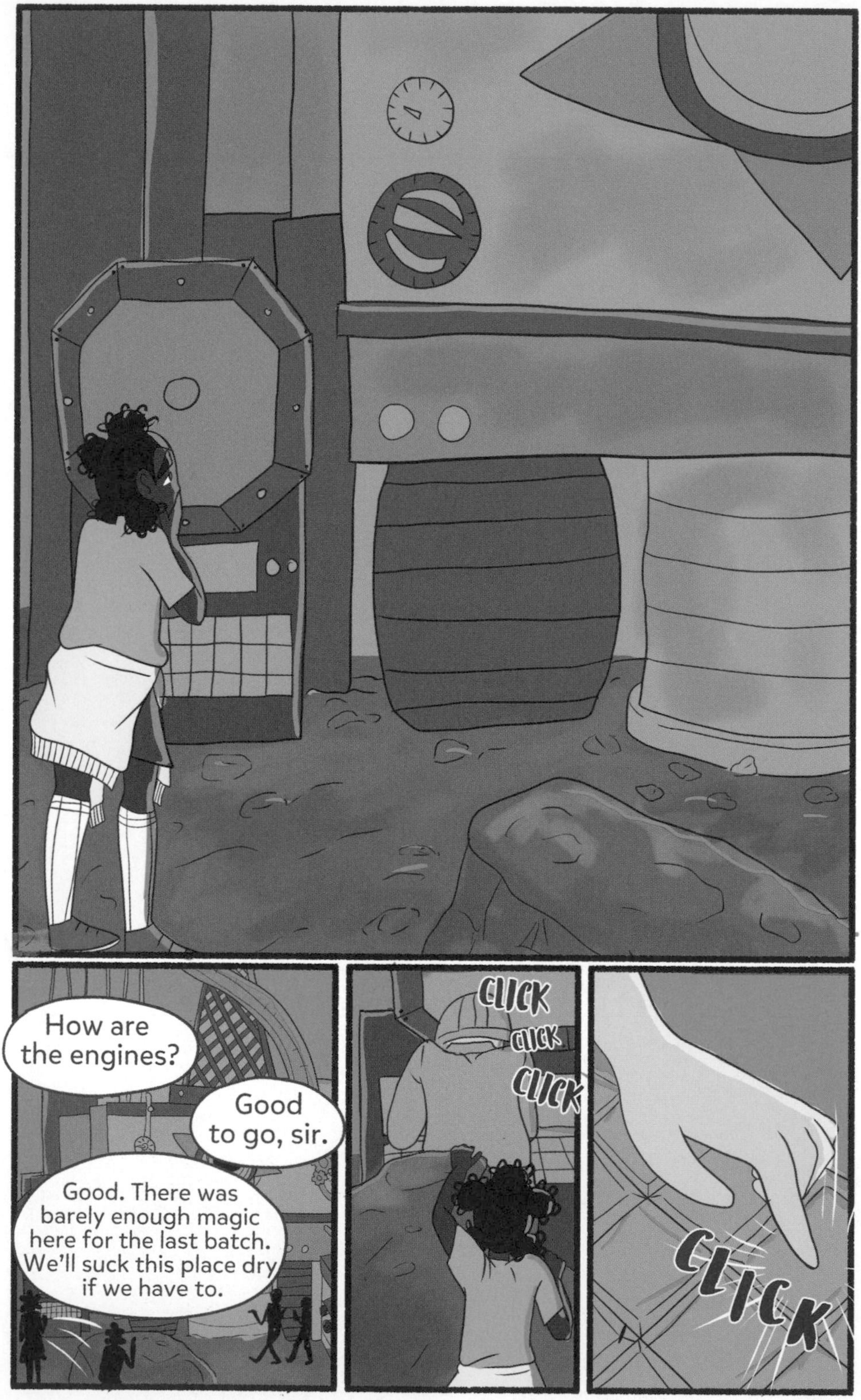
How are the engines?
Good to go, sir.
Good. There was barely enough magic here for the last batch. We'll suck this place dry if we have to.
CLICK
CLICK
CLICK
CLICK

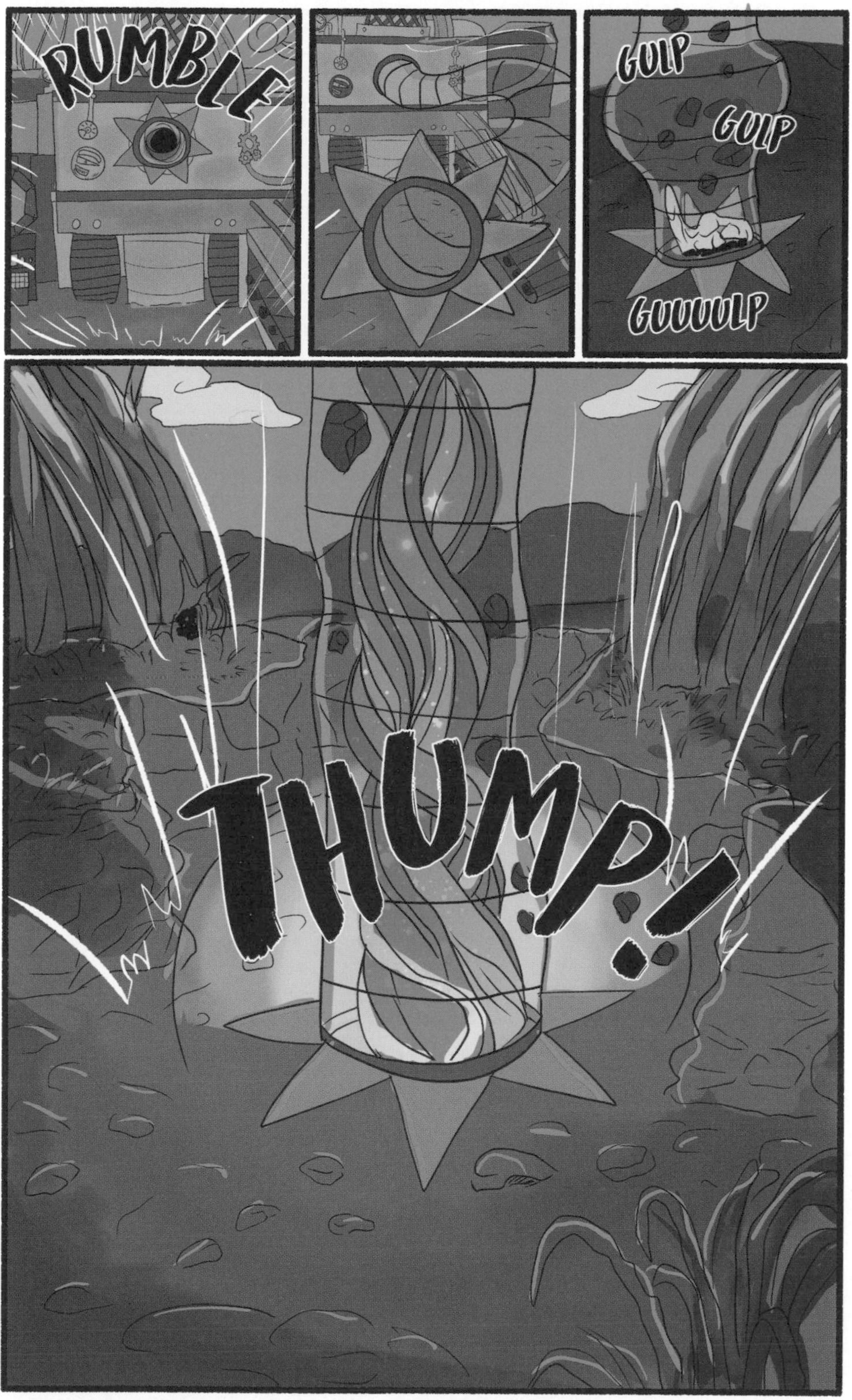
RUMBLE
GULP
GULP
GUUUULP
THUMP!

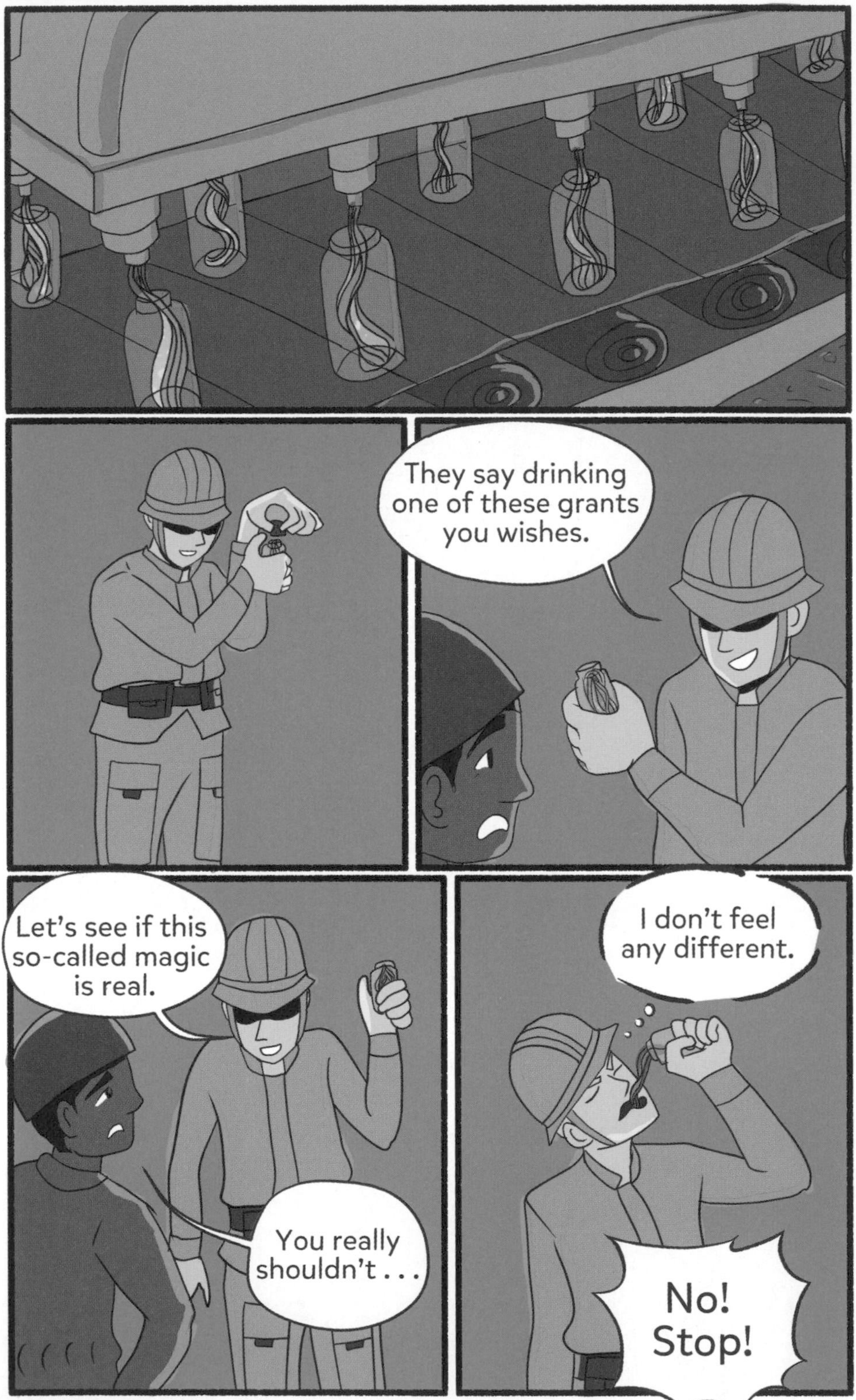
They say drinking one of these grants you wishes.
Let's see if this so-called magic is real.
You really shouldn't . . .
I don't feel any different.
No! Stop!

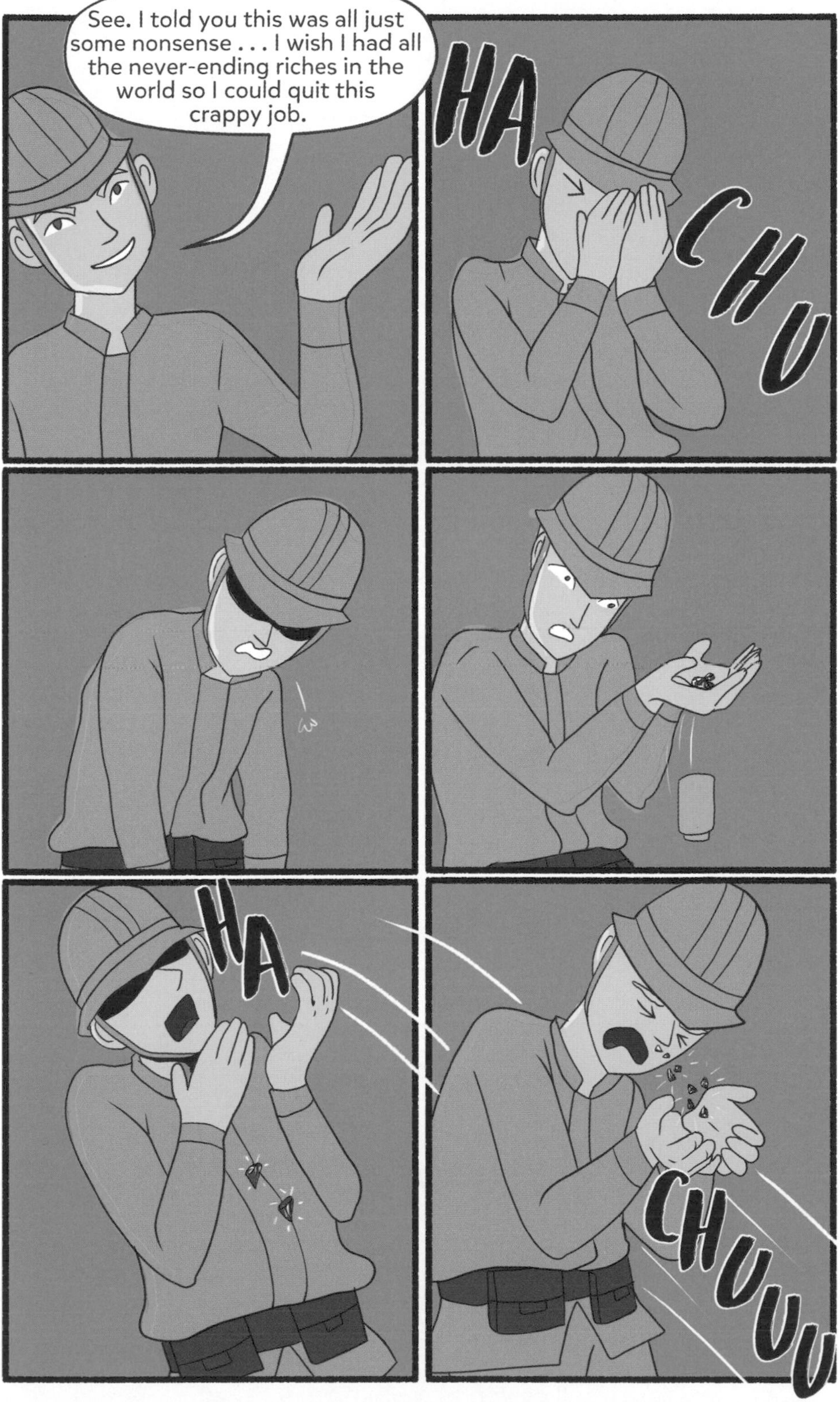
See. I told you this was all just some nonsense . . . I wish I had all the never-ending riches in the world so I could quit this crappy job.
HA
CHU
HA
CHUUU

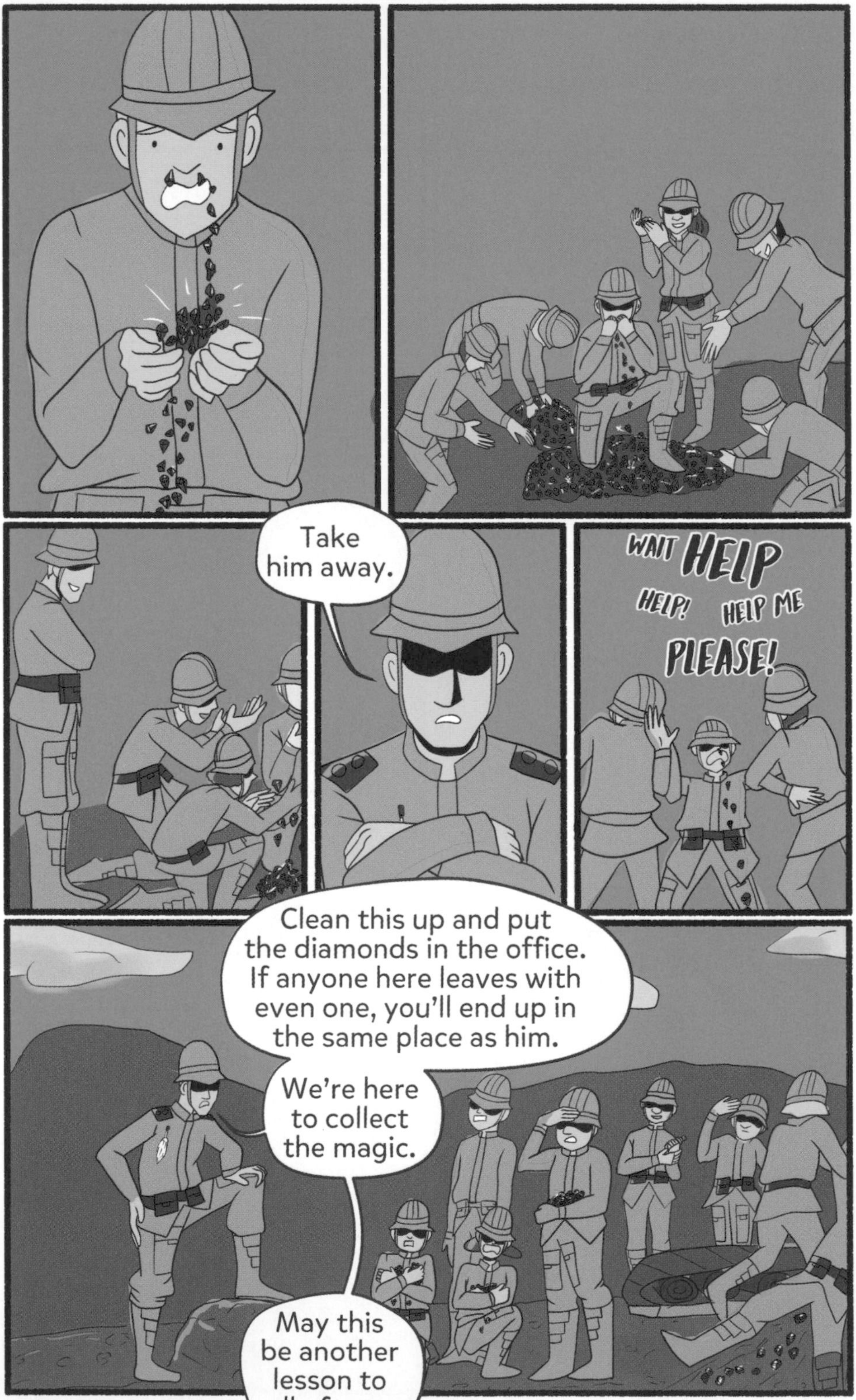
Take him away.
WAIT HELP
HELP! HELP ME
PLEASE!
Clean this up and put the diamonds in the office. If anyone here leaves with even one, you'll end up in the same place as him.
We're here to collect the magic.
May this be another lesson to all of you.

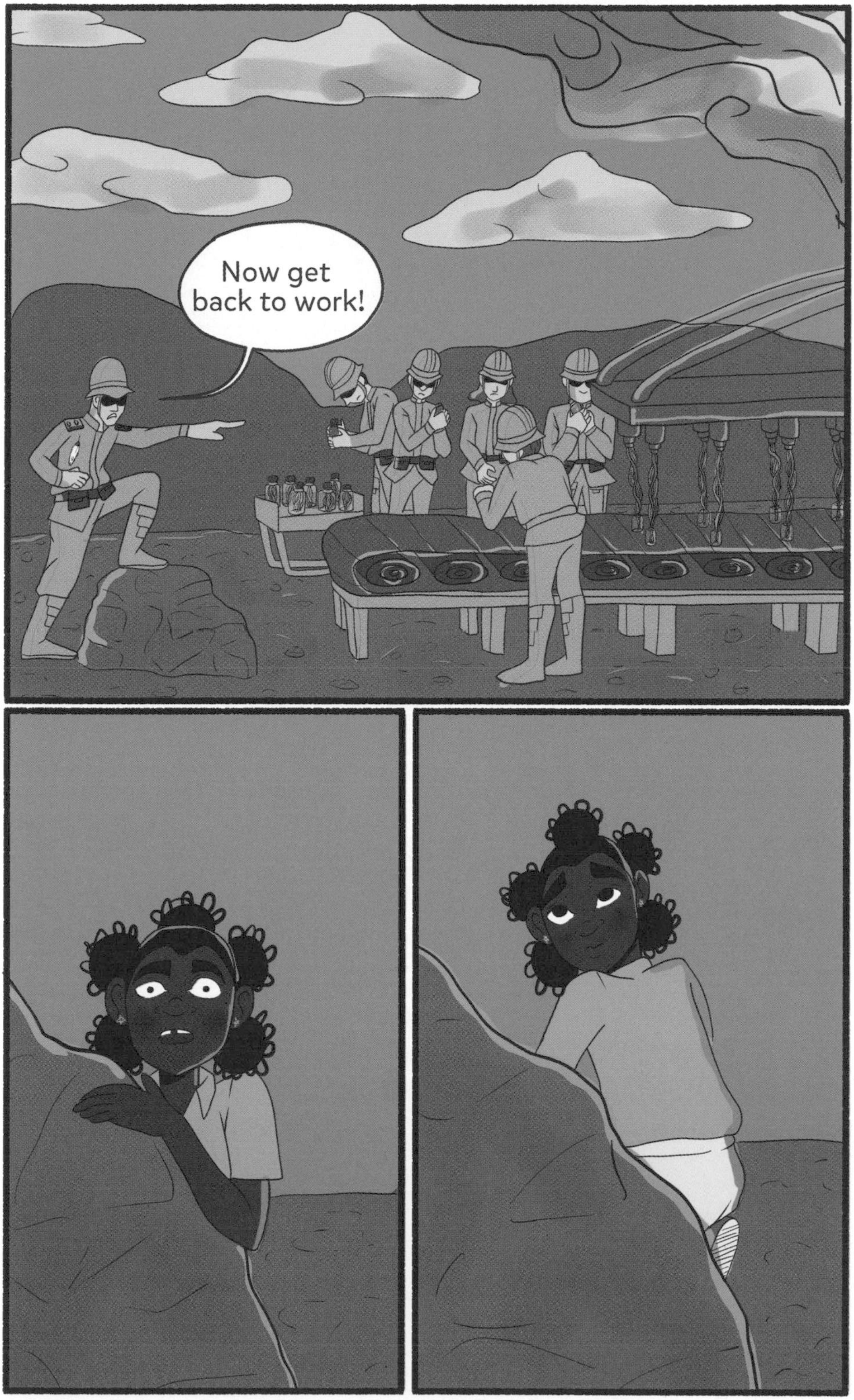
Now get back to work!

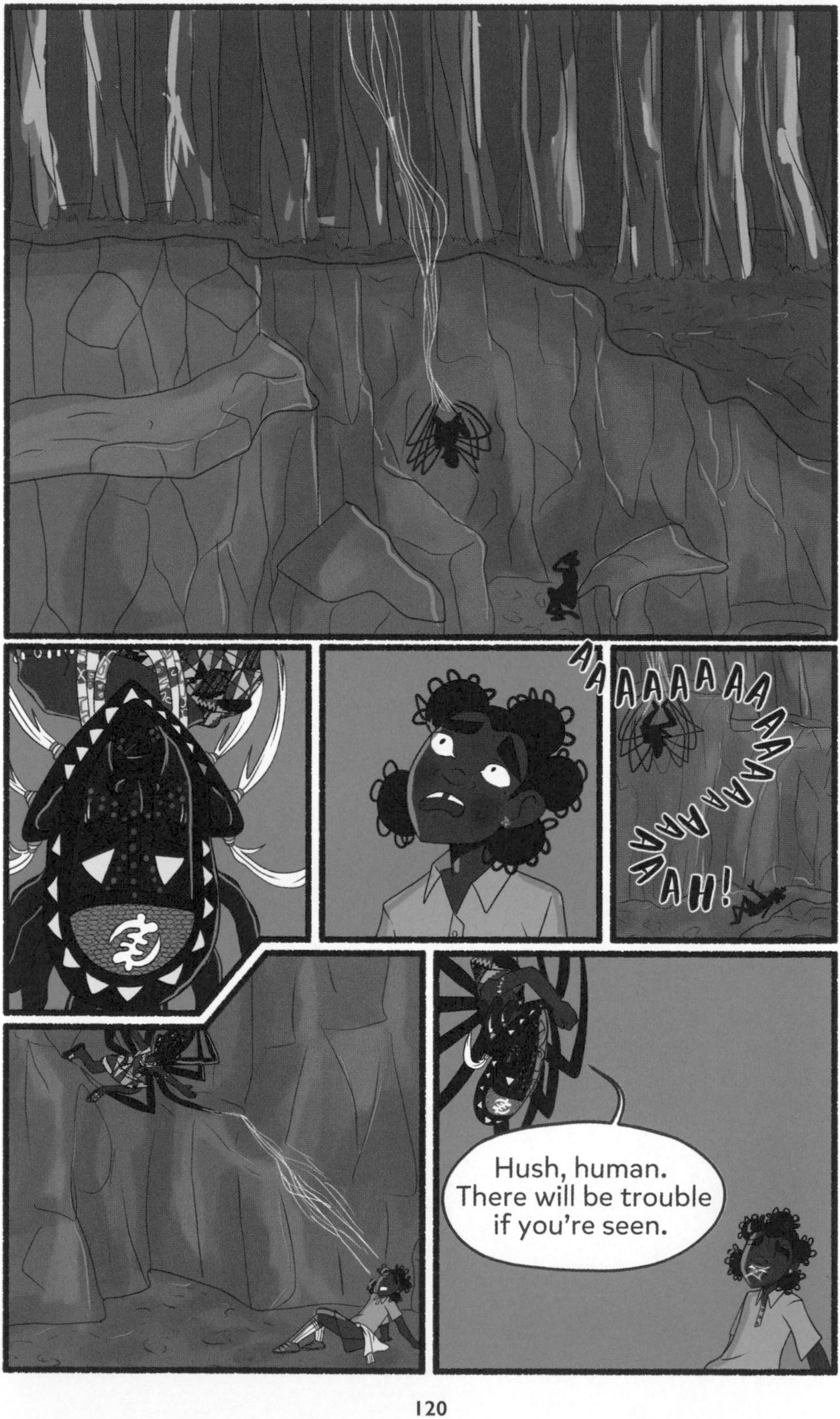
AAAAAAAAAAAAAAAAAAAAH!
Hush, human. There will be trouble if you're seen.

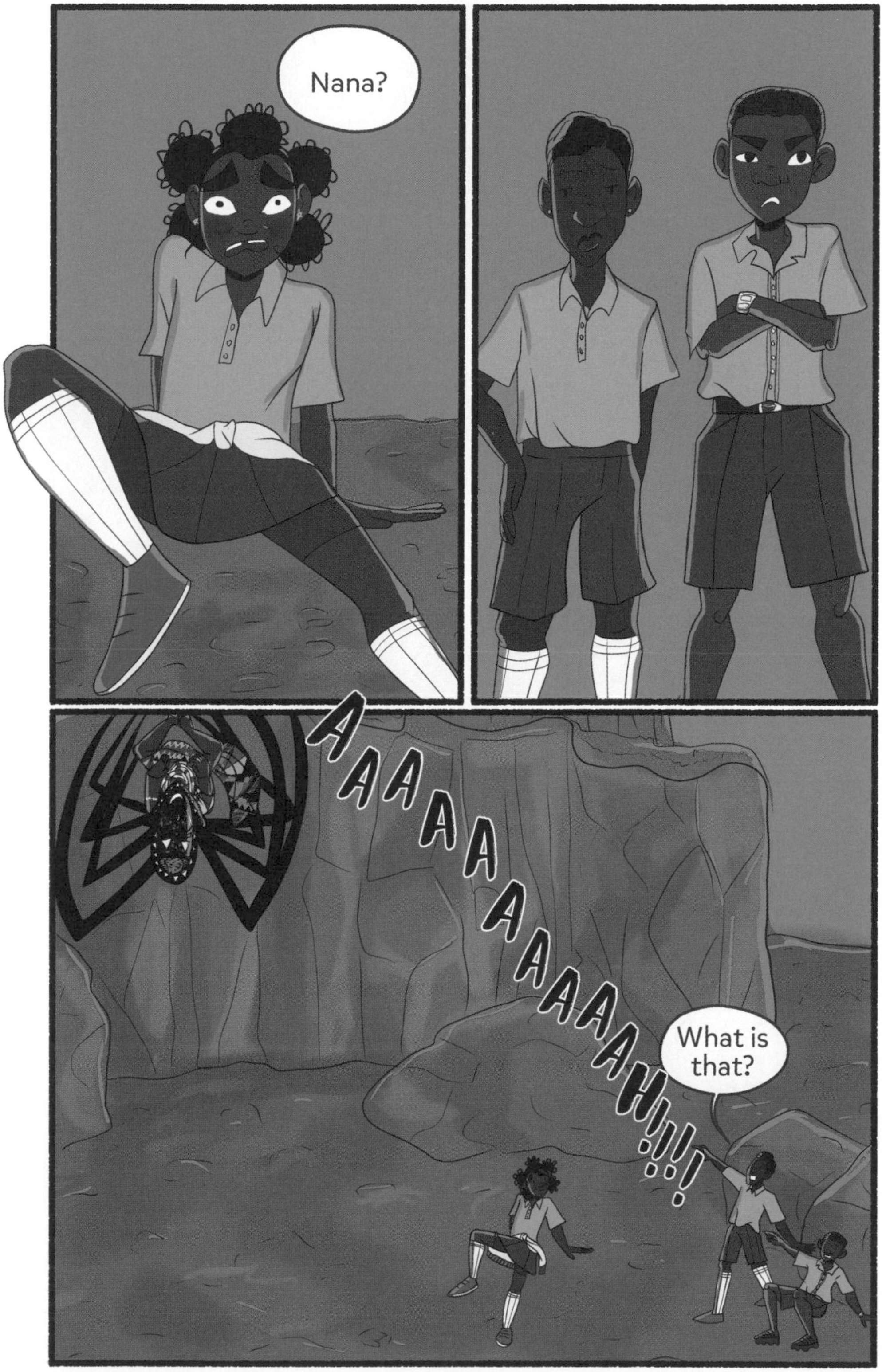
Nana?
AAAAAAAAAAAAAAH!!!!
What is that?

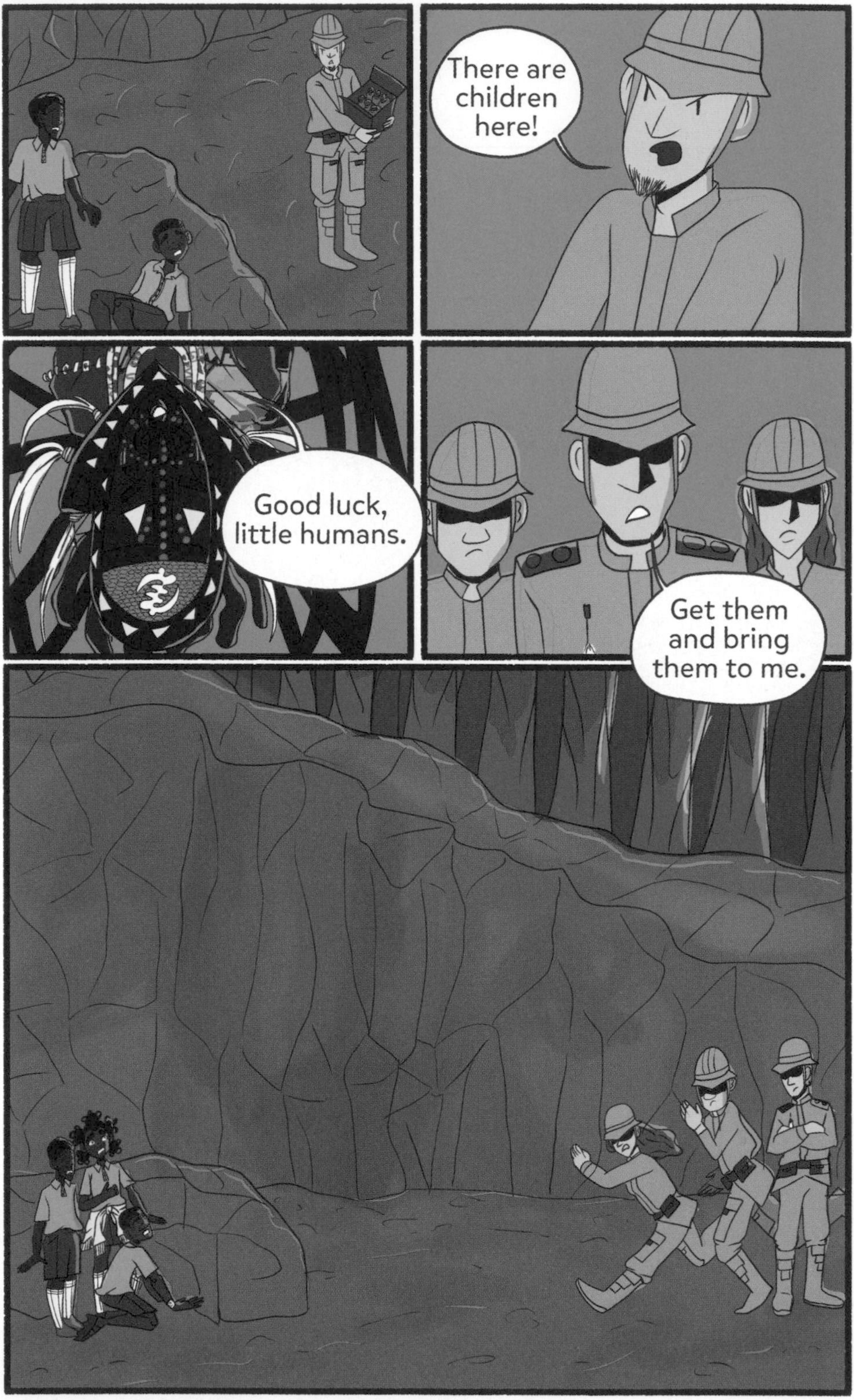
There are children here!
Good luck, little humans.
Get them and bring them to me.

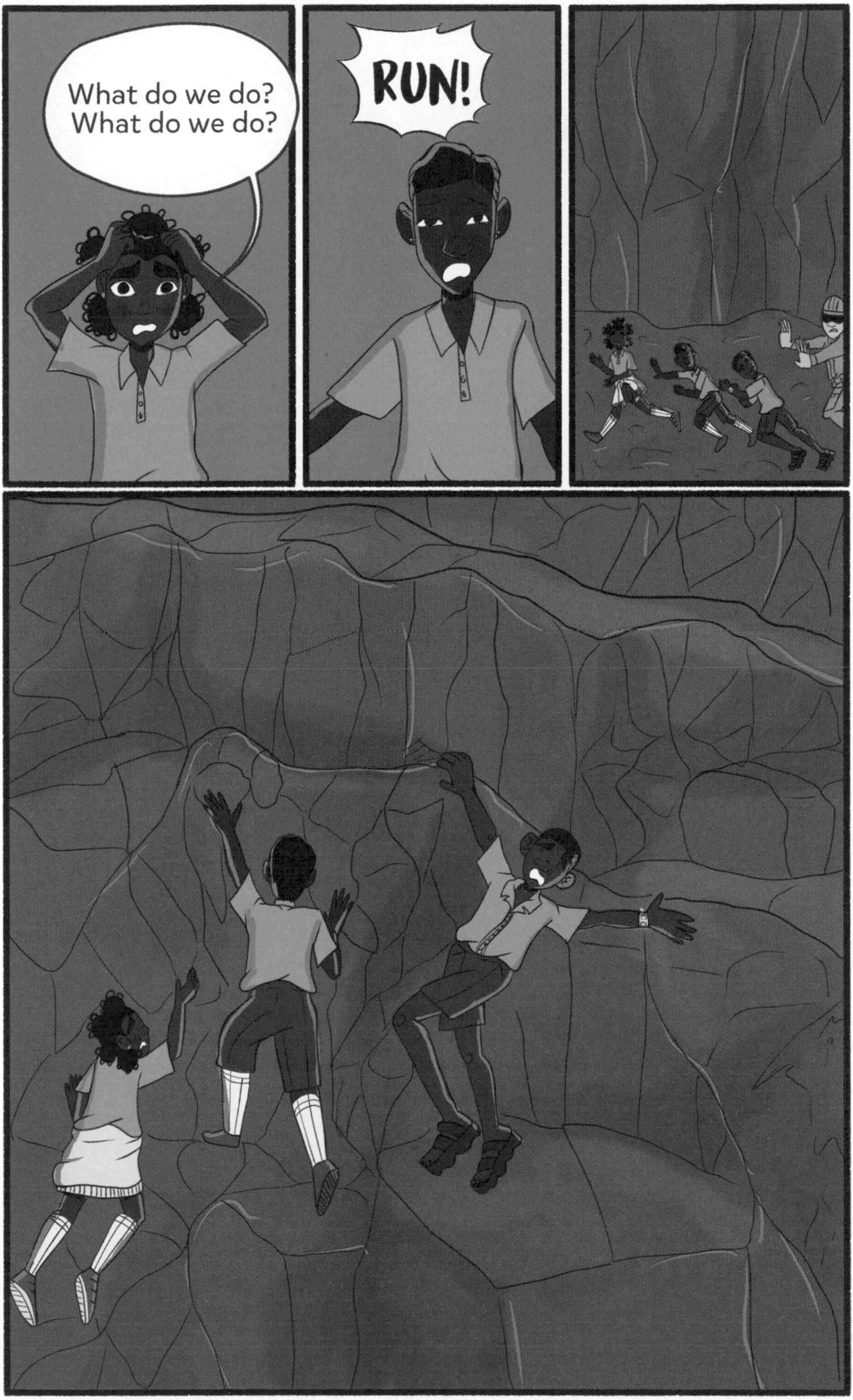
What do we do?
What do we do?
RUN!

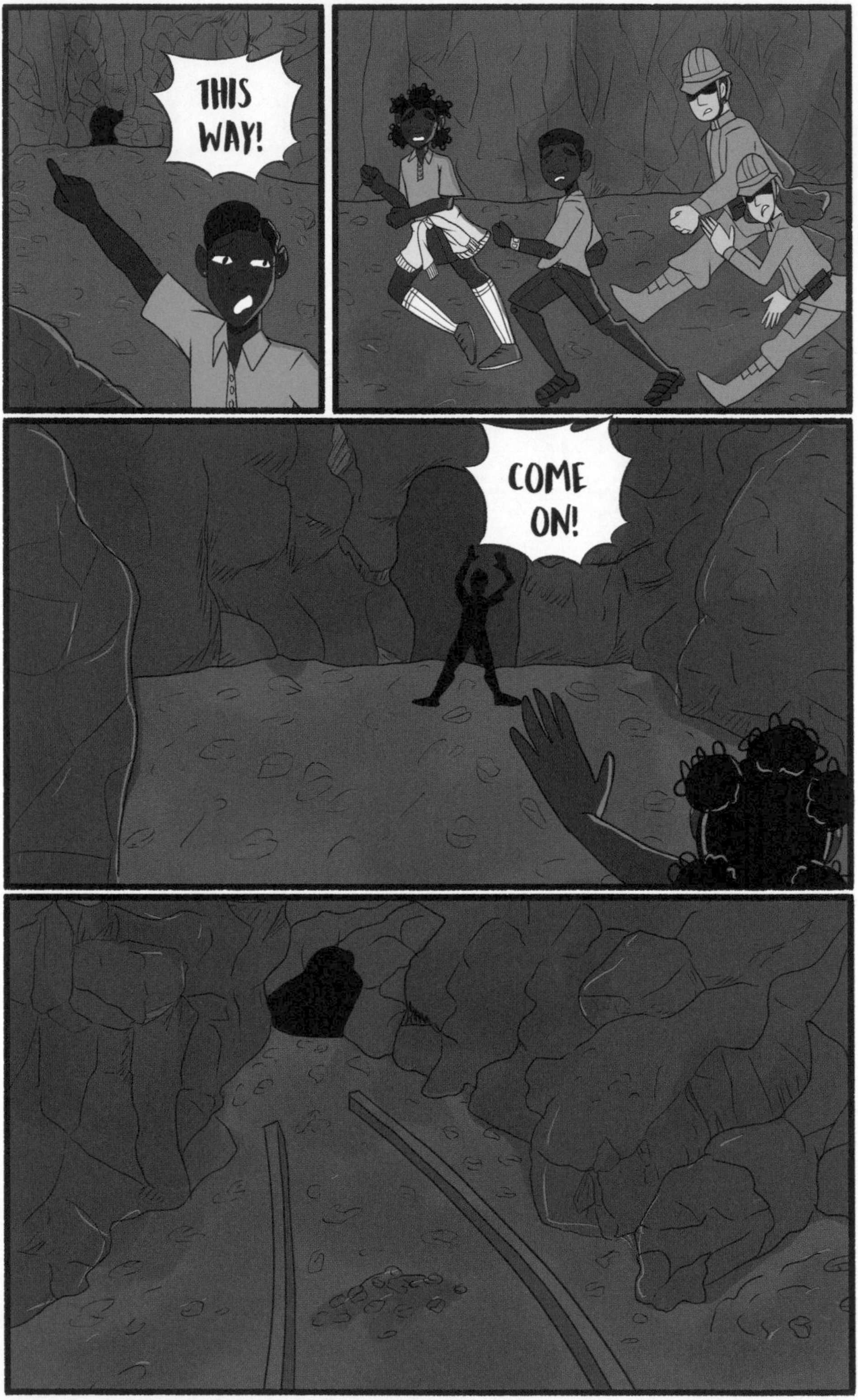
THIS WAY!
COME ON!

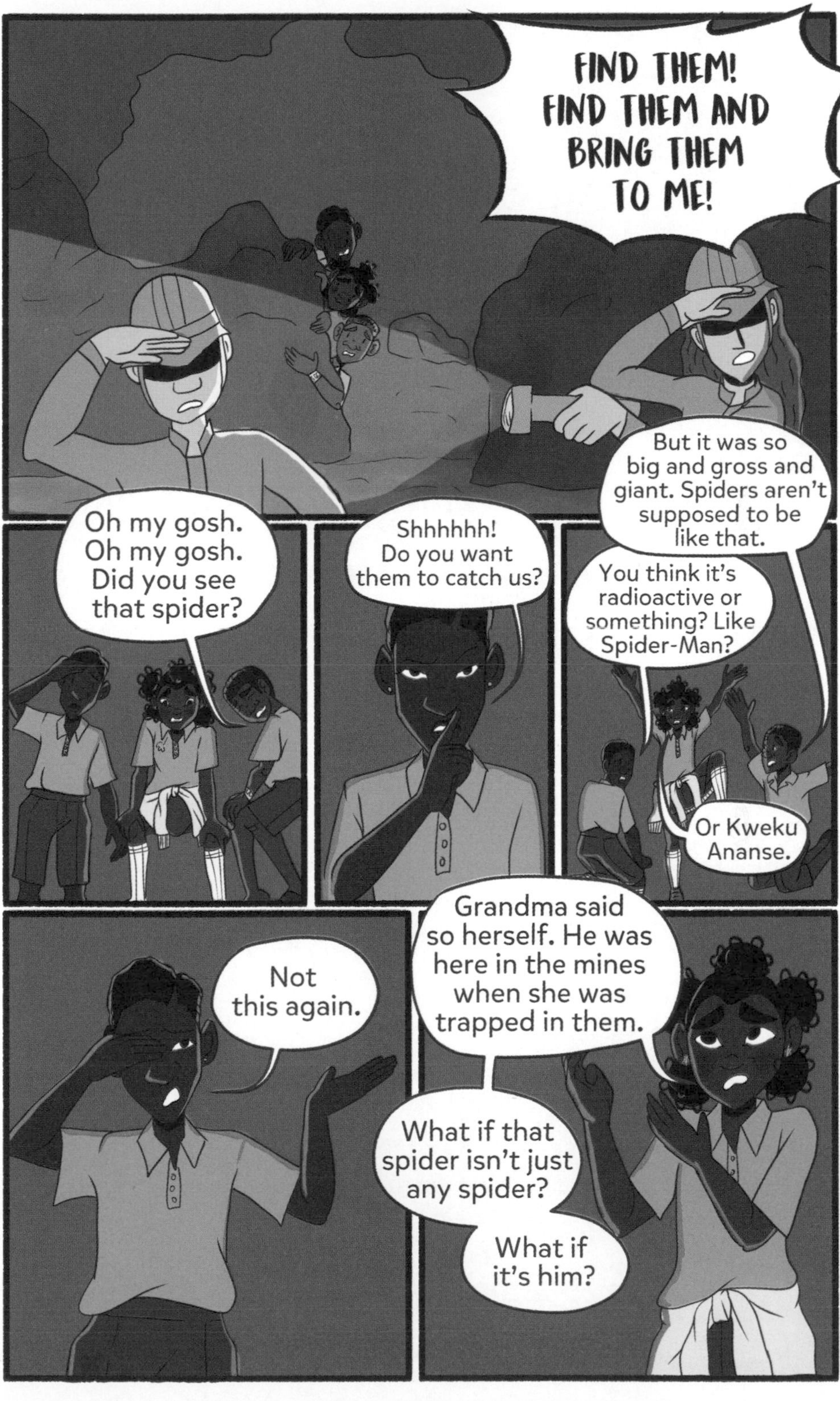
FIND THEM! FIND THEM AND BRING THEM TO ME!
Oh my gosh. Oh my gosh. Did you see that spider?
Shhhhhh! Do you want them to catch us?
But it was so big and gross and giant. Spiders aren't supposed to be like that.
You think it's radioactive or something? Like Spider-Man?
Or Kweku Ananse.
Not this again.
Grandma said so herself. He was here in the mines when she was trapped in them.
What if that spider isn't just any spider?
What if it's him?

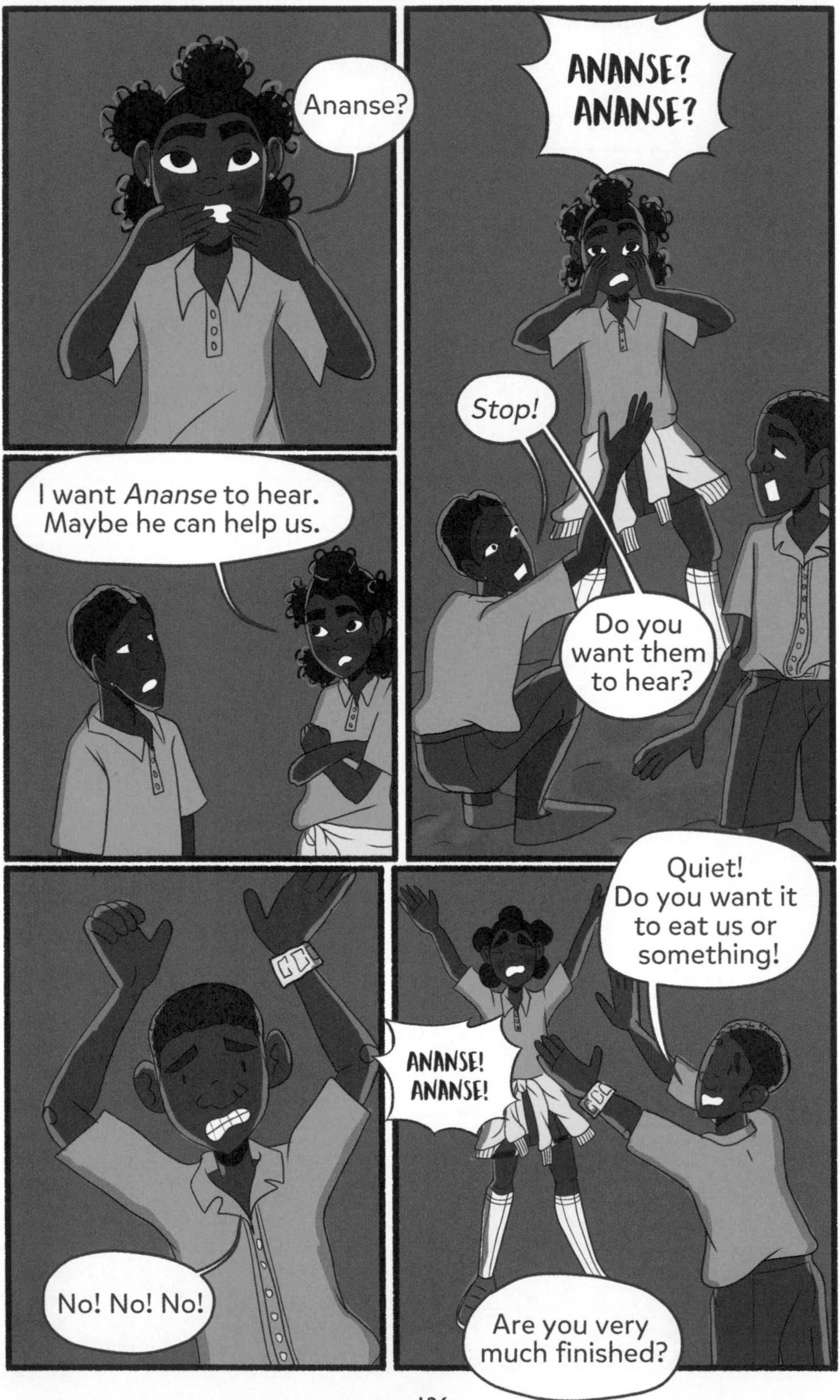
Ananse?
ANANSE? ANANSE?
I want *Ananse* to hear. Maybe he can help us.
Stop!
Do you want them to hear?
No! No! No!
ANANSE! ANANSE!
Quiet! Do you want it to eat us or something!
Are you very much finished?

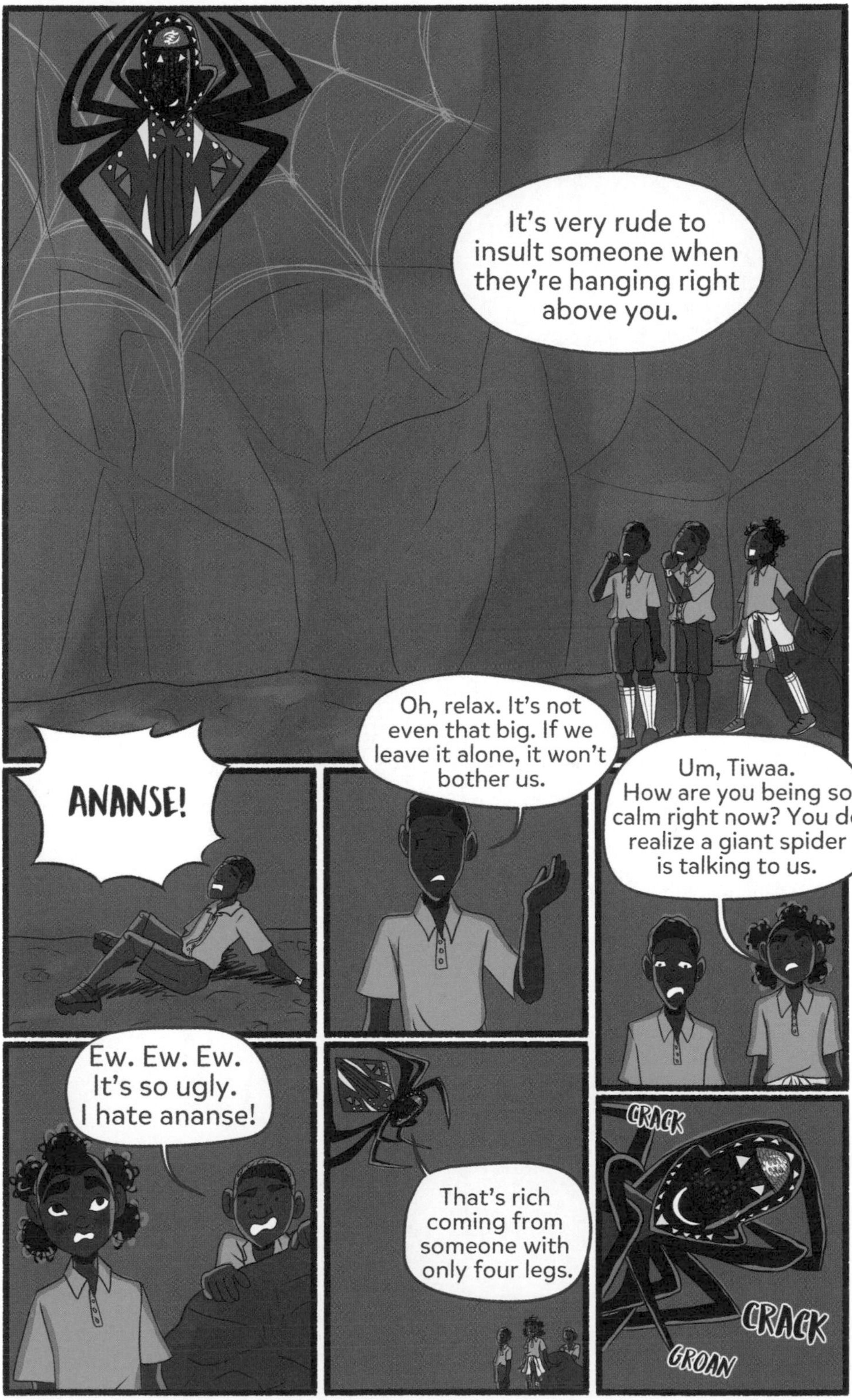
It's very rude to insult someone when they're hanging right above you.
ANANSE!
Oh, relax. It's not even that big. If we leave it alone, it won't bother us.
Um, Tiwaa. How are you being so calm right now? You do realize a giant spider is talking to us.
Ew. Ew. Ew. It's so ugly. I hate ananse!
That's rich coming from someone with only four legs.
CRACK
CRACK
GROAN

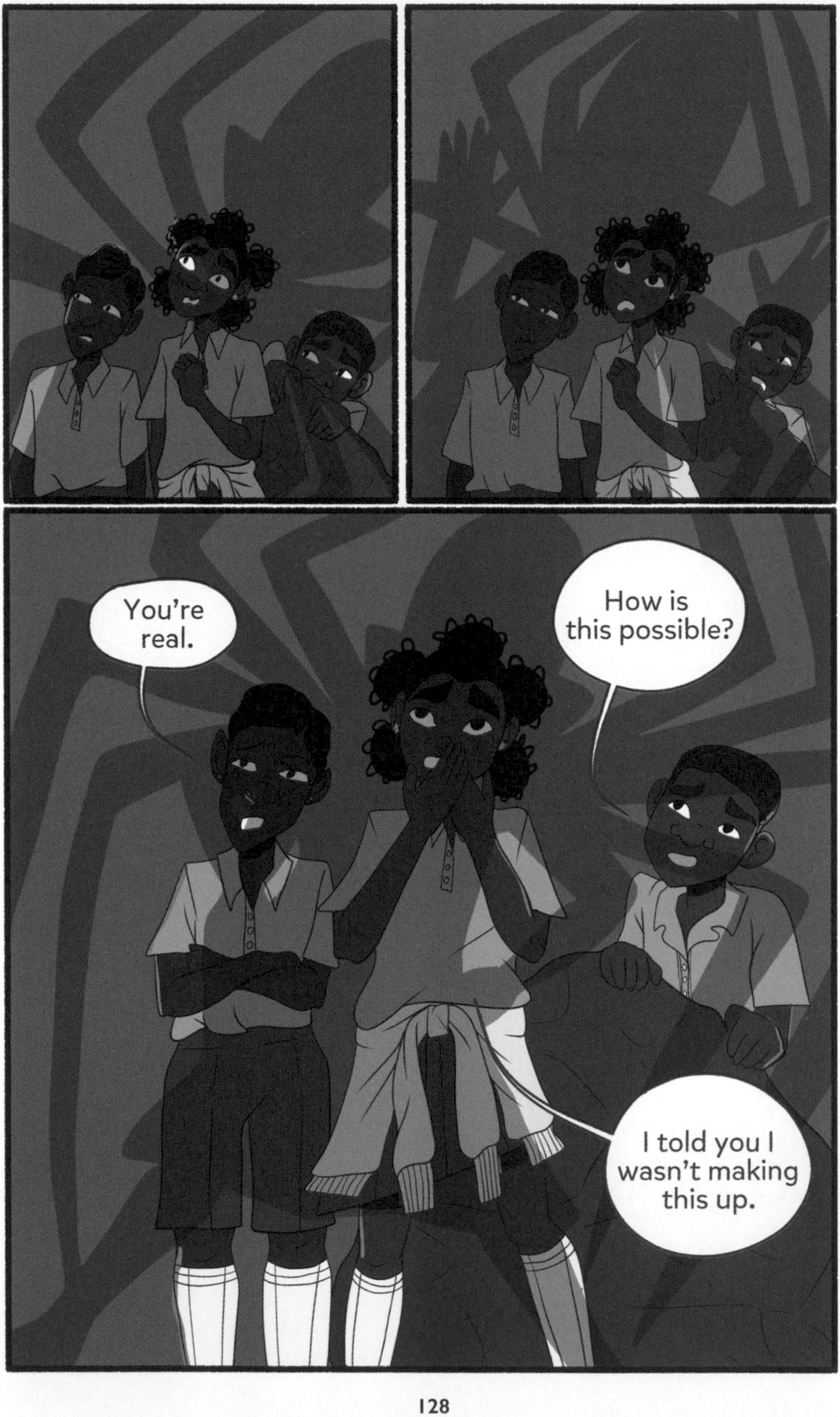
You're real.
How is this possible?
I told you I wasn't making this up.

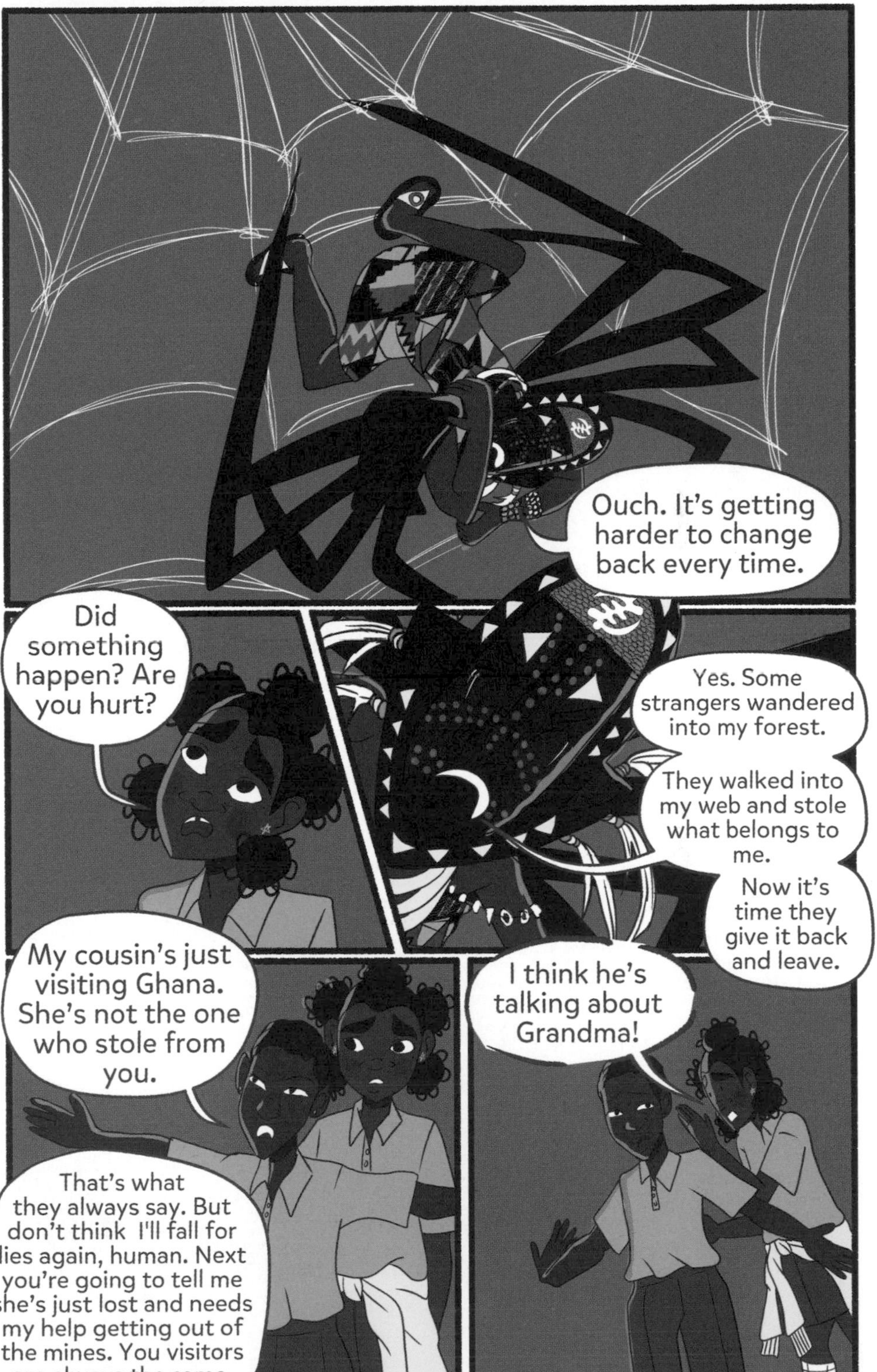

Ouch. It's getting harder to change back every time.
Did something happen? Are you hurt?
Yes. Some strangers wandered into my forest.
They walked into my web and stole what belongs to me.
Now it's time they give it back and leave.
My cousin's just visiting Ghana. She's not the one who stole from you.
That's what they always say. But don't think I'll fall for lies again, human. Next you're going to tell me she's just lost and needs my help getting out of the mines. You visitors are always the same.
I think he's talking about Grandma!

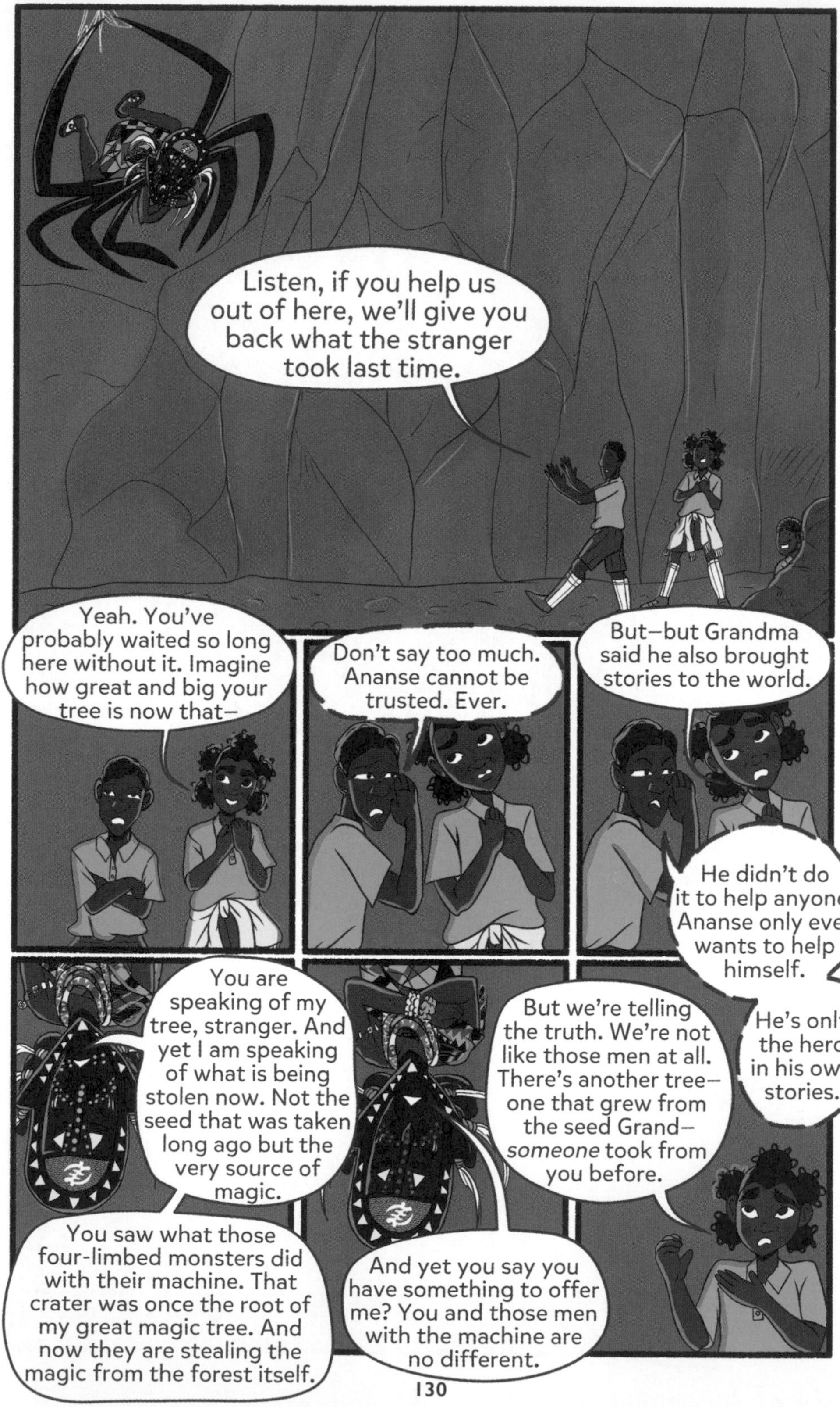

Listen, if you help us out of here, we'll give you back what the stranger took last time.
Yeah. You've probably waited so long here without it. Imagine how great and big your tree is now that—
Don't say too much. Ananse cannot be trusted. Ever.
But—but Grandma said he also brought stories to the world.
He didn't do it to help anyone. Ananse only ever wants to help himself.
He's only the hero in his own stories.
You are speaking of my tree, stranger. And yet I am speaking of what is being stolen now. Not the seed that was taken long ago but the very source of magic.
You saw what those four-limbed monsters did with their machine. That crater was once the root of my great magic tree. And now they are stealing the magic from the forest itself.
But we're telling the truth. We're not like those men at all. There's another tree—one that grew from the seed Grand—*someone* took from you before.
And yet you say you have something to offer me? You and those men with the machine are no different.

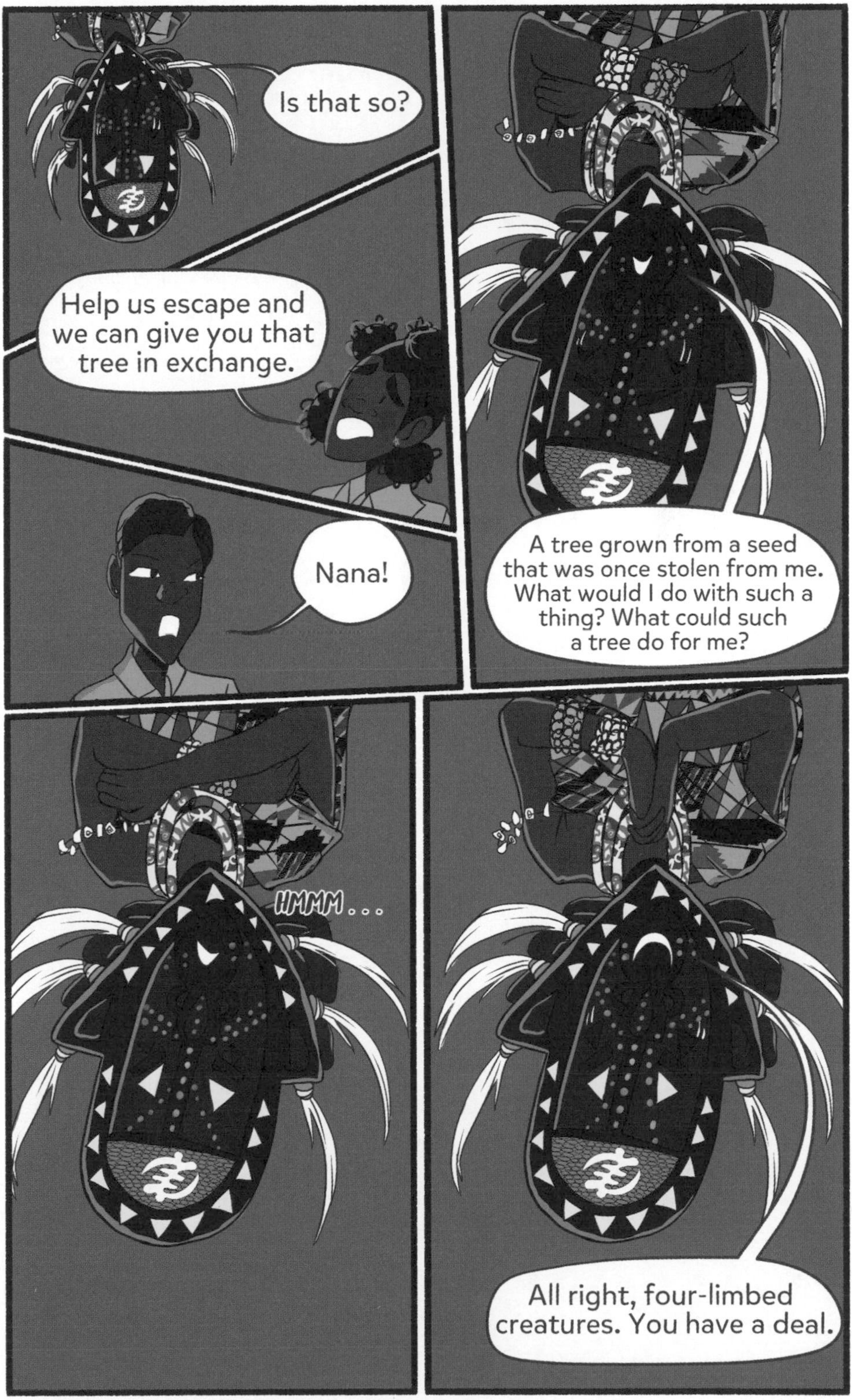

Is that so?
Help us escape and we can give you that tree in exchange.
Nana!
A tree grown from a seed that was once stolen from me. What would I do with such a thing? What could such a tree do for me?
HMMM...
All right, four-limbed creatures. You have a deal.

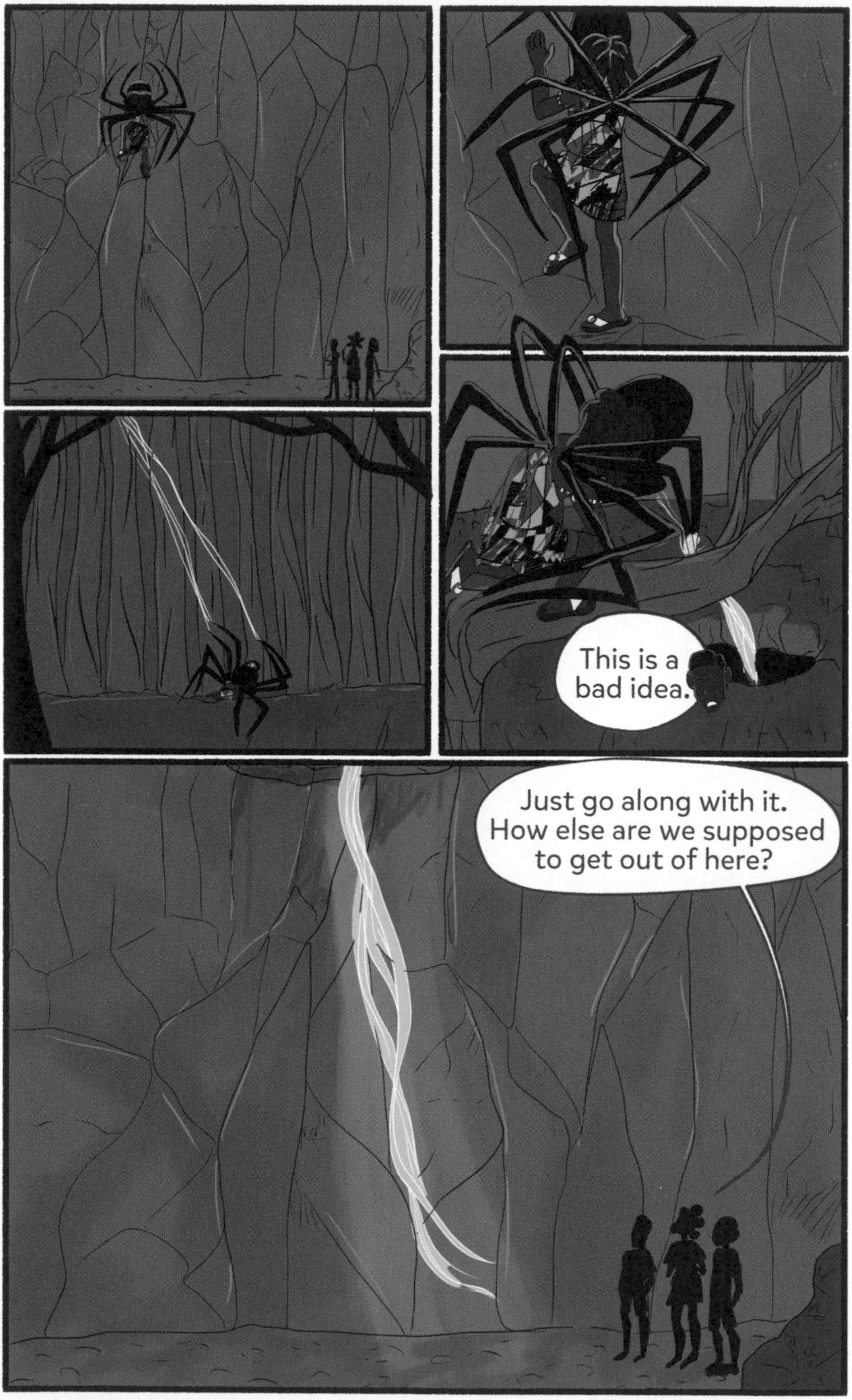
This is a bad idea.
Just go along with it. How else are we supposed to get out of here?

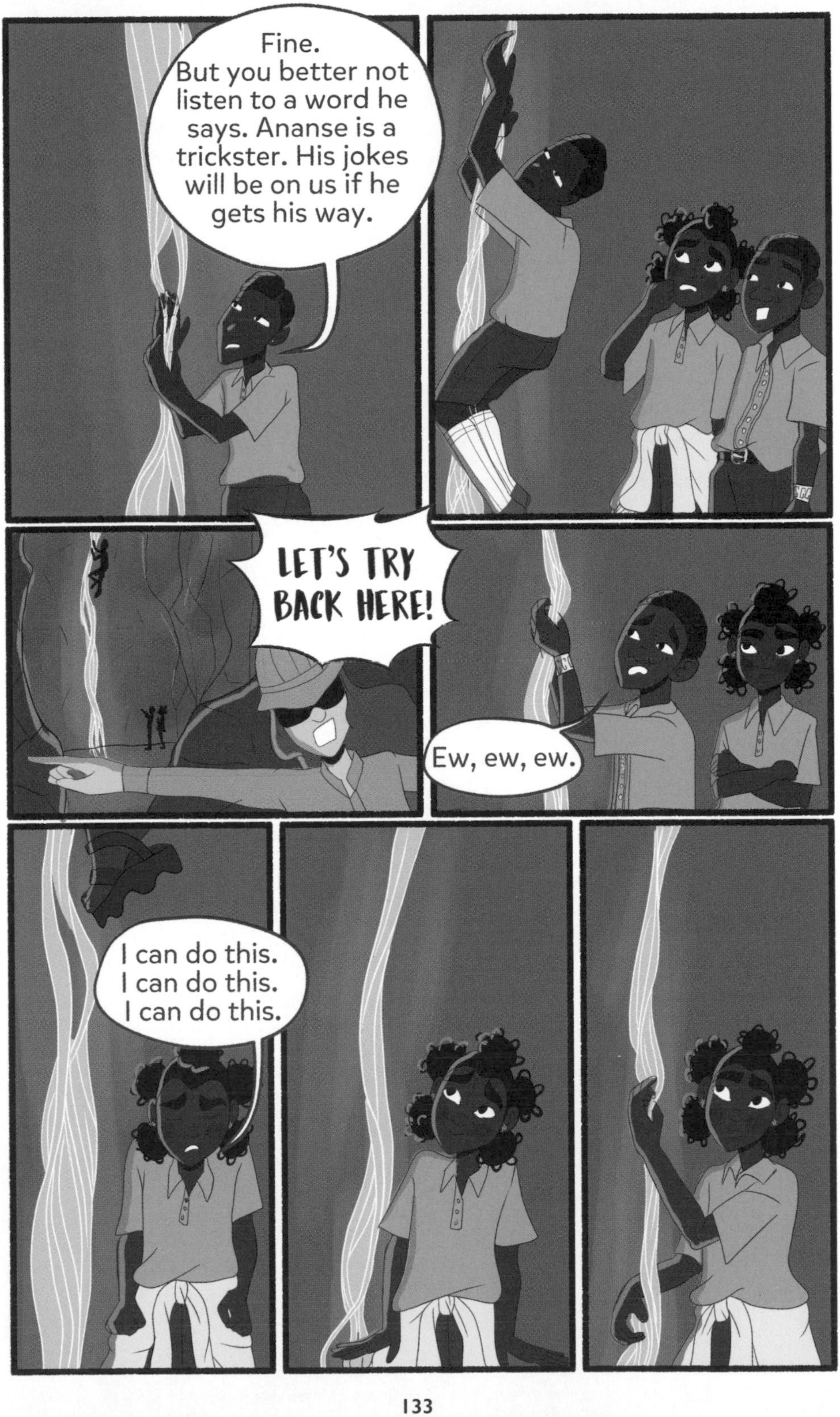
Fine.
But you better not listen to a word he says. Ananse is a trickster. His jokes will be on us if he gets his way.
LET'S TRY BACK HERE!
Ew, ew, ew.
I can do this.
I can do this.
I can do this.

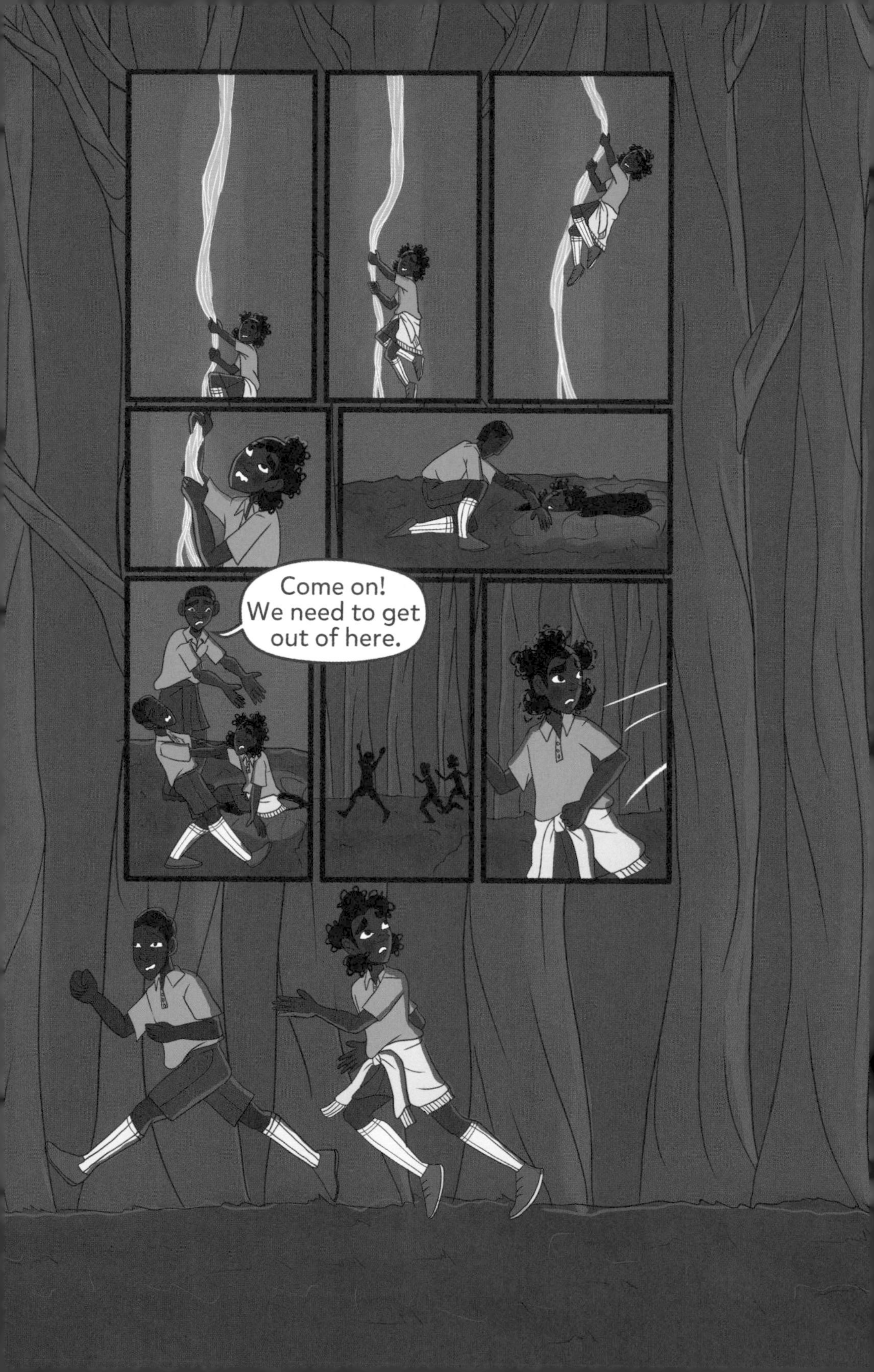
Come on! We need to get out of here.

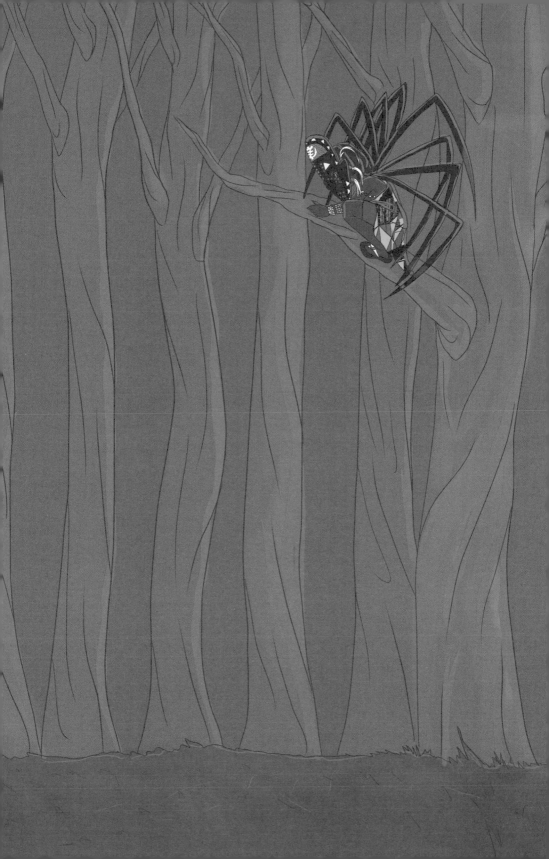

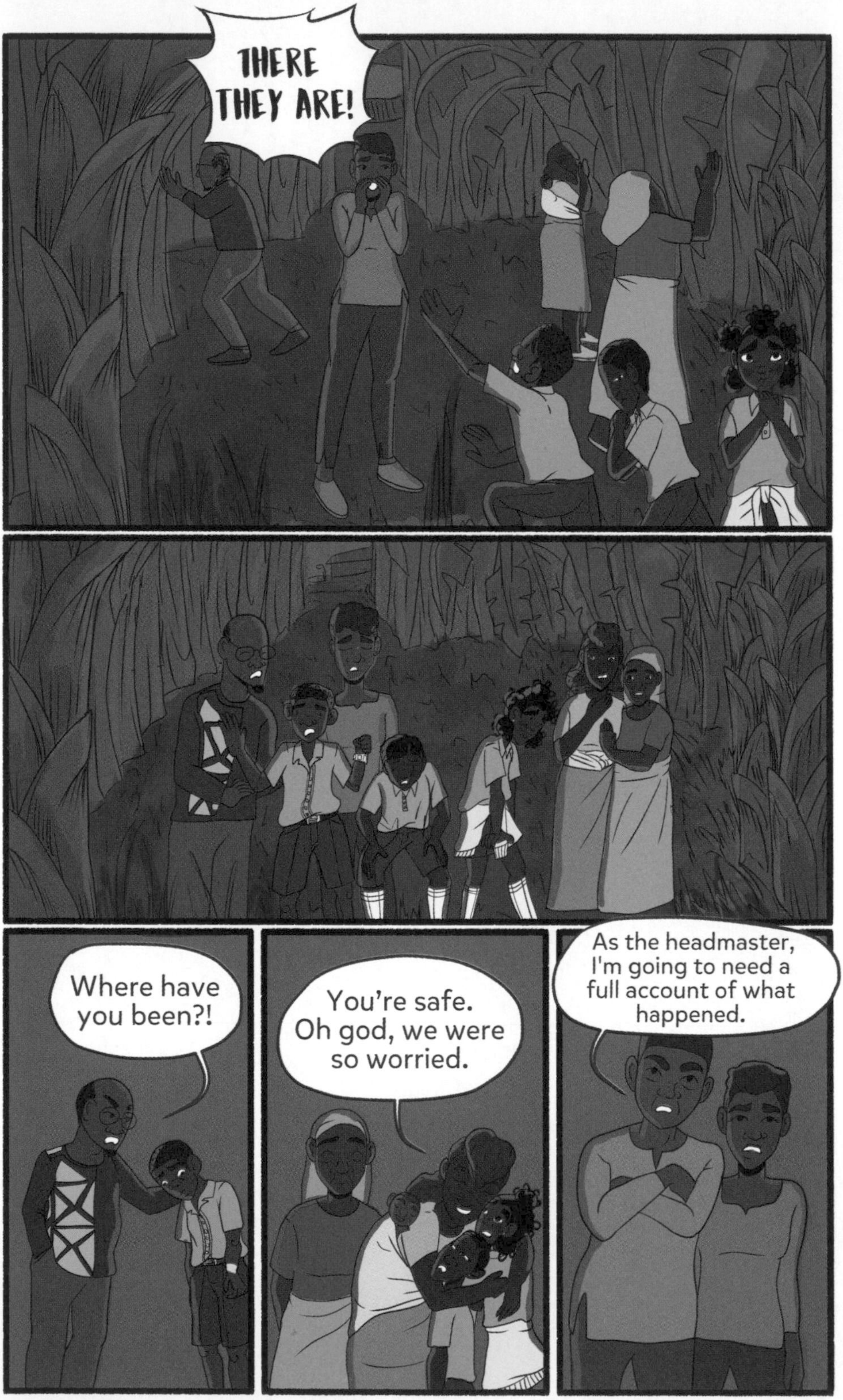
THERE THEY ARE!
Where have you been?!
You're safe. Oh god, we were so worried.
As the headmaster, I'm going to need a full account of what happened.

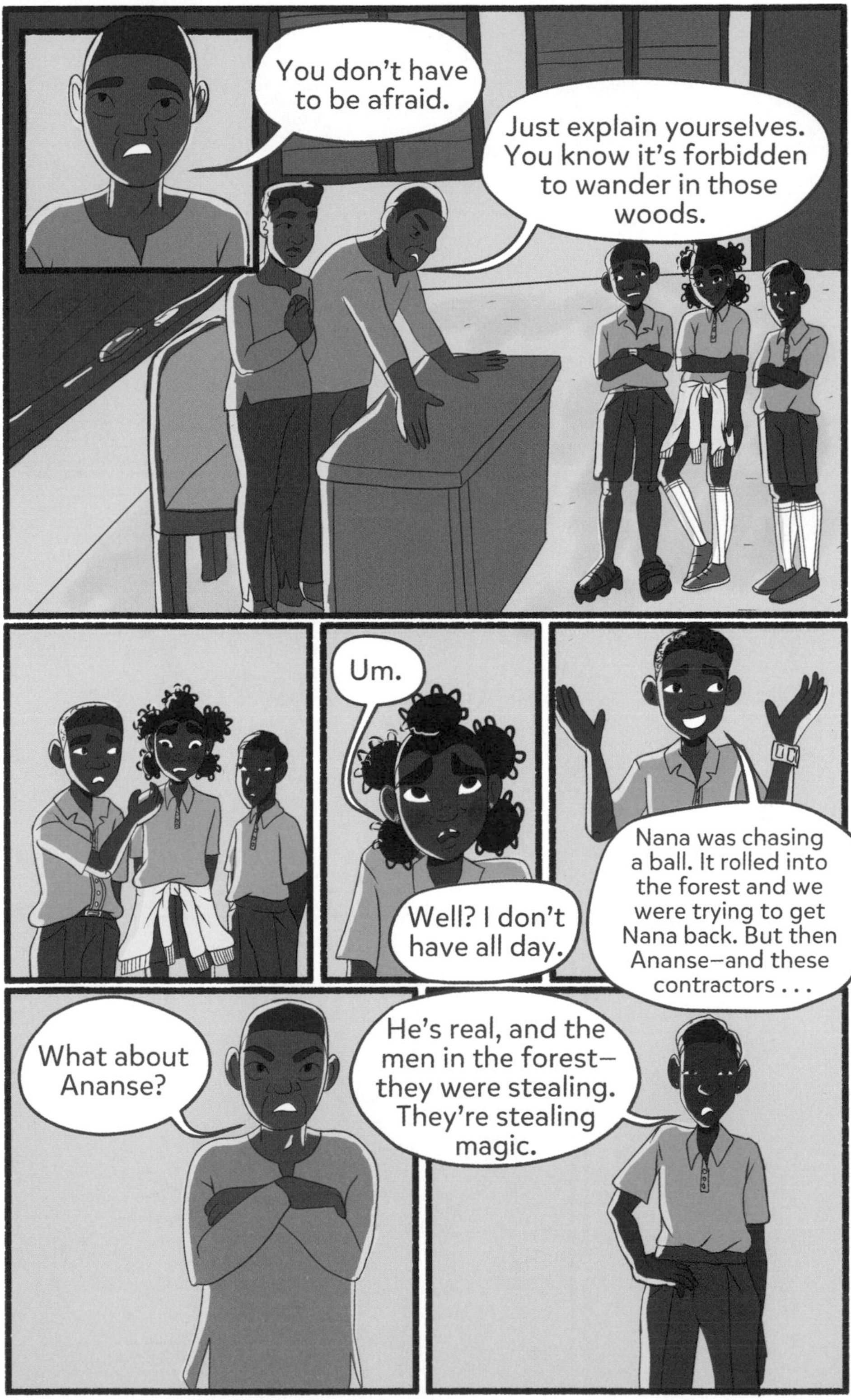
You don't have to be afraid.
Just explain yourselves. You know it's forbidden to wander in those woods.
Um.
Well? I don't have all day.
Nana was chasing a ball. It rolled into the forest and we were trying to get Nana back. But then Ananse—and these contractors . . .
What about Ananse?
He's real, and the men in the forest—they were stealing. They're stealing magic.

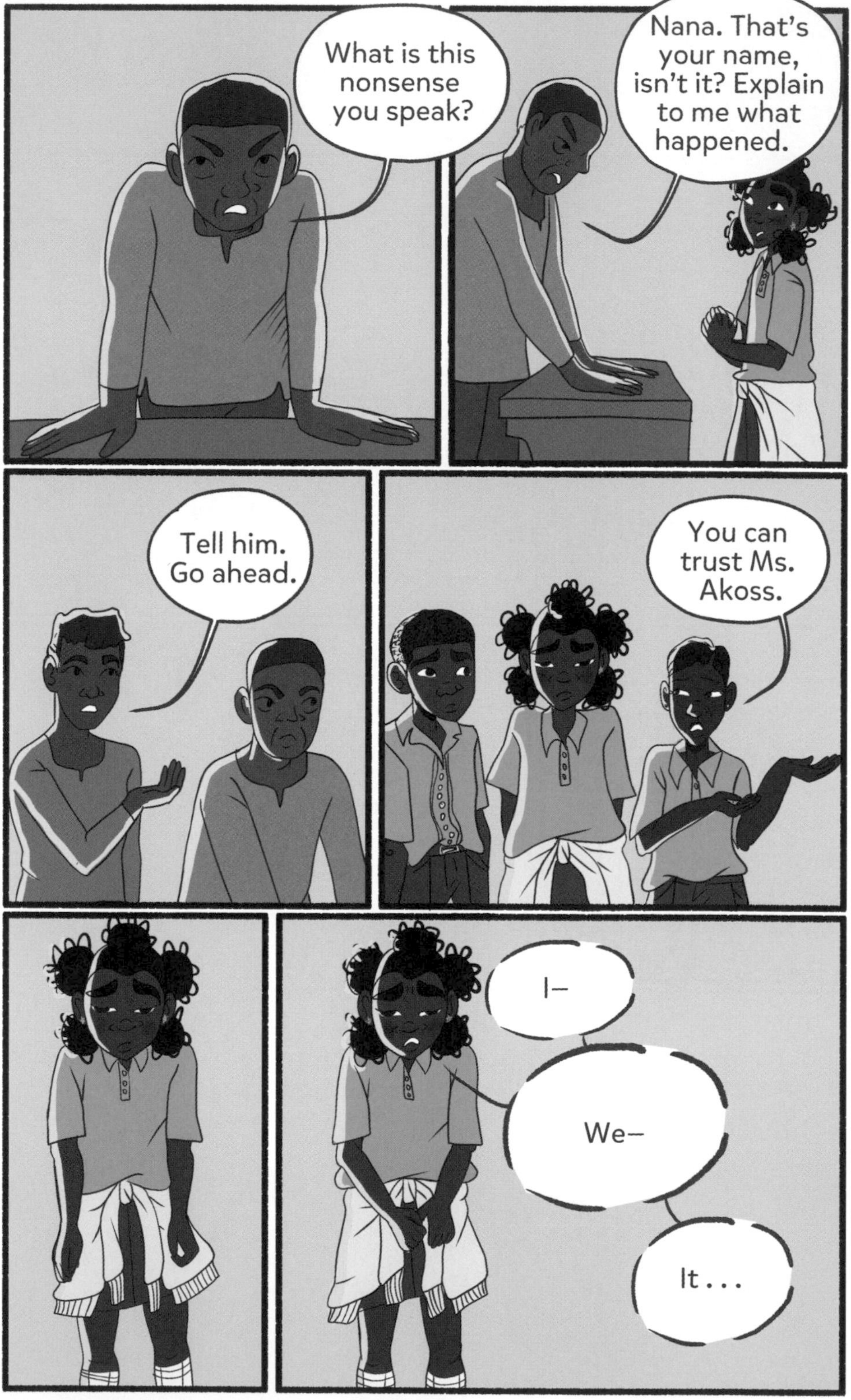
What is this nonsense you speak?
Nana. That's your name, isn't it? Explain to me what happened.
Tell him. Go ahead.
You can trust Ms. Akoss.
I–
We–
It . . .

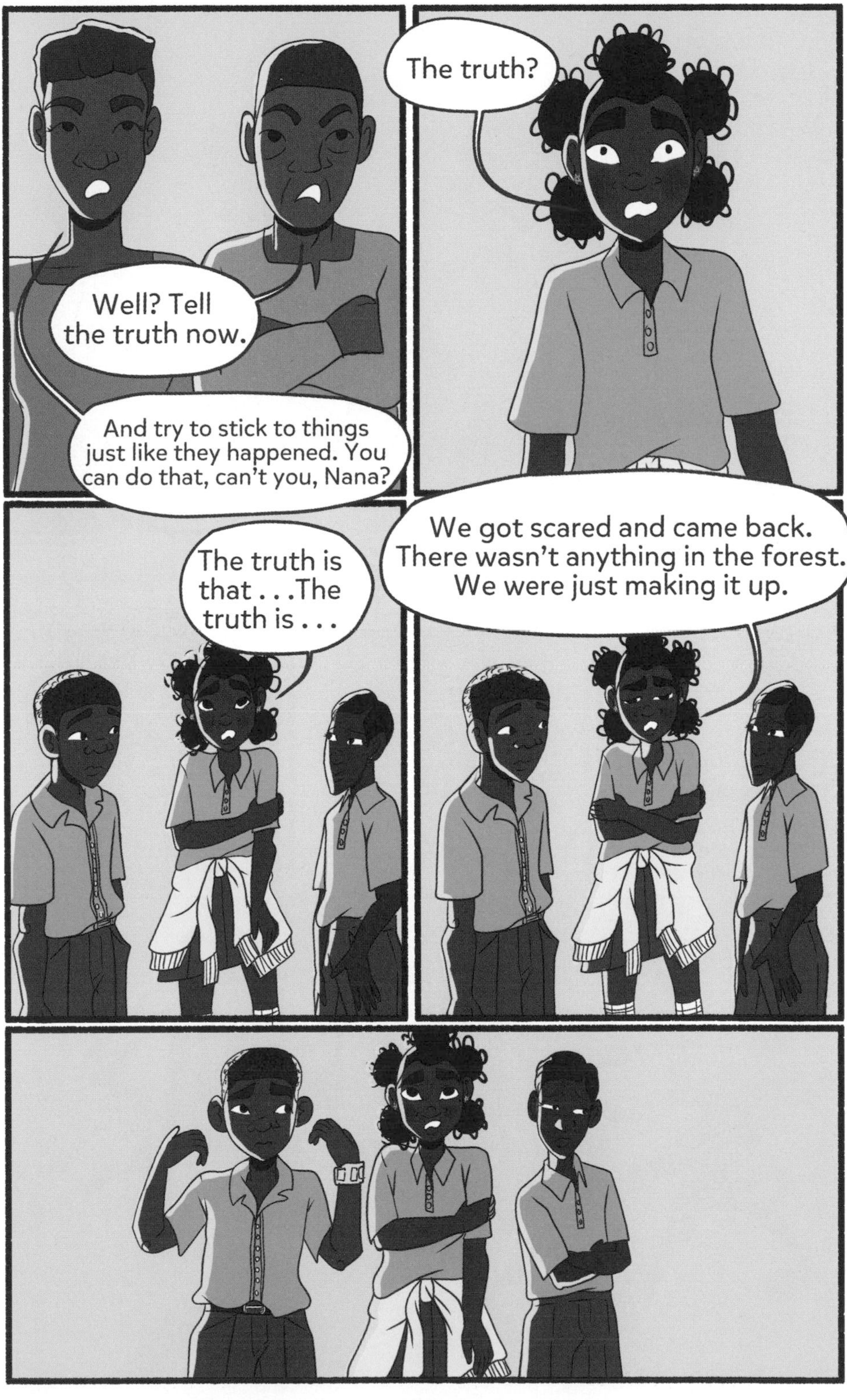
Well? Tell the truth now.
And try to stick to things just like they happened. You can do that, can't you, Nana?
The truth?
The truth is that . . .The truth is . . .
We got scared and came back. There wasn't anything in the forest. We were just making it up.

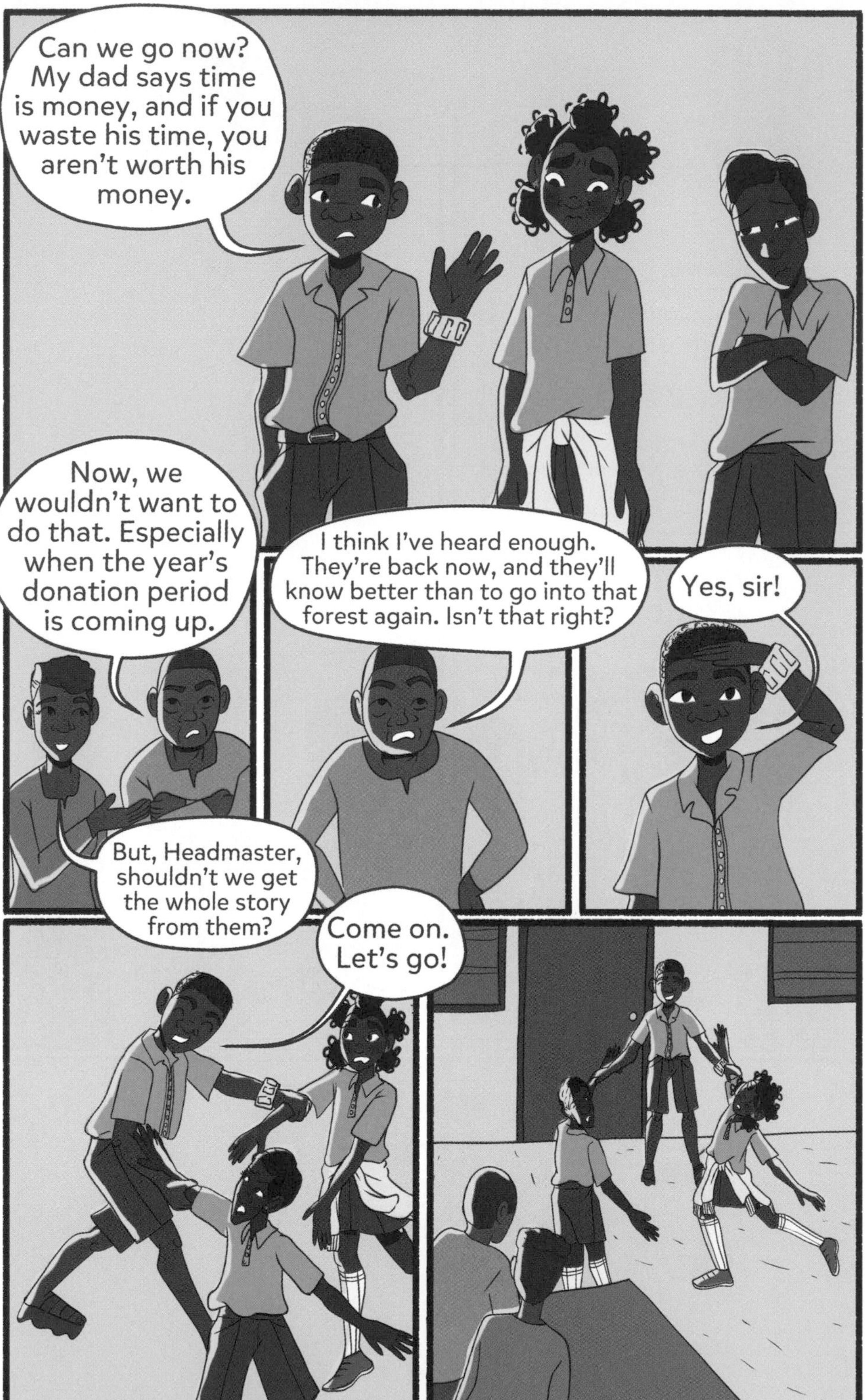
Can we go now? My dad says time is money, and if you waste his time, you aren't worth his money.
Now, we wouldn't want to do that. Especially when the year's donation period is coming up.
But, Headmaster, shouldn't we get the whole story from them?
I think I've heard enough. They're back now, and they'll know better than to go into that forest again. Isn't that right?
Yes, sir!
Come on. Let's go!

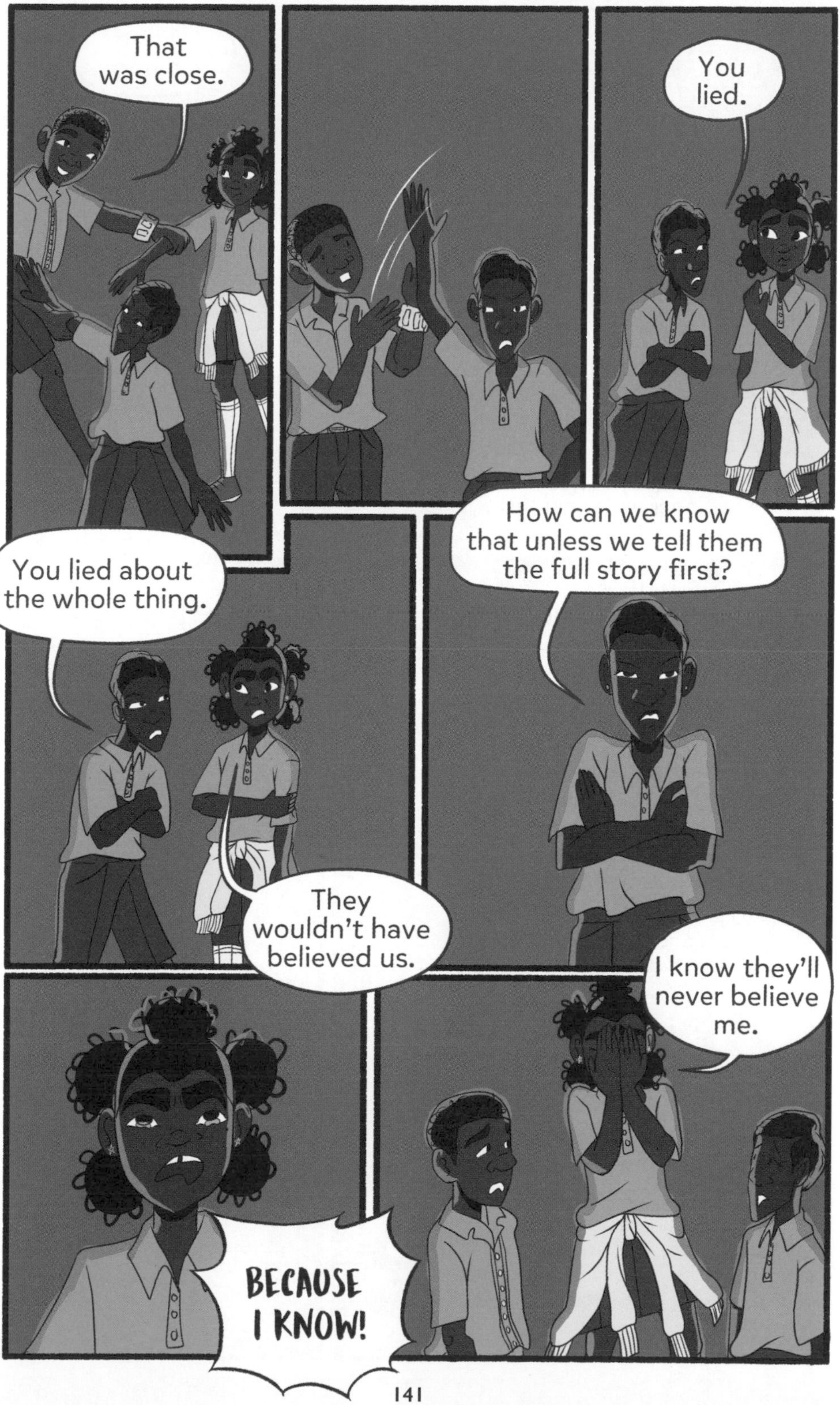
That was close.
You lied.
You lied about the whole thing.
They wouldn't have believed us.
How can we know that unless we tell them the full story first?
BECAUSE I KNOW!
I know they'll never believe me.

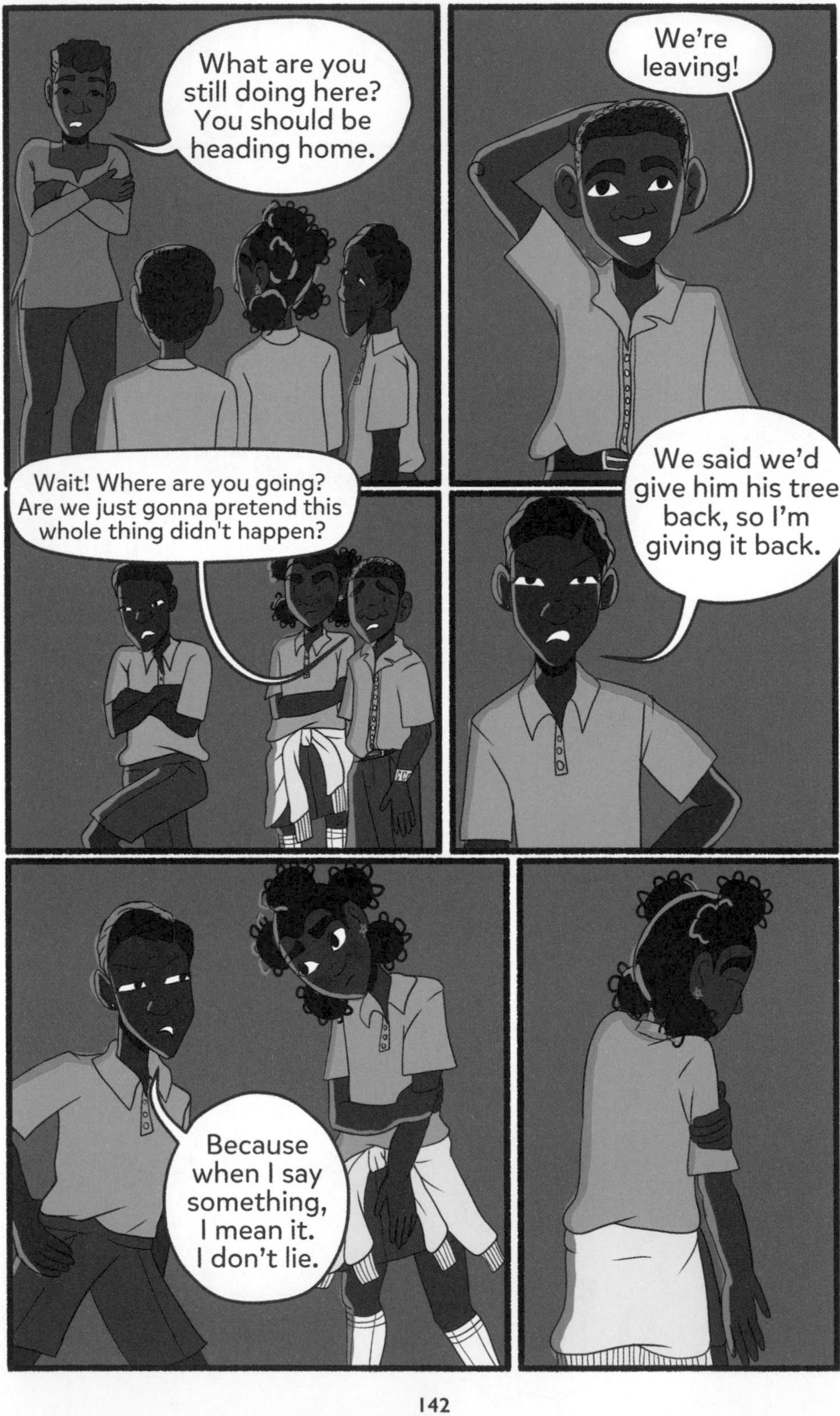
What are you still doing here? You should be heading home.
We're leaving!
Wait! Where are you going? Are we just gonna pretend this whole thing didn't happen?
We said we'd give him his tree back, so I'm giving it back.
Because when I say something, I mean it. I don't lie.

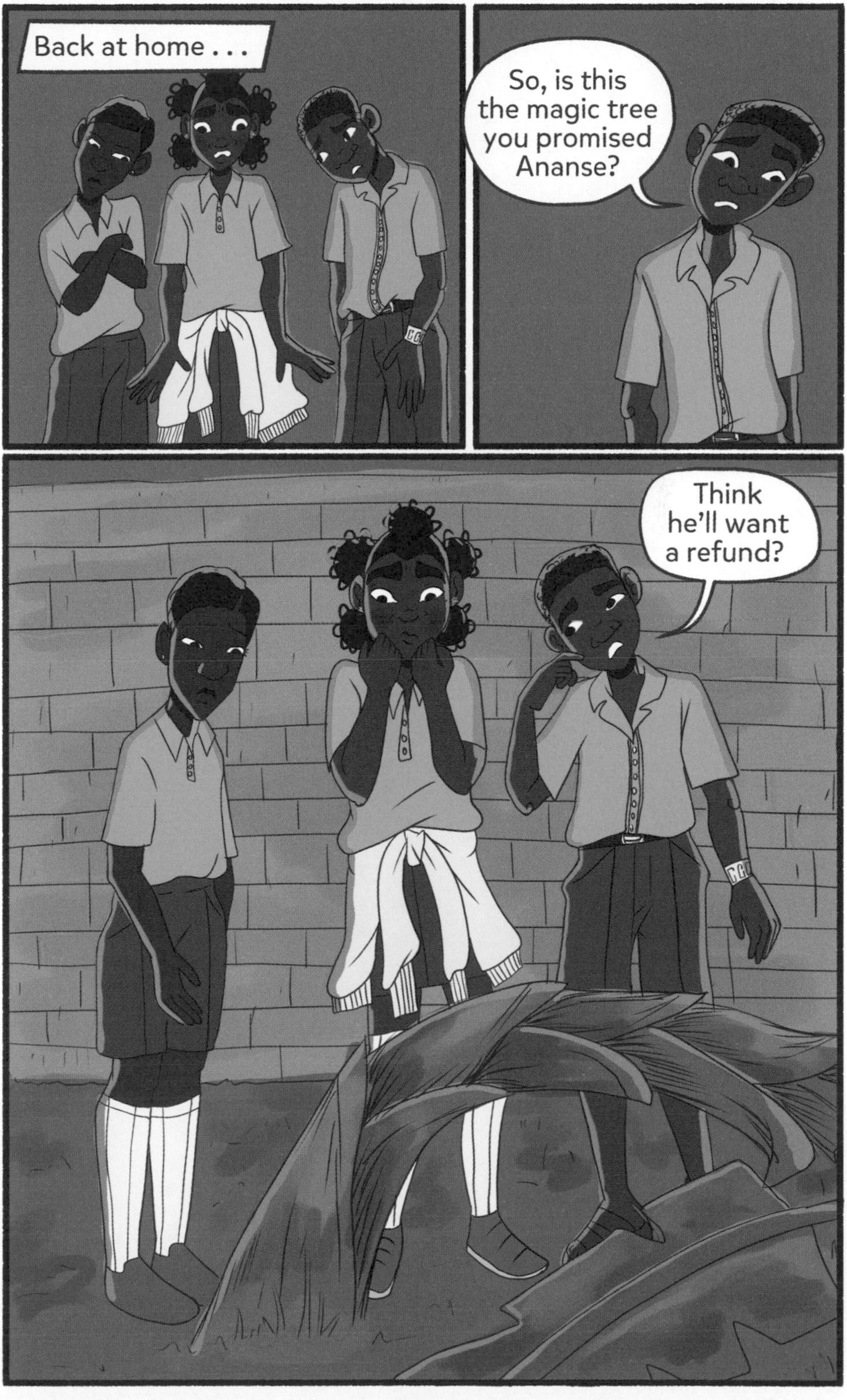
Back at home . . .
So, is this the magic tree you promised Ananse?
Think he'll want a refund?

Chapter 7

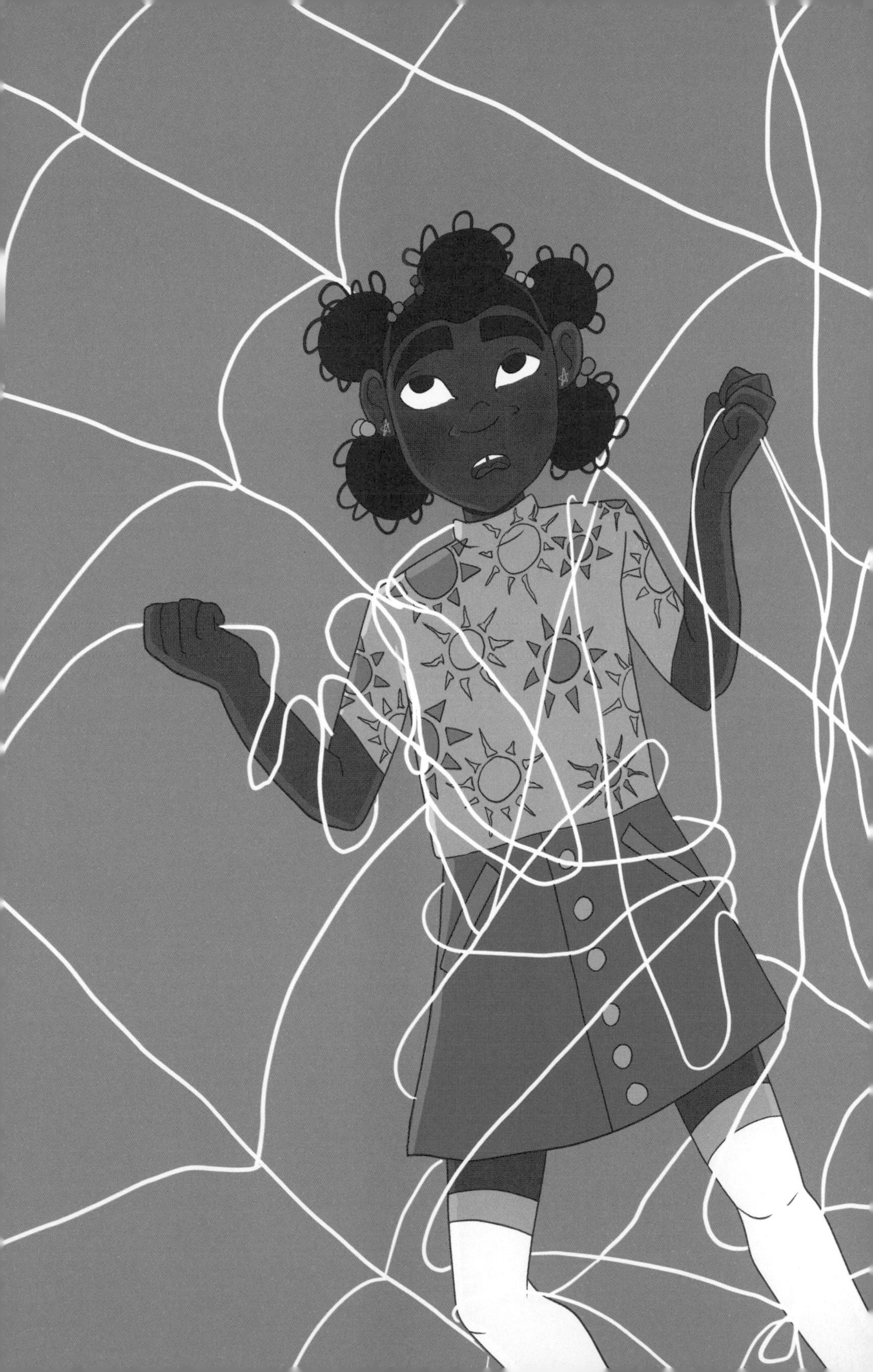

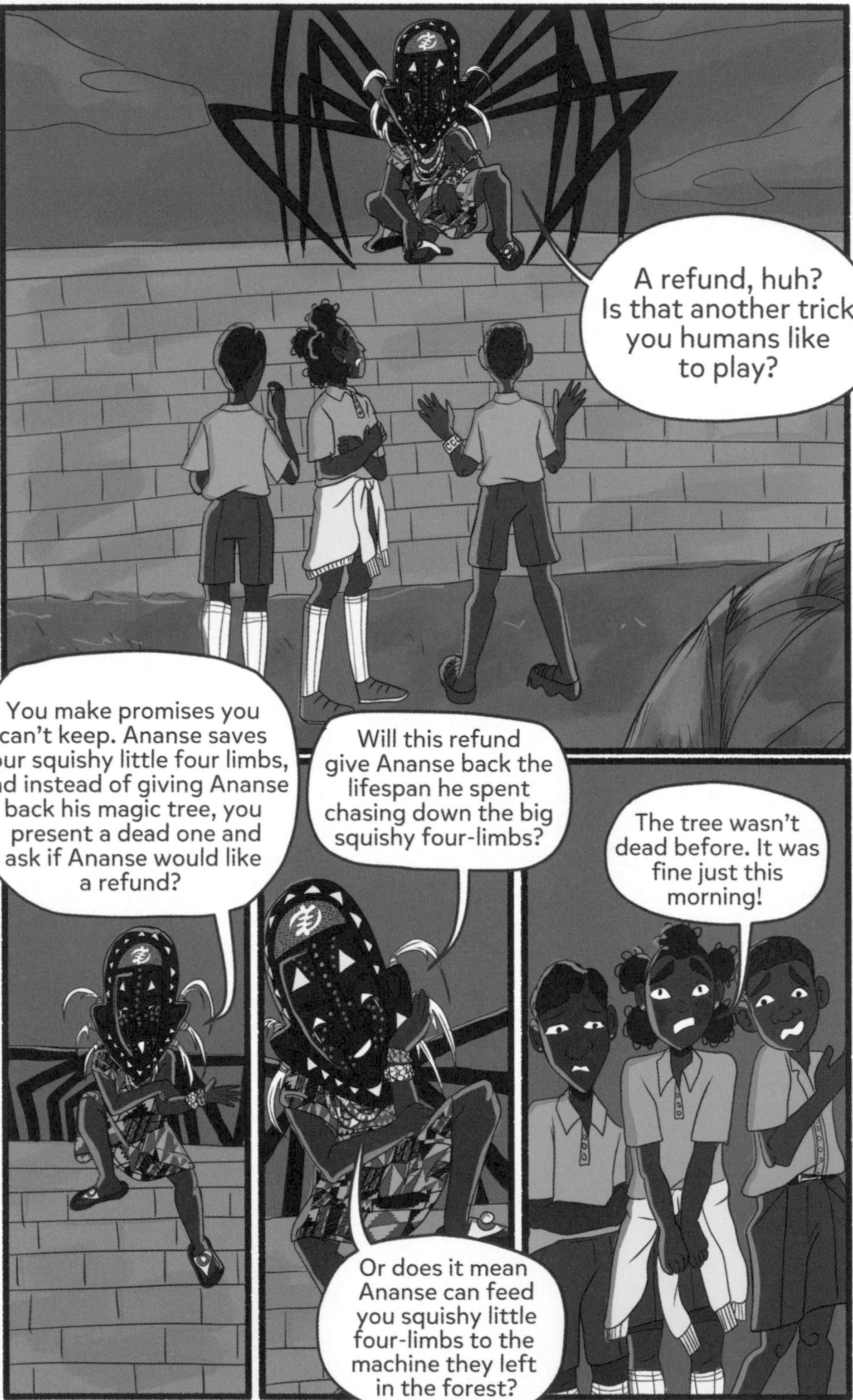
A refund, huh? Is that another trick you humans like to play?
You make promises you can't keep. Ananse saves your squishy little four limbs, and instead of giving Ananse back his magic tree, you present a dead one and ask if Ananse would like a refund?
Will this refund give Ananse back the lifespan he spent chasing down the big squishy four-limbs?
Or does it mean Ananse can feed you squishy little four-limbs to the machine they left in the forest?
The tree wasn't dead before. It was fine just this morning!

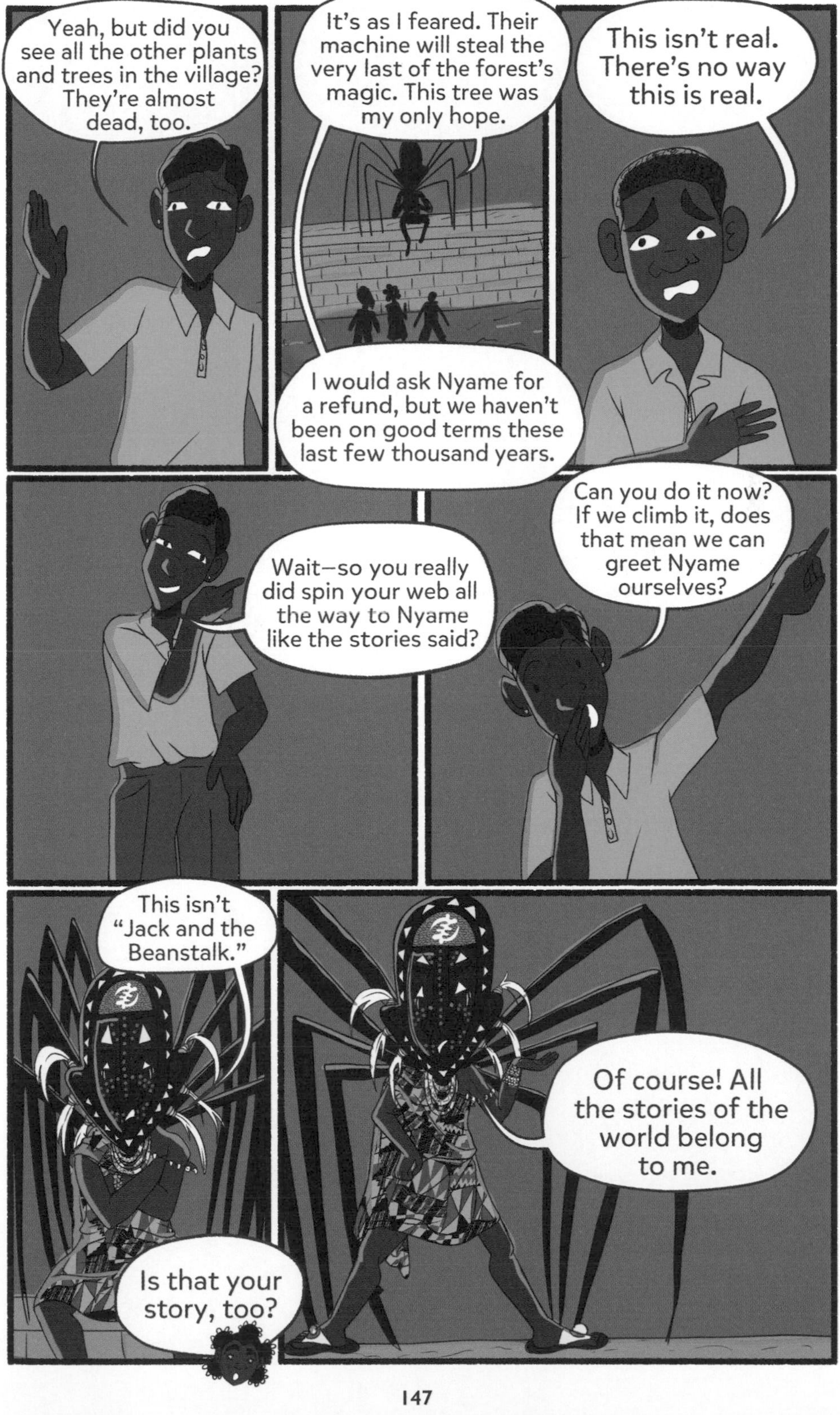
Yeah, but did you see all the other plants and trees in the village? They're almost dead, too.
It's as I feared. Their machine will steal the very last of the forest's magic. This tree was my only hope.
I would ask Nyame for a refund, but we haven't been on good terms these last few thousand years.
This isn't real. There's no way this is real.
Wait—so you really did spin your web all the way to Nyame like the stories said?
Can you do it now? If we climb it, does that mean we can greet Nyame ourselves?
This isn't "Jack and the Beanstalk."
Is that your story, too?
Of course! All the stories of the world belong to me.

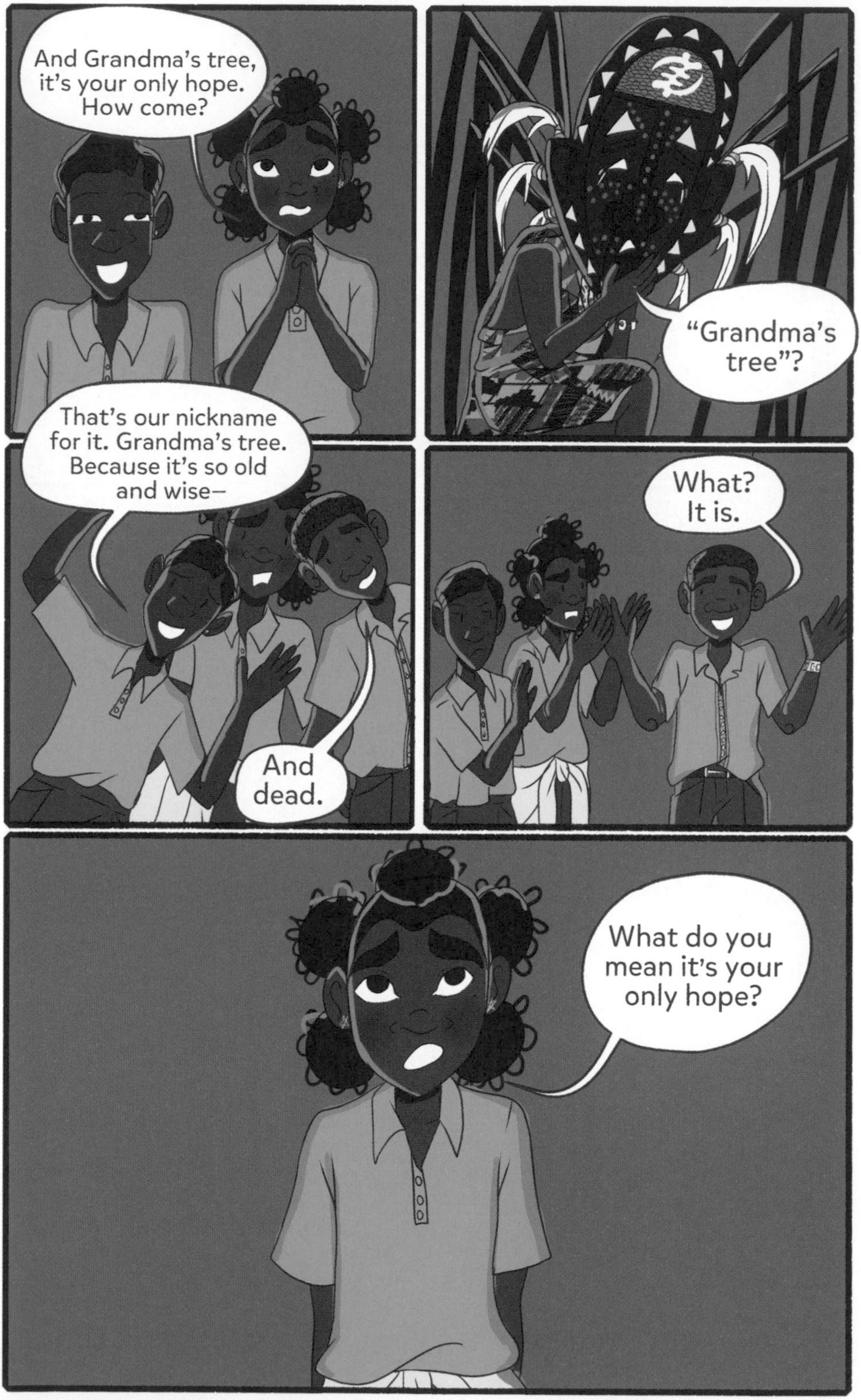
And Grandma's tree, it's your only hope. How come?
"Grandma's tree"?
That's our nickname for it. Grandma's tree. Because it's so old and wise–
And dead.
What? It is.
What do you mean it's your only hope?

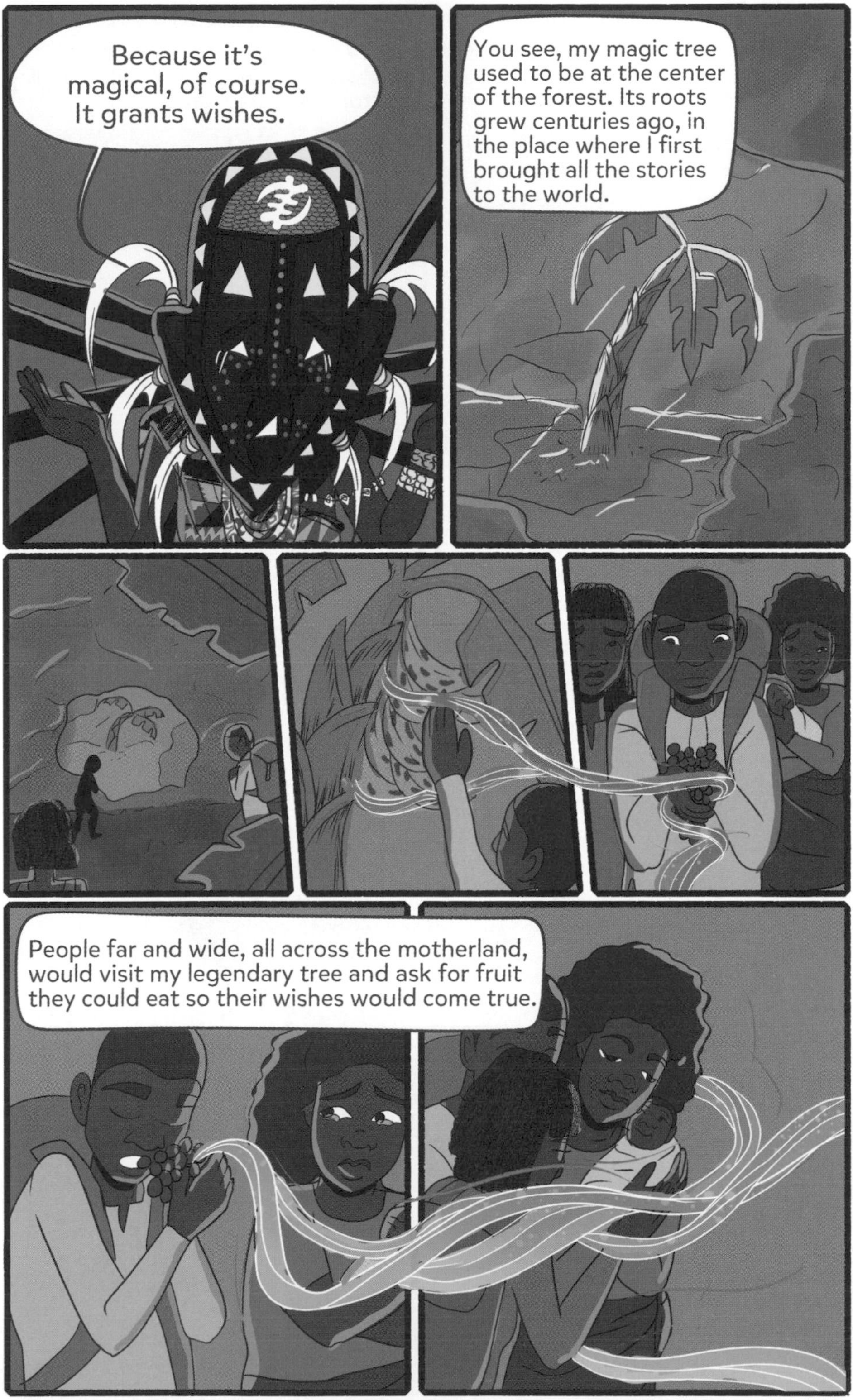
Because it's magical, of course. It grants wishes.
You see, my magic tree used to be at the center of the forest. Its roots grew centuries ago, in the place where I first brought all the stories to the world.
People far and wide, all across the motherland, would visit my legendary tree and ask for fruit they could eat so their wishes would come true.

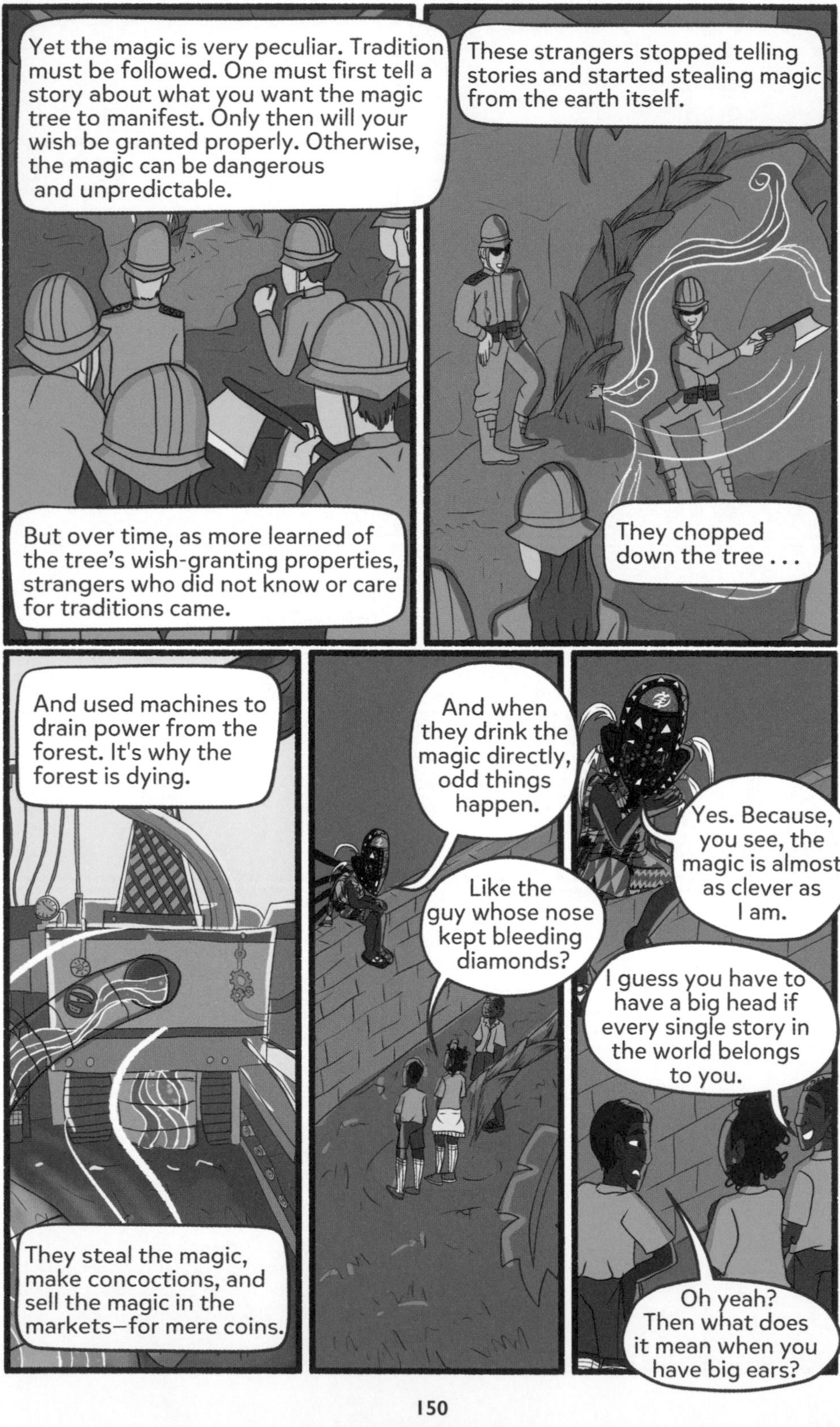
Yet the magic is very peculiar. Tradition must be followed. One must first tell a story about what you want the magic tree to manifest. Only then will your wish be granted properly. Otherwise, the magic can be dangerous and unpredictable.
But over time, as more learned of the tree's wish-granting properties, strangers who did not know or care for traditions came.
These strangers stopped telling stories and started stealing magic from the earth itself.
They chopped down the tree . . .
And used machines to drain power from the forest. It's why the forest is dying.
They steal the magic, make concoctions, and sell the magic in the markets—for mere coins.
And when they drink the magic directly, odd things happen.
Like the guy whose nose kept bleeding diamonds?
Yes. Because, you see, the magic is almost as clever as I am.
I guess you have to have a big head if every single story in the world belongs to you.
Oh yeah? Then what does it mean when you have big ears?

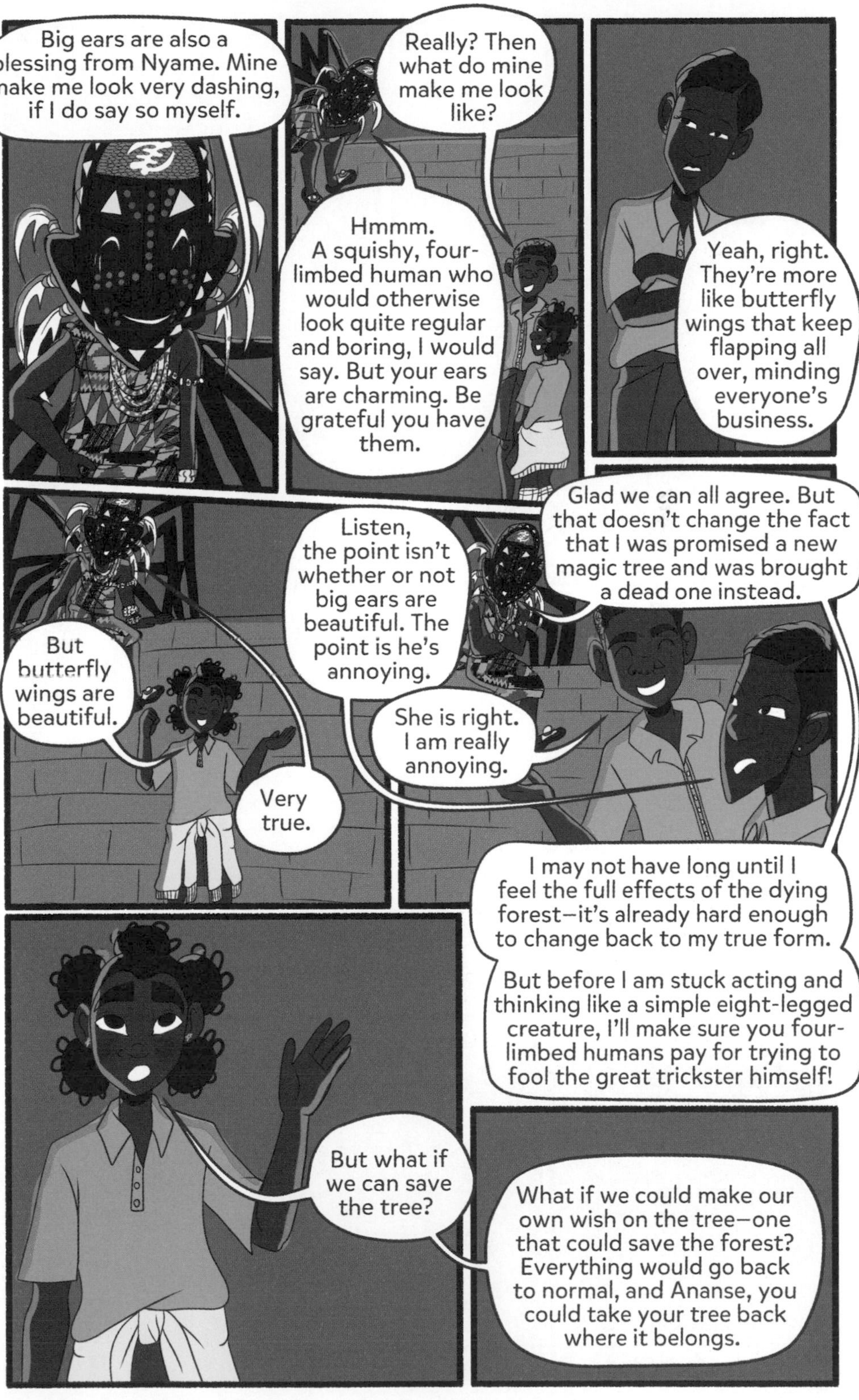
Big ears are also a blessing from Nyame. Mine make me look very dashing, if I do say so myself.
Really? Then what do mine make me look like?
Hmmm. A squishy, four-limbed human who would otherwise look quite regular and boring, I would say. But your ears are charming. Be grateful you have them.
Yeah, right. They're more like butterfly wings that keep flapping all over, minding everyone's business.
But butterfly wings are beautiful.
Very true.
Listen, the point isn't whether or not big ears are beautiful. The point is he's annoying.
She is right. I am really annoying.
Glad we can all agree. But that doesn't change the fact that I was promised a new magic tree and was brought a dead one instead.
I may not have long until I feel the full effects of the dying forest—it's already hard enough to change back to my true form.
But before I am stuck acting and thinking like a simple eight-legged creature, I'll make sure you four-limbed humans pay for trying to fool the great trickster himself!
But what if we can save the tree?
What if we could make our own wish on the tree—one that could save the forest? Everything would go back to normal, and Ananse, you could take your tree back where it belongs.

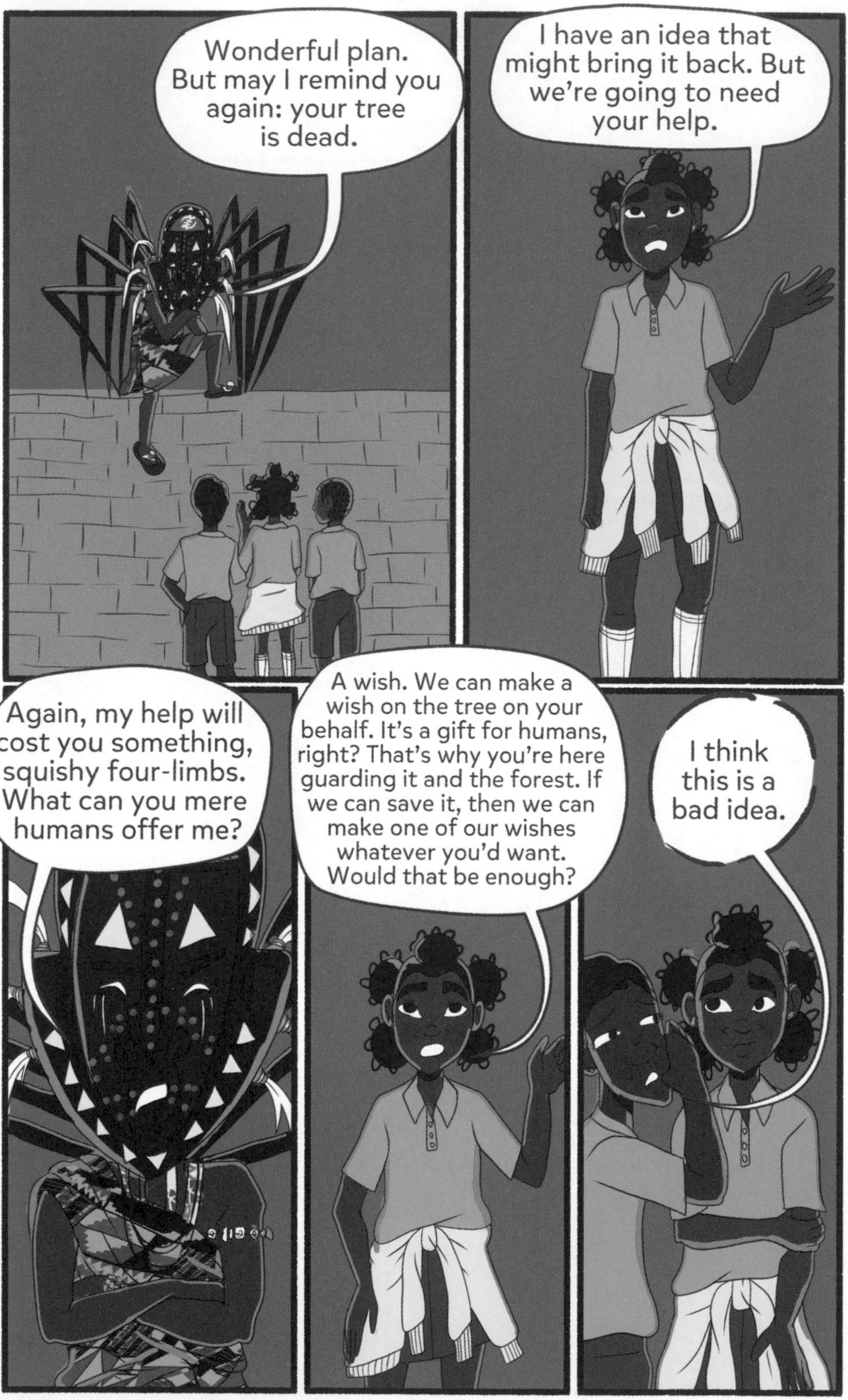
Wonderful plan. But may I remind you again: your tree is dead.
I have an idea that might bring it back. But we're going to need your help.
Again, my help will cost you something, squishy four-limbs. What can you mere humans offer me?
A wish. We can make a wish on the tree on your behalf. It's a gift for humans, right? That's why you're here guarding it and the forest. If we can save it, then we can make one of our wishes whatever you'd want. Would that be enough?
I think this is a bad idea.

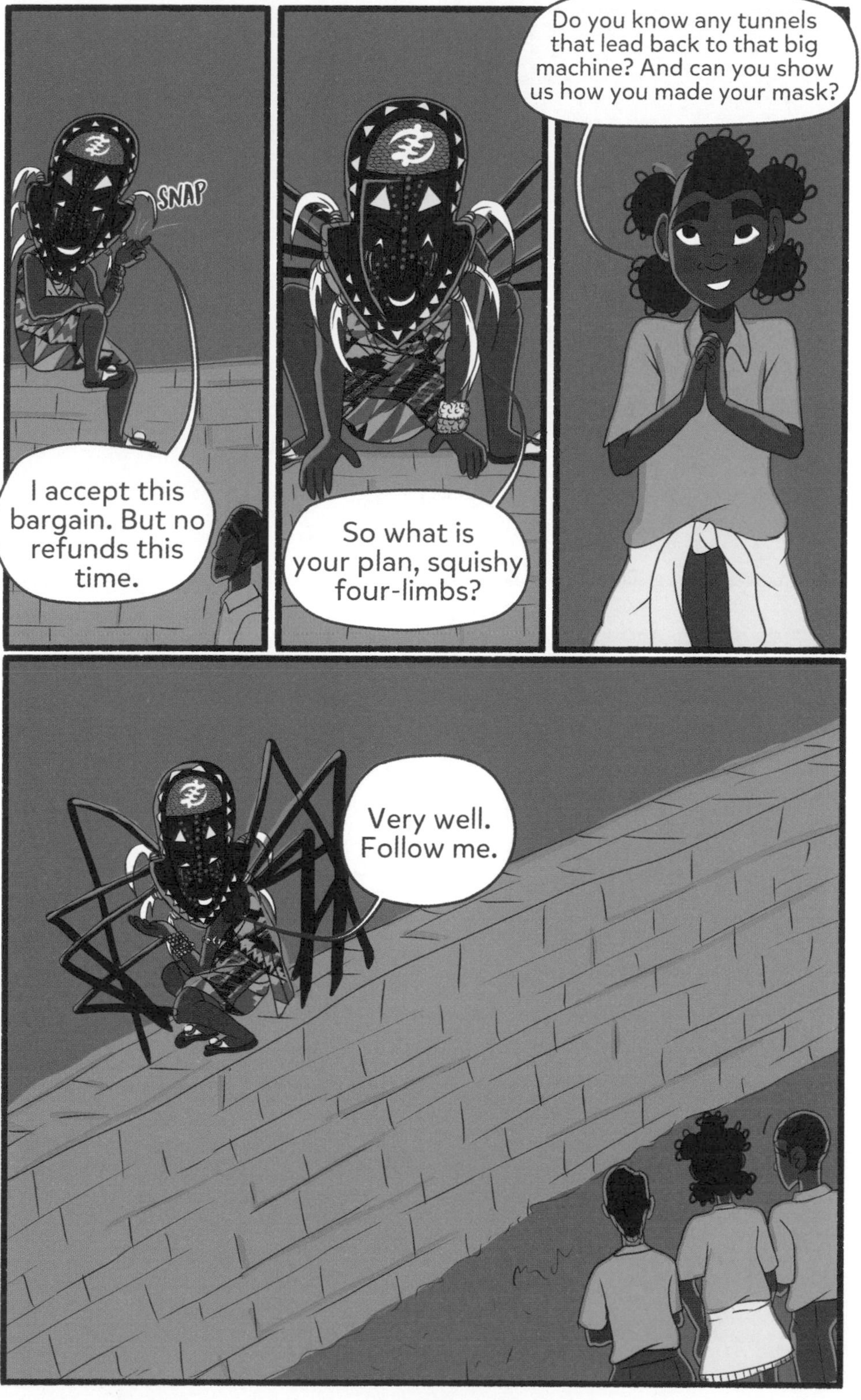
SNAP
I accept this bargain. But no refunds this time.
So what is your plan, squishy four-limbs?
Do you know any tunnels that lead back to that big machine? And can you show us how you made your mask?
Very well. Follow me.

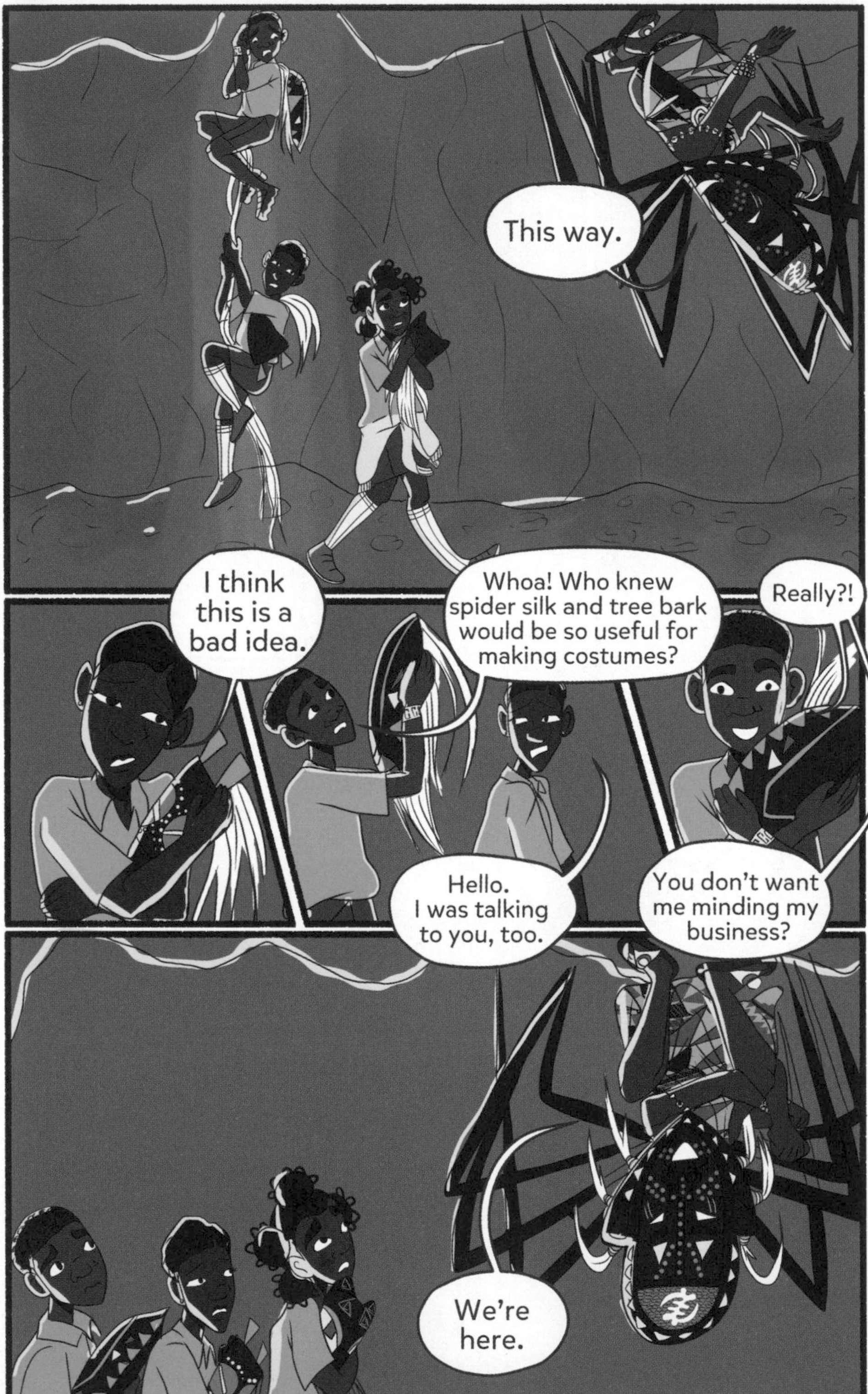
This way.
I think this is a bad idea.
Whoa! Who knew spider silk and tree bark would be so useful for making costumes?
Really?!
Hello. I was talking to you, too.
You don't want me minding my business?
We're here.

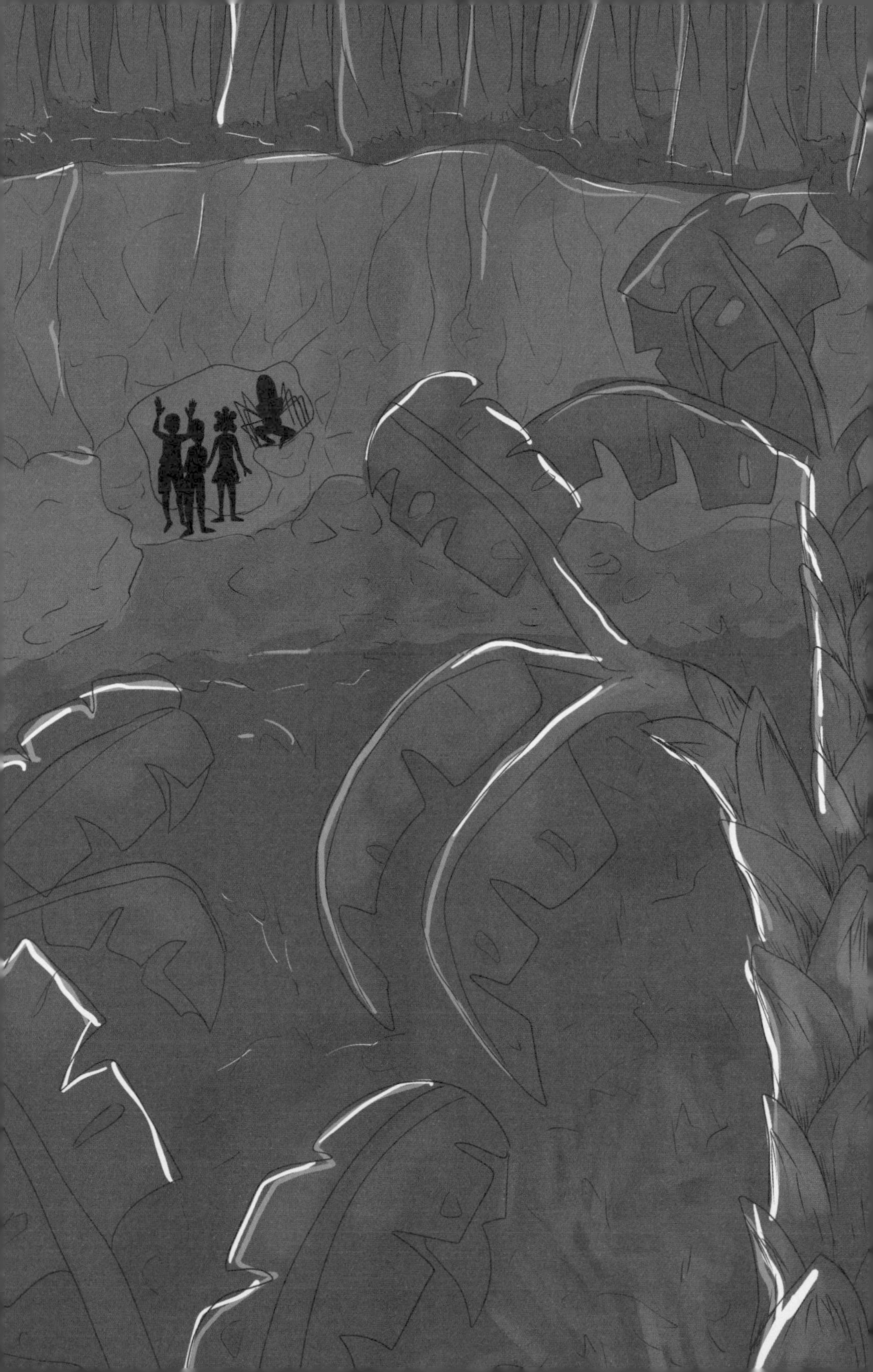

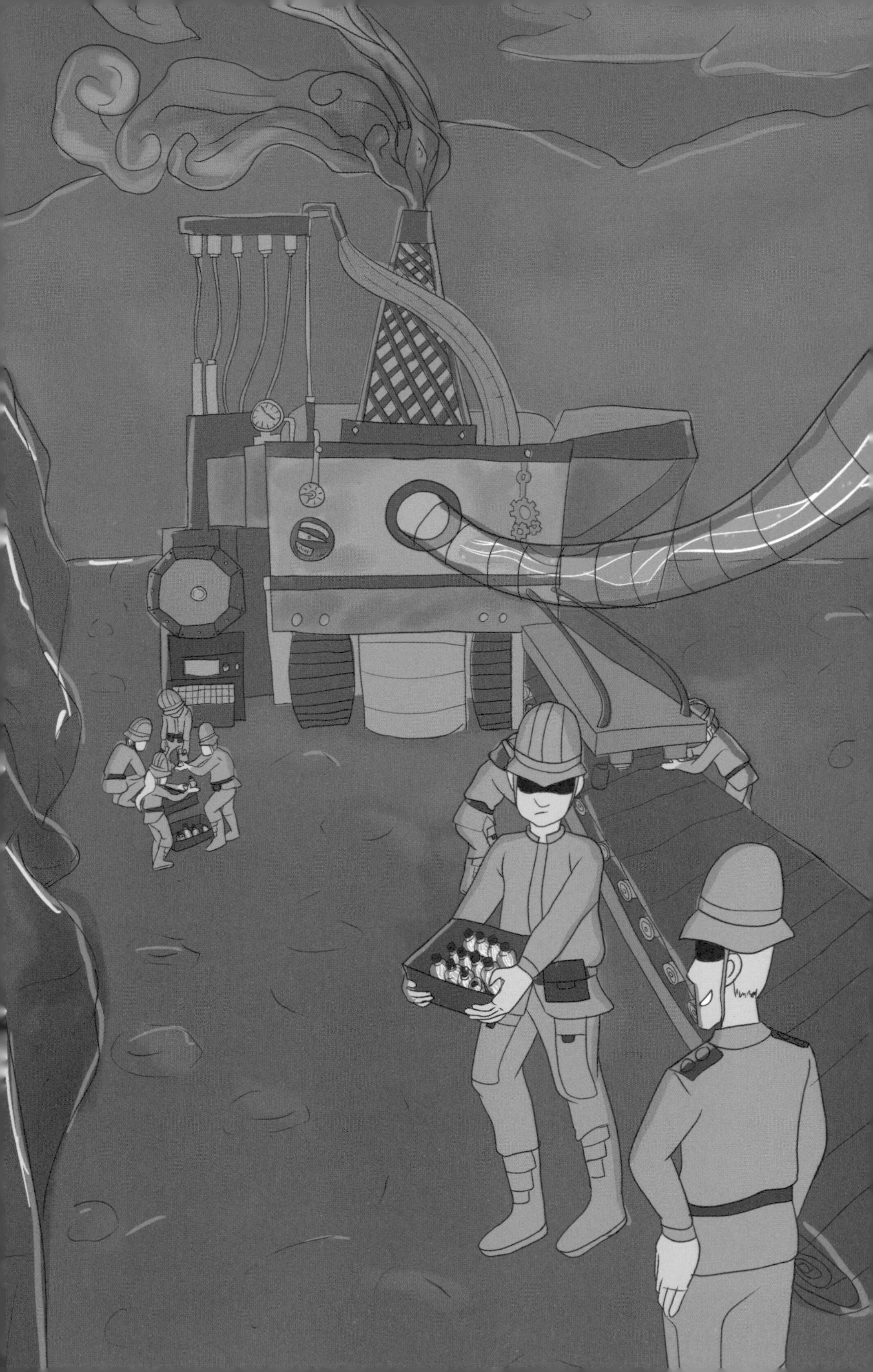

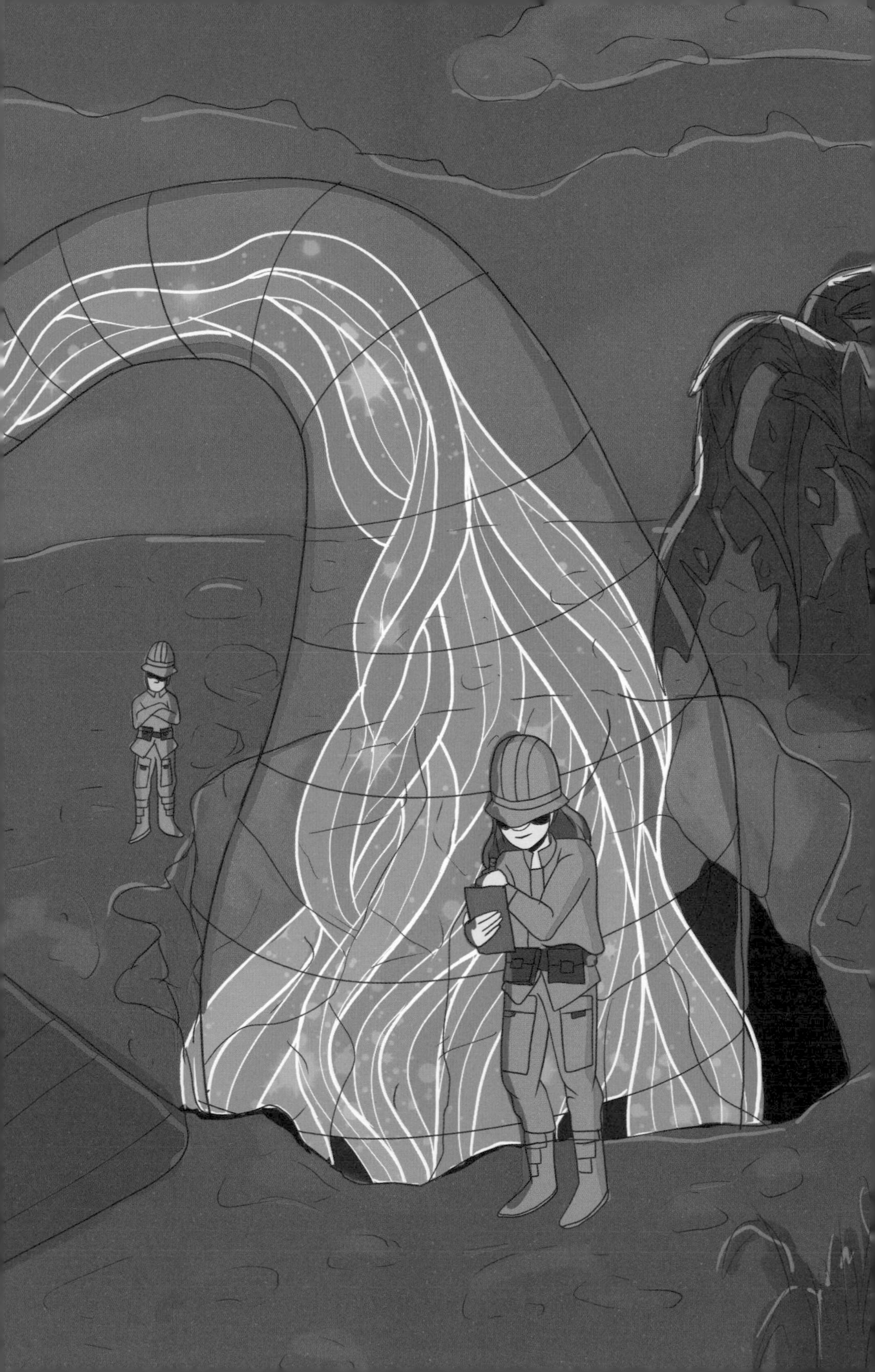

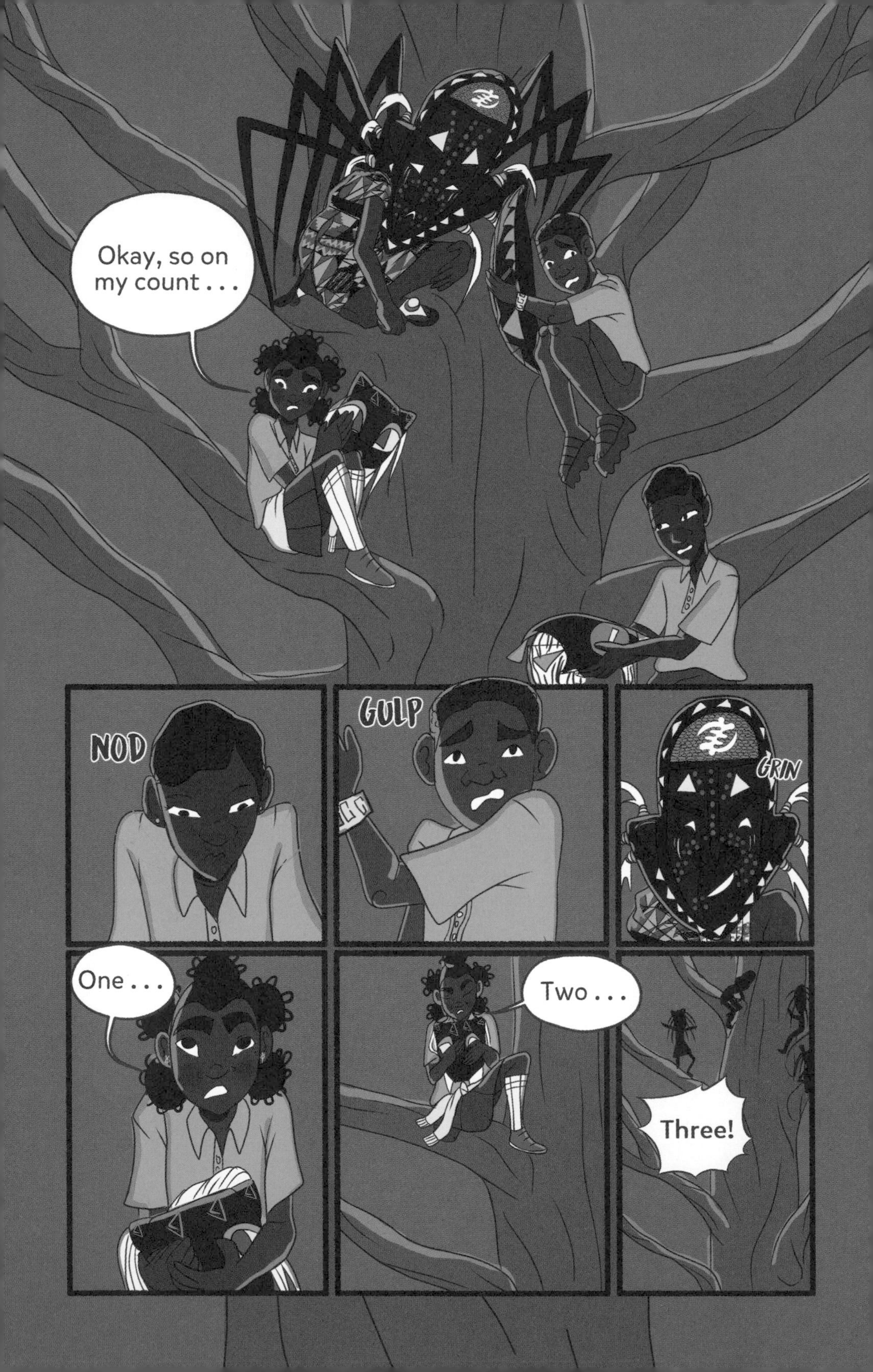
Okay, so on my count . . .
NOD
GULP
GRIN
One . . .
Two . . .
Three!

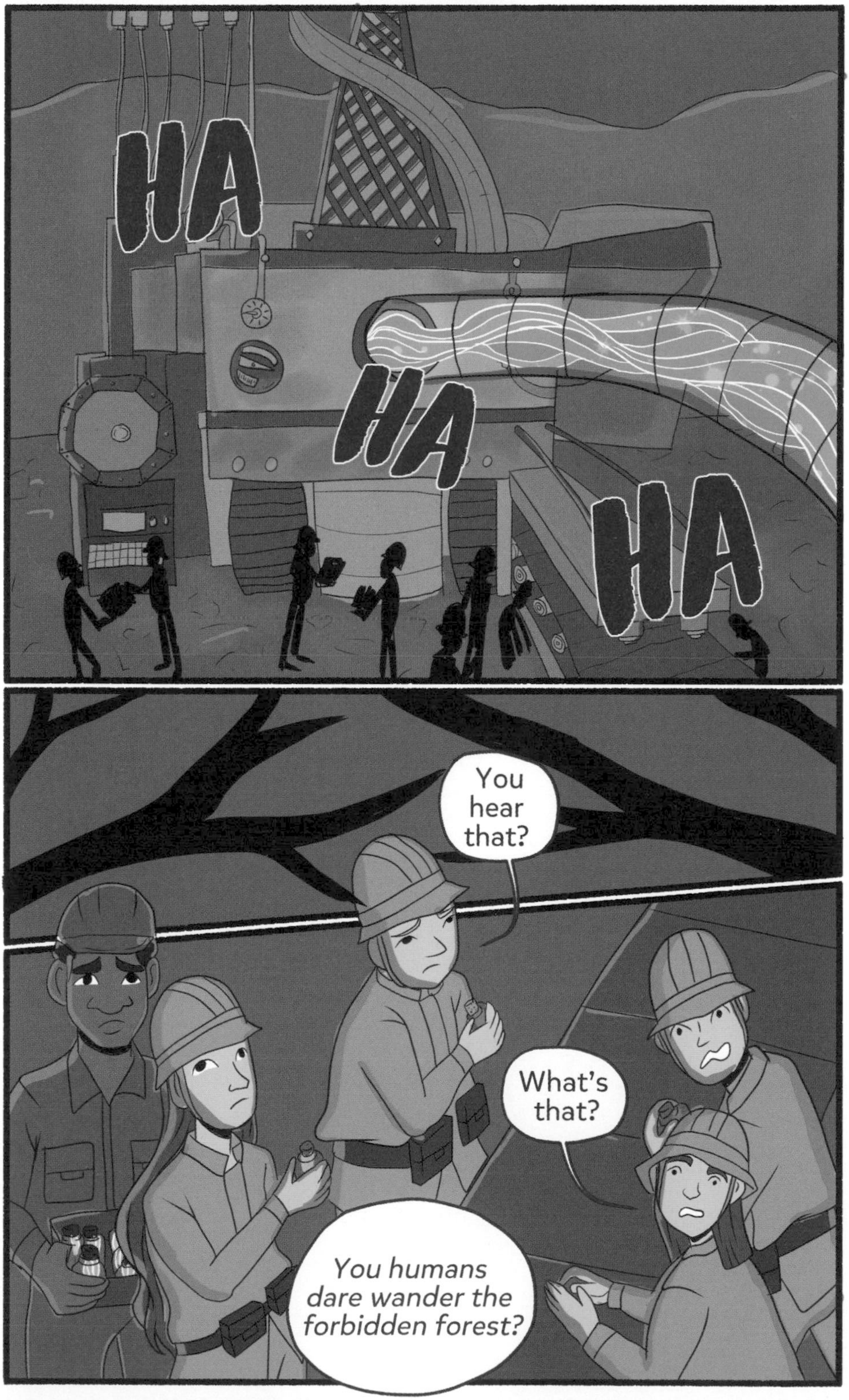
HA
HA
HA
You hear that?
What's that?
You humans dare wander the forbidden forest?

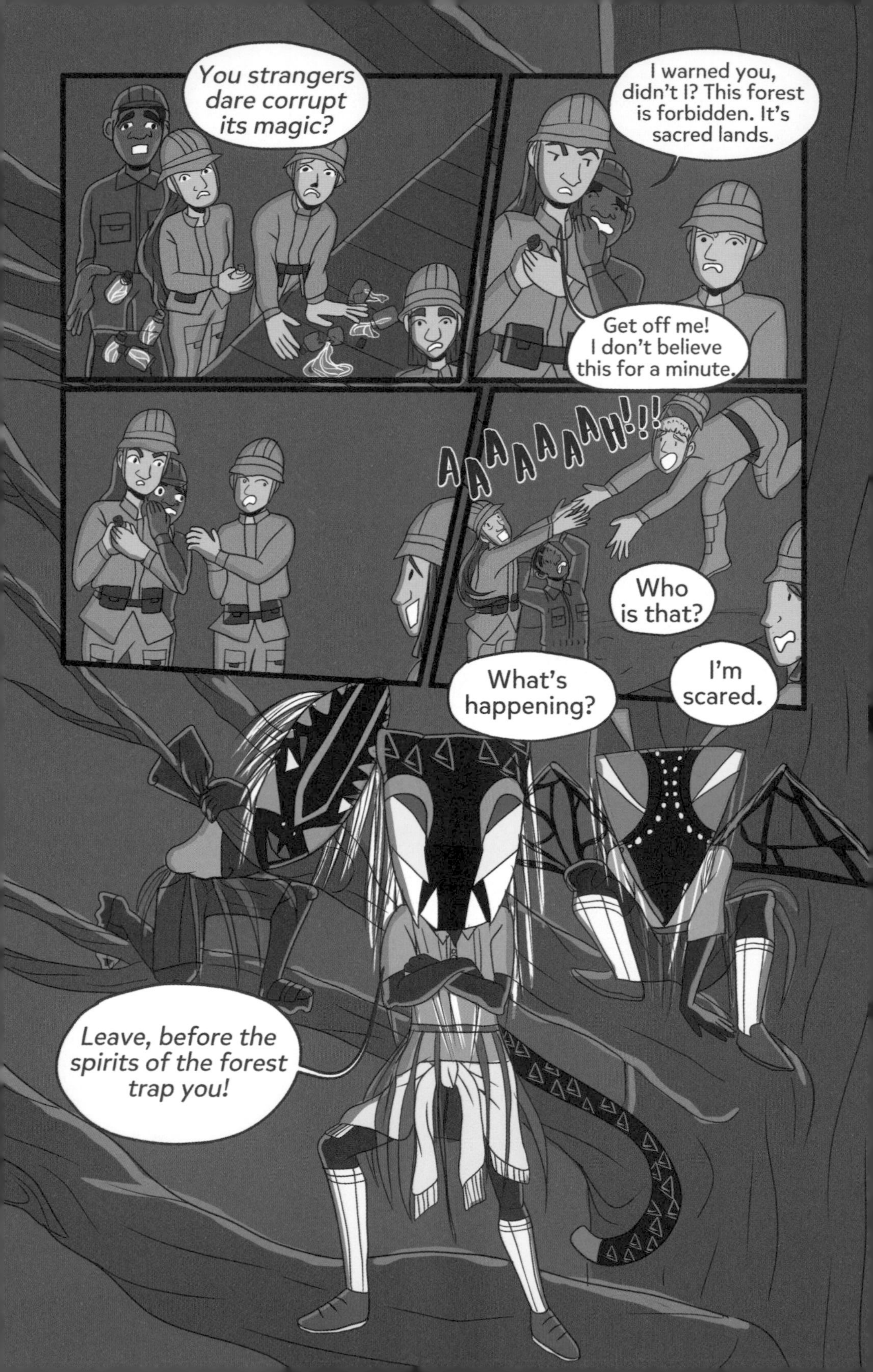
You strangers dare corrupt its magic?
I warned you, didn't I? This forest is forbidden. It's sacred lands.
Get off me! I don't believe this for a minute.
AAAAAAAAH!!!
Who is that?
What's happening?
I'm scared.
Leave, before the spirits of the forest trap you!

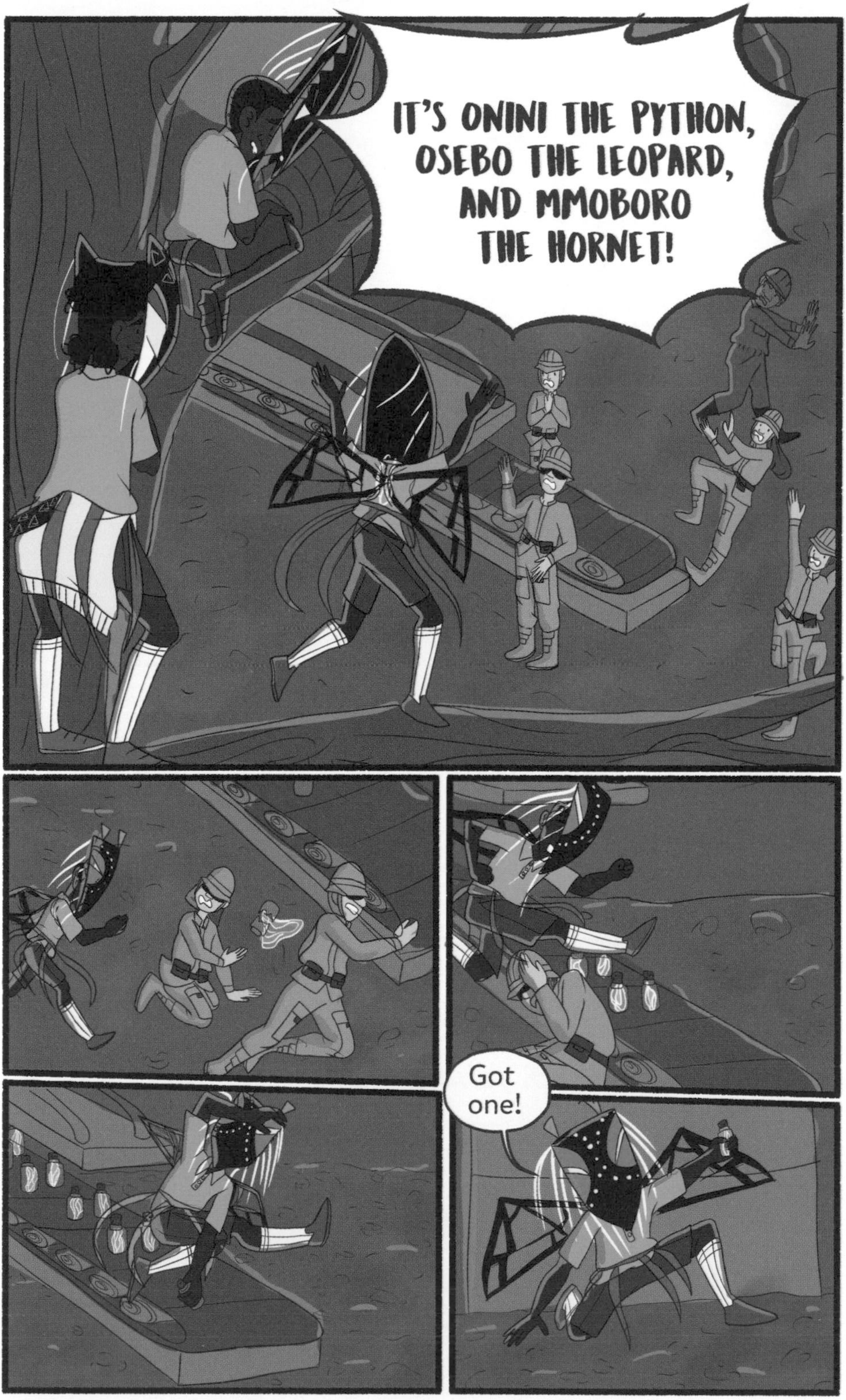
IT'S ONINI THE PYTHON, OSEBO THE LEOPARD, AND MMOBORO THE HORNET!
Got one!

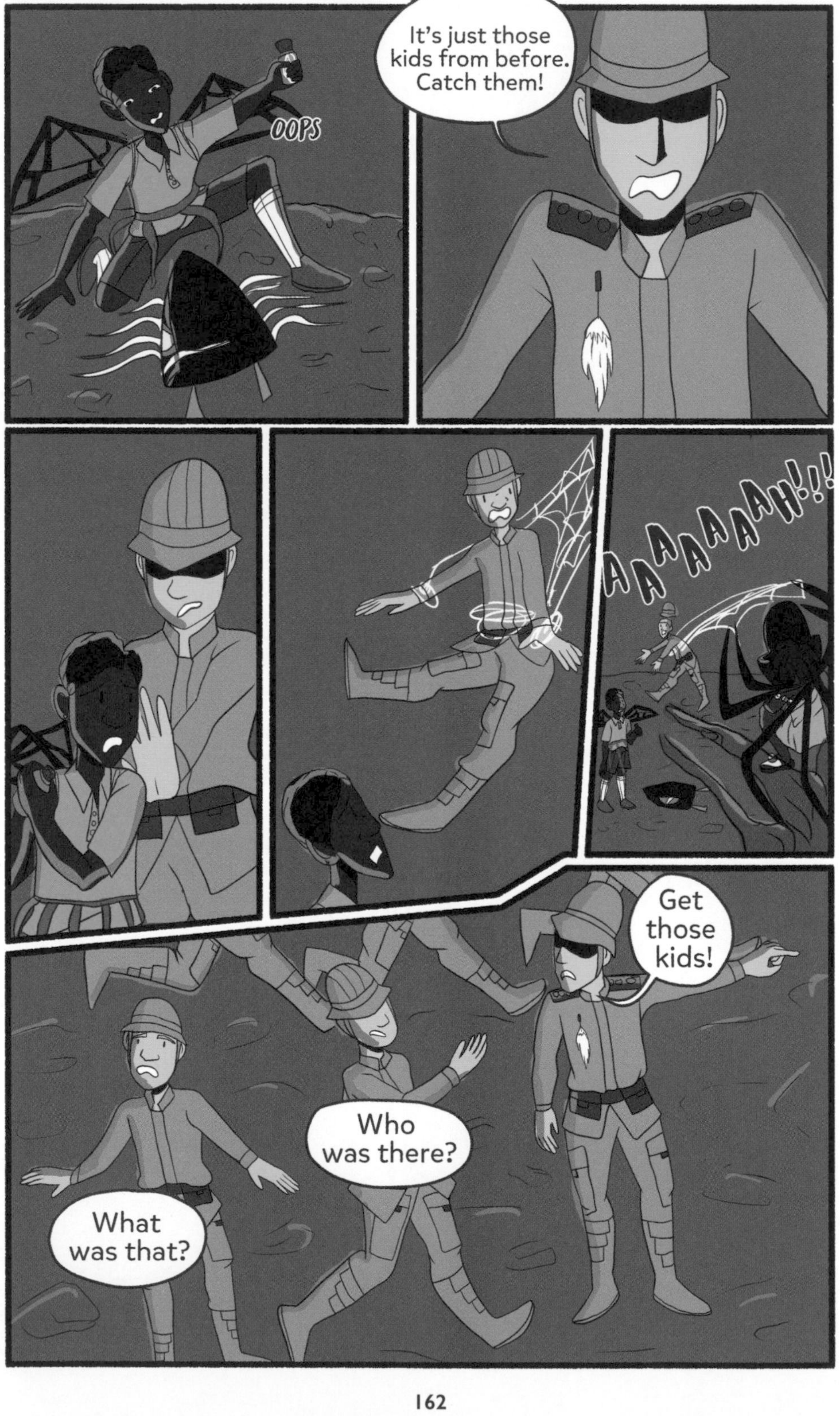
OOPS
It's just those kids from before. Catch them!
AAAAAAAAH!!!
Get those kids!
Who was there?
What was that?

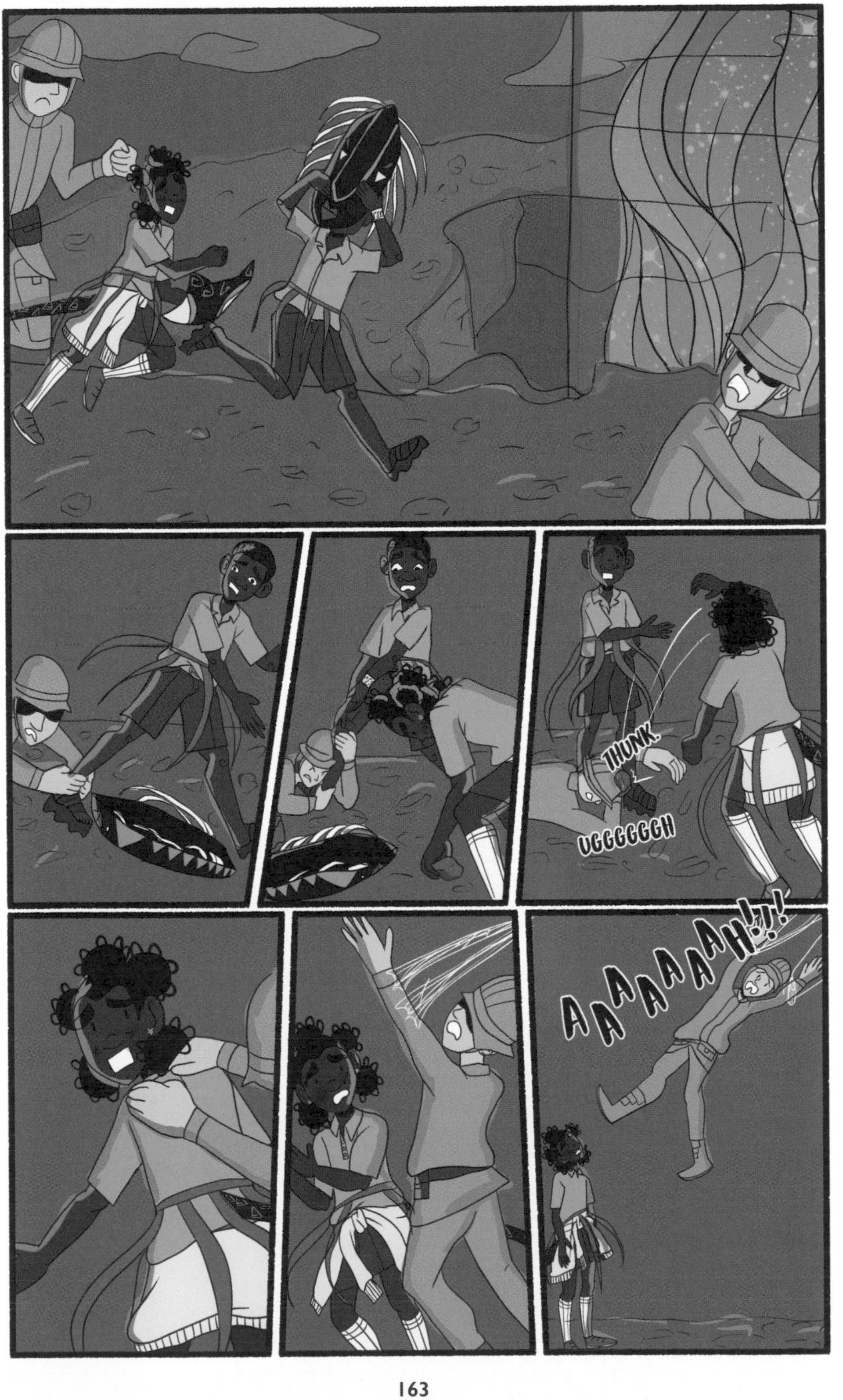
THUNK.
UGGGGGGH
AAAAAAAH!!!

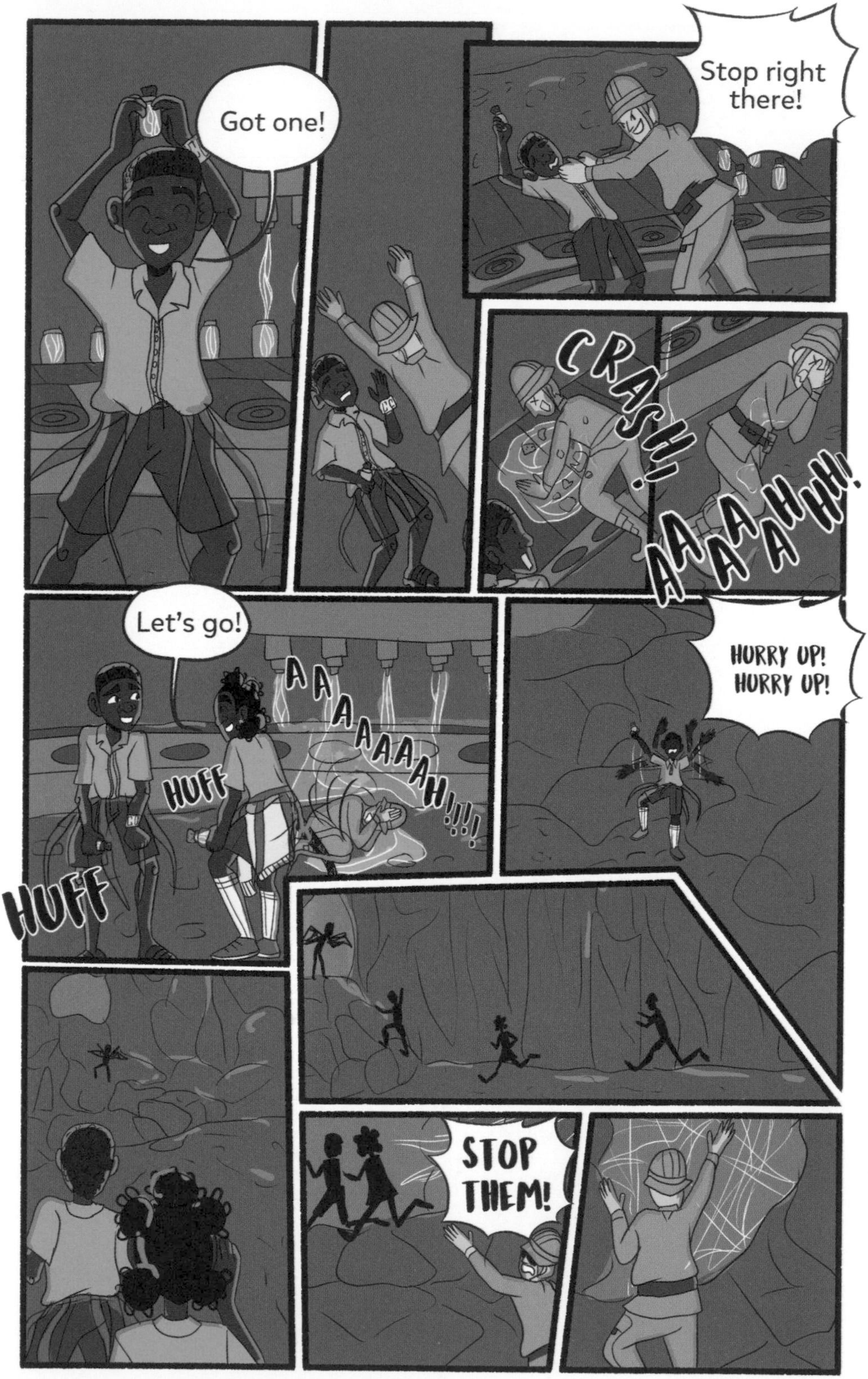
Got one!
Stop right there!
CRASH!
AAAAAHH!!
Let's go!
HUFF
HUFF
AAAAAAAH!!!!
HURRY UP! HURRY UP!
STOP THEM!

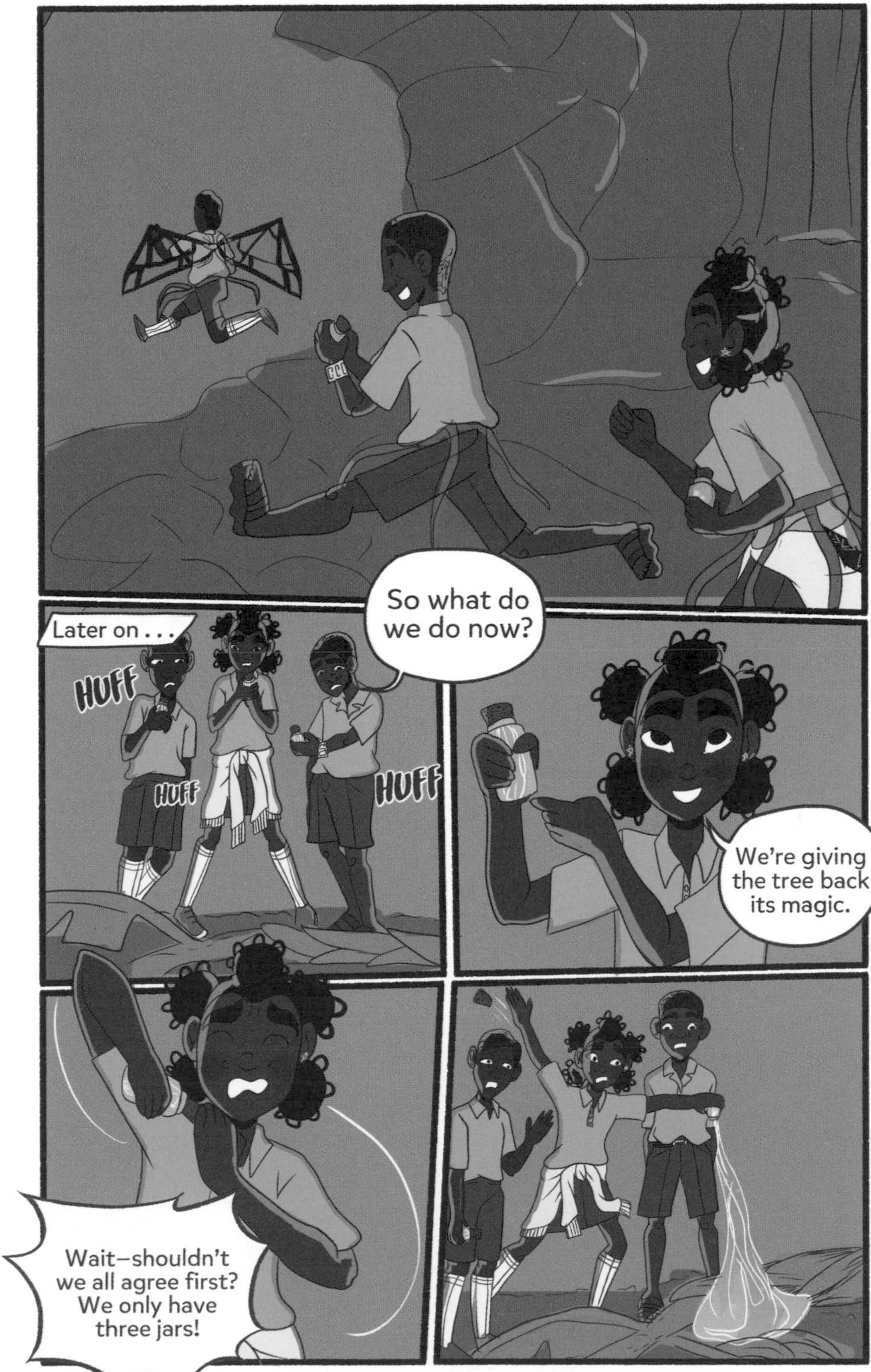
Later on . . .
HUFF
HUFF
HUFF
So what do we do now?
We're giving the tree back its magic.
Wait—shouldn't we all agree first? We only have three jars!

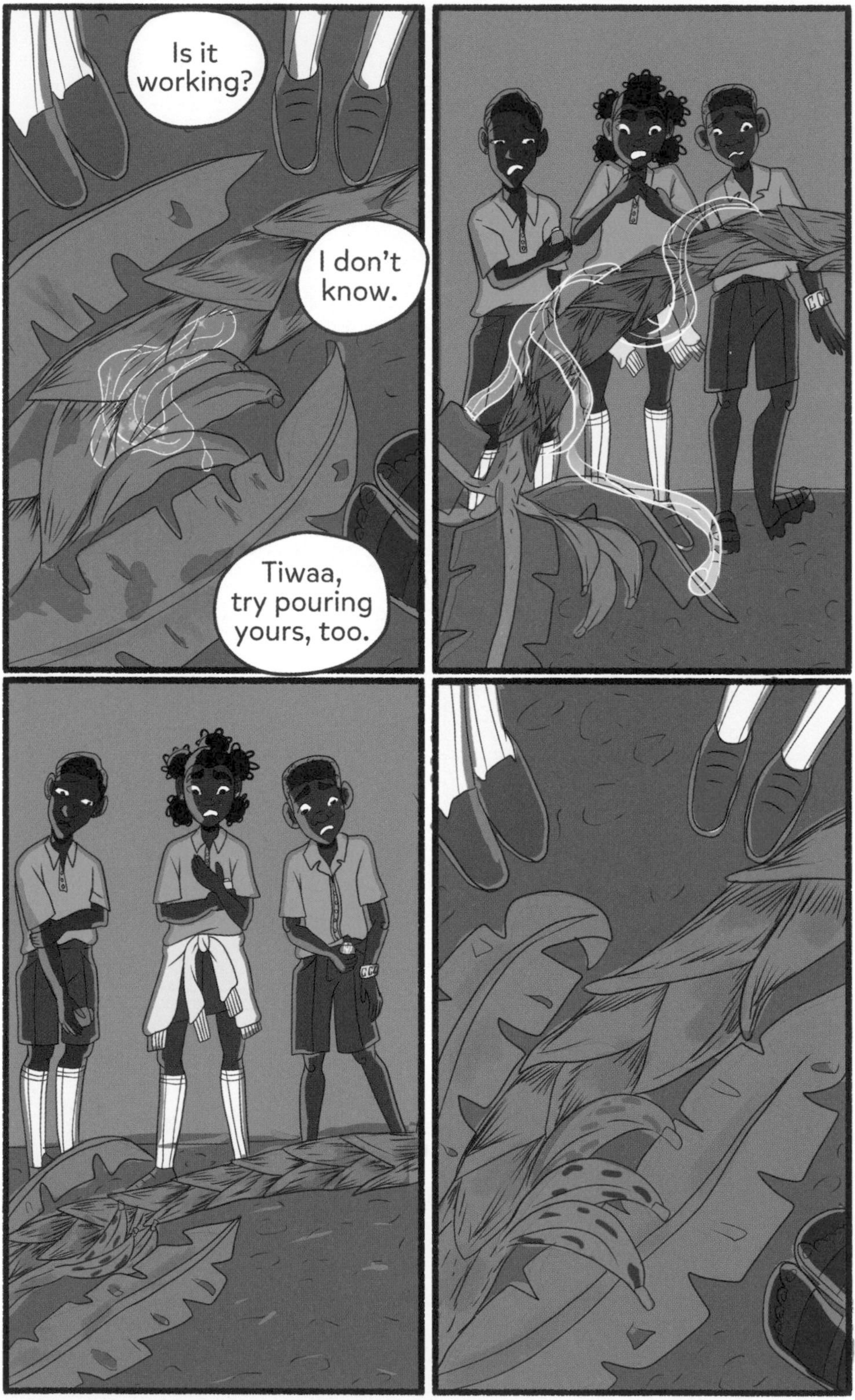
Is it working?
I don't know.
Tiwaa, try pouring yours, too.

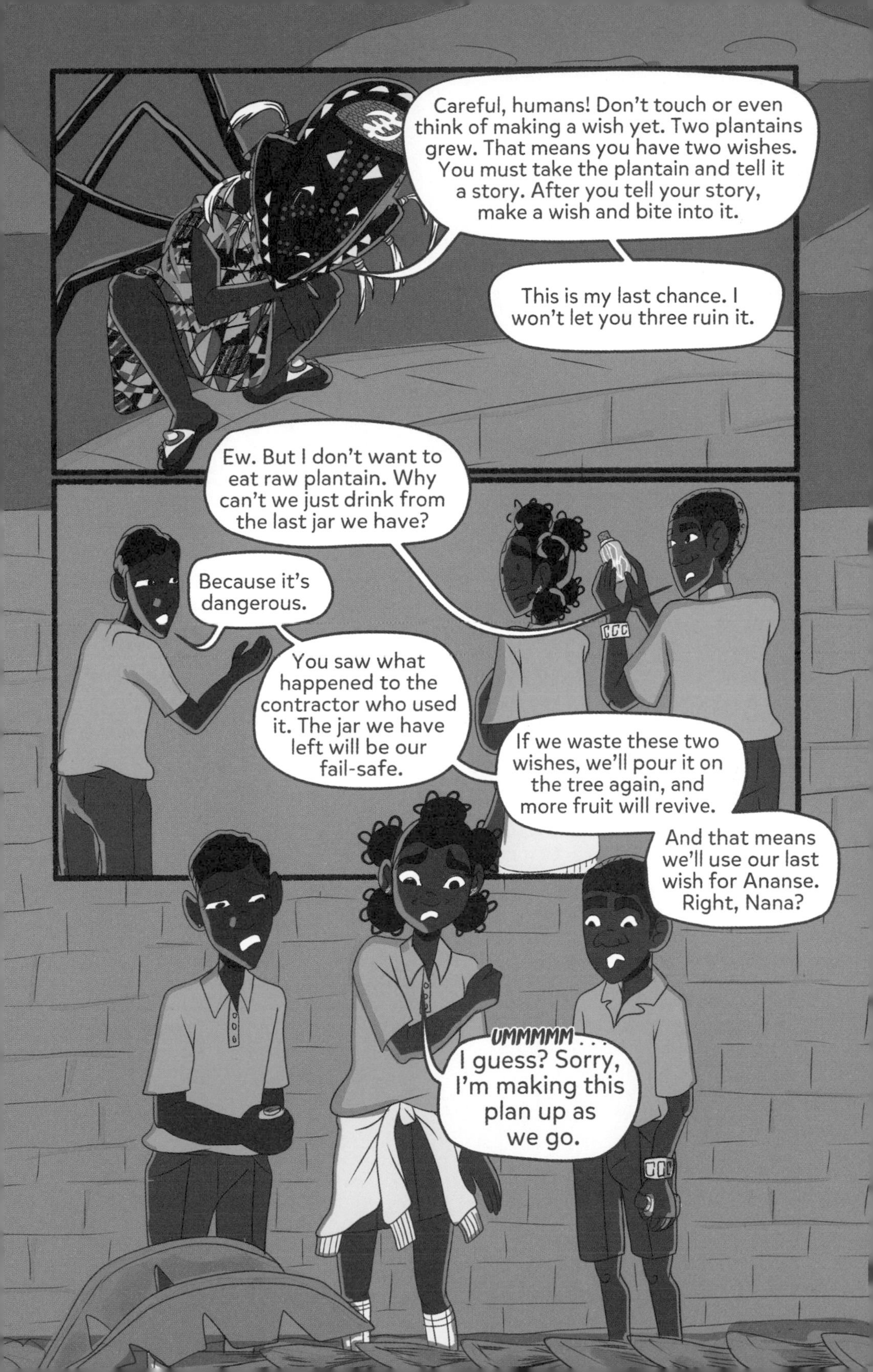
Careful, humans! Don't touch or even think of making a wish yet. Two plantains grew. That means you have two wishes. You must take the plantain and tell it a story. After you tell your story, make a wish and bite into it.
This is my last chance. I won't let you three ruin it.
Ew. But I don't want to eat raw plantain. Why can't we just drink from the last jar we have?
Because it's dangerous.
You saw what happened to the contractor who used it. The jar we have left will be our fail-safe.
If we waste these two wishes, we'll pour it on the tree again, and more fruit will revive.
And that means we'll use our last wish for Ananse. Right, Nana?
UMMMMM . . . I guess? Sorry, I'm making this plan up as we go.

Okay, but who is going to get the first wish if there are only two?

Let's rock-paper-scissors it.

Uh, what?

She means like Ampe. Except American.

So no clapping and jumping, just hand shapes?

Yup.

Rock, paper, scissors . . .

SHOOT!

I guess it's between you and me.

ROCK

PAPER

SCISSORS

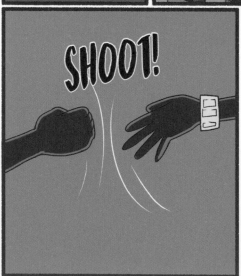

SHOOT!

I win.

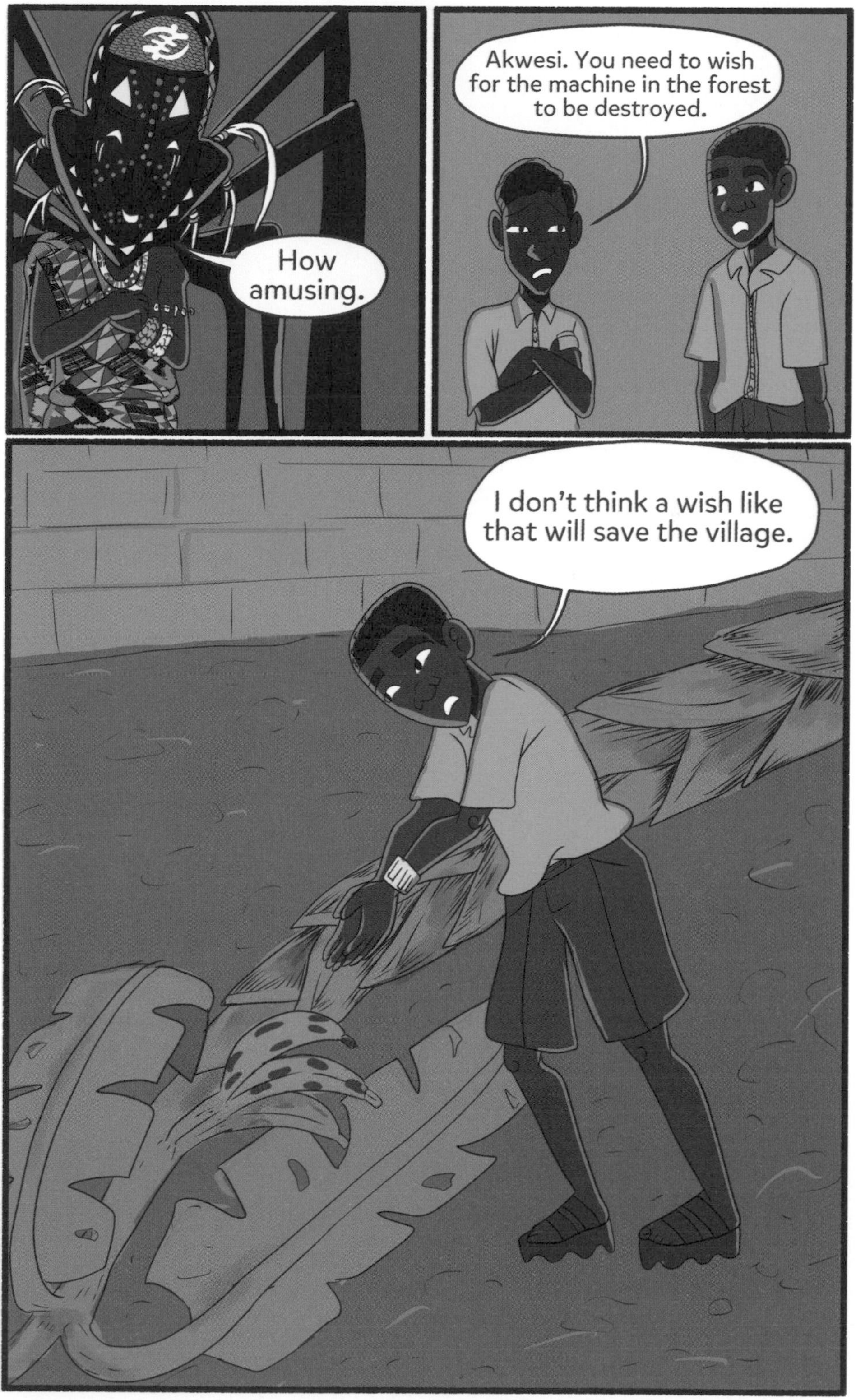
How amusing.
Akwesi. You need to wish for the machine in the forest to be destroyed.
I don't think a wish like that will save the village.

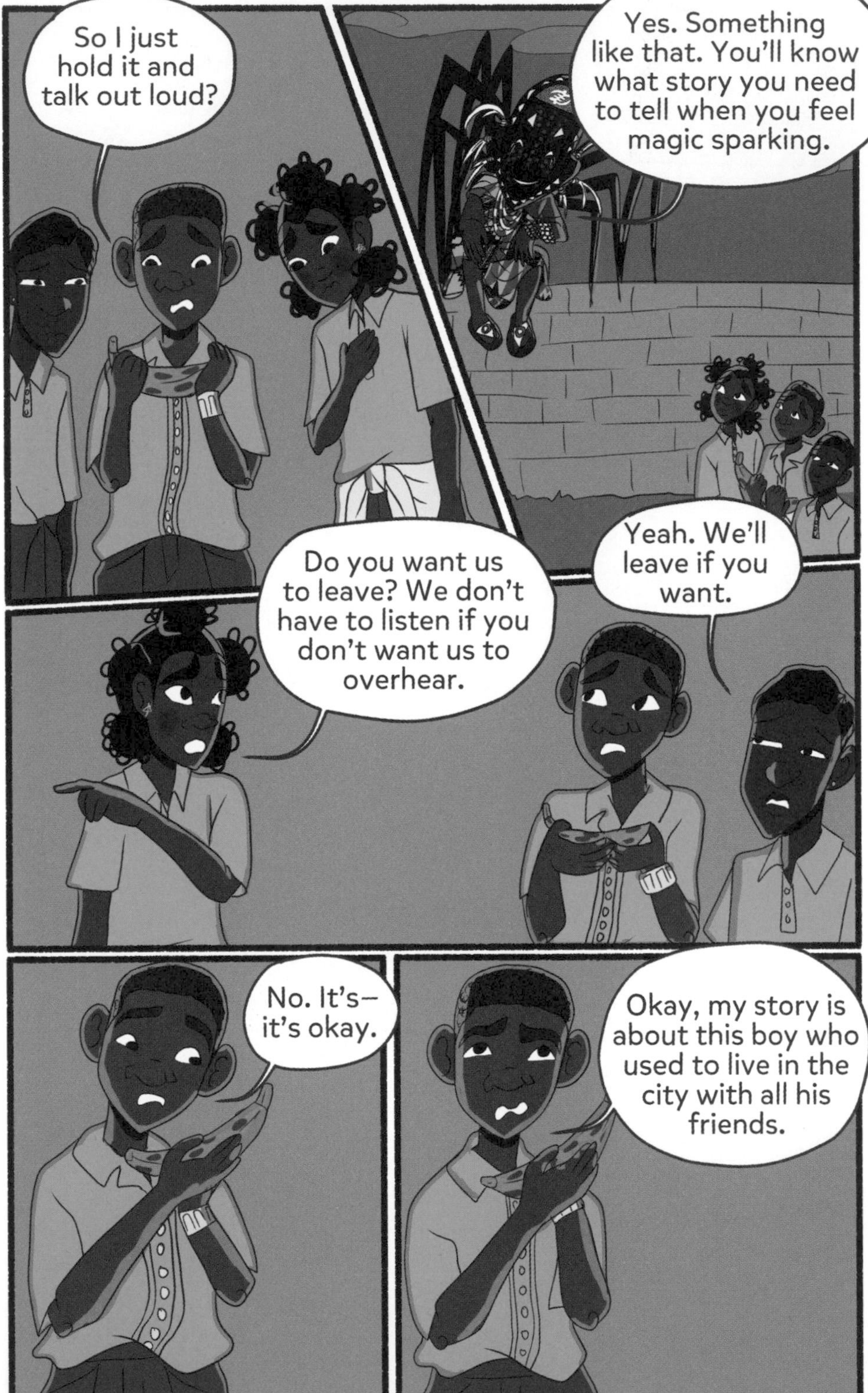
So I just hold it and talk out loud?
Yes. Something like that. You'll know what story you need to tell when you feel magic sparking.
Do you want us to leave? We don't have to listen if you don't want us to overhear.
Yeah. We'll leave if you want.
No. It's—it's okay.
Okay, my story is about this boy who used to live in the city with all his friends.

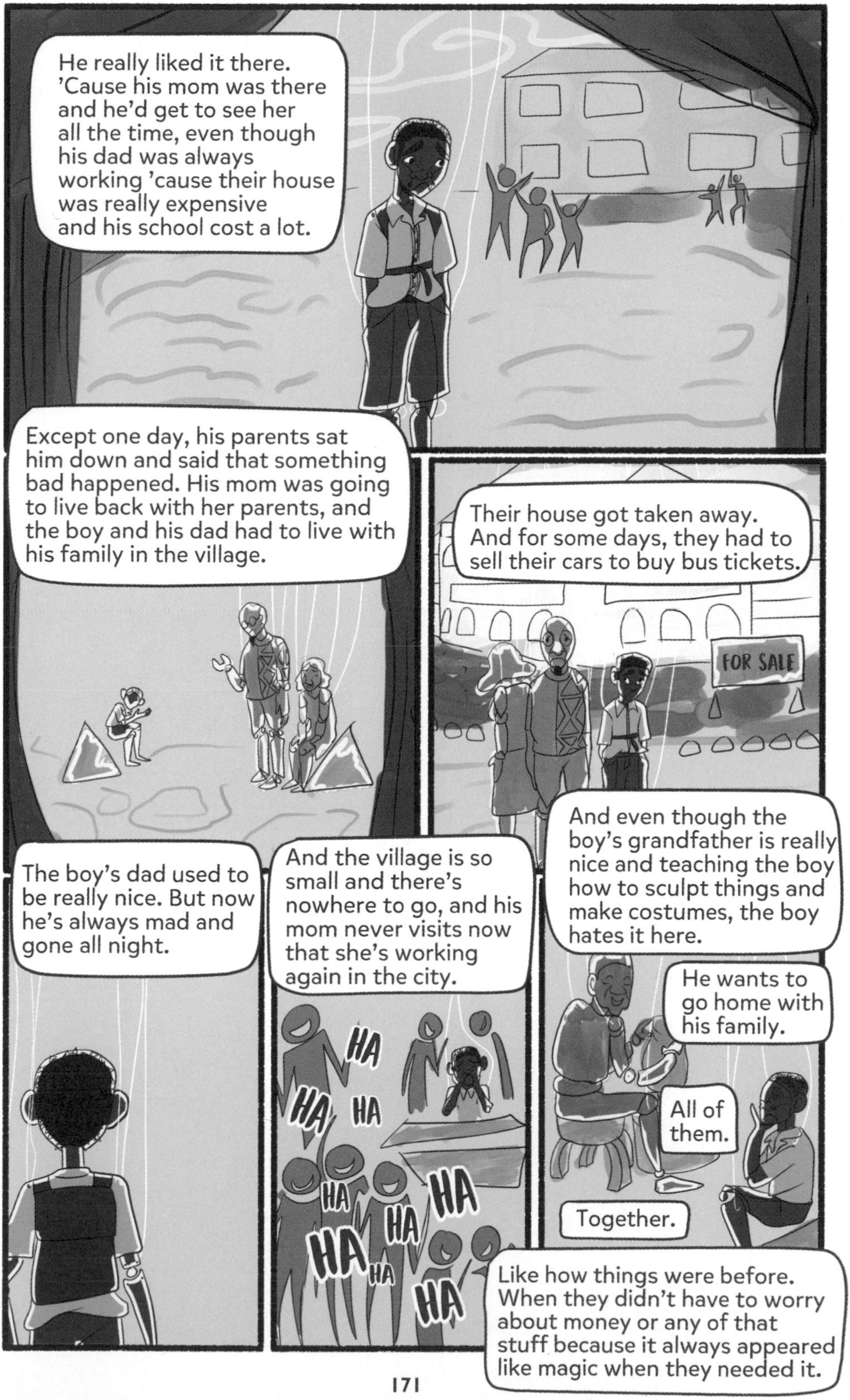
He really liked it there. 'Cause his mom was there and he'd get to see her all the time, even though his dad was always working 'cause their house was really expensive and his school cost a lot.
Except one day, his parents sat him down and said that something bad happened. His mom was going to live back with her parents, and the boy and his dad had to live with his family in the village.
Their house got taken away. And for some days, they had to sell their cars to buy bus tickets.
FOR SALE
The boy's dad used to be really nice. But now he's always mad and gone all night.
And the village is so small and there's nowhere to go, and his mom never visits now that she's working again in the city.
HA
HA
HA
HA
HA
HA
HA
HA
HA
And even though the boy's grandfather is really nice and teaching the boy how to sculpt things and make costumes, the boy hates it here.
He wants to go home with his family.
All of them.
Together.
Like how things were before. When they didn't have to worry about money or any of that stuff because it always appeared like magic when they needed it.

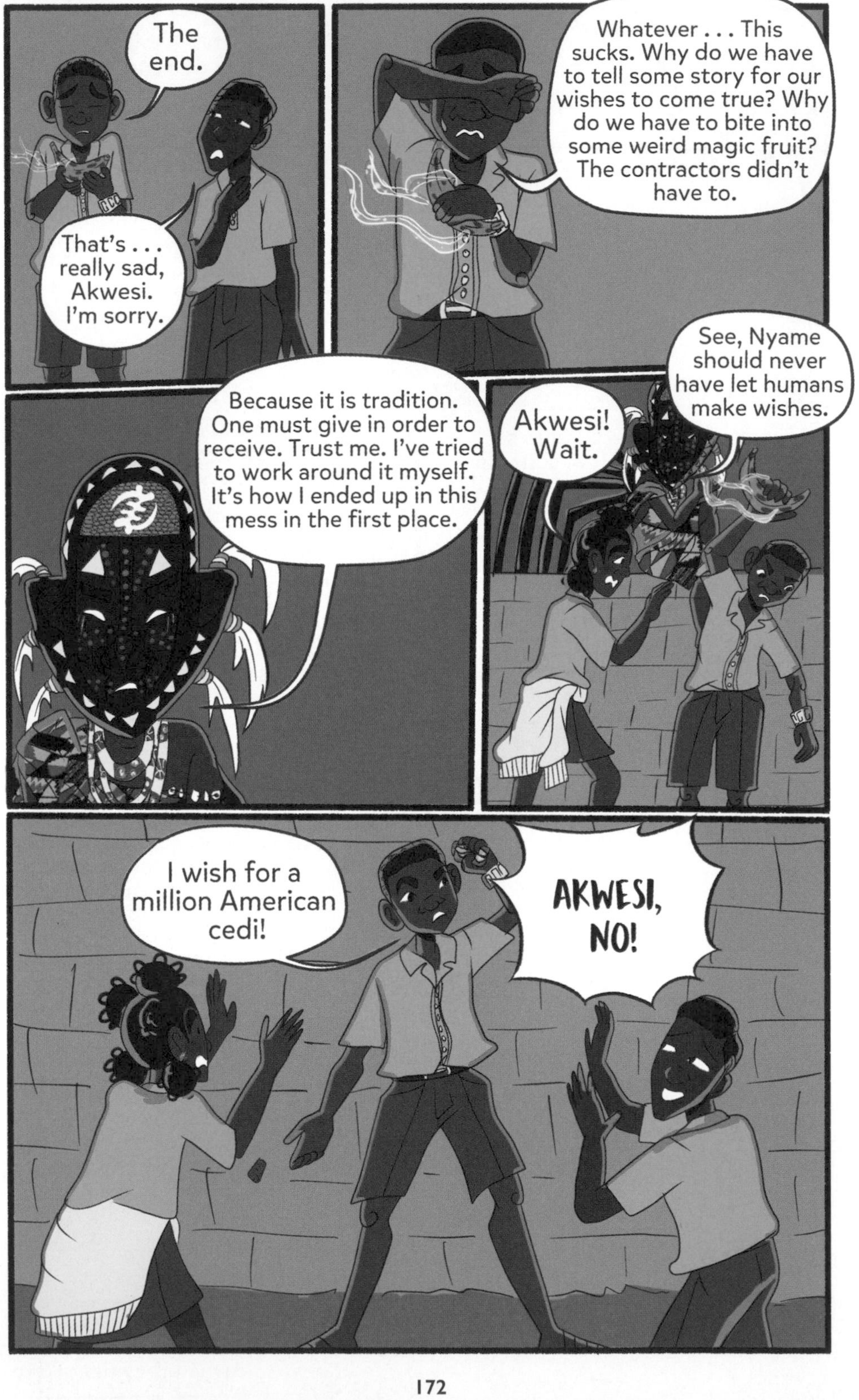
The end.
That's . . . really sad, Akwesi. I'm sorry.
Whatever . . . This sucks. Why do we have to tell some story for our wishes to come true? Why do we have to bite into some weird magic fruit? The contractors didn't have to.
Because it is tradition. One must give in order to receive. Trust me. I've tried to work around it myself. It's how I ended up in this mess in the first place.
See, Nyame should never have let humans make wishes.
Akwesi! Wait.
I wish for a million American cedi!
AKWESI, NO!

Chapter 8

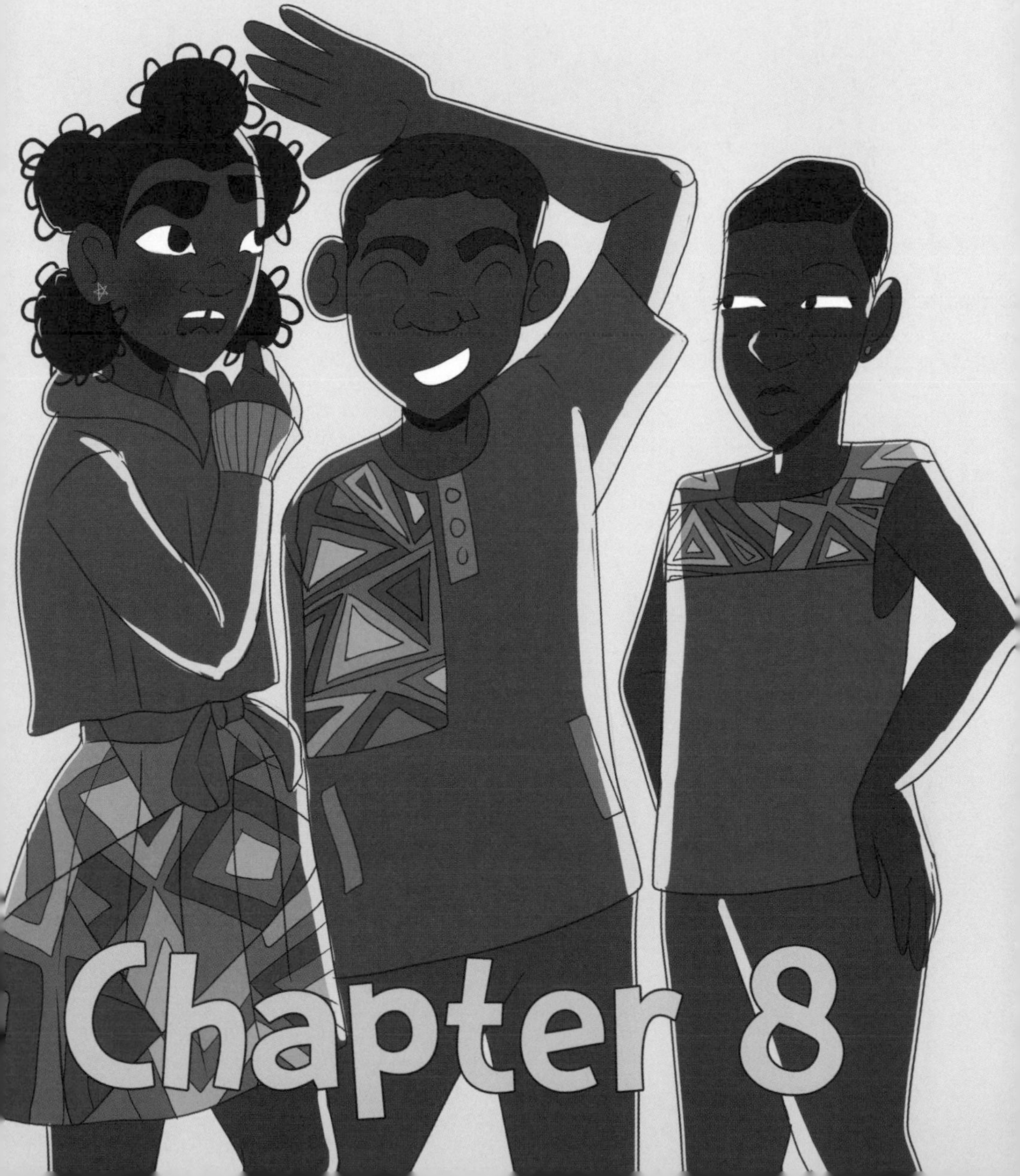

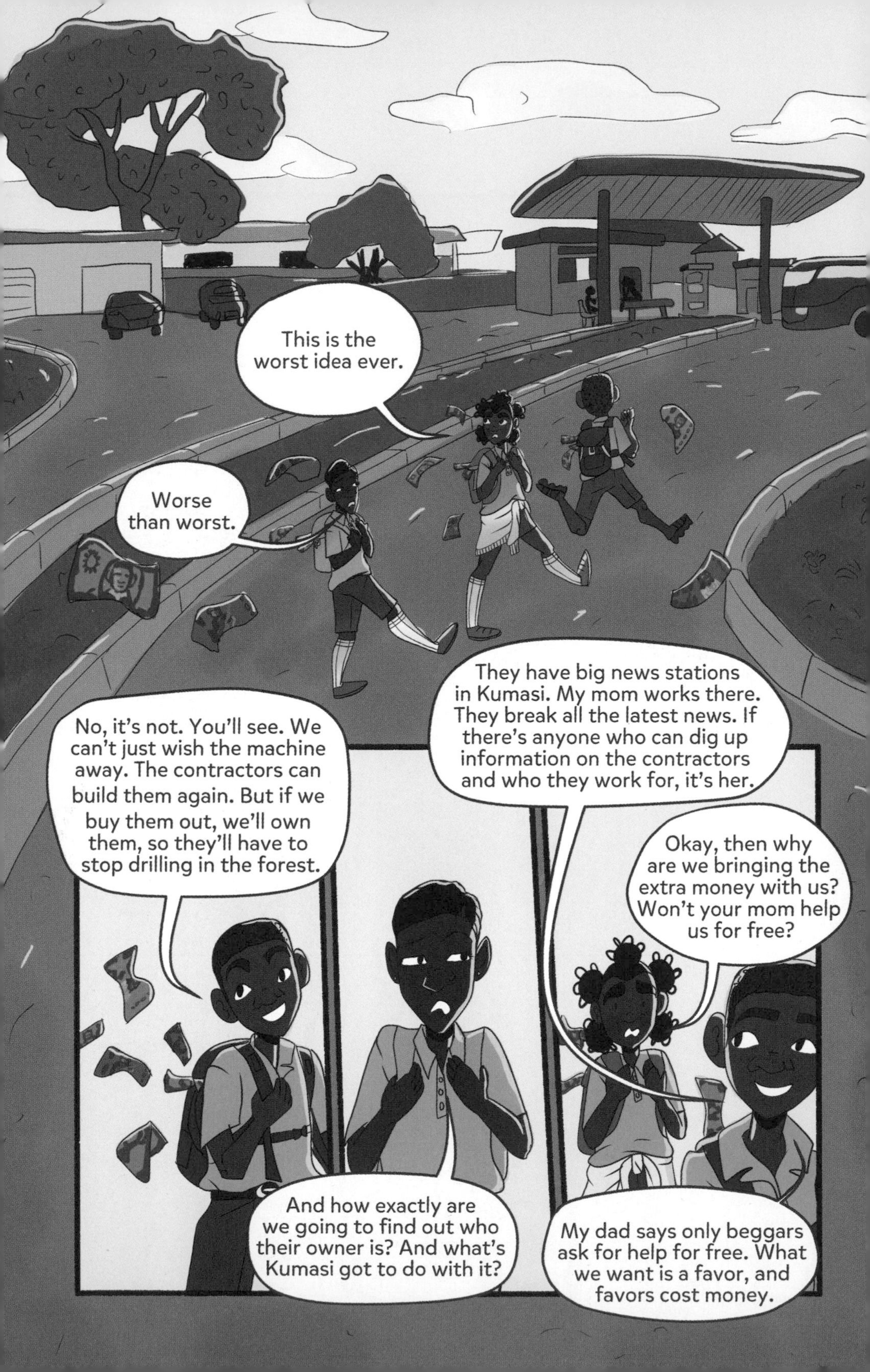
This is the worst idea ever.
Worse than worst.
No, it's not. You'll see. We can't just wish the machine away. The contractors can build them again. But if we buy them out, we'll own them, so they'll have to stop drilling in the forest.
And how exactly are we going to find out who their owner is? And what's Kumasi got to do with it?
They have big news stations in Kumasi. My mom works there. They break all the latest news. If there's anyone who can dig up information on the contractors and who they work for, it's her.
Okay, then why are we bringing the extra money with us? Won't your mom help us for free?
My dad says only beggars ask for help for free. What we want is a favor, and favors cost money.

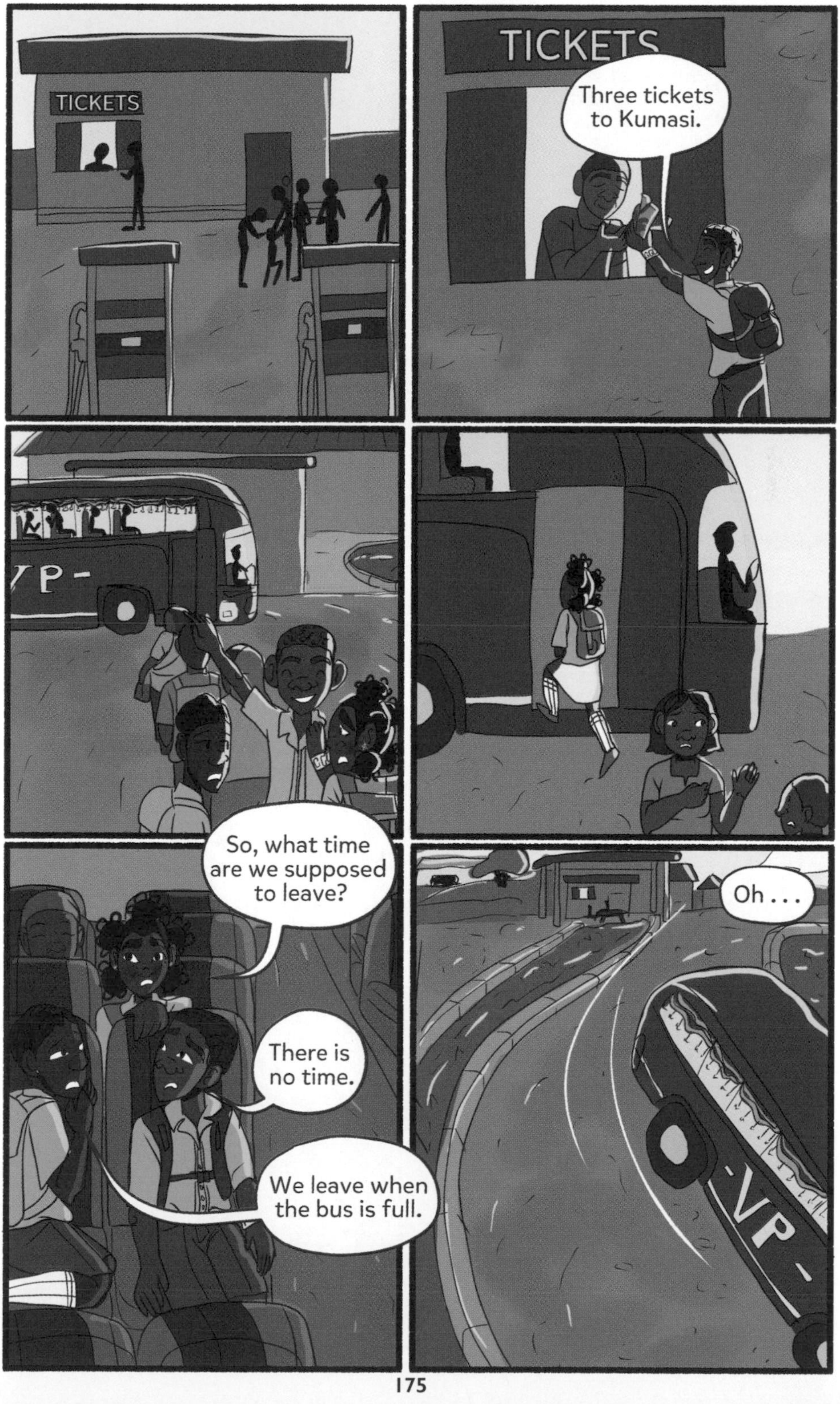
TICKETS
TICKETS
Three tickets to Kumasi.
VP-
So, what time are we supposed to leave?
There is no time.
We leave when the bus is full.
Oh . . .
VP

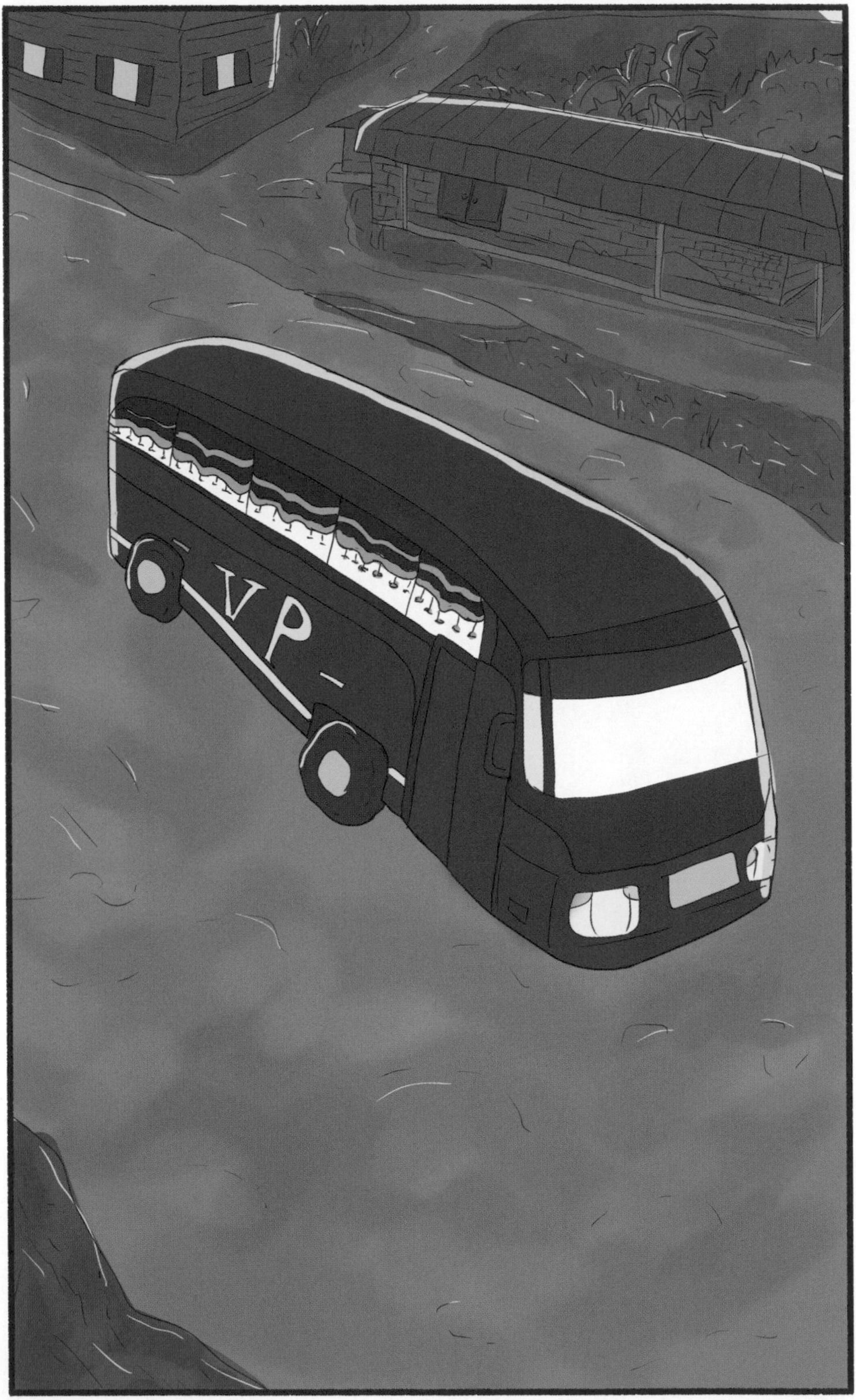
VP

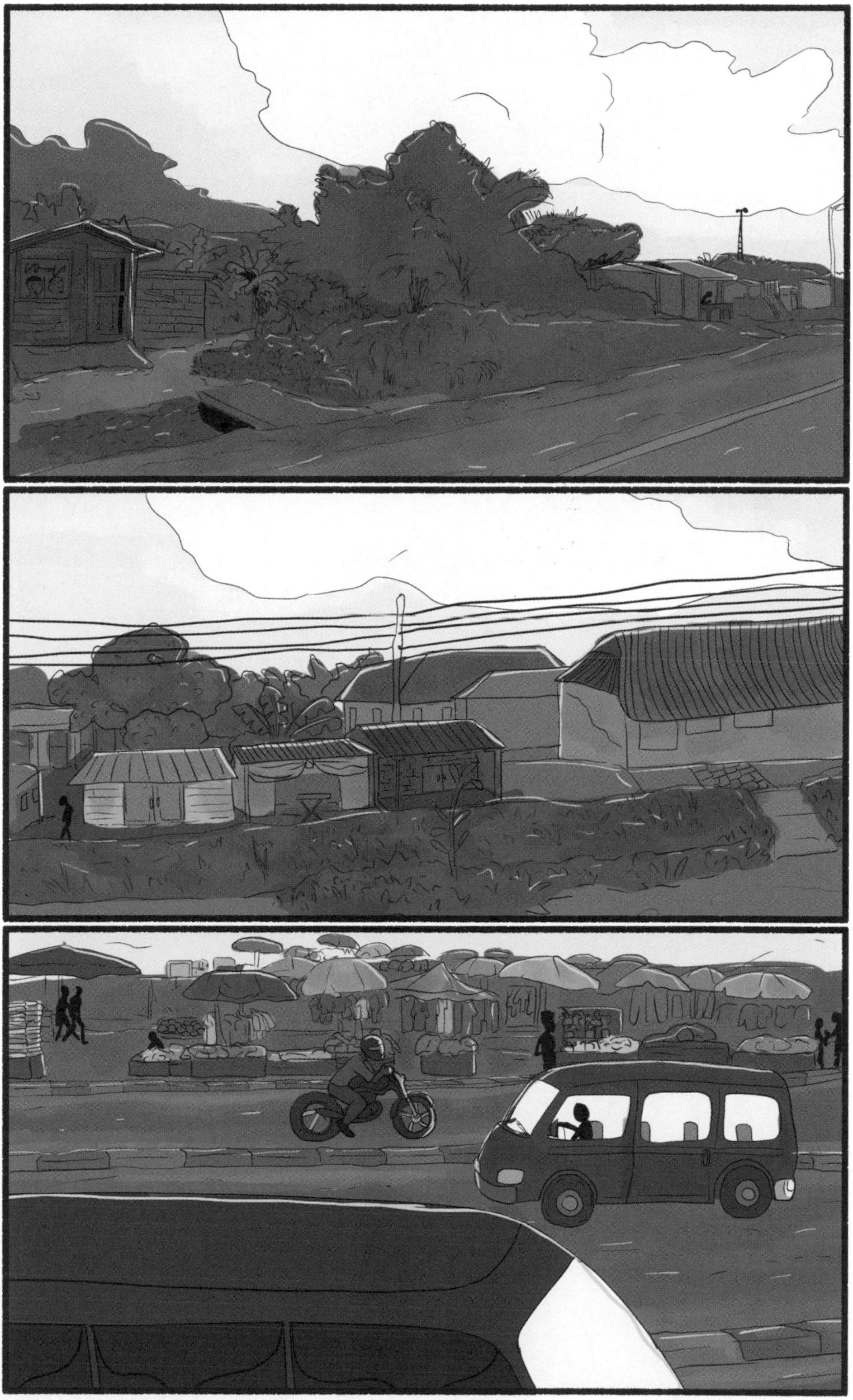

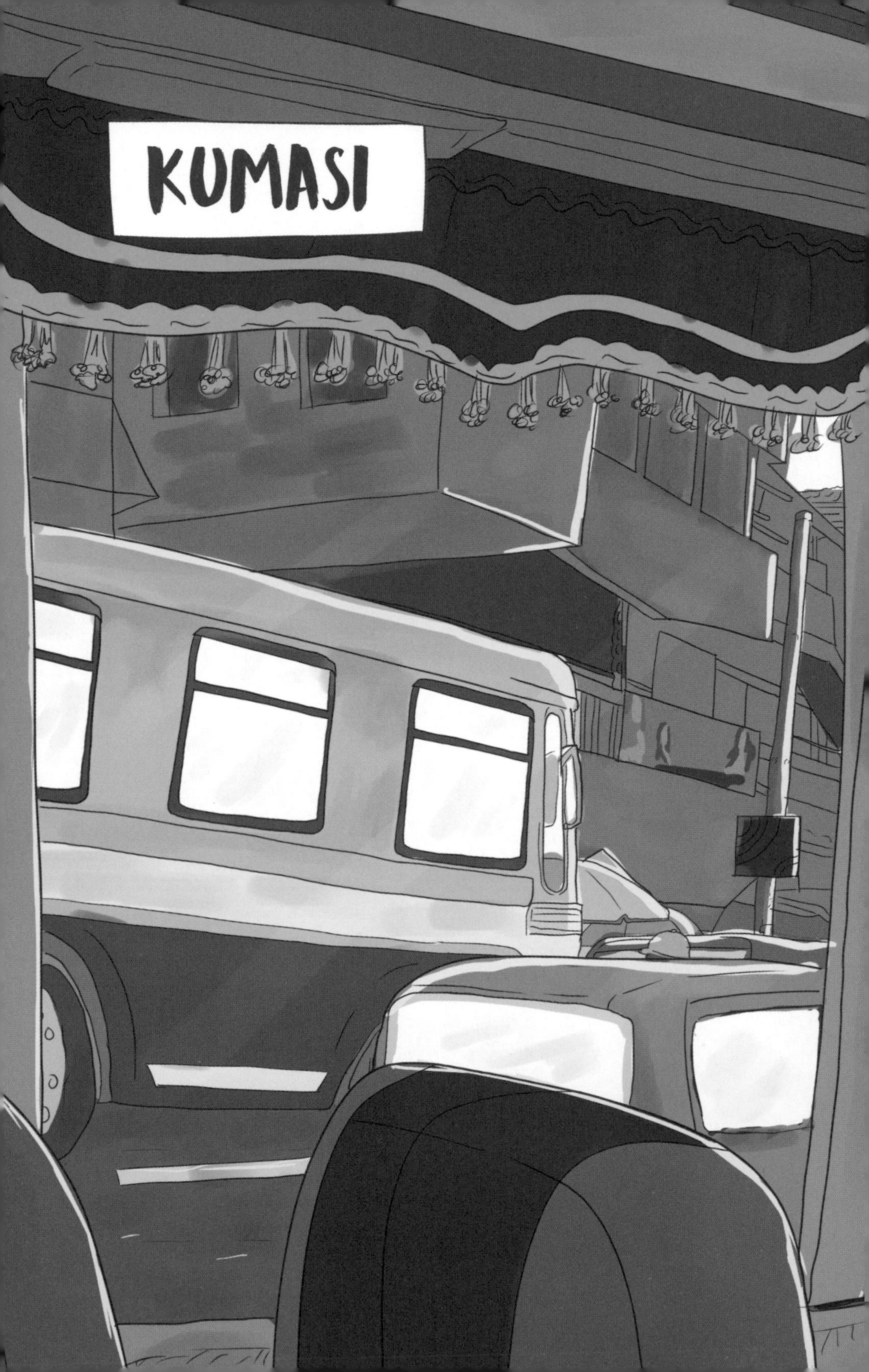
KUMASI

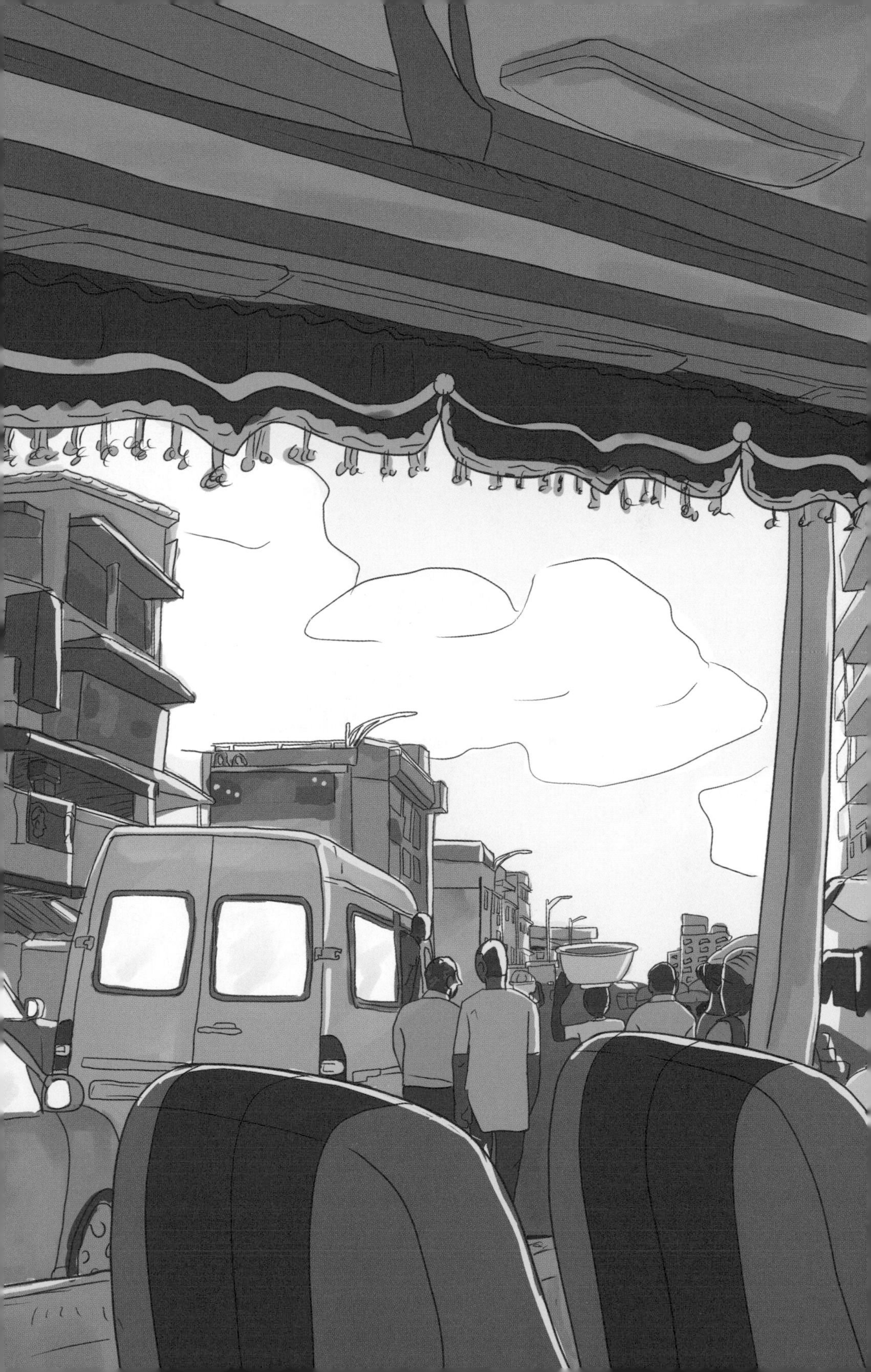

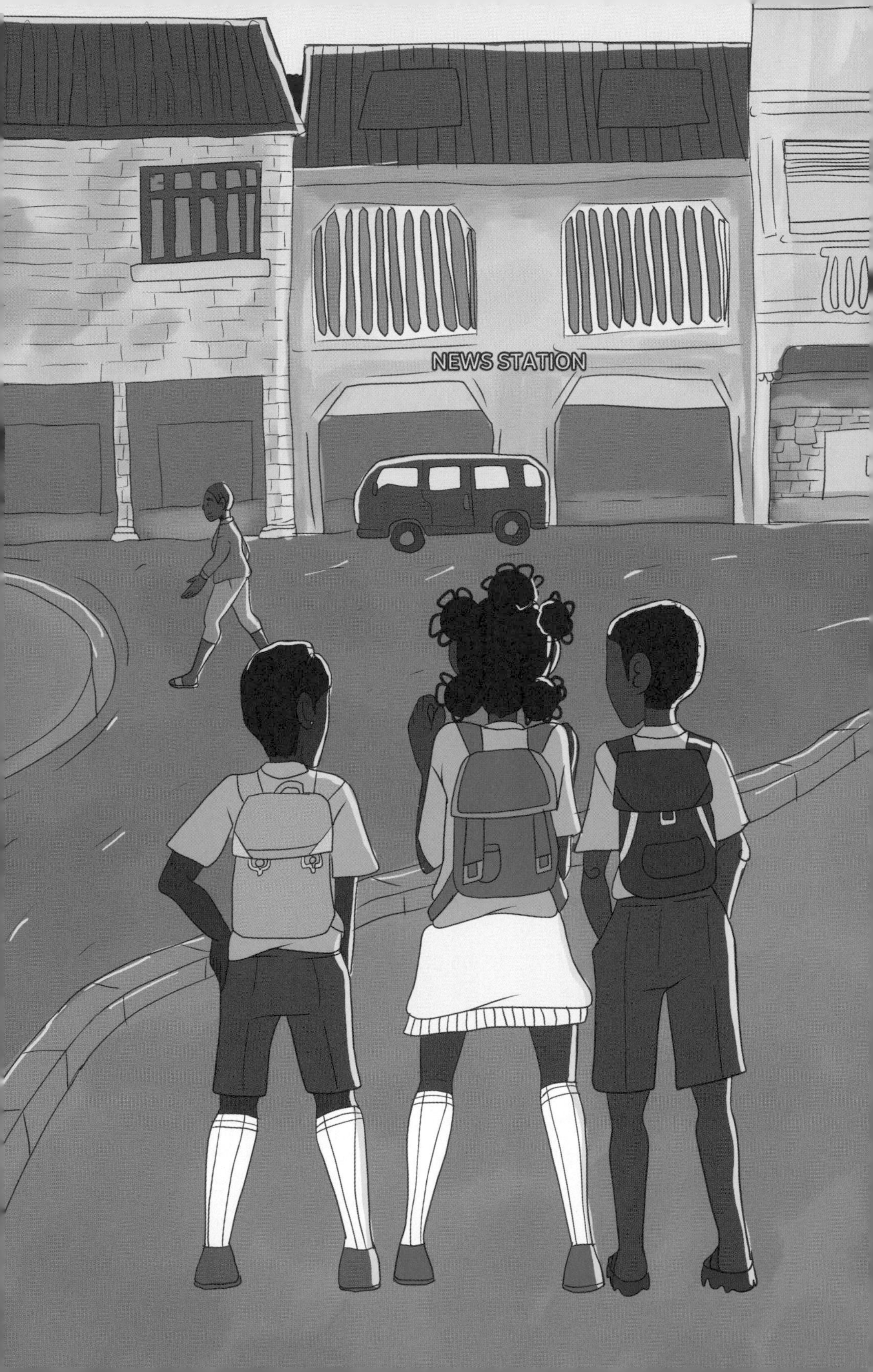
NEWS STATION

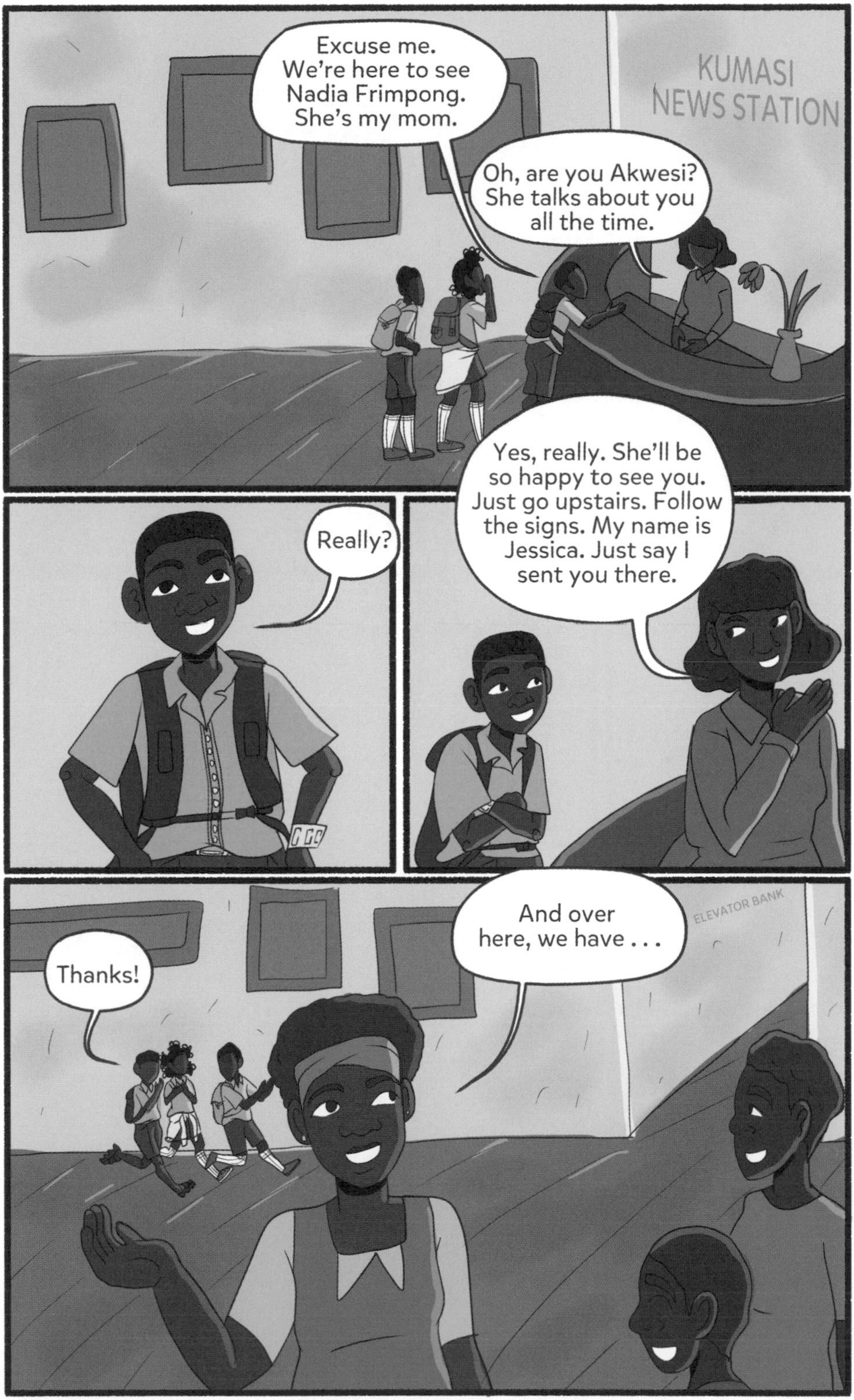
KUMASI NEWS STATION
Excuse me. We're here to see Nadia Frimpong. She's my mom.
Oh, are you Akwesi? She talks about you all the time.
Really?
Yes, really. She'll be so happy to see you. Just go upstairs. Follow the signs. My name is Jessica. Just say I sent you there.
ELEVATOR BANK
Thanks!
And over here, we have . . .

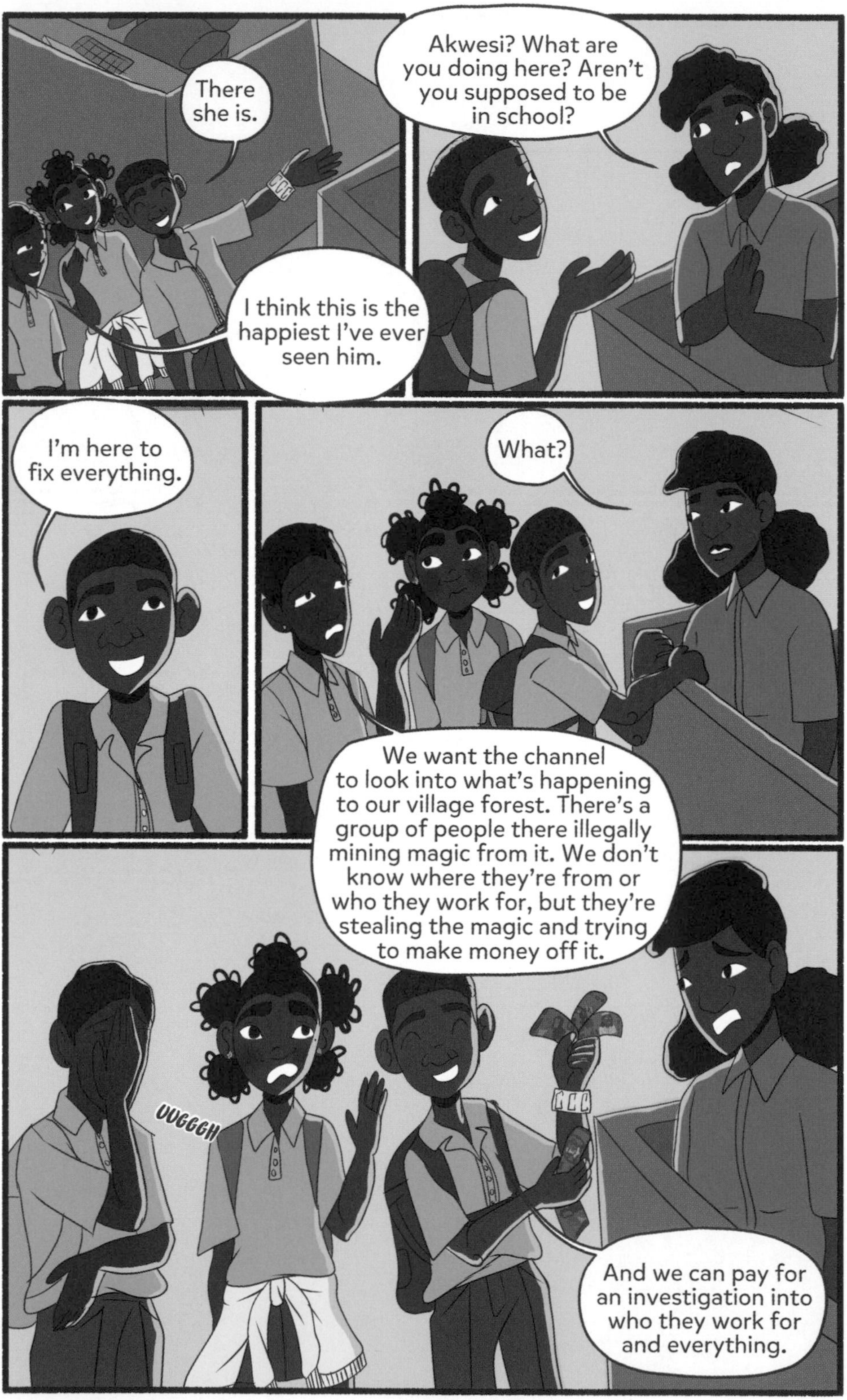
There she is.
Akwesi? What are you doing here? Aren't you supposed to be in school?
I think this is the happiest I've ever seen him.
I'm here to fix everything.
What?
We want the channel to look into what's happening to our village forest. There's a group of people there illegally mining magic from it. We don't know where they're from or who they work for, but they're stealing the magic and trying to make money off it.
UUGGGH
And we can pay for an investigation into who they work for and everything.

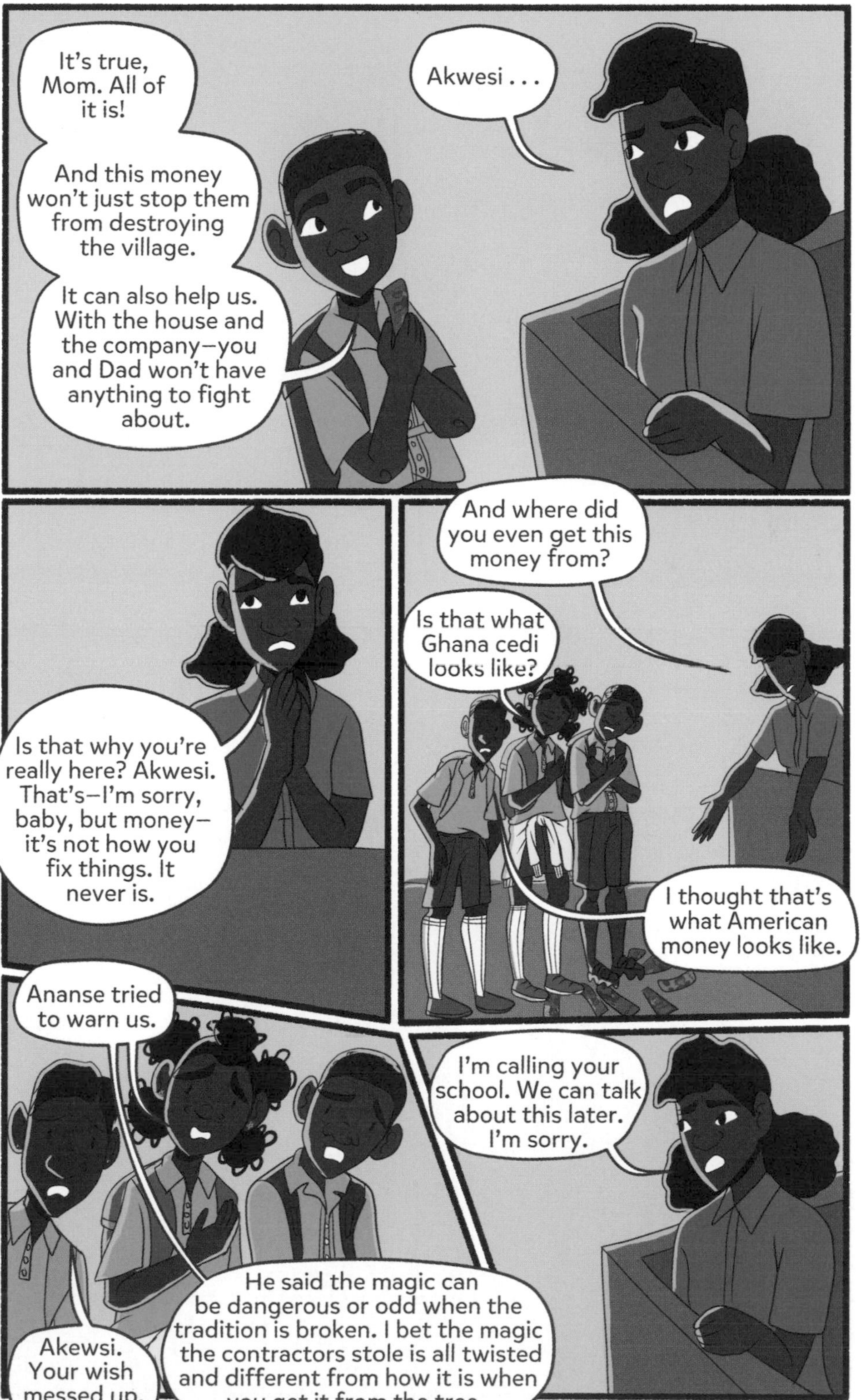
It's true, Mom. All of it is!
And this money won't just stop them from destroying the village.
It can also help us. With the house and the company—you and Dad won't have anything to fight about.
Akwesi . . .
Is that why you're really here? Akwesi. That's—I'm sorry, baby, but money—it's not how you fix things. It never is.
And where did you even get this money from?
Is that what Ghana cedi looks like?
I thought that's what American money looks like.
Ananse tried to warn us.
He said the magic can be dangerous or odd when the tradition is broken. I bet the magic the contractors stole is all twisted and different from how it is when you get it from the tree.
Akewsi. Your wish messed up.
I'm calling your school. We can talk about this later. I'm sorry.

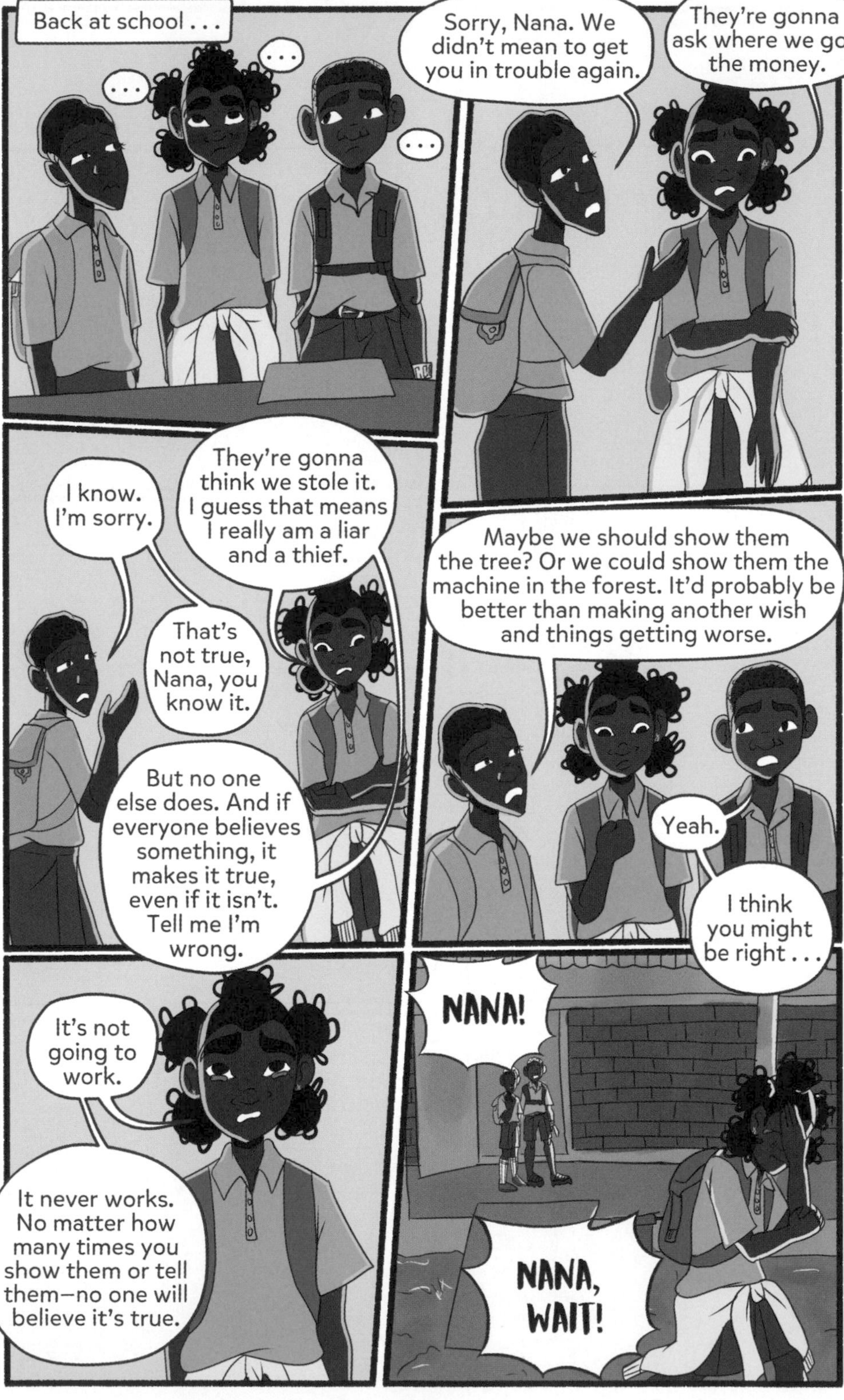

Back at school . . .
. . .
. . .
. . .
Sorry, Nana. We didn't mean to get you in trouble again.
They're gonna ask where we got the money.
I know. I'm sorry.
They're gonna think we stole it. I guess that means I really am a liar and a thief.
That's not true, Nana, you know it.
But no one else does. And if everyone believes something, it makes it true, even if it isn't. Tell me I'm wrong.
Maybe we should show them the tree? Or we could show them the machine in the forest. It'd probably be better than making another wish and things getting worse.
Yeah.
I think you might be right . . .
It's not going to work.
It never works. No matter how many times you show them or tell them—no one will believe it's true.
NANA!
NANA, WAIT!

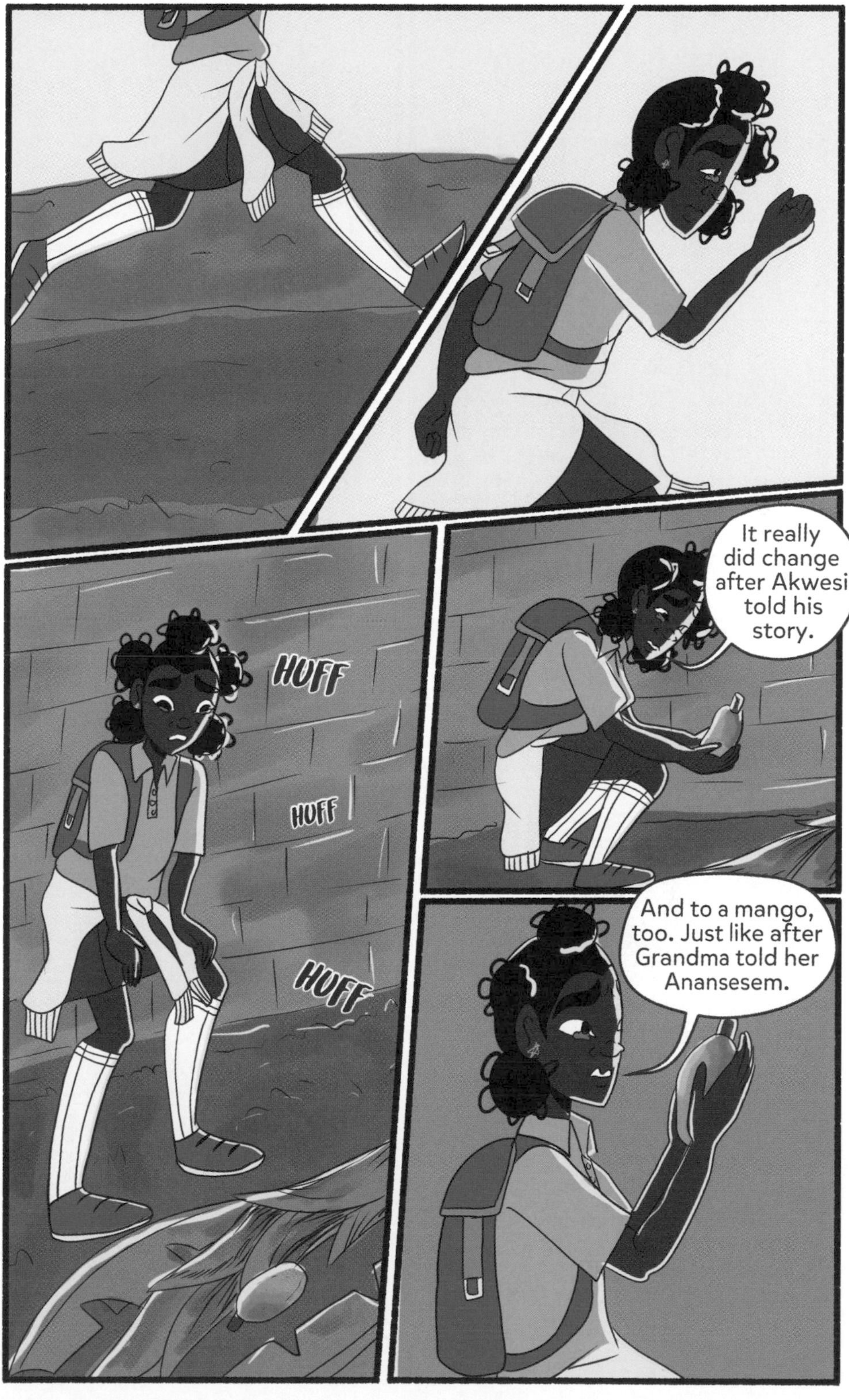
HUFF
HUFF
HUFF
It really did change after Akwesi told his story.
And to a mango, too. Just like after Grandma told her Anansesem.

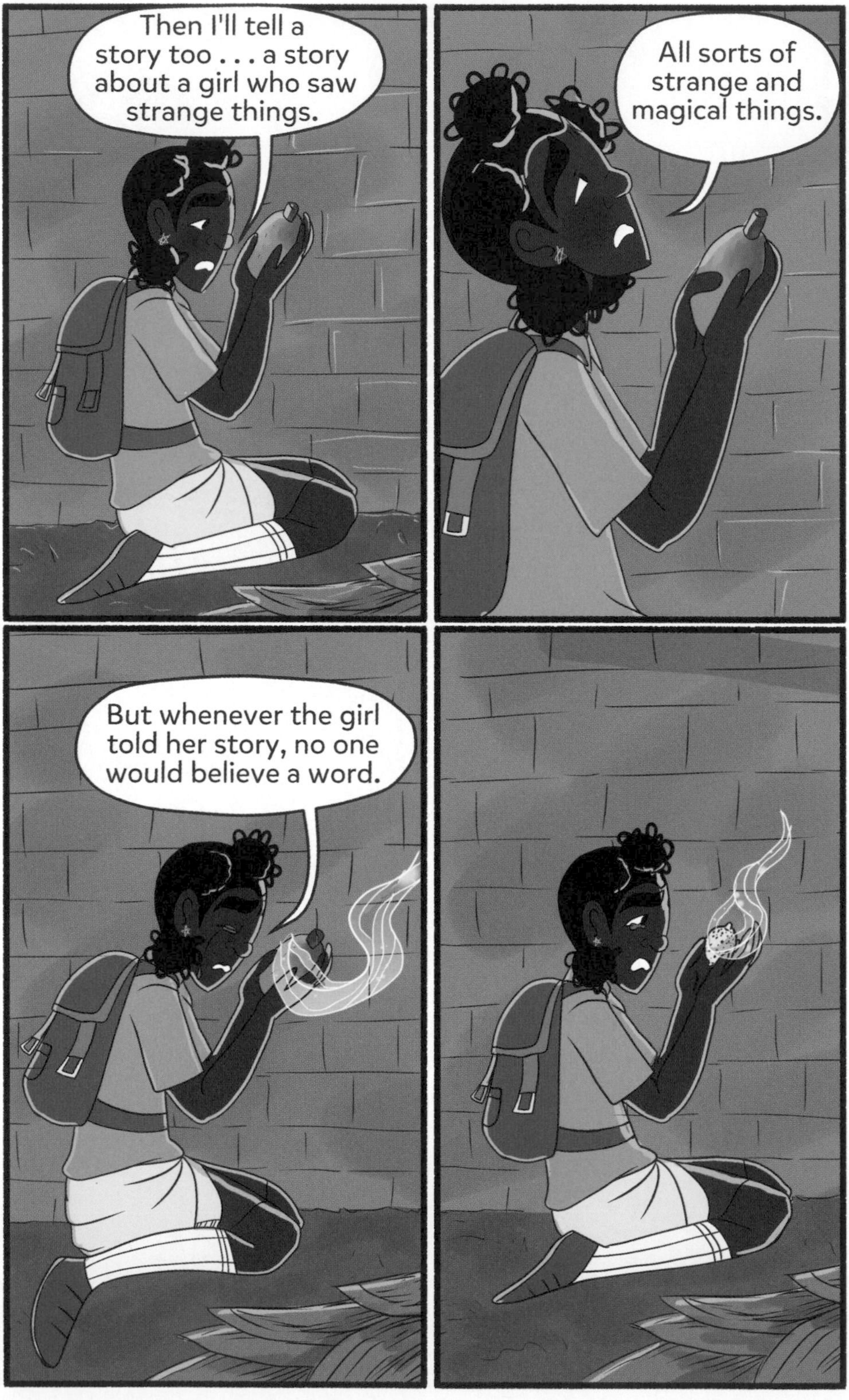
Then I'll tell a story too . . . a story about a girl who saw strange things.
All sorts of strange and magical things.
But whenever the girl told her story, no one would believe a word.

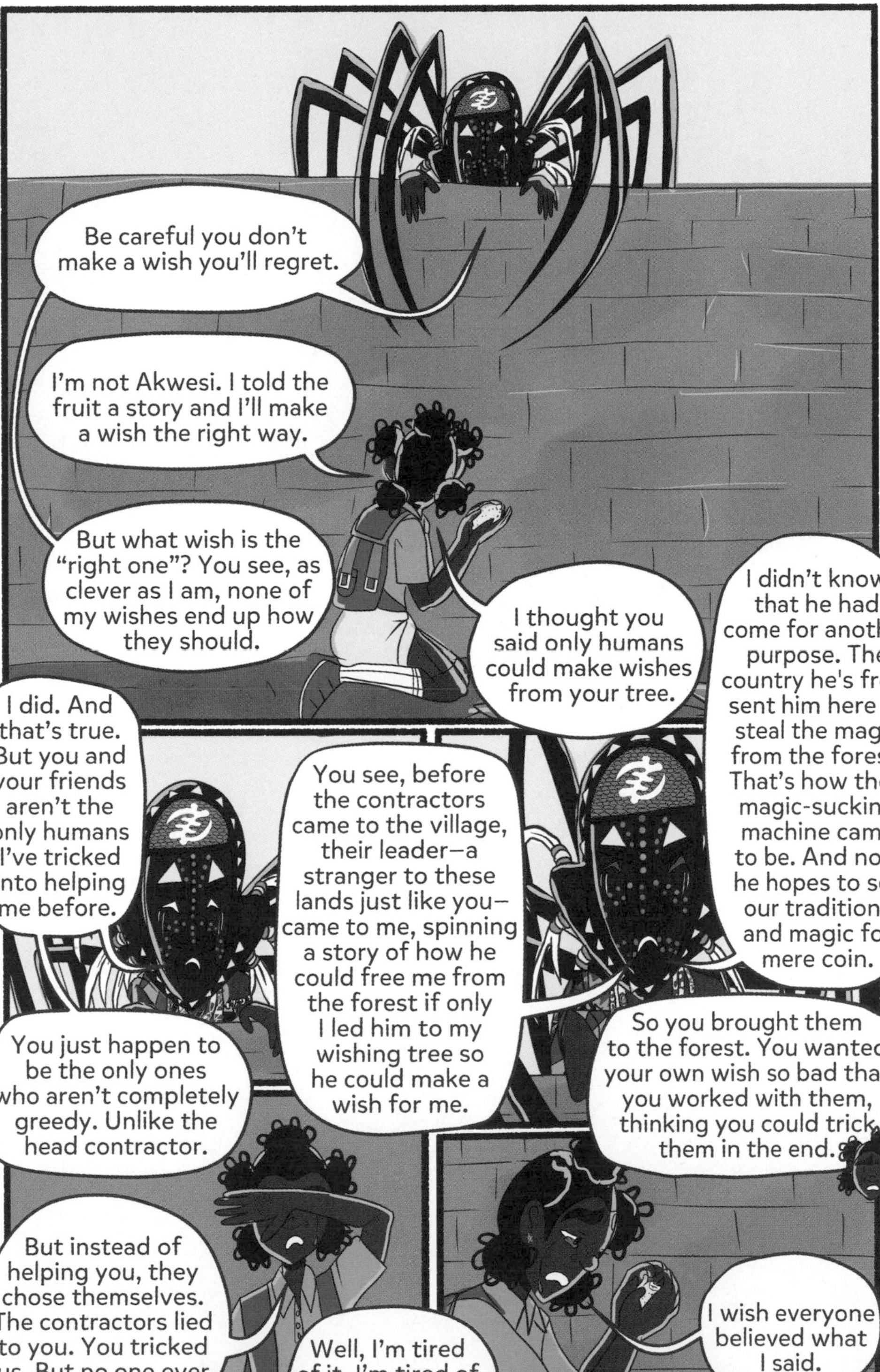

Be careful you don't make a wish you'll regret.
I'm not Akwesi. I told the fruit a story and I'll make a wish the right way.
But what wish is the "right one"? You see, as clever as I am, none of my wishes end up how they should.
I thought you said only humans could make wishes from your tree.
I did. And that's true. But you and your friends aren't the only humans I've tricked into helping me before.
You just happen to be the only ones who aren't completely greedy. Unlike the head contractor.
You see, before the contractors came to the village, their leader—a stranger to these lands just like you—came to me, spinning a story of how he could free me from the forest if only I led him to my wishing tree so he could make a wish for me.
I didn't know that he had come for another purpose. The country he's from sent him here to steal the magic from the forest. That's how their magic-sucking machine came to be. And now he hopes to sell our traditions and magic for mere coin.
So you brought them to the forest. You wanted your own wish so bad that you worked with them, thinking you could trick them in the end.
But instead of helping you, they chose themselves. The contractors lied to you. You tricked us. But no one ever believes me.
Well, I'm tired of it. I'm tired of never being listened to.
I wish everyone believed what I said.

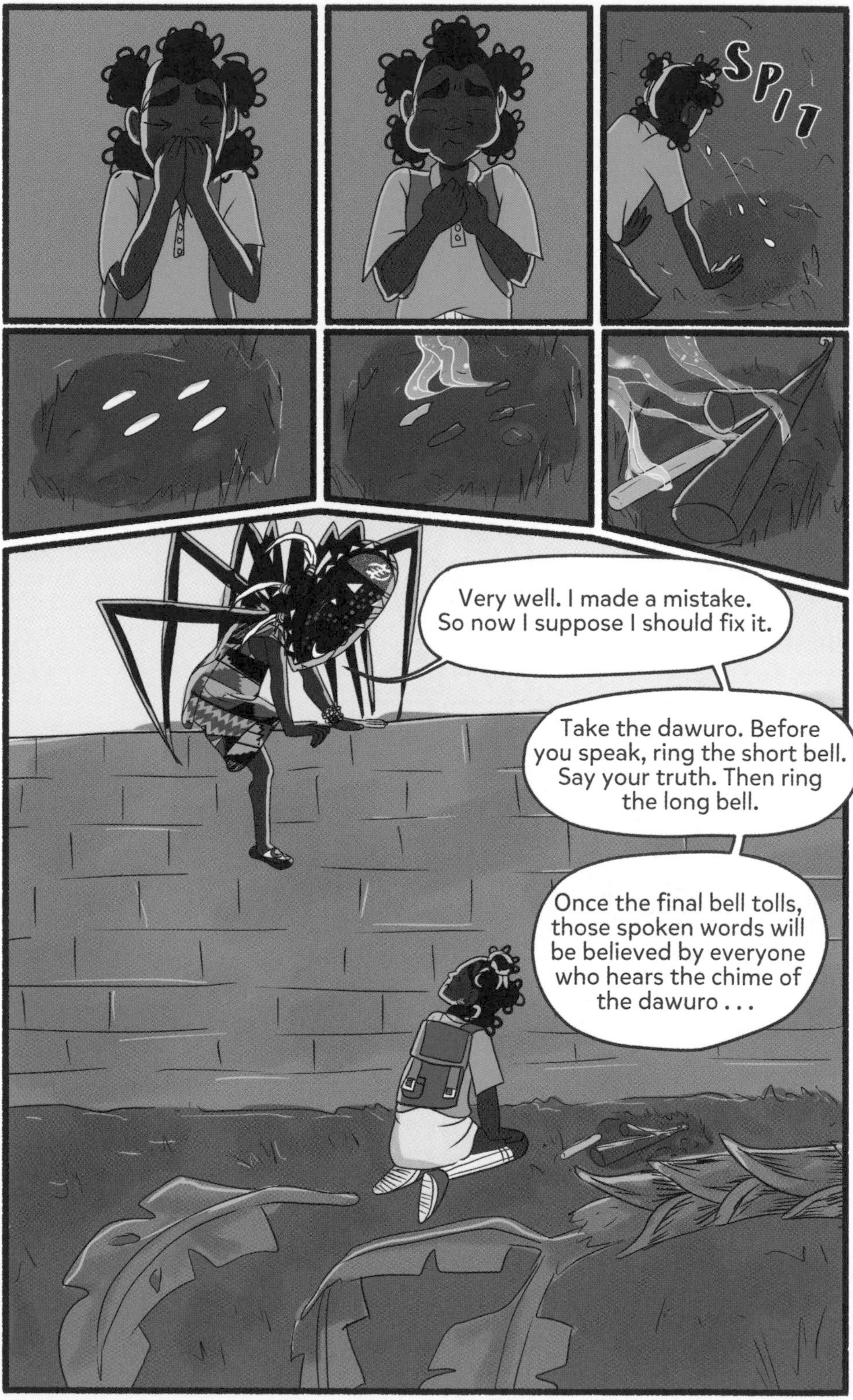
SPIT
Very well. I made a mistake. So now I suppose I should fix it.
Take the dawuro. Before you speak, ring the short bell. Say your truth. Then ring the long bell.
Once the final bell tolls, those spoken words will be believed by everyone who hears the chime of the dawuro . . .

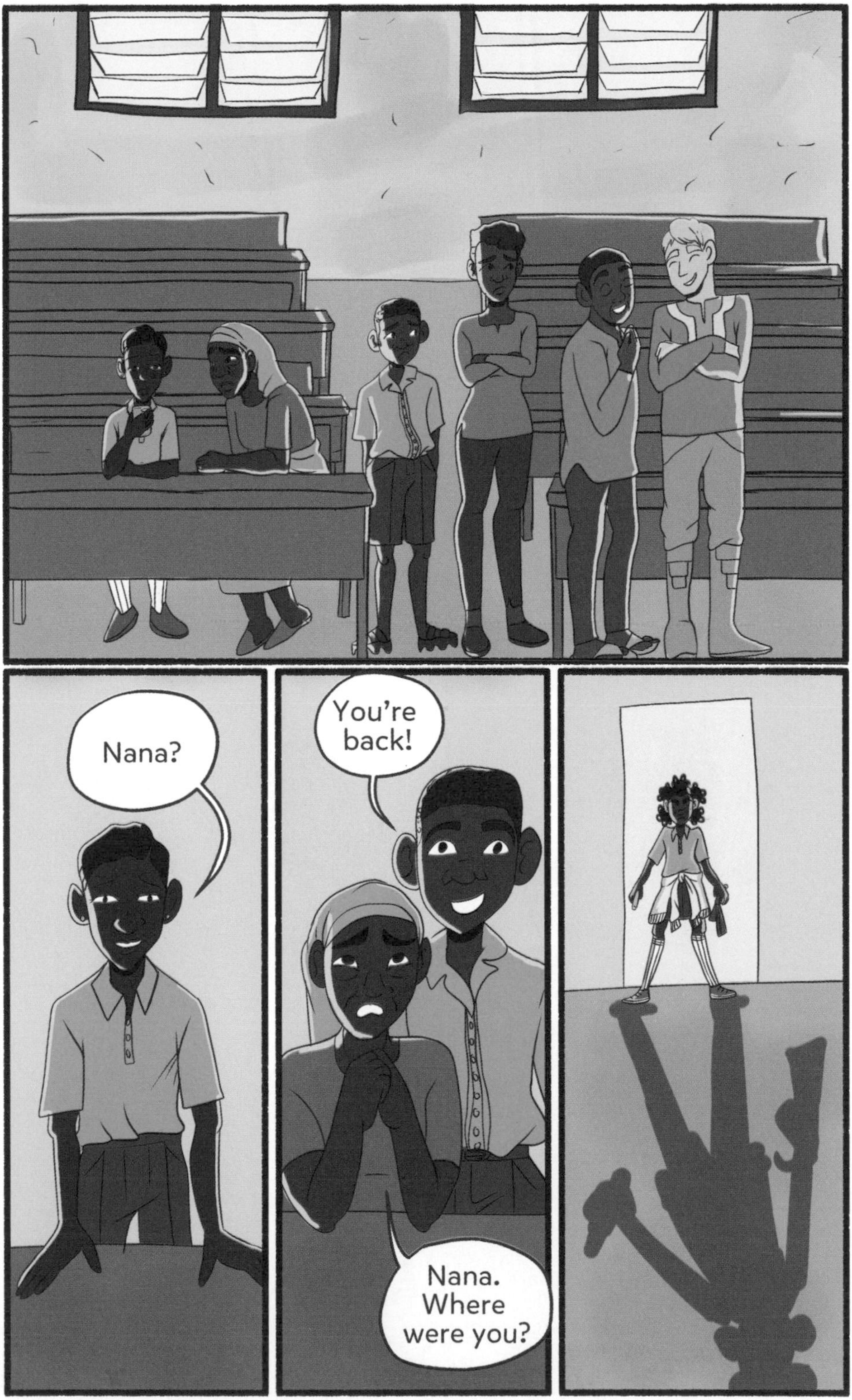
Nana?
You're back!
Nana. Where were you?

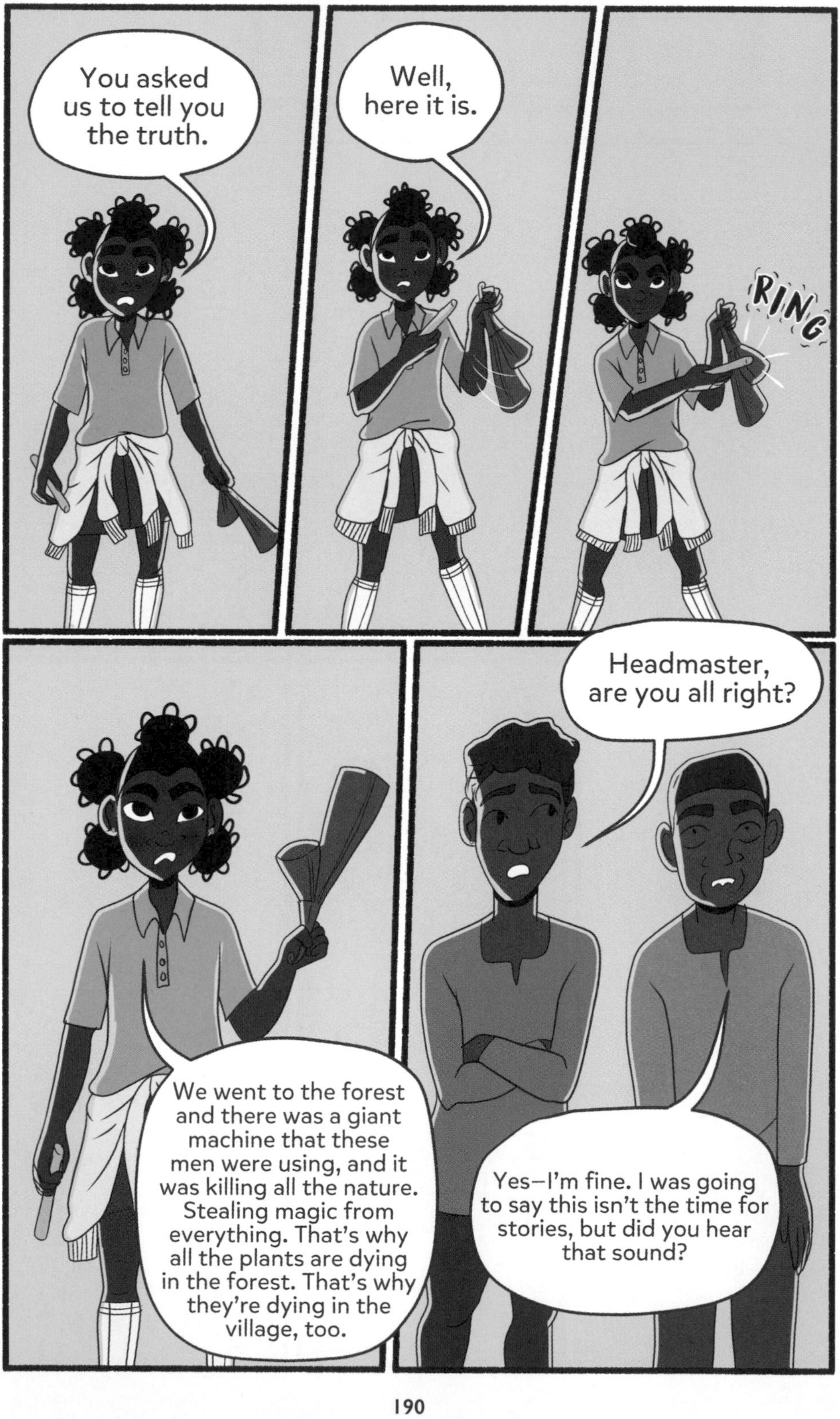
You asked us to tell you the truth.
Well, here it is.
RING
We went to the forest and there was a giant machine that these men were using, and it was killing all the nature. Stealing magic from everything. That's why all the plants are dying in the forest. That's why they're dying in the village, too.
Headmaster, are you all right?
Yes—I'm fine. I was going to say this isn't the time for stories, but did you hear that sound?

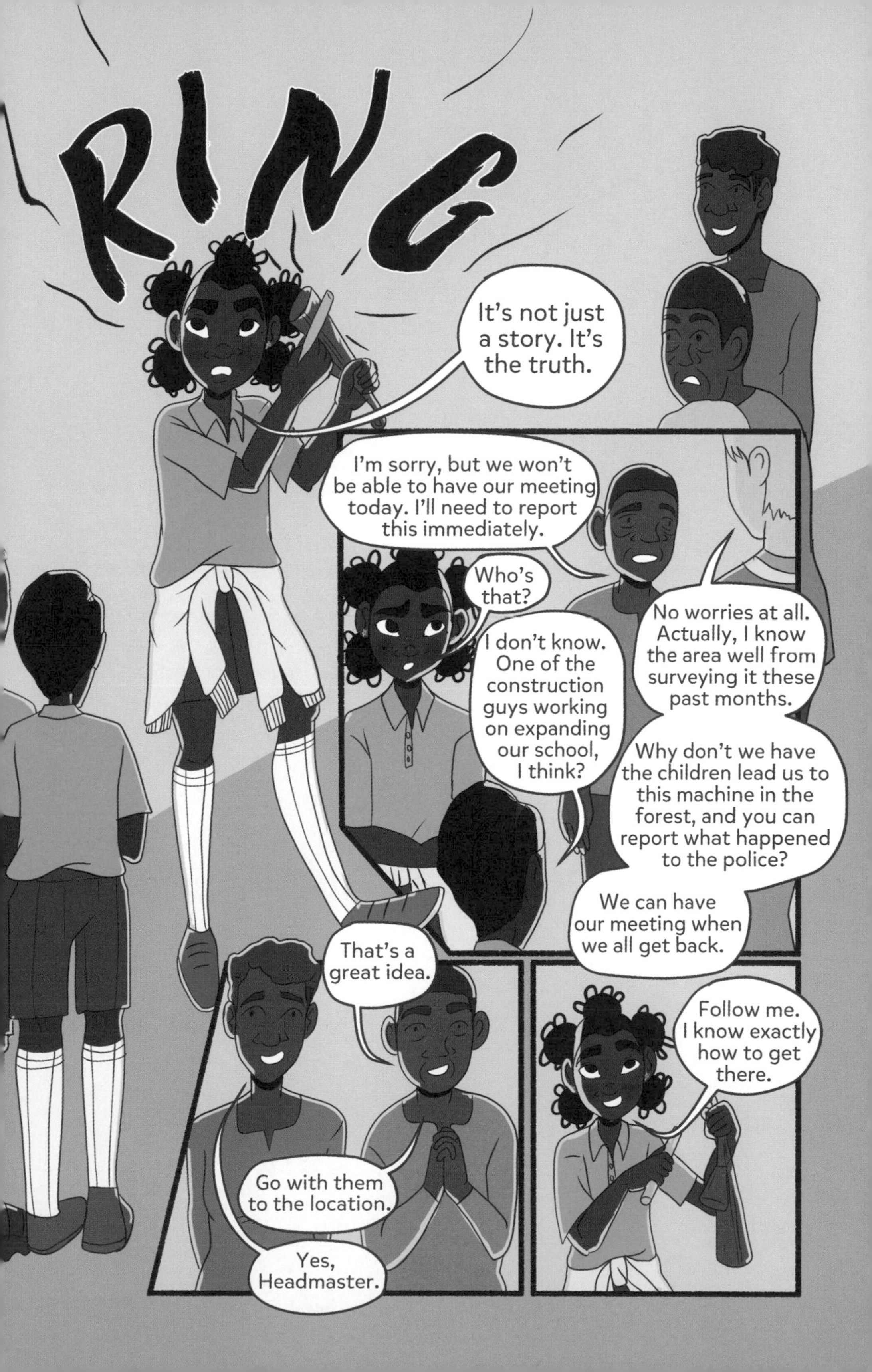
RING
It's not just a story. It's the truth.
I'm sorry, but we won't be able to have our meeting today. I'll need to report this immediately.
Who's that?
I don't know. One of the construction guys working on expanding our school, I think?
No worries at all. Actually, I know the area well from surveying it these past months.
Why don't we have the children lead us to this machine in the forest, and you can report what happened to the police?
We can have our meeting when we all get back.
That's a great idea.
Go with them to the location.
Yes, Headmaster.
Follow me. I know exactly how to get there.

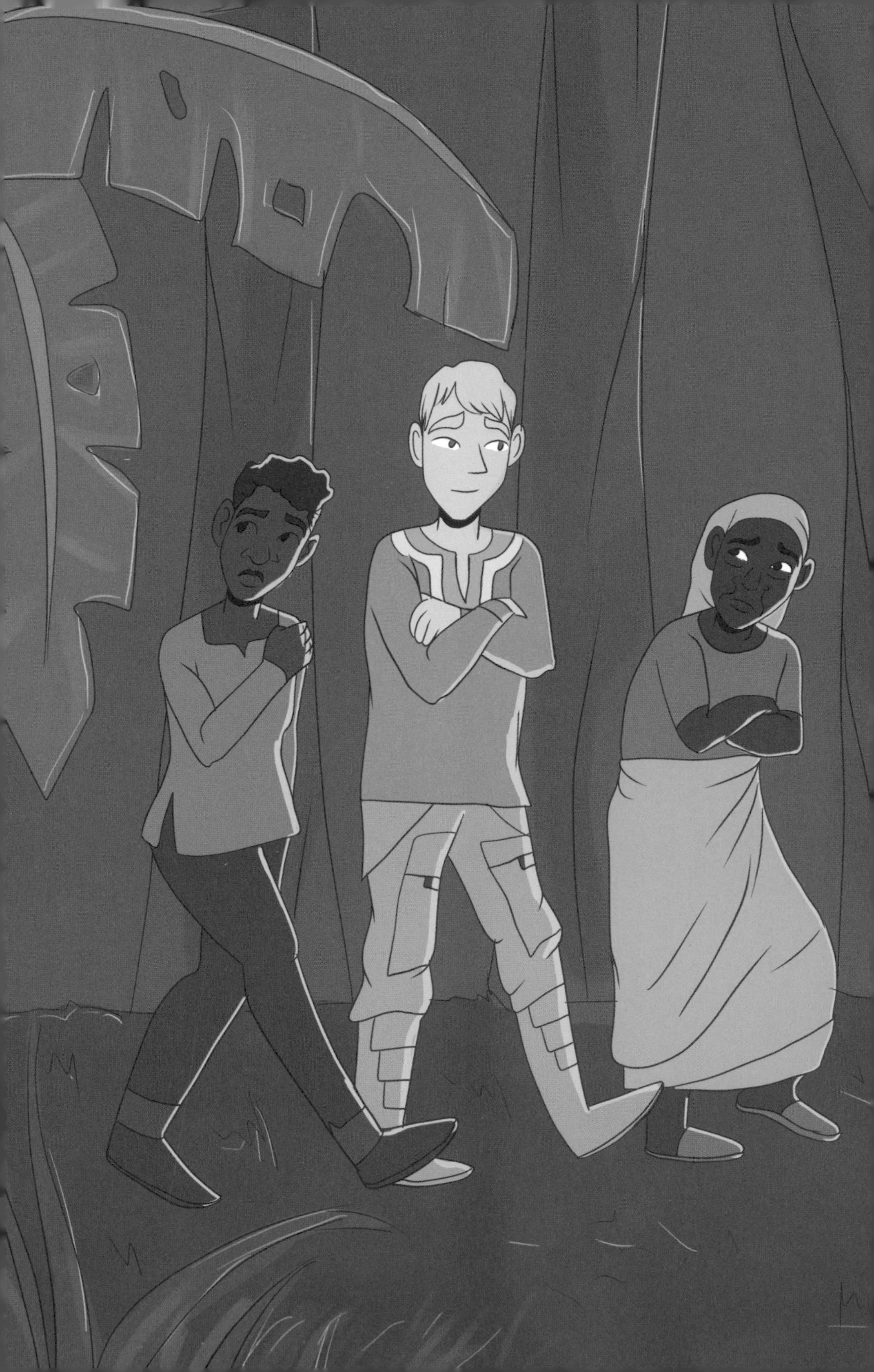

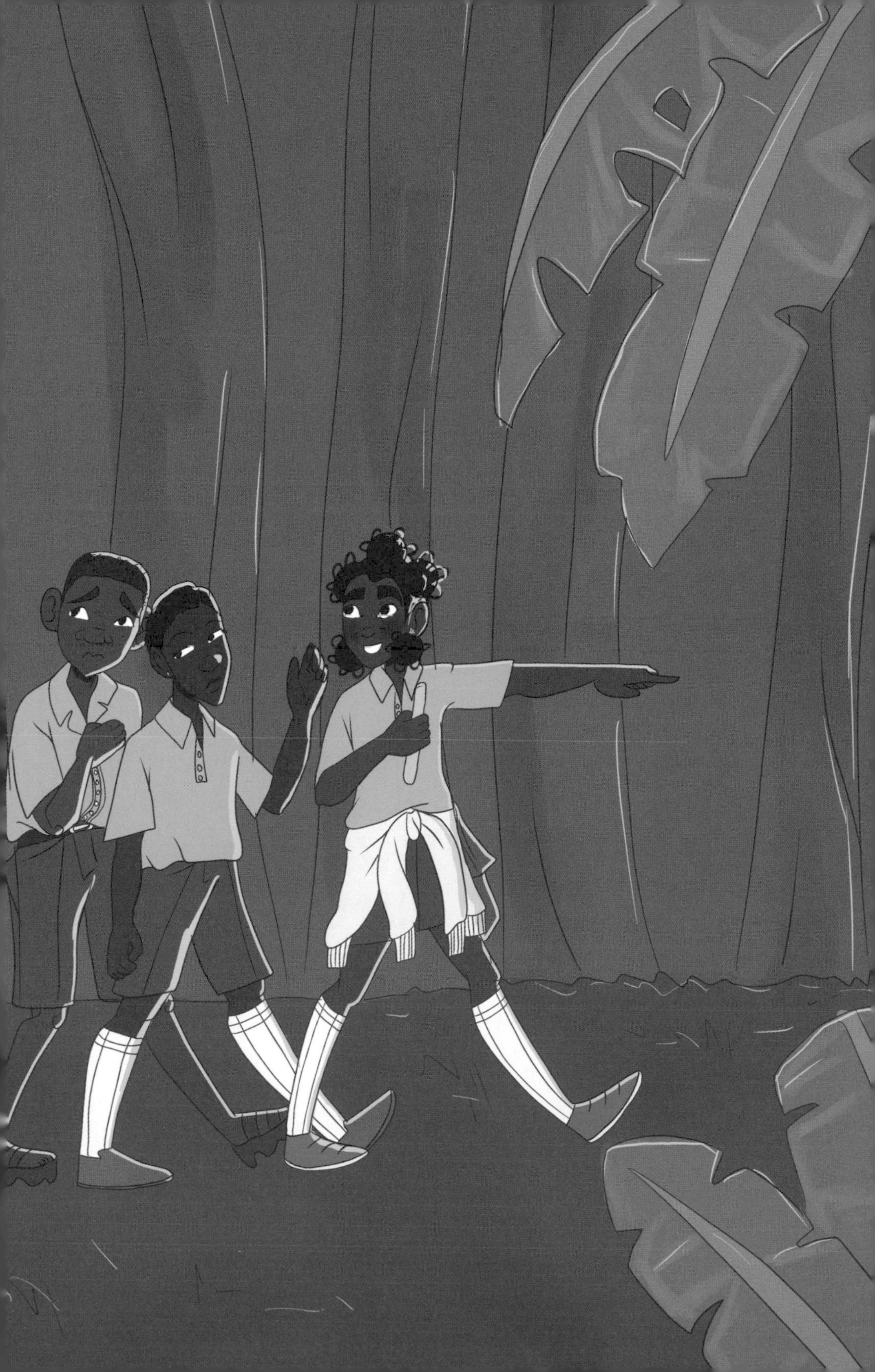

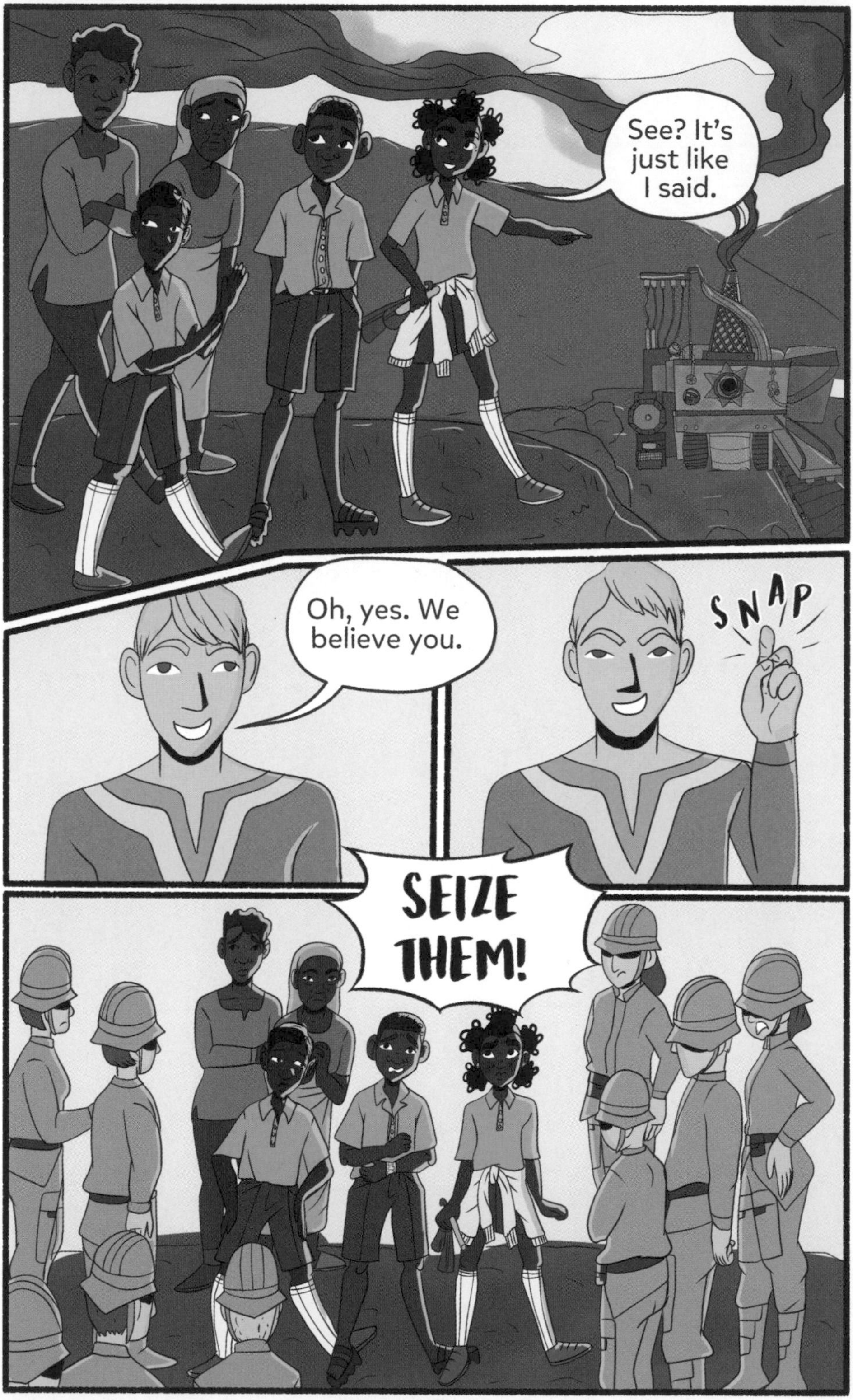
See? It's just like I said.
Oh, yes. We believe you.
SNAP
SEIZE THEM!

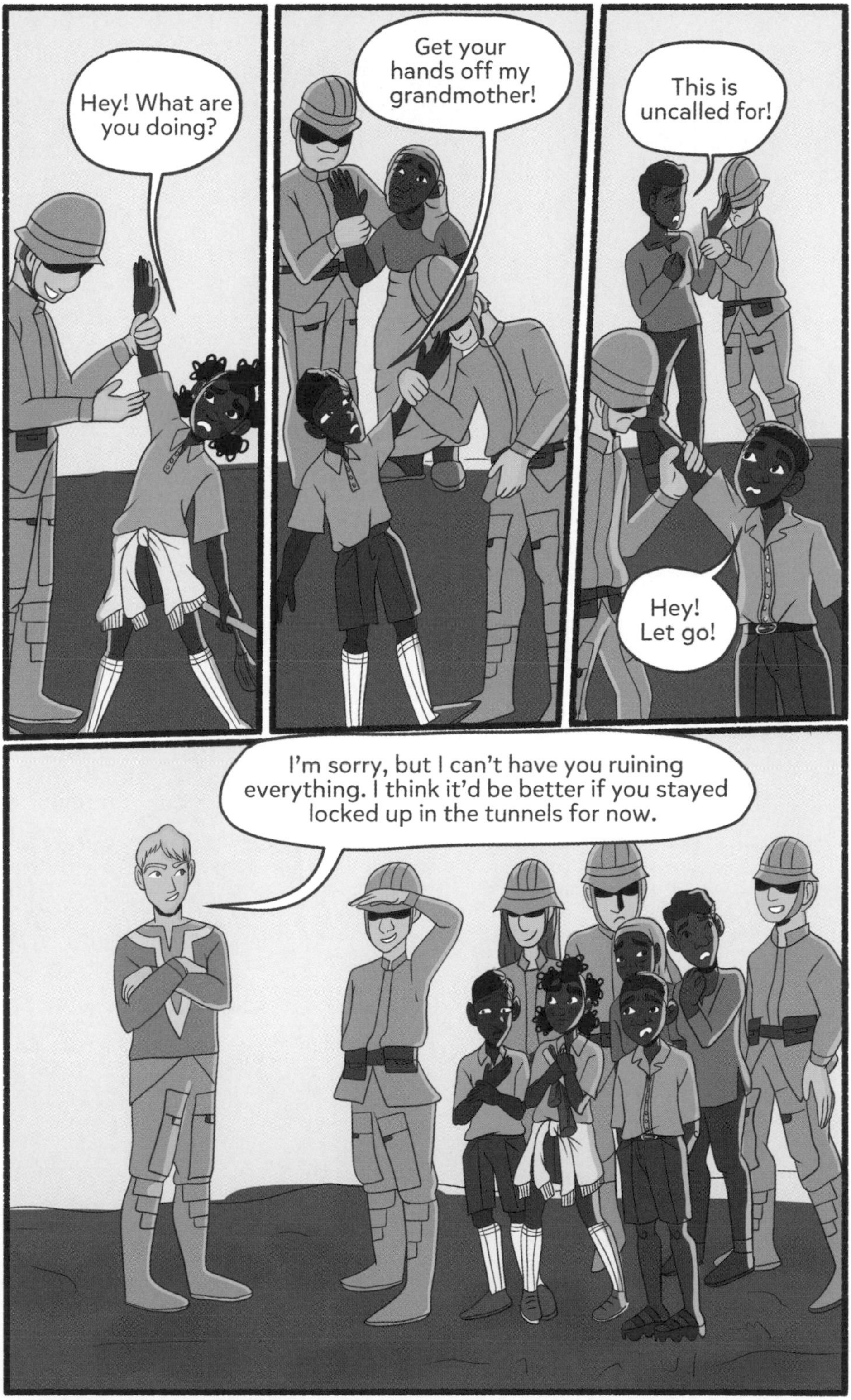
Hey! What are you doing?
Get your hands off my grandmother!
This is uncalled for!
Hey! Let go!
I'm sorry, but I can't have you ruining everything. I think it'd be better if you stayed locked up in the tunnels for now.

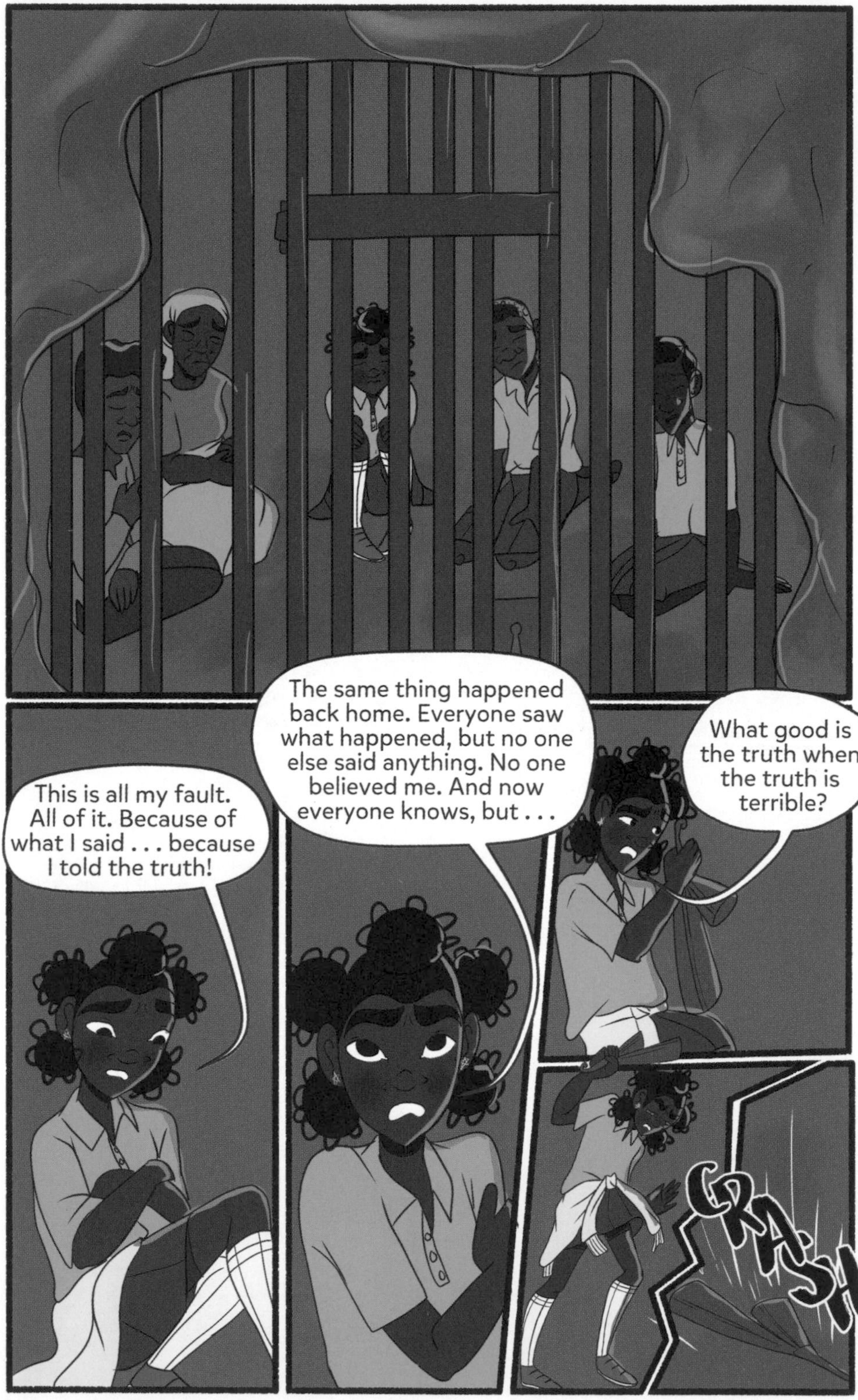
This is all my fault. All of it. Because of what I said . . . because I told the truth!
The same thing happened back home. Everyone saw what happened, but no one else said anything. No one believed me. And now everyone knows, but . . .
What good is the truth when the truth is terrible?
CRASH

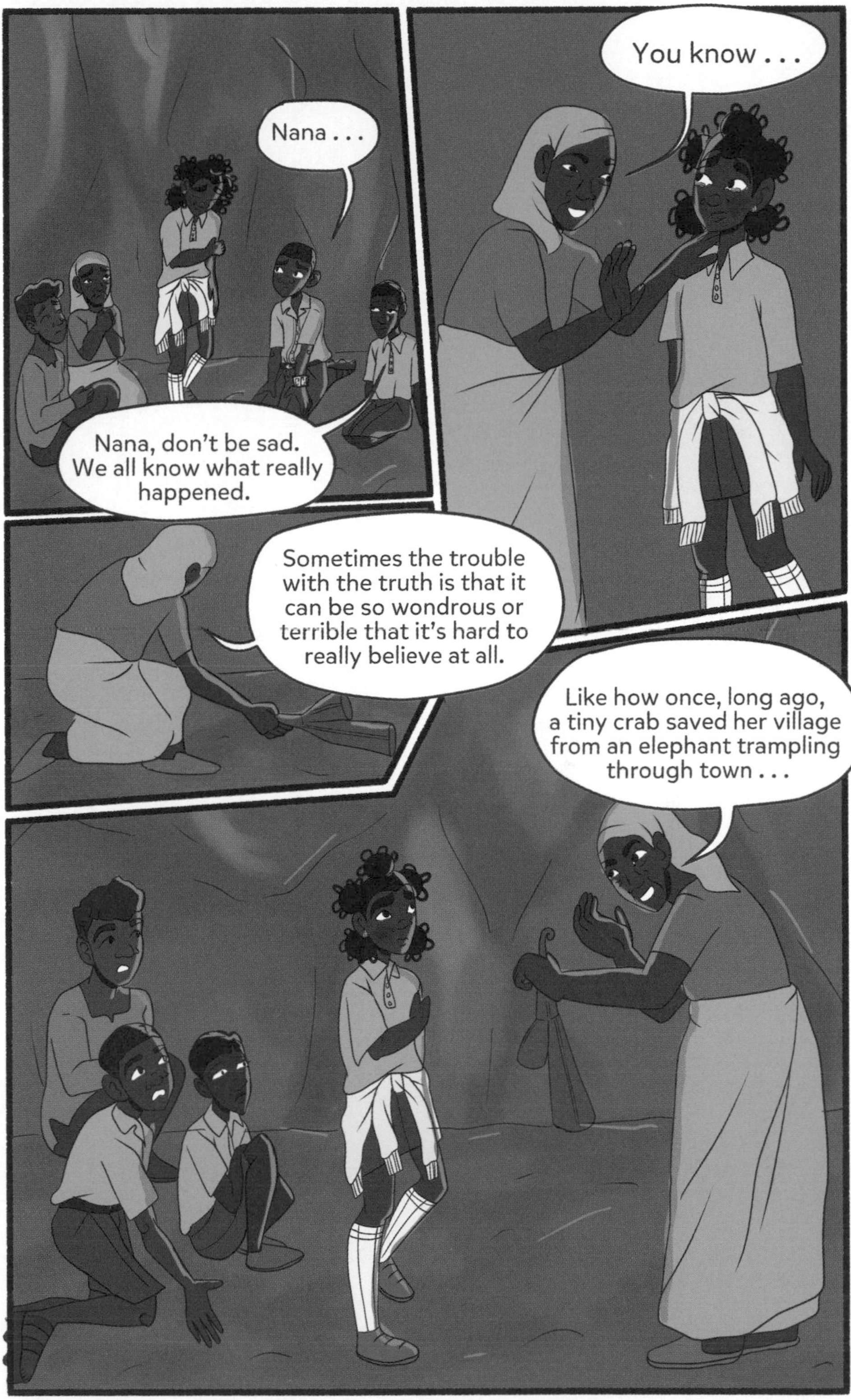
Nana . . .
Nana, don't be sad. We all know what really happened.
You know . . .
Sometimes the trouble with the truth is that it can be so wondrous or terrible that it's hard to really believe at all.
Like how once, long ago, a tiny crab saved her village from an elephant trampling through town . . .

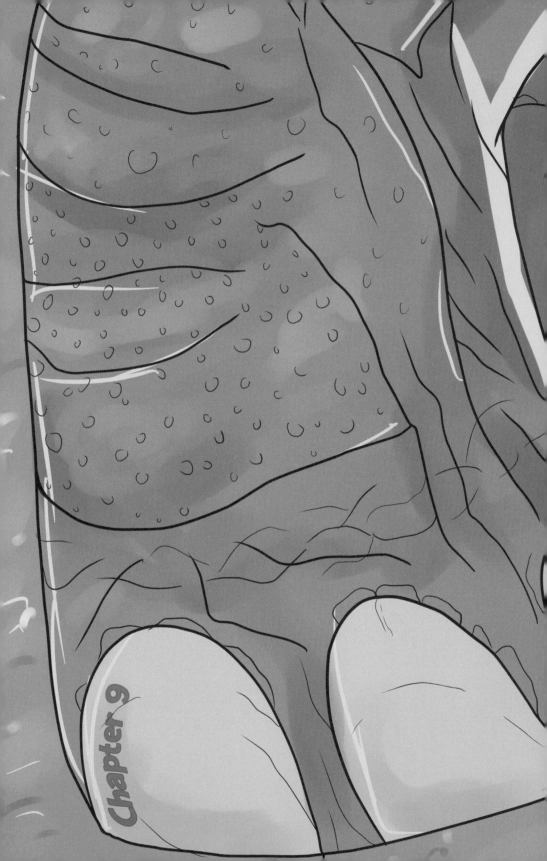

Chapter 9

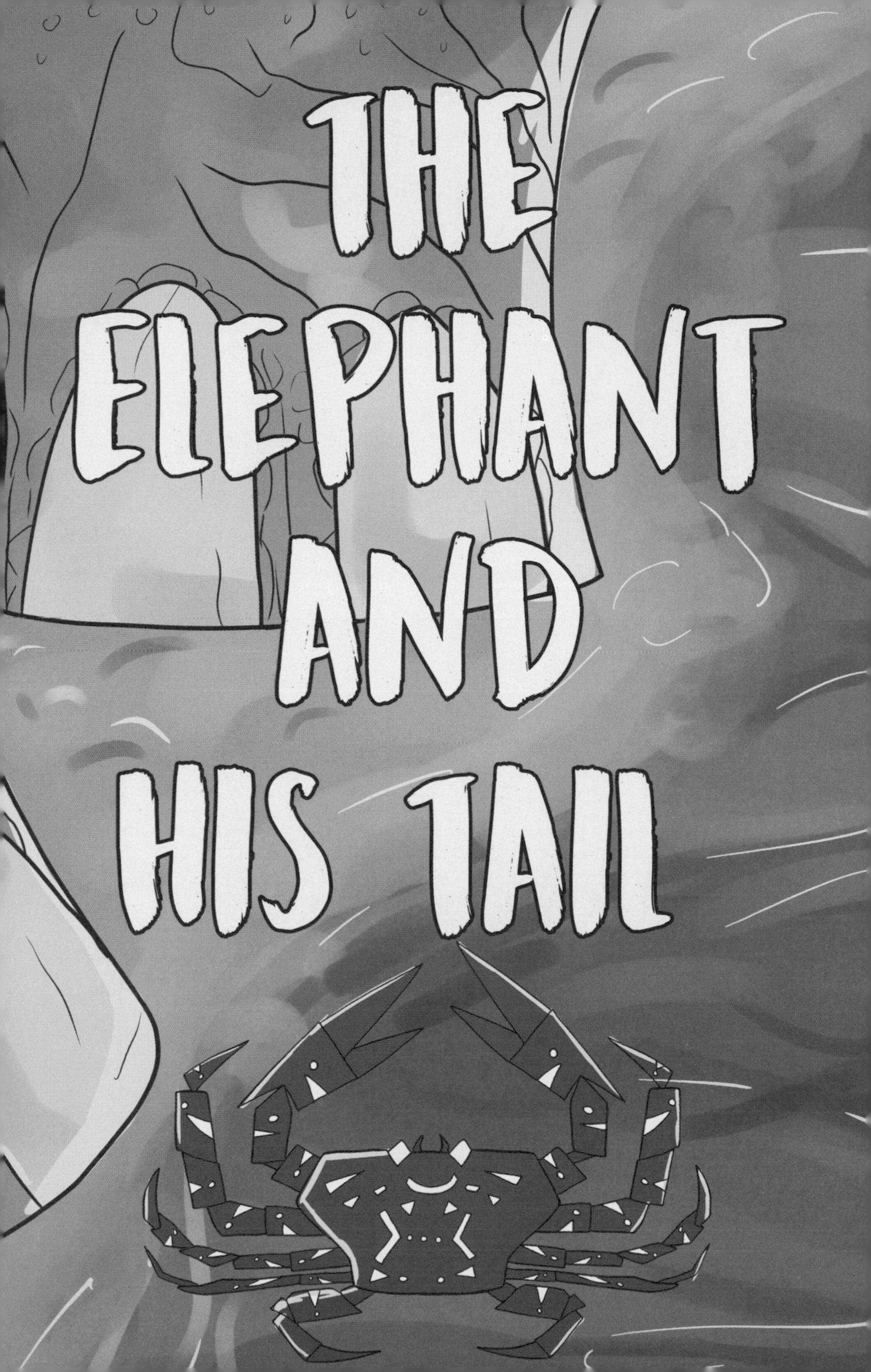
THE ELEPHANT AND HIS TAIL

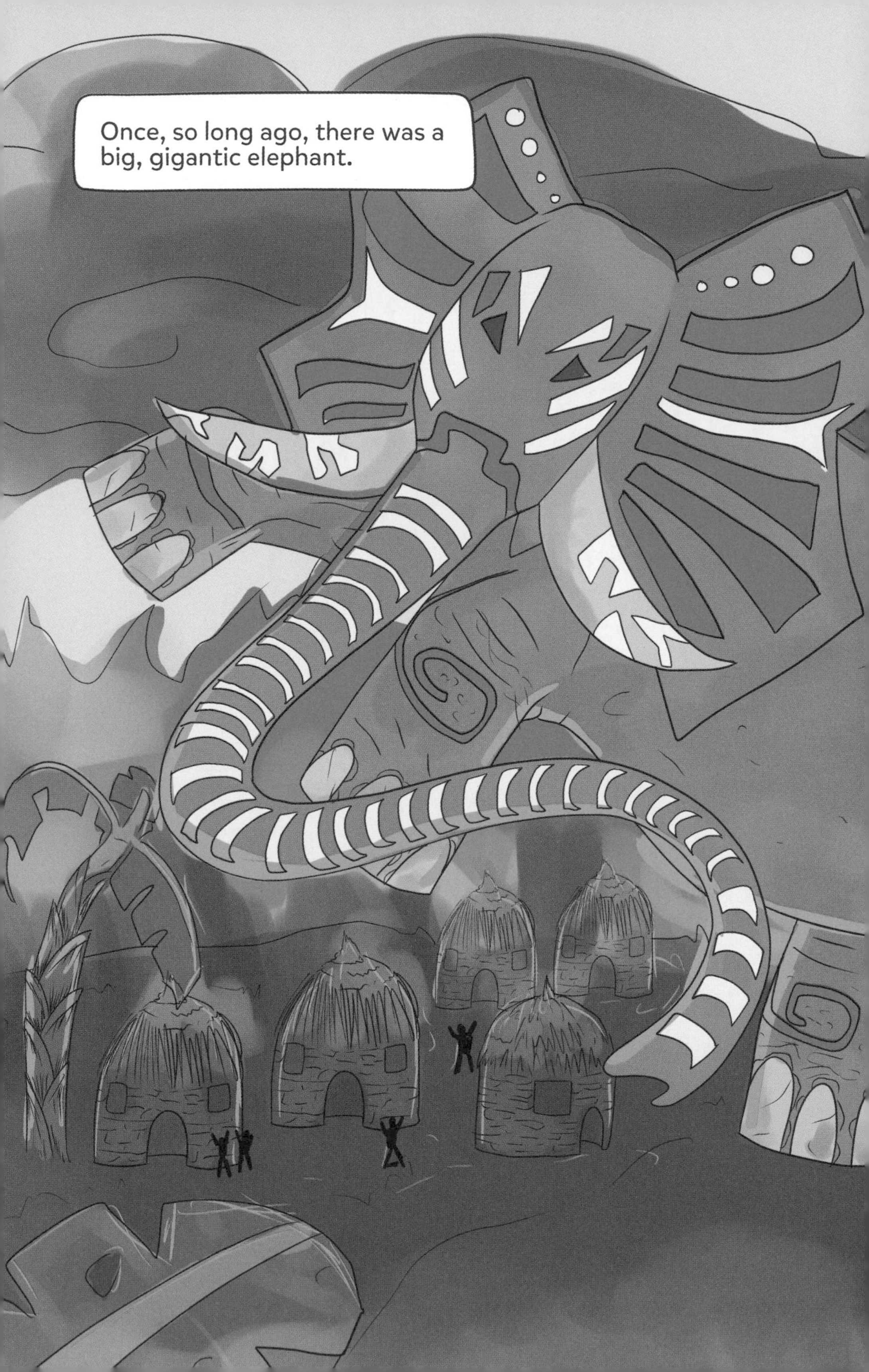
Once, so long ago, there was a big, gigantic elephant.

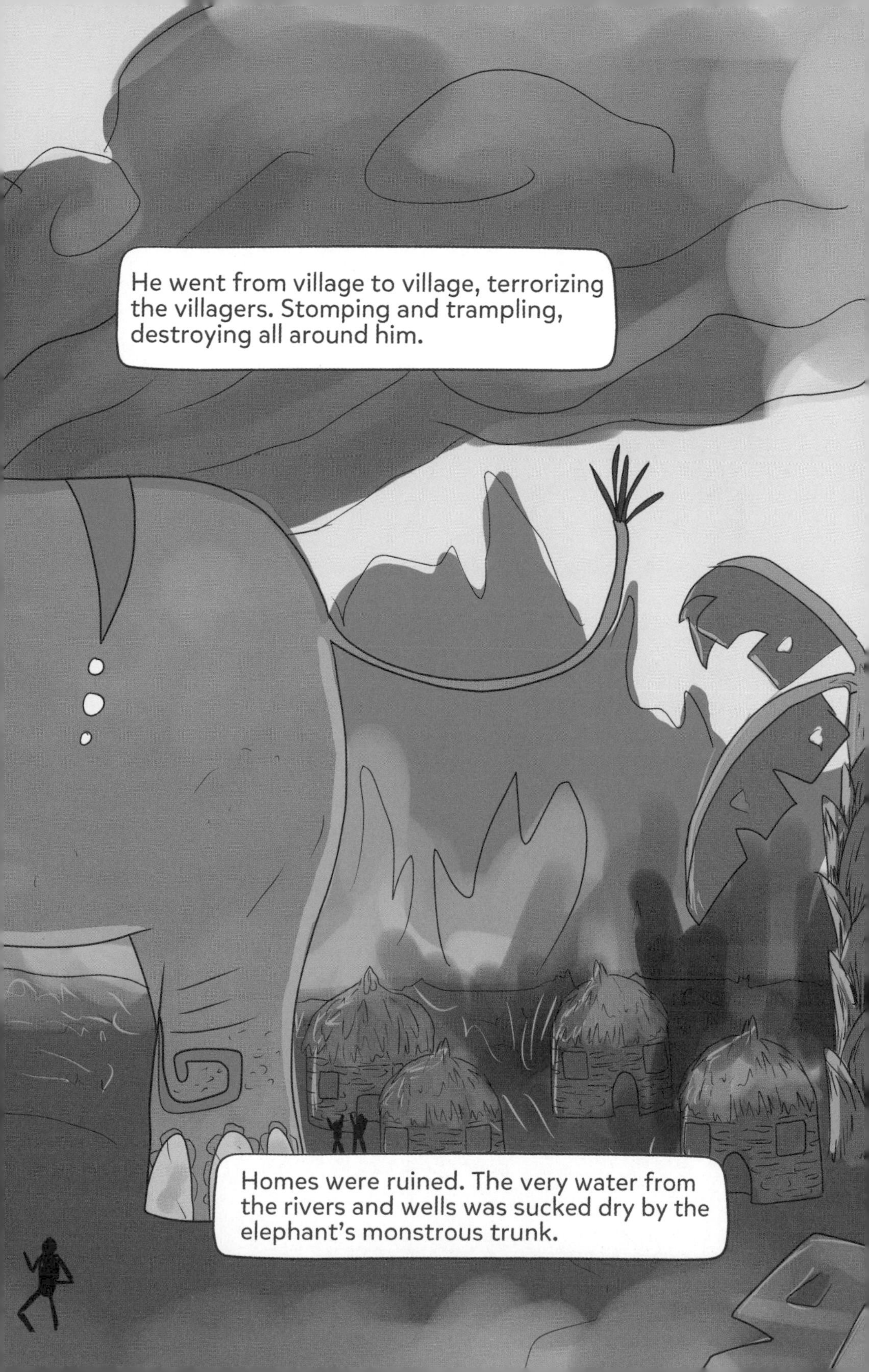
He went from village to village, terrorizing the villagers. Stomping and trampling, destroying all around him.
Homes were ruined. The very water from the rivers and wells was sucked dry by the elephant's monstrous trunk.

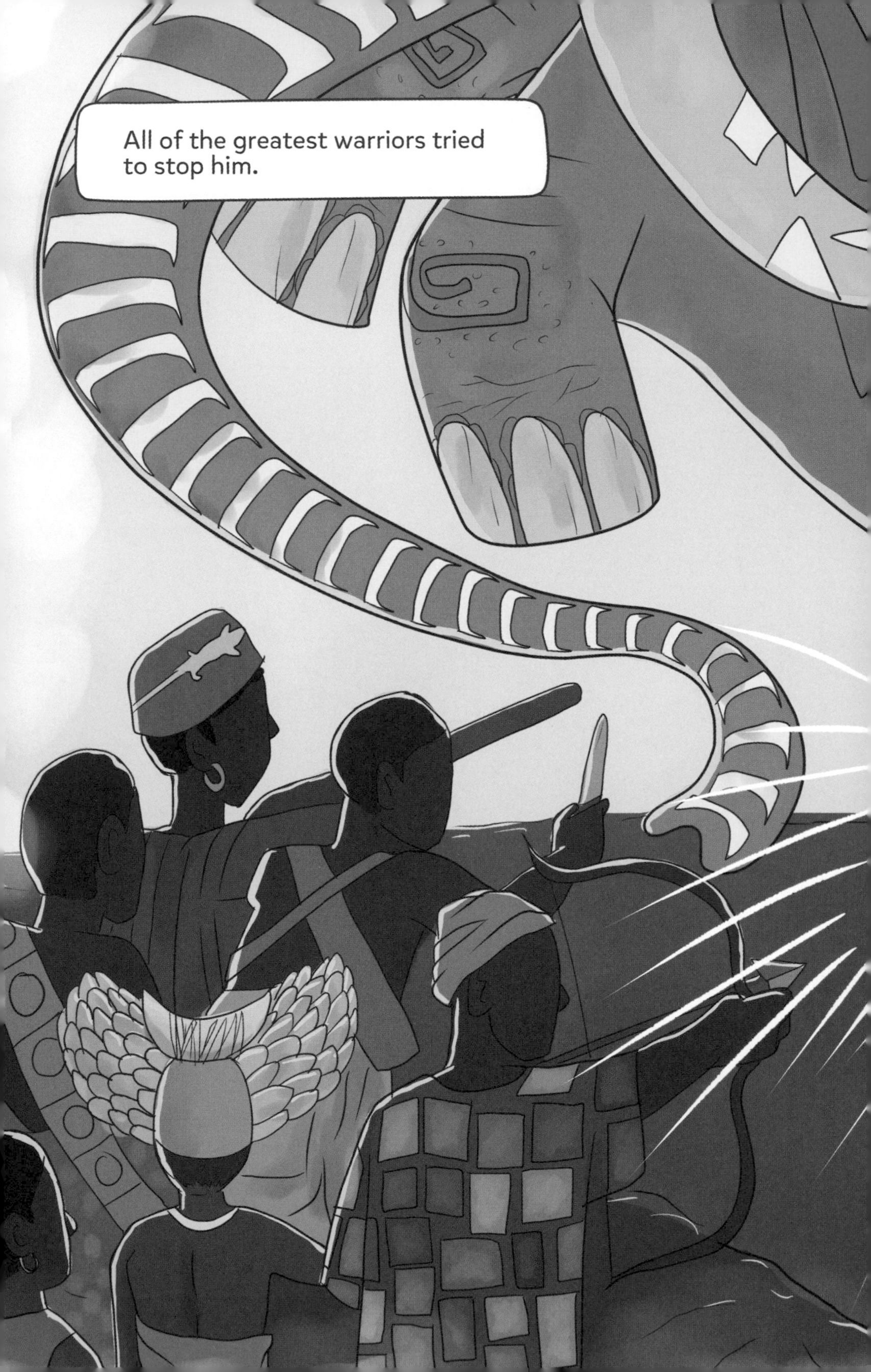
All of the greatest warriors tried to stop him.

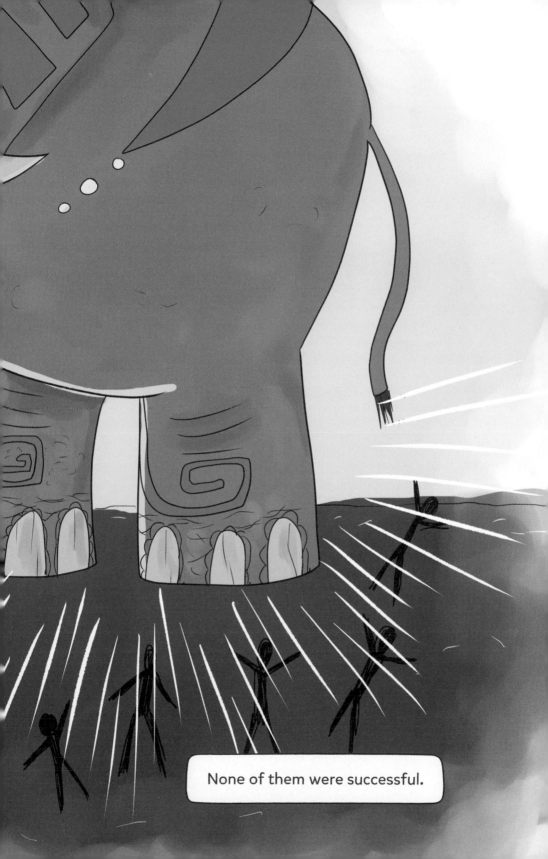

None of them were successful.

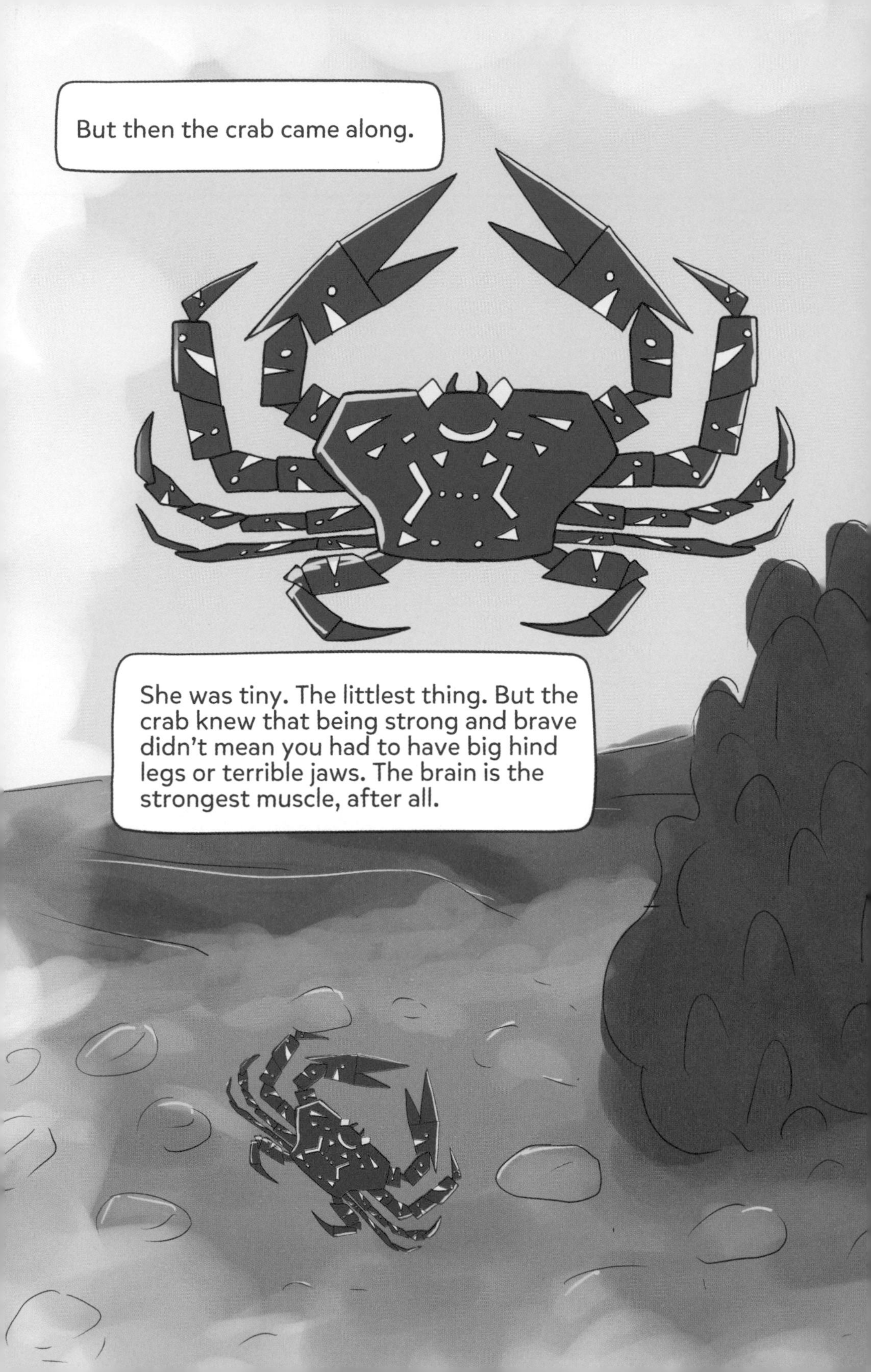
But then the crab came along.
She was tiny. The littlest thing. But the crab knew that being strong and brave didn't mean you had to have big hind legs or terrible jaws. The brain is the strongest muscle, after all.

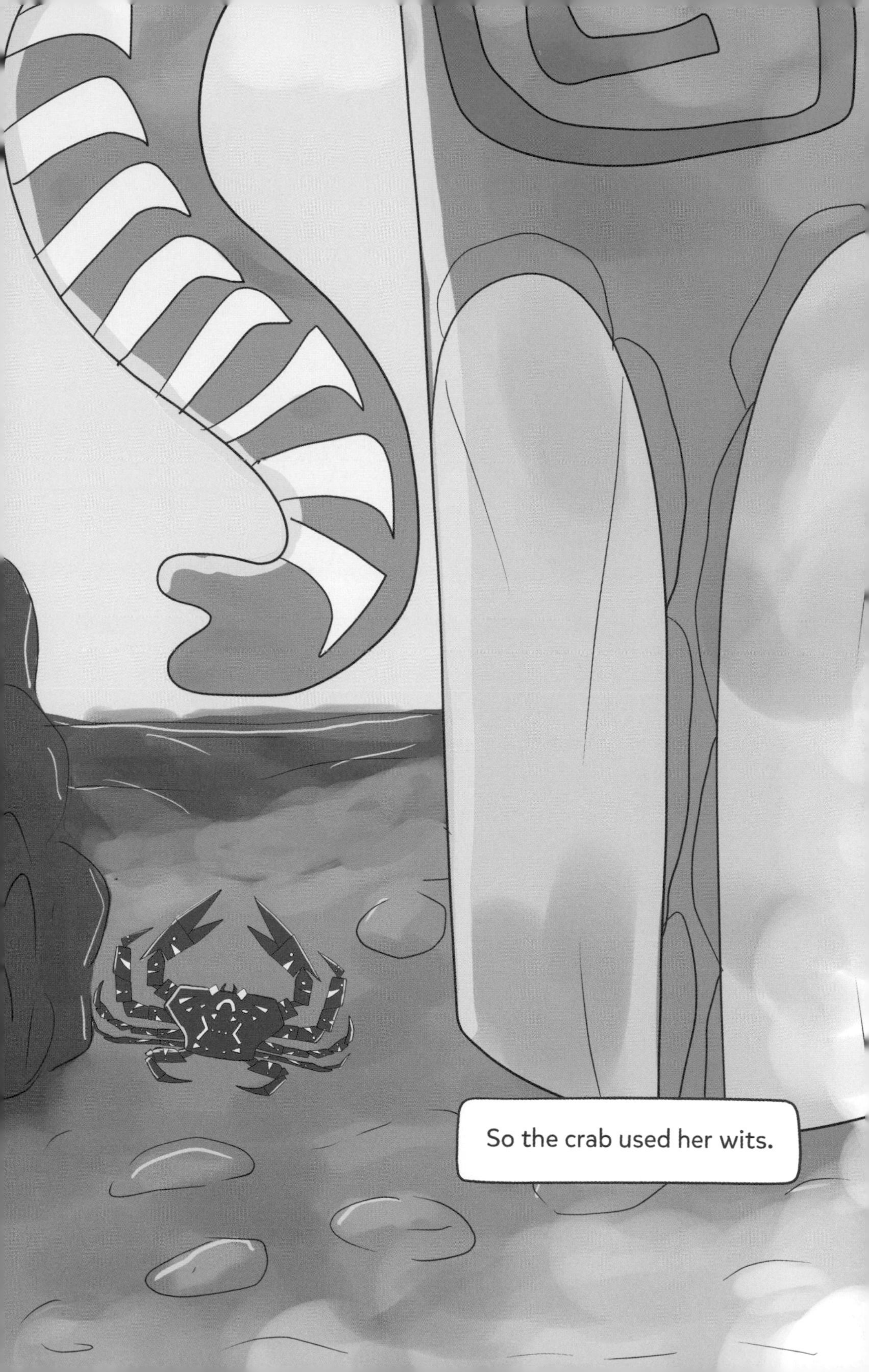
So the crab used her wits.

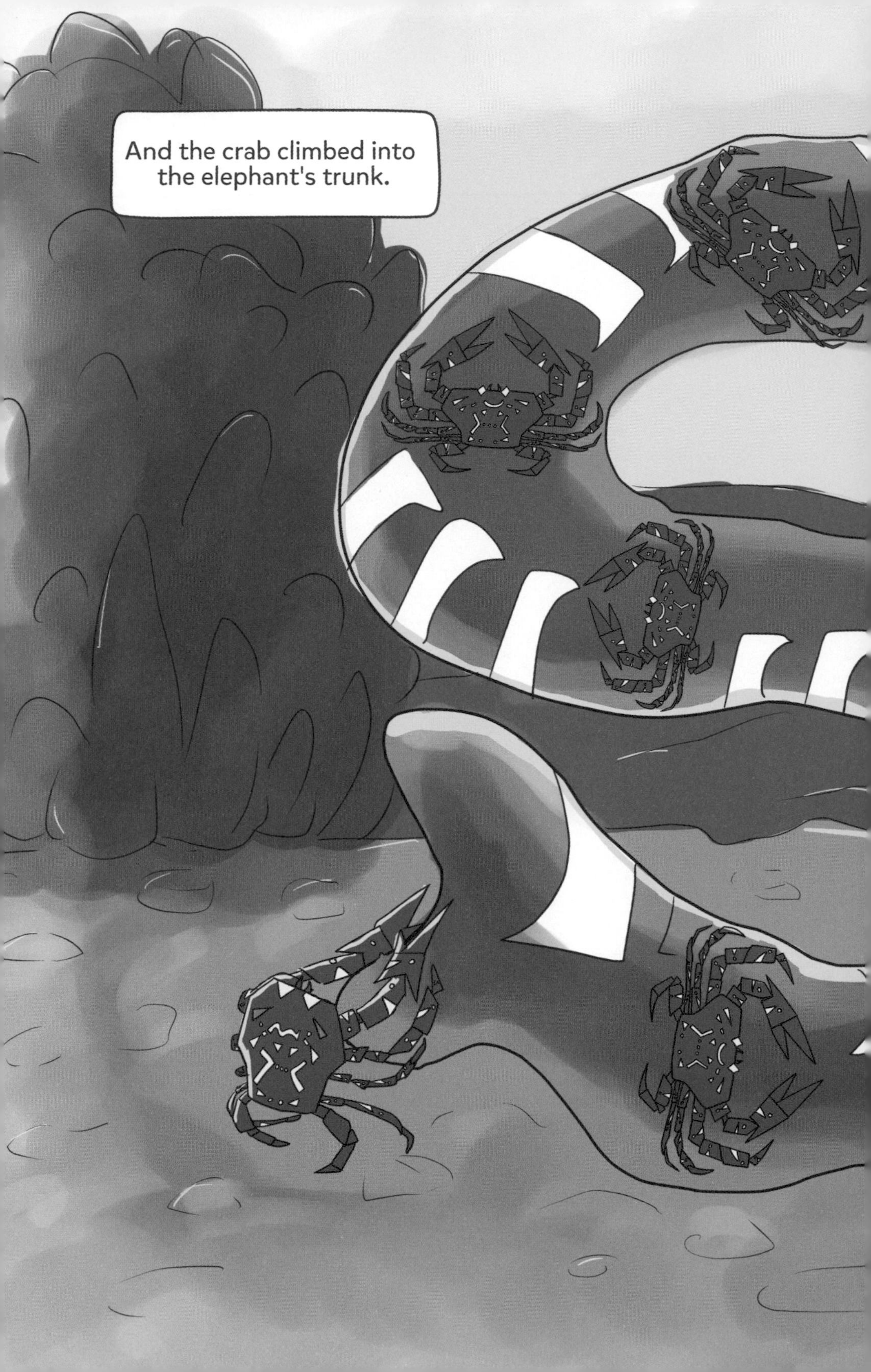
And the crab climbed into the elephant's trunk.

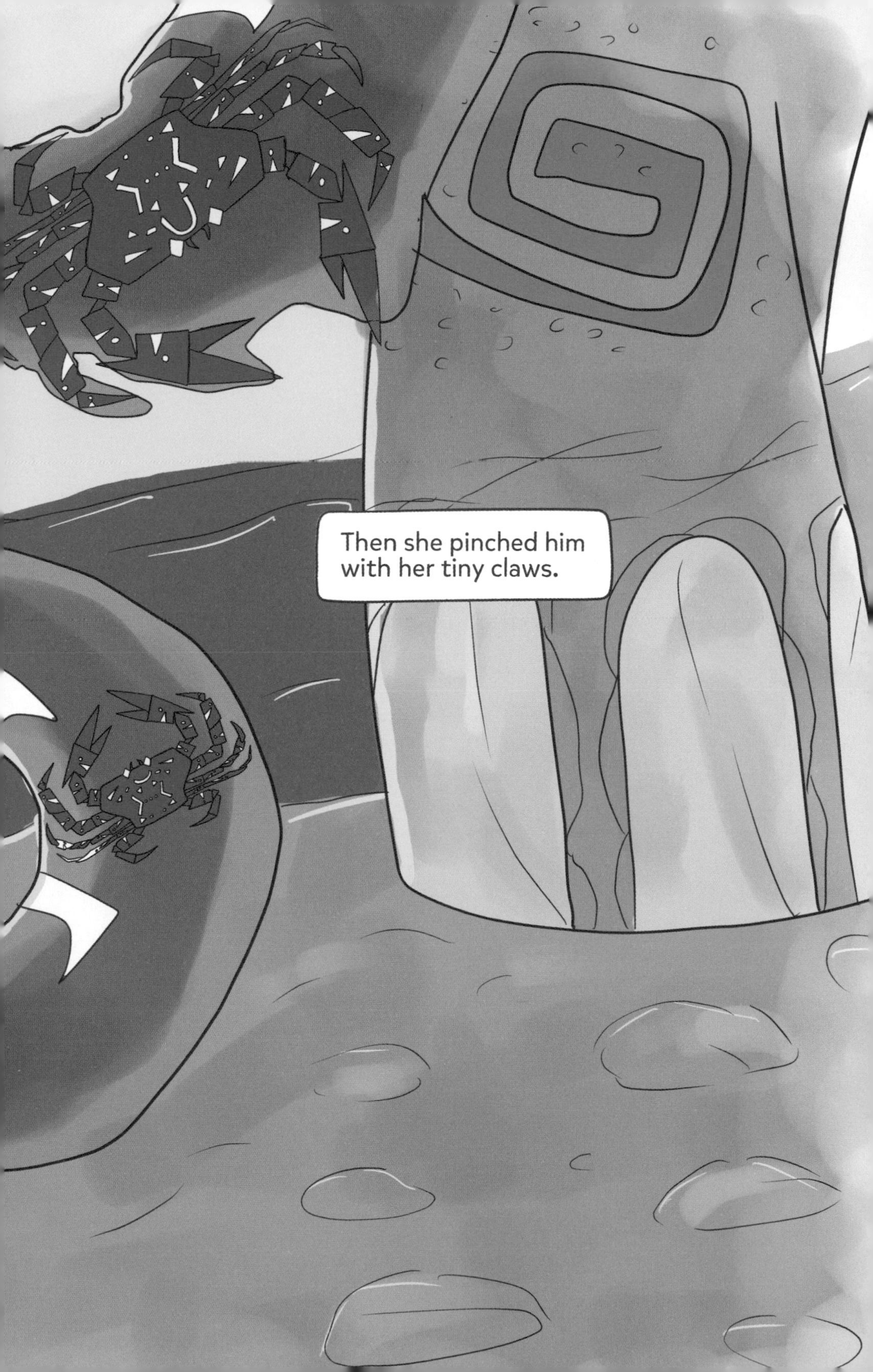
Then she pinched him with her tiny claws.

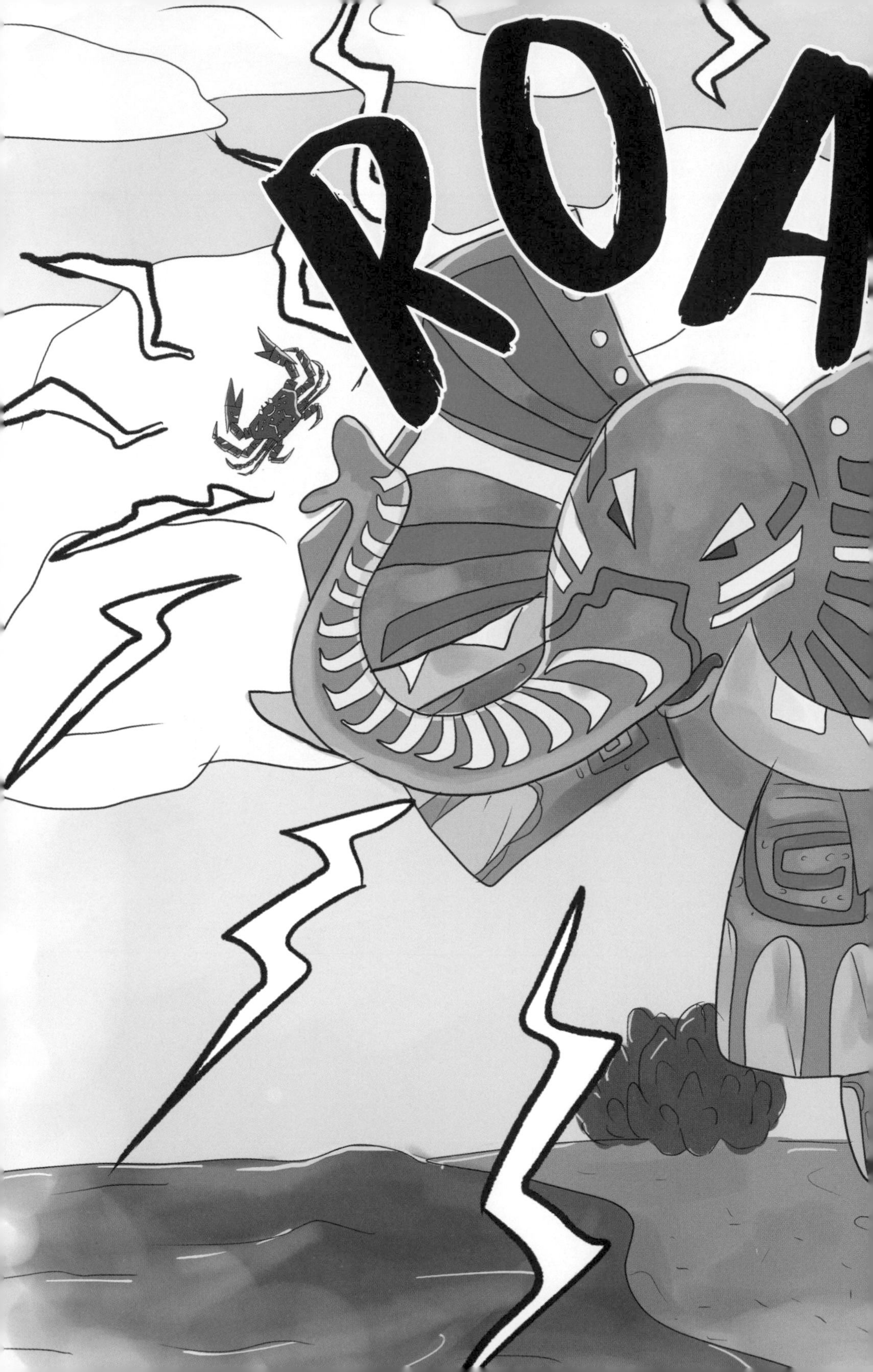
ROA

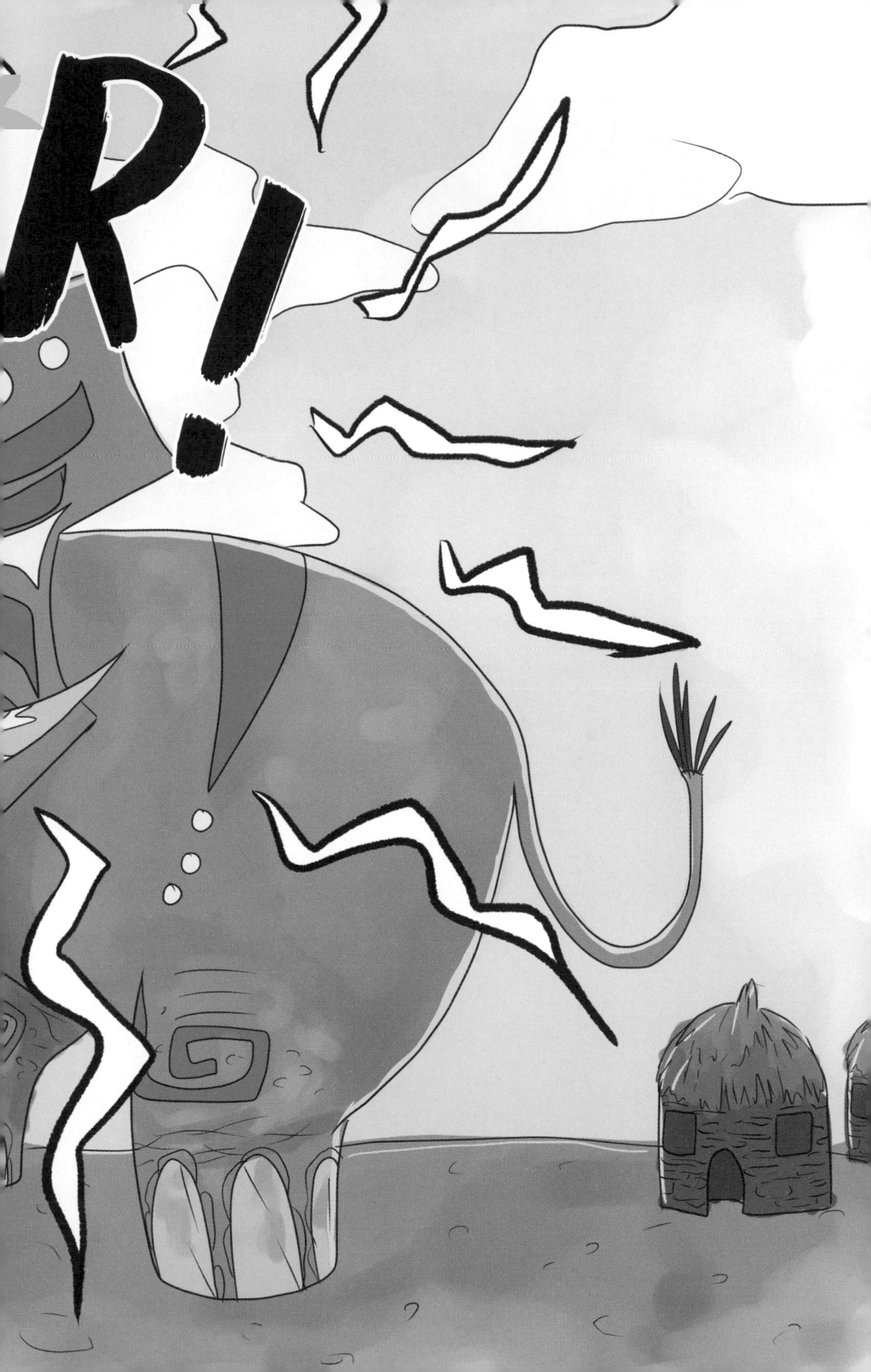
R!

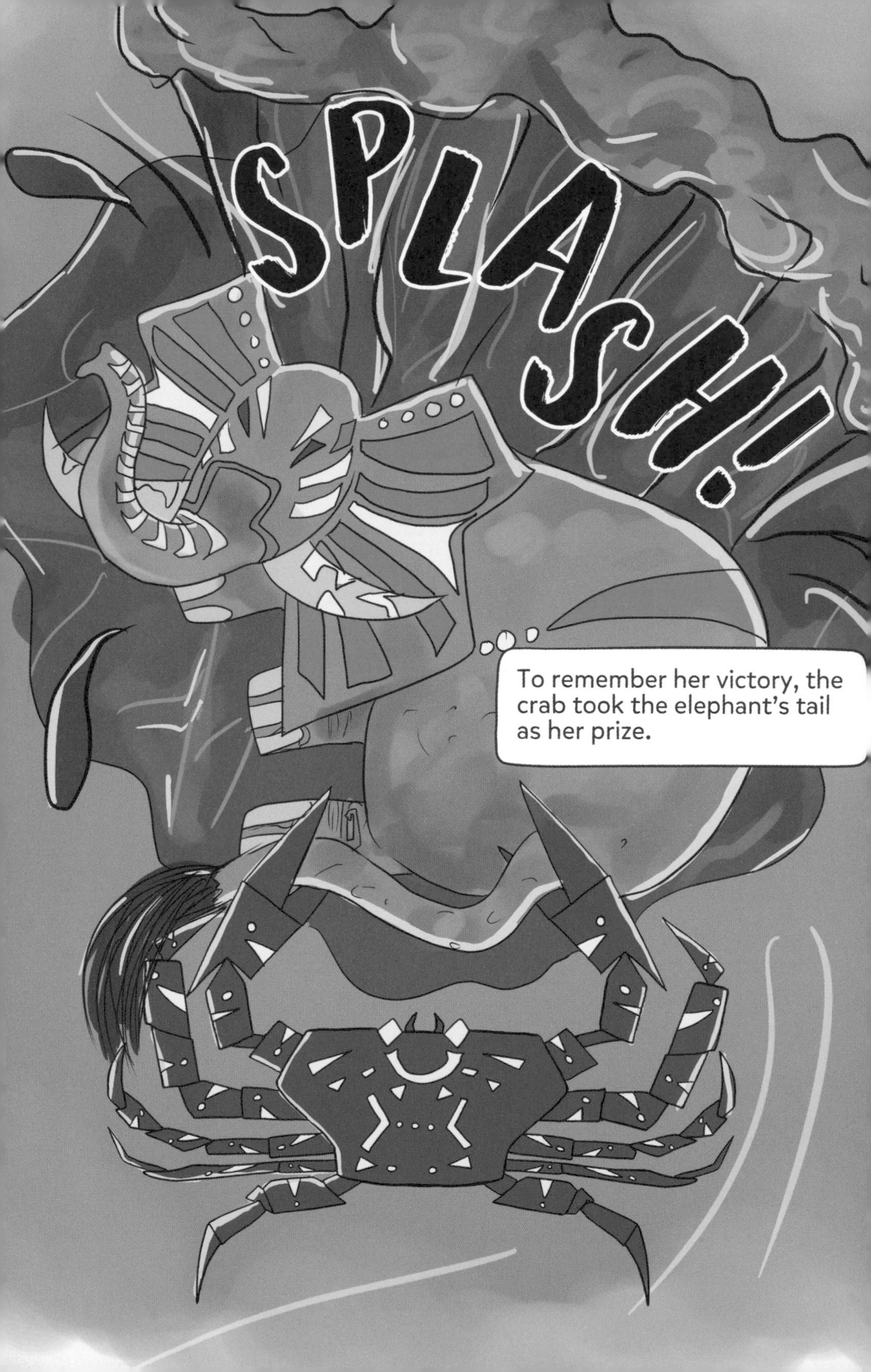
SPLASH!!
To remember her victory, the crab took the elephant's tail as her prize.

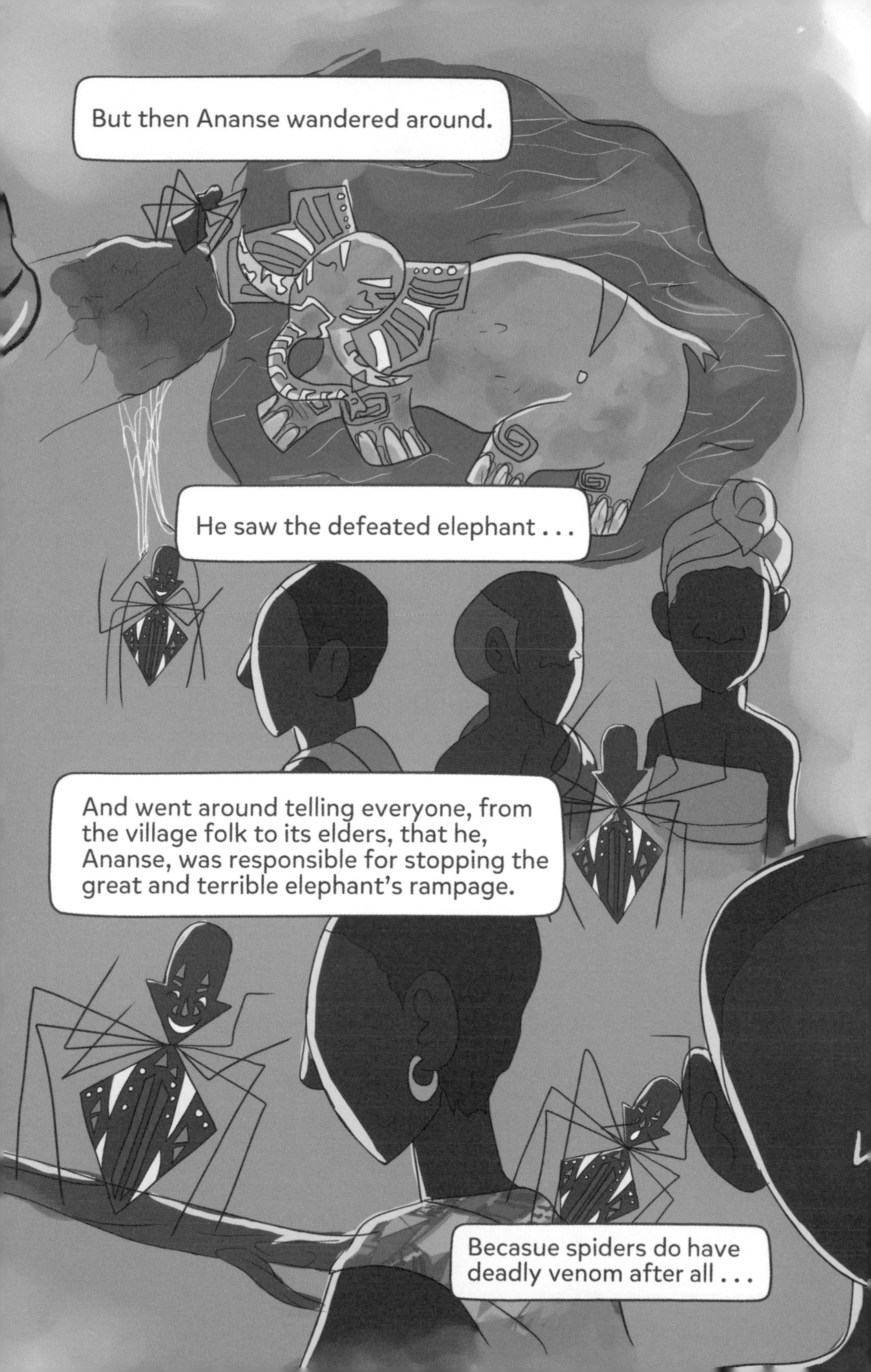
But then Ananse wandered around.
He saw the defeated elephant . . .
And went around telling everyone, from the village folk to its elders, that he, Ananse, was responsible for stopping the great and terrible elephant's rampage.
Becasue spiders do have deadly venom after all . . .

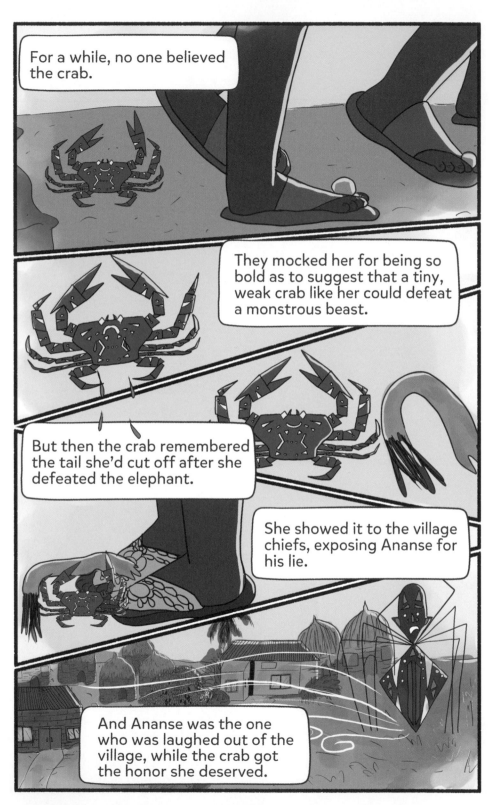

For a while, no one believed the crab.

They mocked her for being so bold as to suggest that a tiny, weak crab like her could defeat a monstrous beast.

But then the crab remembered the tail she'd cut off after she defeated the elephant.

She showed it to the village chiefs, exposing Ananse for his lie.

And Ananse was the one who was laughed out of the village, while the crab got the honor she deserved.

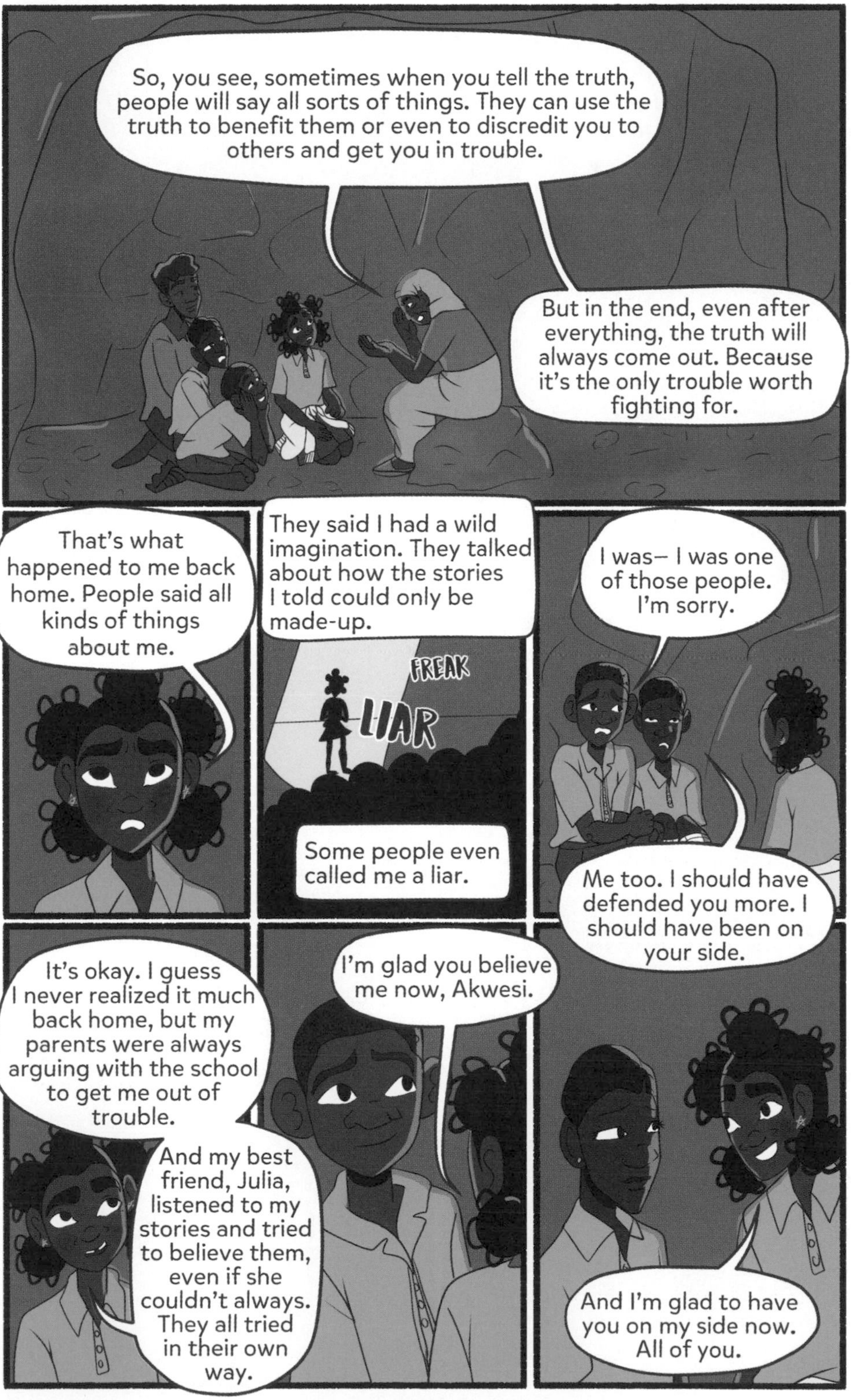
So, you see, sometimes when you tell the truth, people will say all sorts of things. They can use the truth to benefit them or even to discredit you to others and get you in trouble.
But in the end, even after everything, the truth will always come out. Because it's the only trouble worth fighting for.
That's what happened to me back home. People said all kinds of things about me.
They said I had a wild imagination. They talked about how the stories I told could only be made-up.
FREAK
LIAR
Some people even called me a liar.
I was– I was one of those people. I'm sorry.
Me too. I should have defended you more. I should have been on your side.
It's okay. I guess I never realized it much back home, but my parents were always arguing with the school to get me out of trouble.
And my best friend, Julia, listened to my stories and tried to believe them, even if she couldn't always. They all tried in their own way.
I'm glad you believe me now, Akwesi.
And I'm glad to have you on my side now. All of you.

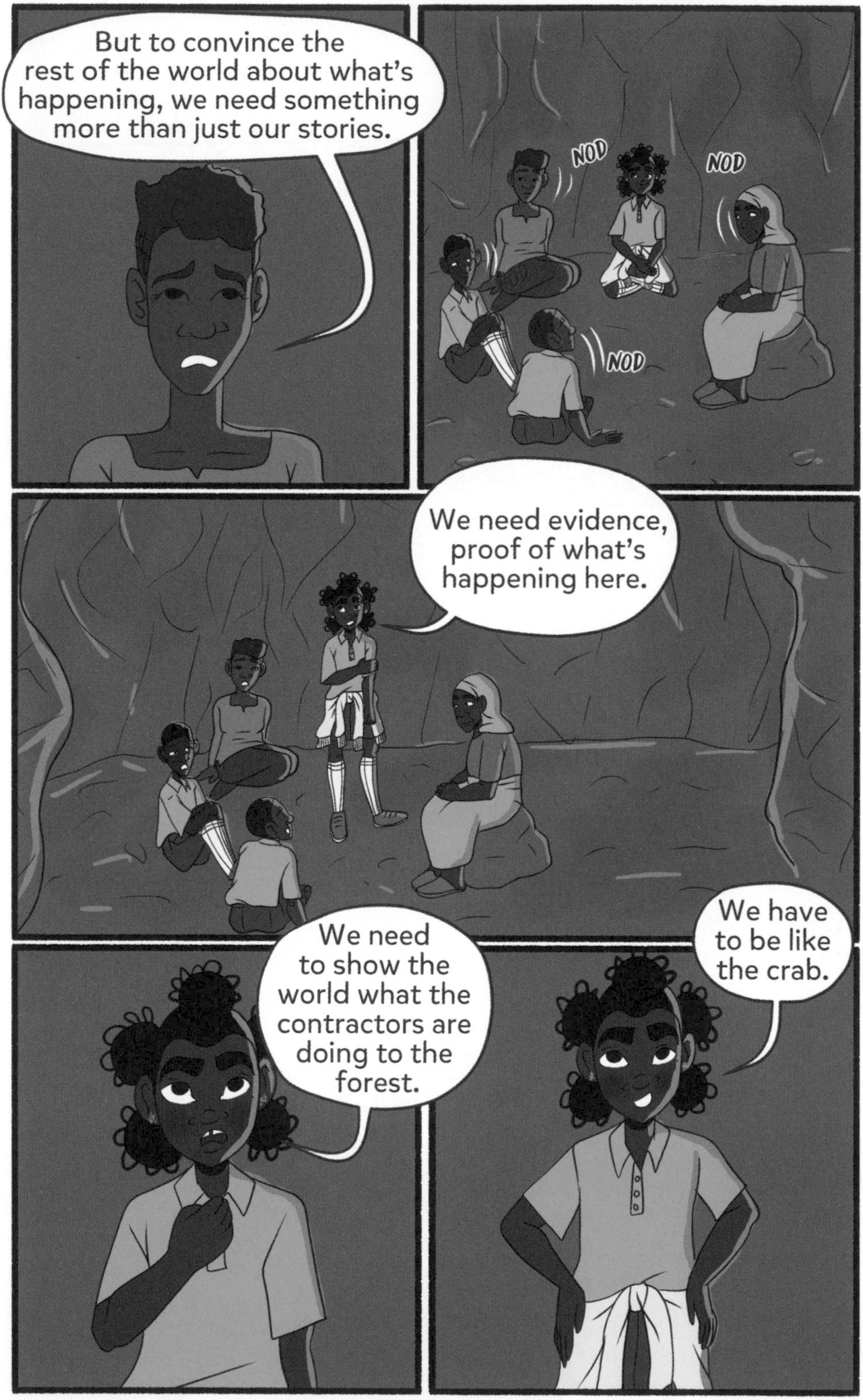

But to convince the rest of the world about what's happening, we need something more than just our stories.
NOD
NOD
NOD
We need evidence, proof of what's happening here.
We need to show the world what the contractors are doing to the forest.
We have to be like the crab.

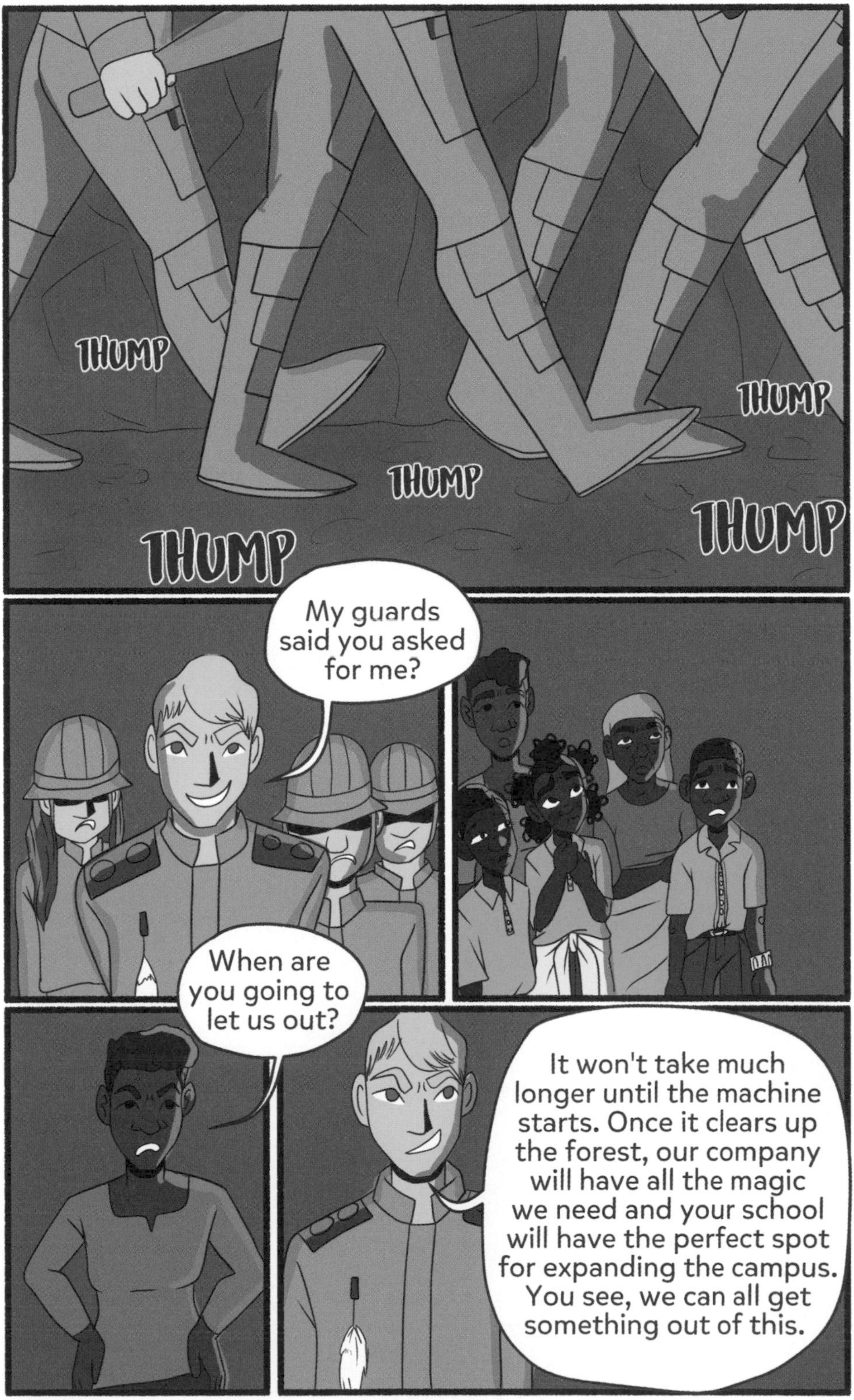
THUMP
THUMP
THUMP
THUMP
THUMP
My guards said you asked for me?
When are you going to let us out?
It won't take much longer until the machine starts. Once it clears up the forest, our company will have all the magic we need and your school will have the perfect spot for expanding the campus. You see, we can all get something out of this.

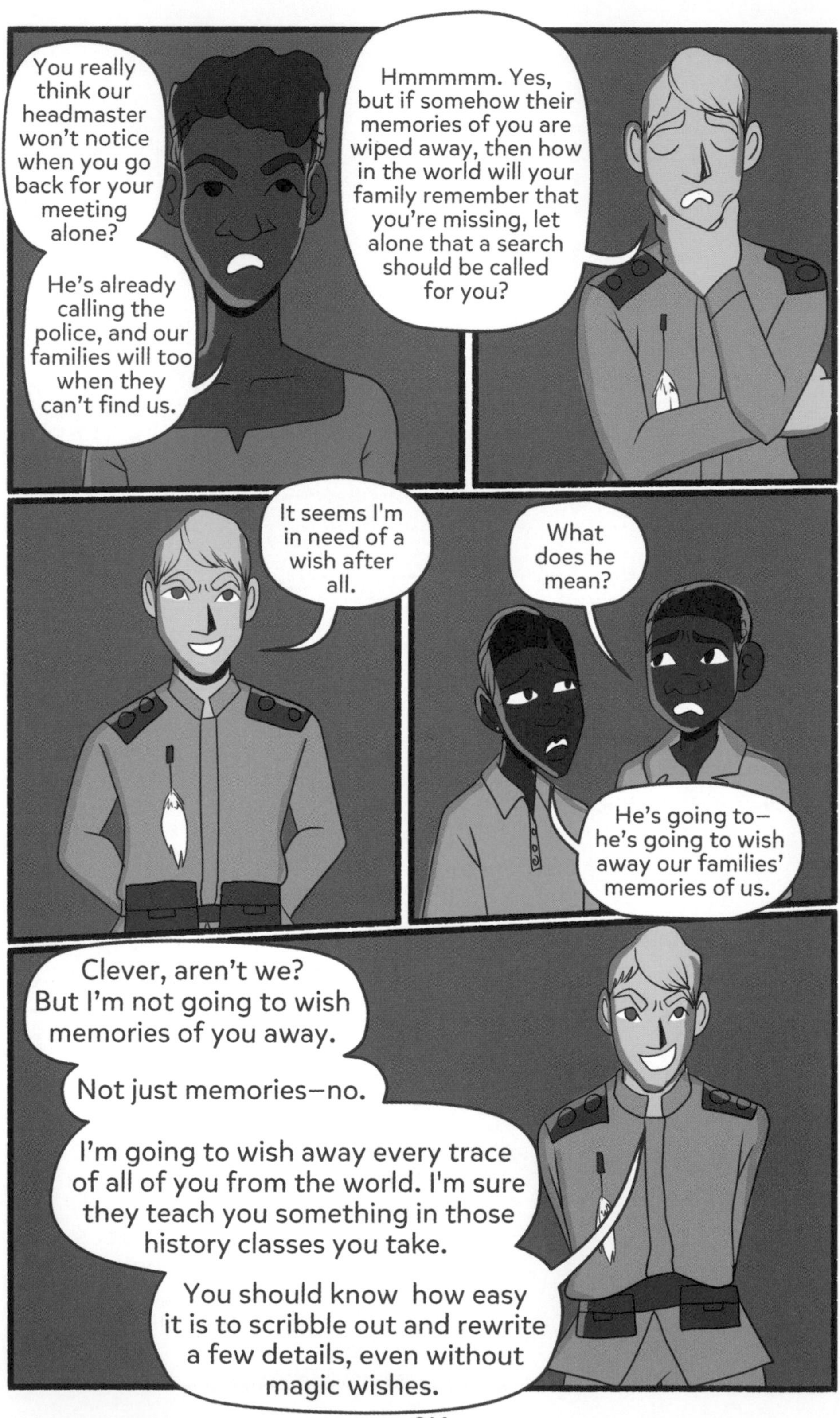
You really think our headmaster won't notice when you go back for your meeting alone?
He's already calling the police, and our families will too when they can't find us.
Hmmmmm. Yes, but if somehow their memories of you are wiped away, then how in the world will your family remember that you're missing, let alone that a search should be called for you?
It seems I'm in need of a wish after all.
What does he mean?
He's going to—he's going to wish away our families' memories of us.
Clever, aren't we? But I'm not going to wish memories of you away.
Not just memories—no.
I'm going to wish away every trace of all of you from the world. I'm sure they teach you something in those history classes you take.
You should know how easy it is to scribble out and rewrite a few details, even without magic wishes.

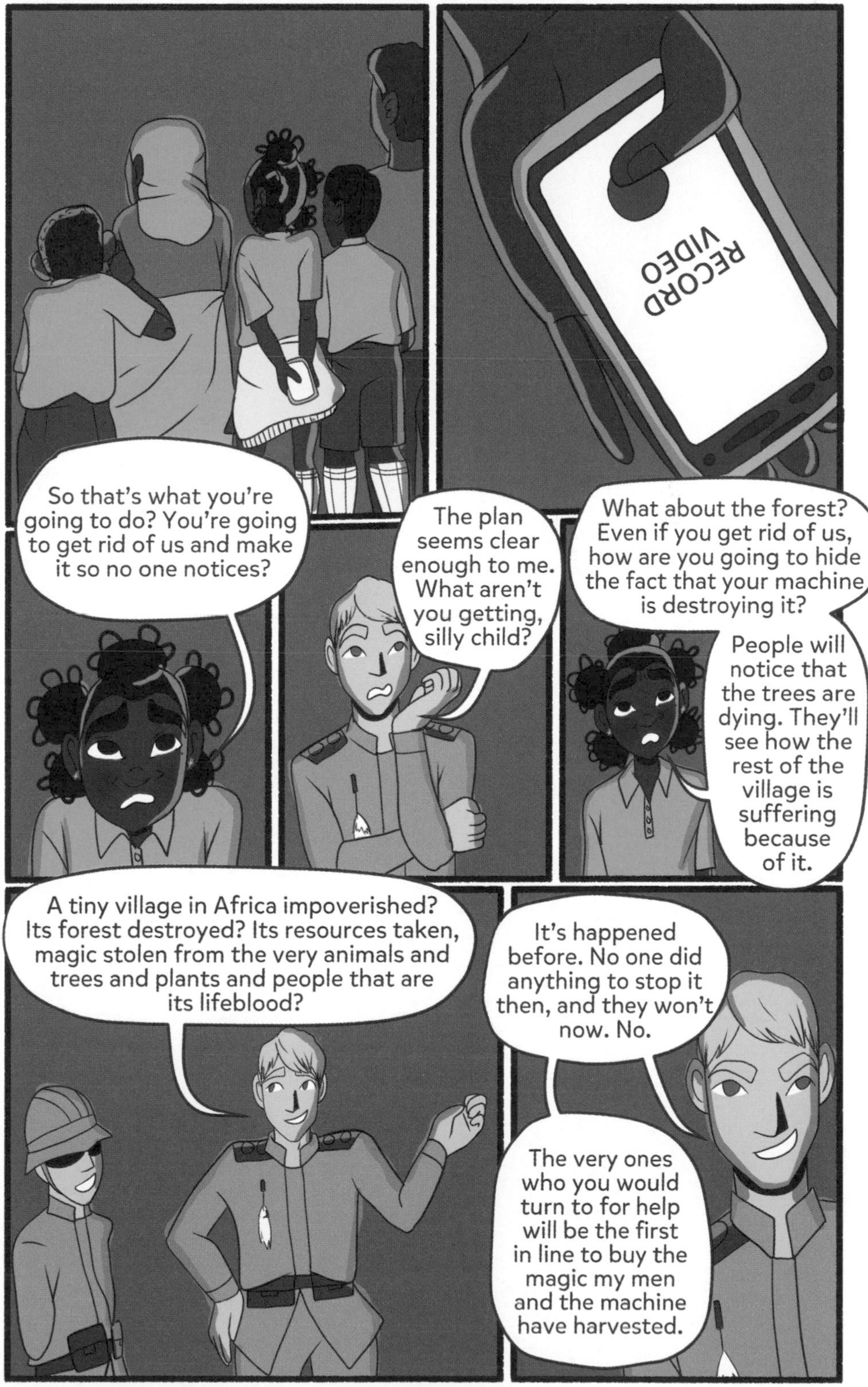
RECORD VIDEO
So that's what you're going to do? You're going to get rid of us and make it so no one notices?
The plan seems clear enough to me. What aren't you getting, silly child?
What about the forest? Even if you get rid of us, how are you going to hide the fact that your machine is destroying it?
People will notice that the trees are dying. They'll see how the rest of the village is suffering because of it.
A tiny village in Africa impoverished? Its forest destroyed? Its resources taken, magic stolen from the very animals and trees and plants and people that are its lifeblood?
It's happened before. No one did anything to stop it then, and they won't now. No.
The very ones who you would turn to for help will be the first in line to buy the magic my men and the machine have harvested.

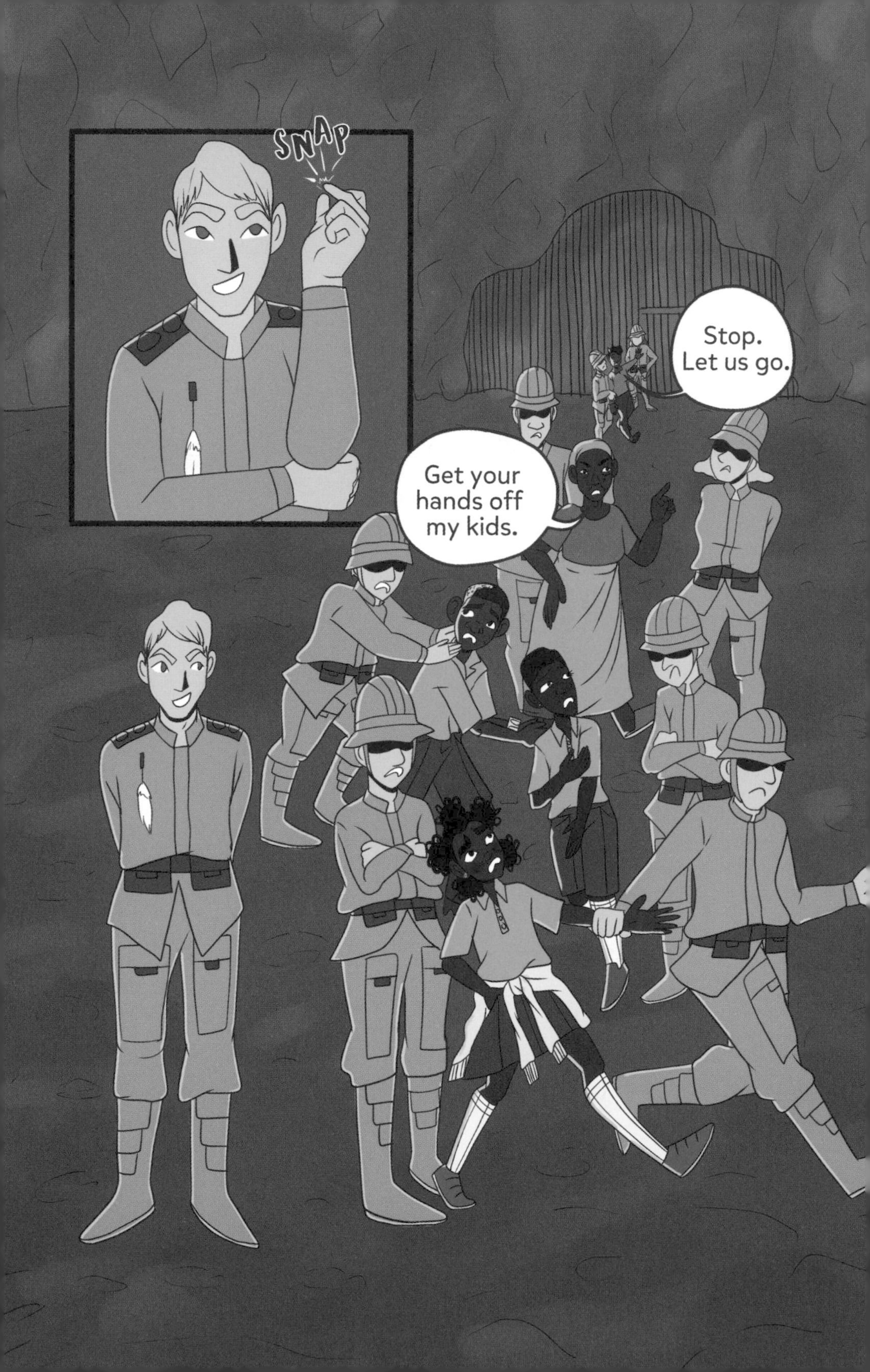
SNAP
Stop. Let us go.
Get your hands off my kids.

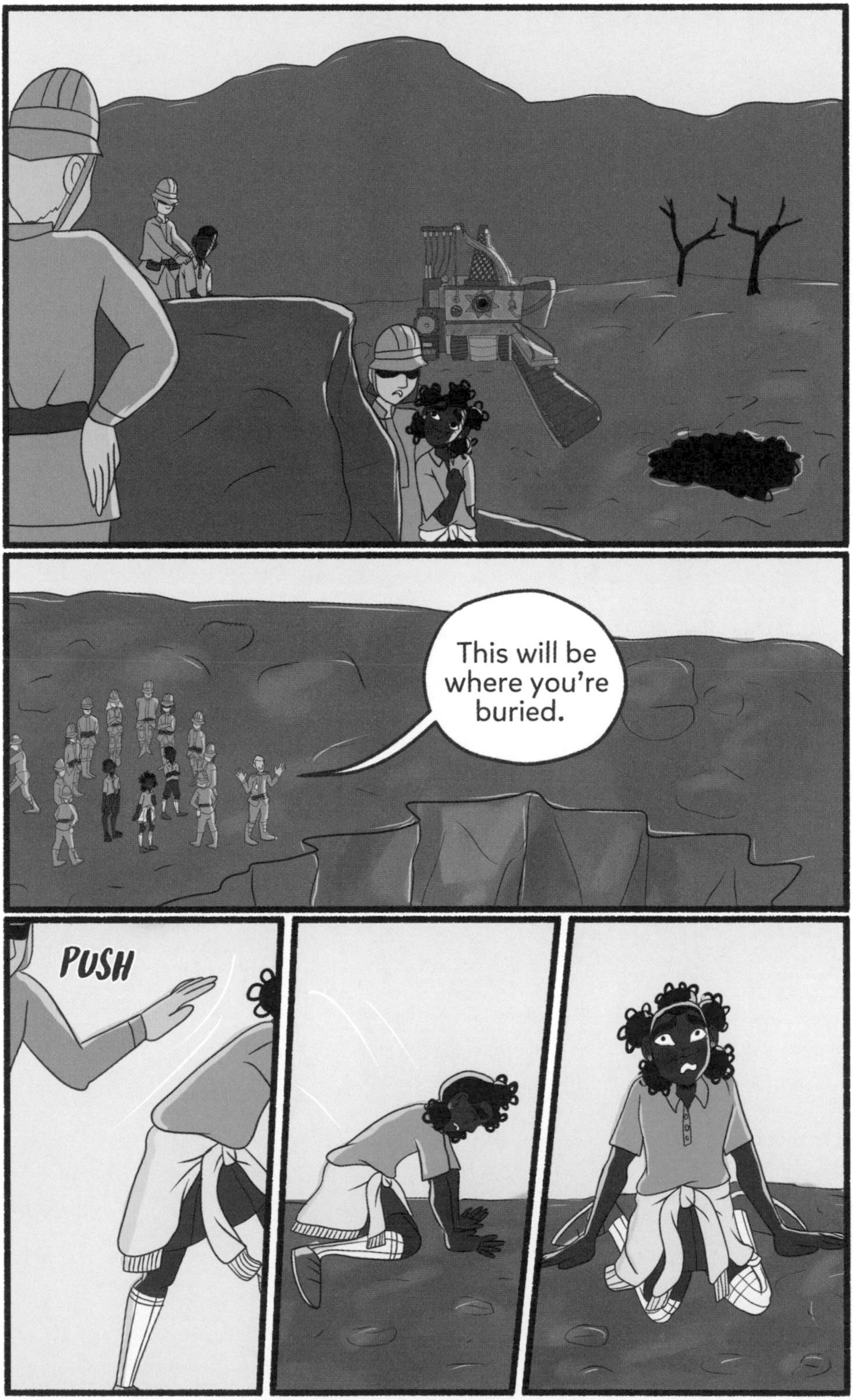
This will be where you're buried.
PUSH

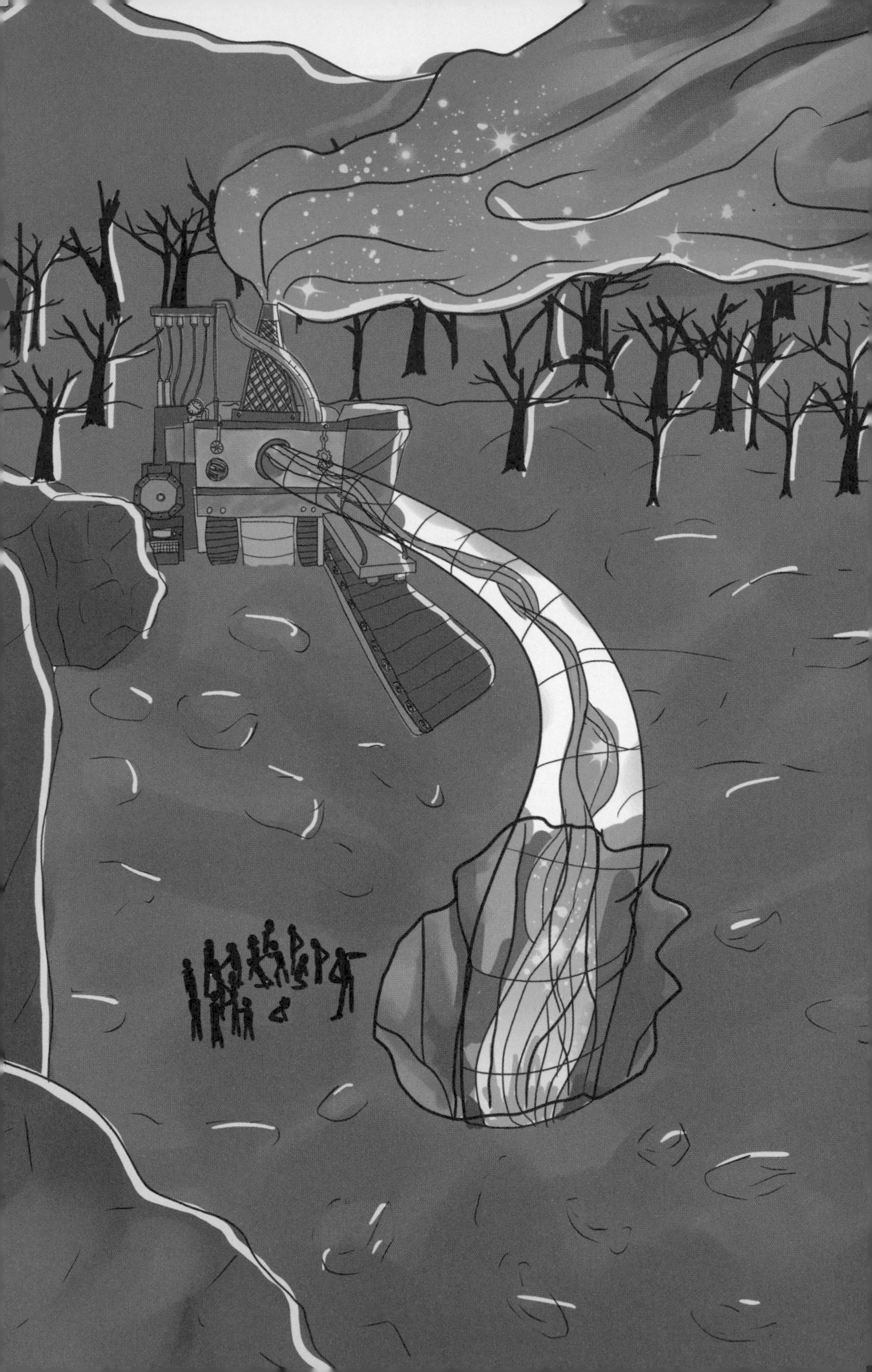

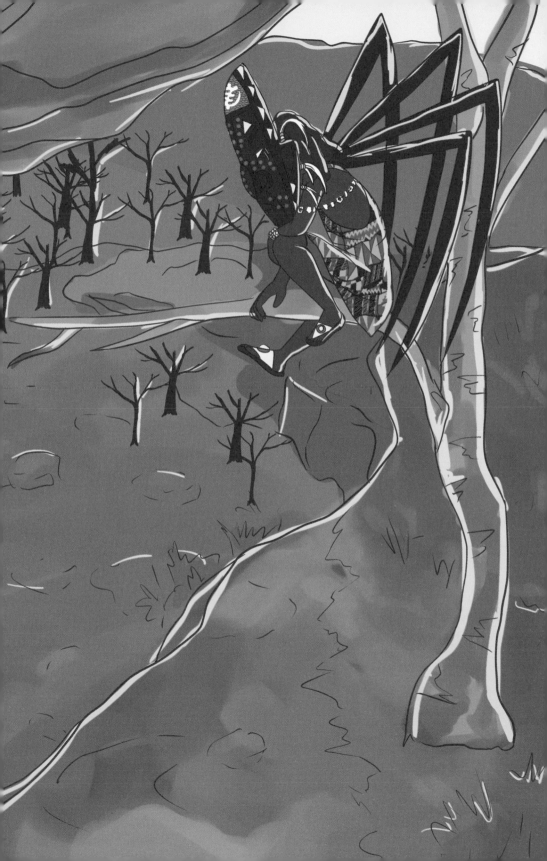

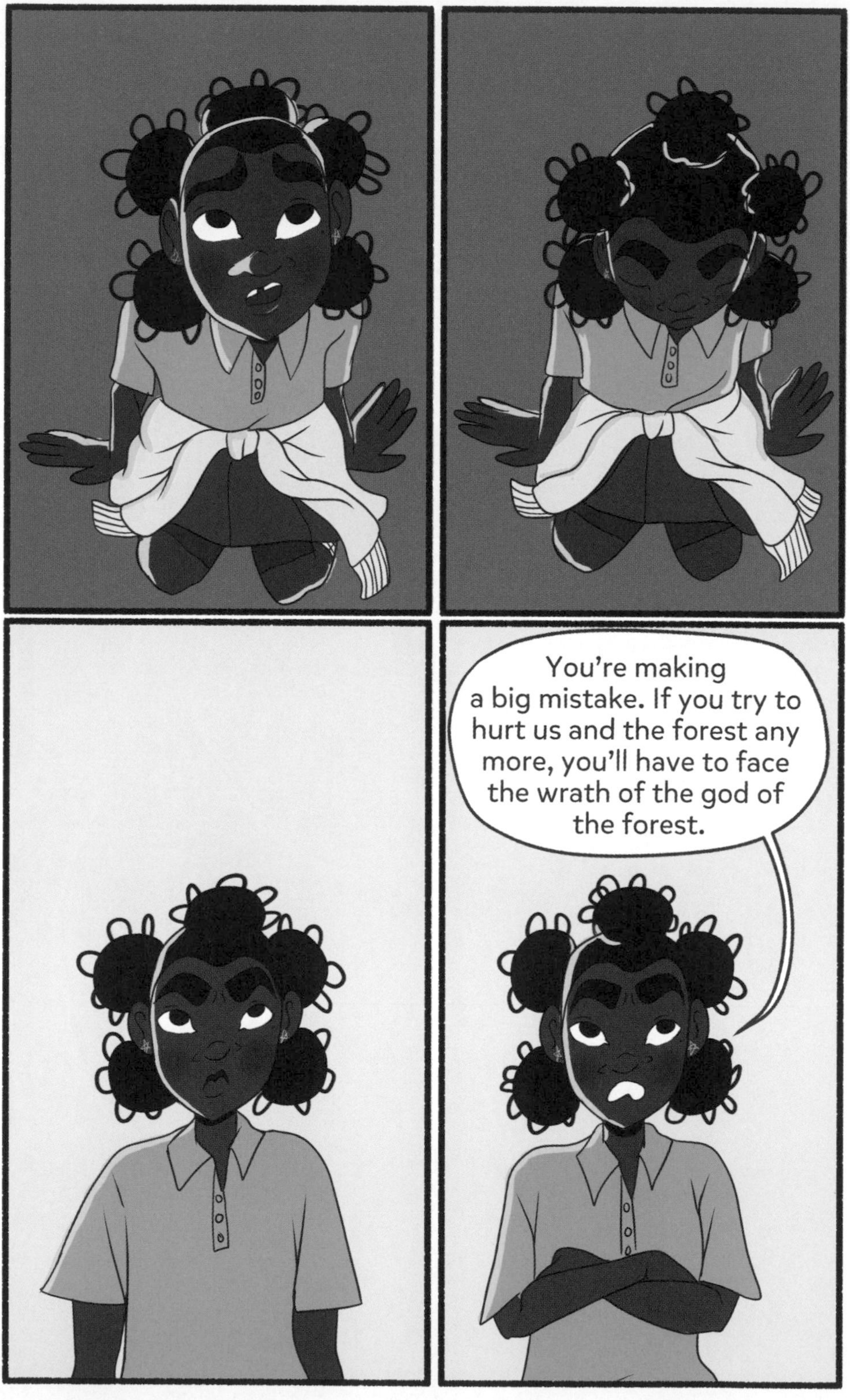
You're making a big mistake. If you try to hurt us and the forest any more, you'll have to face the wrath of the god of the forest.

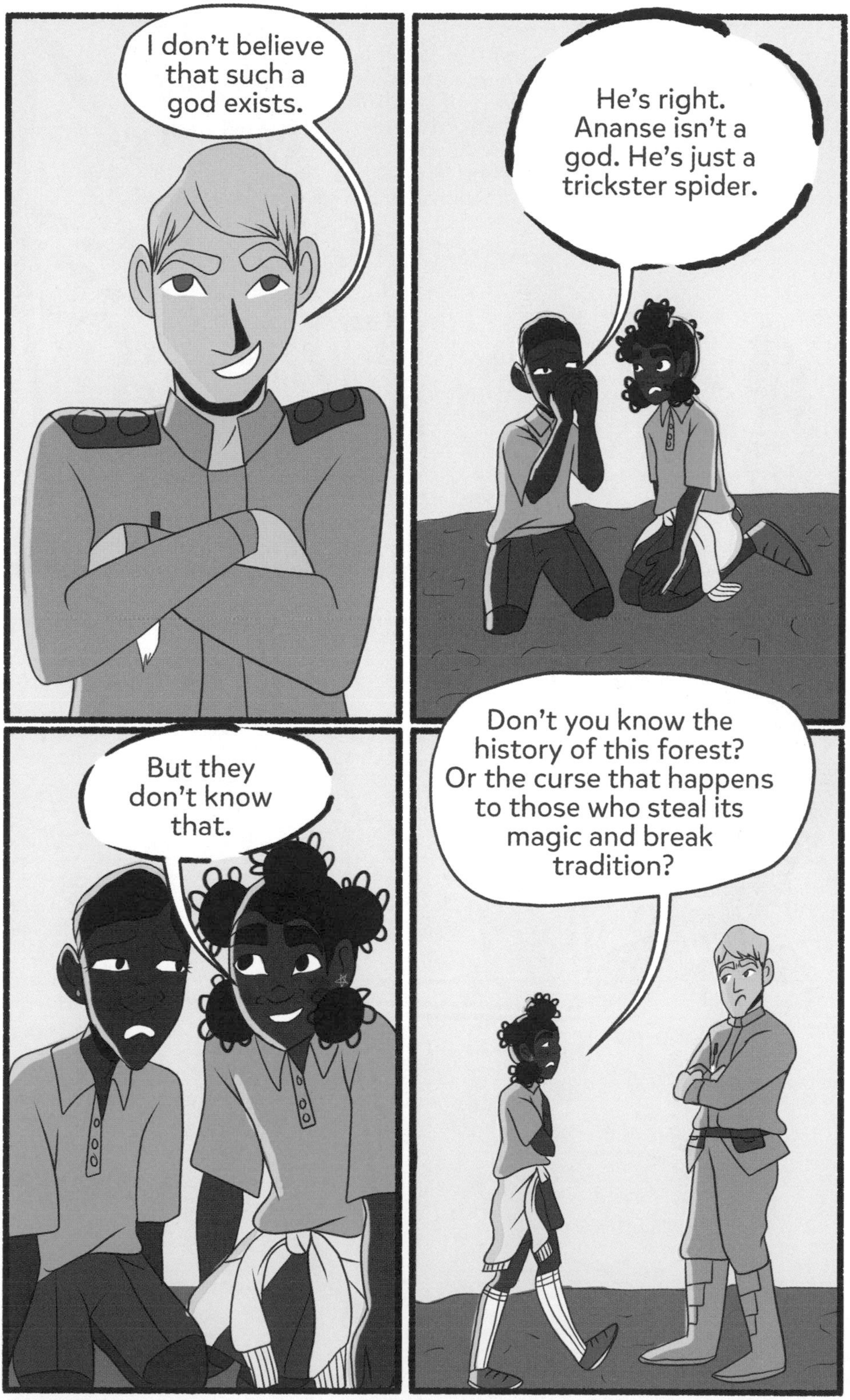
I don't believe that such a god exists.
He's right. Ananse isn't a god. He's just a trickster spider.
But they don't know that.
Don't you know the history of this forest? Or the curse that happens to those who steal its magic and break tradition?

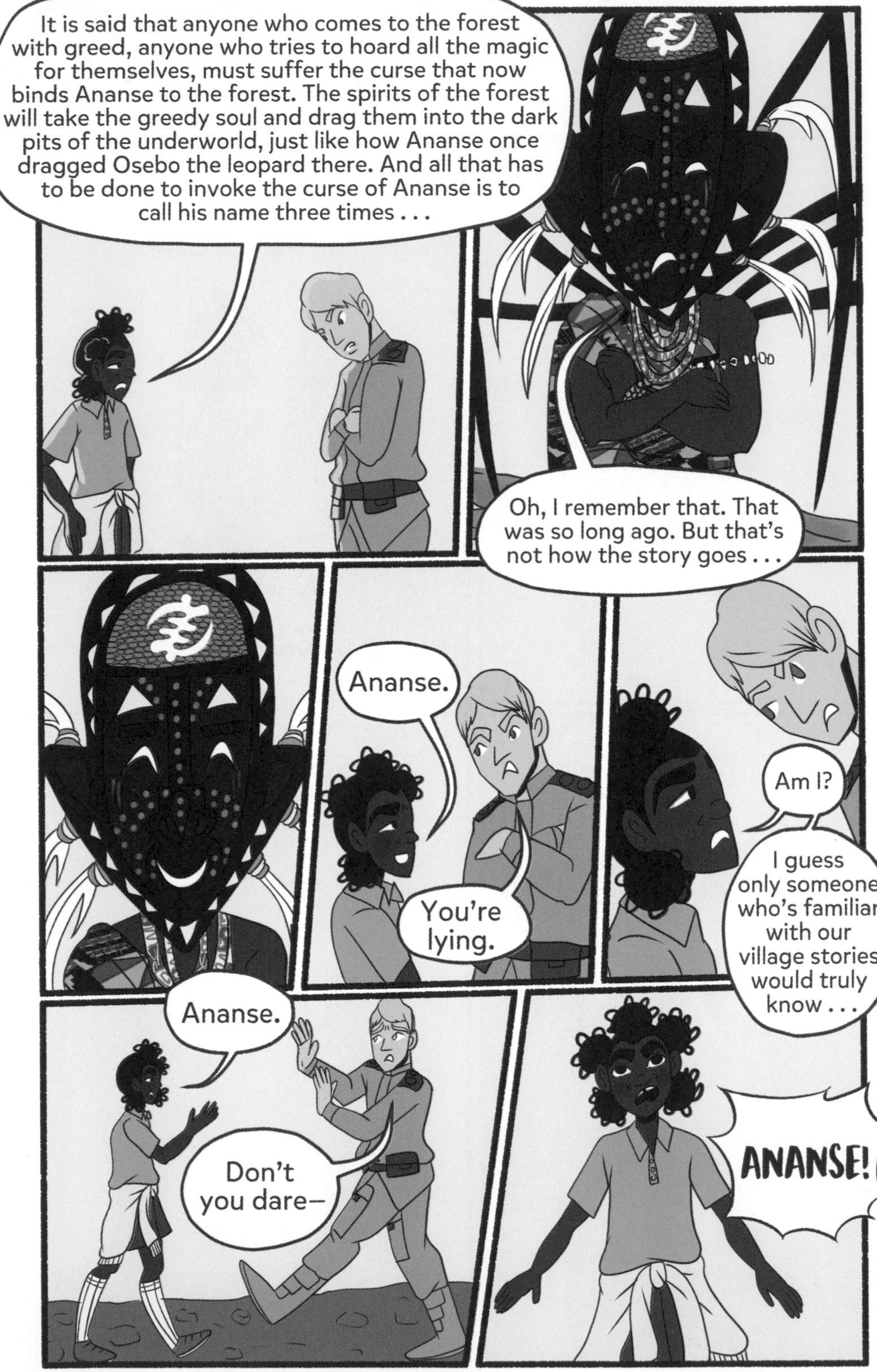
It is said that anyone who comes to the forest with greed, anyone who tries to hoard all the magic for themselves, must suffer the curse that now binds Ananse to the forest. The spirits of the forest will take the greedy soul and drag them into the dark pits of the underworld, just like how Ananse once dragged Osebo the leopard there. And all that has to be done to invoke the curse of Ananse is to call his name three times . . .
Oh, I remember that. That was so long ago. But that's not how the story goes . . .
Ananse.
You're lying.
Am I?
I guess only someone who's familiar with our village stories would truly know . . .
Ananse.
Don't you dare–
ANANSE!

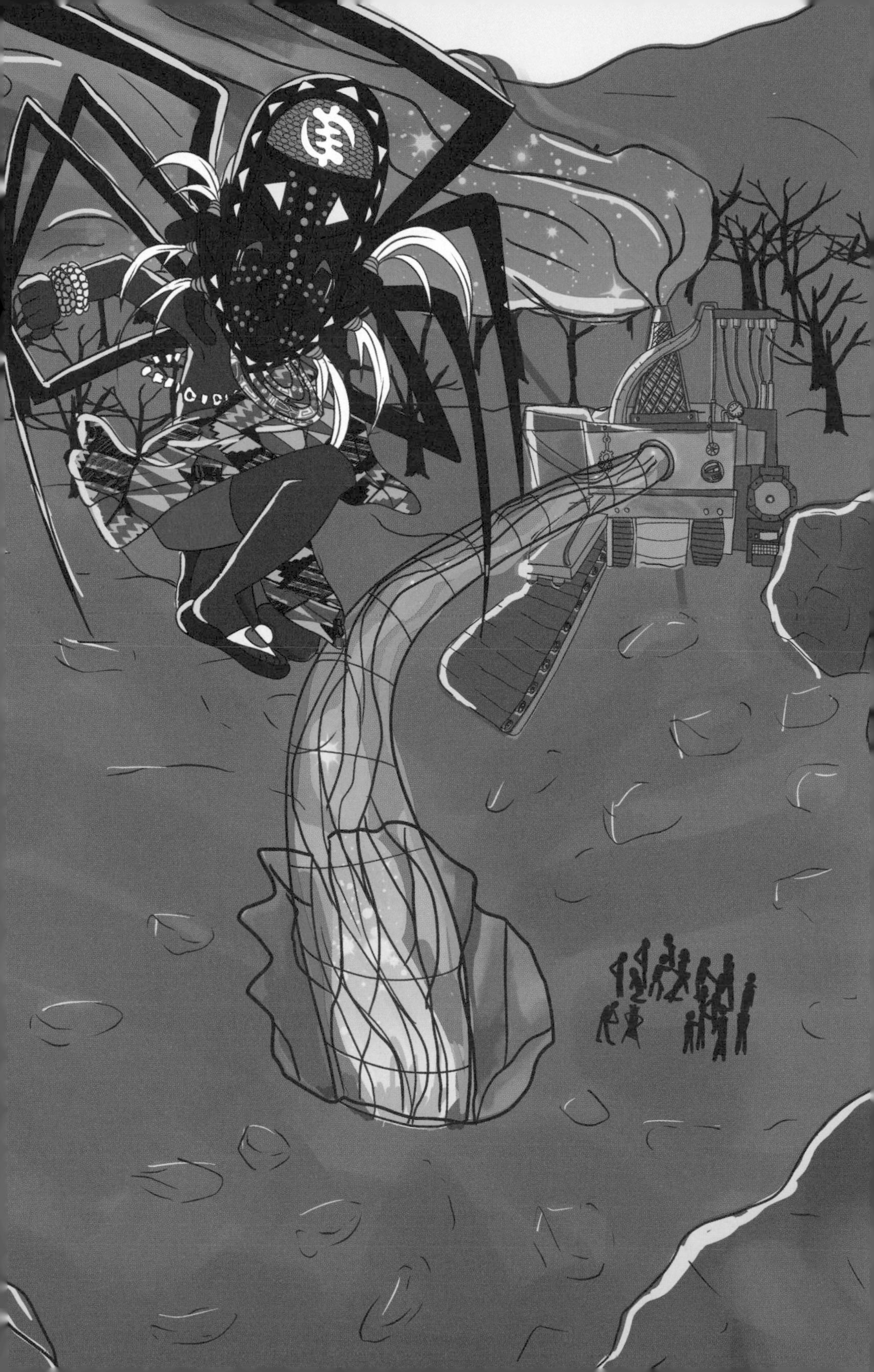

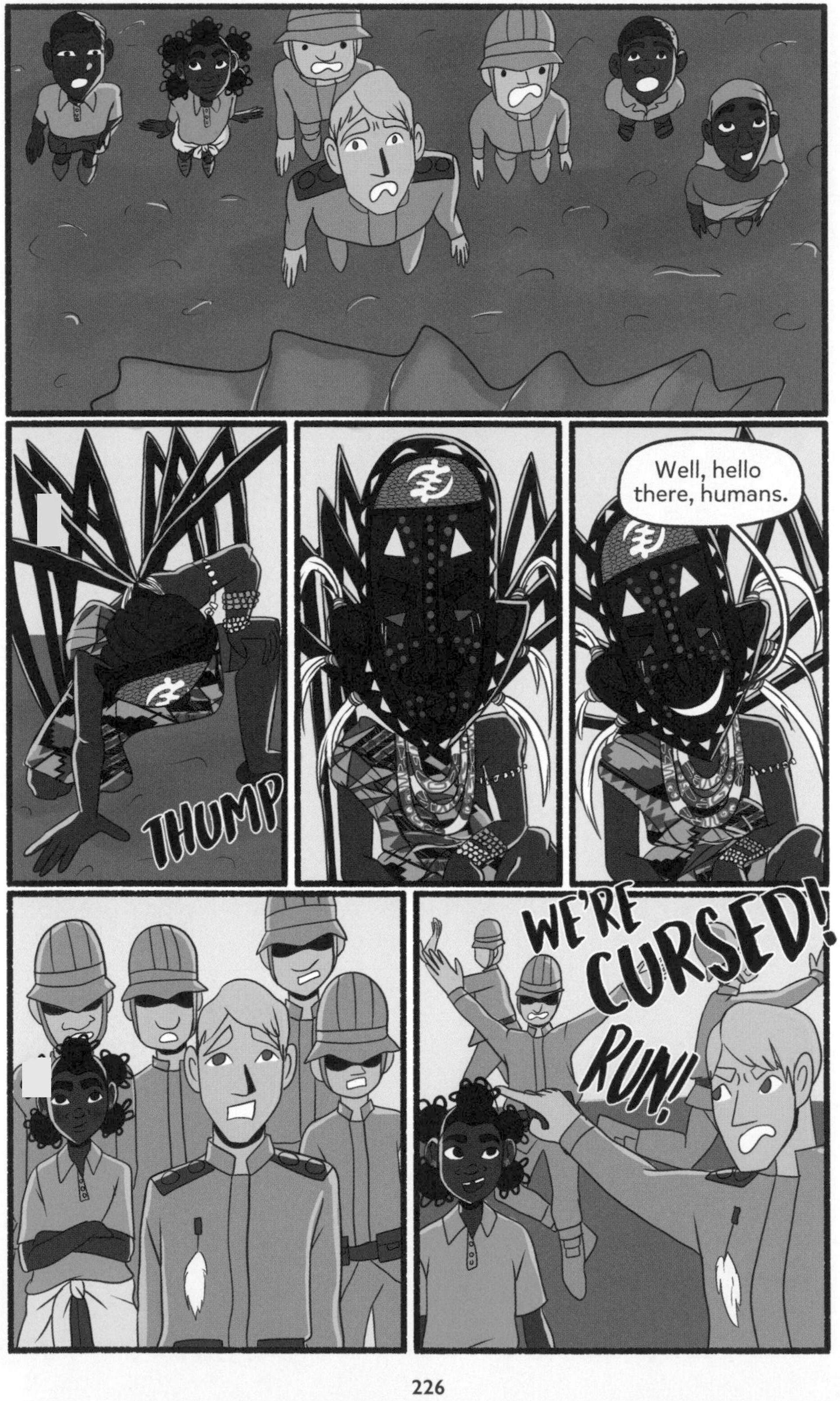
THUMP
Well, hello there, humans.
WE'RE CURSED!
RUN!

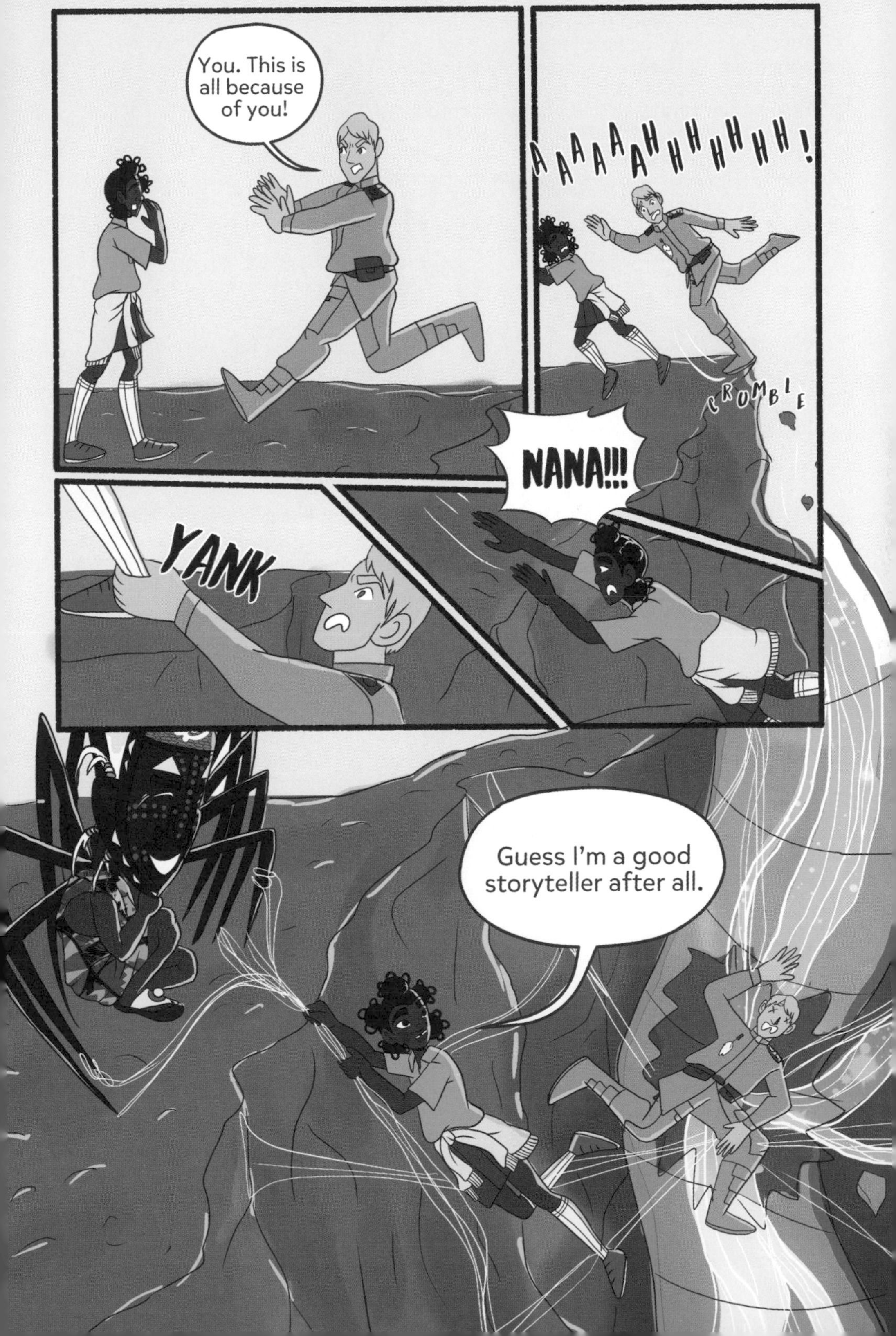
You. This is all because of you!
AAAAAHHHHHHH!
CRUMBLE
NANA!!!
YANK
Guess I'm a good storyteller after all.

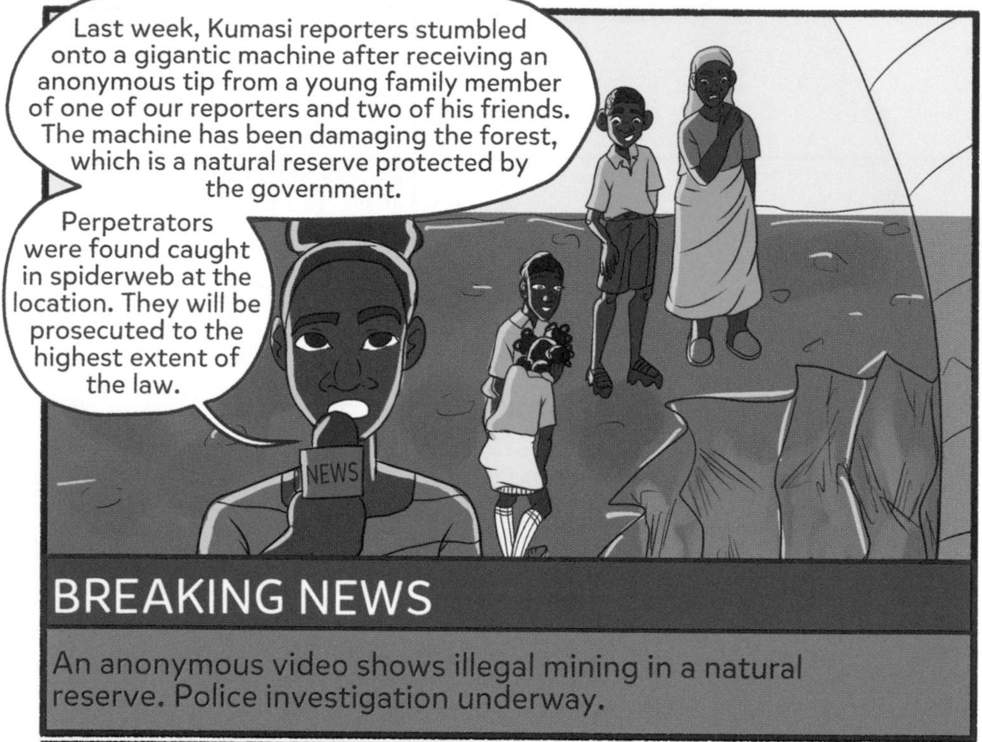
Last week, Kumasi reporters stumbled onto a gigantic machine after receiving an anonymous tip from a young family member of one of our reporters and two of his friends. The machine has been damaging the forest, which is a natural reserve protected by the government.
Perpetrators were found caught in spiderweb at the location. They will be prosecuted to the highest extent of the law.
NEWS
BREAKING NEWS
An anonymous video shows illegal mining in a natural reserve. Police investigation underway.

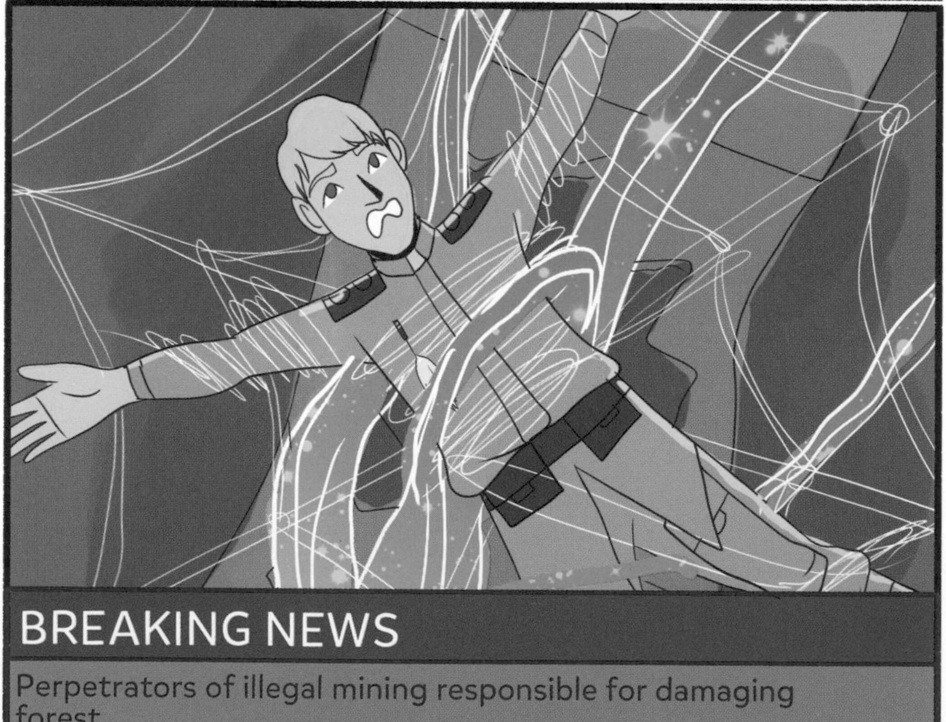
BREAKING NEWS
Perpetrators of illegal mining responsible for damaging forest.

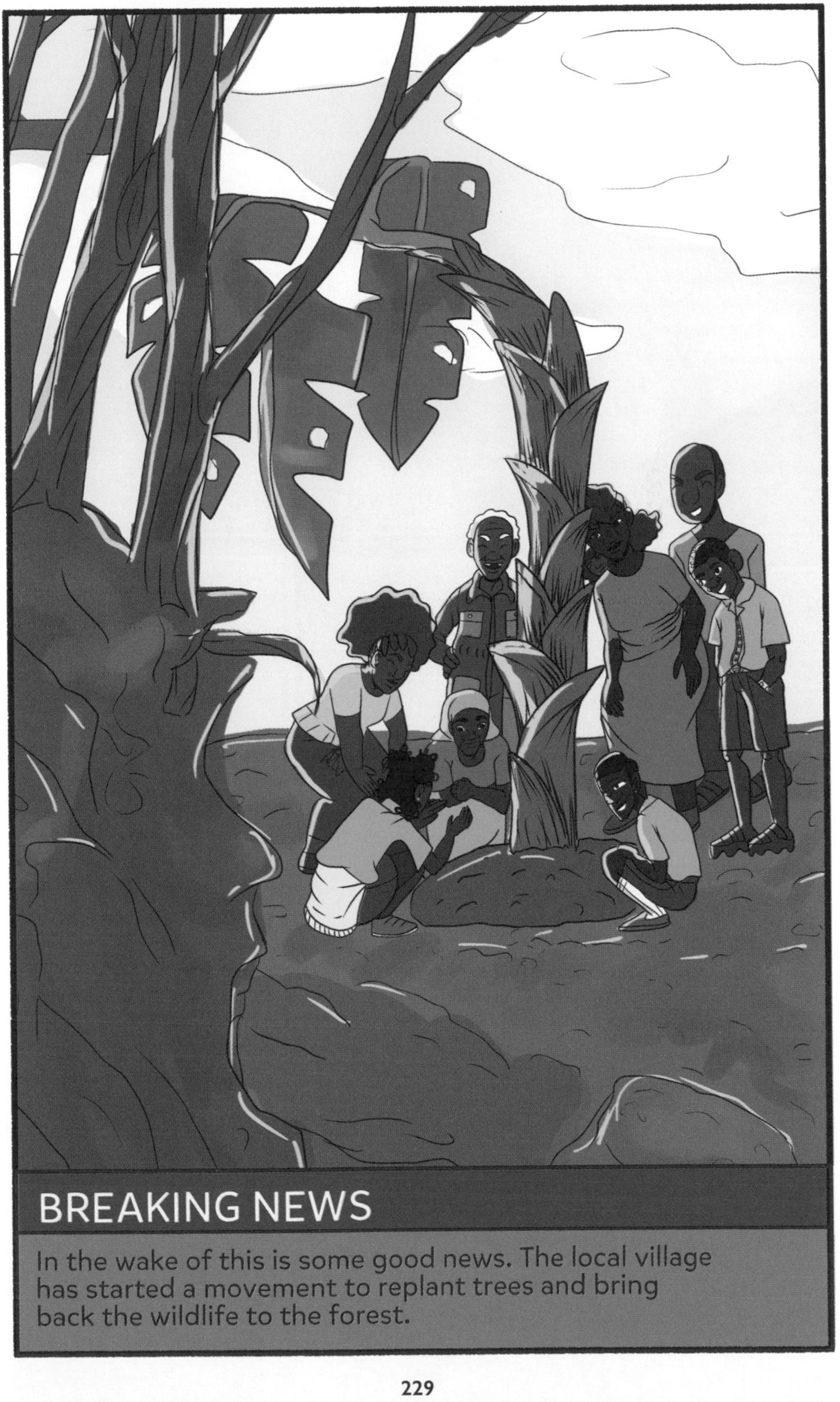
BREAKING NEWS
In the wake of this is some good news. The local village has started a movement to replant trees and bring back the wildlife to the forest.

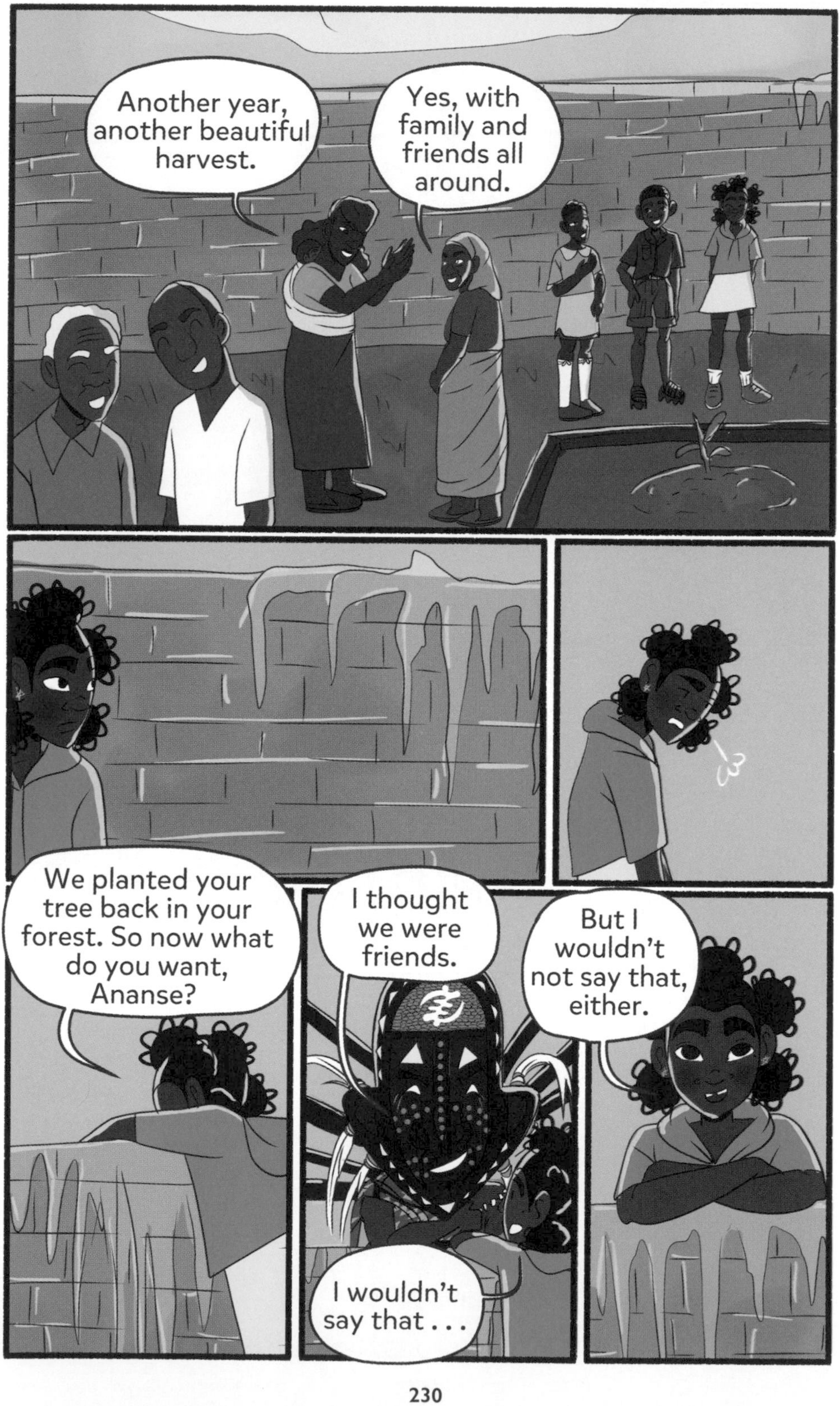
Another year, another beautiful harvest.
Yes, with family and friends all around.
We planted your tree back in your forest. So now what do you want, Ananse?
I thought we were friends.
I wouldn't say that . . .
But I wouldn't not say that, either.

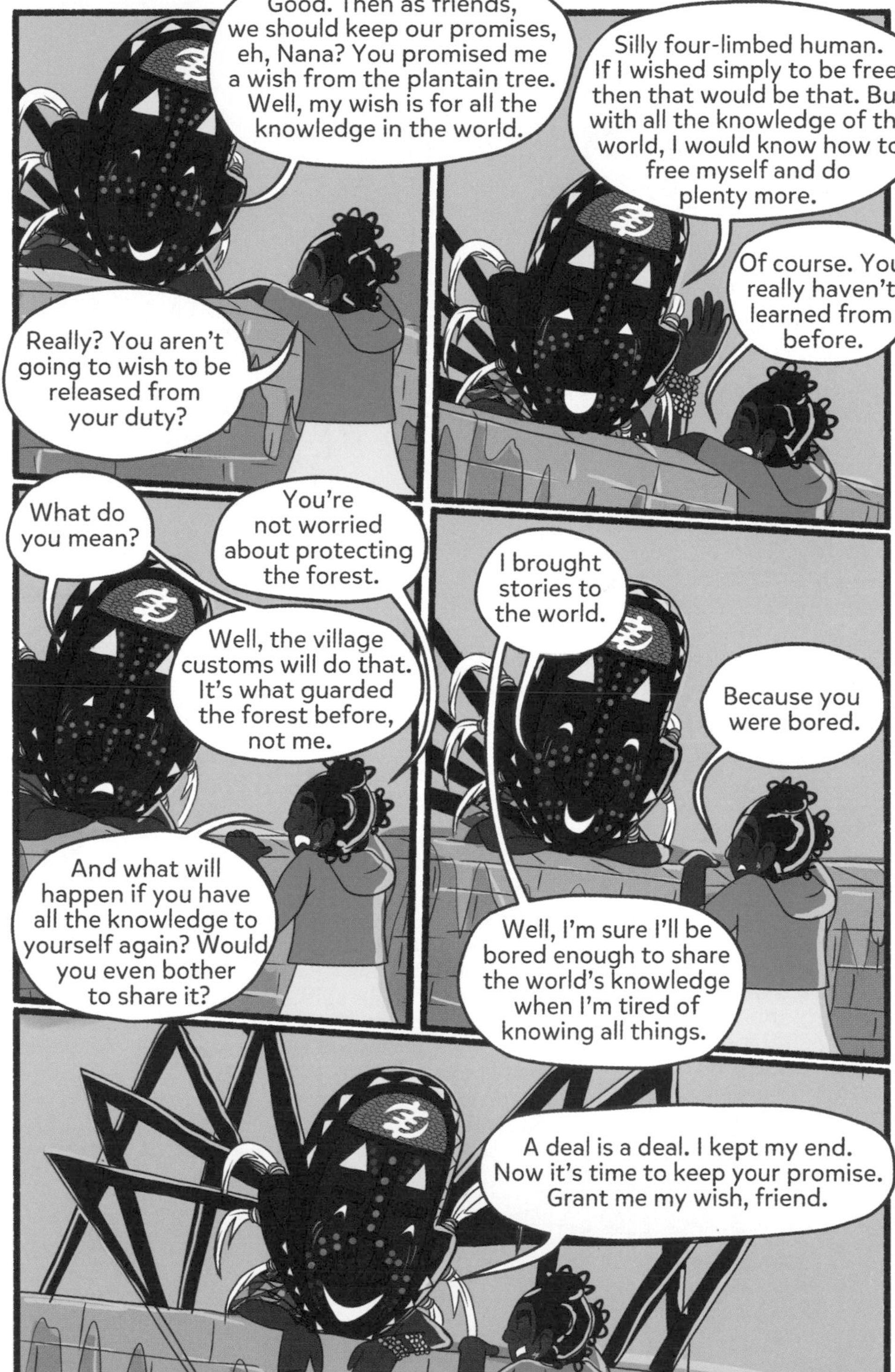
Good. Then as friends, we should keep our promises, eh, Nana? You promised me a wish from the plantain tree. Well, my wish is for all the knowledge in the world.
Really? You aren't going to wish to be released from your duty?
Silly four-limbed human. If I wished simply to be free, then that would be that. But with all the knowledge of the world, I would know how to free myself and do plenty more.
Of course. You really haven't learned from before.
What do you mean?
You're not worried about protecting the forest.
Well, the village customs will do that. It's what guarded the forest before, not me.
And what will happen if you have all the knowledge to yourself again? Would you even bother to share it?
I brought stories to the world.
Because you were bored.
Well, I'm sure I'll be bored enough to share the world's knowledge when I'm tired of knowing all things.
A deal is a deal. I kept my end. Now it's time to keep your promise. Grant me my wish, friend.
. . . Fine.

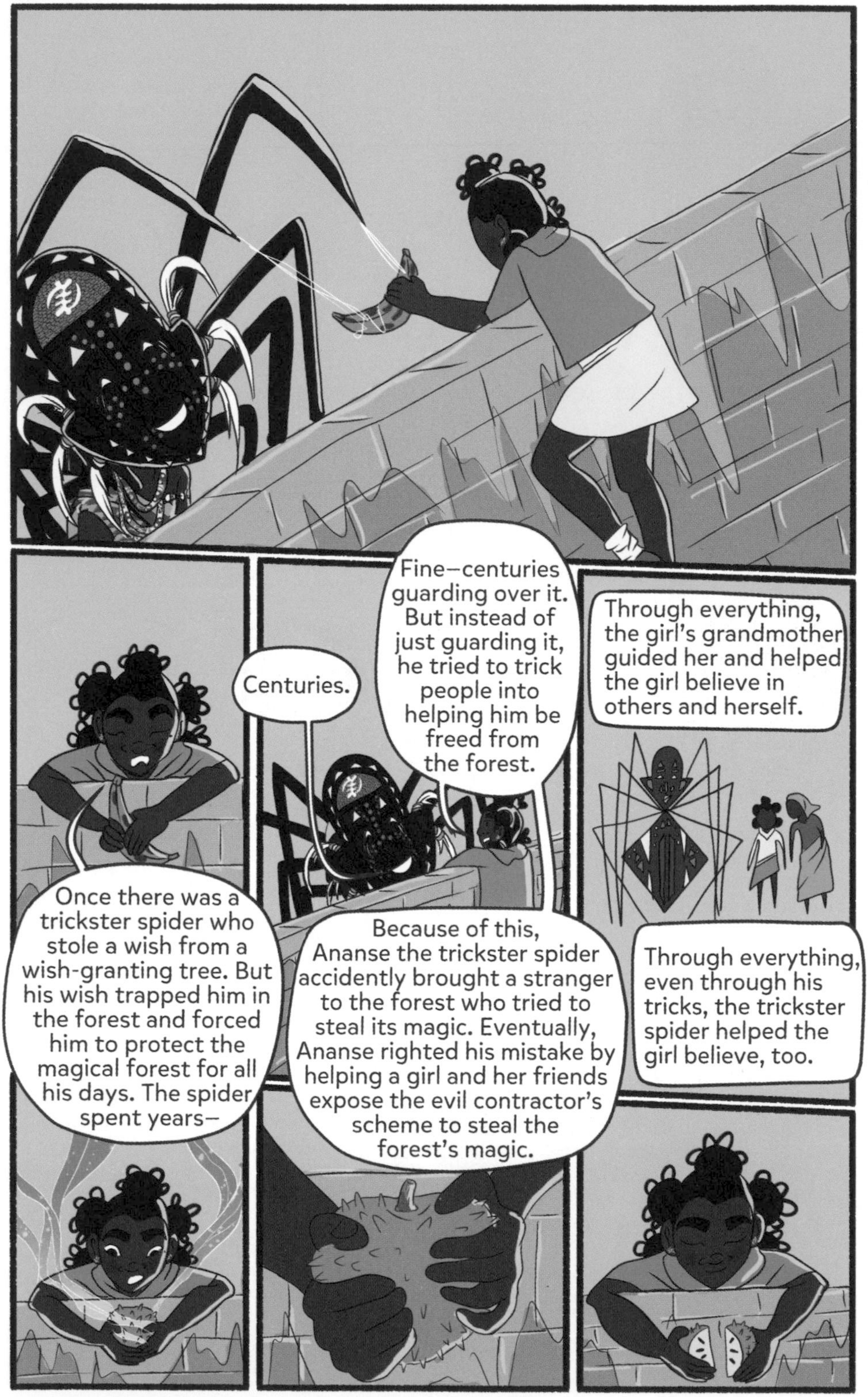
Centuries.
Fine—centuries guarding over it. But instead of just guarding it, he tried to trick people into helping him be freed from the forest.
Through everything, the girl's grandmother guided her and helped the girl believe in others and herself.
Once there was a trickster spider who stole a wish from a wish-granting tree. But his wish trapped him in the forest and forced him to protect the magical forest for all his days. The spider spent years—
Because of this, Ananse the trickster spider accidently brought a stranger to the forest who tried to steal its magic. Eventually, Ananse righted his mistake by helping a girl and her friends expose the evil contractor's scheme to steal the forest's magic.
Through everything, even through his tricks, the trickster spider helped the girl believe, too.

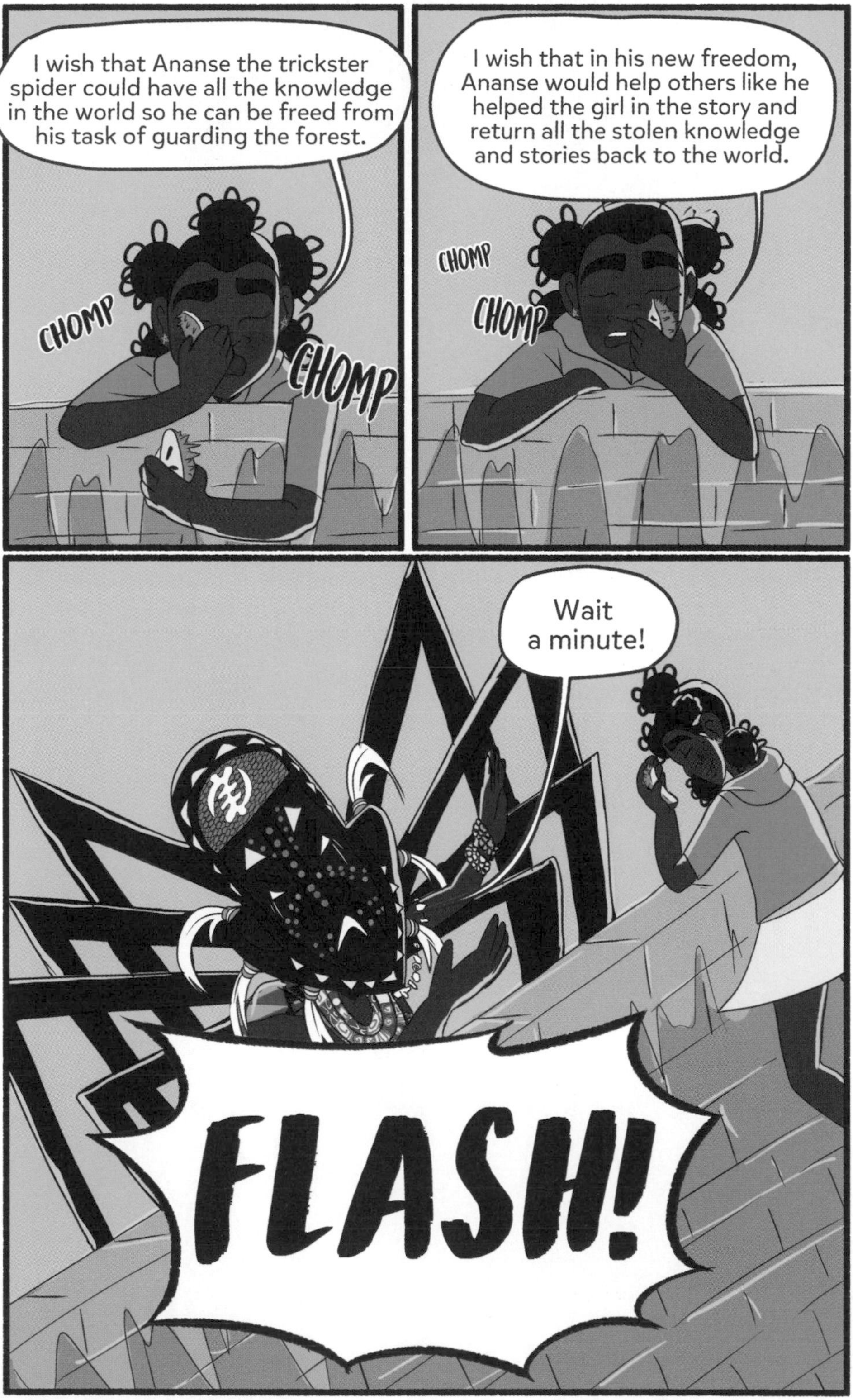
I wish that Ananse the trickster spider could have all the knowledge in the world so he can be freed from his task of guarding the forest.
CHOMP
CHOMP
I wish that in his new freedom, Ananse would help others like he helped the girl in the story and return all the stolen knowledge and stories back to the world.
CHOMP
CHOMP
Wait a minute!
FLASH!

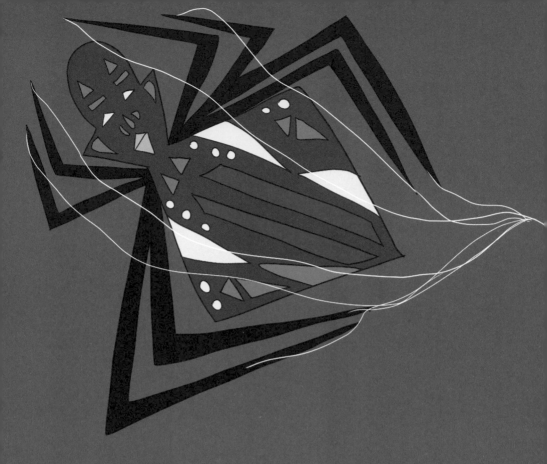

Chapter 10

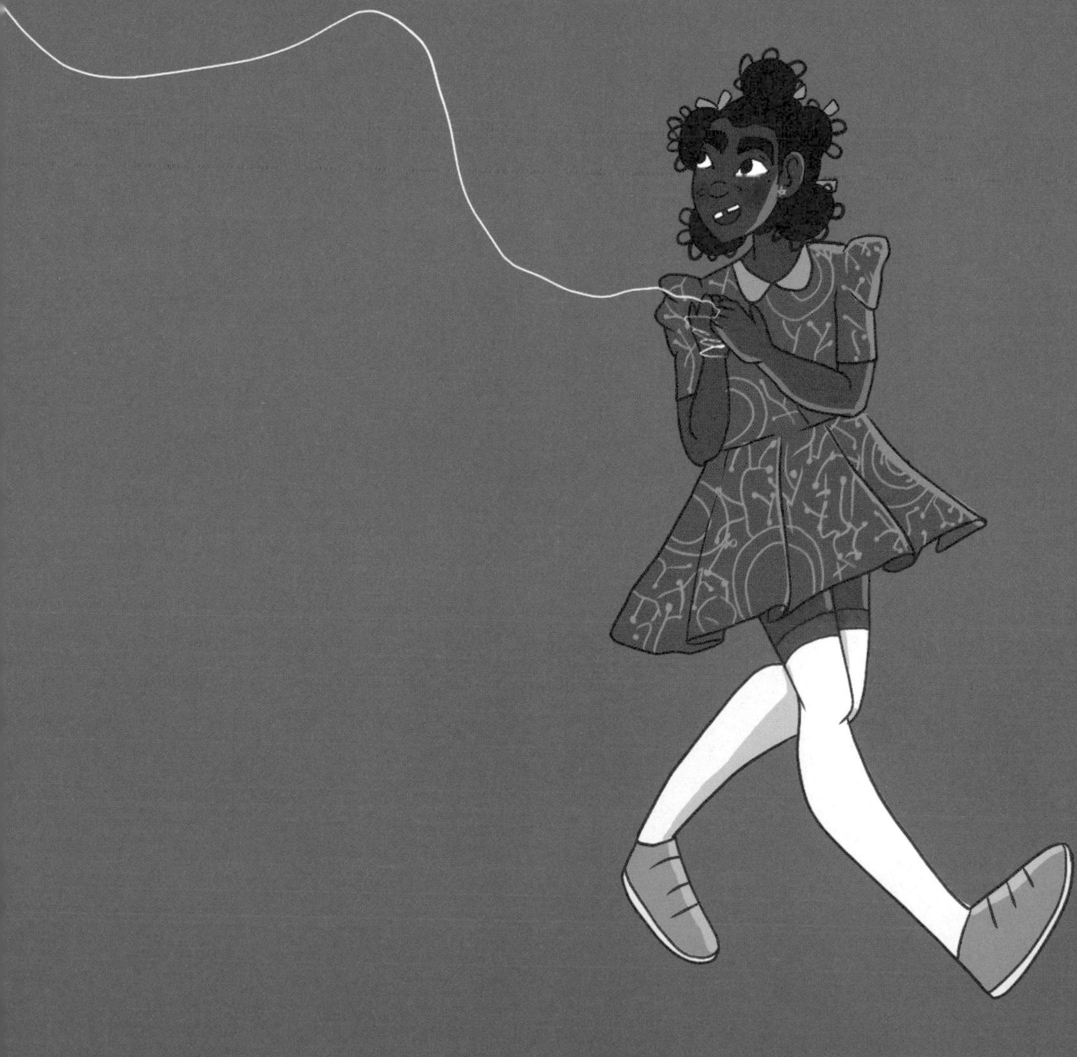

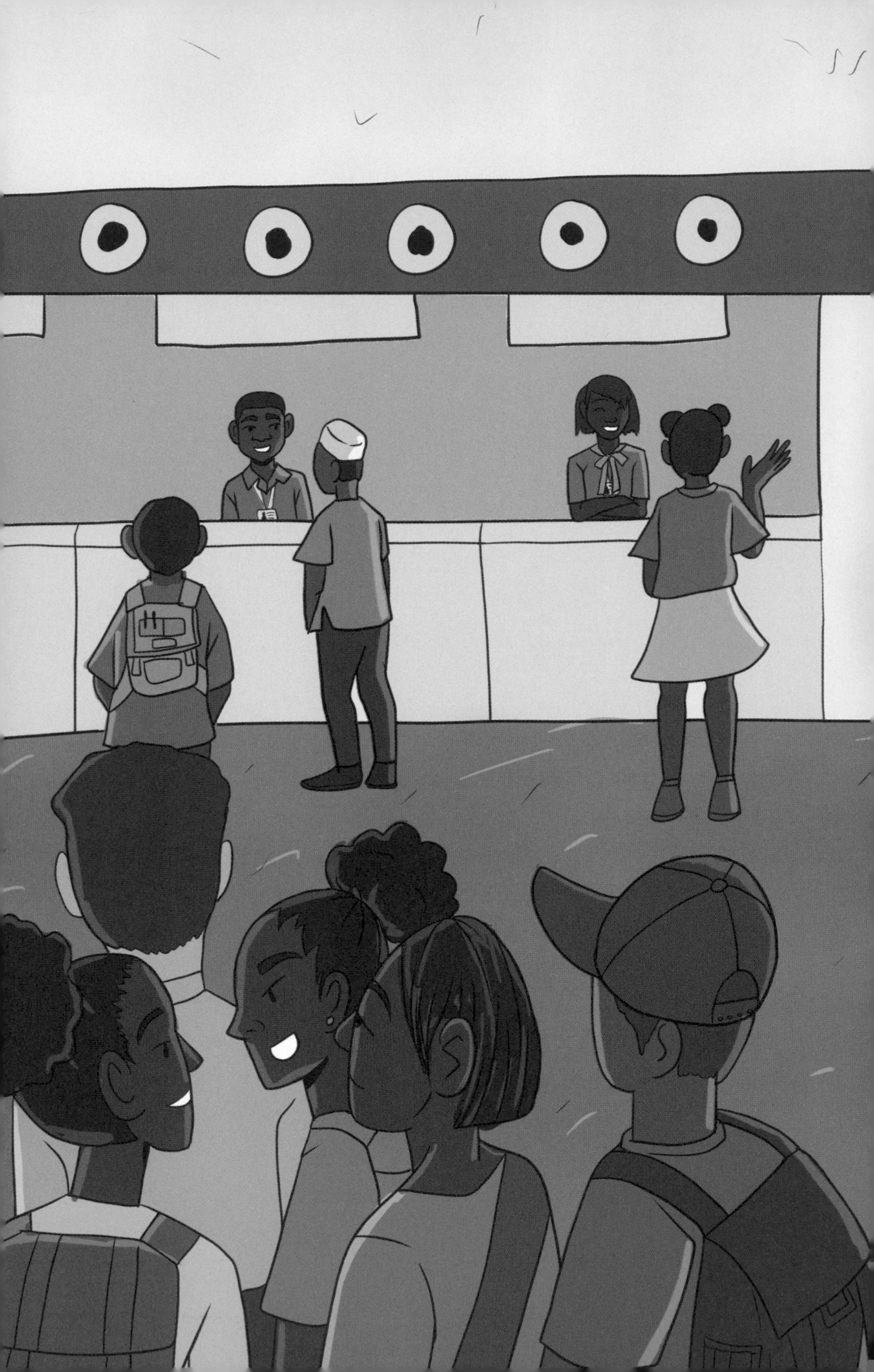

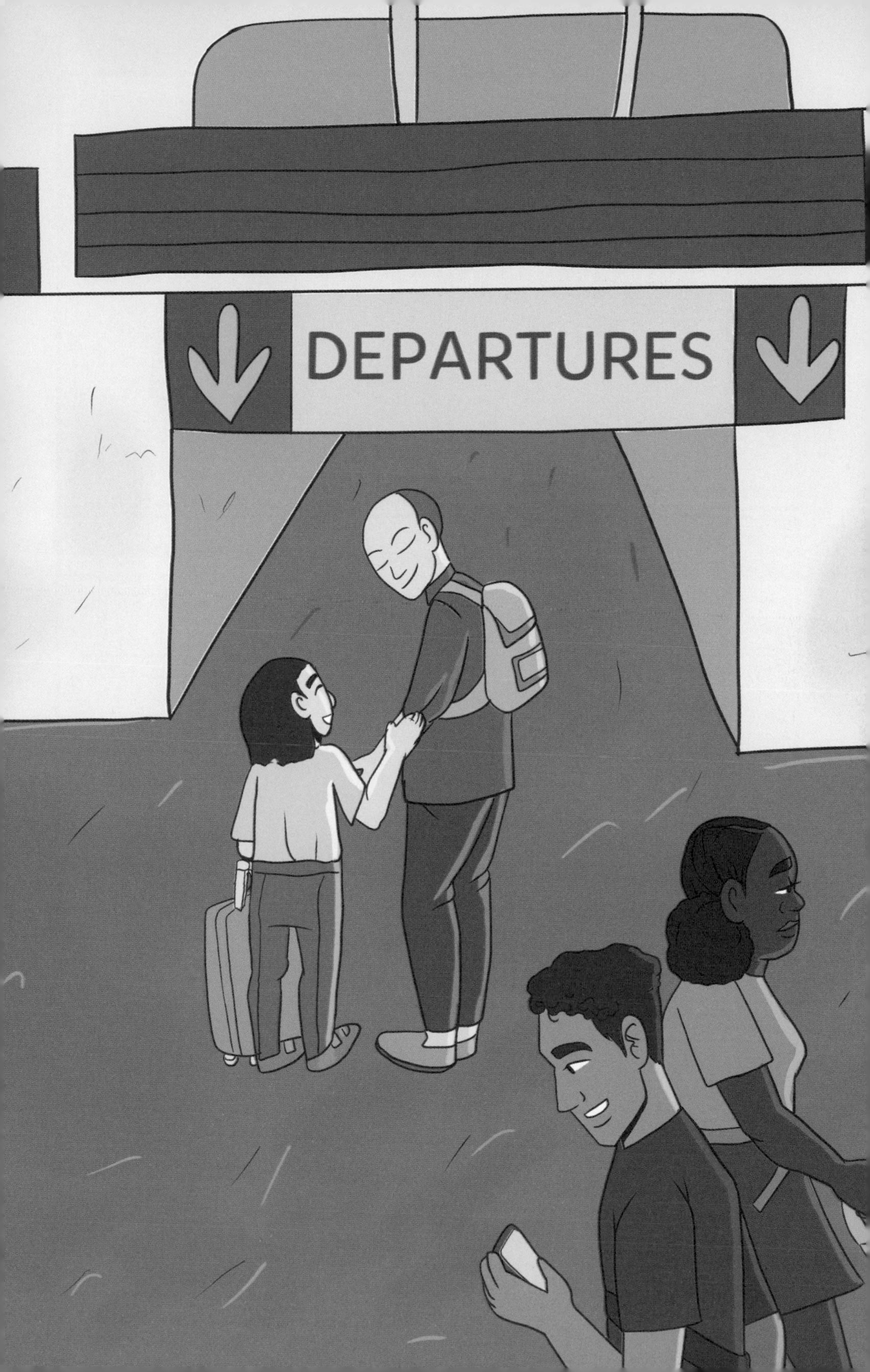
DEPARTURES

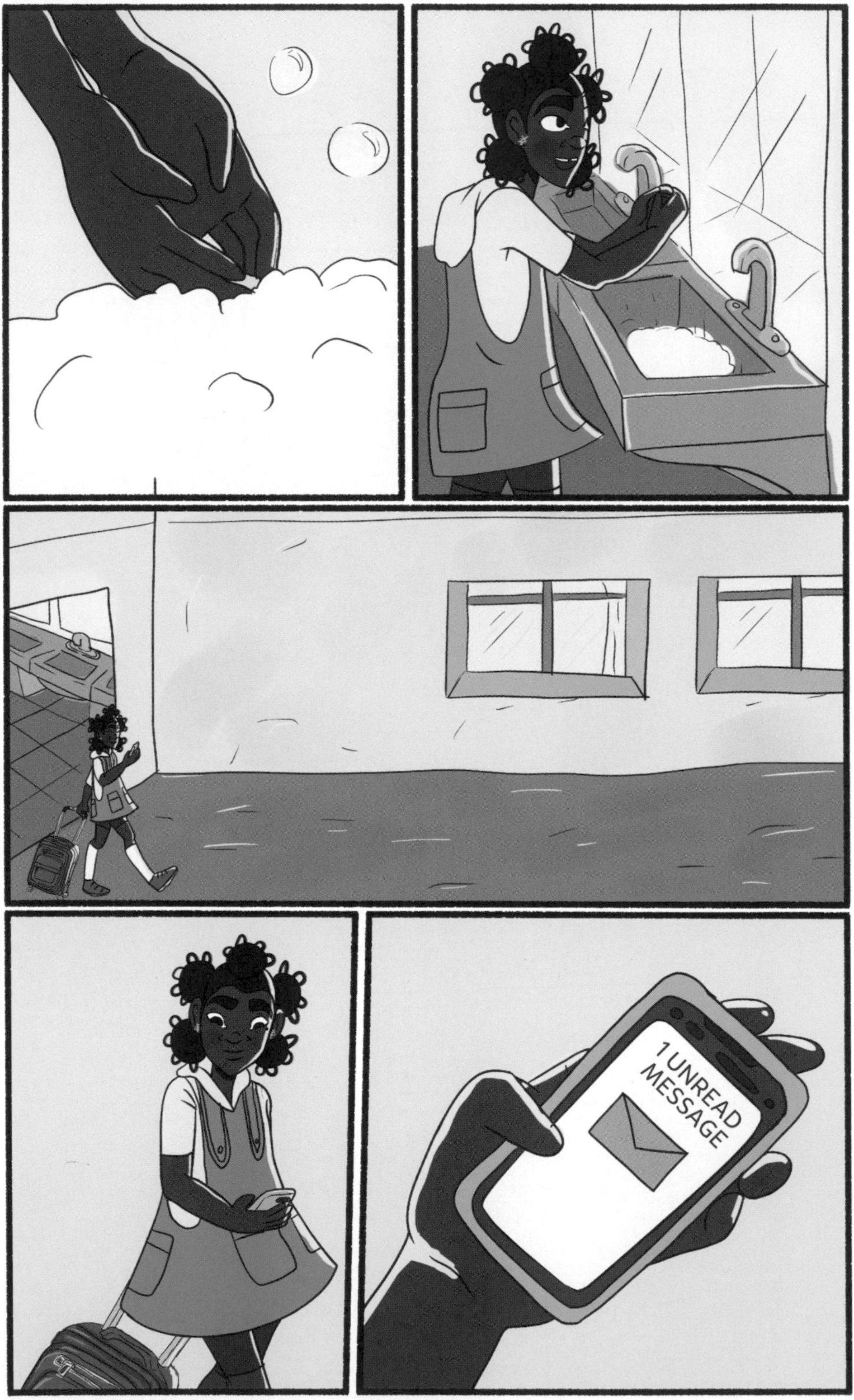
1 UNREAD MESSAGE

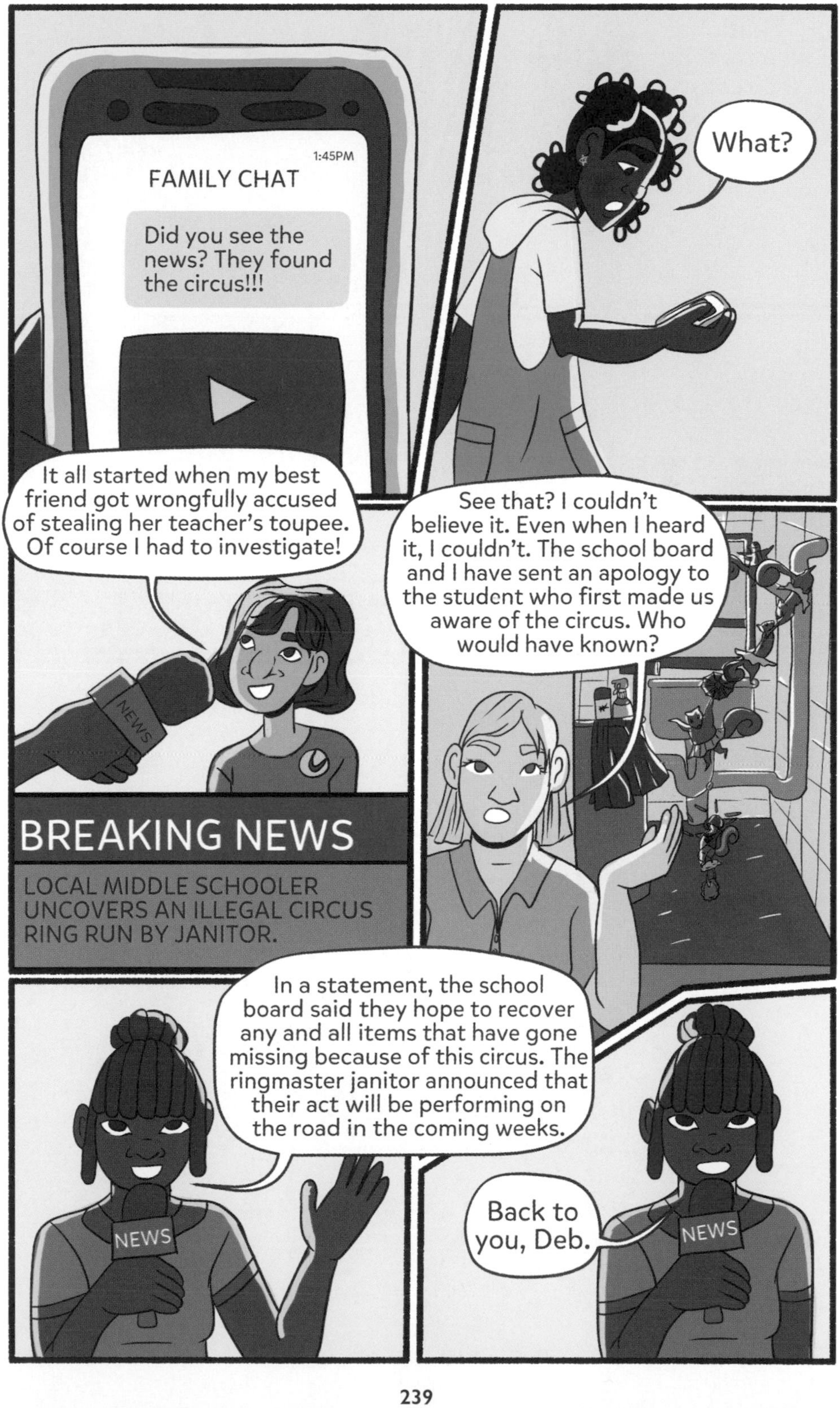
1:45PM
FAMILY CHAT
Did you see the news? They found the circus!!!
What?
It all started when my best friend got wrongfully accused of stealing her teacher's toupee. Of course I had to investigate!
NEWS
BREAKING NEWS
LOCAL MIDDLE SCHOOLER UNCOVERS AN ILLEGAL CIRCUS RING RUN BY JANITOR.
See that? I couldn't believe it. Even when I heard it, I couldn't. The school board and I have sent an apology to the student who first made us aware of the circus. Who would have known?
In a statement, the school board said they hope to recover any and all items that have gone missing because of this circus. The ringmaster janitor announced that their act will be performing on the road in the coming weeks.
NEWS
Back to you, Deb.
NEWS

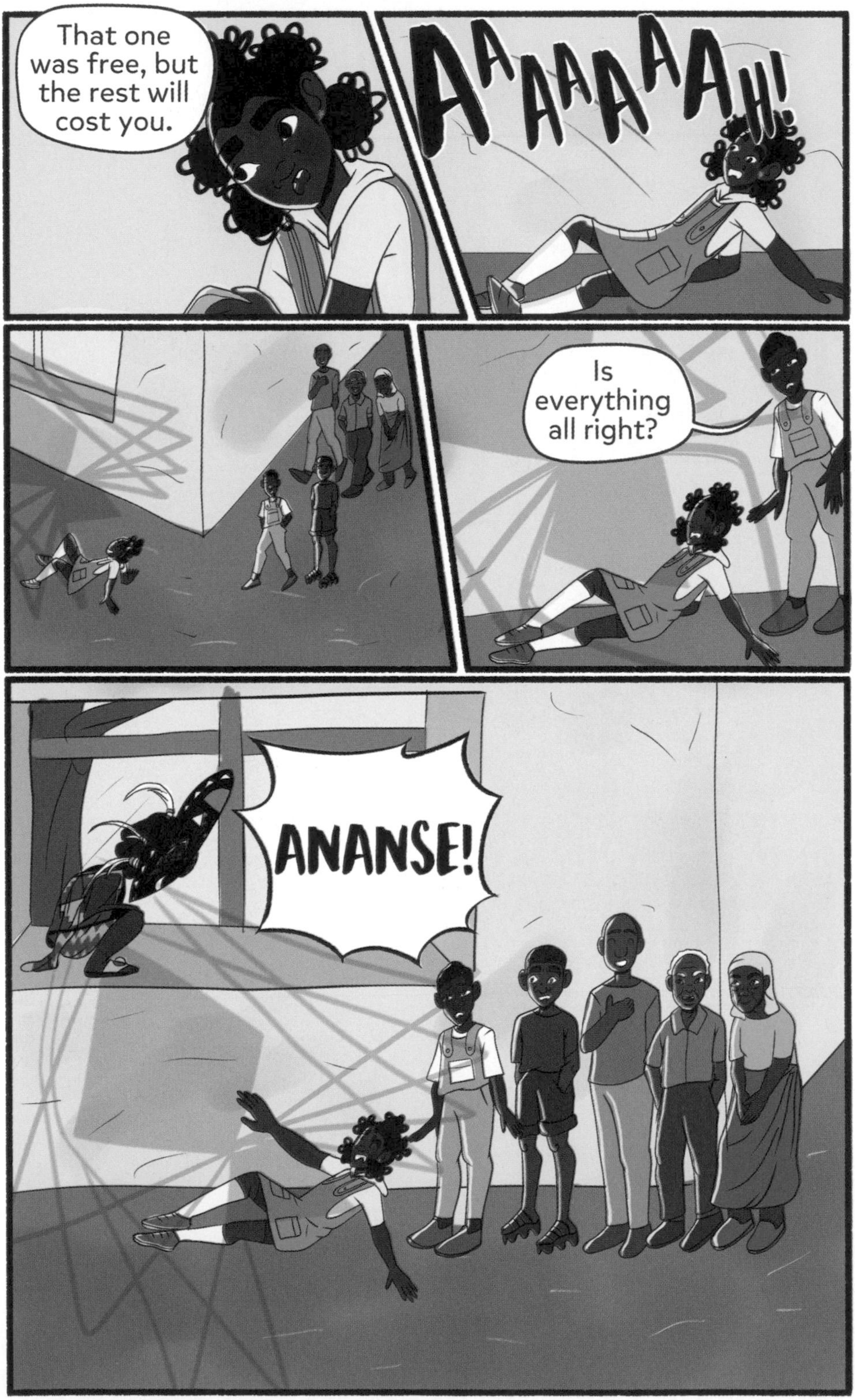
That one was free, but the rest will cost you.
AAAAAAAH!
Is everything all right?
ANANSE!

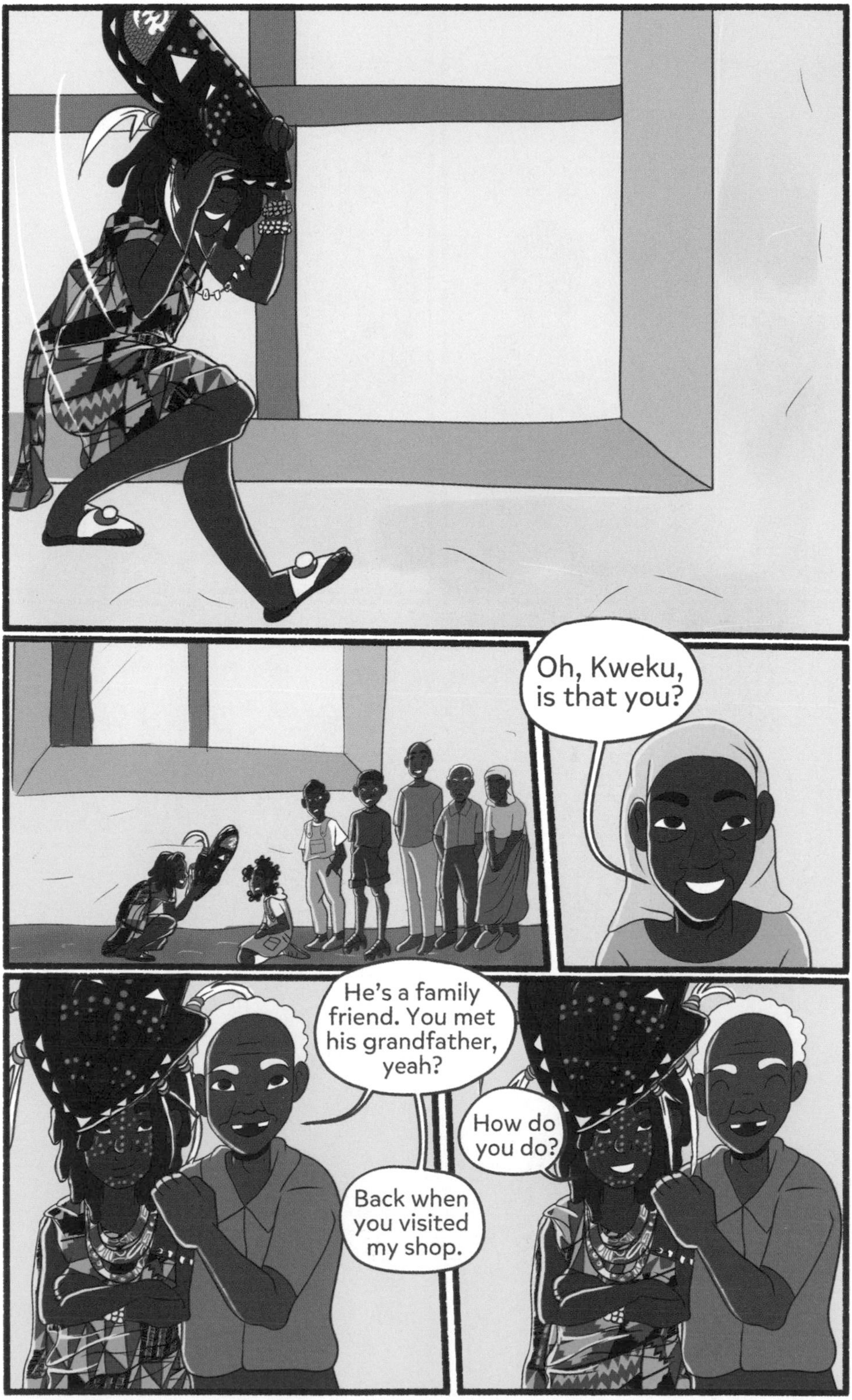
Oh, Kweku, is that you?
He's a family friend. You met his grandfather, yeah?
Back when you visited my shop.
How do you do?

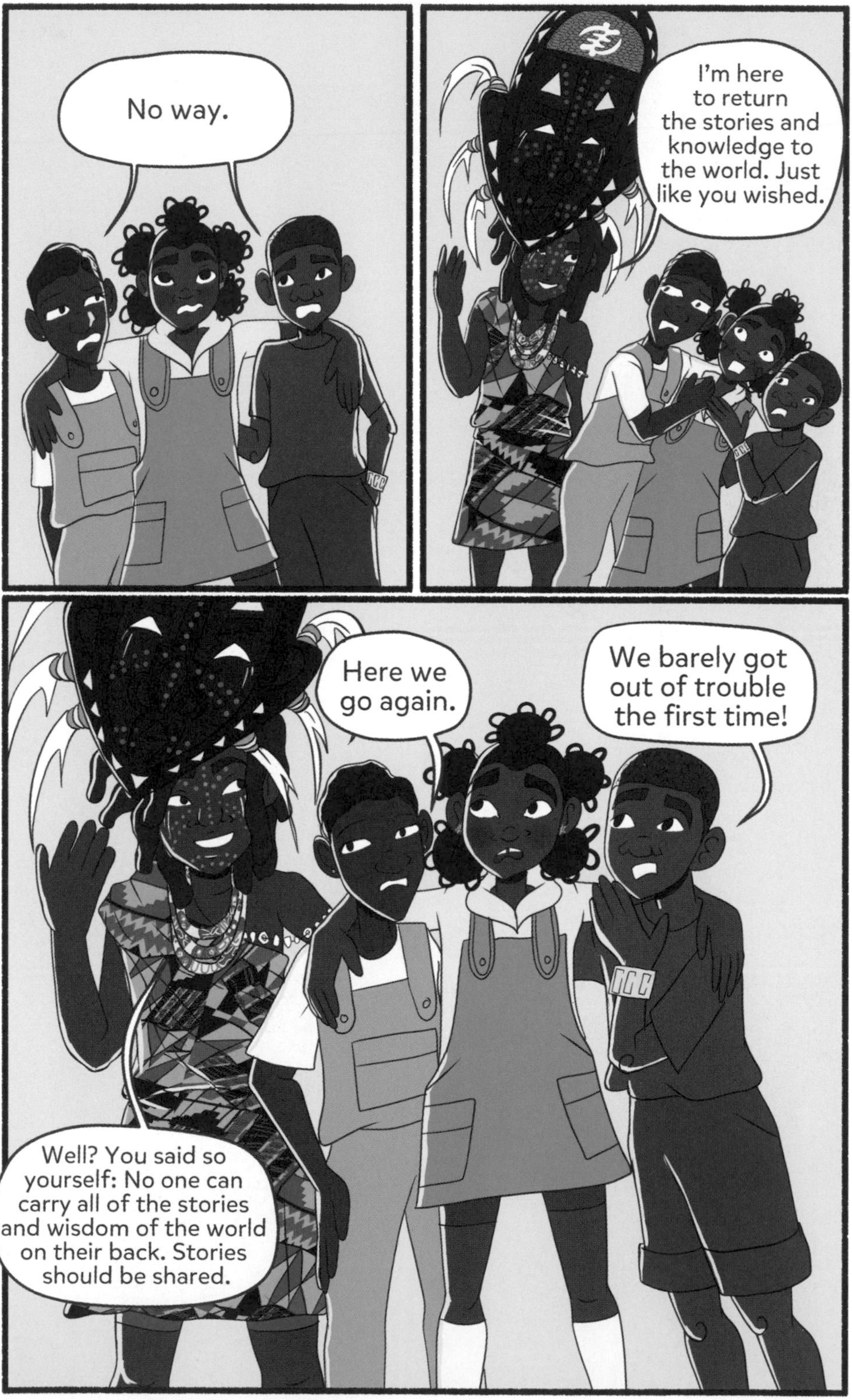
No way.
I'm here to return the stories and knowledge to the world. Just like you wished.
Here we go again.
We barely got out of trouble the first time!
Well? You said so yourself: No one can carry all of the stories and wisdom of the world on their back. Stories should be shared.

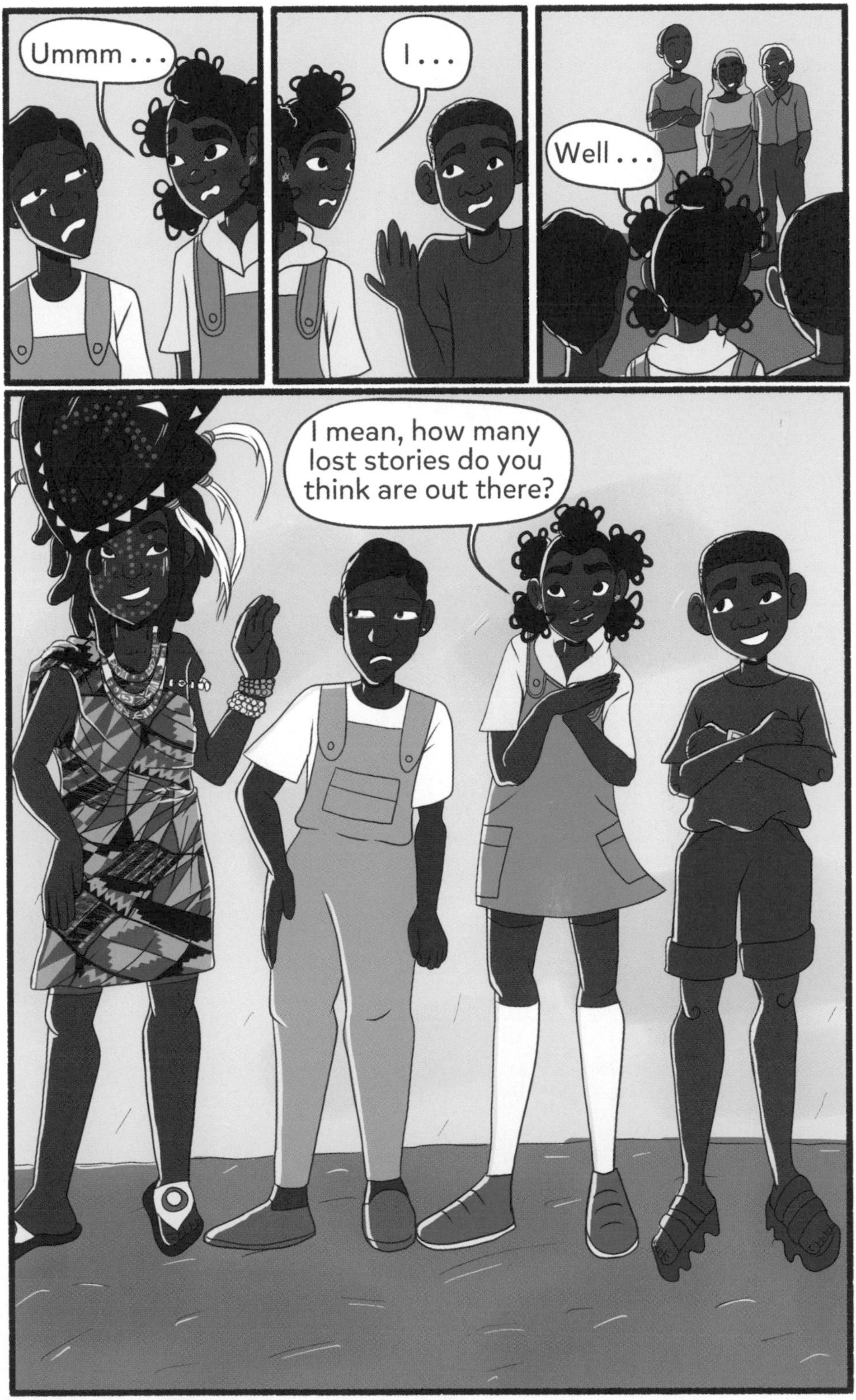
Ummm . . .
I . . .
Well . . .
I mean, how many lost stories do you think are out there?

AUTHOR'S NOTE

Before Ananse brought all the stories to the world—before writing even existed—the tradition of oral storytelling played a pivotal role in African culture. These were tales whispered around campfires, lessons passed along from elders, and lyrics woven into songs. In *Fibbed*, I recount the story of "Ananse and All the Stories of the World," "The Elephant and His Tail," and "Ntikuma and the Magic Drum"—Ananse fables (the last of which is the inspiration for Nana's discovery of the magic in the village forest) that I grew up with and came to learn while writing Nana's story. Like the stories themselves, the history of the mythical spider of African folklore is rich and compelling.

In the Akan language, *ananse* is the word for *spider*. The first known "Ananse stories" came from the Asante, the ethnic group I hail from, who are native to the Ashanti region of present-day Ghana. Considered to be a clever creature whose craftiness outmatches other animals, the spider Ananse almost always proves to be victorious through his quick wit and antics. Traditional stories are generally called "Anansesem" or "Ananse stories," even when the hero is not necessarily Ananse. These stories were passed on from older generations to younger ones as a way of instilling moral lessons.

Ananse stories spread beyond the Asante to other Akan-speaking peoples. And when Africans were enslaved by Europeans, these stories were brought to the Caribbean and the United States. In some of the African, Jamaican, and American versions of Ananse stories, the trickster spider is still usually called "Anansi," but in the southern parts of the United States, storytellers changed "Ananse" to "Aunt Nancy."

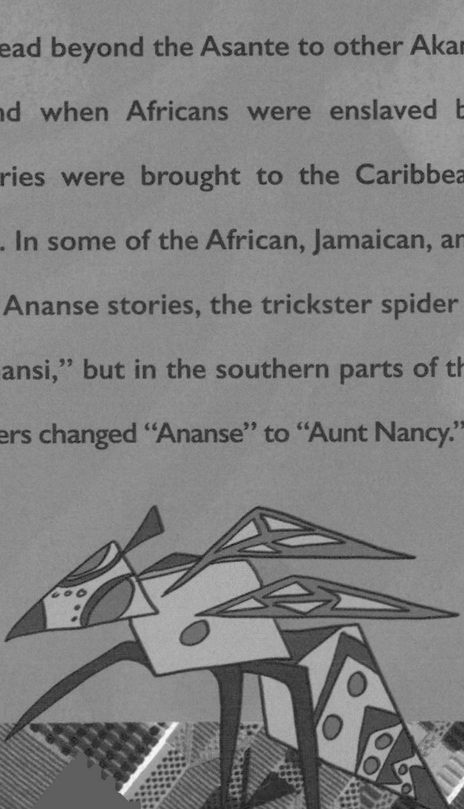

In *Fibbed*, I use the Akan spelling of Ananse, but I also bring my own twist to the many portrayals of Ananse, whom I draw as a young boy rather than the traditional depictions of a grown man with a wife and children. Through writing and drawing *Fibbed*, I feel so grateful to be one of the many storytellers bringing Ananse to a new generation.

—Elizabeth Agyemang

Dawuro—also known as the dawuruta—is a double metal bell used by the Asante. Traditionally, the bell has many uses and the sounds indicate different meanings. When used for official announcements, every town has a different way of playing the dawuro. But not just anyone can ring the dawuro. In order to ensure the authenticity of the message, a specific individual in each town is designated to ring the dawuro. The dawuro is also used as musical accompaniment during adowa dances, ceremonial dances performed during funerals and public social events.

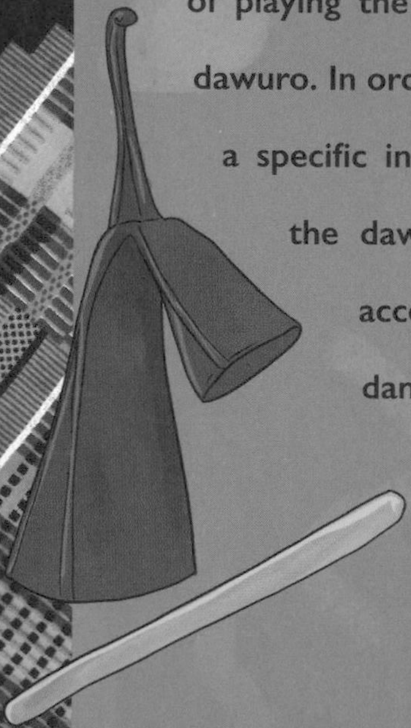

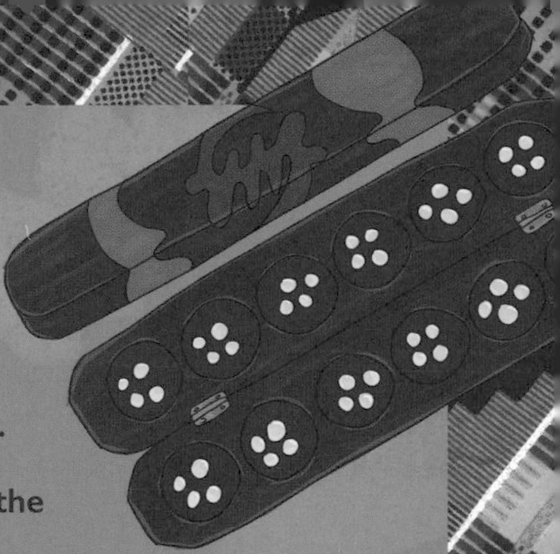

Oware is an important arithmetic game that is played throughout Africa and the Caribbean. Considered the national game of the Ashanti city-state, oware is said to derive its name (which means "they marry") from an Asante legend about a man and a women who played the game endlessly and—in order to stay together and continue playing—married. Spectators play an important role in oware, discussing the game and advising the players. Historically, oware is regarded as a game of the kings of the Asante and Denkyira kingdoms, and was used in the coronation ceremonies of the kings of some African communities.

For more reading on Ananse, check out *Ananse Stories Retold: Some Common Traditional Tales* by L. Gyesi-Appiah.

ACKNOWLEDGMENTS

Behind every story are the people who help bring it to life. Thank you to my brilliant editor, Ruta Rimas, for believing in my story, for meeting my vision with encouragement, and for having an extraordinary vision of your own that helped me bring Nana's journey to life. You are absolutely incredible, beyond creative, kind, and thoughtful, and I feel so lucky to work with you and have you in my corner. Thank you to my wonderful agent, Suzie Townsend, for always being such a passionate and kind advocate for my stories. Thank you to the team at New Leaf; Dani Segelbaum, you are absolutely amazing.

Thanks to the team at Razorbill. Deborah Kaplan, you're truly a wonder to work with, and I feel so grateful to have your design know-how and expertise to help drive this ship. Thank you to publisher Casey McIntyre and many thanks to managing editor Jayne Ziemba for all your work in helping bring this book to life. I truly appreciate having your expertise to help rope all the bookmaking pieces together. Thank you to Gretchen Durning for being an absolute delight to work with.

To my designers, thanks to Danielle Ceccolini for helping to bring this book to life, and special thanks to Samira Iravani and David Cardillo for all your support and patience, and for bringing so much joy into this incredibly intensive process. Thanks to Marinda Valenti, Delia Davis, Sola Akinlana, and Bethany Bryan from the copyediting team. Many thanks to Anna Elling from publicity. A world full of thanks to Felicia Frazier and Debra Polansky from the sales team.

And before Nana's story came to be, there were the people who helped inspire it. I want to thank my parents and my siblings for all the stories they told and for encouraging me to keep telling stories that inspired Nana's journey. A world full of thanks to my father and mother for going over my Twi and helping me with the proverbs. Thank you, Uncle Amos, for your wisdom. To my cousin Prince, I'm beyond grateful for afternoons spent sending audio messages back and forth. Thank you for asking locals about my questions when I couldn't be there in person and for helping translate the Twi throughout the story. Thank you to my little cousins Natasha, Jessica, and Stephanie for showing me what elementary school is like in Ghana. Thank you to Ama for sitting with me and my siblings at the fire outside and telling us our first Anansesem when we returned to Ghana for the first time since we immigrated. To all my family, thank you for always inspiring me.

And to you, dear reader, thank you for picking up this story and going on this adventure with Nana!